THE WILD AUSTRALIA STORIES

OMNIBUS EDITION VOL 1

JENNIFER SCOULLAR

PILYARA PRESS

ISBN: 978-1-925827-40-8
Pilyara Press
Melbourne

Billabong Bend (The Wild Australia Stories - book 3)

Turtle Reef (The Wild Australia Stories - book 4)

Journey's End (The Wild Australia Stories - book 5)

Wasp Season (The Wild Australia Stories – book 6)

Fortune's Son (The Tasmanian Tales - book 1)

The Lost Valley (The Tasmanian Tales - book 2)

The Memory Tree (The Tasmanian Tales - book 3)

BRUMBY'S RUN

THE WILD AUSTRALIA STORIES - BOOK 1

DEDICATION

To those who help the brumbies. To those who rescue, train and rehome them. To those who campaign to improve their management in the wild. To those who work to raise their profile as part of Australia's heritage, and also as wonderful riding and companion horses

It lies beyond the Western Pines
Towards the sinking sun,
And not a survey mark defines
The bounds of "Brumby's Run"

Brumby's Run
by Banjo Paterson

PROLOGUE

'Choose, Mrs Kelly,' says the doctor. 'The adoptive couple is here to collect the child.' He leans in close and lowers his voice. 'They're concerned there's a problem.'

Well, wasn't there? If this didn't count as a problem, then nothing ever would. Mary smiles at her sleeping twins. How to decide? There is no way, it's Sophie's choice. She could play eeny, meeny, miny, mo? Or rock-paper-scissors with the doctor? He wins, and Charlene might go. She wins, perhaps Samantha? The doctor puts on a sympathetic expression. 'Of course, if you've changed your mind . . .'

'No,' says Mary, with hoarse haste. 'I haven't.' It would be difficult enough raising a single baby. She plucks one, then the other, of her dark-haired daughters from their shared crib, and cradles them in her arms. She inspects their faces. All the clichés make sense to her now. They do have button noses, and rosebud mouths that purse sometimes in sleep. They are utterly perfect, and she can't choose. She can't even tell them apart.

'Mrs Kelly.' Mrs Kelly. Why is he calling her that? There is no Mr Kelly. A sop to his own sense of propriety, perhaps? 'If you need more time, perhaps the couple can come back.'

No, that will prolong the agony. She just requires some sort of a sign, some indication of what to do next. The left-hand twin parts her lips in a delicate yawn. The room grows airless. With infinite care, Mary raises the baby that lies in the crook of her other arm, her right arm, and offers her to the doctor.

'Are you sure?' he asks.

Of course she isn't sure. There is no certainty any more, and there never will be again. The world is a senseless place, filled with random acts of cruelty and prejudice, but she nods anyway. As he receives the right-hand baby from her, she yawns too. A misgiving, cold as death, stalls Mary's heart. The doctor checks the infant's wristband. She wills time to stretch. She counts the seconds it takes for him to cross the floor, to reach the door, to vanish with her baby. She consciously commits each detail of the scene to memory. Mary looks down at the single, sleeping baby in her arms. Is it Charlene or Samantha? What if she's given away the wrong child?

'I'll rub him down myself,' said Sam.

Brodie gave her a lascivious look. 'Sure you don't want a hand?' He chewed on a piece of straw. It dangled limp from the corner of his fat lips.

She slammed the stable door in his face, causing Pharaoh to start. Brodie mooched off. Sam hung up the horse's hay net, stuffed it full of his favourite lucerne, and kept some hay aside to make a wisp. Her deft fingers twisted the leafy stalks into a long, thin rope. Then she gathered the top end into two loops and wound the remaining string back through to form a solid pad of hay. 'Ready, Pharaoh?' The big chestnut lent his body towards hers. 'One, two three …' She began to strap his neck with long, regular slaps. The tempo increased as she found her rhythm. Pharaoh tensed and relaxed, tensed and relaxed, in time with Sam's movements, and she slipped into a kind of meditative trance. The horse was not the only one to benefit from such an isometric workout. By the time she'd worked her way along his back and rump on each side, girl and gelding were both spent.

Sam sighed in satisfaction. Summer was just a week away, and life was good. Her eighteenth birthday and the endless exams of Year Twelve were behind her now. The future stretched invitingly ahead –

a future where her mother wasn't in charge of every aspect of her life. Since Dad had taken up his overseas posting a couple of years ago, it had been just her and Mum, rattling around in their big old house together, getting on each other's nerves. A white Christmas, and a month with her grandparents in France, was just what the doctor ordered. Fingers crossed Dad could talk Mum into going back to Dubai with him. The prospect of coming home alone was too perfect to contemplate. She'd be able to spend each spare minute with Pharaoh, preparing for the summer dressage trials. And maybe, without Mum interfering all the time, she might even find herself a social life.

'Samantha?' Her mother peered over the stable door. Whatever was she doing here?

'Just a minute.' Sam hid the wisp, so Pharaoh wouldn't eat it, and went out into the stable yard. Her mother's always pale complexion had turned ivory, and her eyes were red, like she'd been crying. But that was impossible. She never cried. 'What's wrong, Faith?'

'I wish you wouldn't call me that. It's not natural.'

Sam was ready with a smart remark, then thought better of it.

Her mother seemed genuinely distressed.

'Get cleaned up, Samantha. We need to talk.'

'You can't talk to me when I'm dirty?'

Faith heaved a great sigh. 'Don't be difficult, darling. Get changed and meet me at the car. We'll do lunch.'

Sam was starting to worry. She was already halfway through her mushroom risotto, and Faith had barely said a word. Her salad lay untouched. Sam reached across and stole a cherry tomato and an olive from her mother's plate.

'Mum? You said we needed to talk.'

Faith gave a tremulous sigh and met Sam's gaze. 'There's no easy way to say it, so I'll just say it.' A dramatic pause. 'You mustn't hate me, Samantha.' What on earth was she on about? 'Promise me?'

Sam wanted to argue the absurdity of making a blind promise, but her mother's expression silenced her. 'I promise.'

Faith's clasped hands trembled, just a touch, where they lay on the white, linen table cloth. 'Samantha.' A deep breath. 'Your father and I adopted you as a newborn.' Odd shivers fluttered like moths across Faith's shapely neck. 'We couldn't have children, you see.' Her eyes lost focus for a moment and she corrected herself. '*I* couldn't have children.'

It felt like all the blood had drained from her head and formed a sickening pool in her stomach. Sam's chest grew tight. Why was her mother saying this? Was she sick? Delusional? Sam had known for a long time that something was wrong. She'd found pills in Faith's upstairs bathroom and looked them up on the internet. Anti-depressants. But this? It didn't make any sense.

'I'm sorry for calling you Faith,' Sam said, struggling to understand her mother's words. 'Instead of Mum. Some girls at school were doing it with their mothers. I suppose they thought it sounded more grown up, or something.' Sam gave an encouraging smile. 'Of course you're my mother.'

A brief ripple of relief flitted across Faith's face. She reached for Sam's hand with icy fingers. 'Thank you, darling.' Her voice was taut. 'You're right, I am your mother, in every real sense of the word. Your birth certificate says so, doesn't it?' She paused, and tears tracked down her pale cheeks. 'But I didn't actually give birth to you, I'm afraid.'

Sam withdrew her hand and placed it in her lap. She examined her mother's face. There was no trace of artifice. She tried the adoption hypothesis on for size, dared to examine it. Plenty of times, as a teenager, she'd imagined she didn't belong to her parents, had even hoped that she didn't. But that was just wishful thinking. Wasn't it?

'What do you mean? Where did I come from, then?'

Faith took a very deep breath. 'Your birth mother lived in a small country town, in the north-east of the state. Currajong. She was unmarried, Samantha, and quite poor. She relinquished you as an act of self-sacrifice, to provide you with a better life.' Faith fanned herself with the menu. Beads of sweat appeared on her flawless forehead. 'She was just a girl . . . only seventeen.'

Faith fixed Sam with cool green eyes. Sam had always envied her mother those startling green eyes. Her own were the same dark brown as her father's. Tea arrived, and Faith poured herself a cup, her hand steadier now. 'This is extraordinarily difficult, darling. You have no idea.'

Sam gasped for air. Faith had always skirted around the story of Sam's birth, protesting that it was something she didn't like to talk about. *'I can't explain it. Quite an out-of-body experience. It felt like somebody else was giving birth to you.'* There was also a lack of physical resemblance between them. It had always bothered Sam, but she'd put it down to taking after her father in a big way. Faith was petite and fair. Sam was tall and leggy, with the slender strength of a natural athlete. Her sable hair always threatened to escape its tie and fall in unruly waves around her shoulders – quite a contrast to Faith's neat blond bob. These differences seemed suddenly imbued with a dreadful significance. Sam fought against a rising suspicion that her mother was telling the truth. 'I had a right to know all this a long time ago,' she said, in a faltering voice.

'Please, Samantha. I'm telling you now, aren't I?'

The ground shifted beneath Sam's feet and a million questions raced through her brain. 'I need to know everything,' she said. 'Times, dates, places . . . people. I can't promise I won't be angry. I deserve to be, if I want to be.' Sam heard the high panic in her voice. 'Who am I?'

Faith looked around uneasily. 'Darling, you're making a scene.'

So that's why Faith had brought her to this popular restaurant for lunch. There'd be less chance of any histrionics. It was like a public dumping. 'I want to go home,' said Sam. 'To talk. But first, answer me this. Why are you telling me now? Why is it suddenly the right time?'

Faith looked unsure again. She clung to the edge of the table, as if it might somehow anchor her to safety. Several times she opened her mouth to speak, then wavered. 'There's more,' she said at last. 'You are . . . you're a twin.'

A twin? Now this was plainly ridiculous. They were back in the territory of delusion. Sam wondered if she was asleep, and began to run through the techniques she used to wake herself from conscious dreaming.

'Apparently,' continued Faith, 'your sister is very ill and wants to see you. Her mother – your birth mother – contacted me.' She spoke too fast, as if the words were loathsome, or poisonous, and she wanted to spit them out before they killed her. 'You don't have to do this, Samantha. We don't even know these people.'

The sharp sting of impending tears stabbed Sam's eyes, her nose, her throat. It was like she was seeing her mother for the first time. 'And whose fault is that?' She grabbed her bag from under the table and ran out the door.

The most important meeting of her life, and she was running late. Faith had offered to come along, but Sam had sensed her reluctance. In the end she'd gone off in a cab by herself, under a gloomy sky. It was probably for the best. This was something she needed to do alone. The car swished through the rainy streets. Sam stared out the window, stomach knotted tight in anticipation. She was about to meet a sister she'd known about for less than twenty-four hours.

The hospital was enormous and confusing, a rabbit warren of corridors and lifts and doorways. Preoccupied people rushed this way and that, everybody certain of where they were going – everybody except her. A fat woman pushed a teenage girl towards her in a wheel-chair. Could that be her mother? Her sister? She turned to watch them pass, and cannoned into an orderly. 'Lost?' he asked. Sam nodded, and he steered her to a reception area.

When she gave her name, the receptionist reached for the phone. 'Samantha Carmichael here to see you.' She gave Sam a warm smile. 'He'll be down in just a moment.' Who would be down? Sam stood, ill at ease, wondering what to do. An escape out the front doors was at the top of her favoured list of options.

A tall Asian man in a suit emerged from a nearby lift and looked in her direction. He beamed when he caught sight of her, and hurried over. Sam stood awkwardly and took a few tentative steps towards him. 'Samantha Carmichael.'

He grasped her extended hand and shook it energetically. 'No need for introductions, Miss Carmichael. I know exactly who you are.' His smile was kind. 'I'm Professor Andrew Sung, head of the acute myeloid leukaemia program, and the diagnostic molecular haematology laboratory. If you'll please come with me.'

Sam followed him back into the lift, up to the tenth floor, and into a large room. It was some sort of lounge, with sofas and low tables and a flat-screen television on the wall. A loud gasp came from the corner, from a woman standing near a coffee machine.

Sam turned and knew she was looking at her birth mother. She blushed with shame to think that she'd wondered about the person pushing the wheelchair. Did she think she wouldn't know her own flesh and blood? Sam had never seen anybody that looked so much like her before. It hurt more than she could have imagined.

Professor Sung took the woman by the hand and led her over to Sam. 'Samantha Carmichael, this is Mary Kelly, your birth mother.'

'Hello.' It was all Sam could manage, a shy hello.

Mary Kelly was an attractive woman, with a high forehead and even features. Sam had calculated her age, from the scant information supplied by Faith. Mary looked much older than her thirty-five years, looked at least as old as Faith, and Faith was almost fifty. Mary's hair, russet and wavy, was streaked with grey. Her eyes were set in dark rings, and fine, vertical wrinkles pinched her lips. The impression was one of tarnished beauty. Her eyes though were Sam's own, and at the moment they were very wide indeed.

'Samantha,' said Mary. The word sounded like a prayer on her lips. 'You're so very lovely . . . and so very kind to come.'

Mary looked at Professor Sung, and Sam saw something pass between them. He gave Mary a tight-lipped nod. 'There's a good chance, yes,' he said.

'A good chance?' said Mary. 'There's more than a good chance. I couldn't tell them apart when they were born, and I doubt if I could now, except for Charlie being so skinny and all.'

Sam pricked up her ears. Her sister's name was Charlie. Sam seized onto this new piece of information, as if her life depended on it. Charlie. That was a boy's name. It must be short for something. Charlotte, perhaps. She explored the word, tried to conjure up an image based on the name.

'This is too perfect,' whispered Mary. A great smile transformed her face. It shed its shadows and creases, its worry and care. It was suddenly clear that she had once been a great beauty.

Sam tore her gaze away from this stranger who was her mother. 'A good chance of what?' she asked.

'We mustn't put the cart before the horse,' said Professor Sung. 'This is a lot for Samantha to take in. However, since time is of the essence…Would you like to meet your sister?'

'I should bring her something,' said Sam, in a sudden panic. 'At least some flowers.'

The professor shook his head. 'Your sister has a suppressed immune system. She can't have flowers, or fruit. Nothing like that.'

Time was of the essence, the doctor had said. How sick was her sister? Was Charlie going to die, before she even got to meet her?

Mary and the doctor were talking to each other in low whispers.

'Is my sister okay?' said Sam in a sudden panic. 'What's wrong with her?'

Mary burst into tears. Professor Sung placed a hand on the woman's shoulder, but she kept on crying. 'Samantha?' He gestured towards the door. 'Let's have a talk?' Sam trailed out of the room after him, leaving Mary behind.

Professor Sung led her to an adjacent waiting room and indicated for her to sit down. He pulled a chair over and sat facing her. His expression was kind, concerned. 'I'm a haematological oncologist, which means I'm a doctor with special training in the diagnosis and treatment of blood diseases, especially blood-cell cancers.'

'Is that what my sister has? Cancer?'

He nodded. 'Yes. It's something called CML – chronic myeloid leukaemia.' There was a practised pause in his spiel. Leukaemia. That was bad. Sam's friend's little sister had died from leukaemia. Sam felt a sudden shiver down her spine.

'When someone has CML, the bone marrow produces too many white blood cells. They interfere with normal blood production and cause anaemia, bleeding and bruising, that sort of thing.'

'Can't you do something for her?' asked Sam. She wanted to say Charlie instead of *her*, but she couldn't find the courage. To say *her* was horrible. She was ashamed to refer to her sister like that.

'Your sister is in what we call the accelerated phase of the illness. She's had the standard treatments, but nothing has worked. It's unfortunate she wasn't diagnosed earlier, but her family live in quite a remote, rural area. Her symptoms weren't recognised until they became debilitating, and by then the disease was advanced."

'Is she going to die?' asked Sam. Her phone rang, Faith's number. Sam turned the phone off mid-ring.

'We're a long way from that point,' said Professor Sung. 'But I'll explain a little more after you've seen your sister.' He stood, and Sam did likewise, following him back to the lounge room.

Mary was clutching her arms nervously, pacing back and forth. 'I'm going to duck out for a cigarette.'

Sam was aghast. 'You're not coming with me?'

Mary shook her head. 'Charlie might want to see you by herself, just to start with. I'll be back in jiffy.' Before Sam could protest, she hurried off to the lift.

'I'm afraid Mary can barely last twenty minutes between smokes,' said Professor Sung. "The stress of Charlie's illness doesn't help.' Sam didn't know anybody who smoked cigarettes. Such a stupid thing to do. She felt a sudden burst of anger. It was inconceivable that she was related to that woman. Maybe they had it all wrong. Maybe she shouldn't even be here.

As they walked down the corridor, Professor Sung asked a lot of questions about Sam's health. 'Your sister's ANC count is low, so it's important that you don't have a cold, or anything like that. She's highly vulnerable to infection right now.'

Sam nodded, wondering what he was talking about. 'ANC count?'

'It stands for *absolute neutrophil count*,' he said. 'An estimate of a person's infection-fighting white blood cells.'

They walked into a ward, and stopped at the nurse's station. A middle-aged woman looked up from her notes, and did a double take. She looked from Sam's face to the doctor's, and back to Sam. 'Oh my Lord,' she said. 'Charlie's sister.'

'Do I look like her, then?' asked Sam, excitement mounting in her chest.

'That you do, dear. That you do. I'm Colleen.'

'This is Samantha,' said Professor Sung. 'Could you fix her up with a mask and gown, please?' Colleen took Sam's temperature and asked her to wash her hands. After she'd finished, Sam donned a disposable gown, popped on a mask, and followed the professor into a nearby hospital room.

There was a window, a steel hospital bed, and a figure on the bed. That must be her sister ... that must be Charlie. No matter what happened next, her sister would never be just *she* or *her* again. Sam held her breath as she approached, barely daring to believe she was in the same room as her sister. Tubes sprung from Charlie's chest and left arm, attached to a dangerous looking silver machine. It loomed beside the bed, like a Dalek out of Doctor Who. Charlie's eyes were closed, and she was motionless.

'What does that machine do?' asked Sam. She didn't know why she was whispering.

'That's a leukapheresis machine, filtering out abnormal white blood cells.' The doctor observed her concerned expression. 'It's quite painless.'

A soft toy frog, Kermit green, sat on Charlie's bedside table. There were more frogs on the windowsill, some in zip-lock plastic bags. Ceramic frogs, plush frogs, wooden frogs. Sam dared to focus on the figure in the bed. Charlie wore faded Chinese pyjamas and a colourful scarlet headscarf. A beautiful scarf, vibrant and out of place in the functional sterility of the hospital room. Charlie's eyes opened suddenly and she reached for a remote control, turning off the tiny television mounted on a swinging arm above the bed.

Sam got her first good look at her sister. Why did Colleen say that they looked alike? There wasn't much of a similarity, was there? Maybe Sam couldn't see past Charlie's gaunt eyes and sunken cheeks. Maybe she just didn't want to. It was frightening to imagine herself looking that sick. Then Charlie smiled and the resemblance was plain. 'Take off your mask,' said Charlie. 'Just for a minute, so I can see you.' Sam looked at Professor Sung, who nodded. Sam slipped the mask off. 'You're Samantha,' said Charlie. She swung her legs over the side of the bed, and started to sit up.

'Whoa there,' said Professor Sung. 'Not so fast.'

Sam hurried over and instinctively reached for her sister's back. It was strange being so close to Charlie – like looking into a magic mirror in which your reflection had a mind of its own.

'This is the coolest thing,' said Charlie. She was frail, but her voice sounded strong. 'I've been dying to meet you all my life.'

'You knew about me?'

Charlie nodded. 'I've been wanting to find you for years, but Mum said that wasn't right. She said that it was your decision to make.'

Sam smiled bitterly. Her decision, except that she'd never even heard of Charlie. At least Mary had had the decency to be honest with her daughter. Her own parents had taken it upon themselves to erase Sam's entire history. She was sure that it was only Charlie's illness that had made Faith relent. Otherwise she may have never learned the truth. 'My parents didn't tell me about you. I didn't even know I was adopted. If I'd known …' There was no way to finish the sentence. This was all too new, too much.

'That sucks. We could have had so much fun tricking people. Nobody would have been able to tell us apart,' said Charlie. Sam was unconvinced and it must have shown. 'I haven't always looked this ill,' Charlie said indignantly. She took a photo out of her bed-side drawer and handed it to Sam, who shook her head in disbelief. It was a photo of herself, dressed in jeans and a check shirt. She was riding a horse she didn't recognise, a compact bay with a baldy face. The most amazing thing of all was what she was doing. She was chasing a cow.

'That can't be me,' said Sam, confused. 'I've never even seen that horse, or those clothes . . . or that cow.'

Charlie laughed, a healthy belly laugh that suited her wide smile, but not her skinny frame. 'No, it's not you. It's me, last year before I got sick.' She pulled a few more photos from the drawer – school ones, childhood ones, more on horseback.

Sam stared in disbelief at the images. 'We look the same; exactly the same.'

'That's right,' said Professor Sung. 'You may not have immediately recognised the resemblance, partly because Charlie is so unwell, but partly because it is sometimes difficult for us to see ourselves as others see us. But trust me, the likeness is striking … and I hope it can be more than that. I hope it can be life-saving.' He took Sam's hand in his. 'Charlie's very best hope of a complete cure is to receive a syngeneic stem-cell transplant. That's a transplant from an identical twin. Very few people have such an option.' He patted her hand gently.

Sam slowly took in his words and their significance. She turned back to her sister, and saw Charlie's brown eyes, so much like her own, so full of hope.

'Perhaps we could talk a little more outside?' said Professor Sung. She couldn't leave yet! She'd just got there and had so many questions, so much she wanted to ask Charlie. But Professor Sung insisted. 'You two can catch up again later,' and with that he whisked her out the door.

Samantha sat next to Mary in a small room off the ward. Professor Sung sat opposite. 'Would you like me to explain things, Mary?'

'Would you?' said Mary. 'I don't have the words.'

Professor Sung gave her a brief smile and turned to Sam. 'As I said, Samantha, Charlie's best hope of recovery is a stem-cell transplant from a close relative. We've already tested your mother. Not a good match, I'm afraid.'

For a moment, Sam thought he meant Faith, and wondered why she would have consented to such a thing. Faith wasn't renowned for her charitable nature. 'If you wouldn't mind, could you stop calling Mary Kelly my mother? It's disconcerting. My mother is Faith Carmichael.'

Professor Sung held up his right hand, like he was going to swear on the Bible. 'You have my word.'

'And if Mary isn't a match, what about me? I could be one, couldn't I?'

Professor Sung gave her a pleased smile. 'You could be, Samantha. You could be a very good match indeed. Would you be willing to undergo some medical checks?'

'Of course.' said Sam. She wasn't about to forgo her lost sister just when she'd found her. 'Ready when you are.'

Mary put a hand over her mouth. Her eyes grew large, creasing her forehead like corrugated cardboard. 'You're an angel.' She moved to embrace her.

Sam dodged away from the woman's outstretched arms. 'I may not be suitable.'

'We're about to find that out,' said the doctor.

Sam spent the rest of the afternoon undergoing a battery of tests, and replaying the scene in Charlie's hospital room, over and over. She hadn't even said hello, or goodbye. She hadn't asked Charlie how she was. She hadn't hugged her or said what a miracle it was to meet her. She'd made a complete hash of it. The desire to see her sister again grew hot and insistent. When the final test was complete, Sam hurried back to the oncology ward, terrified that Charlie might die before she could talk to her properly. Colleen waylaid her with a gown and mask before she rushed into the room.

Charlie was sitting up, and the Dalek was gone. She wore a

different headscarf – emerald-green this time. It perfectly matched her stuffed toy frog.

'Hello, Charlie.' Sam walked over to the bed, and pulled up a chair. It was good to see her sister alone, and without the tubes tying her to the silver machine. 'How do you feel?'

'Not too bad,' said Charlie, with that sunny smile again. How could she look so happy? 'I'm freezing and there's an awful tingling feeling in my mouth, but it's not too bad. How are you, Samantha?'

It was an oddly formal question. 'People call me Sam.'

'Right. Sam. How does it feel, to know you've got a sister?' Charlie looked suddenly unsure. 'Are you okay with that?'

What a question. 'I'm thrilled,' said Sam. 'I always wanted a sister.' Charlie's expression remained unchanged. 'I'm not just saying that. I wanted a sister so badly, it was like . . . like I knew I should have had one.' Yes, that's how it was. Faith had said how lucky Sam was that she didn't have to share anything, when all she really wanted to do was to share everything. And she'd never really talked to Dad about it. How could she? Even before he moved to Dubai for his diplomatic posting, he was never home, and when he was, he was busy. So her desire for a sister had become a private wish, unexpressed though fervent. Something to dream about.

'We always thought you knew,' said Charlie. 'That was the deal when the Carmichaels took you. Mum said they were supposed to tell you.' Charlie swallowed hard and looked lost. 'They were supposed to tell you about us.'

Up until then, it hadn't occurred to Sam that her father was also complicit in the deception. Everyone she trusted had betrayed her. 'Well, they didn't.' Sam looked away trying not to cry. 'Can you tell me about your life?' she said, to change the subject. 'If you feel up to it?'

'I was about to ask you the same question.'

'I asked first,' said Sam. 'Who's the horse in the photo, for starters?'

'That's Tambo,' said Charlie. 'I broke him in myself, when they ran in the brumbies. He's one of the best campdraft horses in the district.'

'He's a brumby?' Sam looked at the photo again. 'He's beautiful.'

'There are lots of beautiful brumbies,' said Charlie. 'People don't realise how good they are.'

'I have a horse too,' said Sam. 'Pharaoh. A five-year-old Warmblood gelding. We do dressage together.'

'Dressage?' said Charlie. 'Now that's some fancy riding. People say twins have a connection. Maybe with us it's horses.'

Maybe. It was unlikely, though, that horses had played as central a role in Charlie's life – or in anybody else's life for that matter – as they had in hers. Horses had rescued Sam from a lonely childhood, a smothering mother, an absent father; they had been her sanctuary and her ticket to freedom. Anything worth knowing, she'd learned from the back of a horse.

Colleen came into the room. 'Time for your shower, Charlie,' she said. 'And it's time for you to go, Samantha. I expect we'll see you tomorrow then?'

Tomorrow? Sam nodded. Tomorrow and every day after that. Nothing mattered more than Charlie. Charlie reached for her hand and squeezed it. 'Will you really come tomorrow?' she asked.

Sam leaned down and kissed her sister's drawn cheek. 'Just try to stop me.' It was a wrench to leave the room. Sam hurried to the lift, faint with emotion. Mary was a little way down the corridor, waving madly. Sam didn't acknowledge her. Instead she slipped down the stairs, taking them two steps at a time, before escaping from the hospital into the rain-drenched afternoon.

How to make her mother understand? 'Even if I'm a perfect match,' said Sam, 'and even if Charlie recovers quickly, she's still going to be in hospital for weeks, maybe months. I can't go anywhere for a while.' Didn't Faith realise how important it was for Sam to spend time with Charlie?

'But I've already bought the tickets,' said Faith, 'and arranged the itinerary. Dad's going to meet us there.' Sam shook her head. 'But you love France, darling, and your grandmother is expecting you.' Faith gave her a particularly intense look. 'She's eighty this year . . . it may be the last time.'

'Don't give me that,' said Sam. 'Mamie will outlive us all. And yes, I do love France, but I can't go now.'

'You're punishing me for protecting you,' said Faith. Sam struggled against a rising tide of resentment. 'I always had your best interests at heart.'

'Maybe you thought you were protecting me, but you weren't. You were lying to me, that's all. You and Dad.' Sam had spoken to her father on the phone earlier in the evening. What she'd hoped for was a proper apology, and some attempt to explain why he'd made a lie of her life. What she got instead was a flat denial of her right even to know. She would have preferred excuses.

'Things would be better all around if it hadn't got out,' he'd said, as if that was that. 'And this whole debacle proves my point.'

Easier for who? *This is about me, not you, Dad,* she'd tried to say. If he'd had his way, she'd probably still be in the dark, dying sister or not. She had to give Faith some credit. At least she'd found courage enough to do the right thing in the end.

'I knew this would happen,' said Faith. 'I knew I'd lose you someday.'

'You're not losing me, Mum. I love you, and I'm your daughter, no matter what. I just can't go to Europe right now, that's all. There's nothing to stop you from going.'

'Maybe I will,' said Faith in an injured voice. 'Don't you go falling for this Mary woman. Remember I'm the one who's loved you all these years.' There was an undercurrent of real anxiety in her mother's voice.

Sam blinked back the start of tears. 'I won't fall for Mary. I don't know if I even like her. But I have to be around to help Charlie recover – and I want to get to know her. It's about time, don't you think?'

Faith eyed Sam suspiciously. It had been an emotional morning for them both. Sam had demanded answers, and for once Faith was well and truly on the back foot. Endometriosis, she'd said. Nobody could imagine how she'd suffered. And a diagnosis of premature ovarian failure at thirty-two. 'You were the answer to all my prayers, Samantha. Daddy's too,' She poured herself a glass of shiraz and wrinkled up her face, like the wine wasn't good enough, but then nothing was ever good enough for Faith. 'I loved you from the very first moment,' Faith said simply. 'I had no idea, actually, that I could love somebody like that.' She took a sip. 'And now you stab me in the heart.'

Sam sighed, frustration and sadness clouding her mind. It was too much to expect, apparently, for her parents to see that this wasn't about them. 'Mum, you know that's not fair. I'm going to bed,' said

Sam, 'and I'm going to the hospital first thing in the morning. And I'm not going to France.' She tried to make the stairs before her mother could play the victim again.

'Fine,' called Faith, raising her voice and following Sam from the room. 'Do as you please.'

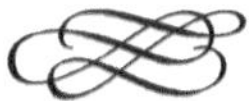

They were a match. Genetically identical. Sam sat quite still as Professor Sung told her the marvellous news.

He handed her an information leaflet. 'HLA stands for human leukocyte antigen,' he said. 'It's a marker the immune system uses to recognise which cells belong to your body, and which ones don't. A good HLA match between donor and recipient is vital to the success of a stem-cell transplant.' Sam waited expectantly, encouraged by the broad smile spreading across his face. 'A transplant between identical twins, such as yourself and Charlie, guarantees complete HLA compatibility.'

Sam was hesitant. 'So this means?'

'There's an excellent chance of a complete cure. Really excellent.'

'Does Charlie know?'

'I told Charlie and Mary this morning.' The mere mention of Charlie's name provoked in Sam an unsettling craving. The pull of her sister was strong, and Sam rose to leave. He gestured for her to sit back down. 'I want to be sure you understand the process. For the next few days, starting from today, you'll receive injections to stimulate stem-cell production; to encourage their movement from your bone marrow out into your bloodstream. Meanwhile Charlie will receive high doses of chemotherapy, to destroy her diseased cells and make way for your new ones. If all goes well, we'll harvest your stem cells one day next week in the morning, and transfer them to Charlie that same afternoon. Do you have any questions?'

Only a million, but Sam shook her head. The details didn't matter. The only thing that mattered was Charlie getting well. The universe had narrowed its focus to that one pinpoint of light, that one wish. Professor Sung gave Sam an appointment card. 'You're booked in at the Apheresis Unit at eleven-thirty for your first G-CSF injection today. Will your mother be coming along?'

'I asked you not to call Mary that,' said Sam.

'I don't mean Mary. I mean your adoptive mother.'

For a moment the term made no sense. 'I don't need Faith's permission,' said Sam. 'I'm over eighteen.'

Professor Sung frowned. 'Only just, Samantha.' Of course. He knew how old Charlie was, so he knew how old she was too. How strange. 'The injections have some side effects, and I want somebody with you, to make sure you get home in one piece.'

'I'll be fine …' she began.

'No, no,' he said, holding up his hand. 'I'm the doctor, and I say you need a support person. Either I ring your mother, or Mary can look after you. Take your pick.'

Mary. She was a complete stranger. What use could she be? But things between Faith and Sam had gone from bad to worse lately. 'Fine,' she said, with a little eye roll that masked her apprehension. 'Mary then. Can I see Charlie now?'

Professor Sung nodded. 'Just remember, the chemotherapy will take it out of her. Don't stay too long.'

Colleen ushered Sam into the room, then closed the door. Charlie was connected once again to the ubiquitous battery of machines. A murky-looking fluid flowed through the central line, like a poison aimed straight at her heart. Charlie lay very still, eyes closed, listening to an iPod with headphones, flicking at it with her fingers. Sam watched her sister unawares – curious and guilty all at once. Charlie looked older, smaller, shrunken. Sam could blow her away with one breath; she needed weighing down. A black head-scarf patterned with scarlet salamanders and snakes coiled about her head.

Sam moved to the foot of the bed, into her sister's field of vision, and touched her leg. 'Hello, Charlie.' Charlie took out the earphones and grinned. The transforming effect of her smile was remarkable, like she'd switched on her life force. It shone brightly from her hollow eyes, and Sam answered Charlie's smile with one of her own. 'We're a goer,' she said, giving her sister the thumbs up.

Charlie nodded, face flushed palest pink with pleasure, and shifted position in the bed. It cost her a noticeable effort.

Sam experienced a stab of sadness, mingled with frustration. It was so unfair. She wanted to take off her mask, go for a walk with her sister, run with her, ride with her. They deserved at least that. Her parents had stolen their past, their right to a shared childhood, and now this cancer threatened to steal their hope for a common future. Aggravation must have shown on her face.

Charlie's smile fell flat, and she looked away. 'It's okay if you don't want to do the transplant. You can change your mind.' Her sister's voice was alarmingly weak, but Sam recognised the spiny prickle in the tone. It was too often in her own.

Sam pulled up a chair close to Charlie. 'Just try to stop me.'

Her sister's smile returned and she reached out her hand, bony and pale. An angry rash, like rope burn, extended from wrist to forearm. It disappeared beneath the sleeve of her unflattering flannel nightgown. Her sister deserved better. How far up did the ugly rash go? Did it cover Charlie's thin chest, her breasts? Did it hurt? Sam tried to think something to say, a message of tenderness, but before she could find the words, Charlie gave her hand the faintest squeeze. The back of Sam's neck tingled.

'Thank the Goddess you're a match.' It was Mary's voice. She rushed to embrace Sam, clearly reaching for some sort of connection with her long-lost daughter. She wouldn't find one. Sam felt nothing for this woman; this woman who'd given her life, then given her away.

Mary turned her attention to Charlie and moved over to the bed without a word. She caressed Charlie's cheek, unwound the serpent headscarf, and pulled out a new one from a plastic bag in the bedside drawer. Sam flinched at the sight of Charlie's naked scalp. With ritual concentration and loving precision, Mary twisted the fresh scarf to shield her daughter's skull. It had a paisley tadpole design, rich teal in colour – almost aquamarine – with long ties and elastic at the nape. It was gorgeous, and a perfect fit.

An unexpected jolt of jealousy left Sam breathless. Was she jealous of Mary for her unspoken bond with Charlie, a bond born of years spent together? A painful stab of insight suggested it might be the other way around. That she might be jealous of Charlie for having had her real mother for her whole life. No, that was absurd. Faith was Sam's real mother. Despite all her flaws, she loved Sam, and Sam loved her. Sam mumbled goodbye and hurried from the room. Charlie's swift, disappointed glance stayed with her for a long, long time.

CHAPTER 5

Drew cantered towards the mob of horses and raised his rifle. A shot punched the frosty air, then another. The herd turned tail and galloped for the ridge line. He glimpsed a flash of hides through the branches: buckskin, grey and the usual bays and browns, perfectly camouflaged, blending with the trees. He'd been right. There was a mob of brumbies roaming Maroong Mountain.

Drew urged Clancy across the creek. Man and horse trotted alongside the rusted barbed wire that marked the boundary between Kilmarnock Station and Balleroo National Park. He spotted the big blue gum on its side, toppled in last week's storm. It had lain low ten metres of fence line, and hoof marks churned up the ground on both sides of the breach. Too late to do much tonight. Best come back on a bike in the morning.

Drew toyed with the idea of telling his father about the mob, but it would just stir up trouble. He and Bill were at odds about the brumbies. To his father they were nothing but pests, eating good grass that should be saved for fattening cattle. Things would be different if Gramps was still alive. He called wild horses the *spirits of the high country*, admiring their beauty and independence. He'd scoffed at Bill for his hostility, saying he had no heart, no feeling for the land. Drew had always marvelled at his grandfather's courage. Nobody else ever dared stand up to his father.

Drew peered through the darkening bush, but the horses were long gone, back up the mountain. Feed was scarce on the higher slopes this summer. They'd be back. But there'd be no more brumby running for Drew, no matter what Bill said. He'd joined his dad on a run last summer. Never again. For years he'd longed to go along, but had stayed away out of deference to his mother's wishes. It was only after she left that he'd joined Bill and the boys on a weekend trip up the mountain.

Mum had always called it cruel, and she was right. Drew hadn't understood, had thought her too sentimental. It wasn't as if they were shooting horses from helicopters, like they did in some parts. His father and the other brumby runners were financial members of the Alpine Feral Horse Management Association. They had permits to remove brumbies from the park. It was all above board, just a sport – a true test of horsemanship, and from all accounts, exciting as hell to boot.

Drew didn't like to think back on the experience. The first unsettling thing had been the dogs. Two of Dad's loudmouthed kelpies came along, as he'd expected. But the other blokes, four contract brumby runners he'd never met before, had brought monsters. Bull Arab hunting dogs, weighing in at fifty kilos each, with heavy heads and muscled bodies; trained to hold wild boars for the bullet. Permits called for the dogs to be muzzled, but who was to see, that high up on the range?

The six of them had headed out from Kilmarnock Station, setting an easy pace up to base camp. They climbed spurs, framed by stringy barks and peppermint gums, stairways to alpine flats where cattle and horses had grazed for generations. The herds of red and white Herefords were gone now – driven off the mountain by reluctant cattlemen when concerns were raised about damage to the high country from hard-hoofed animals. A few mobs of scrubbers evaded the musterers and lived on in this remote place. And so, of course, did the brumbies.

They'd risen at dawn to a cold fire and skins of ice on the water in the billies. Drew watched the men fit heavy-duty motorbike knee-pads beneath their jeans. His dad had thrown him some gear, and he'd copied the others. Leather chaps strapped from crotch to ankle and synthetic rubber gloves completed the outfits. He could barely clamber onto Clancy, stiff-legged and weighed down by his modern brumby-runner's armour. Perversely, they wore no protection at all on their heads – just their customary Akubras. With ropes slung over shoulders and spurs gleaming, the riders were ready.

The dogs ranged ahead of the horses. 'Your horse is everything in this game,' his father told him. 'It needs to stay level-headed, and be able to look after itself as well as its rider. It needs disc brakes, power steering, and it needs to jump like a kangaroo.' The other men rode rangy thoroughbred types with hogged manes – fit and lean and just a bit mad. Their saddles were specially designed with outsized kneepads, grooved at the base. To hold a plunging wild horse, the rider looped the rope around this groove to stop it from slipping.

Drew played with his catching rope while they searched for the brumbies. The aim was to unsling it from shoulder to hand in about two seconds. It needed to be strong enough to snub a wild stallion to a tree, stiff enough to hold the noose in shape, and fine as a lady's finger. Bill had indicated a white and brindle dog, nose to ground, leading the pack. 'That's Bess,' he'd said. 'She's our finder.' Even the other dogs seemed to be watching her. If she took off, so would the riders.

Without warning, Bess flushed a mob of brumbies, and the riders went after them at full tilt, tearing over logs and through trees. Hoofs flung out stones as the horses scattered into the tangled forest. The dogs soon caught up with a small, fat mare – lame and obviously pregnant. She stumbled. A black dog latched onto her head and brought her down. A man leapt from the saddle and snatched a home-made headstall from the bundle on his pommel. The plaited hay band was cheap and hard to break. But it was also thin, like wire, and cut into the mare's skin when she struggled.

The man kicked the dog and made it let go. The mare struggled to her feet. Her left ear was bleeding, almost torn in two. She turned to flee, but was pulled up short, snubbed to the ghost-white trunk of a twisted candlebark by the halter. Fear and pain transformed her into a writhing, rearing, raving thing. The man mounted and waved for Drew to ride on, leaving the horrified mare to fight her invisible demons alone.

Clancy trembled beneath him. Drew hadn't signed up for this. He bit his lip, soothed his horse with uncertain words, and cantered after the others. Similar scenes repeated themselves all that dreadful day, up and down the mountain. The contract runners were suicidal in their determined pursuit of their sport, chasing at breakneck speed through bogs, over rocks and between trees. Never had the old saying *a rider's grave is ever open* made more sense, but adrenalin had got the better of them all. Drew smashed his knees against trees, and didn't even feel it. Only later at home, looking at his purple, swollen legs, had he appreciated the true value of those kneepads.

Drew had finally roped a swift bay colt, elated at first by the capture. The hard nylon catching rope locked onto a large leather eye to prevent the horse from choking, but still the colt laboured to breathe, and struck out with wild, panicked forefeet. It reared over backwards and lay still. One of the other men jumped down, haltered the prone yearling and secured him to a tree. 'He'll be on his feet by the time we get back,' he told Drew. Drew wasn't so sure.

By dusk, six brumbies stood tied to trees. Bill shot dead a young foal, injured by the dogs as it tried to return to its captured mother. His father also shot dead the mob stallion. The big black had turned on Bess and snapped her front leg in a rage as it tried to protect a roped mare. Drew leapt from the saddle and knelt to comfort the whimpering dog. For all he knew, they'd shoot her too. Normal bush rules about fair treatment of animals had for some reason been suspended on this gloomy mountainside.

'I'll take Bess back,' Drew had offered. 'If you don't need me,' he'd added, trying not to sound too keen. There'd been a brief discussion between the men. Finally his father had nodded assent, and helped haul the bitch astride Clancy's saddle. She'd whined and wagged her whip of a tail in thanks. Drew had stroked her head, grateful to the dog for giving him an excuse to escape. On the way down the mountain he passed the bay colt he'd caught. It was standing now, sweating and shivering, forefeet splayed and hanging back on the taut tie rope. Not a bad sort. Maybe Bill would give him a go at breaking it in. Further on, Drew passed the pregnant mare with the ripped ear. She lay dead, head at an impossible angle, neck broken in her furious attempts to free herself.

Drew hadn't stopped when he reached the camp, as his father expected him to. He'd kept right on down the mountain. How naive he'd been, how foolish. It wasn't like Bill to pull any punches, and he hadn't. Drew just didn't think brumby running would have turned out to be so brutal a process. He had a better idea of how the rest of the trip would go now, the idealised scenes wiped from his imagination. Bill and the other men would collect the haltered brumbies and chase them ahead on ropes back to the campsite. There they'd be tied to trees, while the men went and caught more brumbies over the next few days. Bill had said the brumbies were offered food and water, but Drew couldn't imagine those traumatised animals eating or drinking anything. At the end of the weekend, the men would retrieve their Toyotas, fitted with stock crates. They'd use a boat winch to drag the frightened horses onto the trucks, and take them to the stockyards at the showgrounds in town.

When Drew finally caught up with Bill after the weekend, the news was worse than he'd imagined. It turned out that whole group of brumbies had gone to the doggers, even the swift bay colt Drew had his eye on. No, he wouldn't tell his father about the brumbies on Maroong Mountain. Good luck to them.

He whistled up Bess and they headed for home, south across Snake Creek. The dog trotted on ahead of Clancy, nose to ground. Her lamed leg made her useless as a hunting dog, so the contractors had let Drew keep her. Bess was loyal, with a surprisingly gentle nature, and she made a nice change from Dad's hyperactive kelpies and heelers.

Drew passed a sagging bush gate, the back track into Charlie

Kelly's place. For a moment he contemplated making the trip down to the house, to see if she was home. He missed Charlie. She was a headstrong, faithless pain in the arse, but she was also a lot of fun. He missed their bush races, Charlie always cheating, cutting corners to win. He missed her dropping by to demand help with a fence or a calving cow. Missed how she always somehow turned everything into Bill's fault. She wasn't far wrong there. Truth was, Drew was still half in love with Charlie. They'd gone out for a while last year, until he'd discovered the hard way that Charlie preferred rodeo cowboys.

Her mother, Mary, ran a motley, inbred herd of crossbred Angus breeders on Brumby's Run. Her heart had never been it, and now Charlie and Mary had been gone for weeks. Mysterious, how they'd just disappeared like that, without a word. Max, one of Mary's dodgy mates, was supposed to be looking after the place. Max owned the second-hand dealer's yard at Tallangala, and Drew had seen his wreck of a truck coming and going a few times. But not lately.

Come to think of it, Charlie had been avoiding Drew even before she left, keeping to herself. Maybe Mary was in some sort of trouble with the law? She'd struggled more than once to stay on the right side of it. Bill called her trash. There'd been convictions for drunk driving, some petty fraud, a drug charge. Charlie might come to Drew for help around the farm, but she would never have come to him if her mum was in some kind of a mess. She was too damned proud. If he didn't hear something soon, he'd ride on over to the house. Take a look, keep an eye on things for Charlie till she got back. After all, wasn't that what neighbours were for?

The daily injections Sam received in the week prior to the transplant had left her ill and in pain, with a throbbing deep in her bones, like her core was cracking. Her head ached, her stomach ached, and she vomited up her food. Mary made sure Sam was safely in a cab home after each day, and she often fell asleep in the back-seat, overcome with fatigue.

Faith was there to meet the cab outside the house each afternoon, fussing around Sam and insisting she rest. Sam knew she meant well, but the double dose of mothering from Mary and Faith just added to her exhaustion.

Fearing she had the flu, Sam presented to Professor Sung. 'It's the shots, not a virus,' he told her. 'The side effects will dissipate within a few days of the last dose. You're not infectious, if that's what you're worried about. You're no threat to Charlie.'

A swift flush of shame had burned Sam's cheeks. Charlie. What were a few side effects compared to what her sister was going through? She silently put up with the dizziness, the nausea, the cramping in her limbs in the days that followed. At night, she lay awake and concentrated on mobilising stem cells from the centre of her bones – like a general, rallying her troops. She galvanised them, made them multiply, burgeon, pile up and up on themselves until they spilled through the bone-marrow barrier and crowded into her bloodstream.

If Faith noticed her daughter wandering about the house in the early hours, unable to sleep, she didn't say anything. If she saw Sam in the garden at the compost bin, quietly disposing of her morning bowl of fruit and muesli, she didn't ask. She seemed afraid to mention Charlie or the treatment at all.

Mary, on the other hand, had made an effort to find out about the effects G-CSF injections might have on donors. She knew that they hurt, for one thing. This is going to sting, the nurse had said when she gave Sam the first one. Sting? Biting fire ants swarming over her stomach was more like it. The nurse was cheerful, peremptory, distracted. It was Mary who noticed the tears that Sam tried to squeeze back.

Mary waited for the nurse to leave the room after the injections, then produced a little pot of greenish gold salve. She leaned forward and gently lifted the front of Sam's shirt, reeking of tobacco smoke. Sam screwed up her nose and touched Mary's arm, ready to push her hand away, but Mary shushed her and applied the goo to Sam's burning stomach. It brought instant relief. Sam relaxed back on the hard hospital trolley. 'What is that stuff?'

'Organic aloe and calendula balm,' said Mary, offering Sam the little pot. It looked homemade, and had pretty orange petals floating in it. 'Your mother doesn't make it, then?'

What a question. Faith didn't make anything, except a spectacular entrance. Sam couldn't tell if Mary was being sarcastic. If only she knew more about the woman.

'I'll give Faith the recipe, shall I?' Mary sounded sincere enough.

'Tell me how you made it,' said Sam. A test. For all she knew, Mary had whipped around to the nearest pharmacy and bought the stuff. That's what normal people did.

Mary looked thoughtful, like she was actually trying to remember. 'Pick two cups of marigold petals at noon on a sunny day, so they're not the least bit damp ...'

'Marigolds?' asked Sam.

Mary nodded. 'Calendula, edible marigolds. Our garden at Brumby's Run is full of them.' Sam imagined a picturesque cottage, with a rambling herb garden – chooks and flowers and fruit trees. She wanted to ask Mary about her home, about her life, not about the stupid ointment. 'Put the petals into a small saucepan of sweet almond oil and heat for, oh, an hour or so? Add a cup of fresh aloe vera jelly.' Mary paused, and looked hard at Sam. She seemed to be deciding how detailed the instructions needed to be for her townie daughter. 'You get that by scraping out the inside of the leaves,' said Mary slowly, as if talking to a young child.

'Go on,' said Sam, fascinated.

'Strain it all through a square of cheesecloth, unbleached cheesecloth. Warm the mixture again in a saucepan, with quarter of a cup of melted beeswax, until it's smooth. Tell your mum to pour it into sterilised jars, just like she was bottling fruit – and she can mix in a few petals for colour if she likes before she seals them.' Sam was speechless. 'Would you like me to write it down for her?' asked Mary.

Sam burst out laughing. There was obviously nothing normal about Mary. She'd passed her test with flying colours. 'I'm not laughing at you,' said Sam swiftly, concerned by the hurt on Mary's face. 'It's just funny thinking about Faith bottling fruit, or going to so much trouble over anything, let alone something you could just go out and buy.'

'Oh, but you can't buy this,' said Mary earnestly. 'It can only be made by a mother or a grandmother for their child. There's a slightly different recipe for fathers, but they don't often seem to bother.' Sam smiled, unsure if Mary was making a joke. How could she remain so . . . so heartfelt and preposterous at the same time? 'The magic of a mother's love is the active ingredient,' said Mary. 'That's why it worked so well for you.'

Sam turned the strange little pot of ointment around in her hand, like an object from another world. It promised to be a very steep learning curve indeed with this woman, her birth mother.

Mary was equally attentive to Sam's other ills. Ginger tea for the nausea. Nettle soup for the yawning ache in her bones. Mary could identify the problem with one glance. 'Here, take a couple of these,' she said one day as Sam sat outside Charlie's room, waiting for her sister to wake. Mary offered two little sticky tablets, looking like miniature rum balls. 'They'll help with the headache, sweetie.' Sam's head *was* pounding, too furious for analgesic relief. Mary fetched a plastic cup of water, and Sam swallowed the odd little pills without question.

Mary's treatments had proved at least as effective as conventional remedies. But what she liked most about these odd cures was hearing how Mary made them. Sam never wrote them down, and Mary didn't seem to expect her to. She was a little girl listening to fairy stories. 'I suppose you want the recipe?' Mary asked after Sam had swallowed the pills, and Sam nodded. 'Let me see . . . two tablespoons each of dried valerian, chamomile, peppermint, and rosemary. Then the active ingredient – extract of feverfew.' There was always an active ingredient, usually something rather dark-sounding, like skullcap tincture or devil's shoestring. 'Grind them together.' Mary mimed the actions. 'Blend with enough bloodwood honey to bind. Break off pill-sized pieces and roll into balls. Then store them in a tightly sealed tin, on the sill of an open window overnight.'

'Why do you put them by an open window?'

'So they can absorb lunar peace,' said Mary simply.

Marvellous. Sam imagined the country cottage. She felt she knew it quite well by now. Mary, working the mortar and pestle in a sunny kitchen, fragrant with fresh herbs. Charlie, sitting at the rough-hewn timber table, eating scones with homemade blackberry jam, warm from the wood stove. As Sam's headache lost its grip, she imagined out the window to the herb garden. A mountain beyond. She'd not got so far before. A gum-tree gully, a rough paddock of native grass and bright alpine daisies. Some wide-horned cattle. Herefords, was that what Charlie had said? And a herd of wild horses, escaping up the distant hillside, necks arched, manes and tails streaming in the breeze.

By the time the course of injections was finished, Sam had a complete picture of Brumby's Run in her head. Charlie and Mary hadn't been much help. They couldn't even show her a photo. Mary's phone was ancient, too old to take pictures and Charlie's phone was broken. Mary talked a lot about her herb garden, but that was all, and the intensive chemotherapy had laid Charlie so low she could barely speak. Sam spent every spare minute at the hospital, willing her sister to get well, craving the day when she could talk to Charlie properly.

CHAPTER 7

Charlie looked up as two people entered the room. Mum and Sam? With those ridiculous gowns and masks on, it was never immediately obvious who anybody was. A figure leant over her. 'How are things, sweetie?'

Mum asked the most stupid questions. How did she expect things to be? The deadly routine was killing Charlie. She dreaded waking up just to take a gazillion more pills. If she turned on the TV, she was too weary to keep track of the program. She couldn't see the sun, didn't even have a window. Breakfast had looked crappy, and she wouldn't have eaten it even if she could. She was so tired she'd gone back to sleep, and woke up puking her guts out. Nurses come in and out of her room taking vitals – blood pressure and temperature and a million other things – God knows how many times a day. She felt awful all the time and didn't see anybody except Mum and Sam. Had it only been a week since she'd started on this high-dose chemotherapy treatment? It felt like months. The days were a miserable blur, and she wanted to rip out the central line snaking from her chest, delivering its cell-destroying venom. Rip it out and break its back. Charlie wanted to say all this, but she could hardly speak at all. Her mouth was like sandpaper, and she had ulcers all over her tongue, inside her cheeks, even down her throat.

'I'm fine, Mum,' she said.

Mary placed a few ice chips and a little lozenge in her mouth. 'Peppermint, powdered ginger and violet petals,' she said, for Sam's benefit. Her brand-new sister was quite taken with Mum's mumbo-jumbo. It was a pity Mum couldn't whip up a herbal remedy for leukaemia.

Sam reached for her hand. 'I can't wait for tomorrow.'

Charlie nodded. Tomorrow, the fifth of December, was D-Day, peripheral stem-cell transplant day – the day she'd begin to get her life back.

Sam yawned. It was a bit of an anti-climax really. She was hooked up to the Dalek machine that had so frightened her the day she'd first met Charlie, just ten short days ago. Not that the machine was any fun, but it wasn't all that bad either. Not compared to the horror stories people liked to tell about the alternative – surgical bone-marrow donation. That involved an enormous needle, sucking a litre or more of warm liquid marrow from deep inside your hips. Sam clenched her pelvic floor involuntarily just to think of it.

That same afternoon, Sam's stem cells were transplanted into Charlie. Sam waited anxiously for news. When Professor Sung came to see her, she knew it had gone well – the doctor couldn't stop beaming. The transplant had been textbook perfect. Mary performed some sort of pagan ritual of thanks in the hospital car park, with chalk circles and burning beeswax. Charlie was exhausted, but smiled weakly at Sam when they were finally able to see each other. 'Here's to a shared future,' she said.

The only person who didn't seem overjoyed with the news was Faith. 'I can't understand why you didn't want me there,' she said that evening after Sam arrived home. 'I'd have been your support person. But no, you had to go straight to that Mary woman.' This last remark came with a theatrical flourish.

Sam took a deep breath. 'It was something I needed to do, Mum. Mary was only my support person in hospital. You've been here for me the whole time at home.' And about as supportive as a wet dishcloth, thought Sam. 'And anyway, it's given me a chance to get to know Mary.'

Faith snorted her displeasure. 'And what's she like then, this Mary?'

Sam wouldn't answer. Couldn't answer. Mary was a contradiction. She'd never met anybody quite like her. Sometimes Mary didn't seem any older than Sam herself. Sometimes she was selfish and childish. Sometimes she was patient and wise. She was far too direct. At times she was just plain rude, especially if she had a complaint about Charlie's care. Sam smiled. Faith would approve of Mary's fearless advocacy on her daughter's behalf. She had scant respect for hospital rules and regulations. She'd been thrown out, more than once, for smoking in the toilets. But when she wasn't with Charlie or Sam, she spent her time reading to children in the paediatric ward, or visiting a growing army of elderly patients who didn't seem to have any family. None who cared, anyway. Mary never seemed to have any money, except to buy cigarettes and Charlie's beautiful scarves. Sam had bailed her out a few times already – ten dollars here, twenty dollars there, but she didn't mind. Although Mary never had enough money, she always had enough time for her daughters.

'She's nothing like you,' Sam said to Faith. 'It's difficult to explain.'

'Hmm,' said Faith sniffily. 'I'll take that as a compliment, shall I?' She swept out of the room and began clattering about in the kitchen. Being at the hospital, although frustrating and worrying, was no hardship compared to being at home. Since Faith had revealed the truth about Sam, she had grown brittle, defensive – paranoid, even. And for someone who'd rarely cried before, she was making up for lost time. Despite claiming she wanted to help, Faith had turned the whole thing around so that she was the victim. The victim of an unfeeling, ungrateful daughter, willing to toss her aside after eighteen years of love and self-sacrifice. This dynamic allowed Sam no leeway to ask the questions she most needed answers to.

What Sam wanted most was to sit down for an entire afternoon and hear her mother's side of the story. She fantasised about it, and even wrote a list of questions in her journal. How had Faith found Mary? Had she wanted both girls or not? Why had she wanted a closed adoption, a confidential arrangement allowing for no interaction between birth mothers and their children? Had she ever wondered about Charlie? The list was endless. And of course, the most burning question of all - how could she justify having never told Sam the truth? In Sam's fertile imagination, this illuminating afternoon always ended up with Faith's teary apology. An *I'm sorry* would go a long way to help make this mess right. Of course, Faith didn't really do *sorry*, but for once Sam wouldn't be emotionally blackmailed into taking the blame.

Sam spent more and more of her time at the hospital. She abandoned the few friends she had. She even neglected her horse, Pharaoh, ringing the stables and telling them to turn him out.

'But he's in top condition,' protested her coach. 'You can't spell him now. You'll miss the national squad trials.'

'I won't be trying out for the squad,' said Sam. 'And I'm quitting as coach of the juniors. Just do as I say, please.'

'Fine,' her coach said. He sounded disgusted. 'But I'll have to clear it with your mother first. She pays the bills. It will mean cancelling your training contract and altering Pharaoh's terms of agistment.' He hung silent on the end of the phone for a long time. 'Are you sure you want to do this?' he said at last. 'It's a waste of a fine young horse, at the top of his game.'

'I'm sure.' Sam ended the call. She had no time for Pharaoh right now. She had no time for anybody but Charlie.

Charlie grew stronger each day, and as her strength grew, so did her willingness to talk about life back home in Currajong. She was a born storyteller. 'Brumby's Run is simply the most beautiful place on earth,' she told Sam. 'Just wait until I show you. A thousand wild acres in the shadow of Balleroo Range, half an hour's drive from town. At its highest ridge line, on the edge of the national park, you might as well be on the roof of the world. It's magic. The air is magic. The view is magic.' Charlie's eyes shone with a vitality Sam hadn't seen before. Her voice took on a compelling quality. 'To the north there's Maroong Mountain, a granite monolith like Uluru. Parts of it are covered with cypress pine forests. That sort of disguises it, but it's bigger than Uluru; almost twice as big.' Sam tried to picture it. 'There are rock pools with rare frogs at the top. I love frogs.'

'Who knew?' said Sam with a smile, looking around the amphibian-themed hospital room.

'When it rains, streams spill off the bluff, turning the rock to molten silver, and there are permanent waterfalls as well. Balleroo is an Aboriginal word for *rain god*. I'll take you there in spring when the snows melt. Show you the platypus in Snake Creek, and the lyrebirds at Wagtail Gully, and the Powerful Owl nest in the hollow candlebark above the home dam. God, I miss it.' Telling stories seemed to settle Charlie, helped alleviate what Sam sensed to be a growing homesickness. Sam spent whole afternoons listening to tales of brumbies and musters and rodeos. 'When I was twelve,' said Charlie, 'I got lost chasing steers in the foothills. Had to camp alone overnight near the creek, and I swear I saw a panther come down to drink.'

'A panther?' asked Sam. 'How?'

'Oh, there are panthers in the mountains all right. Some say they're descended from mascots released during World War II by visiting American servicemen.' Charlie smiled. 'Of course, I was just a kid. It might have been a big wild cat. We do get some whoppers around Balleroo.'

'You were allowed to go off by yourself at twelve?' asked Sam.

'Sure. Went on my first muster when I was ten. I was a pretty feral kid.' It was hard to imagine this frail sister as feral. 'Half the time Mum never knew where I was, or what I was doing. Wagged school as often as I went.'

What a life. The thought of that much freedom was intoxicating. Charlie had more independence at ten than Sam did now. Faith had been, and still was, a helicopter mum. Sam's eighteenth birthday had so far made little difference.

Sam was torn between love and frustration every time she thought of Faith. She knew Faith had added Valium to her daily pill cocktail. *To calm my anxiety,* she'd said. Well if that was its purpose, the drug was a dismal failure. Faith, always highly strung, now seemed to live on the rim of hysteria. Sam had been keeping informal track of the stash of tablets in the upstairs bathroom. They were disappearing faster than ever before. Perhaps she should tell her father? But Dad could be so judgemental where Mum was concerned. Best not give him anything that could be used as ammunition.

Sam surprised herself by beginning to cry. Her mask served as a shield, so Charlie didn't immediately notice. Perhaps she could stem the tears in time – she didn't want to explain to her sister, didn't know how to explain.

Charlie extended a fragile arm and took her hand. 'What's wrong?'

Too late. Sam's words came all in a rush. 'Your life sounds so perfect, idyllic ...' she said. 'I wish I was you.'

Charlie squeezed her hand with newfound force. 'That's the nicest thing anybody ever said to me.' Her expression grew puzzled. 'And the silliest. I'm half dead. Bald. Stuck in Melbourne for another two months, or even longer. When I do get home, I'm not supposed to have contact with pets. I live on a bloody cattle station, and I'm not supposed to have contact with animals. How's that going to work? Tambo's probably half-starved or cleared off with the brumbies. Mum's broke, and you wish you were me.'

'You've had freedom,' argued Sam. 'An authentic life. I'd forfeit a lot to be able to say that. I've been so protected, it feels like I haven't lived.'

Charlie released Sam's hand. 'I haven't asked you much about yourself. You've been so interested in me. Maybe I've been rude. Truth is, I didn't much feel like hearing about your big house and rich friends and fancy school. I don't blame you or anything; I'm happy for you. But Mum and me, we've had some really tough times. I sometimes wished she'd given me away to the posh family, instead of you.'

'You wouldn't have liked it,' Sam assured her. 'Believe me. My mum would drive you mad.'

'My mum already has,' said Charlie. 'You don't know her.'

A twinge of bitterness caught in Sam's throat. That was hardly her fault.

Charlie continued, oblivious. 'She makes a big show of all her herbal concoctions, but she drinks like a fish, smokes like a chimney and blows what's left over on the pokies. And the men? Damn, there've been that many of them. None of them lasted, of course.' Charlie looked sad and angry at the same time. 'Mum loves me, don't get me wrong, but she's dysfunctional as hell.'

'My mum takes pills,' said Sam, like it was some sort of contest for who had the worst mother. 'That's just as bad. She's kind of clingy and cold at the same time. And Dad doesn't even live with us.'

'So your folks have split up?' asked Charlie.

'No, Dad's an ambassador. He's lived in Dubai for the last three years.'

Charlie whistled approvingly. 'Some cushy job. Why didn't you and your mum go too?'

'It's like living in an oven for eight months of the year, and women don't have much freedom. Mum refuses to live over there, and I can't blame her.' This wasn't the entire truth. Sam had witnessed enough blazing rows between her parents over the years to guess there might be more to the separate living arrangements. 'But Dad went anyway, and sort of forgot about me. We speak on the phone sometimes, but I only see him twice a year.'

'At least you have a dad,' said Charlie. 'Mine was a ratbag. Shot through when Mum was pregnant.' She stopped short.

'Um . . . that ratbag would be my birth father too, remember?' said Sam. They burst out laughing.

'Listen to us,' said Charlie. 'We're a pair of jealous bitches.'

'We should do the prince and the pauper thing,' said Sam. 'We should swap lives.'

Charlie suddenly knelt up on the bed and yanked out the tube attached to her central line. Amber fluid spattered across the white hospital spread. With a deft twist she tossed her headscarf to the floor, exposing an ugly red rash. Her inflamed scalp looked as thin as eggshell. She spread her pale arms high and wide above her head, as if in supplication to some terrible god. The dramatic pose accentuated her wasted frame and gaunt features.

'I think people might spot the difference,' said Charlie. 'Don't you?'

CHAPTER 9

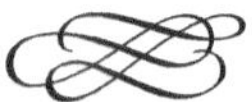

The counselling session was Professor Sung's idea.

Sam wasn't a default pessimist, but her gut told her this wasn't going to work. 'My mother's impossible,' she'd confessed to him on more than one occasion. 'One minute she's obsessed with hearing about everything that's happening at the hospital. Next minute she doesn't want to know, and accuses me of abandoning her if I even mention Charlie.'

Professor Sung had nodded, his eyes wise and understanding.

'There is an implicit tension in the relationship between Mary and Faith,' he said. 'Whether they admit to it or not, adoptive parents often feel secret jealousy, or even anger toward birth parents, and vice versa.'

'There's nothing secret about it with my mum,' said Sam.

'Faith has done all the hard work of parenting, and now worries an interloper might take over your affection. This rarely happens – but the fear is still there. It's quite natural.' Sam had almost argued the point. She was the one who'd done all the hard work. Being Faith's trophy child hadn't been easy. 'I'll schedule a group counselling session,' he'd said.

They'd arrived early. Faith's hair had been done especially for the occasion, cut in an immaculate geometric bob. She wore a plum silk shirt, Donna Karan slacks, and sat in the waiting room with her back to the wall and a good view of the door. Sam sat one seat away. The room was otherwise empty of people, though the air was thick with anticipation.

They heard Mary before they saw her. A little sing-song chant grew louder as she approached. There was a jangle of bangles and there she was, standing larger than life at the doorway, in a flowing white skirt and beaded peasant top. Purple-polished toes poked from fringed leather sandals. She wore flowers in her untidy hair – daisy chains woven into an olive turban headband.

Faith glanced at Sam with a look of horror, then wrinkled her nose as the combined odour of tobacco and incense wafted in. Sam couldn't help but grin. 'Sam,' said Mary, her eyes lighting up. 'I've got something for you.' She produced a jar. 'Lemon bath salts. Wonderfully calming.' Sam acknowledged the gift with a nod, intrigued to see what would happen next. Turning her attention to Faith, Mary enveloped her in a huge hug. Faith recoiled, like the little cat in the old Warner Brothers cartoons, trying to escape Pepé Le Pew's malodorous embrace. 'And for you,' said Mary, when she finally released Faith, 'my famous anti-ageing cream.' Sam gasped out loud. 'For those of us who want to pretend that we didn't have a forest fire of candles on our last birthday cake, eh?' said Mary with a laugh.

Faith's face contorted, like she was struggling with something. In the end she forced a smile and took the proffered jar. 'You're Mary?' she asked, as if she was hoping there'd been some mistake. Mary nodded and beamed. Faith inspected the jar. 'Homemade, then?'

'Of course it's homemade,' said Mary. 'Only the best for my Sam and her family.' Faith visibly flinched at the *my* Sam. Mary couldn't be doing a better job of alienating her if she tried. 'You take two ripe cucumbers, skin and all. Half a ripe avocado, a few leaves of mint, almond oil and a cup of rainwater. Oh, and a good dash of Friar's Balsam.' Faith grimaced. 'Shall I write down the recipe?' asked Mary. 'You could mix some up yourself. That little jar won't last you long.'

Sam began to suspect that Mary's motives were not pure. Faith was fastidious about her appearance and horrified about growing old. She'd had a brow lift, lip lift, eyelid lift and attended quarterly appointments at one of Melbourne's most exclusive aesthetic-surgery clinics. She'd even presented Sam with a rhinoplasty gift certificate for her sixteenth birthday. 'Now you'll be able to do something about that nose,' Faith had said brightly.

'Mum,' she'd said. 'My nose is fine.'

'Well, of course it is, darling. It's beautiful, just like you. But at the moment it turns up at the tip. Weren't you saying that you'd like it a little straighter? A little more classic in profile?'

'No, Mum,' she'd said. 'That was you saying that. Leave my nose alone.'

Faith was forever chasing eternal youth, and she would not react well to the suggestion that she needed wrinkle cream. Not well at all. Sam was gloomier than ever about the forthcoming counselling session.

A smooth-looking woman emerged from a hallway and summoned them into another room, where they seated themselves in a semi-circle on comfortable chairs.

'I'm Sandra,' the woman said with an unctuous smile, and made the introductions. 'I'm here to help you all find a new equilibrium.' Everybody looked blank. 'We'll begin with you, Faith.' Faith blinked. Sandra put on a serious face. 'Adoptive parents often have powerful negative feelings about a child searching for their birth family. We're here to help you work through those feelings.'

Faith bristled. 'Samantha never searched for her birth family.'

'That's because she didn't know she had one,' said Mary. Petals from her wilted headband floated to the floor. 'Sam was supposed to know about me and Charlie all along.'

'We're not here to argue,' said Sandra evenly.

'Why didn't you tell me, Mum?' asked Sam.

'I thought it would be . . . less complicated, and in any case, your father wouldn't allow it.' There was a catch in her throat. 'Victor was adamant, and since he'd arranged the whole thing, well . . . he said it was to be a closed adoption.'

Less complicated. That was a good one. This was about as compli-cated as it got.

'Where is Victor?' asked Sandra. 'It would have been very useful for him to come.'

'He's . . . he's overseas,' said Faith.

'There *was* no closed adoption,' said Mary, with a real edge to her voice.

Sandra rose to her feet, shaking her head and positioning herself between the two women, who were now glaring at each other in open hostility. It was the first time Sam had seen Mary drop her serene, earth-mother persona.

'Adopted children are nearly always hungry to know their own personal stories,' said Sandra. She smiled encouragement. 'Would I be right, Samantha? Is that what you want?' Sam nodded. Sandra looked pleased and resumed her seat. 'Equally, birth parents and adoptive parents often want to hear from each other. Want to gain a complete picture of their child. To fill in the blanks, as it were. It's a gift only you can give each other.' Nobody spoke. 'Right then, let's start with you, Mary. I'm sure Samantha would like to hear the circumstances that led to her adoption. Only tell us what you're comfortable with.'

It was pretty much as Faith had said back at that awkward lunch almost three weeks ago. Mary had been an unmarried teenager, barely able to provide for one child, let alone two. Sam hung on every scrap of information. Mary's mother had died in a tractor accident when Mary was just three, leaving her to be brought up by her father, Jock Kelly. He'd been a lazy, uninterested parent, by the sound of it, who'd pulled Mary out of high school to help him run the farm. 'Dad died of lung cancer the year before the girls were born,' said Mary. 'I worked Brumby's Run by myself after that . . . but I was never very good at it.' She shrugged. 'Should have sold the damn place, but I promised Dad before he died that I'd hang on if I could. So like a sentimental fool, I kept my word to the old bastard.'

'Tell me about my real father,' said Sam, her breath coming fast.

'It's not a pretty story, my sweet,' said Mary. 'His name was Robert Smith. Some sort of travelling sales rep. I left messages on his phone to tell him that I was pregnant, but he never called back. My final message was when you twins were nearly due. Said I'd have to relinquish one baby if I didn't hear from him. Never a word. It did my head in, Sammy, it really did.' How desperate must Mary have been. So young, just seventeen. Sam struggled to put herself in Mary's place. 'The adoption agency found a suitable couple the same day I approached them. All I knew was their name, Mr and Mrs Carmichael, and that they had loads of money.'

'Would you like contact with your birth father, Samantha?' asked Sandra. 'Is that something you'd welcome?' Faith looked horrified.

'Maybe,' said Sam. 'Mary, tell me more about Charlie. What was she like before she got sick?' It was a question that she'd been dying to ask.

'You wouldn't know it to look at Charlie now,' said Mary. 'But she's always been a bit of a devil. Skipping school, running off into the mountains after brumbies. Disappearing for days at a time, to who knows where, with who knows who.' Faith frowned at Mary's words. 'But in spite of that, your sister has a heart of gold.' Mary smiled at Sam. 'Just like you, sweetheart.'

'Samantha recently completed her final school exams,' said Faith, sitting up a little straighter. 'She did very well, I might add, and has been accepted into a Commerce degree at Melbourne University. My daughter always took her education seriously.'

'What choice did I have?' said Sam, suddenly angry. 'You made me study day and night. You wouldn't let me go anywhere except music lessons or the stables. My friends were never good enough. You wouldn't let them come over, wouldn't let me go to their places. I always felt so isolated.' It was Mary's turn to frown.

'You have friends. What about Cate?' said Faith, in a grasping- at-straws kind of voice. 'I always liked Cate.'

'You only liked Cate because she's Randolph Fox's daughter. You used to go on about it all the time, how she was heiress to a media empire. It's just a fluke that I liked her too. Now that she's gone away to that stupid school in Switzerland, I don't have a single friend left in Melbourne.'

'Darling, you know that's not true. And besides, that was a marvellous opportunity for Cate,' said Faith. 'Le Rosey is one of the most exclusive schools in the world. Cate will rub shoulders with the Getty's and Rothschilds.'

'You're such a snob, Mum. I'm surprised you didn't send me off as well. Oh, that's right – it would be too difficult to live your life vicariously through me if I was in Switzerland.' Sam was shocked at herself. Had she really said all that? Had her bitterness finally found so loud a voice?

Sandra said something about one person talking at a time, but nobody paid her any mind.

'Poor darling,' crooned Mary. She reached over and patted Sam's hand. 'When Charlie's right, you come home with us to Brumby's Run. We'll show you how to have some fun.'

Faith rose to her feet. In spite of her petite frame, she seemed to tower over Mary. 'How dare you! You're not fit to look after your own child, let alone mine. What sort of mother lets her child miss school and run wild like that?'

'At least I didn't lock her up like a nun!' retorted Mary. 'If you'd had something else to occupy your time – like a job, maybe – my girl could have had a normal childhood. Sam says you've never worked a day in your life.'

Faith shot Sam a swift, disappointed glance. Mary looked at her too, like she was expecting her to take sides. 'Shut up!' said Sam, her voice rising. She jumped to her feet. 'Shut up both of you! I'm not anybody's child. I'm eighteen, I'm an adult, and I don't have to put up with any of this crap.' With one last contemptuous stare, she marched from the room.

'Goodnight, Charlie. Sleep tight.' Sam tossed her phone onto the bed and stared out the window. It was late, the new moon already high in the sky, but she wasn't tired. Sam had told her sister all about the disastrous counselling session. They'd dissected it between them, word for word. Having Charlie was like having a best friend and a shrink all rolled into one. They shared everything about their lives. Well, perhaps not everything. There was one topic Sam had steered clear of: boys. She had the impression that Charlie knew quite a lot about boys. Sam had never even had a date. The very idea would have sent Faith into a tailspin. It was a prime example of just how cosseted she'd been. So Sam quickly shut down any talk of Charlie's love life, whenever it raised its embarrassing head.

The phone rang. Dad. 'How's tricks, Sammy?'

'Charlie's getting better every day.'

'Good, good.' The pause that followed seemed interminable. 'Are you okay?' he said at last.

'No, I'm not,' she said. 'And neither is Mum.'

'Well, there's not much I can do from over here, Sammy. We'll thrash things out at Mamie's.'

'No we won't. I already said, I'm not coming to France.' There was another long silence on the end of the line. 'Dad, why didn't you tell me about Mary . . . about Charlie?'

'It's complicated, sweetheart. There are things you don't know.'

'Obviously.'

This time the silence lasted so long that she thought he might have hung up.

'Your mother isn't answering her phone.'

'She's had a rough day.'

'Well, just tell her I rang. Tell her I love her.'

'Okay.'

'Thanks, Sammy. Love you too. You know that.'

'Bye, Dad.' The end of the call came as a physical jolt. She tasted tears although she didn't know she was crying.

Sam slipped out to the landing at the top of the staircase. Classical music played – a sad flute solo – and a light shone from the lounge room. Sam padded downstairs. Faith stood staring out the window at the dark garden, a near empty wineglass in her hand. 'Mum?' Faith started. 'Dad's been trying to call you.'

'Has he?' Sam followed her mother into the kitchen. Faith opened the fridge and reached for a bottle of Shiraz. Her glass knocked against the bench and broke into three pieces. Faith tried to put them back together with shaking hands.

'Don't, Mum,' whispered Sam. 'You can't fix it.' She eased the broken glass from her mother's grasp, cutting herself in the process. Blood dripped from her finger, mixing with the spilt red wine. It hurt more than she expected it to.

In an hour Faith would be gone – flown to Paris. Sam concentrated on the road, on finding the airport turnoff, steeling herself against her mother's constant stream of words. 'You mustn't move those two into our house while I'm away,' said Faith, her voice taut with anxiety. 'This is so hard for me, Sam. I can't have Mary taking over my home as well as my daughter.'

Sam's grip tightened on the wheel until her knuckles were white. Careful now. Faith would soon be in France. A long month away, breathing space for them both. 'Why would you think I'd do that, Mum?' she said. 'I never said anything about them moving in.'

'I've done my research. Charlene won't be able to return to that backwater with her mother, not for ages. They'll need ongoing treatment in the city, and they'll be looking for somewhere to stay. Don't tell me Mary Kelly can afford to pay for accommodation here in town?'

'I don't know if she can afford to or not. It's none of my business, and even less of yours.'

'As soon as they know I'm gone they'll work on you,' said Faith. 'That Mary is a gold-digger, you can see it a mile off. She'll try to take advantage, and with you so naïve ...' Faith shook her head in disgust.

'I wish you'd change your mind and come with me. We could take a later flight?'

'For the umpteenth time, Mum, I'm not coming.' Faith let out a great sigh.

Sam repeated the secret mantra beneath her breath – jabberwocky, jabberwocky, jabberwocky – a psychological ploy she used to trigger a calm response in the face of extreme provocation. 'You're right about Charlie not being able to go home. She needs to stay in Melbourne for a couple of months. But don't worry, the Leukaemia Foundation are putting her up in an apartment. Mary's already there.'

'She is?' asked Faith. 'You've seen it?'

Thank God. The airport was in sight. Not long now. 'Yes,' said Sam. 'I've seen it.'

'Where is it?'

'In East Melbourne somewhere.'

'What's it like?' asked Faith.

'Nice,' said Sam warily. 'Room for one patient and one carer. There's a rooftop gym, and a pool. Even an organic grocery store nearby.' She was about to say what a fan Mary was of organic produce, but bit her lip in time.

'Why on earth didn't you tell me? Don't I deserve to know anything?'

Past long-term parking, swinging around towards the international terminal. 'You get upset when I mention Mary,' said Sam. 'I didn't want to upset you.'

'Why?' demanded Faith.

'What a stupid question!' said Sam. 'I didn't want to upset you because I love you.'

'You do?' Faith's face softened and she reached a hand out to stroke Sam's arm.

'Yes, I do love you,' and then, under her breath, 'God knows why,' But Faith didn't hear. 'I'll see you off Mum, then I'm going out to the stables. It's been ages since I saw Pharaoh.'

For some reason, her mother seemed in a sudden hurry. 'No need, just let me out here.' Sam swung into the passenger drop off lane and helped Faith with her bags. 'I'll be fine,' said Faith, taking charge of her monogrammed Louis Vuitton luggage. 'Call you when I get to Mamie's — and have a lovely Christmas, darling.' Sam embraced her in a mighty hug, like the bear hugs she used to give when she was small. Faith's face lit up in a smile. 'You'll crush my suit,' she complained, but they both knew she didn't mean it. They both knew this was the very best possible note on which to say goodbye.

Sam watched her mother stride off on her ridiculous heels, holding her breath until Faith disappeared into the crowd. Sam tossed her keys in the air and caught them with a deft flourish. Finally she could start living her life, her way. She couldn't wait to tell Pharaoh.

'That horse?' said Brodie. 'That horse ain't here.'

'I can see that for myself.' She'd checked his stable, yard and all the private turn-out paddocks. No sign of Pharaoh. Sam waited in vain for an explanation. She'd have to spell it out. 'So, where is he?'

A slow, sleazy smile spread across Brodie's pinched features. 'Dunno, Miss. All I know is that horse is gone. Some bloke loaded it onto a float yesterday and took off. Ain't seen it since.'

'That's not possible.' Why was she wasting her time, talking to this creep? He probably couldn't tell one horse from another, and there were half a dozen chestnuts at the stables. Perhaps Pharaoh was in the wrong loose box? Sam turned to go.

'Sal says your mum sold that horse.'

Sam stopped short. She swung around, her stomach coiled in nasty knots. 'What did you say?'

Brodie's face creased into a malicious grin. 'Nothing.'

'You said Pharaoh's been sold.'

'Did I, Miss?'

He deserved a good slapping. Instead Sam sought out Sally, the stable manager. She was in the office, on the phone, a mug of coffee in hand. Her cheerful face fell when Sam came in. 'I have to go,' said Sally, ending the call in obvious haste. Her expression toughened. It looked like she was preparing for a fight. 'I'm sorry, Sam.'

So, it was true. 'Where he is?' Sam's voice broke with emotion, with rage and grief and disbelief.

'Pharaoh's gone to Andrew Wolf,' said Sally. 'He was most impressed with him. You should be proud.'

Sam wanted to scream, accuse, demand to know how Sally could have done it. How she could send Pharaoh away, cast him into the unknown, without Sam's affection and protection. How Sally could face work and phone calls and coffee, all the while knowing that this moment must come. The moment when she'd have to confess the terrible thing she'd done.

'Get me his number,' said Sam, her voice hard. Sally looked unsure for a moment, then handed Sam her phone. Sam scrolled through the numbers, found Andrew's and rang it. The conversation did not go well.

'Sold by mistake, you say? I don't think so. I have the signed transfer papers.'

'My mother signed those. She doesn't own Pharaoh. I do.'

'According to the papers,' said Andrew in an infuriatingly pompous tone, 'Faith Carmichael was the horse's registered owner. She told me about how you'd lost interest. It happens all the time,' he said, as if he understood everything. 'You girls discover boys and, well, horses take a back seat, don't they?' Sam tried to speak, but Andrew talked over her. 'Shame to see Pharaoh going to waste like that.' There was a long silence. Sam got the dreadful feeling that there was no point trying to defend herself against Faith's wicked allegations. 'Are you saying this isn't your mother's signature on the transfer?'

Sally sipped her coffee while Sam explained that Faith was Pharaoh's owner in name only. 'I haven't lost interest. That's ridiculous. I broke him in myself when I was fifteen, and I've been the only one ever to ride him.'

'That's not quite true,' said Sally in the background. 'Rachael worked him sometimes.'

Sam ignored her. 'Please, that horse is my life! You have to send him home. You just have to.' Her voice was a stammer. 'I didn't even get to say goodbye.' But it was no use. Andrew just kept repeating that

Faith had signed the transfer, rubbing it in again and again. Rubbing in her mother's wicked betrayal. Sam threw down the phone and fled. She had to talk to Charlie.

Charlie rewound her outlandish scarf, a colourful cane toad print this time. 'Mothers are like that,' she said, sagely. 'They rip out your heart one minute, and then expect you to keep right on loving them the next. If she's anything like my mum, she'll twist this around until it's all your fault.'

'Mary does that too?'

Charlie nodded, swung her legs off the bed and stood up. She still looked so frail. If only they could leave the damned hospital and go to a bar or something. Drown their sorrows, make a plan to get Pharaoh home. But it was clear from one glance that Charlie's recovery was going to be long and slow.

'Can't you just buy him back?' asked Charlie. 'Isn't your family loaded?'

'I've tried,' said Sam. 'The buyer won't budge. And anyway, there's a limit of ten thousand on my credit card. That's not nearly enough.'

Charlie whistled. The sound was surprisingly strong and melodious. 'How much is Pharaoh worth, then?'

'A lot more than that. It's ironic, isn't it? I spend all year training him, and now he's worth so much, I can't afford him.'

Charlie pulled a tissue from a frog-shaped box, gently lifted her sister's mask, and wiped the tears from her face. The gesture was as sweet as it was unexpected.

'I'm going to miss him so much.' Sam's words erupted in short gasps, like she'd been winded. 'He was all I'd ever wanted. How will I live without him?' Charlie murmured soft words of consolation, but her expression of sympathy only provoked in Sam a further flood of self-pity. 'There's nothing left,' she managed, between sobs. 'Dad's away, and he's always been too busy for me anyway. I don't have any proper friends. Except for Cate, and she's gone too. Pharaoh was it . . .

all I had. There's nothing left for me here in Melbourne. Nothing at all.'

Charlie reached out, stroked Sam's hair and shushed her. 'There are lots of horses back home in Currajong.' She said it in an odd tone, as if the remark was imbued with some secret significance.

Sam blew her nose behind her mask, a great honking blow. 'So?'

'So, you go home to Currajong for Christmas. Home to Brumby's Run.' Charlie slipped from bed and fetched a box from the cupboard. Beneath some action shots of Charlie campdrafting lay a battered stockman's hat. Charlie handed it to Sam. 'For you. My lucky Akubra. Try it on.' Sam did as she was asked, catching her reflection in the mirror. She looked just like the girl in the photographs. 'You already said that there's nothing for you here,' said Charlie. 'The house back home is empty, and the stock need checking. Mum asked Max to look in on the place, but he's a dodgy old bastard. You'd be doing me a favour.' Charlie pointed to the horse in the pictures. 'Tambo could use some TLC.' Sam took a long look at the photos.

'Well?' asked Charlie, with a broad smile. 'What do you say?'

Bill pushed aside the half-finished plate of bacon and eggs. 'Mary Kelly is a failed hippy, not a farmer. She's got no bloody idea.'

'Fair call,' said Drew, 'but why should her stock suffer for it?' He could feel the hot rush of blood to his temples, something that was happening all too often lately. 'We can't just let them starve.'

'They'll manage until the autumn break,' said Bill, with a dismissive wave of his hand. 'And anyway, what exactly do you propose that I do about it?'

'It's your fault in the first place,' said Drew angrily. 'You've leased every bit of good land she has for a song, pushed her cattle into that rocky top corner. That's mongrel country. Not enough grass up there for goats.'

'Nobody put a gun to Mary's head to make her sign that lease.' Bill gulped the last of his tea, and wiped his mouth with the back of his hand. 'If she's overstocked, that's her problem.' He stood up and stalked away, thereby declaring the subject closed.

Drew started to clear away the dishes. Mai, their housekeeper, appeared from the kitchen. 'I do that,' she said. He nodded. 'I decorate?' she asked. 'Mrs Chandler always have me decorate on Christmas Eve.'

Christmas Eve. If Mum was here the place would be groaning with ornaments and lights and the biggest cypress pine Bill could find. There'd be the smell of roasting pork and homemade plum pudding. Chocolates and lollies and bonbons. Extravagantly wrapped gifts spilling from under the fragrant tree. Melinda, Steph and Mum, arguing and giggling, a joyous confusion of perfumed hair, pretty clothes and flashing, Santa Claus earrings. His sisters could always make Dad smile. But Mum was spending Christmas in Sydney this year, with her new bloke and the girls. She'd asked Drew to join them, but he wouldn't leave Dad on his own. He was beginning to regret the decision. Without Mum's festive energy, the day would be just a poor copy of Christmas.

Drew looked at Mai's expectant face. 'Decorate if you want,' he said.

'No tree?' she asked.

'No, Mai,' he said, and grabbed his hat from a peg by the door. 'No tree.'

After breakfast, Drew finished bolting the new rails on the round yard, then he and Bess took a run into town. The day was stinking hot, the bitumen on the road already sticky. He picked up fuel and a few things at the produce store: oats, layer pellets, dog kibble. Lunchtime found him at the pub, asking questions.

'Mary Kelly?' said Kevin, behind the bar. He wore a hat sprouting Christmas reindeer antlers. They waved when he shook his head. 'Who knows where she is?'

'In jail?' suggested Harry, the town mechanic.

'Best place for her,' said a dour-looking man.

Drew sighed and ordered the mixed grill. Mary was unpopular amongst some of the older cattlemen, who judged any unmarried mother harshly. She'd been just a teenager when she inherited Brumby's Run following her father's early death. Jock Kelly had been a lazy drunk, who'd neglected his land. For years Jock's lower pastures had acted as a weed reservoir. They'd infected neighbouring properties with a flourishing cornucopia of invasive species, infestations that Mary in turn had also mainly ignored. Waterways choked with willow and Cape broom. Purple paddocks of Patterson's curse. Bridal creeper, blackberries and boxthorn. Horehound, periwinkle and ragwort. Brumby's Run seemed to spontaneously generate every noxious weed known to man.

The Department of Environment had issued Mary with a string of infringement notices, none of which she'd complied with. Fines accumulated, totalling thousands of dollars, but you had to hand it to Mary – she'd argued no capacity to pay, and requested that her fines be converted to community service in lieu. Mary never paid a cent. But she did establish a glorious herb garden for the old folks at the Tallangala nursing home. In desperation, neighbours slashed and sprayed Mary's paddocks themselves. Bill became the main catalyst for the intervention. By the time he'd finished, Brumby's Run was as clear of invasive weeds as his own Kilmarnock Station. The whole exercise had not won Mary any friends.

There was a long list of other grievances. Common boundary fences weren't maintained. Mary ran up accounts all over town, and came up with bizarre excuses not to pay. *A baby magpie has flown into my house, and I have to stay home to feed it. Or all names are put into a hat. If I pull out yours, you get paid. If not, I'm afraid you must stay in the hat until next week.* Drew's personal favourite was when Mary argued she suffered from multiple-personality disorder, and the contract for sale of goods had been made with a personality that she wouldn't be seeing for a while.

By contrast, the local alternative life-stylers loved Mary, and frequently sought her out for her encyclopaedic knowledge of herbal remedies. Even the odd station-owner's wife had been known to surreptitiously pay her a visit. Still, it was unlikely that Mary earned much money that way, and she certainly didn't make a living from beef. Drew couldn't remember the last time he'd seen a pen of Kelly cattle go through the sale yards. Whatever could have happened to her and Charlie?

Bess howled from the pub verandah. Drew wrapped up a burnt

sausage for her in a paper serviette that was covered in pictures of snowy pine trees and gold angels. 'Merry Christmas,' he said to nobody in particular, and finished his beer.

Outside, Bess swallowed the snag in one gulp. He secured her in the back of the ute, then headed out of town. It was time to get some answers.

The rusty wire gate of Brumby's Run hung off its hinge. Drew dragged it open, and drove up the rutted track to the house. A car was parked next to the house. Not Mary's car, but a late-model Volkswagen. It looked like a shiny blue Christmas beetle.

Drew parked the ute and lifted Bess down from the tray. Nose to ground, she trotted to the front door, scratched at it and disappeared inside.

'Hello,' said a girl's voice. 'You're a big girl. Where did you come from?'

It was Charlie's voice – and then again, it wasn't. Drew nudged his way inside. Charlie kneeled by the stove, hugging Bess tight. When she looked up, when she looked straight at him, he couldn't pick at first what was so different about her. Then it hit him. Everything . . . and nothing. Her hair was the same rich brown, with the same slight wave. Yet it was a shorter cut, layered and stylish; fashionable, even. Her figure boasted the same full breasts and slim waist, the same long legs. But her clothes were all wrong: tailored shirt, tapered pants, riding boots. Where were the worn jeans and faded T-shirt? One thing was certain, though. This new Charlie looked a million dollars.

'Where the bloody hell have you been?' Drew asked.

She looked uncertain, bewildered. Charlie was many things, but uncertain had never been one of them. 'You might have me confused with my sister,' she said in a hesitant voice. Her pretty mouth moved in an unusual way, rounding out each vowel with particular care, and clipping the consonants. It was Drew's turn for confusion. Charlie gave Bess one last hug and stood up. She extended a slim arm. 'I'm

Samantha.' Drew just stared, open-mouthed. She let her arm fall to her side. 'Charlie's sister. We're twins.'

'What are you playing at now, Charlie?' he said, shaking his head. 'Gone and got yourself a makeover?' He walked around her, nodding approval. 'It sure does suit you.'

'I'm not Charlie Kelly,' she said firmly and with great poise. 'My name is Samantha Carmichael.' A hesitation, like nerves had the better of her, then she flushed like a schoolgirl. It was absolutely charming. 'People call me Sam for short.'

This gorgeous girl might be the spitting image of Charlie, but she sure as hell didn't act like her. Argue with Charlie, and she was likely to jump on you like a wildcat. Drew shook his head. It was such an absurd story though. A pile of luggage lay on the kitchen floor. Expensive-looking luggage. Could she be telling the truth?

'Now that I've introduced myself,' said the girl, 'just who, exactly, might you be?'

She had perfectly even white teeth. Charlie had a little gap. Drew took off his hat and slapped at a fly on the table. 'You're fair dinkum,' he said at last.

She nodded. 'I'm fair dinkum.'

The phrase sounded foreign on her tongue. No doubt about it, this girl was not Charlie. 'Okay, I'll bite. Where is she?' Drew was intrigued, fascinated by this non-Charlie. So beautiful, so classy. He couldn't take his eyes off her. 'And where did you spring from?'

'My sister wants her whereabouts to remain confidential for the time being,' she said with preposterous formality. 'Her mother, Mary Kelly has expressed a similar wish.'

Drew raised his eyebrows, and moved closer to Sam. He looked furtively around, as if he thought someone might be listening, then leaned in close. 'They're in jail, aren't they?'

'Of course they're not! Now, would you please leave?' The girl who wasn't Charlie escaped out the door, marched past the house and started up the hill. Drew followed as if drawn on a string, with Bess bounding after.

Sam stopped by the closed gate of the dam paddock. She turned around and tossed her head, seeming surprised and annoyed all at once to see him there. They locked gaze. She had Charlie's eyes – eyes that burned right into you. 'Who are you?' she asked again.

'Apologies, m'lady.' Drew bowed low. 'Your neighbour, Andrew Douglas Chandler, at your service.' She scowled, but there was the hint of a smile behind it. 'You may call me Drew.'

She played along, and offered her hand. 'A pleasure, sir.' Drew kissed it instead of shaking it, noticing the manicured nails and smooth fingers. This was no Charlie. They turned at the sound of a piercing neigh. A bay horse with a white face cantered down the hill towards them.

'Tambo!' said Sam with a delighted smile. Drew looked at her quizzically. 'I recognise him from a photo Charlie showed me.' The horse skidded to a halt at the gate. 'He's so thin,' she gasped. It was true. His neck was skinny, like a snake. Each rib stood out in stark relief, and his rump was hollow and bony. 'The poor thing.' Sam took off her belt, put it round the horse's neck, and opened the gate. 'Come on, Tambo.' He snatched hungrily at the fresh grass outside the fence. Sam put her nose to him, breathing in his warm, equine smell, like it was an expensive perfume. Then with some urging, she persuaded Tambo to follow them back down to the house.

Sam turned him into the overgrown garden, rubbed his ears fondly, then fossicked around in the tumble-down hay shed. Drew trailed after her. Nothing but a few spoilt bales of coarse grass hay. She squealed as two big rats scuttled off, then kicked the mouldy hay and fixed Drew with those liquid amber eyes. 'Where can I find some fodder?'

'No worries,' said Drew. He whistled Bess, and lifted her into the tray of the ute. 'I'll rustle you up a few bales from home.'

'Are those oats?' asked Sam, spying the sacks in the back.

Drew nodded. He backed the ute up to the cavernous shed. 'Consider it a Christmas present.' He turfed a bag to the ground.

'Thank you,' she said, 'but won't the rats get it there?' Sam used a broken broom to dust off some forty-four gallon drums along the back wall. 'What about putting it in one of these?' Drew hopped out, heaved the heavy sack onto his broad shoulders, and deposited it into the nearest bin. He could feel her eyes upon him as his muscles strained with the load. 'Thanks,' she said. 'That's very generous of you.' He was a sucker for flattery, especially from a beautiful girl. 'I'll need some chaff too,' she said, '… and maybe linseed?'

'I'll see what I can do.' It gave him an excuse to come back, after all. 'You staying on for a bit, then?'

She nodded. 'For several weeks. I'll be running the farm.' He looked down at his boots, in an attempt to hide his amusement. She was too damned cute. 'Did I say something funny?' He shook his head. 'Is Brumby's Run not a farm? Or is the joke that I will be in charge?'

It was a bit of both, really. Why the hell couldn't he stop smiling? Maybe better to change the subject. 'There's never much in Mary's fridge at the best of times. How about I bring back some steaks, along with the chaff?' She considered the matter for the longest time. It annoyed him, how he was hanging on her decision.

'I'd like that,' she said at last, her eyes meeting his. He took off down the track, feeling like he'd won the lottery, and wondering why.

Sam watched Drew's utility spin its wheels, take off down the drive and disappear. She'd never met anyone like Drew Chandler before. He was good looking, no doubt about it. Tall and broad-shouldered with smiling green eyes and a square, determined jaw. There was a suggestion of lean muscle through his torso where it met his narrow hips. But it was more than that. His body would be the envy of any fake tanned Toorak gym junkie, yet he carried himself without a hint of vanity. Drew moved with natural animal grace, like a splendid wild colt, unconscious of his own beauty.

Sam turned back to face the house. No beauty there. It was nothing like she'd imagined. No pretty portico, no shuttered timber casements, no bullnose verandah. Just a tumble-down shack of weathered timber and rusted roofing iron. Torn fly screens flapped against dirty windows. Piles of junk lay strewn alongside the drive: wheel rims, rusty tools and rotting posts. Tambo picked his way around old fencing coils, snatching at tall grass growing through the wires. It was a depressing sight.

She went back inside and explored the house, still thinking of Drew. A tiny entrance hall, lined with chipboard shelves that overflowed with books. A tiny kitchen with a peeling linoleum floor, grimy walls and an ancient stove without a range hood. The filthy fireplace in the lounge room was clogged with ash. Sam opened the window wide, and screamed when a large black crow appeared from nowhere and landed on the sill. It only flapped off with the greatest reluctance when she shoved it with a worn out broom. She opened the fridge and gagged. It had been turned off, but left closed. The interior, together with a few items of unidentifiable food, was a mass of stinking green mould. Quickly she slammed the door shut, feeling the tingle of tears. What a dump. Her bags still lay in the corner of the room. She could still leave, if she wanted to. But maybe the bedrooms would be better.

She moved gingerly down the hall. The first room on the left must have been Charlie's. A single iron bed beneath the window. Bare mattress. Shabby wardrobe. A low timber-pattern laminate dressing table, with a cracked mirror and gold plastic handles. Sam thought of her own bedroom back in Melbourne, furnished in French provincial style to remind her of Mamie. Sheets of fine Irish linen. Goose down pillows in French lace slips graced the ornate lime-washed bed. Her lovely oaken armoire, carved with roses and boasting hammered brass handles. Her burnt-oak commode, of graceful serpentine design. On her walls, prints of roosters. She liked roosters.

Not as much as Charlie liked frogs, though. Her dusty bedroom was full of frogs: figurines, toys, pictures. And cowboys. Posters of nameless cowboys, brooding at the camera or riding bucking horses. She took a closer look. One image was particularly arresting: an Ashton Kutcher lookalike, astride an enormous bull in what looked like mid-flight. In the corner was an autograph. *To Chaz. Forever Spike xx.* The cowboy seemed to be, unaccountably, looking straight at the camera – posing for the shot instead of concentrating on his perilous ride. He seemed to be looking straight into her eyes.

Sam reread the dedication. Was this rodeo rider cowboy Charlie's boyfriend? She hadn't mentioned him, or Drew either. The only local Charlie had mentioned was an awful man named Bill, who owned Kilmarnock Station, the property next door. Apparently he'd bribed Mary to lease him most of Brumby's Run. Charlie was still furious about it. Said her mother didn't have a clue. Said it didn't leave them enough land for their own stock. The lease was due to expire, though. Charlie hoped that with Mary off in Melbourne, distracted, out of contact, they could get their land back. It was Sam's job to inform this Bill character that the current contract would not be renewed, and he'd need to muster his cattle off Brumby's Run by new year. Maybe Drew could give her some advice.

Sam dumped her bags in the next room along the corridor, clearly Mary's room, on the only bed that was made up, and went off to investigate the bathroom. It wasn't too bad, by comparison to the rest of the house. The toilet, however, was unusable. Was there an outside loo? There was, in an alcove off the back porch. Spiderwebs festooned the ceiling, and squares of newspaper hanging from a nail made a sorry excuse for toilet paper, but it was cleaner than the one inside.

She sat down, wary of creepy crawlies. When she pressed the flush button, nothing happened. Sam groaned. The toilet could wait. Her first priority was to clean that kitchen.

Heading back inside, she turned on the sink taps. Nothing. Great. Grabbing two large pots, she went outside and filled one from the galvanised-iron rainwater tank behind the house. The water teemed with mosquito larvae. Sam made a face and went back inside. She flicked a light switch. No electricity. She tried calling Charlie. No reception. What was she going to do? Sam thought for a moment, then rummaged around in the kitchen cupboards until she found a strainer. She took it outside and tried pouring the water through its fine wire mesh into an empty pot beneath. It worked. The strained water was free of wrigglers, a small victory. Back in the kitchen, she put the pots on the stove, and turned it on. It took a minute to confirm that nothing was happening. Of course not. The stove was electric. Determined to remain positive, she found a plug, emptied the pot into the sink, dusted off a bottle of detergent, and started washing dishes in cold water.

Through the cobwebbed window, the sun was sinking below the timbered ridge-line. It burnished the forest a dramatic red and gold. There was a special quality to the light up here in the mountains. The beauty and serenity of the scene buoyed Sam's spirits. It didn't matter that she'd forgone the comforts of her old life. In this untamed place she'd gained much more than she'd lost; she'd gained her freedom.

The crunch of wheels on gravel. Drew? She ran outside to see a twin-cab four-wheel drive. A substantial middle-aged man, with square shoulders, got out and started towards her, holding a document wallet. 'Where's your mother?' he asked in a terse voice. Sam remained silent. 'Never mind. Just make sure she signs these.' He handed her the wallet. Sam took it, still staring. This must be Bill. She should say who she was, but he was so stern, and her story so unlikely. She dreaded going through the absurd spiel all over again, so instead she just nodded. Bill seemed satisfied. 'I saw Bushy today. He's got a yarding of brumbies. Wants you to turn up eight o'clock sharp, Monday. Otherwise he'll get somebody else.' With that, he left.

Sam opened the folder. A lease for land, signed by William Chandler. Chandler. Drew's last name was Chandler. There was such a lot she didn't know about this place.

Sam and Drew sat out the back on kitchen chairs. It was almost dark, and a welcome breeze had chased away the oppressive heat of the day. Steaks sizzled on the barbecue. Drew cut slabs of white bread, and spread them thickly with butter. Faith didn't allow real butter in the house. Said it hardened your arteries and made you fat. Sam tried a piece of the bread. Delicious. Drew turned the steaks, his sleeves rolled up over muscled forearms, and handed Sam a can from the esky in the back of the ute. Beer.

'I'm not a huge fan of beer.' She handed it back. 'Do you have anything else?'

He cracked the can himself, and gave her an amused look, his white teeth bright in the dusk. 'Sorry, m'lady.' Then he lit the kerosene lamp and hung it from the clothesline. The white- hot mantle burned with unexpected brilliance.

'Thanks for all this,' she said.

He flashed that smile again. 'Keep the barbie until you've sorted out your power problems. At least you'll be able to cook.'

'Won't your father mind?'

Drew shot her a curious look. She pulled out the lease document from her bag and handed it over. He glanced at it, gave it back, and slipped the steaks onto odd plates she'd found in the kitchen – not her mother's fashionably mismatched antiques, but cheap ceramics, cracked and chipped.

'Mary won't sign the lease,' said Sam. 'Not this time.'

'Fair enough.' He slapped the meat between slices of buttered bread 'Sauce?'

'Who's Bushy?' Sam cut the fat off her steak and gave it to Bess.

'Town horse breaker,' he said, between mouthfuls. 'Works at the racecourse. Top bloke, is Bushy.' Drew certainly didn't waste words.

'Your dad told me to be there at eight o'clock sharp, Monday morning.'

'Dad thought you were Charlie?' She nodded. Drew whistled. 'Probably no point denying it. He'd have thought you were pulling some sort of scam.' Drew absentmindedly traced two fingers along the steel frame of his chair. Sam wondered how they would feel on her skin instead. 'Shame though. Your sister's been aching to get that job. It'll kill her to miss out.' He threw Bess some gristle. 'Tell you what,' he said. 'Why don't I ride over in the morning and give you a tour of Brumby's? You do ride, don't you?'

She nodded and told him about Pharaoh. Drew sat quietly as she spoke, his dark eyes gleaming in the kerosene light. She liked how he listened – really listened, nodding encouragement every now and then. 'He was sold by mistake,' she finished.

'Tough break.' He put a consoling hand on her arm. Every nerve of her skin felt exposed where he touched her. When he pulled his hand away, she wished he hadn't.

'Think I'll take you up on that beer after all,' she said.

After dinner, he helped pack up the few dishes, and handed her the kerosene lamp. 'Good night, Sam,' he said, drawing close. 'Will you be okay here, on your own? It's a tough way to spend Christmas Eve.'

She bit her lip, tempted to say, 'No, stay here with me.' But she barely knew him – and surely he had plans. Instead she said, 'Good night, Drew. Merry Christmas,' and watched his tail lights retreat down the hill, growing smaller and smaller until they vanished.

There was no moon, but stars shone large in the night sky, in a way they never did in Melbourne. Sam made her way through the dark house to Mary's room. She lay down and turned out the lamp. How odd, to curl up in the bed of her birth mother for the very first time. The pillow still smelt of rosemary and thyme.

Frogs croaked a loud chorus outside. For how many years had Charlie drifted off to this frog-song lullaby? Sam's heart ached with the shapeless loss of what she'd never known, and despite the beer buzz it took a long time for sleep to come. When she finally closed her eyes, Drew's face and the sound of his voice stayed with her. This was going to be a most unusual Christmas.

Drew chained Bess up by the back door. 'Bit far for you, old girl.' He fondled her ears and offered a lamb shank. The dog whined and gave the bone a half-hearted lick. Poor compensation for missing a day out on the range.

They'd made a perfunctory exchange of gifts that morning – him, Mai and Dad. It was a dismal scene. Mai had escaped afterwards to spend the day with relatives in Wodonga. Bill was off to Christmas lunch at neighbouring Brigalow Station. He'd expected Drew to tag along. 'It's a fine thing,' Bill grumbled, 'when your own children can't be bothered with you on Christmas.' Drew had excused himself from the breakfast table, his appetite suddenly gone.

Sam was towelling her hair dry by the water tank when he arrived, Tambo by her side. Singlet top, denim shorts showing off long, shapely legs. Pale legs. Her complexion was like alabaster, her arms, her graceful neck. All white. Drew tried to recall Charlie's nut-brown tan, and failed. Even Sam's voice didn't sound so different this morning. He was getting used to this gorgeous new Charlie. 'Merry Christmas,' said Drew, swinging down from the saddle. Well, well, well - very nice. She'd lit right up at the sight of him.

'Merry Christmas!' Sam came running and hurried straight past him. It seemed his horse was the attraction. 'What's her name?' she asked, stroking the red-roan mare's nose.

'Chiquita.'

Sam ran her hand appreciatively down her shoulder. 'Quarter horse?'

Drew nodded. 'Dad's a fan.' He combed a burr from Chiquita's chestnut mane with his fingers. 'I don't go along with him there. Give me an Aussie stock horse every time.' The mare stamped her foot, as if in disagreement. 'Charlie used to back me on this one. To hear her tell it, riding quarter horses was tantamount to treason. Un-Australian, she used to say.'

Sam gave him a strange look. 'Charlie's not dead.'

'So you said.'

'Then perhaps you could stop referring to her in the past tense.'

'Did I?' He tied Chiquita to the fence. 'Have you had breakfast?'

'I didn't feel like stale Froot Loops without milk,' she said. 'You?'

'I had a dingo's breakfast.'

'What's that?' she asked.

'A yawn, a piss and a good look around.' Sam made a face at him as an impatient Tambo shoved her in the back with his nose. 'He's keen to get going,' said Drew. 'Been shut up in that dustbowl of a paddock for too long.'

Sam looked doubtfully at the gelding's scrawny frame. 'Do you think he's up to it?'

'My oath,' said Drew. 'A brumby like him will run all day on a sniff of feed.'

'He's not shod.'

'His feet are neat and hard. He won't be needing shoes – not out here in the bush.'

Sam looked doubtful. 'If you say so,' she said. 'Give me a minute to change.'

'Righto.'

Ten minutes later she emerged looking like a magazine model, wearing jodhpurs, an ivory shirt, gleaming boots, and carrying a stock saddle. Drew whistled in admiration. She sure was something to see.

Beneath the hint of a blush she looked a little lost. 'I found this inside.' She heaved the saddle onto a rail. 'Is it Tambo's? Will it do, Drew, do you think?'

He nodded, liking the way his name sounded on her tongue. 'Want some help?' She had the surcingle back to front, and the breastplate upside down. 'Thought you knew about horses,' he teased. 'Or do you just dress the part?'

Sam put her hands on her hips. 'I've never used this kind of saddle. I use a straight-flapped dressage one back home.' She frowned. 'Or at least I used to, when I still had a horse to ride.'

Drew came over, deftly fitted the surcingle and breastplate, then slapped the pommel. 'This here's a handmade Tony Gifford Jubilee Poley,' he said. 'Specially made for campdrafting. The flap's shorter than usual, cut a little more forward. You can shorten up your stirrups and get your leg right on the horse.' He pointed to the kneepad. 'See this angle? Your thigh fits snugly, but you can still get up out of the saddle. Charlie won this little beauty at the King of the Mountains festival last year. It's the town's annual big bash.'

'I'm very honoured to use it, then.' She pulled a black riding helmet from a bag at her feet. Jesus. She'd cop a serve if anybody around here saw her wearing that. Still, she might need it. Tambo had a cold back. Sam strapped on the helmet and mounted. The horse took off, pigrooting down the driveway. She rode well, sitting out the half-hearted bucking display with ease.

Drew swung into the saddle and they headed up the hill at a brisk canter. When they came to the dam paddock, Drew reined his horse in. 'Tambo's a champion at opening gates. Just push him forward, use your legs.' Sam did as he said, leant forward and unlatched the gate. 'Now back up, swing his quarters around. No, hang onto the gate. Back up again, and there, you're done.' Sam's horse stood facing him on the other side of the closed gate.

Sam grinned. 'Tambo just executed a perfect turn on the forehand.'

'A what?'

'A turn on the forehand. The basis of all lateral work in dressage. The horse's inside leg steps under his body. It encourages correct engagement.'

'What, like this?' Drew moved Chiquita up to the gate, performed the same deft manoeuvre, and joined Sam on the other side.

'Just like that,' said Sam, smiling. 'Charlie warned me that Tambo would seem green compared to the horses I'm used to.' She leant forward and patted his neck. 'I must remember to tell her it's not true.' They started up the hill, walking fast on a loose rein, without breaking into a jog. 'You know what we're doing now?'

'As far as I can tell, nothing,' said Drew.

'We're doing an extended walk. *The horse covers as much ground as possible without haste, and without losing the regularity of his steps,*' she recited. '*The rider allows the horse to stretch out his head and neck without losing contact with the mouth.*'

'Tambo's a good walker, I'll give you that,' said Drew, mystified, 'but we're still just bloody walking.'

'There's walking, and then there's walking,' said Sam. 'Look.' She turned around, and pointed to their hoof prints in the dusty track. 'In the extended walk, the hind feet touch the ground clearly in front of the footprints of the forefeet.' He nodded. It was as she said. Sam forged on uphill, a smug smile on her face. Lesson one. With this girl, straightforward things could quickly get complicated. It certainly made things interesting.

The sun rose ever higher into a sky of flawless blue. Drew and Sam followed the winding creek upstream. Grassy clearings opened up around each bend. Three grey kangaroos stood like statues, before bounding away at the riders' approach. Sam cantered forward, then lost them in the forest of peppermint gums.

'Did you see that?'

'Roos,' said Drew. 'So what?' A small mob of fat Herefords, red and white, calves and cows, raised their heads from the tall grass, then trotted away from the riders. Tambo pricked up his ears and sidled sideways, impatient with the bit.

'They're just how I imagined them,' said Sam. 'I thought you said Brumby's Run was short of feed?'

'Those cows are in good nick, I'll give you that,' said Drew. He swatted a stinging fly from his arm. 'Trouble is, they're not yours. They're Dad's. He leases these creek flats. It'll be a different story higher up.'

The track led upwards through a ragged thicket of tea-tree to a rusted gate. In sharp contrast to the lush country they'd just ridden through, the land beyond the gate was starved-looking land, bare of grass. Grey clay showed between patches of woody scrub. Even unpalatable stringybarks told the tale of hungry stock – their trunks chewed and ragged, some ringbarked completely.

A sorry herd of black baldies picked their way across the barren hillside. The rotting carcasses of a cow and calf stank out the air. Drew frowned. He trotted up the hill to take a closer look at the herd. The cattle were no more than skin and bone.

'They're starving,' said Sam, staring open-mouthed at the walking skeletons.

Drew sized up the herd. 'Get behind them,' he said. 'We're going to push the mob further up the hill.'

Sam did as he asked, a distressed look on her face, and the herd made its faltering way towards the ridge top. It was painful to watch. Drew rested them frequently, allowing the weakened cattle time to catch their breaths. It was more than an hour before they saw the northern boundary fence — the fence that separated Kelly land from Balleroo National Park. In stark contrast to Brumby's Run, the park boasted sunburned seed heads, swaying above a carpet of summer pasture. A bare strip ran the length of the fence, where famished stock had pushed their heads through, wrapping hungry tongues around each precious leaf or blade of grass within reach. It was a sorry sight.

Drew swung forward at a canter, scouting the boundary, searching for something. There, by that patch of black cypress pine – a crude bush gate, just wire and droppers, fastened to a tree with baling twine.

Drew slashed the hay band, dragged the gate wide and urged Sam to help press the stock through. The starving animals rushed the opening, bellowing low, propping a few metres into the park and snatching at the grass with desperate urgency.

'Won't they run away?' asked Sam.

'Run?' Drew snorted. 'Take a look at them.' They sat on their horses and watched the cows for a while. 'We'll move them to your lower paddocks once Dad gets his cattle out. In the meantime, they could use a good feed, don't you think?' Sam nodded, open-mouthed, still staring at the skeletal beasts. 'Come on,' said Drew. 'Let's pick up the rest of them.'

That morning Sam got a crash course in mustering. She was a dead-set natural. Of course, it helped that she was riding a top stock horse. Tambo could have just about done the job on his own. But not all the cattle were as poor as that first lot, and more than once Drew wished he'd brought a stockwhip. His dad said riding out without your whip was as bad as riding out without your pants. One mob of lively steers really gave them a run for their money. Tambo may have been thin, but he was keen as mustard, eagerly running down each breaking beast, swinging it hard back to the herd. At first Sam sat straight in her saddle, glued to it, body swaying in graceful time with Tambo's props and turns. Sexy? Yes. Gorgeous? Undoubtedly, but perhaps not the best seat for running rough stock through the bush.

Drew reined left, gathered a cow and young calf from their tea-tree hide, and steered them towards the herd. Sam galloped Tambo across the facing gully. That was better. Her legs had slid forward into traditional stockman position. Lying flat over Tambo's wither, she drew level with a beast and expertly shouldered it back into the mob, like she'd done it all her life – just as Charlie would have done.

He cantered over. 'We'll make a cowgirl out of you yet.'

Sam's face shone with excitement and triumph. She leaned over and stroked the horse's neck. Her breasts swung down a fraction, changing the contours of her buttoned shirt in a fascinating way, sending a shiver of desire right through him. Watch it, boy, he told himself.

'It was all Tambo,' she said, but he could tell she didn't mean it. There was pride behind her words, a small conceit. He nodded approval and urged his mare after the mob, guiding them uphill towards a second gate in the boundary fence.

By noon, maybe fifty cows and calves were feasting on the national park side of the fence. It was good to see the hungry cattle filling their bellies, but there were so few of them. How many were there meant to be? Whatever the number, they'd been left to fend for themselves for far too long. Guilt made him shift uneasily in the saddle. How could he have known that the Kellys would just take off like that, without a word of where they were going or when they'd be back? He watched Sam follow an inquisitive calf up the faint, rocky track. She knew where her sister was – knew, but for some reason wasn't telling. It was most mysterious.

Drew trotted after Sam. 'Come on,' he called. 'I want to show you something.' He took the lead, winding his way through the stringy-bark and tea-tree, pushing his mare up the stony slope. The muffled thud of Tambo's unshod hoofs sounded close behind him. The approaching horses flushed out a bold daytime fox, sleek and fat as butter. It darted downhill.

'Foxes and dingoes will be having a field day,' said Drew. 'There's good pickings for scavengers at Brumby's.' He reined Chiquita in, regretting his words as soon as they were uttered. The path widened, and the horses walked two abreast. Sam didn't look at him, staring straight ahead between Tambo's pricked ears. 'I'll tell you something you don't know about foxes,' he said.

'How about I tell you something you don't know about them instead?' said Sam. 'Where are there more foxes, do you think? Per square kilometre, I mean. Here? Or in Melbourne?'

'Here,' he said. 'They're bloody everywhere. What would a self-respecting fox be doing in town anyway?'

'Wrong. Urban environments are full of garbage. Highly beneficial for foxes. Towns support population densities up to ten times greater than rural areas.'

'Is that so?' said Drew. 'Well, since you're such an expert, perhaps you can explain this. Out bush a while back, I saw this pretty little vixen tearing bark off a tree with her teeth. Should have shot her, I suppose, but instead I just watched, quiet like, so as not to scare her. She carried a mouthful of bark down to the creek, and backed into the water, until all I could see was her black nose, and the strips of bark between her teeth. She stayed stock still for a few minutes, then dropped the bark and let it drift off downstream. Jumping back onto the bank, she gave herself a bit of a shake and trotted off, happy as Larry.'

'That's the strangest thing,' said Sam. 'I can't imagine why a fox would behave in such an odd way.'

'Thought a smart girl like you could figure something like that out.'

She cracked a smile, the kind that set a bloke dreaming. 'Do *you* know?'

Drew nodded. 'That little fox was getting rid of fleas. See, as she backs into the creek, they jump forward, to get out of the water. Eventually they all jump onto the piece of bark between her teeth, and she lets it float off, so the fleas get a chance for a bit of white-water rafting.'

'No.' Sam laughed. 'I don't believe that for a minute.'

Drew tipped his hat. 'True story.' Then he cantered off, with Sam chasing close behind.

Their path intersected with the old stock route used in years gone by to bring the mountain cattle home. Almost there. An ancient hut appeared through a curtain of gum leaves. It had a rusted tin roof, corrugated-iron rainwater tank, a crumbling chimney at one end, and a rough porch at the other. 'Dead Man's Hut,' said Drew. A creek bubbled from beneath rocks nearby, spilling past the ramshackle building into a chain of clear pools.

Sam and Drew tethered their horses to a rail of the bush timber yard. Sam loosened Tambo's girth, then pulled the saddle off altogether. 'It's hot,' she said. 'Might take him for a swim.'

Now that was a tantalising prospect. Sam sat down on a split log bench near the door. Drew hesitated for just a moment before unsaddling his own horse. How could he resist? He pulled a water bottle from the saddlebag and sat down close beside her.

'Drink?' She took a swig. Water trickled down her neck and delicate cleavage. His groin ached at the brief pressure of her thigh against his.

'Why is it called Dead Man's Hut?' she asked.

'You don't want to know.'

'Looks like it's straight out of *The Man From Snowy River* movie,' said Sam, in a delighted voice. 'And I'm Jessica Harrison.' She ran her fingers along the warm grain of the timber seat. 'I'm rebellious and reckless.' And sexy and gorgeous, thought Drew. Don't forget gorgeous. He had a mind to say it out loud.

Sam stood up and struggled with the rusty lock. Drew pressed close to her warm body, reached around, pulled back the bolt and pushed the door open. Inside was a rickety bunk with worn horsehair mattresses, a dusty table and a blackened fire-place. A bridle, green with age, hung on a nail, and a few rusted tins of bully beef stood along a splintered plank shelf.

'It's charming,' said Sam.

Drew saw nothing charming about the gloomy interior. He saw only isolation and loneliness.

'Imagine living up here, waking up to that.' Sam pointed down the valley, past the ridge of candlebark and wattle, to the rolling hills below. A glittering stream meandered through the river flats in great loops. The sun caught it, transforming the winding watercourse into a chain of shining, silver crescents. 'Well?' asked Sam.

'It's nice,' he admitted, feeling foolish. It wasn't his custom to reflect on the scenery.

'Nice?' scoffed Sam. 'It's more than nice. It's stunning!' She heaved a great sigh. 'You're so lucky to live here.'

Lucky? This place was home, and he loved it, but he'd never thought of himself as lucky to be here. Quite the contrary. It was duty that bound him to these mountains. His two older sisters were long gone, drawn to Sydney like moths to lamps, building careers, hunting for husbands, escaping the tyranny of their critical father. Even his mother was gone. Last year when Mum left to visit her plugged-in Sydney daughters, she'd never come back. A long-distance divorce, and his father hadn't seemed to flinch.

And him? Well, his heart wasn't in the cattle business. Horses were his passion, especially Australian stock horses; a beautiful breed of tough, intelligent animals exemplified by the Walers – station-bred horses turned war horses, renowned as the finest cavalry mounts in the world. Drew's dream was to build up a quality herd of studbook mares, purchase a stallion or two with Abbey heritage and found his own line of stock horses. A line with particular emphasis on temperament, to suit a wide range of riders, of varying abilities. He wanted to run treks into the spectacular high country, showcasing the versatility and kind nature of his horses. Drew had saved up to buy Clancy as a colt for just such a purpose – the foundation stallion for his future herd.

Bill, however, had no patience for his son's dreams. *Kilmarnock is a cattle station, always has been and always will be*, he'd said.

Drew came home one day to find Clancy gelded.

I won't have any ill-bred stallion running around, harassing my mares. And that was that. Things at home would be run Bill's way, or no way at all. Plenty of times Drew had wanted to chuck it in. Station hands talked about the money to be made in the mines out west. But paternal expectation is a powerful thing, and Drew was the only son . . . There was just so much a man could take though, and Drew's patience was wearing thin.

Sam removed her helmet, looked at him and smiled. 'Don't you ever take off that cowboy hat?'

He shrugged one shoulder. Truth was, he rarely did. 'It's not a cowboy hat. It's a stockman's hat.' His dad was the cowboy hat fan. Big and black, ten-gallon style with a high crown, pencil-rolled brim and studded, buckled band.

'It looks like a cowboy hat to me.' Sam reached up, snatched it from his head and tossed it onto the grass. She laughed and crouched down to retrieve it, dark hair parting at the nape. He wanted to kiss the pale skin of her neck.

'How pretty.' She picked up the curled crescent of a gum leaf. A small green frog sat in its centre, no more than three centimetres long. Contrasting black stripes extended from its nostrils, right over its eyes and head like a costume mask. Its back was striped a stylish emerald and brown. Tiny discs decorated its digits and webbed toes. Sam jumped as a surprisingly loud series of low whistling notes burst from the tiny amphibian. 'Do you know what species it is?'

'Of course.' Drew leaned in close for a better look, close enough to feel the light heat of Sam's body, and to catch a scent of her perfume; strange and exotic and marvellous. 'It's a species of frog.'

Sam laughed. 'I bet Charlie would know.'

'I bet she would, at that.' It had been the first mention of Charlie for a while. 'Do you have a boyfriend?' asked Drew suddenly. 'Back in ... back in wherever you come from?'

She met his gaze. 'No.' Her reply came swift, bold and unequivocal

Hallelujah. 'Come on.' He took hold of Sam's right hand, helping her to her feet. 'Your sister would never forgive us if we let anything happen to that frog.' He didn't let go of her hand as he led her to the ferny creek behind the hut. Truth was, he didn't want to ever let it go.

'Goodbye, Mr Frog,' said Sam, setting it free. The little creature launched itself into a pool, paddled away to a clump of reeds, and sat watching them.

'You're left-handed,' said Drew. 'Like Charlie.'

'Of course,' said Sam. 'We're identical – physically, anyway.'

It was just too intriguing. She looked at him with those tawny eyes of hers, like tiger eyes, and the desire to touch her overwhelmed his caution. On an impulse he spread his arms in invitation, and willed her to him. It worked. She moved into his embrace like it was the most natural thing in the world, her body soft and warm in his arms. He folded her in, lowering his head to her lovely mouth for a kiss. But her response was stiff, uncertain. Resistant. Then it dawned. Perhaps she hadn't done this before? After all, this girl was no Charlie. She had class. You wouldn't find her behind the chutes at a rodeo, beneath some hotshot bull rider. His kiss turned from ardent and probing, to tentative and tender. He drew back and Sam pressed in against him, her eyes locked on his.

'I've never met anybody like you before,' he said softly.

'Of course you have,' Sam said, smiling. 'What about my sister?'

Drew shook his head. 'Charlie's not like you. She's feral – crazy even.'

Sam pulled away and gave him a penetrating look. 'She doesn't seem crazy to me.'

'Well, she is – and she likes rodeo cowboys way too much.' Why were they talking about Charlie? He wanted to talk about Sam. 'Why didn't she ever mention you?'

'I don't know,' said Sam. 'Why didn't she ever mention you?'

'She didn't?'

'No. But she mentioned your dad. He's a complete bastard, apparently.'

Chiquita whinnied loudly. Drew and Sam looked around to where she and Tambo were tethered beside the yard. The roan mare stood at attention, head high, ears pricked towards the gully. It was then they heard it. A close, trumpeting neigh. Chiquita shivered in her skin, pawed the ground and raised her tail.

A buckskin horse emerged from the stringybark trees. He marched with arched neck and a bold, high-stepping gait, right up to the restive mare. Could it be Jarrang? Chiquita reared and squealed; the high, insistent squeal of a mare in season. Drew leapt up and darted for her head. Too late.

The brumby stallion laid his ears flat back as Chiquita's reins snapped. His head snaked to her flank, biting hard. Drew yelled and tried to force himself between the horses. The buckskin lunged straight at him, all bared teeth, slashing hoofs and wild, rolling eyes. The bugger. Drew ducked beneath the rail, and watched as the stallion half drove, half cajoled his mare across the clearing. The pair disappeared at a gallop into the trees. Tambo neighed and danced at the end of his reins.

'Damn!' Drew glanced at Sam, standing wide-eyed by the yard. Then he swung bareback onto Tambo, and took off after Chiquita.

The horses headed straight up the hill. The buckskin knew what he was doing. He kept to the trees, staying between Drew and the mare, lashing out with both hind feet whenever Drew came too close. It was all Drew could do to keep pace with him. When they reached the ridge's rocky spine, Chiquita faltered. It was a precipitous place, and treacherous underfoot. She swung back around into the open. Drew rode at right angles to intercept her, pushing Tambo into her shoulder and grabbing her trailing reins. The buckskin wheeled, but Drew had hold of her now. He spun Tambo around, drew his horses to a halt and faced the stallion. Drew was certain of it now. This was Jarrang, Charlie's orphan foal, all grown up.

Jarrang retreated in a series of small, defiant rears, right back to the escarpment. Tambo and Chiquita stood with heaving sides, but the brumby stallion seemed unfazed by the uphill gallop. He'd matured into a striking horse, about fifteen hands, with the deep chest, short back and good length of rein so typical of early Walers. The type of horse that might even impress Drew's father – if his father didn't know Jarrang was a brumby, that was. What Drew needed was a rope. Jarrang reared again and boxed the air, as if reading Drew's mind. Drew leaned down to stroke Chiquita's damp neck. 'Come on, girl. Let's get you home.'

They turned to go. The buckskin screamed with anger. In a surprise move he thundered back and shot past so close that Drew could have touched him. Startled, Chiquita rose high on hind legs, and Drew impulsively wound her reins around his hand. Bad move. Tambo leapt forward. Chiquita hung back and wrenched Drew to the ground. Even then he didn't drop the reins, but Jarrang was determined to have his mare. He galloped straight for Drew, ears flattened, forcing him to dive for cover. Swiftly the stallion urged Chiquita on, nipping at her wither. With a dreadful, sinking feeling, Drew watched the horses scramble up the scree and vanish behind a rocky overhang.

For a moment he feared he'd lose Tambo as well, but the bay seemed to understand the stallion would not welcome his company.

He stopped short at the base of the stony slope and played hard to get for a few precious minutes, before allowing Drew to mount. There was no point giving chase. Those horses were long gone. Drew spat on the ground in disgust, and headed back to the hut. His dad would be furious. Merry Christmas, indeed.

Eight o'clock, Monday morning. 'So, you're Charlie.'

Sam nodded uncertainly, as if she didn't believe it herself. Don't say a word. Her voice would give her away more than anything. She'd been practising talking like Charlie – trying to speak from the back of her tongue and limiting lip movement a little. And she needed to speed up her speech, and run the words together a bit more. It was like giving herself elocution lessons in reverse. Thank goodness Bushy didn't seem to expect her to talk.

Sam had never met an Aboriginal person before. Bushy wore a funny, old fashioned hat – an iron-grey fedora, like Indiana Jones might wear – along with moleskin trousers, an ancient tweed jacket and a black tie. Quite an eccentric look.

He extended his hand and she shook it, limp-wristed, willing her own hand not to shake. His grasp was firm and Sam wished she'd applied more pressure. Bushy scrutinised her, hawk eyes peering from a weathered, leather-skinned face. As with an old saddle, it was impossible to guess his age. Fifty? Seventy?

'You're a bit pasty for a country girl,' he said. There was no answer to that. This was never going to work. Why on earth had she thought she might pass for her sister? 'You've a way with horses though,' he said. 'That's what they say.' Bushy gestured for her to follow him. 'We'll soon see if it's true.'

In the corner of the showgrounds stood a stockyard, and in the corner of the stockyard stood a frightened palomino colt with a flame-shaped star. His eyes were wary, his head held high, forefeet balanced in readiness to flee left or right as circumstance demanded. 'There's a little brumby for you,' said Bushy. 'Straight off the mountain. Passive trapped, so he's not been hurt.' He picked up a rope, and they climbed through the rails into the yard. 'That colt is as frightened as you'd be if you were stuck in a room with some fella from outer space. That fella might be friendly, or he might want to have you for supper.'

Sam jumped as a noose snaked out from Bushy's hands and landed neatly over the horse's head. The colt screamed and reared, battling the pull on his neck. 'Leave it loose to start with. Prove you mean no harm.' Bushy handed Sam the rope. 'I want you to halter-break that brumby.' He took a pouch of tobacco and papers from his pocket, and proceeded to roll a smoke. 'You've got half an hour. Do that, and the job's yours – and you get to name the colt.'

Sam felt sick. She'd be exposed for the fraud she was. But before giving up she considered her task. Hadn't she broken in Pharaoh herself? However there'd been a team of trainers on call, and he'd arrived at the stables as a well-behaved youngster, with perfect ground manners. A far cry from this wild, fearful creature. Still, the basic principles were the same, and she was wearing Charlie's lucky hat to boot. How difficult could it be? Sam cautiously shortened the rope. She'd never used a rope on a horse before, but the stiff noose held its shape, and the large leather eye seemed designed to prevent choking. The palomino fought against the slightest pressure. Sam kept up a firm, light contact, letting the stout rails do the work of containment for her. Dust choked her throat and her pulse was racing. The line lightly slipped and slid along the horse's flanks and over his rump as he twisted and turned. After a minute or two he seized upon a new way to escape his captor, plunging round and round the yard with wide, rolling eyes, searching the rails for any weakness. But no matter how he tried, he couldn't evade Sam's quiet touch. His first terror gone, the colt lowered his head and turned to face her.

'Good,' called Bushy from outside the yard. 'You're halfway there.'

Sam spat the dirt from her mouth and checked her watch. She'd better be. Only fifteen minutes left. Sam controlled her anxiety, allowing the golden colt to settle down, to appreciate that the rope around his neck was no threat. What now? She played it by ear, swinging the rope softly, slow and rhythmic, so it brushed his muzzle, his cheek, then up to his ear. He flinched, but didn't move, watching her. She crooned a sing-song stream of reassuring words. 'There's a boy, stand up, I just want to pat you.'

'Pat him?' yelled Bushy from the side. He roared with laughter. 'That's a new one.'

Sam ignored him. She forgot about the time. Each nerve tingled in tempo with the palomino's racing heart. She steadied her breathing, and the colt steadied his. Then he relaxed his jaw and yawned. Sam smiled and moved right up to his shoulder, crooning all the while, unable to believe her luck. He examined her with his velvet muzzle, taking her in, the taste and smell of her. She looped the rope into a rough halter and slipped it over his nose, stroking his shivering neck all the while.

'You still gotta lead him,' called Bushy.

Sam backed up, in line with the colt's forefeet, and flicked the rope end. He moved smartly around the yard at a trot. Sam relaxed her body and the brumby dropped back to a walk. With infinite patience Sam approached his shoulder, coiling the rope as she went, keeping pace with him. Soon she had the colt following her around the perimeter of the yard, just as calm as could be.

She glanced up at Bushy, heart banging with pride. He nodded. 'You'll do. Turn him loose.'

Sam punched the air, letting out a whoop of excitement. The brumby reared, causing the halter to tighten on his nose. He thrashed violently from side to side. Sam dropped the rope and ran for the rails. Bushy slipped into the yard, picked up the line and urged the horse into a canter. When he slackened the rope, the colt turned to face him, and Bushy released him with one expert flick of his wrist.

'It's wise not to get ahead of yourself with any horse,' he said, chuckling. 'Especially a wild brumby.'

'Do I still get the job?' asked Sam, breathless.

Bushy took an extra long look at her, as if he was contemplating a difficult question. 'You do,' he said at last. 'Come back after lunch.' The palomino pranced and neighed. 'You got a name for him?'

'Phoenix,' she said without hesitation. 'I'll call him Phoenix.'

Sam climbed up on the rails, and watched the young brumby buck his way around the yard. 'It's a new start for us both,' she whispered.

Sam sat in her car and tried calling Charlie again. Her phone had been dropping out badly ever since she'd arrived. Maybe there'd be better reception out here at the showgrounds. Even when she did manage to get through, all calls went through the hospital switch-board. A conspiracy of nurses seemed determined to thwart any attempt to talk to Charlie. Her sister was either asleep, or having tests, or having showers or having lunch. Didn't they realise these calls were important? Charlie must be going insane, wondering how things were going. 'One moment please,' said a voice, and then, miracle of miracles, she was through.

'Sam?' Charlie sounded excited, and much stronger than Sam remembered. 'Tell me absolutely everything.'

Sam launched into a report of her four days so far at Brumby's Run, guided by Charlie's enthusiastic inquisition. But an odd thing was happening. As she told her story, she found herself editing the account in little ways. Or maybe they weren't so little. Bill, for instance. He'd mistaken her for Charlie and she'd let the impression stand. How could she explain that? How could she convey, on a shaky phone line, how difficult it was to swear that you weren't who somebody assumed you were? But she hadn't deliberately misled Bill – not like she'd done with Bushy. When Sam got to that part, she told Charlie that she'd taken the job with Bushy in order to hold it for her when she came home. This was true, after all. Totally true . . . and Charlie had been thrilled to hear it. Any misunderstandings could be cleared up later. And then there was Drew. She mentioned how helpful he'd been – but not the toe-curling kiss they'd shared. She tried to talk casually about him, sure Charlie would be able to see through her nonchalance. But her sister was caught up in her own problems.

'Remember, don't tell anybody I'm sick,' said Charlie. 'They feel sorry enough for me around Currajong already. You should hear them. Poor little Charlie, having a mother like that. A drunk. A druggie. Running around with all those men. No wonder she turned out like she did. Sanctimonious jerks. I couldn't stand any more pity! And anyway, Bushy might think I won't be up for the job.'

'Don't worry,' said Sam, feeling faint. 'Nobody knows.'

'What about Drew? What have you told him?'

'That you're away on confidential business,' said Sam. Charlie thought that was funny. She laughed, loud and strong. There was something about the laugh that Sam hadn't heard before, a disturbing quality. It took her a while to pick it. Charlie's laugh was sounding too much like her own.

'He must be mad with curiosity,' said Charlie finally, a note of immense satisfaction in her voice.

Now it was Sam's turn to ask questions. It turned out that her sister's recovery was proceeding beautifully. She'd be home in a couple of months, touch wood. 'You've saved my life, you know that?' said Charlie, just before the line dropped out for good.

Sam went over the conversation in her head. Her gaze wandered to the imposing blue peaks of the Balleroo Range, to the clear azure sky, to the beautiful brumby dancing in the stockyard. A satin bowerbird, in splendid blue-black plumage, swooped on spilled oats outside Bushy's feed shed. Its odd creaking cry sounded like the opening of a long locked door. 'No, Charlie,' said Sam, as she started the car. 'I think it's you who's saved mine.'

CHAPTER 14

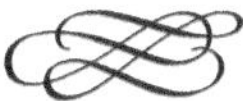

Bill tossed the last hay bale down. Drew fielded it and stacked it on the tray of the truck. Monday afternoon, and he still hadn't told his father they were losing the lease for Brumby's Run. The opportunity was staring at him over breakfast. Bill had been on the phone to Tom about stocking rates for next year, but Drew hadn't mustered up the courage. What was worse, his father was talking about buying in more cattle.

'I want you to inspect those Benambra weaners for me next week,' Bill said as he dusted off his hands. 'Make sure they bring in the bloody lot, so they can't hide the tail.' The *tail* was the inevitable percentage of poorer calves in any yarding. Bill had been caught out last year, buying a motley, weedy mob based on an unrepresentative sample of yarded stock. It was Drew who'd warned Bill against them, so there was a certain irony in Bill's words of caution. 'And don't act too keen. Buying paddock mobs is like playing poker, and you've never been much good at poker.' Bill walked away whistling, looking pleased with himself.

'Yeah, yeah,' muttered Drew to himself. Gloom gathered over him like his own, personal cloud. Why shouldn't Dad look pleased? He'd had a win, no doubt about it. Thanks to the recently elected state government, cattle were going back into Balleroo National Park –as a trial to start with. A phone call that morning confirmed the stock would mainly come from Kilmarnock. It didn't hurt that Bill and the new environment minister were old school mates. So now Bill had plans to move the cows and calves from Brumby's up into the park, and put a few hundred new weaners onto Mary's land. Drew needed to tell his father to back off before things got out of hand — and he needed to do it soon.

Drew was ready to jump in the cab when Bess began to bark. Sam's bright-blue beetle was scooting up the drive. From his vantage point at the hay shed, he watched his father stride down to meet her. After a minute or two Bill raised his voice and Sam retreated to her car. With a dismissive wave of his hand, Bill marched back to the house. Drew headed down the hill at a run. Charging around the corner of the verandah, he cannoned headlong into his father coming the other way. Too late - the beetle was heading off. Drew mumbled an apology to his father and tried to appear offhand.

'The Kellys are back,' said Bill. 'Hate to think how they got their hands on a car like that.' He shook his head. 'The girl, Charlie — she was just here.' Bill gave Drew a shrewd look. 'Don't you go getting keen on her again, son. She's not for you.' Drew took a long, steadying breath. Just ignore him, don't give him the satisfaction. 'Know what she said?' Bill gave a hollow laugh. 'She said Mary won't renew the lease.'

Drew put on a look of suitable surprise. 'Well that scotches the cattle buying trip then.'

'It bloody well doesn't!' barked Bill. 'Mary will come round. You're still going, right after you round up those damned horses and get Chiquita back for me. I'm not losing my top mare to some mongrel stallion, not like Don Campbell did at Jindabyne.' Yes. The little issue of Dad's mare. 'I'm sending Ted to repair the yards up at Dead Man's Hut. Then I want those brumbies run in.'

'What do I do with them?'

'Shoot them, dog them, I don't care - just get Chiquita back.' Bill walked off, still looking pleased with himself. Drew remembered the horror of running the brumbies last year on Maroong Mountain. One thing was certain. This time things would be done differently.

The sun blazed low in the western sky when Drew set off for Brumby's Run. He'd packed a box with Christmas leftovers: cold meat, salad, half a pavlova, mince pies and fresh fruit. A bottle of wine sat on ice in the esky.

This was Drew's second try today. The first time, he'd gone by just on spec and Sam hadn't been home. He'd hightailed it out of there, scared she'd catch him on his way out and think him desperate. This time he'd had enough sense to try her mobile and score himself a proper invitation. Sam was waiting for him outside the house wearing Charlie's clothes: jeans, plaid shirt and an Akubra. She looked tired and happy, her skin flushed, her face sunburned - even prettier than he remembered. Bess scrambled off the tray to meet her before Drew had a chance to lift the dog down.

Sam had put up a card table under the peppercorn tree out back, set with plates and cutlery. Charlie's pet crow cawed from a low branch, causing Sam to jump in fright. 'That's Condor,' said Drew, throwing the friendly bird a piece of ham. 'Charlie hand-raised him when Dad shot his parents. Poor little fella must be missing her something shocking.'

'I had no idea,' said Sam. 'And to think I've been chasing him off.' Sam held out a piece of bread by way of apology. The big black bird received it with great dignity. 'Condor - that's an unusual name.'

'You know what a nature nut Charlie is,' said Drew. 'Condor's named after those big American vultures, cause he's a bit of a scavenger. And by the way, don't let Charlie hear you calling Condor a crow. He's an Australian raven, apparently, although I'll be buggered if I can tell the difference.'

Drew produced the wine and poured it into tumblers that had once been jam jars. 'A toast,' he said. 'To bringing Chiquita home.' They clinked glasses, and locked eyes. Hers sparkled in the twilight, and he wanted to pull her into his arms again, but dressed like that, with her sister's Akubra and all – the resemblance to Charlie was too disconcerting.

'Don't you ever take off that cowboy hat?' he asked. She smiled, tossed it off, and they tucked into the food. He told Sam about the plans to retrieve Chiquita.

Can I help?' she asked. 'After all, I'm a professional brumby breaker now.'

Drew went to speak and stopped himself. He'd better watch it; he'd almost called her Charlie. 'You fooled Bushy?' He supposed it wouldn't have been that hard. Bushy had never met Charlie. He'd only recently arrived as a replacement for the last horse breaker, a man whose penchant for hard liquor had got the better of him. Bushy had settled on Charlie for the job by word of mouth alone, for she had a formidable local reputation as a horsewoman.

Sam's tone was instantly defensive. 'You said yourself that it would kill Charlie to lose that job.'

'Maybe so, but you can't go around town masquerading as your sister forever.' She didn't respond. The truth was, Sam probably could get away with it if she kept to herself, at least for a while. The resemblance was striking, and for the past few years the Kellys had been on the outer. Mary's unconventional lifestyle and erratic behaviour had seen her marginalised from the mainstream Currajong community. Over time she'd been frozen out of the Parents and Friends Association, the garden group, the picnic race committee. Unfortunately, this prejudice had extended to Charlie.

It had started with a few girls at pony club, deriding her and her brumby mounts with vicious barbs. *Trust a feral to ride a feral* or *Since when were donkeys allowed at rallies?* or *Is Charlie wearing those clothes for a bet?* It didn't matter to hot-headed Charlie that the bullies were in the minority. One cruel remark was enough to set her off. She was kicked out of the club after terrifying one of her tormentors with a stockwhip. Things grew worse as she got older. The insults became more personal, and were no longer confined to the horse she happened to be riding. *Why does Charlie look so confused? Oh, that's right*

— it's Father's Day or *You must have been born on the highway because that's where most accidents happen.*

Charlie always gave as good as she got. *It's a shame to ruin such beautiful blonde hair, by dyeing your roots black* and *If the zombie apocalypse comes, you'll be safe – they eat brains.* When the others pushed her too far, she just jumped them. Drew had no doubt they were jealous of this stunning girl who could ride the pants off the best of them. No wonder Charlie had grown up to be a loner. Horses and the bush became her closest companions. Romantically, she favoured the kind of superficial relationships she could find with the travelling picnic race jockeys, or cowboys on the rodeo circuit. Drew had found that out the hard way.

'What happens when Charlie comes back?' he asked. The uncomfortable silence grew, and it soon became obvious that Sam did not intend to respond to his question. For some foolish reason he felt compelled to point out a few more home truths. 'And you've got other things to worry about besides Charlie. No electricity means no running water, no flushing toilets.'

'Anything else?' Sam's tight lips belied the cool tone of her voice.

'No fridge, no lights, no way to cook, or to charge your phone. Does the landline work?'

Sam shook her head. 'Cut off too, just like the power. I paid the bills and tried to reconnect, but I need Mary's passwords, and she's forgotten them . . . but it's fine, Drew.' There was something about the way Sam said his name that made it sound important. 'I can manage.'

She was pretty resourceful for a city girl, he had to give her that. Drew fondled Bess's floppy ears, and questions crowded back in. Where the hell were Mary and Charlie? And why wouldn't Sam say? She really was the most fascinating girl, tough and naive at the same time – a beautiful contradiction .

Drew couldn't resist any longer. Should he try to kiss her again? What if she pulled away? He took off his hat, reached across slowly, watching her, and smoothed the tangled hair back from her dirty face. He'd been thinking about doing that all day. Their faces were almost close enough to touch – but something was holding him back. Sam broke eye contact and the moment passed.

'Admit it, Sam,' he said. 'You need me. Tomorrow I'll rig you up a generator.' She really did have the cutest nose. 'If you run it for a few hours in the evening, at least you'll be able to cook and have a shower.' The corners of her mouth turned down. 'What's wrong?'

'I didn't think I'd have to cook. I thought you were going to bring me dinner every night,' she said with a straight face.

'That could be arranged, m'lady,' he said. 'Very easily. But you'll still need a shower.'

Sam fingered her top button. 'I could skinny-dip in the dam.'

Drew reached for the bottle of wine, not trusting himself to look at her. 'You're a tease, Samantha. You know that?' He topped up her glass, trying not to imagine her naked. 'Perhaps you're more like your sister than I thought. And if you think a dip in the dam will get you clean, then you're not accounting for the mud. And then there's the whopping great water bugs. They bite something shocking. The mozzies will eat you alive, and a big yabby could nip your toe clean off. Not to mention the snakes.'

'What do you mean, more like my sister?' asked Sam, suddenly serious.

'I just meant she could be a flirt too. All girls can be. Sometimes I think they can't help it.' Sam moved away and started picking strawberries off the pavlova. Terrific, now he'd offended her. Perhaps if he changed the subject. 'So you talked to Dad?'

Sam nodded and ate the last strawberry. 'I told him we're not renewing the lease, and that his cattle have to be out by the end of the week.'

'It's not that simple,' said Drew. 'He won't listen to you. It has to come from Mary.'

Sam shrugged. 'Without a lease his cattle are trespassing. I'll call the police if I have to.'

'What,' said Drew, 'with your stock wandering loose all over the national park? That could backfire badly.'

'I don't know,' said Sam. 'Maybe I'll just chase them out myself. Can't you talk to him?'

'Won't do any good,' said Drew. 'He doesn't listen to me either — never has. As I said, you'll need Mary. Could you get her to ring my dad?' Sam shuffled her feet and avoided his gaze. 'Or doesn't Mary know? Is ending the lease something you and Charlie have cooked up between you?'

Sam turned on him. 'That's none of your business, and don't you dare tell your father.' He made a show of packing up the picnic. 'What on earth was I was thinking? You're the last person I should be talking to about this.'

Drew stood up. 'Fair enough.' He put on his hat. 'I'll be around tomorrow with the generator.'

'Don't bother,' said Sam, glaring. 'I don't need your help.' She was holding onto Bess like she meant to confiscate her.

Drew nodded, almost said something, then changed his mind. He'd royally stuffed this one up. Drew whistled and Bess wriggled from Sam's arms. Then he tipped his hat and left.

Friday already and Drew still hadn't been back. Each day after work as Sam tidied the yard, or washed the windows, or cleared out the hay shed, she listened for the sound of his wheels on the drive. At night she lay in Mary's bed and wondered if Drew was wondering about her. How did these things work? She'd regretted her harsh words just as soon as they were out, but it seemed the damage was done. It had been a stupid idea to discuss the lease with Drew in the first place. He was Bill's son, after all. She'd given Charlie a solemn oath to get back Brumby's Run. Yet if Bill found out that Mary didn't want it back, he'd never move his stock.

Sam stroked Tambo's nose as she fed him a carrot. 'Well, boy, it looks like it'll be just you and me seeing in the new year together.'

Her first week of working for Bushy had passed much too quickly. Each morning she rose at the clear light of dawn, and made coffee and instant porridge on a portable butane cooker she'd bought from the produce store in town. 'No point trying to put that on the account,' the man had told her. 'Your mum's three months' late on payments as it is.'

'No worries, George.' She'd learned his name from Bushy, who, oddly enough, didn't seem to turn a hair when she asked him such questions. What's the butcher's name again, Bushy? I forgot. Where's Duffers Lane? Who can I get some lucerne hay from?

'Can I have a copy of that overdue account please?' she'd asked George. He'd narrowed his eyes and complied. 'I'll fix that up for you now if you like?' Sam had said, to his obvious surprise and pleasure. She'd done the same all over town, paying off accounts at the grocer, the butcher, the service station. Who'd have thought that you could buy petrol on account? But Mary had managed it.

'You and your mum must have come into a bit of money, then?' said Harry at the service station as he checked her oil and water. It was a remark she'd heard all too often this past week, and the townsfolk's curiosity made her wary. Sam avoided people as much as possible. It wasn't hard. She loved her work, and she loved being home at Brumby's Run, cleaning up the house or weeding the garden in preparation for Mary and Charlie's return. She was far too busy to feel lonely.

Every day after breakfast Sam washed the dishes outside at the tank, tossed Tambo a few biscuits of hay and headed for the racetrack. The historic course at Currajong doubled as the showgrounds and was picture perfect, nestled at the edge of the forest on the outskirts of town. There were usually a few trainers and gallopers on the track when she arrived. She'd learned to slip into the jockey rooms to grab a quick shower and leave her phone charging, hidden behind a bench. Then she joined Bushy for a cup of tea and hot, buttered raisin toast before they started the day's work.

Close to forty brumbies stood in the stockyards: weanlings, yearlings, two-year-olds and a few mature mares. These horses, along with many others, had been trapped high in the range as part of a concerted federal push to remove them from national parks. Most went for slaughter, but a rescue organisation, the Brumby Coalition, had selected the most promising horses for rehoming. A wealthy sponsor had engaged Bushy to assess the brumbies, and teach them a few ground manners prior to their auction at the picnic race-day in a month's time. Ryan, a serious, bespectacled young man from the organisation, visited occasionally to ensure the horses were progressing well. They had lessons in leading, tying up and standing quietly for grooming; lessons in picking up feet for the farrier, and loading into floats. All the essentials for any self-respecting horse. Sam had soon found her favourites among them: the greedy, taffy gelding with the wall eye who seemed determined to eat her hair, the sweet chestnut filly who tried so hard to please – and then, of course, there was Phoenix.

Bushy had assigned the palomino colt to her as a personal project. It was a relief to know that Phoenix wouldn't go through the sales next month along with all the other brumbies. 'You started him,' said Bushy, lips clinging to the inevitable roll-your-own. 'Now you better finish him.' Each morning he coached her. Working with the colt generated in Sam a fierce, possessive pride, akin to that first thrill of working with Pharaoh. Sometimes she felt disloyal, as the pain of losing Pharaoh lost some of its bite.

Phoenix raised his head, and nickered at her approach. 'Hello, gorgeous,' she said. 'Was that welcome for me, or for this bucket of feed?' Sam slipped into the yard beside him. The colt nosed the fingers of her extended hand, snuffling low. She reached out and buried her hand in his snowy mane, stroking his neck, his nose. The strength of their connection was palpable. Phoenix lowered his head, blinking evenly as she emptied chaff and oats into the old tyre feeder. Long pale lashes framed his big amber eyes. She liked how his ears swivelled independently of each other, simultaneously keeping track of her and any movement outside the yard. Tracing the muscular definition of his graceful neck, she admired the range of colours in his sleek summer coat. Silver, blonde and chestnut – combining to create the illusion of spun silk. She couldn't wait for the day she would ride him.

Sam picked up a comb and tamed his mane, no longer a tangle of knots and twigs. Instead it tapered neatly down his neck, like a fashion accessory, designed to lift and float, to add beauty and symmetry to his outline.

Grabbing a handful of hay, she wove a wisp. Fingers flew in practised precision. She could almost have been back at the stables in Melbourne, about to put Pharaoh through his paces. Caught in this pleasant dream she leaned back and thumped the wisp down on the colt's neck.

Phoenix exploded in a flailing flurry of hooves, climbing the air. Sam ducked under the rail as he tore to the far side of the yard and stood watching her, all rolling eyes and stamping forefeet.

'What the hell did you do there?'

Bushy's voice. A cold nose nuzzled the back of her hand. Bess? She turned to see Bushy shaking his head, with Drew grinning beside him. Sam showed Bushy the wisp and tried to explain. 'It's a massage pad made by plaiting hay. You slap it along a horse's neck, shoulders and rump to tone his muscles.'

'Well, that's a damn fool idea,' said Bushy. 'Phoenix? He ain't no tame city pony. You belt him with that, he'll more than likely belt you back.'

'I wasn't belting him!' protested Sam.

'Sure seemed like it to me.' Bushy indicated the outraged colt. 'And to him too, by the looks of it.' He picked the wisp up off the dusty ground and grunted. 'Waste of good hay.' Phoenix snorted in loud agreement. 'You get that fella back and groom him up proper.' With that, Bushy walked off in disgust.

Drew shuffled his feet and tipped his hat forward a little. He was trying unsuccessfully to hide the broad smile on his face. 'Morning.' Why did he have to be here, of all people? To see her dressed down like a foolish schoolgirl. Still, in spite of her embarrassment, she was glad to see him. 'Good morning,' said Sam, and went to retrieve the fractious colt.

Drew eyed Phoenix approvingly. 'He's a nice sort.'

'Come to check up on me?' she asked. At least he'd stopped smiling – almost.

'Dad sent me over with a couple of two-year-olds for Bushy to break. You did know he works for Dad too, didn't you?'

Sam spun around. Phoenix half-reared at her swift movement, as if he thought she might give him another thumping. 'Well, of course I didn't,' she said in a loud stage whisper, looking around to make sure Bushy was out of earshot. 'How was I supposed to know that?'

Drew shrugged. Whose side was he really on? If Bushy worked for Bill, and she worked for Bushy, then it meant she was indirectly working for Bill herself. It was an unsettling thought. Phoenix decided Sam's fit of madness had passed, and returned to his feed bin at a high-stepping trot. He sent her flying with a cross toss of his head, and she landed seat first in the dust. Drew helped her up, holding her hand a little longer than necessary. A sudden panic gripped her. She had to do something or say something, right now, to show him she was still interested. She couldn't bear for the moment to be lost.

'I'm sorry about the other night, Drew. You were right about Mary,' said Sam. 'She does mean to renew the lease. It's Charlie who doesn't want to.' *Don't forget to send the contract to me, will you, sweetheart?* Mary had said before Sam left. *It's very important, I'll post the signed documents back for you to give to Bill.* But Sam hadn't given them to Bill. Instead, she'd burned them on the barbeque.

'No worries.' Drew trailed a hand idly along the fence. It felt like he was trailing his fingers up and down her spine. He looked thoughtful, as if he was trying to make up his mind about something. 'I'm having a shot at catching Chiquita tomorrow,' he said at last. 'Going to run the brumbies into the yards up at Dead Man's Hut.' He drew a line in the dust with his boot. 'Sure could use some help.'

'Really?' asked Sam. 'You mean me?'

Drew leaned against the top rail and watched two horses go around the track. 'Dad won't be causing you any problems for a while. Came off his bike yesterday and smashed his leg. Nasty break. It'll lay him up for ages.'

'I'm sorry,' said Sam, although she wasn't. She had no sympathy for Bill.

She must have sounded as false as she felt, because Drew held up his hand. 'I never agreed with him leasing your land in the first place. Fact is, nobody will make a decent go of Brumby's until our cattle are gone. Dad knows that.'

Phoenix was watching the gallopers too. Nerves twitched beneath his satin coat.

'It's New Year's Eve,' Sam said, 'and the lease ends today. I sent your dad a text last night. Told him to move his stock out by tomorrow, or I will.' It had been an empty threat. Her beginner mustering skills would never stretch to moving hundreds of cattle by herself.

Drew raised his brows. 'Then I suppose you'll be needing some help.'

This was too perfect. Without thinking, Sam threw her arms around Drew's neck in a swift, grateful hug.

Phoenix approached the rails, allowing Drew to stoke his muzzle. The colt reached over, snatched the hat from his head and cantered off, thrashing it from side to side like a terrier shakes a rat. 'Cheeky bugger,' said Drew with a laugh. Sam ducked into the yard, played a short game of tug of war, then came back with the hat, complete with teeth marks. Drew looked at it ruefully. 'It's had a hell of a hiding.' He shook it a few times. 'You know, Dad's old school. Can't abide texts. You should hear him. *If something's worth knowing, it's worth saying face to face.* He could go forever without checking his phone. You sure you sent it?' Sam nodded. 'I reckon that's fair notice then.' Drew slapped the hat back onto his head. 'Tell you what, I'll make sure he gets the message – after we've moved the cattle, that is.'

'Deal,' she said, smiling. Why had she ever doubted him?

'Let me take you out tonight,' he said. 'There's a few parties on.'

For a moment Sam was tempted. A night out with Drew was more than she'd hoped for. But then reality set in. 'Do you really think that's a good idea? Who would I go as? Myself or Charlie? I might be able to fool the traders in town, but I'd never fool friends, people I'm supposed to know.'

'Why are you pretending to be Charlie anyway?'

'I don't know. I didn't set out to,' she said. 'I just went along with everybody. It was so much easier than having to explain.'

'In the short term, maybe. But not in the long run.' Drew gave her a knowing, sideways glance. 'I think it's more than that. I think you're enjoying yourself.'

'That's ridiculous,' said Sam. 'You think I enjoy having to watch every word? Enjoy not even being able to go out on New Year's Eve in case I give myself away?'

'Yep,' said Drew, with an infuriating smile. 'Admit it. It's exciting, isn't it? Fooling everybody? There's the thrill of not being found out, of living a double life. It's like being undercover, or a spy or something. My guess is your old life was kind of tame.'

Why did he always have to do that? Call her out, embarrass her just when things were going well? Still, she'd learned her lesson. No more hasty words this time. She wanted Drew to help muster the cattle out, didn't she? So she mustn't put him off. But a nagging internal voice challenged her to be honest with herself. Sam examined the dusty ground for answers. Who was she kidding? She wanted a lot more than that.

Bushy appeared from around the corner, halters in hand. 'Hey, Drew. You going to stand yakking to Charlie all day, or come help unload those horses?'

'I'll be over later with that generator,' Drew said in a low voice. 'We'll see in the new year together, eh? I've got some ideas you might be interested in.' She nodded, feeling her flesh goosebump in anticipation.

'Come on, fella,' called Bushy. 'Any slower, you'd be in reverse.' Drew tipped his hat to her, a delightfully old-fashioned gesture.

'Until tonight, m'lady.'

Sam waved goodbye to Bushy.

'See you next year,' he said, and laughed at his own joke. For once, Sam was leaving work on time. All week she'd stayed long past knock-off. There was always plenty to do and see. She might give a nervous yearling some extra handling, or head over to watch the thorough-breds on their evening gallops. Not tonight though.

As Sam reached the car her phone chimed - a message from Faith. She hadn't forgiven her mother for Pharaoh, not by a long shot. How could she? How could she ever pardon such a base betrayal? She'd sent Faith a brief text on Christmas Day, but that was all. By contrast, Faith had bombarded her with phone calls. When they went unanswered, Faith wrote text messages as long as her arm. These missives were full of apologies. Good, so they should be . . . but the apologies were weak and full of excuses. Sam read her mother's latest offering.

I'm sorry, Samantha. It was wicked of me to sell Pharaoh. Faith should have stopped right there. Sam could have almost accepted such a simple, heartfelt admission of guilt. *But you were always so busy with Charlene,* she continued foolishly. *So busy with Charlene, and that Mary woman. You certainly had no time for me. You had no time for Pharaoh. You'd absolutely deserted us, Samantha. I honestly thought the horse would be better off with Wolfe.* Sam deleted the message.

These sorts of stupid, selfish rationalisations only served to harden Sam's heart. 'Get Pharaoh back,' Sam had said bluntly on the one and only occasion she'd answered Faith's call. 'Then we'll talk.' Faith responded with a message avalanche, detailing the extraordinary lengths she'd gone to, trying to do just that. But apparently Wolfe wouldn't budge. *He's set on a berth in the Olympic squad, and he thinks Pharaoh is the horse to take him there. It's such a compliment to your training, Samantha.*

That was true. A wonderful compliment with a poison arrow at its heart. So her family communications had been confined to Dad and Mamie. She'd spoken to her father a couple of times, and he'd been surprisingly supportive. He'd asked after Charlie, and had even been solicitous about Mary. He'd promised to give her a generous monthly allowance while she was in Currajong. But he still refused to discuss the adoption. That talk would have to wait until they stood face to face.

Sam stopped at the little Currajong supermarket on the way home for supplies. It wasn't a supermarket in the normal sense of the word at all. No endless, gleaming aisles and self-checkout lanes. It was a traditional general store, doubling as the post office. Its old-world charm would have been more appealing if Sam didn't always have to be so careful. Every time she went to town, every time somebody looked at her with recognition in their eyes . . . every time somebody called her Charlie, Sam's heart was thumping in her throat.

'What are you up to tonight, Charlie?' asked Marjorie, the kindly middle-aged woman at the checkout. Sam had learned her name from the tag on her ample bosom.

'Staying home.'

'That doesn't sound much like you. Is your mother back?'

'Not yet. She's still working in Melbourne.' This was her new line. She hoped the idea of Mary working didn't sound too preposterous, and it helped explain where the money had come from to pay off the bills. The money that had actually come from Sam's own dwindling bank account.

Sam wandered down one aisle and back up the other. She bought cheese, a jar of olives and another of sun-dried tomatoes. A tub of French onion dip. Crackers. Some cherries and grapes. There wasn't much vegetarian fare on offer, but a diet of barbecued meat had begun to pall. She walked out with her purchases and felt the first plop of fat, summer rain. To the east, dark clouds boiled higher and higher, warning of an approaching storm. Looked like they'd be eating inside tonight. On an impulse, Sam dashed back inside. Braving Marjorie's curious stare, she bought a box of tea-light candles, a pair of plastic wine glasses and a bag of ice. Then she headed for home, nervous anticipation churning her stomach. Sam thought of her sister, still languishing at the hospital in Melbourne. She must call later in the evening to cheer Charlie up and wish her a happy new year.

Raindrops ran down the windows and drummed on the tin roof as Sam did a final check. Everything was ready for Drew's arrival. The formerly filthy kitchen shone with shabby chic and smelt of lavender. Sam placed the last marigold into the jug-cum-vase that adorned the tiny table. A faded sky-blue curtain, washed and line-dried, stood in for a regular table cloth. The antipasto platter spilled over with the last of the season's sweet cherry tomatoes, and looked suitably festive. A jam jar of billy buttons and silver snow daisies sat on the sill. Sam peered past it to see Drew pull up and lift Bess from the tray of his ute. Finally! She dashed outside, heedless of the pouring rain, or of seeming too eager.

'Hello.' Sam raised her voice above the noise of rolling thunder. 'Why do you always lift Bess down like that? She must weigh a tonne.'

'She's got a bung leg,' he said.

The massive dog ran over and buried her wet nose affectionately between Sam's knees. Drew heaved something that looked like a motor off the tray. The power of him showed in his upper arms, as they strained with the load. Drew stashed it on the narrow verandah, then squatted down to make an adjustment. His sodden shirt was translucent, the colour of flesh. The crouch accentuated the length of his back and the strength of his thighs. Sam knelt down beside him, shivering. Heat radiated through his wet clothes. He smelt of horses, earth and saddle leather. She moved closer until their bodies touched. The motor thing must be the generator. Sam almost regretted that candlelight might not be the only light tonight.

Drew dashed back to the cab and emerged with a white paper parcel and a wine bottle. Fish and chips and champagne. Bess shook herself in a rainbow of spray. The pair ran inside laughing, leaving soggy Bess complaining on the porch.

'It's the cleanest I've ever seen this kitchen,' Drew said, an expression of wonder on his face. Sam just smiled, suddenly shy. Drew looked her coolly up and down, and she felt her pulse quicken. 'Will I set up the generator?'

'Let's eat first.' Dusk was gathering around them, reaching dark fingers through the window. Time for the candles. Her arm stretched for the matchbox on the table.

'Allow me.' Drew covered her hand with his own, and extracted the box from her curled palm. Round the kitchen he went, lighting the tea lights, one by one, until the room was bathed in a soft, romantic glow. The act seemed imbued with special significance. It was a ritual, and he the high priest.

Drew pursed his lips and blew out the match. Seconds ticked by. She waited with bated breath. Then his arms were round her, sure and hard, the most natural thing in the world. Drew lowered his mouth to hers, and she parted her lips to taste him. The kiss was so sensuous and slow that Sam wished it might never end. Was this love? This dizzy warmth, this flush of desire, this feeling that her body knew exactly what it was doing?

Drew pulled away first. 'Jesus,' he said. 'That was a bombshell kiss.' He reached up to gently run his knuckles down her cheek. 'You don't know your own strength. Or was it beginner's luck?'

'All beginners need to practise,' she said, and tugged him back to her, amazed by her own boldness.

Bess ruined the mood. The dog's determined scratching had finally paid off, and she burst into the kitchen through the flimsy screen door. Bess and Drew dived as one for the parcel of fish and chips on the table, and rescued it just in time. The aroma of wet dog replaced the fragrance of lavender. 'Bad dog,' said Sam, but her tone was not scolding. She sank to her knees and hugged the happy hound.

Drew laughed. 'Yeah, that's the way to tell her off.' He reached for Bess's collar.

'Let her stay,' said Sam. 'It's her new year's eve too.' Bess barked in approval.

'I thought three was a crowd?' said Drew, but Bess was already following Sam to the esky, smiling and waving her whip of a tail.

'Does she like bacon?'

Bess whined in assent and swallowed two rashers in one gulp, before Drew's withering stare sent her slinking into the corner. The big dog squeezed behind a bucket, designed to catch drips from the leaky roof, then curled up tight as if she hoped she might become invisible.

'Come on. Let's eat,' said Drew, 'before she cons you into feeding her our dinner, as well as our breakfast.' Sam gave him a searching look. Breakfast? Was that a statement of intent, a circuitous request? An offer?

Drew didn't appear to appreciate the significance of his remark. He went about dividing the portions of battered fish and steamed dim sims. He made two mounds of lukewarm soggy chips. Sam poured the sparkling wine into the new glasses, and proposed a toast to the new year. They each took a sip.

'I've got another one,' Drew said. 'To us.' He leant across and kissed her again.

The last thing she felt like doing now was eating. Nonetheless Sam tried a chip. It wasn't until the food hit her palate that she realised how hungry she really was. Fresh air and hard work had piqued her appetite. The chip was warm and creamy on the inside. Salty. Yummy. The fish tasted even more delectable. A search of the pantry turned up a bottle of white vinegar and some soy sauce for the dim sims. It was, quite simply, the most delicious meal of her life.

Drew topped up her glass. 'So what's the plan?'

'Plan?' What exactly was he asking her? 'For tomorrow? Is that what you mean?'

'I meant your long-term plan. The big picture.'

'I don't suppose I have one,' she said.

'Are you staying on?'

Did he want her to, was that it? Was he asking her to stay? 'Maybe.' She didn't mention the commerce degree awaiting her in Melbourne.

'When will Charlie be back?'

Why were they suddenly talking about Charlie? This wasn't what she'd expected, an inquisition. It caught her off guard. 'A couple of months . . . when she's well.'

'So, she's sick?'

Damn, there was no denying it now. The implication of her words had been plain. Sam nodded miserably. Her first real slip. 'Where's the shame in that?' asked Drew, sounding puzzled. 'Why all the secrecy?'

'Charlie doesn't want people feeling sorry for her.' Sam was just making it worse. The charm of the evening was fast evaporating. She was stuffing it all up. 'I'm sorry. I'd rather not talk about my sister.'

But Drew wasn't about to let it drop. 'That's Charlie for you. Too much pride in one direction, and not enough in another.'

Sam experienced a tight twinge of envy. She hated to hear Drew talking about Charlie with such easy familiarity. Talking like he knew Charlie better than she did. Confirming all she'd missed, these past eighteen years. And she hated to think of Charlie, alone with Drew, so many times. A sharp gust of wind blew out the tea lights on the table, and the marigolds had closed their bright petals.

'Exactly how well do you know my sister?'

'Charlie and me? We go way, way back.'

That was the wrong answer. A loud clap of thunder made Sam jump. Bess whined in fear and came to lay her head in Sam's lap, but Drew remained unphased. 'I've got an idea to run past you,' he said. 'A way to make a living from this place, until you can afford to restock.'

A business proposition, now? What was this evening really about? She poured herself the last of the wine. What she wanted most was a big tub of chocolate ice-cream and a spoon.

'Trail rides,' said Drew. She rewarded him with a blank look. 'Trail rides,' he repeated, as if she hadn't heard him the first time. 'There's a string of ten horses and ponies going at Gidgee. The bloke's been keen to sell them for a while, with no luck. He plans to put them through the Currajong horse sale. I'll bet if you made him an offer, you'd get the lot for a song.'

'Why would I want to do that, exactly?'

'Hang on,' said Drew. He disappeared outside and returned with dripping hair and a six-pack of beer. The romantic mood was fast disappearing. 'Want one?' Sam shook her head. Clearly Drew did not intend for this to be a dry argument. 'Your mum will be skint when she gets back, that's a given.' Sam hesitated, then nodded. How strange to hear Mary referred to as her mother. 'She relies on Dad's lease fees and not much else. Without them, she'll need some sort of replacement income.'

'What about the cattle? Can't she just sell some?' asked Sam. 'Isn't that how it works?'

Drew snorted and shook his head. 'There's maybe fifty head, all skin and bone. It'll be six months before those calves are fit for sale, and you can't put cows that poor straight back in calf.' Drew stood up and began to pace around. 'Want to know what I'd do?' Perhaps she'd have that beer after all. 'I'd cull the bulls and chopper cows. Wean the calves. Winter down any cows you want to keep. Then buy new bulls and restock slowly. Problem is, it all takes money. That's where the trail rides come in.'

'Chopper cows?' asked Sam.

'Old, sick, infertile. Bad mothers. Cows that have twins and can't raise them both. Cows that don't have a calf each year.'

'And what, they're killed?'

A draught extinguished more candles, casting Drew into shadow. 'Well . . . yes,' he said. 'There's no retirement home for cows.'

'No, I suppose not.' Bad mothers. There was no equivalent penalty for bad mothers in the human world. Absurdly, Sam imagined Mary and Faith as cows. Would they qualify as choppers? Forfeit their lives for terrible parenting? It was unfair to kill a cow because she couldn't get pregnant. Faith couldn't get pregnant. Mary couldn't raise both twins. Sam's head swam with conflicting emotions. It hadn't occurred to her that she might be required to make decisions about the practical operation of Brumby's Run.

'I want to keep all the cows for the time being,' she said. 'Give them another chance.'

Drew's expression grew soft. 'We've a way to go before we make a farmer out of you. Tell you what, you keep the cows. But you'll have to cull the bulls. That herd is inbred enough as it is.'

'Deal,' said Sam.

Drew pulled her to him. 'What is this?' he asked, with the hint of a smile. 'Feminism for cows?'

'Maybe.' She certainly didn't have the heart to steal their calves away, and then send those poor, starved creatures to be slaughtered. Not yet, not after all they'd endured. She pictured her cows wandering lush paddocks in spring, growing fat, new calves gambolling at their feet. 'Maybe I'm just not cut out for the cattle business.' The idea of running trail rides certainly seemed a far gentler way to earn a crust.

'You're a hypocrite, Sam. You know that, don't you?' said Drew. He threw an olive in the air and caught it in his mouth. 'I didn't see you turn your nose up at my steaks.'

'It's true, I do eat meat. I try to eat free range though, no intensive pork or chicken or grain-fed beef. It's not the death of an animal that I object to, as long as it's humane. We all have to die sometime. My problem is with a life of suffering.' She cracked open the beer. 'I don't think I'd normally have a problem with selling cattle. Those ones of your dad's, for example – they looked completely content. Death isn't so bad, is it? Not after a happy life.' It mattered that he understood her. 'Our cows have suffered so much,' she said. 'I want them to have some happiness.'

Drew relit a candle. 'Fair enough,' he said, with a decisive nod. 'We'll have them knee-deep in clover, literally. Dad's been saving your eastern flats for winter feed. All sown down to rye and clover. We'll move the poorer cows in there and they'll be happy as free-range pigs in mud,' he said, 'I guarantee it.'

'Perfect.' She wanted to add, *enough with the talk*. Wasn't he ever going to kiss her again? On an impulse Sam laid her hand on his chest, feeling the firm muscles beneath. She slipped her fingers between a button, felt the warmth of his skin, the beat of his heart. He fixed her with eyes intense with desire, and one by one undid her own buttons, big fingers fumbling a little. She smiled encouragement, the blood rushing in her ears. He leant in close, landing a flurry of tiny, whispery kisses over her face and neck. Now his tongue was in her ear, his hands running over her bra, the swell of her breasts, pausing on a hardening nipple, stroking her sensitive belly. Sam's legs went weak, and her skin burned beneath his touch. A delicious feeling swelled deep between her thighs, a sensation of exquisite sweetness. She sighed as his hands encircled her waist.

With a loud whoosh, the storm sent a whipping surge of wind through the kitchen, extinguishing every candle. The sudden darkness was complete. So was the silence. 'Come to bed,' whispered Drew, taking hold of her hand. She quivered with the anticipation of his touch in the dark.

But as Drew urged Sam to her feet, the dull throb of a motor sounded in the distance. Gradually the noise grew louder and louder. A car was coming, its headlights visible now through the window, brightening the room enough for Sam to find the torch in the cutlery drawer. She hurriedly buttoned up her shirt as Bess launched herself out the back door, baying like the Hound of the Baskervilles with Drew hot on her heels. Sam checked the time on her phone. Ten to twelve. Friends of Charlie's, maybe, come to ring in the new year? Should she hide? Too late. She heard a heavy thud outside and shrank back from a shadowy male form that loomed in the door. Not Drew. Taller and fair-haired, but with the same thin-hipped, broad-shouldered silhouette.

Torchlight lit the man's face, making it ghostly, like a Halloween mask. Sam shivered in spite of the warm night air and fumbled for matches. She lit a candle while the stranger watched. He looked puzzlingly familiar. Had she seen him in town, perhaps? No, Sam felt sure she'd have remembered a face so striking.

There was a mathematical formula for beauty, or so she'd read. The golden ratio. The divine proportion. Something about the distance between mouth and nose, the width of the lips, the height of the cheek. In this man's handsome face, the formula was made flesh. His blue eyes held her own with a disturbing intensity, supremely confident, a little arrogant, like those of a young lion. Currajong certainly knew how to grow good-looking men.

'Chaz,' he said. 'Long time no see.'

She had it. The poster cowboy. Drew pushed past him. 'Hey, man,' said the cowboy, extending his hands with palms upheld. 'It was an accident.'

'What was an accident?' asked Sam.

'The bastard tripped me.' In the faint candlelight she could see mud caking the front of Drew's shirt and smudging his nose.

The cowboy surveyed the candle-filled kitchen with the manner of a man who'd been drinking, but was not yet drunk. 'Very romantic.' He flicked the useless light switch and clicked his tongue. 'Or did your mum just not pay the bill?'

Drew shouldered the stranger. 'Get out, Spike.'

'I'd say that's Charlie's call, wouldn't you?' He had the kind of eyes that ran up and down a woman's body like a searchlight. Drew waited, looking at Sam expectantly – waiting for her to back him up.

'Yes,' she said at last. There was a simmering tension between the two men that she couldn't read. 'Would you go, please?'

Spike pricked up his ears. 'Since when did you start bunging on a voice, Chaz?' He came closer, examining her with curious eyes. It was like a physical touch. She felt vulnerable, exposed, but deliciously so. It was no use, she couldn't fool him.

'You've confused me for my sister,' she said, hearing her voice falter. 'I'm Samantha. Charlie is away.' Now for the disbelief, the doubt, the astonishment. Comprehension was the last thing she expected, but there it was, plain on his face.

'My mistake.' He spoke in a low, modulated tone, at times a half-drawl. No two ways about it, Spike's voice was very sexy – and not just his voice.

'Completely understandable,' she said. 'Charlie and I are identical twins.'

Spike shot Drew a look. 'Man, what a beautiful dream.' Drew sprang forward and Sam instinctively moved between the two men. 'You're not going to kick me out, are you, Samantha?' Spike checked his phone. 'Not at five minutes to midnight, in the rain, on New Year's Eve?' He took off his hat and put it on the table, as if it might anchor him to the room.

'That's exactly what she's going to do,' said Drew. He rammed the hat back onto Spike's head and gave him a helpful push.

'Okay, okay,' said Spike. 'No need to shove.' He removed his hat, inspected its shape, and replaced it with a flourish. 'If you want, Samantha, I'll come over tomorrow and set that generator up for you. No point just having it sit there for clumsy folk to trip over, now is it?'

'Get out,' snarled Drew. Bess growled in low agreement.

Spike gave Sam a dazzling smile. 'Do me and yourself a favour, will you, sweetness? Dump this clown.'

Then he was gone. The headlights retreated down the hill, and the tiny kitchen was theirs once again. But the mood was spoiled, the air heavy with Drew's anger.

'You don't like him?' asked Sam.

'Spike's a jerk.' Drew arched his back, hands clasped behind his head 'You told him your name. Why him?'

Sam shrugged. 'He already knew I wasn't Charlie.' She checked the time. Five past twelve. 'Happy New Year.'

'Happy New Year.' A single candle flickered on the table. Sam tried her best to suppress a yawn, suddenly overcome with fatigue.

'You're tired,' said Drew. 'I'd better go.' He gave her a chaste kiss on the cheek. 'See you first thing in the morning.'

She nodded, feeling crushed. If only Spike hadn't arrived. Now everything was somehow changed.

He whistled Bess and the pair disappeared out the door, braving the storm.

Sam swapped the half-full bucket beneath the leak for an empty one. The anticlimax was almost unbearable What had she done wrong?

She tipped the water into the sink and washed up the few dishes, mind still too busy for sleep. She wiped down the benches, covered the remainder of the cheese platter with cling wrap, and put it on ice in the esky. Lightning lit up the sky and the trees outside the window. It lit up Tambo's dark form in the yard above the house.

For the first time since being at Brumby's Run, Sam was genuinely lonely. She picked up the candle and headed for the bedroom, replaying every detail of the evening over and over in her mind. She thought of Drew, and then of Spike – of the overt hostility between them. What was it, she wondered, that they weren't telling her? It was only in the wee small hours of dawn, as she finally drifted off to sleep, that she remembered she hadn't rung Charlie.

Charlie scoffed the rubbery scrambled eggs, the tough toast, the cold tea. In the process of tearing the top from a tiny container of long-life orange juice, she managed to tip the lot down her front. Not a very auspicious start to the new year. She swore and dabbed at the spill with the scrap of paper napkin provided. Being no bigger than a postage stamp, it wasn't much use. She wiped the stain with the sheet instead. What she wouldn't do for a real breakfast right now. Charlie's head sank back onto her pillow, eyes closed, and let her imagination take flight. Fried eggs on slabs of thick white toast, smothered in butter. Rashers of juicy bacon. Tomato halves, grilled until their skins turned black. Pan-fried field mushrooms.

The ringing phone jolted her back to reality. Charlie snatched it up. 'Sam?' she said. 'At last! It seems like ages since we've talked.'

'Not so long,' said Sam. There was a defensive note to her sister's voice. 'Happy New Year. I did try to call last night. Couldn't get through, though.'

Charlie didn't challenge the remark. Mobile phone reception was unreliable in Currajong, but it still sounded like an excuse. The possibility that she was being lied to unsettled her, even if it was only a little white lie. Sam was supposed to be her window on the world back home, yet in the last eight days they'd hardly spoken.

'Happy New Year to you, too,' said Charlie. 'How are things? How's Tambo?'

'Tambo's fine,' said Sam. 'I'm riding him up to Dead Man's Hut today to help Drew run in some brumbies. A wild stallion stole one of Bill's mares.'

Charlie squeezed her eyes and held the phone away from her head. She could still hear the small, indistinct prattle of Sam's voice, but thankfully could no longer make out the words. They conjured up far too clear an image of all she was missing. Charlie took a deep breath and returned the phone to her ear before Sam realised she'd been away.

'. . . decide what to do with them once we get Chiquita back. What do you think?'

'So, you're yarding the Maroong Mountain mob?' asked Charlie.

'Yes,' said Sam. 'I suppose they're the ones.'

'Big buckskin stallion? Cocky as all hell?'

'Yes,' said Sam. 'It sounds like him.'

'That's Jarrang,' said Charlie. 'I love that horse. You let him go, Sam.'

'Drew might have other ideas. His father doesn't want us to release them.'

'I don't give a damn what Bill wants,' said Charlie, her voice rising. 'Just let him go, along with a couple of mares for company. Otherwise he'll keep on stealing station horses.'

'I'll try,' said Sam. 'More importantly, how are you doing?'

'I'm getting out next week. Moving into the apartment with Mum.' Professor Sung had told them last night. Apparently her recovery was progressing perfectly. Charlie was sceptical by nature, but it was true that her appetite had returned with a vengeance, and she was feeling stronger every day. 'Your stem cells really packed a punch, Sam.'

'That's fantastic! How long before …' Charlie heard a man's voice in the background. 'Sorry,' said Sam. 'Got to go. Drew's here. I'll call you tonight and let you know how we went.'

Charlie's mouth went dry. No, Sam couldn't go yet. Their phone call had just started. 'Remember what I told you,' said Charlie. 'Look after Jarrang. We're old friends.'

'I'll remember,' said Sam, and then she was gone. Charlie hurled the phone to the floor. What she wouldn't give to be home right now, joining the hunt for Bill's lost mare, galloping the wild slopes of the Balleroo Range. Silent tears flooded her face. She used the sheet to mop them away, then extracted the set of painted pagan prayer beads from her drawer. Sitting cross-legged on the bed, she worked to clear her mind of envy and longing, like her mother had taught her, then repeated the familiar chant.

My blood, my bone, my body, is healing now, healing now. The goddess force is in me. She heals me now, heals me now. Strength of day, strength of night, give me strength beyond my sight.

The prayer's comforting words worked, as they always did, to soothe away the anxiety and unravel the taut threads of her nerves. Get well. That's what she needed to do now. Get well and return to Brumby's Run. Get well and reclaim her life.

CHAPTER 17

A flock of crimson rosellas exploded from the trees into a sky of perfect blue. Clancy pawed the ground as Drew swung into the saddle. 'Wear that riding helmet or you're not coming,' he said over his shoulder. Sam had taken to wearing Charlie's lucky hat recently.

'Won't the others think it's a bit strange?'

'Who cares what they think? Put it on or stay here.'

Sam looked like she was about to argue. Then she apparently thought better of it, threw Tambo's reins over the fence, and ran back for her helmet.

Drew wasn't quite sure how to act around Sam today. There had really been something between them last night – hell, they were about sixty seconds away from consummating that something. But then Spike had shown up. Talk about déjà vu hitting Drew over the head with a mallet. It might be with a different girl, but it was close to the bone. Sam and Charlie, Charlie and Sam – it was all too weird to be falling in love with Charlie's twin, especially when Sam wouldn't tell him what was really going on. And look at what happened when Drew fell in love with Charlie herself – not exactly a ringing endorsement for either girl. He pushed his feelings to the back of his mind and tried to concentrate on the task at hand. Once they got going, he'd be right.

Sam came back with her helmet, and there was a noticeable tremble in her legs as she mounted. Tambo had broken into a sweat. The horse sensed Sam's excitement, sidling sideways and playing with the bit. Although still early, the day was already uncomfortably warm. A shimmering haze rose above the purple peaks of the range, adding a silvery surrealism to the scene.

Since meeting Sam, Drew was seeing the world with fresh eyes. He paid attention now. He paid attention to the sound of the creek on its way down the mountain, to the subtle fragrance of the bush, to the pictures in the clouds. What would a stranger make of this view? He guessed they'd be pretty impressed. But most of all, he paid attention to Sam. Her laugh, her frown, her childlike wonder in the world. He loved just watching her ride. The way her hips swayed in time with her horse. The way her slim arms reached down occasionally to hug Tambo's neck. He imagined those arms wrapped around him instead. Her very presence heightened his senses, making life infinitely more exciting.

'Ready?' asked Drew. Sam had Charlie's stockwhip on the saddle. 'You know how to use that thing?'

'No, but I'll learn.' Sam adjusted her stirrups. 'Charlie said to let the brumby stallion go.'

'Did she now?' Drew grinned. 'That's cause her and Jarrang, they're old mates. Charlie raised him from a baby after he was separated from his mother during a storm. She couldn't have been more than twelve years old. I weaned one of our foals and lent her the brood mare, hoping it might adopt the little colt. Nothing doing. Instead it tried to kick his head in. So Charlie milked that damn mare like a dairy cow, morning and night for months, and bottle-raised Jarrang.' Drew slapped a fly off his thigh with his hat. 'That little colt was a good sort. I said she should geld him and keep him for herself. But Charlie hasn't got a practical bone in her body. Said he wouldn't be happy in captivity.' Drew didn't put the rest of his thought into words; didn't say that Jarrang would be a lot happier in Charlie's paddock than in the knackers' yard. If the federal government had its way, a knackers' yard was where all the park brumbies would end up.

'So what do we do?' asked Sam.

'Tell you what,' said Drew. 'If we run in Jarrang, you can have him. Let him go if you want, or keep him for when Charlie comes home.' Sam nodded. 'Come on,' he said. 'We've got horses to catch.'

They cantered up the hill, past the dam, heading for the northern boundary of Brumby's Run. Drew had constructed 200-metre-long wings – ring-lock wire fencing, disguised with hessian chaff bags – to funnel the brumbies into the yards at Dead Man's Hut. He was pleased with the job. It helped that Chiquita was no wild horse. Since Christmas he'd left the big yard open and generously supplied with salt licks and hay. Hoof prints and vanishing feed told Drew she'd led the mob inside more than once. They'd be less wary now. Still, if he missed them the first time, they'd be on to him. You only got one chance with brumbies.

When they reached the old stock route, they saw five riders approaching at a spanking trot, stock whips slung by their side. Two eager blue cattle dogs trotted behind. Drew reined Clancy in and waited.

'Who are they?' asked Sam.

'That's Tom Ward, our head stockman. Bushmen don't come any better than Tom. The other four are contract brumby runners.'

'Why's that one got a rifle?' asked Sam. Drew thought back to his own disastrous experience running brumbies the previous year, and prayed she wouldn't wind up just as disillusioned.

'If a horse breaks a leg, we'll have to shoot it,' he said honestly. 'It's the kindest thing.' Sam stared in open astonishment and his stomach lurched with doubt. There was fear and apprehension in her large eyes now, and he was the one who'd put it there. Drew suddenly wished he hadn't brought her along.

'G'day Tom,' said Drew, as the lead rider reached them. Tom pulled up his horse and leaned his elbow on the horn of the saddle while he rolled a smoke. A crashing sound in the scrub provoked the two heelers into a mad flurry of barking. A small mob of fat black baldies, tails held high, broke from a stand of tea-tree and lumbered into the bush. Tom silenced the dogs with a word and stared at Drew. They were Kelly cattle. He must have missed them when he mustered the herd home to Brumby's Run. Their presence would not go unreported.

'Those brumbies aren't too far away,' said Tom. 'Spotted them yesterday, in the clearing below Waratah Spring. Me and the boys will circle round and try to get above them.' He nodded towards Sam. 'You and the girl hold down the flank. We'll make plenty of noise for you.'

'Righto,' said Drew. Tom and the others veered left off the track, heading uphill through the trees, while Drew and Sam rode on to the hut. The brumbies had been there, and recently. Hay was trampled all about. So far, so good. The new wing fences hadn't spooked them.

Drew led Sam to a position fifty metres along the northern wing. 'Tambo knows what to do. Just stay put and stand your ground.' He pulled the stockwhip from her saddle and offered it. Sam took the coiled lash, holding it as cautiously as she might a snake. 'You'll hear the horses coming a mile off. Don't let them past.' Sam nodded, face flushed with either excitement or fear. 'You okay?' He put his hand on her arm.

'I'm okay,' she said, and inexpertly brandished the whip. It slithered across Tambo's wither, making him shiver. Drew gave what he hoped was an encouraging smile, then rode down around the yards and hut, and back along the southern edge of the trap.

It was a waiting game. He could just make out Tambo further up the mountain, tucked amongst a patch of snow gums. Far enough back to escape detection unless the brumbies headed straight for him. An hour passed. Little pestering flies crowded the corners of his lips and eyes. The sun swung higher and higher. He cleared his mind, allowed the silence to seep in, a kind of meditation. An hour passed. Clancy stamped his feet, weary of the morning vigil. Their plan required the patience of an ambush predator. Tambo remained motionless, statue-still on the hill above the yards. Two hours passed. The sun grew fierce. Drew had backed Clancy beneath the shade of a black wattle. The horse dozed sporadically, resting a hind foot. Drew's left foot insisted on going to sleep.

He felt them before he heard them. A certain low vibration, travelling through Clancy's body into his own, alerting them both. In the distance came the faint cries of men and the drumming of hoofs. Careful now. Don't show yourself without cause. Let the mob momentum carry the horses right through to the yards. The noise grew louder. A volley of whip cracks told him they'd tried to make a break. Drew didn't breathe until he was sure they were still on track. Then, bursting over the brow of the ridge, he saw them.

An avalanche of horses in full flight, flanked either side by riders, was heading straight for the trap. There was Chiquita in the lead, and Jarrang bringing up the rear, galloping dangerously close to the lower hessian fence. Dust plumed in their wake, and hammering hoofs dislodged rocks that rattled and rolled down the mountainside. Clancy trembled beneath him. Drew didn't need Sam's *looking through another's eyes* strategy to appreciate the spectacle. By anyone's yardstick it was a magnificent sight.

The mob thundered closer. In another minute they'd be past him. Tom trailed close to Jarrang. The stallion's pace lacked the panicked quality of the other brumbies. Instead, he moved with a watchful, confident grace. If any horse broke rank, it would be him.

As the mob drew close, Clancy's excitement got the better of him. He raised his head and let out a long, trumpeting neigh. The sound quivered right through his body, through the saddle, through Drew. Without missing a beat, Jarrang veered into the hessian wing, tearing it apart at a join only metres from them. Clancy leapt forward and flung himself into the stallion's shoulder. For one bone-jarring moment it seemed all three of them might come crashing to earth. But as Drew recovered his balance, he plied the stockwhip with all his might and sent Jarrang hurtling back down the hill after the herd, with Tom hard on his heels.

The horses approached the open gate and the riders slackened their headlong pursuit. Nobody wanted Bill's mare to hit the yard at a dangerous gallop. With perfect timing, first Chiquita, and then the brumbies surged in at a slow canter. They milled around, shapes blurred by dust, in search of an escape route. But the trap was already sprung, the slip rails in place.

Drew glanced around for Sam. There she was, trotting back down the hill. Somehow she'd swapped her helmet for Charlie's hat. Sam joined him by the yards. They dismounted and surveyed their catch. Twelve horses in all. Jarrang kept a close eye on the humans, like he was assessing what danger they might pose. His mares and youngsters had arranged themselves facing the other way at the back of the yard. They presented a solid row of round rumps. When Sam moved around the yard, the brumbies quietly rearranged themselves, maintaining the maximum possible amount of distance from her.

The two heelers emerged from the bush, wild-eyed and panting. They trotted up to Drew, tails wagging, and he leant down to pat the spent animals. Dogs were worth their weight in gold on a mountain muster. Where thick trees or scrub might turn a rider, dogs could run right through and set a breaking beast back on course.

Tom led his horse over. The gelding was lathered in sweat and caked with dust. 'We had a bugger of a job finding them. You did well to hold that buckskin.' Drew nodded in recognition of the compliment. Tom didn't give them lightly. 'We'll leave the mob overnight to settle down. Cut Chiquita out, will you, and yard her separately. The trucks will be here in the morning.'

Drew nodded again. 'How about I pick Chiquita up this evening,' said Drew, 'along with one of those brumbies? That'll leave ten horses, two trucks' worth. Save you making an extra trip.' Behind Tom's back, Sam pressed her palms together and mouthed a thank you.

'Good idea,' said Tom. 'Want a hand?'

'We'll be right,' said Drew. 'I'll drop the brumby off at the showgrounds after I've taken Chiquita home.'

Tom nodded. 'There's a nice young grey in that lot,' he said. 'A decent size and all. I reckon she'd suit the stock contractors. That stallion too.' He glanced at Sam. 'Charlie.' The barest acknowledgement, then he led his horse off towards the troughs.

'Stock contractors?' asked Sam.

'They supply bulls and bucking horses for rodeos.' Drew didn't like the look on Sam's face. 'Don't worry. I promised you Jarrang, didn't I?'

'What about that grey Tom's talking about?'

'The Brumby Coalition buys any likely youngsters. She'll be fine. Anyway, rodeo horses have a good enough life. Only work for maybe eight seconds a day, two days a week. There are worse gigs.'

Sam looked unpersuaded. 'You said the Brumby Coalition takes the young ones. What happens to the rest?'

'They'll go through the feature horse sale, next picnic race day. The sale I told you about last night – the one where you might be able to pick up that string of good trail horses, if you have a mind to.'

'Will any of these brumbies go for slaughter?'

Jesus. He really didn't want to get into this with her. 'I don't know,' he said. Sam turned and moved off along the rails. Drew followed her, getting his first good look at the captured horses, standing well back so as not to stress them. He spotted the young grey straight away. Tom was right. The mare was no average brumby. Sired by Jarrang, to go by her presence, and the unusual stripes on her hoofs. But she wasn't out of any of these mares. Way too tall for one thing. A three-year-old, he guessed, from Jarrang's first crop of foals. Powerful body, well balanced with great bone. Clean legs. An elegant head, slightly convex in profile, and the most magnificent full mane and tail he'd ever seen. Who might her mother be?

'She's stunning,' said Sam, eyes filled with admiration. 'Can I have her too?'

'You're joking, right?' She didn't look like she was joking. 'Contract runners get to keep the brumbies as part payment for their work,' he explained. 'They'll want them auctioned off at the highest price. It's going to be hard enough explaining when Jarrang goes missing.'

'I'll buy her at the sale then,' said Sam.

'If you want. She's a nice type of filly.' Sam's expression brightened. Drew took another look at the grey. Very nice indeed. Maybe he'd buy her himself as a present for Sam. Chiquita pricked up her ears as Sam offered a handful of hay through the rails. Jarrang bared his teeth, warning the mare not to approach the humans. 'Stay away,' said Drew. 'Just let them settle.'

The other men didn't stick around for long. A shared thermos of tea, a brief rest for the dogs and they were gone. In spite of Drew's admonitions, Sam remained glued to the rails, watching the brumbies. Jarrang watched back. Occasionally he rolled his eyes, or laid back his ears at her. 'I reckon that stallion's the only one in Currajong who can tell straight off that you're not Charlie,' said Drew. Sam smiled at him. She looked extraordinarily beautiful, face flushed pink with happiness, glossy hair escaping from a careless knot at the nape of her neck. 'Come on,' he said, giving himself a swift kick. 'It's time to cut out some horses.'

It didn't prove too difficult to separate Jarrang and Chiquita from the mob. Chiquita had greedy eyes for the bucket of oats, and Jarrang had greedy eyes for Chiquita. When the mare finally slipped past her jealous keeper into the side yard, eager for a treat, he followed in an attempt to retrieve her. Drew stood guard between the two horses and the gate, stockwhip in hand, while Sam secured the sliprails. 'Nothing to it,' she said with a triumphant grin.

They fed the stock and filled the troughs. 'I want to stay here while you get the truck,' said Sam, still staring at the horses.

'They won't disappear, you know, if you take your eyes off them,' he said. Sam didn't answer, didn't even look around. The brumbies had apparently hypnotised her. With the exception of Jarrang, the horses paid no attention to Sam, as if by determinedly ignoring their captor she might go away. A dun foal, the baby of the group, occasionally peeked at the humans from between its mother's legs. The others stood with backs turned, deceptively quiet in the fierce noon-day heat. They could have been a string of riding school horses on a lunchtime break. Only Jarrang remained vigilant.

Drew untied Clancy and swung into the saddle. 'You sure you'll be okay out here by yourself?' She didn't seem to hear him. 'Sam?' At last she turned around.

'What about Jarrang?' she asked.

'I'll pick him up in the truck this arvo, along with Tambo and

Chiquita, drop him off at your place on the way through. Got your phone?'

Sam nodded. 'What will you tell Tom?'

'That I lost him. He'll think I'm a fool, but what can he do?'

'I can't thank you enough,' said Sam. 'Just wait until I tell Charlie.'

Drew wheeled Clancy around. 'Don't thank me too soon,' he said, pointing to Jarrang. 'That one's trouble on four legs. You might be cursing me before too long.'

Sam waited at the yards for Drew. It was hot, too hot. The glare of the sun made her squint. She fanned herself with Charlie's hat. Its broad-brimmed protection hadn't been enough, and a deep flush of heat warned that her nose and cheeks would be painfully red and sunburned by morning. Why hadn't she bothered with sunscreen? Back home, she wouldn't even walk down the street without following her mother's carefully prescribed skincare regime. Yet out here in the bush? In the sun, with the flies and the dust and the heat? Out here it didn't seem important.

At least the heat helped take her mind off Drew. She had no idea what had happened between them. Last night they'd been – well, she'd been – she didn't really know, but she'd been ready to do just about anything for him. And now, while Drew wasn't cold, he was treating her with a certain distance. If only she had someone to talk to about it. Maybe Charlie could help? On second thoughts, maybe not. Sam had the feeling there was history between Drew and Charlie, and she wasn't sure she wanted to know what it was.

She turned back to the horses. Eleven brumbies in all. Jarrang, six mares, three yearlings and the foal. Most were bays, very cob in type, with lightly feathered legs and lots of white markings. Superior height and conformation set Jarrang and the young grey well and truly apart from the rest. The pair were in top condition. From a distance they'd all looked well, with shiny summer coats and fat bellies. But on closer inspection, the others weren't so good. Skinny necks, prominent ribs, jutting hip bones. Their fat bellies more indicative of pregnancy or a load of worms than anything else.

Bushy had dispelled Sam's romantic notions about brumbies. 'It's a hard life, especially for a mare,' he'd told her. 'Pregnant, back to back, when you're no more than a baby yourself. There's droughts and freezing winters. Parasites. Wild dogs take foals and injury's a death sentence. To top it off, them brumby-runner fellas are out to get you.'

Sam came from a world where horses lived in pine-lined loose boxes and sheltered day yards. They ate nutritionally balanced pellet and grain mixes, wore satin hoods and rugs, and travelled in padded floats, with bandaged legs and sheepskin boots. An image of Pharaoh came to mind. What would he make of this harsh, magnificent place? Sweat dripped from her nose. It was so hot that even the ants had gone to ground. Defeated by the sun, she sought out the shade of the hut's little verandah. The plastic water bottle in her saddlebag was warm, its contents unappetising. The creek presented a far more inviting option. Sam checked her phone. Hours yet before Drew would return with the truck.

She slipped from her shirt and jeans, and left them on the porch. Dressed only in bra, panties and riding boots, Sam made her way to the creek. Giant tree-fern fronds filtered the sunshine here, in this cool haven from the dust and flies. Soon her boots lay discarded on the bank. Smooth pebbles and damp river sand lodged between her toes. The stream, when it hit her feet, was painfully cold. She let out an involuntary squeal. Hard to believe that the heat of the air and the cool of the water could exist in such delicious proximity. Soon she was numb to her knees, her thighs, her sensitive waist. Fallen logs, woven together, had created a natural dam. When she stood in the deepest part of the creek, the water reached her breasts. The icy shock made her think of Drew; of his hands, and the charge that had spread through her body at his touch. Enough of that she told herself.

Sam paused mid-stream. The trick was not to imagine the biting creatures that Drew had so kindly alerted her to: the water bugs and yabbies; the snakes? But the creek was clear as glass, transparent as the water in her swimming pool back home in Toorak. Surely she'd spot any danger? Sam ducked down and let her hair fan out on the water. Heaven. She could linger in this shady sanctuary forever.

It was then she saw it — the striped, bronze reptilian head, barely wider than its dark copper body. It slid from the bracken towards the creek, forked tongue flicking in and out, tasting the air. Tasting her? Keep still, wasn't that the advice? She hardly dared to breathe. The snake stopped, frozen like Sam herself, and the pair were locked in a deadly standoff. An intricate pattern of pale cream scales striped its gleaming length. The creature had been hand-painted by a grand master. Was she safe in the water? She didn't know, didn't know enough about snakes, didn't know enough about living in the bush. She should be in Le Midi, relaxing at her grandmother's elegant villa at Provence. Such a safe place, filled with history and art. She tried to imagine it — no yarding of untamed horses, no confusing romantic notions ... no snakes.

But her imagination reached only as far as Brumby's Run. The idea of this wilderness had consumed memories of gentler places. Her calves ached, yet her thighs were numb. For how long could she stand so still? She guessed the patient reptile could outwait her. They stared at each other. Its eyes were twin yellow globes. They blazed with a sort of fire, beautiful and mesmerising. Like being lost staring into flames. She understood how helpless the snake's prey might feel, caught in that hypnotic gaze.

Was that an engine? Surely Drew couldn't be back with the truck yet? Or had fright made her lose track of time? Sam wanted to call out, wanted to scream for help. But that might antagonise the snake. It lay wound in elegant coils on the bank, still intent upon her, to judge by its stare. The sound of the motor grew louder and louder, then stopped. Perhaps she should make a run for it? Or should she just stay still, and wait for Drew to come and find her? The snake raised its head and Sam let out an involuntary scream. It flared its neck a fraction, looked left, looked right, then slid into the pool. Barely breaking the surface tension, it glided towards her in a serpentine pattern, the first quarter of its metre-long body rearing from the water.

A figure appeared at the periphery of her vision. 'Don't move,' said an unfamiliar male voice. For some unlikely reason the voice had a German accent. She couldn't have moved even if she'd wanted too — frozen as she was, legs dead from cold, with the snake closing in. If she took her eyes off it for even a second, she knew it would strike.

'Don't scare her. She won't hurt you if you stay still.' Who was that? And how the hell did he know? The snake lowered its head, so the full length of its bronze body sailed on the surface.

Only centimetres away now, it paused. 'Hold your nerve,' said the voice. The snake reached out with infinite slowness. Sam willed herself to stone, felt the fleeting tickle of a forked tongue on her goose-fleshed arm. She flinched and the snake vanished into the reeds. Sam remembered to breathe again, relief flooding her body and leaving her limp with shock.

A man dressed in khaki stood on the bank. Mid-twenties, slim and athletic-looking, with close-cropped blond hair and serious grey eyes. 'You've had a close encounter with Austrelaps ramsayi. Gravid, I'd guess, by her girth. A rare privilege.' Sam staggered from the pool, all too conscious that she wore only underwear. Her nipples pushed, embarrassingly erect, against the translucent wet cotton of her bra. She wrapped her arms around her chest, convulsed with violent shivers. 'So it wasn't dangerous?' she asked, teeth chattering from more than cold.

'On the contrary.' His tone was clipped and formal, such a contrast to the usual Aussie country drawl. 'Alpine copper-heads are extremely dangerous. Quite capable of inflicting fatal bites.'

'Then why did you say it wouldn't hurt me?' she asked, incredulous.

'They're shy, not usually aggressive,' he answered calmly. 'Bites are uncommon.'

'Uncommon?' repeated Sam. She'd meant the word to drip with

sarcasm, but the stranger either misunderstood or deliberately overlooked her intent.

'Yes, quite uncommon. Even on land, a snake can only strike a distance of half its body length. A snake in water does not have a solid surface to thrust against, so its striking ability while swimming is quite limited. You were probably in no danger.'

She wanted to scream, shout at this idiot, whose only advice during an encounter with a deadly snake was not to scare it. But confronting a strange man while so scantily clad was not ideal. 'Do you mind if I get dressed?'

'Of course not. That would seem prudent.'

Jesus, he really was Mr Literal. The afternoon heat swiftly chased away the chill from her frozen legs. She hurried back, grabbed her clothes and dressed in the privacy of the hut. Why she should be so modest about putting clothes back on was a mystery to her.

'Whose horses?' he asked, when she emerged.

Sam didn't answer. She wasn't quite sure who they actually belonged to, and anyway, shouldn't she be the one asking the questions here?

'Who exactly are you?' she demanded.

The man extended his arm. 'Balleroo park ranger Karl Richter, at your service.' She shook his hand, which was smooth with a gentle grip. 'These are feral horses, then?'

She didn't like the way he said feral horses. The term stripped them of their dignity. 'They're brumbies, with a few saddle horses among them.'

The man looked suddenly stern. 'I suppose you know that a permit is required to remove feral horses from the park?'

She shrugged. 'Sorry, I don't know anything about that. You'll have to talk to Drew Chandler.'

'Chandler.' The ranger rolled the name around on his tongue. 'He owns Kilmarnock Station, right?'

Sam nodded. 'Drew and his dad, Bill.'

'This area is not part of the grazing trial,' said Karl. 'Cattle have been roaming illegally here for weeks. Once I identify their owner, somebody's in a lot of trouble.' He frowned. 'I'm new and don't know the locals yet, but I've been briefed that either the Chandlers or the Kellys are the most likely culprits. Your surname isn't Chandler, is it? Or Kelly, perhaps?'

Sam didn't know what to say, mind spinning through the possible responses, weighing them up. Karl was new here and didn't know folks – that's what he'd said. She could take advantage of that ignorance. 'My name's Samantha Carmichael and I live in Melbourne,' she said. 'I'm just visiting Currajong.'

Karl gave her a searching look, then walked over to the yards and peered through the rails at Chiquita. Jarrang took offence. The stallion laid his ears flat back and, accompanied by a series of ferocious snorts, thundered to the fence. The ranger leaped back. Something in his manner told Sam that Karl knew nothing about horses. 'Christ almighty,' he said. 'You could have warned me.'

'Like you warned me about your deadly snake?' asked Sam.

Karl laughed. 'Touché, Miss Carmichael. I suppose that vicious brute is one of the brumbies?'

Sam ignored his stupid comment. All this talk of permits had her worried. Had Drew run this roundup by the book or not? Could Karl confiscate the mob if their paperwork wasn't in order? What would happen to the horses then? 'No,' she said, quickly. 'That's Jarrang. He's mine, along with the baldie-faced bay. And the golden chestnut mare belongs to the Chandlers.' Karl looked around vaguely. It was obvious that he couldn't identify the particular horses by reference to their coat colours, and anybody with any horse sense would guess Jarrang was no stockhorse. Karl didn't have a clue. Sam almost claimed the grey filly as well, but Drew had been so insistent she must go with the others.

The ranger approached the yards again, wary this time. 'That's ten ferals then. I'll be checking someone holds a valid licence to remove them. Don't misunderstand me, you're doing a good job here, getting rid of them I mean. There's a plan to eliminate wild horses from the park all together. Management's considering an aerial cull.'

'What?' said Sam, with a growing sense of horror. 'You don't mean shoot them?'

Karl nodded. 'It's not an ideal solution, if you ask me,' he said. 'A public relations disaster waiting to happen. But one way or another, the brumbies have to go.' Jarrang reared. Karl backed off with such haste that he stumbled over a grassy tussock and almost fell. 'Well,' he said, regaining his balance. 'If you see the Chandlers or Mary Kelly, let them know I want a word.' He handed Sam his card. 'Now you're dressed, you have a pocket to put it in. How very convenient.' What a nerve. 'Well, it's been a pleasure to meet you, Miss Carmichael. You look quite fetching in your underwear, by the way.' She wanted to slap him. Instead she just watched him climb in his jeep and head off in a cloud of dust.

The scorching sun was already sinking low in the western sky before the truck bumped back up the track. Sam's heart lifted at the sight of it. Drew's face grinned at her from the cab. He'd brought a hamper of choice sandwiches and pastries prepared by Mai, which Sam wolfed down, along with a bottle of warm lemonade.

They loaded Tambo first, then Chiquita. 'How are we going to do this?' asked Sam, pointing to the stallion, who was climbing the rails.

'Why don't you just let him go?' suggested Drew. 'Save yourself a world of strife.' Sam shook her head. She told Drew of Karl's visit, and of the proposal to cull the brumbies. She left out the bit about the snake and being caught in her undies. 'I heard they'd hired a new ranger,' he said. 'The last bloke was a lazy so-and-so, never gave us any trouble.'

'This one seems keen,' said Sam.

'That's a problem then. Okay, let's get Jarrang loaded. We can't have him being used for target practice, can we?' Sam was prepared for a long and difficult fight to get the stallion on the truck. But Jarrang ascended the ramp with surprising alacrity, and began to preen Chiquita's neck. 'He'd follow that mare anywhere,' said Drew. 'And remember, Jarrang was hand raised. He doesn't have the same fear or respect for all things human as a normal, wild-born brumby does.'

Tambo took advantage of Chiquita's close proximity to sniff her flanks, then her tail. He tilted his head up and curled his lip, savouring the mare's scent. The stock crate rattled and shook as a jealous Jarrang made a concerted effort to attack him through the steel partition. Tambo snapped back.

'Tambo's a gelding,' said Sam. 'Why is he interested in Chiquita?'

Drew double-checked the tail gate and grinned 'He can dream, can't he?'

'Will those two fight,' asked Sam, 'when we get them home?'

'Probably,' said Drew. 'Although Jarrang won't be so full of himself without his mares. They'll have nothing to argue about.'

An orange sunset streaked the sky by the time they unloaded the horses at Brumby's Run. The air was still oppressively hot. What Sam wouldn't do for air-conditioning … Drew helped her settle Jarrang and Tambo in adjoining yards. Then he reloaded Chiquita. 'Time to say goodbye to your girlfriend.' The stallion reared. Drew climbed into the cab of the truck and set off down the track. Chiquita and Jarrang exchanged frantic neighs until the truck was out of earshot. Then, just as Drew had predicted, the buckskin fell quiet. More than that, he was positively lounging – head low, ears relaxed, resting a back foot. No male posturing at all.

Tambo boldly touched his nose to Jarrang's. With rivalries apparently forgotten, the stallion pricked his ears in polite acknowledgement, then resumed his nap. Sam burst out laughing, in spite of her exhaustion and headache and sunburn. For some unaccountable reason, she was reminded of New Year's Eve. Maybe men were like that too? Only at each other's throats when you added a girl to the mix? Perhaps Spike and Drew would have behaved like old mates as well, if they'd met down the pub that night, instead of in Sam's kitchen.

CHAPTER 19

This was Sam's first picnic race day. The quiet, almost deserted racecourse where she worked each day with Bushy and the brumbies, had been transformed into a vibrant festival of colour and crowds. She looked warily around, keeping her hat pulled down firmly over her eyes. Such a public outing was fraught with risk. Which identity was she supposed to claim?

'Here you go,' said Drew. 'One roast beef roll and a coke.'

It had been three weeks since New Year's Eve, and there'd been a certain tension between them ever since. Sam had no idea what to do about it. The odd glance, the odd brush of the hand or leg told her that the story wasn't over. Drew remained attentive and helpful, but that was all. Sam was utterly bewildered. Had she done something to make him back off?

In his father's absence, Drew had organised the removal of Kilmarnock cattle from Brumby's Run. They'd spent last weekend mustering the Kelly herd home, watching the cows and calves reclaim the rich pastures and shady creek flats that belonged to them. He'd cut out the bulls, trucked them to the Wodonga saleyards and returned with a cheque made out to *M. Kelly*. Sam had proudly deposited it into Mary's account the next morning. The rush of pleasure and pride provoked by that achievement was in no way proportionate to the small sum involved.

To say thank you, Sam had cooked dinner for Drew. If she was honest with herself, she'd hoped for a repeat of New Year's Eve, minus the interruption. She'd found instructions for preparing a Sunday roast in a dusty cookbook, and had spent an afternoon struggling to understand the mysteries of Mary's ancient oven. The bottom rack seemed barely to warm food at all. The top rack burned everything to cinders. With a great deal of trial and error, she'd turned out a passable meal with all the trimmings. Drew had been full of praise, devoured several helpings, then finished off the tiny tub of toffee ice-cream that barely fitted in her miniscule freezer. He'd complimented her on dessert, as if she'd made it herself. Afterwards they'd played poker for matchsticks, drunk cider until midnight — and still nothing.

She'd been weak with anticipation when, at the end of the evening, Drew had finally gathered her into his arms by the door. But a brief, almost perfunctory, kiss on the lips was all that followed. Then he was gone into the bright night. She'd wandered across to visit Tambo and Jarrang, her mind in turmoil. The stallion had half-reared at her approach, a *levade* equal in elegance to any performed at the Spanish Riding School in Vienna. The moon's orb loomed low on the horizon. Stars pricked the roof of the sky, dazzling in their brilliance, and a warm wind played through the trees. It had been a night tailor-made for romance. What a waste.

'Do you want to watch this?' asked Drew, dragging her thoughts back to the present. He pointed to a sheep-dog display going on in the arena. Sam surreptitiously studied his handsome face in profile. What on earth was she doing wrong?

'Let's eat lunch in the stands,' she suggested. Sam loved the Federation timber and cast-iron grandstand, so full of old-world bush charm. Together they climbed the wooden stairs beneath the broad verandah, weaving their way through the throng to a space near the top. 'Now,' said Sam, as she gazed across the track to the forested mountainside beyond. 'Can we go through the plan one more time?'

'There's not much to it,' said Drew, downing half a hot dog in one bite. 'We meet the bloke before the sale starts and make an offer. Don't worry, I'll suss out the auctioneer on the price first.'

'When do I get to see these horses I'm supposed to be buying?' asked Sam.

'The truck from Gidgee isn't here yet. But like I said,' Drew swallowed the other half of the hot dog, 'I've already checked them out.' Sam couldn't quite believe it. In the space of a month she'd be going from completely horseless, to buying ten in one fell swoop.

Charlie had loved the idea of setting up a trail-riding business. 'Fantastic,' she'd said. 'I know every inch of Balleroo. We could do a ride to Maroong Mountain, with the best view in Victoria. Bluff Falls could be another. What about platypus-watching at Snake Creek Billabong? Or brumby-spotting? Maybe an eco-ride, visiting endangered alpine bogs.'

Sam was pleased to hear the newfound strength and enthusiasm in her sister's voice, but she couldn't help wondering how practical the plan really was. When would Charlie realistically be fit enough to conduct these rides? She'd need a lot of help, and for an extended period. You couldn't run such an operation by yourself. There were costs too, for insurance and registration fees. Permits to ride in the national park. So many rules and regulations to comply with. Would they need to provide food for clients? What about toilets? First aid? Riding equipment? And the most important question of all — what would happen when Sam took up her university course in Melbourne in a month's time? The prospect of leaving Brumby's Run, of leaving Drew, was gut-wrenching.

Drew had dismissed Sam's fears out of hand. 'You can count on me,' he'd said. 'Tom's got Kilmarnock running like clockwork. It's so much easier with Dad away. He makes such a big production of everything. I reckon Tom will manage fine without me for a bit.'

'For a bit?' she'd said. 'We're going to need help for more than a bit.' But that wasn't quite true. It wouldn't be *we*. Soon it would be Charlie alone who'd need Drew's help.

'For longer then,' Drew had responded. 'Let's just concentrate on getting our hands on those horses.' Sam's imagination took flight.

Drew and Charlie, working side by side, building up the business. Riding the wild slopes of Balleroo without her. Sam suddenly lost her appetite. 'You've got a bit of gravy on you,' said Drew. He reached out his hand, dabbing gently at her chin with a paper serviette. Sam shivered, but just as soon as his hand touched her skin, it was gone again.

Drew turned away to hide his frustration. It was maddening. He'd simply reached out to wipe Sam's chin, and had almost wiped away his resolve instead. His resolve not to fall for her. The moment he'd touched her, Drew knew he was in trouble. It had taken all his determination to keep his distance from Sam over these past weeks. She hadn't made it easy. She'd been giving him every come-on signal in the book. The flick of her head, the intense eye contact, the half-smile that promised something good, something wonderful. It took a monumental effort to resist. Then Drew thought back to New Year's Eve, and it was suddenly easy.

That night when Spike had shown up. The night when Drew had remembered why he didn't want to mess with the Kelly girls – or the Carmichael girls, or whatever they were called. Not again, mate, he'd told himself. He'd seen it too many times before, the way girls looked at that puffed-up narcissist. He'd seen it with Charlie. It was the same way Sam had looked at Spike that evening. He'd been about to take her to bed, and next thing she's making goo-goo eyes at Captain Fantastic. And then there was the knowledge that Sam was hiding something from him – like the real reason she was at Brumby's Run, and where exactly her sister and mother might be. It was enough to make a bloke seriously gun shy.

A piercing double whistle blasted him out of his reverie. Speak of the devil. Spike bounded up the grandstand, two stairs at a time, a broad grin on his stupid face. Drew groaned. He'd thought Spike was safely away on the rodeo circuit.

'You two kids having fun?' Spike punched him lightly in the arm.

Drew gave him a sour smile, his hand clenching into a fist. 'Hear you're after Terry Mitchell's horses,' said Spike. 'What's up with that?'

Sam opened her mouth to speak, but Drew's black expression warned her off.

'Don't all talk at once,' said Spike, plonking himself down and lighting a cigarette with maddening slowness. The cold shoulder didn't seem to worry him one bit. He seemed perfectly happy just to sit and stare at Sam.

'Those horses are for Brumby's Run,' said Sam at last. 'We're thinking of branching out into trail rides.'

'We?' asked Spike. 'I do so hope you're talking business partners only.' A loudspeaker announced the next race, the Currajong Ladies Bracelet. Spike blew a series of expert smoke rings. 'And it doesn't hurt that four of Terry's mares are registered Australian stock horses now, does it?' Spike moved closer to Sam. She crossed her legs as he lowered his voice and stage-whispered in her ear. 'Drew wanted a stock-horse stud for Christmas, but Daddy wouldn't buy him one.' He tapped the side of his nose with his forefinger. 'Looks like you're going to be Santa Claus instead.'

'Shove off, Spike,' said Drew roughly, pulling Sam to her feet. 'Or better still, we will.' He bustled her down the steps, out into the throng and over to a grassy spectator mound. Time to change the subject. 'See there?' said Drew, pointing to where transports were pulling up at the stock pens behind the racecourse. 'Your horses have arrived.'

The Mitchell horses milled about the yard. Six mares: two chestnuts, two creams, a brown and a black. Two solid taffy geldings with flaxen manes and tails, and a pair of skewbald ponies with the longest blond forelocks and eyelashes Sam had ever seen. 'They're gorgeous,' she said to Drew, pleasantly surprised. The label of *trail horse* had conjured up an image of worn-out riding-school hacks. One of the ponies came up to the rails and explored Sam's outstretched hand with its warm, whiffling muzzle.

'Knew you'd like them,' said Drew. He was looking pretty smug. 'Those two mares in the corner?' He pointed to the pair of classy chestnuts with white stars. 'They're in foal to Condamine Joe.' She looked blank. 'That stallion is a legend, and he carries a double Abbey cross in his pedigree.' To judge by the excitement on his face, this was something very special indeed. However Spike's words still echoed disturbingly in her ear.

'What use will broodmares be in a trail-riding operation?' she asked. Drew wasn't listening. Instead he was up and over the rail, talking to a stout, elderly man in a blue singlet. Why hadn't they thought this through more carefully? She didn't even know by what name she should introduce herself.

Sam climbed over the fence, and with an apologetic smile to the man, pulled Drew aside. 'Who does he think I am?' she whispered.

'Does it matter?' asked Drew.

'Of course it matters. I'm not committing fraud by signing my sister's name on any transfer papers.' Sam could hear the rising irritation in her voice. 'And what about the cost? What's he asking?'

'You won't believe this.' Drew glanced around as if somebody might be eavesdropping. 'Three thousand bucks for the lot, including all their gear. The sentimental old codger has a mind to keep the string together.'

Sam did some quick thinking. It would leave her with almost no savings, but she couldn't argue with that price. And Bushy paid her a modest wage in cash each week. If it came to the crunch she could always ask her father for money. Equine buying and selling certainly was a different proposition back home in Melbourne. Trials, guarantees, insurance, exhaustive vet checks. That would have been the deal when Andrew bought Pharaoh, but here in Currajong she was contemplating buying ten horses without ever having seen them under saddle. A pig in a poke, as Bushy would say. All she had was Drew's vague assurance that he'd checked them out. It was madness.

Sam looked from the lovely herd to Drew's expectant face, and then back to the herd. She imagined the horses grazing in the paddocks of Brumby's Run. She imagined Jarrang's excitement when he laid eyes on those pretty mares. She drew a huge breath and nodded. 'Let's do it.'

Terry Mitchell heard her and looked hopeful. 'We have a deal then?

Good on yer. You'll never find a finer string at the price. Just promise me they'll get a good home.'

'Of course,' Sam reassured him. 'Will you take a cheque?' She was half-afraid Mary's reputation had preceded her, but Terry just nodded and smiled expansively. She wrote out the cheque, then took possession of the sheaf of transfer papers and service certificates. Sam signed her name as Samantha Carmichael, but Terry didn't bat an eyelid, and continued to happily call her Charlie.

One of the friendly ponies laid its head on Terry's arm. He hugged its neck, burying his face in its bushy mane. Was this tough-looking man crying? 'You be good then, Topsy.' He turned to go, his face crumpled and red.

'Wait,' said Sam. She could see how much these horses meant to the man. 'You can't leave yet. Not before I know a bit about each of them.' She dug around in her bag for a pen and notepad.

A grin cracked Terry's face. 'Well, you've met Topsy, and that,' he said, pointing to the matching skewbald pony, 'is his mate Turvy.' For half an hour Sam listened to Terry talking about his horses like they were best friends. 'Those cream mares, they're wild-caught brumbies. Quietest, most well-mannered horses you could find. And see that liver chestnut by the trough? That's Flicka. She's due in the middle of March. It's her first foal, so she'll bear extra watching. And Jet,' he called to the black mare, who disengaged herself from the herd and walked straight to him. 'Jet, here,' he said, stroking her cheek. 'Jet loves to be at the front of the ride. She'll jog and fuss otherwise, so you may as well let her have her way.'

Sam carefully recorded all he told her. When he was finally ready to leave, he shook Sam's hand, an expression of immense gratitude on his face. 'You treat 'em right, and they'll do the same to you. I reckon they couldn't be in safer hands.' The old man hobbled from the yard without a backward glance.

'That was a good thing you did,' said Drew.

'It was practical, that's all,' said Sam. 'How else would I know that Ruby only stands for the farrier if she gets liquorice?'

Drew's laugh lit up his handsome face and Sam's misgivings fell away. Everything would be okay. She and Drew would make this trail-riding operation a success. His enthusiasm for the deal was infectious. 'Come on,' he said, giving Topsy a final scratch behind the ears. 'The auction's about to start.'

A stand was set up in front of the campdrafting ring where the feature sale was to be held. The sign above it read *National Brumby Association.* Sam browsed the posters and other paraphernalia on display. 'There's a brumby studbook?' she asked the round woman behind the trestle-table counter. 'I had no idea.'

The woman nodded. 'Established in 2007 to promote the Australian Heritage Brumby as a recognised breed.' She introduced herself as Margot, and handed Sam a brochure. *The Australian Brumby Horse Register,* read Sam, *brings to owners the formalisation of the Brumby as a unique breed. It will help to preserve the bloodlines and the heritage of this unique animal, that has developed through natural selection in the wild for more than a century.*

'Do you have a particular interest in brumbies?' asked Margot. 'Or perhaps you own one?'

Sam considered the questions. Two months ago she barely knew what a brumby was. She knew nothing of the world of wild horses. But now? She'd spent the past month working with over forty of them. She supposed that counted as a special interest.

Did she own one? Come to think of it, she actually owned more than one. There was Tambo — technically Charlie's, but as good as hers. And Jarrang? She smiled to herself. Could anybody really own Jarrang? Then there were Terry Mitchell's creamy brumby mares - *her* creamy brumby mares now. She even had the transfer papers in the name of Samantha Carmichael to prove it. After what had happened with Pharaoh, that was a very reassuring thing. And what about Phoenix? Sam had decided some time ago that, sooner or later, the golden colt would be hers. And then there was that graceful grey from Jarrang's mob – she wanted her too. 'Yes,' she answered at last. 'Yes to both questions.'

'You'll want to join then.' Margot handed her a membership form. 'And register your horse.' A registration form landed in her hand. Sam must have looked unsure, for Margot went into a promotional spiel, worthy of the finest infomercial host. 'The National Brumby Association accepts all authentic brumbies into the register, and welcomes anyone interested in preserving our brumby heritage to become a member. All horses that can be verified as coming from a wild herd are eligible. Progeny from authenticated brumbies can also join, and there's an appendix register for part-bred brumbies.' She paused for breath. 'If your brumby isn't registered, please consider joining.'

What could she say to that? Apart from, 'Can I have some more registration forms please?'

Margot beamed. The loudspeaker announced the sale was about to begin. 'Come and see me afterwards if you've got any questions,' said Margot. Sam thanked her and went to find Drew.

Drew and Sam sat on one of the giant hay bales surrounding the campdrafting arena. The auctioneer knocked down the last of Bushy's horses to a local family, and the pretty yearling pranced from the ring. There'd been a surprisingly strong demand for the ground-broken young brumbies, even from interstate. Sam would miss working with them, and was very glad Bushy had held Phoenix over. There was no way she could have afforded to buy the colt now, not after paying for the Mitchell string.

'Want a beer?' asked Drew.

Sam nodded. He jumped down and wandered off towards the bar. The loudspeaker crackled back to life: 'Next we offer a yarding of ten wild brumbies, captured three weeks ago straight off Maroong Mountain.' Jarrang's mob. She looked around for Drew. He wouldn't want to miss this.

Sam felt the weight of somebody scaling the bale behind her, then two hands covered her eyes. She yelped. 'Drew, so help me ...!' But it wasn't Drew. It was Spike.

'Disappointed?' he asked, flashing a winning smile.

'Annoyed is more like it,' Sam said. 'Now shush. I want to see what happens.' The elegant grey mare trotted into the ring. No – it was more like she floated in. Sam had seen that graceful gait before. She racked her brain to think where it had been. National dressage championships, Sydney equestrian centre, Horsley Park. A charismatic, dappled stallion, the first Andalusian she'd ever seen in the flesh, performing the passage – a high-school movement consisting of an elevated and extremely powerful trot. How was it that this brumby mare, straight off the mountain, moved with the same degree of collection and impulsion as had that exotic stallion from Spain? It was like she was dancing on air. An appreciative murmur rose from the crowd and the bidding commenced.

Ryan, the young welfare officer from the Brumby Coalition, made a bid. Sam did sums in her head for the umpteenth time. She couldn't possibly afford to buy again today. No matter. If the mare fell to Ryan she would be in charge of its basic education anyway. Plenty of time to save up for the mare, and for Phoenix as well. Now a rough-looking man to her left raised the bid. Sam peered around Spike, looking for Drew. Her shoulder inadvertently pressed against the bull rider and he responded with a subtle pressure of his own.

Sam moved away a fraction.

Ryan raised the offer, and the other bidder followed suit. A stray kelpie suddenly slipped between the rails and darted for the mare's heels. She exploded in a frenzy of bucking, hurling herself skywards with stiffened legs, spinning like a whirling dervish. The crowd cheered as she turned on the red dog and pursued him from the ring with flattened ears and bared teeth.

'Wayne won't let her go now,' said Spike, leaning close.

'Who's Wayne?'

Spike pointed at the rough man to her left. 'Wayne Clarke from Clarke and Sons. Rodeo contractors. That mare? She's got a mean buck.'

Sam's heart fell. Ryan had to buy her. The magnificent mare had to stay at the racecourse, safe with Bushy, safe with her. She couldn't go to some rodeo. Drew would help. Sam stood up and looked over the crowd milling below the stand. She spotted him wending his way back with drinks in hand. Sam waved both arms in the air. Great, Drew had seen her. He smiled and waved, but he was coming so slowly.

Sam jumped up and down, screaming his name. 'Drew, hurry up!' Some people nearby glared in her direction, but Sam didn't care. 'Quickly!' Couldn't he hear the auctioneer's voice over the loud-speaker. '*Wayne Clarke can see the potential in this young brumby as a bucking horse. He normally gets what he wants, and he wants this grey brumby. Do I hear a new bid?*' Sam already knew the answer; knew that Ryan was on a tight budget and couldn't compete with the cashed-up contractor.

The penny must have dropped for Drew. Too late, he came sprinting towards the stand. A brief scattering of applause, and the mare was knocked down to Wayne Clarke.

Sam sank back down onto the bench and buried her head in her hands.

'Not to worry, princess,' said Spike. 'A good bucking animal's worth its weight in gold to those guys. I've seen horses get a lot worse treatment in show-jumping rings. And don't even get me started on jumps races.' He moved sideways to let Drew through, then moved back before Drew was properly past, jostling him.

Drew shoved back, his face darkening. 'Don't tell me Wayne got his hands on that grey?' He handed Sam the beer. She took the can and nodded dumbly.

'I tried to tell her the horse'll be okay . . . ' Spike started.

'Shut up, Spike.' Drew took Sam's hand, tugged her from her seat and out of the stand.

'Sorry, Sam, but that bloke really rubs me the wrong way.' Drew took a swig of beer. 'And I'm sorry about that mare.' He took off his hat and wiped his brow with the back of his hand. 'I should have been here, should have bid on her myself — they usually leave the best horses until last. But for once, even though it kills me to admit it, I have to agree with Spike. Those rodeo blokes do the right thing by their stock.'

Sam couldn't agree. To her rodeos were blatant exhibitions of animal abuse that had no more place in a civilised society than cock-fighting or bear-baiting. It made her sick to the stomach, thinking of that lovely filly being forced to buck. And to think that she'd been involved in the horse's capture, that she was responsible for delivering her from a life of freedom to one of torment.

The auctioneer announced the next entry. The bay brumby with the inquisitive dun foal trotted into the ring. Sam turned to watch. Thank God Ryan was back in full swing. Bushy stood beside him as he bid against a thin man in a baseball cap. After the mother and foal were knocked down to him, Ryan spotted Sam by the rails and he and Bushy came over to say hello. Another horse entered the arena, an older roan mare this time. 'You'd better get back over there,' said Sam. 'The next brumby's out.'

Ryan made a show of turning his pants pockets inside out. 'I'm done for the day,' he said. 'It's a shame I lost the grey filly. What a beauty.'

'Drew says she'll be okay,' said Sam, doubtfully. 'So does Spike.' She was trying to convince herself as much as Ryan.

Bushy looked grave. 'Normally I'd agree with them fellas,' he said. 'But there's something about that horse.' He shook his head. 'I reckon rodeo will turn that one bad.' Nobody spoke for a bit, depressed by Bushy's gloomy prediction.

'On a brighter note,' said Ryan. 'You guys will have six new ones to work with on Monday.'

'Only six?' asked Sam. 'What will happen to the rest?' She pointed to the roan brumby, standing alert and uncertain in the middle of the arena. 'What will happen to her?'

'We can't save them all,' said Ryan and he turned away.

His words gave her a chill. When the sale was over, Sam returned to Margot at the stall.

'What got you into this brumby thing?' asked Sam.

'I suppose the original inspiration was an author, Elyne Mitchell. Like so many other girls of my generation, I was raised on the Silver Brumby books. When my husband and I bought our first brumbies, the meat truck pulled up behind us. They took the ones that we didn't take. I was horrified.'

Sam looked over at the chain-smoking man with the baseball cap who had just bought the nervous roan mare, and an awful realisation hit her. Mr Baseball Cap was the knackery man.

CHAPTER 20

It took only a week of working alongside Sam each day to completely destroy Drew's resolve. She was drop-dead gorgeous and his body had a mind of its own. At times his longing for her was so powerful that it felt like an illness.

They spent their days testing out the new horses, extending the yards, fixing up the sheds and disposing of truckloads of rubbish. The old place had never looked so good. Sam was always tantalisingly near; standing at the opposite end of a saw plank, or a two-man post hole digger. Having a crack at hoof trimming, bent down right in front of him while he steadied the head of a fractious horse. She was a fast learner, a quick thinker and never shirked a task, however difficult or unpleasant. The more he got to know her, the more he grew to love her. To hell with guarding his heart. It was time to take a risk.

On Saturday he took Sam on a ride, right to the rim of the range. To gaze out from Ram's Head Rock was like being suspended in space. It felt good, sharing that dramatic view with her. To the south the ridges were clothed with virgin forest, as far as the eye could see. To the west a jagged wall of granite cliffs rose like battlements. To the north a silver streamer hung down the cliff. It broke into rainbows of spray on the rocks below, filling a chain of deep reflective pools. A primeval scene. They could have been the last people on earth.

'Stay with me,' he said. 'Stay with me tonight at Dead Man's Hut.' His invitation echoed around the range. Sam studied his face for the longest time. He dreaded seeing reticence or refusal in her eyes. When she finally smiled her assent, he'd wanted to sing.

Dusk was falling fast by the time they reached the hut. Drew couldn't ever remember being so happy. He sat on the ground before the campfire, propped against his saddle, Sam's back between his knees. 'So what do you think of the Mitchell string now?' He lightly combed her silky hair between work-roughened fingers. 'Will they do?'

'They'll more than do,' she said. 'And that ride we took today? Seriously, it's stunning, absolutely magical. People will beat a path to our door for an experience like that.' Drew, leaned forward, gently turned her head, and kissed her, a proper kiss this time, a deeply sexual kiss. She could not have mistaken its meaning, and still her response was warm and eager, a consent not only with her lips, but with her entire body. Easy now. Don't push it.

The two creamy brumby mares nickered in their yard. Drew tore himself away from the kiss and jumped to his feet. 'Relax,' said Sam. 'Jarrang's safely back home at Brumby's Run. He won't be stealing any mares away from you tonight.'

That was true. The brumbies were gone from Maroong Mountain, for now at least, though it wouldn't take long for a new mob to claim Jarrang's deserted territory. Drew wandered over to the yards where the mares stood with high heads and pricked ears, transfixed by some invisible presence in the gloom. An uncertain moon rose behind the peak. It hesitated for a few moments, then throwing caution to the high winds, launched its round orb skywards. Soft light lit the night and gilded the cream mares in polished silver. A snowy owl silhouetted on a twisted branch hooted gently as Drew peered into the dark. Black limbs of trees gleamed pale against the sky, and the ground was striped and patterned in moon shadow.

Drew loved night-time in the mountains. Life seemed less complicated, reduced to its essentials, stripped bare of daytime cares. Its sheer simplicity sometimes scared him.

The deep-throated lowing of cattle echoed through the ghost gums. So that's what had disturbed the mares. Most likely Kilmarnock cattle, part of the trial grazing deal his father had wangled with his government mates. Although there were, he knew, wild bands of scrubbers roaming the range, elusive as phantoms. They bore no brands, endured no whips or dogs. They grew old and died in the shadow of Maroong Mountain instead of in the shadow of the slaughterhouse. Drew's grandfather had believed that bad luck would befall any man who tried to muster in the scrubber herd. Even Drew's practical father had not dared to test the theory. So they had remained for generations as free and untamed as Balleroo itself.

Drew threw the mares a few biscuits of hay, then hurried back to the warmth of the fire, to the warmth of Sam. Drew's body thrummed in anticipation, his every nerve ending alive. He wanted so very much to sleep with Sam, to hold her all night in his arms, to make love to her. He imagined her sweet, soft body cradled naked beside him, and desire welled up in a physical way. But he wanted something else much, much more. He wanted to know who she really was, and how she came to be here with him on this star-studded night, on this magic mountain.

'I'm shivering,' she said on his return. 'Let's light a fire in the hut.'

Drew shovelled up the hot embers and took them inside. With the help of some extra logs, the hut's long-abandoned fireplace soon blazed bright. For the first time in years its cheerful radiance lit up the cracks and crevices in the rough-hewn timber walls. A light that would leave no shelter, Drew hoped, for dark secrets to hide. He buried a few spuds in the coals, found the chops in his saddle bag, and poured cups of black tea from the billy hanging over the fire. Sam lit a candle and dragged the wooden bench over. They sat side by side, staring into the flames, waiting for their dinner to cook.

She laid her head on his shoulder. Drew turned her face and kissed her. He could feel the sudden quiver of her breath, like the heart of a startled bird. He traced her moist lips with his finger. 'Sam?' he said quietly. 'Tell me about you and Charlie. I can't go on with . . . with us, until you level with me.'

A long silence followed his question. She lifted her head and looked at him, boring in with those beautiful brown eyes. 'Is that why you pulled away?' she asked. 'You did — you know you did. After New Year's Eve, after Spike's visit, you seemed ...' She paused, as if struggling to find the words. 'You seemed almost frightened of me.'

It was his turn to struggle. How to explain? That Spike's appearance had stirred up painful memories? That he'd suddenly realised how little he really knew about Sam and her life? She seemed so fresh, so innocent, so guileless. And yet he'd learned in life that things were rarely what they seemed. Sam was, after all, Charlie's sister. He took her delicate hand in his and pressed it to his lips. 'I suppose I was,' he said. 'Frightened of being in the dark. You still haven't really told me what's going on. Where Charlie and Mary are, for instance, and how come nobody's ever heard of you before? Where you come from, and … and how long you'll stay.'

Sam looked away. 'You're right, Drew. I owe you an explanation.' Over a dinner of lamb chops and roast spuds, washed down with billy tea, Sam told him everything. She told him about her solitary childhood, her absent father and controlling mother. About Pharaoh, and how horses had rescued her from a terrible loneliness. About how she'd discovered the reality of her adoption, and of her sister, in almost the same breath. Of Charlie's deadly battle with cancer, and of the procedure that had transformed both their lives.

'Jesus, Sam. That's some story.' Drew sat awhile, trying to digest all he'd been told. 'Come to think of it,' he said, 'Charlie did get pretty skinny last year. Although she's such a tomboy, it was hard to tell. It's not like she wears tight, sexy clothes.' Something in Sam's expression warned him to change tack. 'Will she be all right?' he asked. 'When does she come home?'

'Professor Sung predicts a full recovery, thank God.' Sam sipped her tea. 'As to when Charlie will be home? I don't know. In a month maybe,' she said, sounding oddly unenthusiastic about the prospect.

Drew reached for a log to add to the fire. Sam stopped his arm, with her hand on his. 'Your turn,' she said.

'My turn?' He grabbed the log, tossed it into the hearth, and lit a candle.

'Your turn to tell me about you,' she said.

'What do you want to know?'

'You're being coy,' she said, with a laugh. 'Just start at the start.'

'It's weird.' Drew shook his head, as if in disbelief. 'But thanks to some strange twist of fate, you and I have a lot in common.'

'We do?' She sounded sceptical. 'Certainly not the circumstances of our lives. Me in Melbourne and you …' She swept her arm around. 'You out here.'

He poured himself another mug of tea and stood with his back to Sam, facing the flames. 'I've never told anybody this before,' he said. 'but I'm adopted too.'

'You're kidding me.' Sam sat open-mouthed.

'After my sister Melinda, Mum couldn't have more kids. They wanted a boy. Well, Dad did anyway. My aunt worked for an adoption agency in Wodonga, and kept her eye out. I was born to a teenage mother, just like you were. She wasn't seventeen, though – she was only fifteen, and her parents insisted she adopt me out. The family moved interstate afterwards. To make a fresh start for their daughter, I guess. I've only ever received two letters from my mother. One on my eighteenth birthday, and again last year on my twenty- first. She loves me, she says, but she's married now with two children, a girl and a boy. Her husband doesn't know she had another baby and she wants to keep it that way.'

'What about you?' asked Sam. 'Do you want to keep it that way?'

'Absolutely,' he said. 'She was just a kid. Who can blame her for wanting to live her life?'

'Don't you want to meet your brother and sister?'

'Not now. It might spoil things for her … for them. She promised to tell them when they grow up. Then if we get curious we can arrange to meet up. But right now? It's not that big a deal.' Sam looked astonished. 'I reckon it's different for me,' he said. 'I always knew.

Can't ever remember not knowing. Mum and Dad were up front right from the start.'

Sam stood up and slipped her slim arm round his waist. 'That's it,' she said. 'You knew, so you don't have a trust issue with your parents.'

He cupped her chin in his hand and kissed her, savouring her sweetness. 'No, I don't,' he said. 'Not with my parents.'

Sam cocked her head and regarded him curiously. 'With who then?'

He laughed, trying to keep it light, hoping he didn't sound bitter. 'If you must know, I've had the odd girlfriend or two that I couldn't trust.' Sam opened her mouth to speak. 'I'm definitely not going there tonight though,' he said, holding up his hand. 'What is this? Truth or dare?'

'If you won't tell the truth,' she said, 'perhaps you'd rather a dare?'

'Dare me to make a bed for you,' he said, and pulled a rubber mat from his saddle bags.

'It's like the Tardis in there,' she said, laughing.

'May I present to you the Thermarest 2000, a self-inflating double mattress.' He pulled out its plug, and the core immediately began to plump up.

'You certainly came prepared,' she said.

'Would you rather sleep on those filthy horsehair mattresses?' Drew pointed to the single bunks and went over for a closer look. He peeled the pock-marked surface layer of timber from a bedpost, and held it up triumphantly. 'Borers, m'lady,' he announced. 'I'm afraid occupational health and safety regulations preclude me from allowing you to use these bunks.'

'Kind sir,' she said in mock seriousness. 'I'm a law-abiding girl who wouldn't dream of flaunting regulations.' She stared down at the partly-inflated rubber bed. 'The Thermarest it is, then.'

Drew was down on his knees in a second, blowing great lungfuls of air through the plug to speed up the process. When he'd finished he reached for Sam's hand, anticipation shivering through his veins. She let him pull her down, and he kissed her gently, his lips exploring the contours of her face.

A sudden series of loud thumps and bumps sounded from the roof, accompanied by a blood-curdling screech. Sam rocketed into his arms. He stroked strands of hair from her face, ignoring the excited clenching in his abdomen. 'Possums,' he said, mouthing a silent prayer to the helpful little marsupials. 'Just possums.'

'It sounds more like World War Three.' Sam sat up and looked doubtfully at the roof. 'What are they doing?'

'Mating,' he answered. 'Are you cold?' She nodded, wide-eyed and trembling slightly – whether from nerves or cold, Drew couldn't tell. He stood up, stoked the fire, and fetched some blankets from a pile in the corner. The rooftop hissing and screaming reached fever pitch.

'Truth or dare?' whispered Sam, wrapping a cover around herself. 'And you won't like the dare, so you'd better take truth.'

'Okay, hit me,' he said, settling back down with her on the mattress. 'Truth.'

'Why is this called Dead Man's Hut?'

'You really want to know the story?' She nodded solemnly. 'Okay,' he said. 'I just don't want to scare you.'

'You won't scare me,' she insisted, and moved closer, nestling into his shoulder.

'Once upon a time,' he said, like he was telling her a bedtime story, 'there was a man who packed up his belongings and went to live in a hut he built in the bush.'

Sam stared up at him. 'You mean this hut?'

Drew nodded. 'He was a cattle duffer, by all accounts. Nicked cleanskin calves and grazed his stolen mob around Snake Creek.'

'What was his name?'

'Nobody remembers,' said Drew. 'But he earned himself the nickname Brumby Jack. In fact, they named your place after him. Jack claimed to be the son of Mad Dog Morgan, the bushranger, although nobody knows for sure whether he was telling the truth.' Drew brushed a strand of hair from her face. 'A man alone in the bush for too long can grow a bit peculiar. His imagination plays tricks on him. That's what happened to Jack. He stopped coming into town for supplies, stopped dropping by musterers' camps for a chat. Instead he spent each day riding the range. Rain or shine, even in the winter snows.'

'Why?' asked Sam.

'He was searching for a horse. Jack used to talk about a wild, white stallion, telling anyone who'd listen. He said it led a herd of magic mountain brumbies: brumbies that became invisible when you chased them, brumbies that could fly. Jack became completely obsessed with catching this enchanted stallion, but of course it only existed in his imagination. One day his horse stumbled into Currajong, caked in sweat and bloodied from the spur. They sent riders up to check on the old man.'

'And?' asked Sam, staring at him with rapt attention.

'They found Jack lying out in the yard, a catching rope still clutched in his dead hand. One end was snubbed to a post. The noose end had snapped, like it wasn't strong enough to stand the strain. The churned-up ground told of a terrible fight. Tom's skull was crushed. But this was the strangest thing . . . the gate was shut tight, bound securely with ropes, yet the yard was empty. Whatever killed him had jumped eight-foot rails from a standing start.'

'Or simply flown away,' said Sam, with a faraway look in her eye.

'Don't you start believing in magical brumbies.' His fingers reached for the buttons of her shirt. 'How about believing in me instead?' Was that a shadow or the first flush of arousal darkening her pale skin? He stretched out beside her and they kissed – ardent, but not urgent. They had all night, and he dared not rush a single, extraordinary moment. The smell of perfume and leather, her body soft and fresh, the firelight bright on her face. She closed her eyes and he willed her to open them, willed her to look at him. Drew nipped Sam's ear and her lids flickered back up. Long lashes framing almond eyes, and real desire there. Drew leaned across and blew out the candle. His lips found the hollow of her neck in the dark, and he knew he would remember the curve of her throat and the taste of her skin for all of his life.

. . .

Early morning light filtered through the tiny hut window. Sam stretched and opened her eyes, feeling Drew's sleeping warmth beside her. A possessive arm lay flung over her naked body. It was no dream. She kissed his arm and placed the palm of her hand over his heart. Drew stirred and pulled her close, his eyes still shut, an expression of supreme contentment on his face. She took a deep breath and snuggled further under the covers, moulding her body to his. They were as one. It was hard to tell where her skin ended and his began. Drew looked like she felt: deeply happy.

Later, over mugs of breakfast tea and toast cooked on green twigs before the fire, Drew told her that he loved her.

Sam felt tears come into her eyes – tears of joy, tears of wonder. It was overwhelming. Was she supposed to say it back to him? Was that how it worked? The problem was that she couldn't. Not because she didn't love him. She thought that she probably did, but how to be sure? How to define these new feelings? Mouthing *I love you* seemed just too corny, seemed to trivialise the potent emotions he'd awakened in her.

'It's just the beginning …' said Drew as he rolled up their bed, 'and I'm already so crazy in love with you. I swear, nothing's even come close to this.' He dropped the bed and took her by the waist, kissing her roughly before waltzing her around the hut. His raw energy overcame her in a heady rush. She could feel her body's automatic response and gasped for air. Like on her first abseil, or a rollercoaster ride; the simultaneous thrill and terror of being out of control.

Drew swept her up in another long, sweet kiss that left her dizzy. When he let go she sank down on the old bunk, and shook her head to clear it. He fished around in his magic pudding of a saddle bag and pulled out a little box.

'For you.' He tossed it onto her lap. 'Bought it in Wodonga last week. It's set up and ready to go.' He'd bought her a present? That meant he'd been thinking about her all along. She opened the box. - a new smart phone.

'Thank you,' said Sam, kissing him. 'I love it.' The present could have been a dish mop for all she cared, and she would have said the same thing. It was most definitely the thought that counted.

'You never seem able to get reception with your old one,' he said. 'You'll be able to ring Charlie whenever you want with that. Or your mother.' He laughed at her bemused expression. 'You've got two of those to keep happy, remember?'

Sam made a face. He pulled her in and clasped his strong hands behind her back. 'I don't suppose Charlie's ever got any credit to ring you. How do you think they're managing for money?'

'That's the peculiar thing,' she said. 'They're doing just fine, apparently. Somebody's been making deposits into Mary's bank account. Generous deposits too. According to Charlie, they've never been better off.'

'So Mary's got an anonymous benefactor,' said Drew.

'Looks that way.'

'I bet there's a story there. No wonder she hasn't made a fuss about Dad's money.'

Sam nodded. 'Just as well for us.' She played with her new phone. 'Thank you,' she said again, hugging him. 'You're very thoughtful.'

He nodded. 'I am, aren't I?'

Sam wriggled free and punched him playfully. 'Let's go, you big egomaniac. I can't wait to get home and have a long, long talk to Charlie.'

Mary had met a man. Well, of course she had — she always did. Charlie shaded her eyes from the afternoon sun, and watched from the window as her mother climbed into his battered old Buick. It was disgusting to see her giggling like a girl, flirting and simpering with pony-tailed Carlos. They'd met at the hospital and bonded over cigarettes smoked outside on the street. It was a perfect match. Two ageing hippies, behaving like teenagers, not realising how pathetic and embarrassing they were.

The car drove off. It grew smaller and smaller, turned left around a corner and vanished. Charlie grabbed her giant soft-toy frog and collapsed on the bed in tears. She'd imagined that life in this East Melbourne apartment would have been a big improvement on the hospital. No more gowns or masks or over-the-top hand-washing. No more endless waiting: for engraftment, for blood-cell counts to return to safe levels, for side effects to lessen. But she'd been wrong. This lonely hole in the wall was worse than a prison.

Who would have thought she'd miss the nurses and doctors at that bloody hospital? She even missed Colleen, bossing her around, fussing like a mother hen. Here in the apartment she saw nobody but her mother. Oh, and Carlos of course. She knew the drill. She should, after all these years. Carlos trying to be friends, laying it on with a trowel for her mother's benefit. How many times had she been through this? It could be worse, she supposed. Carlos was a dork and a massive pothead, but aside from that he was inoffensive enough. Some of her mum's past boyfriends had not been so harmless. A suggestive comment here, a hand on her thigh there - gifts of money or alcohol behind her mother's back.

Charlie's phone rang and she lunged for it. 'Sam?'

No, just her mother, asking how she was and whether she needed anything. Charlie braced against the surge of disappointment. 'Crikey, Mum, you just left. What could have possibly changed?' Charlie threw down her phone and it slid under the bed. Good riddance.

She put on the kettle in the kitchenette, and searched through the tea bags in the pantry. Just as she thought – every herbal concoction under the sun when what she really wanted was an old-fashioned cup of plain black tea. No, what she really wanted was a beer. Well, why not? Mum probably wouldn't be back for hours. She'd gone ostensibly to buy a secondhand laptop from some dodgy friend of Carlos. A present, Mary had told her, so Charlie could keep in touch with friends and download music and movies — that sort of thing. First, she didn't have any friends. And second? It was more than likely that the pair would end up in a bar, forget all about the computer, and not return until late at night. City living wasn't good for her mother Charlie had decided. Too much temptation.

On impulse Charlie found her wallet, slipped out the door and descended the steps to the lobby. Though well enough to leave the hospital, her recovery was far from over. Some days she still felt too weak to do much more than sleep, sit up, and walk a bit around the apartment. Her only outings so far had been back to the hospital for tests.

According to Professor Sung it could take six months before she was ready to resume normal activities. 'During this period your white blood-cell count may be too low to provide normal protection against the viruses and bacteria encountered in everyday life,' he'd explained. 'You must therefore restrict contact with the general public. Crowded movie theatres, supermarkets, department stores – these are places you must avoid during your recuperation. Often patients like to wear protective masks when venturing outside the home.'

Stuff that. Charlie emerged from the double doors onto the street. At first the rush of human traffic made her dizzy and a little afraid. There was nobody to lean on. But bit by bit she found her land legs. The late-afternoon sun shone mellow and bright. It relieved the constant chill that still plagued her bones. Her reflection in the mirror of a shop window was frightening in its frailty. Look straight ahead, aim for that bottle shop on the corner, she told herself.

The attendant peered at her. 'I *am* eighteen,' she said.

'I'll need some ID, love.' Charlie fished around in the wallet for her learner's permit. This would be her first legal purchase of alcohol. It was wonderful to be treated as a normal person again. She bought a six-pack of beer, headed for a park beyond the bottle shop and removed her shoes. The grass was soft between her toes. She lay down and buried her face in the soil. It had no fragrance. Chemo had destroyed her sense of smell, perhaps. Or was it the city smog that had rendered the natural world odourless? Whatever the case, this artificial patch of green, surrounded by countless square hectares of concrete, had no discernible scent at all.

Charlie approached a stunted Eucalyptus ficofolia, a red flowering gum tree in sparse bloom, its trunk ridged and deformed by a tight cement collar around its base. Charlie stroked its rough bark and plucked a leaf. The scent of eucalyptus was faint and far away. 'Like your home forest,' she whispered. Charlie settled down, beer in hand, with her back propped against the sad gum tree. It must have been peak hour, to judge by the increasing flow of pedestrians on the street. 'Well,' she said companionably, draining the first beer and opening another. 'You might be a sorry excuse for a ficofolia, but you look a damn sight happier than those buggers.' She toasted the tree.

Shadows lengthened. Occasionally Charlie moved around the trunk to a new spot, seeking out the low slanting rays of the descending sun as it swung westwards. It would be lost below the city sky-line well before it set. She removed her head scarf, exposing her fuzzy scalp, and swigged the beer. Passers-by cast disapproving glances her way. She smiled and raised her bottle. 'Cheers,' she shouted, enjoying herself for the first time in a long time.

Charlie cracked another beer. 'Where are your birds?' she called. 'What sort of a park are you without any birds?' How long had it been since she'd seen a bird? Charlie didn't count flying rats like Indian mynahs and sparrows and pigeons. The city was infested with them. She meant real birds.

As if summoned by her thoughts, a ragged black raven alighted on a rubbish bin just metres away. Charlie knelt up with a sharp, excited sigh, and it responded with an almost human sounding *aarr, aarr, aarrrrr*, the last note long and drawn-out. 'Hello, Mr Raven. You remind me of a very good friend.' The bird hopped to the ground, walked closer, and inspected her with striking ivory eyes. It looked so much like Condor. For a moment Charlie believed that by some miracle he had found her, but when she reached out a hand, the raven flew away.

Charlie hurled the bottle after it and stumbled to her feet. 'It's easy enough for him,' she complained to the tree. 'He can just fly away whenever he likes, back to the bush.' She gave the tree trunk a swift hug. 'Not so simple for us now, is it?'

'Are you all right?' asked a dreadlocked young man who'd stopped to watch her.

Charlie grabbed the three remaining beers of her six-pack. 'No,' she said. 'I'm not.'

The man walked over, retrieved her scarf from where it lay on the grass, and handed it to her. Then he picked up the scattered empty bottles and threw them in the bin.

'You know what?' said Charlie, rewinding her scarf and giving him the once over. 'You're pretty hot. Want to go for a drink?'

It was after nine o'clock when she finally arrived home. Mary was furious.

'Where in heaven's name have you been?' she demanded. 'I've been worried sick!'

Charlie wondered for how long her mother had even been home. Not long, she thought. There was only one butt in the ashtray. 'I've been for a drink,' said Charlie, 'with an ever so nice young man. It was fun.'

'You're drunk,' said Mary.

Charlie ignored the comment, although there was plenty of truth in it. 'Did you get my laptop?'

'No.' Mary sounded suddenly cagey. 'Something came up. Carlos will bring it round tomorrow.' Charlie knew exactly what had come up. She could smell the pot on her mother's clothes. Mary lit a cigarette, stood back and took a long look at her. 'You're not supposed to go out yet. You know your cell counts are still low. Did you kiss him? What if you catch an infection?'

'No, Mum, I didn't kiss him. I only just met him. Who do you think I am - you?'

Mary frowned, purse-lipped. She was such a hypocrite. About men, about everything. How could her mother have the nerve to lecture her about health when she smoked a pack a day, and the rest?

'Suit yourself,' said Mary, looking wounded. 'Next time, although I hope there won't be a next time, take your phone with you.' Charlie looked around for it. 'It was under your bed,' said Mary, taking it from her pocket. 'Sam's been ringing. We had a lovely chat, although she was worried about where you were, of course. She said she'd ring back later.'

Charlie snatched the handset from her mother's hand, just as it rang. She marched off to the bedroom with the hard kernel of a headache germinating within her skull. She'd had some monsters lately, and all that beer could only make matters worse. She really was an idiot. Charlie checked the caller display. 'Hi Sam, how're things?' she asked. 'No, I'm fine. Surely I can go out once in a while without everybody making a big production out of it? Tell me about Brumby's Run. I've been dying to hear.'

She listened to her sister's excited stories of life back home; of working with Bushy and the six mares from Jarrang's mob that had been purchased by the Brumby Coalition, of trying out the Mitchell horses, a different one each evening.

'Drew was right,' said Sam. 'They're all great rides, quiet and responsive.' She was positively gushing. 'The two ponies are a little stubborn at times, but that's safer for kids than being too speedy.' The beer buzz was like a haze in Charlie's brain, a dense swirl of confusion. Sam kept talking. 'Jarrang and Tambo are terrific, although Jarrang is obsessed with the new mares.' The pounding in Charlie's head made it hard to hear. 'You should see him prancing about, so full of himself, showing off.'

A swift shaft of jealousy pierced through the pain. It left Charlie breathless at all she was missing. Her sister's voice faded to a drone. Only the most significant, most important phrases penetrated the white noise. Drew had given her a phone . . . Drew had trucked over hay . . . Drew had reinforced and extended Jarrang's yard . . . Drew had taken her to Bluff Falls . . . Drew this, Drew that. There were too many sentences starting with Drew. She tried to focus, tried to inject some clarity into her thinking . . . The two of us, overnight at Dead Man's Hut. What was Sam saying?

'Drew told me he loved me, and I think I love him too.' Sam fell silent.

As her sister's words sank in, Charlie wailed out loud. 'You can't!' she said, tongue struggling to translate her fear into speech. 'That's my life, not yours. I caught Tambo. I trained him. I raised Jarrang on a bottle. That job with Bushy and the brumbies? That's my job, not yours.'

She heard Sam's sudden, sharp intake of breath. 'But this was all your idea. I've just been trying to help.'

Trying to help? What a cruel joke! How was stealing somebody's life helping them? Well, Sam wasn't the only one who could be cruel. 'Haven't you got enough already?' Charlie spat. 'With your fancy clothes and overseas holidays and university courses? Do you need to take what little I've got as well? Even my boyfriend?'

'Boyfriend?' came the uncertain response. 'How do you mean?'

'Do I need to spell it out?' Charlie knew she was out of control, but fuelled by envy and anger, goaded by alcohol and the skull-splitting ache in her head, she couldn't help herself. 'Bloody hell,' she said with a hollow laugh. 'What a complete bastard. Drew does one twin, then the other. He's living every bloke's fantasy.'

'But how is that possible?' said Sam. 'You never even mentioned him.'

'Would it have made a difference? Everything of mine seems to be fair game for you.'

'Of course it would have made a difference,' pleaded Sam. 'I had no idea, and I'm so, so terribly sorry. Charlie, please calm down. Please? When will you and Mary be coming home?'

'Are you sure you still want me to?' Charlie's voice cracked as she started to cry. 'Maybe you won't want your invalid sister hanging round, cramping your style.'

'Don't say that!' said Sam. Was she crying too? It was hard to tell, so hard to make sense of things with this terrible hammer in her head. 'I'm doing all this for you, for Mary. I can't wait until you're home, you must know that. Charlie, I love you, you're my long-lost sister. I'll never ever let anything come between us, I promise — least of all a man.'

So good to hear those words. So comforting. Sam loved her. Why had she ever doubted it? 'Love you too,' said Charlie. 'But I've got such a splitting headache.'

'Why don't you go lie down?' suggested Sam in a soothing voice. 'Have one of Mary's famous sleeping tonics. Chamomile tea with rose hip and valerian — is that it?'

'And a little milk and honey,' mumbled Charlie. Maybe that was what she needed.

'That's right. Hop into bed, and I'll ring you in the morning.'

'Promise?' said Charlie.

'I promise. Now go get some rest. I love you, Charlie. Don't you ever forget that.'

'I won't,' whispered Charlie. 'Love you too.'

She dropped the phone as her mother came in with toasted cheese sandwiches and a pot of tea. Mary put the tray down, pulled a fresh nightie from a drawer, and tossed it to Charlie.

'Pop into bed, sweetheart.' She turned on the little television. 'There's a documentary about the Spanish Riding School of Vienna. Your sister's been there, hasn't she? Want to watch it?'

Charlie nodded and sipped her hot drink. Aah, Mum's tea always did the trick. Charlie closed her eyes and imagined herself home in the kitchen at Brumby's Run. The pulsing pain in her skull eased, but her head was still spinning, making her dizzy. Eight Lipizzaner horses performed in an elegant indoor school hung with crystal chandeliers. Fairy-tale horses, the last word in animal grace. Charlie's lids grew heavy. She struggled to hold her eyes open. Sam would like this show. How was her sister going, she wondered? She tried to remember when they'd last talked. It had been a while, hadn't it? Perhaps she'd better ring Sam in the morning. And as the splendid snow-white stallions danced across the screen, Charlie fell into blissful, oblivious sleep.

Drew escaped out the front door of the rehab centre at a run. He didn't envy the nursing staff left behind. They were locked, so to speak, in the lion's den. Bill was finally out of the full leg cast that had so infuriated him, but it didn't mean he was free and clear, not by a long shot. 'There are complications,' the surgeon had told Drew. 'Fractures of the tibia can be tricky, and I'm afraid your father's attitude has not helped matters. He's been on his feet against all medical advice. The pressure it put on the cast has compromised circulation in Bill's lower leg. On top of that he has nerve damage that hasn't healed.' The surgeon shook his head. 'Your father needs daily physiotherapy to restore a full range of ankle and knee movement, and the muscle strength lost in traction. If he went home now it would be in a wheel-chair.' Dad was spitting chips, but no amount of complaining was going to fix his leg. He wouldn't be physically involved in the property management side of things for months.

It was hard to feel too sorry for his father. Life had been sweet at Kilmarnock in Bill's absence. Tom had the place running like clock-work, and Drew didn't interfere. They were all happier without the old man breathing down their necks about each little thing, micromanaging his way through everybody's day. And Bill's absence allowed Drew to spend most of his time next door at Brumby's Run.

There was just one cloud on the horizon. Sam. Here it was, Valentine's Day of all days, and there'd been no repeat of the blissful night they'd shared together at the hut. That was more than a fortnight ago now, a fortnight fraught with frustration. It was the most confusing thing. One day they were in love, or so he'd believed. They'd shared the stories of their lives, shared their secrets, shared their bed. Twenty-four hours later, Sam was behaving like it had never happened.

'What's up, Sam?' he'd asked, the first time she ducked away from him. She wouldn't answer. Instead she studiously ignored him, or laughed off his questions. Sometimes she stared at him, as if she expected him to know. But he didn't, and it was killing him – being so close, within arm's reach, but not being able to hold her. Not even being able to touch her.

'This isn't a game, Sam,' he'd said. Was that what she thought it was? 'What the hell's going on?' But she wouldn't say. He wanted to grab her and kiss her til her breath came ragged, until she spat out the problem. Once he'd even caught her looking at him with a certain grim resentment, though it might have been his imagination. It was driving him nuts.

On the surface Sam was still friendly enough, keen for him to help set up the trekking business. Together they'd planned a variety of trips for the trail riders, ranging from two hours up to an overnighter at Dead Man's Hut.

'I can drive up the day before and drop off the camping equipment, stock the hut with hay and food, that sort of thing,' Sam had said. 'That's if I can borrow your four-wheel drive.' He'd nodded. Didn't she realise? What was his was hers. 'Then I can tell them the story of how the hut got its name. We can sit around the camp fire swapping ghost stories. It will be magic.' Drew had nodded, though the only magic he wanted to create at that damned hut was with her. He'd spent sleepless nights trying to figure the whole thing out, and had come to the conclusion that he'd simply moved too fast. It was the only possible explanation. Sam's first time, and he'd barged ahead like a bull at a gate. She'd seemed as eager as him, but maybe he'd been wrong. Maybe she needed time to come to terms with it.

His own first sexual experience had been very different — a dangerous liaison in his fifteenth summer with a woman from the local takeaway shop. She was ten years older, and separated from her violent, jealous partner. Looking back, Drew wondered how he'd survived the affair. He'd plummeted head over heels, and would have risked everything for Darlene Darcy. Correction, he did risk everything for Darlene. He nicked station vehicles in the dead of night to drive, unlicensed, into town. Then he crept from her door before dawn, drove home like a madman and climbed back in his window before his parents woke up. He'd risked his father's wrath by stealing whole days with his lover, when he was meant to be fencing or checking on calving cows. He'd risked becoming the target of her estranged husband; a stupid, stalking brute of a man, who randomly and frequently turned up at Darlene's caravan. It had been the most exciting time of his life. Only a return to St Leonards, his Wodonga boarding school, had succeeded in tearing him away. Drew had maintained his passion through sexy texts, professing undying love with his thumb, sending messages through the ether from his dorm room in the early hours.

The crunch had finally come in the form of a newspaper cutting from the Currajong Gazette, sent to him by his sister with a note that read simply, *A wake up call. That could have been you. Love Melinda.* It seemed there'd been a shooting.

'A 33-year-old man is in a serious condition after being shot twice in the back with a rifle on the main street of Currajong. Shane Darcy of nearby Tallangala has been charged with the attempted murder of Kevin 'Bomber' Wilson. It is believed the victim was confronted after being discovered sharing a caravan with the accused man's estranged wife.'

It was funny, looking back. He'd been gutted about Darlene seeing another man. And he'd been mortified that Melinda apparently knew all about his clandestine relationship. But thanks to the folly of youth, he didn't appreciate that he'd literally dodged a bullet. Later on he heard the news that Bomber Wilson was wheelchair-bound for life, a paraplegic. It was only then that the penny finally dropped, and he realised how fortunate he'd been.

He wasn't going to make the same mistake twice. After that disastrous debut he'd been careful to only date girls without prior attachments. There'd been quite a string. Drew liked women and they liked him. Getting them wasn't the problem — it was keeping them. 'The right girl will come along, soon enough,' said his mother. 'Don't be so impatient for it to happen.'

There was a time last year when he'd hoped Charlie might be that girl. They'd grown up neighbours. He'd helped her with the occasional orphan baby, like Jarrang, for instance. But with him off at boarding school and his family holding the Kellys in such low regard, he'd generally had little to do with the pretty tomboy next door. That all changed when he completed his senior year at St Leonards and returned home to be groomed for his career at Kilmarnock.

The first time Charlie had really registered on his radar, Bill had stormed into the kitchen screaming something about goats in the garden. 'I've got an appointment this morning with my accountant.' His face was like a thundercloud. 'Those vermin better be gone by the time I get back from Wodonga,' he'd said, 'or goddam it, I'll use my rifle.'

Drew had wandered outside to find his mother armed with a broom, pursuing a legion of little angora goats around the garden. 'My roses,' she'd wailed, as the mini mops on legs stripped leaves and blooms from stalks with relentless efficiency. 'Drew, do something!'

Drew had unchained Jock, expecting it would be an easy matter for the kelpie to round up the goats and yard them. But he hadn't counted on one thing. Goats don't herd, not like sheep do. The cute creatures had shot off in singles and pairs, at odd angles, in all directions. He'd grabbed a broom and leaped into the fray. The two of them dashed around like mad things, their shouting adding to Jock's excited barking and the goats' indignant bleating. It had taken forever to collect a group in the corner of the chicken yard. But even then they wouldn't stay put. They seemed to have no respect for humans, no fear at all – charging scornfully past all attempts to block them.

It had soon become obvious that this strategy wasn't going to work. Drew had been loath to bring out the big guns. Dad's tough heelers were liable to make mincemeat out of the petite little goats. But if he didn't do something soon, his mother was liable to make mincemeat out of him.

Suddenly a new sound had joined the general cacophony — the sound of pealing laughter. Drew had turned to see a tall, dark-haired young woman watching them, splitting her sides with mirth. She'd looked familiar somehow. But how could he have overlooked such a beauty? Tanned skin like dark honey. Chestnut hair cut like a pixie's, long on top and short around the back and sides. It had emphasised the length of her graceful neck and her almond-shaped eyes. The most mesmerising eyes — like pale, luminous amber, daring you to look away. Could this be the rude, skinny kid from next door, all grown up? The next minute he lay sprawled on the grass, butted from behind by a small sharp-horned goat that packed a big punch.

'Are you hurt?' the girl asked, rushing over.

'Nah, I'm good,' he'd said, picking himself off the ground. But Drew had soon realised that her professed concern was not for him, but for the goat.

'Hammerhead, you naughty boy.' The wayward goats had lined up to be petted and fussed over by this gorgeous girl. Drew had wanted to get in the queue. Then, like she was some sort of modern day Pied Piper, the animals had followed her meekly home.

After that day, Drew and Charlie had become friends. Her mother, Mary, was always coming up with one mad scheme after another. Like all its predecessors, the angora goat stud didn't last long. Mary couldn't afford the shearer. Then the goats got out and chewed their way through a local blueberry crop. The grower had kept the flock as compensation. Two years later he'd established a thriving mohair operation with Mary's goats.

'How come he could make it work, and we couldn't?' Charlie had asked Drew.

He didn't have the heart to tell her. And anyway, he knew that deep down, Charlie already knew the answer. That her mother never put a sustained effort into anything. That she spent too much time drinking and smoking and fooling around with men. That she'd never make a success at anything unless she changed . . . and that she'd never change. Mary just lurched from one disaster to another, all at her daughter's expense.

From what Drew could figure out, the pair had scraped by for the last few years on little more than his dad's lease fees. Why Bill wanted the extra land in the first place was a mystery. Kilmarnock always turned a substantial profit. Drew had walked in on a couple of blazing rows between his parents on just that subject. Mum accusing Dad of wanting to help Mary – although why that should be a problem, Drew still didn't understand. Mum's favourite preacher at church was always urging the congregation to help their neighbours.

The issue had coincided with the collapse of his parent's marriage. Their relationship had always been adversarial. There'd been fighting for as long as Drew could remember. Mum had been feeling increasingly isolated in far-flung Currajong, and Drew supposed that his sisters' move to Sydney was the final straw. She'd left Drew and Bill to battle it out on their own.

Charlie had always had a way with animals, with horses in particular. When Mary sold their horses to pay the rates, Drew had helped Charlie run in a few brumbies and let her keep Tambo for herself. He'd soon spotted Charlie's talent for riding in general, and campdrafting in particular. Before long she was winning events. She and Tambo caught lifts with Drew and his horse truck to the local competitions. It was a crazy time, a happy time, and he'd fallen hard for Charlie.

But it had been a ruinous romance. Charlie could no more stick with one man than her mother could. Drew had given Charlie a great deal of leeway, suffering a flood of snide remarks and vicious rumours along the way. He'd endured all the gossip that the town could throw at him, and still he'd stuck by Charlie. Stuck by her for months. And then, he'd discovered Charlie and Spike together on the ground, behind the chutes after the Walawai rodeo. More than together …and it was clear it wasn't the first time.

But even this final humiliation hadn't been enough to end his friendship with Charlie. She'd had a tough life, he knew that. Abandoned by her father, neglected by her mother, ostracised by her peers in the town. Of course, Charlie could be her own worst enemy, lashing out at those who tried to help or befriend her. *I'll get you before you get me* seemed to be her chief philosophy. There'd been a couple of other girlfriends since the breakup, but none with Charlie's vitality and spirit – poor carbon copies at best.

Until a miracle had come along. Sam. All of Charlie's beauty, all of her sparkling energy, minus the chip on her shoulder – and with a phenomenal personality of her own. Sam was a girl in a million. If he could just figure out how to get their romance back on track …

Drew pulled off the road into a truck stop, where a cheerful Italian woman was selling flowers from a stall beside a caravan. What were Sam's favourites, he wondered? He picked up an arrangement of natives – scarlet waratahs, flanked by kangaroo paws and bull-rushes. They would have been Charlie's pick, but Sam wasn't Charlie. Drew grabbed a big bunch of red roses as well.

'You want both?' asked the woman. Drew nodded. 'Your sweetheart, she's a lucky girl.'

He gave her a rueful grin and wished Sam agreed with her. Drew drove on, anxious to swing by Brumby's on his way home. He was hanging out to see Sam. A day apart from that girl felt like a week. The Currajong Festival was on this weekend. Was Sam the kind of girl to be impressed by a King of the Mountains title? He wasn't sure, but it was worth a shot. There was one thing he was sure about, however. Nothing and nobody would make him give up on Sam now.

Sam was in the hay shed when Bess bounded in and Drew's head appeared around the door. 'Afternoon,' he said, proffering the bunches of flowers. 'Here I am, reporting for duty.' Sam took them from him, stammered her thanks, then put them aside. He ducked inside, put his hands around her waist and bent his head to hers. The kiss was long enough to stir the butterflies in Sam's stomach, and short enough to leave her hungry for more.

'Don't.' She half-heartedly squirmed from his grasp. 'I'm busy. Thanks to you and your crazy schemes there are about a dozen horses to feed.'

'I'm here to help, aren't I?' He looked briefly irritated. 'Crikey, Sam. You sure do run hot and cold.'

What could she say? He was right, of course. Ever since her sister's surprise phone revelation, Sam was about as confused as a person could be. Drew hadn't changed – keen as ever, helpful, devoted even. He found any excuse to come around. Resisting him took all of her willpower, leaving her frustrated and miserable. Damn Charlie! She'd ruined everything and made Sam's life a misery. The strangest thing was that Drew barely ever mentioned her. When he did, there was no trace of anything but friendly concern in his voice. He was so cavalier that Sam almost doubted Charlie's assertion that Drew was her boyfriend before she left for Melbourne.

Sam had spent a lot of time thinking of ways to suss out the truth of her sister's story. She just couldn't bring herself to ask the question outright. She'd ploughed through all sorts of scenarios, ways to casually raise the topic. She stopped to watch Drew swing a bail over a rail. He moved with an easy grace. She loved the sure sweep of his arm, the angle of his hips. She loved everything about him.

Why on earth couldn't she just come right out with it? Were you sleeping with my sister? If I wasn't here, would you two still be together? Is it me you want, or her? These were the questions she needed to ask, but she was scared she wouldn't like the answers. Scared of looking like a fool. Scared to ruin such a good thing – although it had already been ruined, she thought bitterly.

Her phone rang. Mary. Sam sighed and picked up. 'Hi, Mary . . . Yep, I'm fine, things are good here . . . So Charlie's doing well? . . . When are you coming home? . . . I will. Goodbye, Mary.'

'What's up?' asked Drew. 'How's Charlie?'

Here was her chance. Sam's heart beat faster. She inspected Drew's expression, ready for any trace of deceit. 'What did Mary think,' she asked, 'about you dating Charlie?' There, she'd said it. She wanted to see shock on his face. She wanted him to say that he'd never been with Charlie, and why ever would she think such a stupid thing? She wanted it not to be true — but Drew didn't deny it. He didn't bat an eyelid. He just answered the question, as if it hadn't been laden with hidden meaning.

'Mary hated it when me and Charlie hooked up,' said Drew. 'Beats me why.' He smiled, his green eyes full of humour. He had the most gorgeous smile. 'Bit of a laugh, Mary not approving of me. I reckon it should have been the other way round.'

Sam gulped hard. So Charlie was telling the truth. She was disgusted with herself. What sort of a person hopes to discredit their own sister? If only there was some way to fall out of love with Drew. It really would be so much easier.

Brumbies, Sam had come to understand, were different from other horses in a few fundamental respects. Bushy said it was because they were raised the way horses were meant to be raised, in a herd dynamic, within a settled social structure of equine law and order. Foals stayed with their mothers for a year or more, learning brumby lore, growing up with a firm sense of their own place in the world. 'Those poor little tame horses, I feel downright sorry for them fellas,' said Bushy. 'All that early weaning and not enough mothering – it's a crime.' Sam had learned about attachment disorder in humans. About how the strength of the parent-baby bond affected the emotional health of the child, right through to adulthood. Perhaps it was the same for horses? Perhaps it was the same for her.

A lot of the pampered mounts she'd known back at the Melbourne stables were terribly temperamental – flighty or bossy or downright vicious. By contrast, the wild-caught brumbies were extraordinarily grounded and level-headed. They swiftly embraced their position in the new pecking order. Bushy taught her how to tune into this natural aptitude, how to show leadership but never domination, how to earn the animals' respect. Brumbies treated this way, even high-spirited colts like Phoenix, displayed a touching innocence and willingness to trust. They bonded closely to humans in a way rarely achieved by domestic horses.

Sam rode Phoenix once more around the yard. He was a dream ride: intelligent, spirited and responsive. Pure fire and air. Bushy stood beside the rails, observing the pair with his usual critical eye.

'That'll do,' he said, and Sam brought the colt to a halt. Bushy ran a hand down Phoenix's shoulder and grunted approval. 'You be here by six o'clock sharp tomorrow.' Sam nodded. Tomorrow was the first day of the annual Currajong Festival. It was exciting to be helping with the brumby demonstrations. 'They're trucking in a dozen new horses for the Brumby Catch,' said Bushy. 'I've got a fella coming both days to lend us a hand.'

She dismounted and rubbed the colt's golden neck. 'Do you think he's ready?'

'My oath,' said Bushy. 'He's a smart youngster, that one.'

Sam kissed Phoenix on the nose, and the colt tossed his head at her impertinence. 'Did you say somebody's helping us out tomorrow?'

'Yep. I reckon you already know him. Spike Morgan.'

'Why do we need help?' she said, trying not to squirm. 'What's wrong with me?'

'There ain't nothing wrong with you, girl. You got a hell of a gift with them brumbies.'

'Then why do you want Spike?'

Bushy climbed through the slip rails and took the colt's reins. 'There's a couple of long days ahead of us,' he said simply. 'I could use a top horseman.' For some unaccountable reason he chuckled. 'Go home, Charlie,' he said, and with that he led Phoenix from the yard.

Sam rummaged through the pantry for something to eat. She opened a tin of spaghetti and ate it standing up, cold from the can. Ugh ... she threw the empty tin into the sink and dragged herself back outside. There were still so many jobs to do after she'd already worked a full day at the racecourse. Normally she didn't mind. Normally she willingly launched into the feeding and watering: admiring Jarrang's arrogant displays, laughing at Topsy and Turvy's antics, fussing over the pregnant mares.

Evenings used to be her favourite time. When the sun sank low behind the mountain, she'd finish up, wash her hands and cook a simple meal. An omelette or chicken breast, with fresh salad greens and sweet cherry tomatoes picked from Mary's overgrown garden. She'd fill up a glass from the jug of tank water in the fridge; the sweetest, purest water she'd ever tasted – once the wrigglers were strained out, of course. Then she'd eat at the table under the peppercorn tree, sharing her meal with Condor and the occasional bold currawong.

Or Drew would come around and barbecue some steaks. She stopped herself from smiling at the recollection. Ever since that dreadful phone call with Charlie, Drew's absence in the evenings was like a physical ache. It left her empty, hollowed out. But there was no getting around it. Drew had betrayed Charlie, and by extension Sam herself. He'd admitted it, and hadn't even have the good grace to be ashamed. This was an unfathomable, unbearable fact, and the implications were clear. It meant the death of their relationship. What did Drew think about her pulling back from him? She'd never explained herself. Most probably he'd figured out the truth for himself. How could he have slept with her when he was going out with Charlie? It was a bastard act. It would have been easier if she could have made a clean break of it, excised Drew from her life, but she was still bound to him in so many ways. Without his help there could be no future trail-riding business. She couldn't do it alone. Her impulsive purchase of the Mitchell string would turn into one huge folly, a white elephant, a financial albatross around all their necks. She tried to imagine what Mary might say, returning home with a sick daughter to face no lease income, and the added cost of a dozen extra horses to feed.

Sam gulped down a glass of water, headed for the haystack and heaved a bale onto the rusted wheelbarrow. She looked miserably at its flat tyre, then staggered up the hill towards the dam paddock, casting Drew firmly from her mind. She had more pressing problems. Like how on earth she was going to manage things tomorrow, with Bushy calling her Charlie, and Spike calling her Sam? What a mess she'd made of things. Why the hell had she allowed people to believe she was Charlie in the first place? She was an idiot, plain and simple.

Sam tossed biscuits of hay over the fence at regular intervals, and watched the two ponies boss all the bigger horses out of the way. She turned and trundled back down to the hay shed for a second bale. If only she could get Charlie's voice out of her head. *That's my life, not yours!* Drew had accused her of much the same thing. Accused her of being seduced by the adventure of living a double life – of living Charlie's life. Was he right?

Sam hurled the bale onto the wheelbarrow with such force that it tipped over. She could agonise over motives, or she could concentrate on coming up with a plan to fix things. Because like it or not, she was living in a house of cards, and tomorrow was tumbledown day. Then and there she made a resolution to put things straight, no matter what the cost. Because the truth was, Charlie didn't know the half of it. If her sister was upset now, how would she react to the news that Sam had been impersonating her all over town, however innocently it had begun? Sam grimaced. It didn't bear thinking about.

As Sam hauled the hay back into the barrow, she heard a car pull up in the drive. Please no, not Drew. She couldn't bear the prospect of all those *I told you sos*. What right did Drew have to be so sanctimonious? His deception had been far more deliberate, and far more cruel.

'Charlie? Sam? Jesus Christ, which one are you, darlin'?' Spike strolled around the corner, lithe and languorous, like a well-fed tiger. Sam let out a great, relieved sigh. Spike was one of the few people in Currajong with whom she'd been honest, right from the start.

And what was better, he didn't seem to be the type to moralise. 'I'm

Sam!' she yelled. 'Samantha Carmichael. Any resemblance to Charlene Kelly is purely coincidental.'

'That's not what I hear,' said Spike. He smiled seductively. 'Shove over.' Tossing the bale to the ground, he wheeled the empty barrow down to his truck and inflated the tyre using a portable air compressor he found in the tray. 'How's that?' Sam nodded approval. The wheelbarrow now moved with ease.

'Allow me, princess,' said Spike, marching the hay up the hill. 'I heard Charlie bought Terry Mitchell's horses,' he said, as they fed out the second bale. 'Drew's idea?'

'It was me,' she said, in compliance with her new policy of full disclosure. 'Me who bought them, and I signed my true name, but Terry kept on calling me Charlie and I didn't correct the mistake. So shoot me.' She heard the defiant note in her voice. Why was she angry with Spike? None of this was his fault. 'I've left a great many misunderstandings uncorrected,' she said, trying to sound more contrite.

Spike whistled, smooth and low. 'So I figured.' He cast his eyes over her and the horses. 'Not a bad-looking bunch,' he said. 'Now you've got them, what in the world are you gonna do with them?'

Sam ignored the question. 'I gather we'll be working together tomorrow.'

Spike nodded his head, an amused glint in his intense blue eyes. Sam had never seen eyes quite like them before. The colour of cornflowers, with a luminous quality that made you feel like an animal transfixed by headlights. Electric blue. Bedroom blue.

'Don't worry,' he said, and crossed his heart. 'I won't give the game away.'

She held up her palm. 'No, I'm coming clean about everything tomorrow. I'll explain to Bushy, and anybody else that wants to hear, who I am and how things got so out of hand.'

'That'll be a real shame,' said Spike. 'Folks around town are fans of the new Charlie,' he said. 'She's polite, friendly, reliable. She pays her debts. There's been quite a turn-around in public opinion.' He lit a cigarette. 'I wonder if they'll like Charlie's sister as much. Especially when they find out she's been playing them for fools.'

Sam was stunned. She hadn't thought this through. Of course people would feel tricked – betrayed, even. She didn't want that. She liked the people of Currajong, and apparently they liked her too. Marjorie at the general store had popped a few extra rolls and a jar of homemade blackberry jam into Sam's order last week. 'I always make too much anyway,' she'd said, laughing, dismissing Sam's protests. And there'd been two extra bags of oats in the delivery from the produce store. When she'd told George, he'd simply said, 'Don't worry about it. Just keep on doing a good job with those brumbies. I've got a soft spot for the mad buggers.' Harry at the mechanic's shop had repaired a punctured tyre, then refused payment. 'In appreciation for fixing that account up, love, and for giving my young bloke a lift when he missed the bus on Tuesday.' Dozens of little kindnesses, adding up to a community-wide spirit of acceptance. For the very first time Sam felt like she really belonged somewhere. It was a precious thing, something to be protected and treasured, not deliberately cast aside.

Things had been so perfect. Her time in Currajong, in spite of all the difficulties, had been quite simply the happiest time of her life. Free of Mum and all her dreadful expectations. Free of the pressures of school. Living in the true knowledge of who she really was, and where she came from. Perversely, it felt more authentic being Charlie than it had ever felt being herself. Resentment rippled out across the pond of her thoughts. Resentment for her mother, her father, for Mary. And there was no point denying it - a swelling wave of resentment against her sister. Charlie had accused her of stealing a life. What if it was the other way round? What if Charlie had stolen hers? Maybe she was the one who'd been meant to grow up in this beautiful place. Maybe Charlie had been supposed to live with Faith, and because of some stupid mistake when they were babies, they'd been switched. Currajong, Brumby's Run, the horses . . . Drew. Maybe they were all really meant to belong to her?

'I'll help you finish your chores,' said Spike. 'Then I'll take you for a slap-up meal at the pub.'

The matter was apparently settled. Sam hadn't eaten in town before. She'd not wanted to raise suspicions, but anger made her bold

– reckless, even. She wanted to step out with this gorgeous cowboy, wanted to talk and laugh and drink, to socialise. She wanted to have some fun, without always wondering if she'd give the game away. Tonight she'd be whoever the hell she wanted to be. And for one honest, shameful moment Sam wished that Charlie might never come home.

CHAPTER 24

Spike was in one hell of a hurry. He unzipped the swag. 'Take off your boots and get in.' His voice was low and urgent. Sam did as she was told and lay very still. Though wrapped tight in the sleeping bag, she still felt exposed, like the eyes of the world were upon her. Judging from the sound of shouting voices, they soon would be.

This certainly was a crazy competition. Part of the Currajong Festival, it was like some kind of fast-forward day on the farm. 'In the Station Team Muster,' boomed the announcer, 'a team of two people are required to light a fire, boil a billy, cook an egg and eat it, ram in a steel post and take it out again, split wood, tie a sheep, move a hay bale on a bike, and scull a warm beer, all in six minutes flat. Rafferty's Rules apply, which means they are subject to change at any time and the judges' decision is final.'

Sam held her breath, closed her eyes and waited for the swift kick that she knew was coming. Spike would be on the bike, winding his way back through the poles towards her. The shouting grew louder and finally she felt his toe in her ribs. 'Wake up, princess!'

Sam scrambled from the bag, pulled on her boots and used the kindling and newspaper in their box to light a fire. Yes, it flared with the first match. Sam grabbed the billy and plonked it over the flames, almost extinguishing them in the process. She nursed the fire back to life and cracked the egg into the pan.

Sam glanced up. Spike had reached the fence with the hay bale still safely on the motor bike, and was now tying the legs of a ram he'd caught. Close behind him, Drew and another man leaped into the yard and grabbed a sheep each. The fire was going well now. Sam fanned it with her hat. The egg turned white around the edges and the billy began to steam. Spike said the time-saving trick was to roll up the swag once things were cooking. Sam did just that, strapping it together carefully, keeping an eye on the flames at the same time. A quick look at the other teams showed the wisdom of this strategy. Their swags still lay stretched out on the ground while the cooks fussed over their fires.

Spike sped back, skidded his bike to a halt, almost running over the campfire in the process, then attacked the pile of firewood with an axe. He split the timber in a few sure strokes, then rammed the metal post in like a mad man, until it was in the ground up to the white line. The arena rang to the sound of axes and rammers. All the while, officials wandered about, observing the mayhem with clip-boards and serious expressions.

The third team was out of contention. Their sheep had freed itself from the tie and somehow escaped the yard altogether. Sam sneaked a peek next door, where Drew was yanking his steel picket from the ground in one powerful movement. Cords of muscle stood out on his neck and his shirt pulled tightly across his broad back. He was on his bike a few seconds ahead of Spike. She caught herself in a silent cheer. Wait, who was she barracking for, anyway?

Sam lifted the corner of her egg under the watchful gaze of a judge. Good enough. She scraped it onto the slice of bread, and downed the lot in three gulps just as Spike arrived back from untying their sheep. Drew was already sculling the beer, but his cook hadn't finished rolling up their swag yet. Spike drained the content of his can, hurled it to the dust and punched the air in victory. The crowd cheered, and some triumphant country anthem burst from the loud-speakers. After a brief conference, the officials gave the nod, and declared Team Morgan the winner, while a man with an extinguisher wandered about, dousing the camp fires.

'Congratulations,' said Drew graciously as Sam left the arena. His knock-out smile grabbed at her insides. 'I needed you with me.' Sam braced against a swift stab of shame, trying to tell herself that she had nothing to feel guilty about. Drew shot Spike a poisonous glare, then tipped his hat to Sam. 'If you'll excuse me, I'm on next in the whip crack.'

He disappeared into the crowd, one that seemed far too big for sleepy little Currajong. Sam watched him go and couldn't stop her heart from sinking. Why on earth had she teamed up with Spike? For a bit of fun, like he'd said? That was part of it, but not all of it. A piece of her wanted Drew to feel as jealous and lost as she did.

The King of the Mountains Stockman's Challenge was the Melbourne Cup of bush riding, a weekend-long celebration of traditional skills fast disappearing from an increasingly urbanised world. It was uniquely Australian, and the showcase event of the Currajong Festival. Sam could barely wait for it to start. She'd slipped away early that morning to watch the vet, skills and gear checks that were designed to weed out pretenders. Just as well, as the challenge was potentially perilous. A copy of each entrant's ambulance subscription was a compulsory requirement. There was no doubt about it. When it came to a test of superb all-round horsemanship, the Stockman's Challenge was second to none. Bush men and women competed in six gruelling preliminary events, set to challenge even the most talented riders and their horses. The top ten gained a place in the two final events, the Brumby Catch and the Stock Saddle Buckjump. Spike and Drew were top contenders.

All day the pair had behaved like it was a two-horse race; a head-to-head challenge just between them. Spike had issued his own private challenge to Sam. He'd dared her to go on a date with him if he was crowned King of the Mountain. A proper date. Spike uttered the word *proper* in a slow, sexy drawl with an eyebrow raised. The proposition sounded downright dangerous, and left Sam in little doubt about its implications, but she didn't give herself room to think about that. Spike was more than an instrument of revenge. He was a giddy diversion from her disenchantment with Drew. She was living a modern day fairy-tale – a knight jousting for his lady's hand. It was a wild, romantic notion, and as foreign to the old Sam as it could have possibly been.

Sam had spent most of the day helping Bushy out with the brumby demonstrations on the main arena. But it was hard to concentrate on her work with so many marvellous things going on all around her. She couldn't resist ducking off, and the event which really grabbed her attention was the bareback obstacle course. Competitors not only competed without saddles, but collected extra points if they rode just in halters. Horse and rider teams backed over bridges, jumped hedges, wound their way through hanging obstacles and negotiated tyres and gates – all against the clock. They finished with a thirty-second freestyle opportunity to impress the judges.

She'd been lucky enough to arrive in time to see Drew compete. At an invisible signal Clancy had lain down, flat out on the ground, and allowed Drew to crack a stockwhip over his body. This showed more than good training. It was a remarkable trust exercise for both horse and man. However the most spectacular performance of all was Spike's. Exercising perfect control, he cantered his rangy, coffin-headed chestnut around the course without saddle, bridle or halter – revving a chainsaw in one hand. Spike pipped Drew at the post on points. So did Spike's best mate, a pinch-faced, red-headed stockman named Rowdy. Sam frowned as Rowdy spurred his horse past her, hands harsh on the bit. The three of them would go into the next event neck and neck on the scoreboard.

The elegance and discipline of high-school riding seemed a world away from this rough and ready country carnival. Yet it was impossible for Sam not to connect the two. In the course of the practical events, these stock horses routinely performed flying changes, roll backs, spins and stops that would be the envy of any national dressage-squad hopefuls. And just like in dressage, competition was designed to display the horse's athleticism and ability, while exhibiting the rider's horsemanship. It was a reminder to Sam that modern high-school riding had its practical origins in the ancient cavalry. The same skills that lent a horse grace in the ménage also allowed it to twist from the course of a slashing sabre or maintain the precision of a cavalry charge. Leaps into the air, like the capriole, could have cleared entire lines of enemy infantry at once, while momentary halts, like the levante, perfectly positioned riders for well-aimed sword strokes or musket shots.

An announcement blared from the loudspeaker. 'In a few minutes there'll be a brumby handling display in the main arena for all those interested, proudly sponsored by the Brumby Coalition of Victoria.'

Sam raced back to the yards. Spike was already lunging Allawarra, a pretty piebald filly, in running reins and a roller. They were the picture of calm control. Hard to imagine it was only a few weeks since this young horse had first laid eyes on a human being.

'Sorry,' Sam told Bushy breathlessly. 'Everything's just so interesting. Spike was fabulous in the bareback obstacle – you should have seen him.'

'Spike's a bloody good horseman, all right,' he said. 'Now will you get Phoenix ready? Or is that too much trouble?' Sam apologised again. She saddled the colt and mounted, waiting in the wings with bated breath for Spike to finish his mouthing demonstration. It took her right back to her days of performing with Pharaoh in the dressage arena, the heart in her mouth excitement, just before she acknowledged the judges and commenced her round.

'In you go,' said Bushy, as *The Man From Snowy River* theme music started up. Sam took a deep breath, urging Phoenix forward, cantering around the arena and putting him through his paces. She could hear the appreciative oohs and aahs of the crowd. The beautiful golden colt had a special presence, a certain charisma. Phoenix made Sam feel like a star herself, making it easy for her to throw caution to the wind. He made her reckless. Spike and Drew were both watching from the rails, standing opposite each other.

'This stylish little colt was wild caught off the mountain not two months ago,' said the announcer. 'He's a fine example of the temperament and versatility of some of these brumbies. Let's give him and the little lady a hand.'

Phoenix bowed low, then cantered out to an enthusiastic burst of applause. Now Spike drove Bushy's old Holden ute into the ring. The audience wouldn't believe this next stunt. Sam had barely believed it herself when she'd seen it that morning in rehearsal.

Bushy clambered bareback onto Banjo, his black brumby stallion, and they made their entrance. The announcer cranked back into gear. 'Bushy Nandawarra caught this brumby as a ten-year-old stallion, after it had spent years sneaking into his paddocks to get his stock horse mares pregnant.' There was loud laughter from the crowd.

'So what you're seeing here today is a horse that spent the first decade of his life untouched by human hands. He's a real tribute to the disposition of these brumbies, ladies and gentlemen. Banjo is a registered sire with the Brumby Studbook. Those foals by Bushy's stock horse mares, incidentally, are all appendix-registered brumbies now. And I might add they're fetching good prices, and competing nationally in campdrafts and barrel races.'

Banjo had an extensive repertoire of tricks. He could count, play fetch, and answer questions by nodding or shaking his head. He lay down on command, sat up like a dog, and amused children by pulling the saddle cloth off with his teeth every time Bushy turned his back to fetch the saddle. He reared on cue, and even balanced on a tractor tyre while wielding a stock whip held in his mouth. The most amazing trick of all was when Banjo casually jumped onto the tray of the ute, and stood there calmly while Spike drove a lap of honour around the arena. 'This bloke will put float companies out of business!' the announcer said. Bushy and Banjo galloped from the ring to the sound of thunderous applause. It really was an astonishing act.

Next a clown with a performing mule entered the ring to the laughter of children. 'Go on with you,' Bushy said, as Sam looked longingly across the showgrounds. 'I won't need you for a while.' Sam thanked him and dashed off. Past the yabby-burger stand. Through a throng of tiny boys wearing too-big cowboy hats. They already had the swagger. There was still so much on: a tent-pegging display by the

Australian Light Horse Association, a shoeing competition, the cross-country obstacle course. She couldn't possibly see it all. Sam settled down to watch Drew in the Patterson Packhorse, part of the Stockman's Challenge. 'This challenge,' said the announcer, 'shows our younger generation how things were done before the tray-back truck.'

Drew had to load up a packhorse, ensuring the packs were evenly balanced, lead it from Clancy through an obstacle course, maintaining the balance of the load, and then unsaddle – all in a fifteen-minute time limit. He completed the event with ease, and Sam felt a surge of pride.

Spike was next in the line of competitors. He saw Sam at the ropes, dismounted in a single leap and was suddenly beside her. 'A kiss for luck,' he said. Before she knew it his lips had found hers, eager and insistent. When she pulled away Drew stood nearby, watching, face black as thunder. Spike grinned, saluted him and swung back on his horse.

She burned with embarrassment, unable to stand the accusation in Drew's eyes, and slipped off into the crowd. She was playing with fire. The two men were still behaving like personal rivals. It was a competition within a competition, and if she was honest with herself, it was flattering to think she might be the prize. Problem was, she couldn't decide who she wanted to win. Her head was with Spike . . . but her heart was with Drew.

Next up was the stock-handling challenge. Sam watched a man and dog briefly chase some cows around the arena. What was the point of it? A middle-aged woman sitting beside her must have noticed Sam's confused expression. She introduced herself.

'I'm Faye. Is this your first Stockman's Challenge?' she asked. 'You look a bit puzzled.'

'I am,' Sam admitted.

'Shall I explain the rules?'

'Please.'

A new challenger, Rowdy, entered the ring, and Faye talked Sam through the round. 'He leads his horse in and ties it up. Then the five-minute time limit starts.'

'Five minutes for what?' asked Sam.

'He walks over to the yard – that's called the camp – and is scored on cutting out three unmarked steers on foot. If he lets out more than three, or any marked ones, he's eliminated.' Sam noticed that some of the cattle had different coloured splashes of paint on their shoulders or rumps. 'Then he mounts up and signals for his working dog to be released. The rider and dog have to move the steers through the gate and into that little yard.'

A red heeler loped from the pen, eyes trained on the cattle. At a nod from Rowdy, it sank low to the ground and a rough dance commenced between the man and beasts in the arena, all to the staccato beat of a cracking stockwhip. After a few minutes a bell rang, signalling that the competitor had failed to complete the course in his allotted time. Sam flinched when Rowdy surreptitiously kicked his dog.

'Thanks,' said Sam. 'It's much more fun to watch when you know what's going on.'

Faye smiled and patted her hand. 'You look so much like Charlie Kelly, dear. You must be related.'

A shiver ran up Sam's spine. What was she doing, admitting to some random stranger this was her first challenge? Admitting she didn't even know the rules? There seemed nothing for it but to fess up. 'I'm Samantha, Charlie's sister.'

'Lovely to meet you, Samantha,' said Faye. 'I heard you were in town.' She had? Faye pointed to Spike, leading Bailey into the ring. 'That's my son over there.'

Great. Spike had told his mother who she was, after promising to keep her secret. Who else had he told?

'Spike and Charlie used to be … very close.' Faye reached out to pat her hand, but Sam subtly moved it away. Unbelievable. Spike too? Did she have to get everything second hand from her sister? Sam felt the press of people around her like a threat. It had been foolish to come here today.

She excused herself and returned to the yards. Bushy was mixing up feeds. 'I'll do that,' said Sam and snatched his bucket. What on earth had she been thinking? Best stay close to her brumbies and avoid the crowds.

It was harder to avoid Spike, who came strutting over with his self-importance and tight jeans. 'I'm leading on points, honey.' She ignored him, and readied Allawarra for the three o'clock show. Spike broke into a passable rendition of *The Winner Takes It All*.

'Don't you go writing off the competition yet,' said Bushy. 'Drew'll give you a run for your money.'

'I'm ten points ahead of Chandler.' Spike threw Sam his most devastating smile. 'Ready for that date? I've got tickets for Lee Kernaghan tomorrow night.'

'You told your mother,' she hissed beneath her breath, flashing furious eyes at him.

'Told her what?' he asked in a loud voice, sounding genuinely puzzled. Sam shushed him. He shrugged his shoulders and led the filly onto the arena.

When her turn came to ride Phoenix, she pleaded illness. 'I'm dizzy and have a stomach ache. And a headache,' she added for good measure.

Bushy gave her the once-over and looked unconvinced. 'Spike better do it then. Go home and come back in the morning. You're no use to me sick.' He took the reins from her and led Phoenix to the gate.

When Spike finished the mouthing display, he had a quick word to Bushy and sprang onto the golden colt. Sam felt a pang of guilt and stopped to watch. It was clear Phoenix resented the unfamiliar rider. He fought Spike's hands, tossing his head and clenching his jaw to avoid the action of the bit. Their work out may have looked smooth enough to the uninitiated, but to anybody with a modicum of horse sense the tussle between horse and rider was obvious. Phoenix refused to bow on exit, tensing his neck, instead of yielding and flex-ing. When Spike persisted, the colt reared in defiance; a dramatic exit, but not at all what Bushy had intended. Sam rushed over to the sweat-ing, agitated colt, and stroked his neck while Spike dismounted.

'What did you mean,' he asked, 'when you said I told my mother?'

Sam looked around to ensure Bushy wasn't in earshot. 'About me. You told your mother about me.'

'I didn't, I swear.' Spike kicked the dust. 'I didn't tell anybody.'

'Will you get that ute in the ring?' yelled Bushy as he rode past on Banjo.

Spike nodded and extracted a set of car keys from his pocket. 'If my mum knows something, she didn't hear it from me.'

Now Sam was more confused than ever. If Spike was telling the truth, it meant other people in Currajong knew who she was. And if that was true, why hadn't they called her on it? A wave of paranoia washed over her. The crowd applauded Banjo, who was responding to questions with graceful nods or shakes of his head. If only her own questions could be so easily answered. She remembered the poster of Spike on Charlie's bedroom wall, signed with love. Sam breathed deeply and steadied her nerves. What great taste in men she and Charlie had. Go home, Bushy had told her. It was the best advice she'd had in a very long time.

CHAPTER 25

Sunday morning. The snorting, wide-eyed colts for the Brumby Catch made their hesitating way out of the truck and down the cattle ramp. They'd been brought in from Balleroo last spring, turned out into good paddocks and left alone until today. All were fat and fit, perfect for the event to be held later on that day. They clustered at the far end of the yard in the characteristic way of wild horses, presenting a solid row of rumps to onlookers. A call was made over the loudspeaker for the top ten finalists to draw their brumby.

Sam sipped her coffee, bleary-eyed, and watched Drew stride across the arena to the judges. Spike strolled after him. It would take more than one coffee to get her started this morning. She'd spent a sleepless night. How to sleep with so much riding on today's outcome? Drew may be out of bounds, but the truth was she was still in love with him. She'd hated seeing the hurt and anger on his face when Spike kissed her. Did she really want to pursue this thing with Spike? It would be a rebound fling, entered into for all the wrong reasons. But then maybe that was just what she needed.

The announcer was explaining the rules of the Brumby Catch over the loudspeaker. They seemed designed to make success impossible. A brumby colt would be turned loose into the arena from the bucking chutes. The mounted competitor was required to halter the colt and have it leading within two minutes. Two minutes. Impossible. Sam turned to help Bushy with the morning's demonstration. 'Is the catch hard on the brumbies?' she asked.

'It's a darn sight harder on the catcher,' he said. 'I've seen colts break a man's leg with a well-aimed double-barrelled kick, then be back with their heads down, eating hay, just as soon as they're back in the yards.' Bushy bridled Banjo. 'See that bay over there?' He pointed to a neat little horse ridden by a teenage girl. 'One of last year's Brumby Catch colts. I broke him in no worries. Top pony club horse, that one. You couldn't do that with a traumatised horse.'

'So they won't go for meat?'

'Not this lot,' said Bushy. 'All of them fifteen colts already have buyers waiting.' Sam walked back around to get a better look at them. None of the colts were a patch on either Jarrang or Phoenix. What fine studs those two would make.

After the demonstration Sam raced to find a good seat, for the Brumby Catch was about to begin. There was a real buzz of excitement in the stands. The first colt had a surprising turn of speed and outran Rowdy. His brief time was up without him even getting close with the halter.

The second colt demonstrated what Bushy had said about the event being tough on the catcher. The big chestnut considered offence to be the best form of defence, and spent the time doing handstands, his hind feet lashing out with such ferocity that he was soon back in the yards. The competitor was allowed a reserve draw. His second brumby wasn't much better, flattening ears and snapping at the unlucky rider's horse, who was understandably loath to get too close. The challenger exited the ring for the second time with no score.

Drew was up next. His colt was fast, but Clancy was faster, maintaining pace with the brumby, shoulder to shoulder. Within the allotted time and to Sam's utter astonishment, Drew managed to drop the halter over the colt's head and lead it in triumph around the arena. It was a peerless display of horsemanship – or so she thought.

Then it was Spike's turn. He'd drawn a tough black with a wicked temper. Sam now appreciated that Bailey, Spike's ugly, square-headed horse, was miles better than he looked. He dodged a barrage of nasty kicks and courageously remained neck and neck with the surly brumby. Spike had the black haltered and led off the arena with time to spare. No other contestants completed the challenge. Spike and Drew had rocketed to the top of the points table.

The grey brumby huddled at the far end of the stock contractor's yard. Sam dreaded the prospect of seeing the mare buck, and her nerves were raw. Drew slipped in beside her at the rails, and she jumped like a startled colt. 'That horse is named Demon now,' he said. 'Rowdy's drawn her in the buckjump. Already got herself a reputation, apparently.'

'Demon?' Sam shook her head. 'Can't we do something? She looks so miserable.' The other horses appeared relaxed enough, resting hind feet, nibbling at hay, pretty much ignoring the spectators. By contrast the grey was the picture of tension: erect ears, high arched crest, muscles taut in neck and jaw.

'No, *we* can't,' said Drew. 'Why don't you ask Spike to help you?' He marched off towards the bucking chutes. It didn't matter. Sam wasn't barracking for him anymore, or for Spike either, for that matter. She was barracking for Demon.

Sam hoisted herself up and perched on a top rail, with a good view of the horses being run into the laneway. 'Riders must use the same saddles they've used during previous challenge events,' boomed the announcer. 'Riders must stay on for eight seconds and crack their stockwhip at least once.' Eight seconds? That wasn't long. Maybe this wouldn't be so bad after all. 'Judges award equal points for riding skill, and for degree of difficulty of the bronc.'

It jarred to hear the lovely brumby being referred to as a bronc. The grey didn't belong here. A month ago she'd been living wild and free on the range. Then by some random twist of fate she'd ended up a bucking horse. She might have escaped, or gone to Ryan. She might have been gently tamed and found a loving owner. Was the mare's story so different to Sam's own? Mary had sent her away from where she belonged, away to live with Faith. It had changed who she was. Yes, she and the brumby mare were common victims of a haphazard, indifferent universe. The futility of it all sickened her.

Sam had never seen a saddle-bronc competition before. The first horse to enter the chute was liver chestnut with a wild eye. Drew appeared, carrying a simple hackamore that bore a broad leather noseband and rope lead. He climbed the rail and slipped the head-gear onto the gelding. Next came his saddle, fitted with a curious back cinch. A leather strap lined with sheepskin was fitted around the horse's ticklish flanks. Drew lowered himself into the saddle, wearing nothing on his head but a stockman's hat.

Sam closed her eyes at the foolish irony of it all. Riders of the little motorbikes in the novelty Stockman's Muster had all worn safety helmets. So had the cross-country competitors. But in this most dangerous challenge of all? Of course not. They wouldn't want to spoil their macho image, would they? Someone handed Drew his stockwhip and he signalled for the gate. Sam was sick with fright.

The gelding's mouth yawned wide, and he exploded from the chute in a bone-jarring succession of high, stiff-legged leaps. It was a primal scene – man against beast. Eight seconds suddenly seemed like a very long time indeed. Drew clutched the rope in his left hand, raised the stockwhip high in his right, and the arena rang with whip cracks. In spite of her fear, Sam found herself cheering along with the crowd. Drew seemed to retain his balance by magic, adjusting his body as if he could anticipate his mount's every move. It was an amazing display of horsemanship. Sam felt sure she'd have been unseated by the first buck. A horn sounded and the pickup rider sprang into action, cantering beside the bucking horse, allowing Drew to grab his saddle and jump clear. Sam felt weak with relief and pride.

Surprisingly, the gelding continued to buck after Drew stood safely back on the ground. The pickup rider caught the horse's rope rein, leant down and released the flank strap. Only then did the gelding calm down. So, it wasn't the rider that the bucking horses objected to. It was the flank strap.

'And he's made eight seconds, so let's have a big hand for Drew Chandler riding Nightstalker.' Sam joined in the applause. A gust of unseasonably cold wind caught up willy willies of dust and chased them across the arena, causing people to grab their hats. Sam shivered, buttoning her shirt right up to the neck, and pulling her cuffs over her hands. Spike sat on the rails of chute number two, above a powerful paint horse with a hogged mane. The loudspeaker crackled so much that Sam missed the beginning of the announcement. All she caught was, '. . . Spike Morgan riding Switchblade.'

Spike tossed away his cigarette, settled in the saddle and fixed his stirrups firm under the arch of his heels. The horse reared and launched itself at the fence, knocking a man off the walkway. Spike kept his seat. At a nod the gate swung wide. For a few moments Switchblade stalled and just stood there, to the amusement of the audience. Then he dropped his head to the ground and erupted from the chute. The horse didn't so much buck as do full handstands, flinging his hind legs above his head past the vertical axis. He bucked so hard and high, it was a miracle he didn't flip right over.

Spike was unbalanced and in trouble from the start. He managed one crack of his whip before Switchblade spun like a top and pitched him over his left flank. As Spike's right foot flew over the saddle, its spur somehow caught on the cantle, leaving him hanging head down, while the horse bucked and plunged. There was a loud gasp from the crowd. Sam grimaced and held her breath as Switchblade cannoned into the fence. Spike wrapped his arms around a post and hung on with grim strength. He jerked his leg free and collapsed to the dust, while the pickup man reached for the horse's rope.

Spike was okay, but he hadn't made his ride. Sam thought it through. He and Drew had been top of the leader board, equal on points, and the buckjump was the last event. That meant the Challenge was now a dead rubber. Drew had won — he was King of the Mountain. Sam sighed. She'd been kidding herself, thinking that she didn't mind who won. The rush of pride and relief she felt at the result told her that.

The loudspeaker crackled into action. 'What a terrific bucking horse this big paint is. Unfortunately Spike hasn't stayed aboard for his full eight seconds. Let's give a big hand for Switchblade.' The crowd whooped and cheered. Spike staggered to his feet and limped from the arena for a medical check. Sam could see her grey mare in chute three, with red-headed Rowdy already in the saddle.

'Next up is Demon, nicknamed The Four-legged Fury.' Demon. Sam wanted to shoot whoever had given the lovely brumby such an awful name. 'Demon has just been bucking for a few weeks, but already this mighty mare has a fearsome reputation. Some horses buck hard and some buck fast, ladies and gentlemen – and Demon does both. Fact is, nobody has so far scored a ride on her.' The mare flung her head around. Sam winced as it slammed into the steel pipe of the chute. 'This horse hasn't come through the Born to Buck program like many others here. She's a genuine brumby. Let's see if Rowdy Clarke can take on Demon today and win.'

The mare reared sideways and Rowdy leaped onto the fence to avoid being crushed. With ears flattened and teeth bared she lunged at him. Men scattered and Rowdy dodged. Easy now, Sam whispered. Take it easy. Back in the saddle, Rowdy gave the signal. Horse and rider exploded from the chute to the deafening strains of *We are the Champions*.

The mare sprang skywards like a spring released. Back arched like a cat, stiff-legged and finishing with a wicked twist. She was a fearful sight. But when she crashed back to earth, Rowdy was still in the saddle. He cracked his whip and spurred in time with her bucks, raking her from shoulder to flank. She foamed at the mouth and launched herself back into the air, screaming. Sam had never heard a horse make such a noise before and was unaware they could. It was a bloodcurdling, devilish sound that set Sam's teeth on edge.

Lightning cracked above the arena, and thunder rumbled in the throat of the darkening sky. The mare ducked and dived. She swivelled and spun. She ruined Rowdy's rhythm, sunfished right, then left, always landing with unforgiving, bone-jarring force. The heavens opened to lashing torrents of rain, turning the dusty arena into an instant mud pit. Rowdy was flying high out of the saddle and in trouble. Sound the horn, for God's sake! This was killing them both. Rowdy collided with the ground and lay winded where he fell. 'And The Four-legged Fury remains unridden,' boomed the announcer over the storm. 'Give this great bucking horse a big hand, ladies and gentlemen. And another one for our courageous cowboy.'

The crowd applauded as a pickup man closed in on the brumby mare. He took hold of her trailing rope, leaned down and released the flank strap. Sam breathed a sigh of relief, and shielded her face from the blinding rain. She could barely see now. Jumping off the rail, she sought shelter beneath the cattle ramp, a position that offered a good view of proceedings. Water and bulldust mixed to muck in her eyes. She wiped it away and turned her attention back to the arena. Rowdy still lay, a soggy heap on the ground near the fence, only a metre or two away. He groaned, looked around for his hat and waved the stockwhip to show that he was okay. The crowd cheered encouragement.

Sam frowned and focused her attention back on the brumby mare. Something wasn't right. It showed in the white of her eye, the angle of her ears, the set of her jaw. A chill ran down Sam's spine and she shrank back from the fence. The mare suddenly whirled and let fly with both hind feet, connecting hard with the tender flank of the pickup horse. It reeled and staggered, losing its footing on the slick surface. The pickup man dropped the halter rope and jumped clear of his horse as it skidded sideways and landed in the mud. In the driving rain it was every man for himself, as the crowd dashed for cover. Nobody seemed to be taking much notice of the mare any more.

The grey spun round and advanced on Rowdy in a series of half rears. He lurched to his feet and cracked the whip in the mare's face. It was then that Demon attacked. She charged at the man with striking hoofs, eyes blazing with hatred, and knocked him to the ground. Rowdy ducked and rolled, but the mare was too fast. Taking aim, she slammed the full force of both forefeet into the back of his head. Was it Sam's imagination, or did she hear the sickening crunch of bone?

The mare snorted, seemingly satisfied with the job, and cantered to the exit. A boy opened the gate and she trotted to join the other horses. It was only now that people seemed to realise the gravity of what had happened. An army of people converged on the fallen man. Two ambulance officers waved them away and knelt to examine Rowdy. Two women ran over with a canvas tarpaulin and held it like an umbrella over the paramedics while they worked. Sam watched, unable to move, horrified and fascinated all at once. Somehow she knew already that Rowdy was dead.

Sam sat in Drew's truck, his oilskin around her shoulders. 'It wasn't the mare's fault,' she said, eyes blurry with tears. 'They drove her to it, they drove her mad.'

Drew shook his head. 'Maybe,' he said. 'But everybody saw what happened.' He handed Sam a coffee. 'That was no accident.'

'It was self-defence, that's what it was,' protested Sam. Drew didn't comment. 'What will happen now?' Her hands were shivering too hard to hold her coffee, so she put it down on the dashboard.

'I spoke to Wayne Clarke,' he said. 'The man's absolutely gutted. Rowdy was his nephew.'

'No,' she said. Could it get any worse?

He nodded. 'They thought they were onto a winner with that mare. She bucked like bloody Curio.'

'Curio?' asked Sam tearfully.

'A legendary grey bucking mare. She featured at the Marrabel Rodeo, way back in the fifties. Unridden for eight years. They say she only worked for five minutes in her whole life. Got those cowboys off with just one buck.' Rain was sneaking in on an angle through a narrow crack at the top of the window. Drew wound it up all the way. 'A horse like that would be worth a fortune these days.'

'Well, our grey isn't Curio,' said Sam, 'and five minutes more of that kind of work would be enough to kill her.' She reached for the coffee and took a trembling sip. 'I asked you what's going to happen.' Drew avoided looking at her. 'Just tell me!' she shouted, furiously wiping away tears.

'She's going to the knackery in the morning.'

Sam slammed her coffee onto the dashboard and ran from the car into the pouring rain. Drew sprinted after, both of them slipping in the mud. He caught her in a fierce embrace. They stood that way, still as statues, for the longest time. Water streamed from their conjoined bodies in rivulets, like flooded creeks off Maroong Mountain.

Was it dark enough yet? Drew pulled the curtains apart and gazed into the night as he heated the milk. Damn — he snatched the saucepan from the stove just as it boiled over. Sam sat slumped on the frayed couch in front of a cheap bar radiator, inconsolable, wrapped in a blanket. Her bare shoulder poked out, pale and smooth, bisected by a black bra strap. He couldn't stop looking at it, fought against kissing it.

'I helped catch her,' Sam managed between shuddering sobs. 'She was beautiful and free and happy, and what did I do? I helped hunt her down, helped sell her to the rodeo, helped send her to the slaughterhouse. They should shoot me too.'

Drew concentrated on the task at hand, tipping milk from the saucepan into two cracked mugs, splashing plenty onto the bench. Bess wagged her tail and lapped up the warm liquid trickling to the floor. Drew stirred in spoonfuls of Milo and some extra sugar to boot, then handed a mug to Sam. She shook her head and turned from him. He put down the cup, pulled her around, forced her to face him.

'Listen to me — they won't kill that horse,' he said with more determination in his voice than he felt.

She blinked back tears. 'Why? What do you mean?'

'Stop crying, drink this, and I'll tell you.' He shoved the Milo into her now compliant hands. 'Drink it.'

Sam took a big gulp, then another. 'Why won't they kill her?' she asked in a voice raw with weeping.

'Because I won't let them. Finish that drink and get into some dry clothes.' He wet his lips with his tongue. 'We're going to steal her back.' Sam's eyes grew large and her mouth fell open. In an instant she was in his arms, soft lips pressed against his. Drew felt a familiar ache in his groin as his fingers traced the soft hollow of her hip. He forced himself to pull away. 'Do you want to do this, or not?'

She granted him one more melting kiss, then ran from the room to get changed. Drew drained his mug of Milo, wanting something stronger. He searched the kitchen cabinets for liquor. Nothing. A framed picture of Charlie riding Tambo lay face down in the cupboard. He examined the girl in the photograph, marvelling at how much she looked like Sam. Hadn't the picture been displayed on the sill last time he'd been here? Why had Sam put it away like that? He slammed the cupboard door shut when he heard Sam in the hall.

'I'm ready,' she announced, a shining, expectant smile on her face. 'What next?'

Good question. Bess shoved her nose between them. He put down a blanket and chained the dog to the table leg. 'You stay here, girl.' He offered Sam an oilskin coat. 'Wear this. It's my sister's.' Sam pulled it on. Drew struggled to open the door against the driving rain. 'Come on,' he said. 'We've got some horse rustling to do.'

It was past midnight when the cattle truck laboured through the rain, back up the rutted track to Brumby's Run. What little gravel there might once have been had been washed away in this deluge. The road ran like a river. Drew tried to angle the truck towards the cattle ramp, and almost lost control as the wheels skidded sideways in the mud. He braked and swore. 'If I try to get any closer, we'll slide down the hill and roll.'

'Well, we'll just have to unload her here then,' said Sam. Sure. Just slip a halter on the mad bugger and lead her down the ramp. 'I'm naming her Whirlwind,' said Sam happily, her face alight in the dim dashboard glow.

The truck shook as the mare reared and kicked. Drew figured the name suited her. Lunatic would have suited her better. What a night-mare it had been, trying to load that horse in the rain and dark. She'd been conveniently yarded on her own, right next to the loading ramp, ready for the doggers to pick up in the morning. And he'd taken his dad's two heelers along for good measure. Those dogs were tough enough to tackle wild scrubber bulls straight from the bush. *How hard could one brumby mare be?* he'd thought. He'd thought wrong.

Jasper whined and wagged his tail. Sam stroked him where he lay on the floor at her feet. 'Will he be okay?' she asked.

'I reckon she's broken his leg,' said Drew grimly.

'It wasn't her fault,' said Sam. 'She was scared.' Scared? They were the ones who should be scared. Whirlwind plunged about in the back and the whole truck rattled.

'Let's get her out, then,' he said, not quite knowing how this was going to work. They climbed from the cabin, shielding their faces from the blast of wind and rain. Drew slipped on a head torch, but its beam was swallowed by the rain a few feet from his face. Why the dickens couldn't the weather give them a break? With a spiteful crack of thunder, the wind redoubled its fury. The one saving grace was that the storm had covered their tracks back at the racecourse.

Drew assessed the situation. It was just as he feared; the truck was a good ten metres short of the yard. There was only one option, one he'd prepared for as a last resort. Drew grabbed his catching ropes and climbed up on the truck. He could hardly see. Just as well she was pale grey and not black. He considered himself a good aim, but it was extraordinarily difficult to throw the noose over a moving, snaking target in the dark and the storm. It didn't help that the horse seemed intent on killing him at the same time.

It was only when Jarrang caught wind of his daughter, and announced his pleasure with a trumpeting neigh that Drew got his chance. Whirlwind froze at the sound. Drew seized the opportunity to cast one, then two ropes over her head. Moments later she erupted in a rearing fury, but by then it was too late. He had her. Drew pulled the Lewis winch out from under Sam's feet, and heaved the chainsaw from the rear of the cabin. Opening the gate, he anchored the winch's snatch block to a large strainer post at the back of the yard.

Sam appeared beside him. 'What are you doing?' she asked anxiously.

'Yarding your horse for you.' He retrieved a length of chain from the floor of the truck and fixed it to the ropes around Whirlwind's neck. Then he attached the winch cable to the chain and started the saw. Its savage snarl joined the roar of wind through the forest. Sam pulled at his sleeve. Drew turned off the saw and handed Sam a torch. 'Point it here, will you.' Why on earth hadn't he taken the bar off at home? Fitting the adapter in the dark was just about impossible. 'Hold these, put them in your pockets or something.' He handed Sam an assortment of washers and nuts. Finally it was done. The chainsaw's power block was bolted fast to the winch.

The penny must have finally dropped for Sam. 'You can't!' she yelled urgently, struggling to compete with the screaming wind. 'She hasn't even got a halter on. She'll choke to death.'

'Got any better ideas?' he snapped, regretting his words as soon as they were uttered. 'Look,' he said, in what he hoped was a more conciliatory voice. 'We can't get the truck close enough to unload her straight through the gate. If we unload her out here without the winch, we'll never hold her. She'll go bush, and the first bugger to find that mare will either give her a bullet or run her in for the doggers. Wayne's bound to post a reward.' She might have been crying again, but it could have just been the rain. He tried to sound more encouraging. 'Those ropes have got big leather eyes so they can't pull too tight, you know that. It might not be pretty, but I guarantee I'll get that horse into the yard, safe and sound.' Sam turned, and stared at the truck. 'I can let her go instead if you want,' he said.

'No,' she said at last. She turned to face him. 'What do you want me to do?'

'Just close the gate once she's through.'

Sam nodded. Drew fired up the chainsaw motor and the winch ground into action. When it had taken up most of the slack in the cable, he lowered the ramp. Whirlwind was huddled at the back of the truck. She didn't react when the ropes first grew taut, but as the pressure increased, she began to fight. The indifferent, galvanised cable maintained its inexorable pull. It tightened around the mare's throat, dragging her, choking the fight from her. She took a step forward, then another, her exhaustion showing. Jarrang neighed again and Whirlwind finally capitulated. She stumbled into the yard.

Sam yelled with delight and rushed to close the gate. Drew heaved a great sigh of relief. He ran to shut off the motor and release the catching ropes from the winch cable. Drew shone the torch into the yard. Whirlwind stood drooping and defeated in the corner. The two nooses had loosened, now the strain was off. It would be safe to leave them on overnight.

'She's shivering,' said Sam, wiping streams of water from her eyes. 'She needs a rug.'

Drew shook his head. 'That horse doesn't need a rug. She needs some peace.' And so do I, he thought, feeling a little sick at what he'd done. He pulled Sam into the truck cabin out of the rain. 'Leave her alone until morning,' he said. 'Promise me?'

Sam nodded. 'I can't believe we did it. Thank you.' She softly kissed his wet cheek.

Drew's skin tingled where Sam's lips had touched it. 'I can't believe it either. Now let's just hope we don't get caught.' There was no way to hide the horse. By a stroke of good fortune, the yards at Brumby's Run were set well back, not visible from the house. But if anybody bothered to come looking, they'd find her. No point worrying about that now, though. It was done, the die already cast. 'I'm going to pack up the winch,' he said. 'Then can we please go inside and get dry for the second time tonight?'

'Of course, your Majesty, Mr King of the Mountain. Yes, we can.' Sam threw her arms around his neck and kissed him properly this time. She radiated warmth and happiness right through her soggy clothes, and he remembered why he'd embarked on this ridiculous escapade in the first place. Maybe she was finally ready to try again with him.

Drew extracted himself reluctantly from her arms and jumped out to get the winch. A soft nose nuzzled his hand. 'Bess? What are you doing out here?' Hadn't he left her in the kitchen? Drew stowed the gear back in the truck, hopped in and started the engine, trying not to step on Jasper in the process. The back wheels spun wildly for a few moments, then somehow gained traction. Thank goodness it was a downhill run to the house.

Drew rounded the hay shed, then slammed on the brakes. The headlights' beam revealed a car parked in the drive. Sam glanced up at him, an expression of horror on her face. Drew put his finger to her lips and shushed her with a whisper. He killed the lights and slipped from the cabin.

It was difficult to see in the dark, but he didn't think he recognised the car. One of those generic Japanese things, a Honda or Suzuki or something. Bess stood on the porch, tail aloft and waving. Why wasn't she barking? The dog ran right up to the back door, and with one scratch of the paw, she was in. Drew jumped back in the truck and parked it out of sight behind the hayshed. 'There's somebody in the house,' he whispered to Sam. 'Stay here.'

'I'm coming with you,' said Sam firmly. She jammed her hat further down on her head and hopped out.

'At least let me go first.' She fell in behind him, and they approached the rear windows. There was a lull in the storm. The shadow of a figure showed through the kitchen blind. They moved around to the front porch. But as Drew reached for the handle, the door opened. It was Charlie.

CHAPTER 27

S am didn't know what to think. Competing emotions made her dizzy. She should be very happy, and she was — in a way. Thankful, certainly, to see Charlie looking so much stronger, although she still had a kind of frail, elfin beauty about her; still looked wrong somehow outside of a hospital setting. Her eyes had grown elegant brows and lovely long lashes. Her hair was an inch or more in length now over her head. If you didn't know she'd been bald, it might have looked like she had a stylish crop, one designed to bring classic definition to her features. It was a great comfort to see this beautiful, healthy version of her sister. But with a jolt, Sam recognised that happiness wasn't on the top of her emotional scoreboard. Disappointment, jealousy, guilt, resentment – these were the clear winners. Charlie's face had filled out, and their resemblance was more disconcerting than ever. Sam was looking into a distorted mirror.

'Aren't you going to say anything?' said Charlie.

Sam pushed past Drew and briefly embraced her sister, feeling meat on her bones for the first time. 'This is such a surprise,' said Sam, meaning *why didn't you ring first?* Charlie started to softly sob. Sam gathered her up in sodden arms, filled with a sudden, fierce, protective love that hunted away all her negative feelings. 'Tell me what's wrong.'

'I got so fed up in Melbourne,' said Charlie, sniffing back tears. 'Honestly, I couldn't stand it for one more minute. What's the point of beating cancer if that shitty city is just going to kill me anyway?' Sam stayed silent and let Charlie talk. 'I've had some terrible fights with Mum. She never gets off my back: don't do this, don't do that. And she's got this new boyfriend. They get stoned all the time.'

Sam couldn't reconcile Charlie's portrait of Mary with that of the woman she'd known in Melbourne. The woman always by her daughter's side, who bought her beautiful headscarves that she clearly could not afford. The woman who concocted homemade herbal remedies, with mother's love as the main ingredient. Sam stroked Charlie's hair. It had the silky-smooth texture of a Siamese cat. She made soothing noises, holding her sister close.

'Come on, you two,' said Drew, 'Get inside. I'll light the fire.' Sam sat Charlie down in the kitchen. Drew caught Sam's eye. Get into dry clothes,' he said. 'You'll be no good to anybody with pneumonia.' Drew was right, she was shaking; whether from cold or emotion, she couldn't tell. Sam ran to the bedroom, threw off her wet things, climbed into pyjamas and tore back down the hall with a mohair rug.

Charlie was sitting at the kitchen table. Drew had a blaze going in the hearth, but she was still shivering. Sam put the blanket round her sister's shoulders. 'Does Mary know you're here?'

Charlie shook her head. 'I finally spat the dummy, and Mum said that if I'd made up my mind, she'd drive me home. She just had to say goodbye to Carlos first . . . she'd only be an hour.' Charlie's eyes blazed with a furious indignation that had chased away any hint of tears. 'Five hours later,' she held up the fingers of a hand for emphasis, 'and she's still not back. Nice one, Mum. So,' she shrugged, 'I drove myself. Mum probably doesn't even know I'm gone.'

So Charlie had driven alone for seven hours, in shocking weather without a licence. Sam was aghast. She'd left her phone behind that morning. Where was it? There, behind the bread. She quickly checked it – five missed calls from Mary and a dozen messages.

'Oh, I think she knows,' said Sam, still reeling from Charlie's sudden appearance. Drew held up the kettle behind Charlie's back, and she nodded for him to put it on.

'I'm a good driver,' protested Charlie, 'and I didn't see one single copper.'

'Thank goodness for that,' said Sam. Charlie yawned. 'Now let's get you something to eat, and then get you to bed.' Sam winced — she was sounding like her mother. 'We'll talk more about it in the morning.'

'I'm not sleepy yet,' said Charlie, like a petulant child. She stood up and looked into the little lounge room. 'The house looks so beautiful and clean. I've never seen it like this.'

Sam swelled with unexpected pride. 'Sleep in Mary's room,' she said. 'You might be more comfortable.'

'No,' said Charlie. 'I've been dreaming of my old bed, my old room.'

Drew placed mugs of tea in front of them. Sam slipped down the hallway and quickly inspected Charlie's bedroom. The posters on the wall, the frogs, the cast-iron bed frame – these were the only original things about it. Sam had bought a new mattress, new bedding, new curtains. She'd painted the grimy walls, and scattered bright rugs over the stained carpet. Charlie's frog collection was displayed on shelves made from bricks and planks, and brightened up with pretty throws. Drew had donated the simple colonial wardrobe with the lovely etched-glass mirror that now stood in the corner. It had been languishing in a Kilmarnock shed for a decade, apparently, ever since his mother refurbished the bedrooms.

Sam had used the old dressing table and wardrobe for firewood. She switched on the antique lamp that stood on the two-drawer timber bedside table, both pieces she'd found at Tallangala's sprawling secondhand-dealer's yard. She smoothed the bedspread, accented with gum-leaf motifs in rich red and green. Frogs featured in the pattern and were embroidered on the pillow cases. What if Charlie didn't like it? It seemed insane to her now, to have tampered with the bedroom without permission.

Charlie appeared in the doorway and Sam held her breath. A stunned look grew on her sister's face as she gazed around. 'It's gorgeous.' Charlie walked about the room, feeling textures, opening drawers. She bounced on the bed, grinning broadly. 'It's like I'm on one of those home makeover shows.'

Sam heaved a relieved sigh. 'I'm glad you like it.' She sat down on the bed beside her sister. 'Are you really well enough to be here? Shouldn't you be near your doctor?'

'I told you, I can't stay in bloody Melbourne. It's driving me insane.'

Drew stuck his head around the corner. 'Supper's up.'

Charlie looked curiously from Drew to Sam. 'Has Drew been . . . helpful?' Sam nodded and smiled, a little too brightly. What was Charlie implying? And for that matter, why weren't Drew and Charlie acting like a couple, if that's what they'd been? She stood up and opened the curtain. Was her face flushed with guilt? Perhaps the cold air by the window would help.

'Sammy?' Charlie hadn't called her that before. Something in the tenderness of her sister's voice broke her heart.

'Let's have that supper,' Sam said briskly, hurrying from the room. In the kitchen they found plates of toasted sandwiches oozing melted cheese, and mugs of Milo.

'Whose car?' asked Drew.

'Mine,' said Charlie. 'Something peculiar's been happening. Somebody's sending me and Mum money. Lots of money. Then this car arrives, registered in my name, with an unsigned *Get Well Soon* card taped to the windscreen.'

'That's crazy,' said Sam, hot cheese squishing out of the corner of her mouth. 'Any idea who?'

'Nope. Mum reckons it must be one of her old lovers made good. Maybe even my dad.' That would be my dad too, thought Sam. It was odd and kind of exciting. A mystery father, showering gifts on Charlie. With a twinge of envy she realised that if this anonymous benefactor was her real father, he may not even know that a second daughter existed.

'Fair dinkum?' said Drew. 'That's some story. You sure Mary didn't just harvest a dope crop or something?'

'No,' said Charlie. 'I'm not sure. Anything's possible with Mum.'

'Why would you say something like that?' asked Sam.

'A few years ago, Drew and I were mustering calves out of the Snake Creek flats,' said Charlie. 'We came across this bloody huge cannabis plantation, half in Brumby's, half in the park. Mum had a real champion of a boyfriend back then. What was his name?'

'Clint,' said Drew, taking the last sandwich.

'Yeah, Clint. What a lowlife. Anyway, Drew and me ripped up the lot and burned it.'

Drew laughed. 'Took us two whole days.'

'We had to stand upwind or get stoned ourselves,' said Charlie. 'You should have seen Clint's face when he discovered the crop was gone. He blamed this mate of his. They got in a fight, Clint got arrested and we never heard from him again.'

Sam was staggered. She wanted to say something, to defend Mary, to demand evidence that she was complicit in Clint's scheme. But what right did she have to even hold an opinion on the past? The story was an unwelcome reminder that she was an outsider here at Brumby's Run. Drew, Charlie, the bush, the town – they shared a history from which she was forever excluded. It was too painful to contemplate.

'If you don't mind, I'm going to bed,' said Sam. 'It's been a big day.' Charlie raised her exquisite new eyebrows, requesting an explanation. 'Drew will fill you in,' said Sam. Of course he would. No doubt they had lots to catch up on. She gave Charlie a hug, and hurried down the hall to her room. No, it was Mary's room. She was just visiting. For the first time in a long time she thought about Faith, about Dad and her grandparents. She thought about university. She'd deferred her course, but now she wasn't so sure that had been a good idea.

Sam could hear low voices in the kitchen still, murmuring, reconnecting. She squeezed her eyes shut and shoved her head beneath the pillow. Sam drifted into troubled sleep, confused about Charlie, desolate about Drew, and trying without success to block out the looming memory of Rowdy Clarke's face.

CHAPTER 28

Charlie had slept on and off for almost twenty-four hours. Each time she'd woken, the sweet, familiar sounds of the bush had lulled her back to sleep. The laughing call of a kookaburra, the distant bellow of a bull, the high roar of wind through the forest — and best of all the dusk to dawn chorus of frogs in the dam. On the second day she'd risen early, rested and restored, just in time to see Sam off to work. Charlie stood out on the porch. She munched a piece of toast and waved goodbye, looking longingly after her sister's car. There'll be time enough, Sam had said, for you to take back the job with Bushy. You're not strong enough yet for a full day's work. Sam was right, although Charlie hated to admit it. Even showering left her spent. She turned back to face the house. The homestead had been transformed, inside and out; gardens weeded, rubbish gone – the front door even sported a fresh coat of paint. It looked fantastic, but the place no longer felt like her own. What on earth was she supposed to do all day? Everything was already done. A sudden movement up at the yards caught her eye and she went to investigate.

The lovely grey mare was not friendly at first. She'd rushed at Charlie with ears pinned back, and threatened her with wicked hoofs. Charlie had studiously ignored her. She'd armed herself with a bag of sliced fruit and a book, put a plastic picnic chair in the middle of the yard, and calmly sat down to read. It hadn't taken long for Whirlwind's curiosity to overcome her caution. Soon she was snuffling the chair, snuffling Charlie, nibbling at the fruit. Charlie had slipped her a piece of apple, and popped another piece absentmindedly into her own mouth. 'Listen to this.'

She read to Whirlwind every day for a week. On the eighth day she tried something different. The mare was standing beside her with twitching ears, while Charlie read to her from Edward Abbey's *Desert Solitaire*.

'Am I boring you?' she asked after a while. The answer, apparently, was yes. Whirlwind's head had drooped. A hind hoof was at rest. Her bottom lip quivered and her eyes were half-closed.

'Let's do something else,' said Charlie. The mare woke with a start and followed her over to the gate. Charlie opened it. 'Come on, then.' She began walking up the hill to the dam. 'Field observation time. You can be my assistant.' Whirlwind stood stock still for a few moments, as though she couldn't quite believe her luck. Then she'd ducked her head and pounded out of the yard, catching up with Charlie and bucking around her in wild, joyful circles. Charlie took her cue from the dappled horse, racing as fast as she could – chasing Whirlwind, and being chased in turn. Her weakened legs seemed to draw strength from the mare's playful exuberance. Vigour returned to her wasted muscles, and she pulled off her top to run in her bra, the sun kissing her skin. When her energy was finally spent, Charlie flopped down in a patch of everlastings. Whirlwind snorted twice and began to graze nearby, occasionally checking in with Charlie, nibbling at her clothes or hair.

Little by little, day by day, the friendship between the girl and the rogue mare grew. Charlie knew about horses. She knew more about horses than she knew about people. And she knew it was only through such a friendship that the damaged mare might heal. A sort of natural wisdom guided her. Wisdom gained during endless days spent riding in the ranges. Like all children, Charlie had had her heroes – role models, people she admired. But unlike most children, they weren't sports stars or pop singers. They were scientists like Jane Goodall and Dian Fossey – pioneering naturalists who immersed themselves in the society of the animals they studied. For them, it was the chimpanzees and gorillas of the central African jungle. But for Charlie, it was the wild horses of Maroong Mountain.

Charlie had learned the hard way that happiness wasn't to be found in the loneliness and exclusion of the schoolyard. Happiness was to be found instead, in the acceptance of the herd. Ever so slowly, with infinite care, she'd insinuated herself into the secret life of the wild horses on the mountain. Charlie may not have been at school, but she was getting an education. She learned the brumbies' waterhole rituals. She won the forbearance of their wise old stallion. She won the friendship of their lead mare, Jarrang's mother. Charlie grew fluent in the language of their bodies and, one by one, the brumbies allowed her to slip onto their backs.

It was through this unique brand of liberty training that Charlie hoped to win over the traumatised mare. No saddles, no bridles, no ropes or round yards. But Charlie wouldn't tell Sam — not yet. This was just between her and Whirlwind.

CHAPTER 29

Charlie wasn't the only one who'd come home. Bill was back too. Back with a nurse, not fully recovered, not able to physically run the property himself. But he was back, and back with a vengeance. He'd never been so impossible, so full of bile. For Drew there was no more time spent next door at Brumby's Run. In the week since Charlie's return, he'd hardly seen Sam. When he phoned, she'd seemed distant. When he dropped by, she was always busy, and Charlie was always there.

Drew remembered Sam's kiss the night they stole Whirlwind. She'd been happy, ready to start off where they'd left off – he was sure of it. What they really needed was some clear air. If Charlie hadn't turned up like she did, who knows what would have happened? Somebody was always getting in their way. Like Bill, for instance. Hijacking every minute of every day. So far Drew had put off telling his father about the expired lease. Why invite trouble? But sooner or later it was bound to come out.

'Mr Bill, he want to see you,' said Mai, as Drew came in for breakfast.

Drew nodded and sat down. 'Those eggs look good.' He grabbed a piece of toast. 'Any chance you could rustle up a few mushrooms to go with them?'

'Mr Bill, he wants to see you now.' Drew took a closer look at Mai. Her eyes were red, and her apron was all bunched up in her hands.

'All right, Mai.' He put down the toast and stood up. She gestured down the hall. Voices sounded from the study. Drew gave her a reassuring smile. 'I'll see what he wants.'

Bill glared at Drew as he entered the room. 'About time.' Tom stood by the door, an expression of pure exasperation on his face. Bill was waving a newspaper about – the latest *Stock and Station*. 'What the hell happened to that Benambra mob I told you to buy? Bob Hunter's got them.' Bill stormed back and forth, as much as a man could storm when sitting in a wheelchair. He rolled over to his desk and searched the drawers, tossing papers and pens aside as he went. Lena, his nurse, gathered the scattered things off the floor.

'And where's the new lease that Kelly woman signed?' He became more and more agitated every second. 'Tom said they turned our cattle out and locked the gates?' Bill shook his head. 'Unbelievable.' He started searching the desk, all over again.

'Dad, stop. Mary never signed the renewal.'

'Makes no difference.' Bill slammed shut the drawer. 'A clause in the agreement states that when the lease expires, it converts to a periodic tenancy. While Mary accepts those lease payments, the contract renews itself automatically each month. She had no legal right to turf out our cattle. I want them back in there first thing tomorrow.'

'Dad.' Drew raised his voice a notch. 'Will you just listen for once? This isn't about the law — it's about what's right. The Kellys need that land for themselves.'

'Mary needs it? What for?' argued Bill, his voice rising. 'That wormy, inbred mob of hers are no better than scrubbers. They're a waste of good feed.' He was shouting now. 'And they'll never earn her an income. I just about keep that woman!' A purple vein throbbed at Bill's temple and Drew began to fear his father might have a heart attack. 'Sucking me dry all these months, without a word? I should brief my solicitor, take her to the cleaners.'

'You mean she's been collecting agistment fees all along?' asked Drew.

'Damn straight,' said Bill.

It hadn't occurred to Drew that his father might keep right on paying Mary, without a signed copy of the renewal in his hand. He was always so tight-fisted.

'Where's Mary?' barked Bill. 'Get her over here. I'll soon sort this out.' He rose from his chair and his face suddenly distorted in pain. Lena sprang forward.

'Mr Chandler. Please don't put weight on that leg. It won't heal right.'

'Stop bloody mothering me!' he yelled, sinking back down. Lena tried to put the rug back onto his knee, and Bill flung it aside, clouting her hard on the leg in the process. She squealed and jumped back. 'And Tom, what's happening with the stock up in the park? You been keeping an eye on them?'

Tom nodded. 'I wish we'd fitted those GPS collars though, Bill. Right now we're in direct breach of our agreement with the state government.'

'Tracking devices for cows,' scoffed Bill. 'What a load of nonsense.'

Drew wasn't listening. He was watching Lena's face. The woman looked absolutely terrified. Somewhere inside him a slow fuse began to burn.

'You imbecile!' Bill was screaming at Tom now, accusing him of not knowing one end of a cow from the other. Lena caught Drew's eye, shrugged and looked helpless. Drew cursed beneath his breath. It was about time someone stood up to his father.

'Tom,' said Drew in a low growl. The two men went on arguing. 'Tom!' Tom stopped in mid-sentence and stared at him, disbelief written all over his face. 'Leave us, please, Tom. I want a private word with Dad.' Tom opened his mouth to speak. 'Leave us, Tom.'

The head stockman shut his mouth and left the room.

Bill looked at Drew like he'd gone mad. 'I'm not finished . . .'

'Oh, you're finished all right,' said Drew, his voice full of controlled fury. 'You're finished fuming and bitching and throwing your weight around. You're finished bullying Mai and Lena. You're finished talking to the most respected head stockman in Currajong like he's a first-year jackaroo.' Drew marched forward and stabbed his father in the chest with a finger. 'And you're finished treating me like a damned slave. If you want to move our cattle back onto Brumby's Run, do it yourself. But if that's your decision, I won't be here to see it.'

Lena cowered in the corner. Bill sat speechless, his eyes popping out of his head. That only happened when he was seriously, seriously angry. Up until now Drew had feared this bug-eyed father, but not today. Today Bill just looked like a sad old man, struggling to keep hold of his shrinking world.

'You have no right —' Bill started.

'It's you who have no right,' said Drew. 'No right to run my life, or anybody else's. You'll drive me off, Dad, just like you did Mum and the girls. I love you, you old bastard, and I don't want to leave Kilmarnock. But if you take back Brumby's Run from the Kellys, I swear, I'm gone, Dad. Gone for good.' He took one last satisfied look at his father's stunned expression, then strode from the room and slammed the door behind him.

Drew took a big breath. His heart was beating like a bongo drum, but he felt like a million dollars. He should have done this years ago, should have taken back the power. Lobbed the ball into dad's court. Stay or go, it was all the same to him now. Not that he'd go too far if it came to that. Not too far from Sam. His gut told him Dad wouldn't call him on this one, but just in case, he'd better head over to Brumby's when Sam got home from work and warn her.

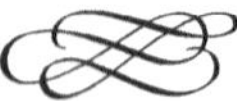

Every morning after Sam went to work with Bushy, Charlie worked with Whirlwind. At first she'd struggled with the exertion, dead tired by lunchtime, crawling wearily into bed for an afternoon sleep. But as each day passed and Whirlwind grew calmer, Charlie grew stronger. She'd started working Tambo too, and today, in this first sparkling week of autumn, Charlie felt ready at last to ride into Balleroo.

Balleroo — the very word was music. Charlie could hardly believe it; she and Tambo together again, sweeping up a grassy slope into the mountains. She could breathe. She was free. Free of doctors, free of walls, free of well-meaning people asking her *Are you okay, Charlie?* in that pointed, exaggerated way, that invited her to respond that indeed, she was not. Charlie was free of everything but the rhythm of Tambo's hoofs on the earth. How good it felt to be physical again. For months her body had seemed like a hostile alien – holding her hostage, attacking her from deep down in her bones, producing nothing but pain. To survive, she'd cultivated such a deliberate disconnect between mind and body that she'd feared it was permanent. But Tambo's world was an intensely physical one, and it required Charlie to be physical as well. Her body moved in time with Tambo's, synchronised to the tempo of his breathing. Her pelvis, her thighs, her heels and hands all spoke to him. She could smell their sweat, their combined heat.

The wasted muscles of her core went to work, keeping her slim frame balanced, bringing it to equilibrium. Tendons tightened in her lower back, her upper leg, all the way down to her toes. Charlie revelled in the sensation. Back in the hospital, she used to wonder if she even had muscles any more. Her fingers played with the reins, keeping delicate contact with Tambo's mouth.

Charlie focused on the mountain, hyper-alert. A rider had to concentrate, lose herself in the present, had to see and hear and smell whatever her horse did. 'Lose myself to find myself,' she whispered. Tambo's ears flickered back at the sound of her voice. Charlie leant down, buried her face in his mane and wrapped her arms around his neck. Tambo stopped and politely waited for Charlie to behave. She laughed and sat upright, breathing in the bush.

A magpie carolled overhead. An old man kangaroo bounded across their path. The soft patter of gumnuts on the ground revealed a feeding flock of red-headed gang-gang cockatoos in the tree tops, and a daytime dingo howled. The fragrance of peppermint gums was sweet and strong. Charlie smiled to think of what Professor Sung would say if he saw her now. *Restrict physical activity,* he'd said. *Avoid animals for fear of infection,* he'd said. What would be the point of living? There was more to a person than blood cells and bones.

Charlie gulped great lungfuls of scented air, and cantered to the top of a ridge clothed with alpine heath and everlastings. Where was that patch of snow gums? They couldn't be far now. There they were, trunks resplendent in splashes of salmon, apricot and peach. How long was it since she'd been to Corroboree Bog? She cast her mind back, past the transplant, past her failed treatments, past the dreadful, desperate days spent hiding her illness from her mother. It had been early spring, just after snow melt. She'd packed a lunch and spent the day taking field notes. It had been an unusually successful breeding season for the frogs in the bog, and she'd found lots of fertile egg clutches. With any luck, she'd find an abundance of healthy young froglings emerging from the ponds.

Ever since she was old enough to ride into the mountains, Charlie had considered herself the keeper of the Balleroo bogs. There was something so hauntingly beautiful and fragile about these primitive wetlands, remnants of the last ice age. Most people couldn't see it. Most people were blind. When the mobile library came to Currajong, Charlie lost herself in private study, in books, in the internet's infinite cloud of knowledge. She became an expert about local landforms, especially the sub-alpine bogs. 'You should study science at university,' the librarian had urged her. 'You're a natural. Not many students engage in all this extra research.' Charlie just smiled. She never studied at school. How could she? She was hardly ever there. It would have been different if they'd taught interesting subjects – like ecology, for instance.

She'd learned at the library that Balleroo's bogs were formed during the Palaeozoic Age, five hundred million years ago. Cradled beneath granite and sandstone peaks, sculpted by glaciers, eroded by rain and snow – each bog had adapted to the particular combination of its own topography and microclimate. Charlie knew each one by the names she'd given them long ago. There was Tree Frog Tarn, Barking Marsh and Bullfrog Bog. She'd found a colony of rare water skinks at Pobblebonk Pond, and even rarer growling grass frogs at Parrot Pools. Her favourite amphibians were the pretty, spotted tree frogs, miniature cousins of the green tree frogs that were popular as pets. Corroboree Bog was a haven for these unique little animals, and she couldn't wait to discover how successful the summer hatchings had been.

Charlie dismounted, aching and stiff from the ride. She tethered Tambo to a tree and walked down through the snow gums. Turning left through paddocks of purple eyebrights and starbursts of hoary sunrays, she reached the fence dating back to the old mountain leases. The hardwood strainer posts were rotten with age; the barbed wire rusted and broken.

Charlie had started down the hill along the old stock route when something made her pause. A prickle along the nape of her neck, like she was being watched. Slowly, very slowly, she turned around.

Only twenty metres away, across the grassy clearing, stood a great red-and-white bull. Charlie gulped the air to calm herself. A skinny black cow with a late calf marched to stand beside it. The cow mooed uneasily. Charlie recognised her by her bright-pink ear tag. That was a Kelly cow. What the hell were Kelly cattle doing way out here in the park? Or any cattle, for that matter?

The big bull pawed the ground and tossed his head. Charlie retreated a few steps. There was something unusual about him; something she couldn't immediately put her finger on. And then it struck her. He had horns. Bill ran poll Herefords, which were hornless. This wasn't one of Bill's bulls. This animal's massive horns curved forward, long and upswept with pointed tips.

The bull snorted, flared his nostrils and trotted a circle around the cow. His hide bore battle scars in place of tags or brands. Charlie's heart lurched when she recognised just what she faced. A wild scrubber bull. He lowered his head to the ground, bellowed, and charged at a candlebark tree. His cow lowed in admiration at the display of strength. Bulging muscles strained against the resistance of the trunk as he scraped his horns from side to side, shredding bark to sawdust. It looked for all the world like he was sharpening his horns.

Charlie glanced around, hoping for her own tree, but she'd left the sheltering forest behind. The old, grassy stock route led down a wide slope to the wetlands, two hundred metres below. She was caught out in the open, with no shelter apart from the rickety fence. Charlie walked backwards down the hill, unwilling to turn around. She sensed that only eye contact was keeping the animal at bay, and it would run her down if she turned tail and made a break.

The bull bellowed a challenge, made a run at her, then stopped to uproot a young wattle. The tree lay over his horns like an Olympic victory garland while he tore at the ground with first one forefoot and then the other, sending clods of clay and clouds of dust sailing over his back and past his flanks. A rumbling battle cry rose in his throat, ending in a deafening roar. This was a bull with something to prove.

Charlie maintained her slow and steady retreat, keeping the tumble-down fence between her and the bull wherever she could.

Until the bull charged. He moved with a cumbersome, rolling gait, but Charlie wasn't fooled. She knew full well the deceptive speed of such a lumbering stride. She turned and sprinted down the hill, hampered by shaky legs and weak muscles, heart hammering in her chest. She tried to judge the proximity of the animal from the sound of his thundering hoofs and rumbling breath. Her own lungs burned now, and it was harder and harder to keep her balance amongst the tussocks of snow grass. Any moment now he'd shove her in the back and trample her to earth. What would it feel like, she wondered? She'd almost lost her life at that hospital in Melbourne. Far better to die on this wild mountain.

Unexpectedly a shot rang out, then another, and another. A bawl of pain and the earth shuddered. Charlie fell down in fright, squeezed her eyes shut and waited. All she could hear was the rush of blood through her body, the thump of her beating heart. Seconds felt like minutes.

Then a quiet voice. 'You're safe. Take my hand.'

Charlie dared to believe she'd survived. She rolled over and there was a man, tall and blond. He wore the khaki uniform of a park ranger, and carried a bolt-action rifle. With a start, she turned to see the bull lying quite dead where he'd speared into the ground, surrounded by blood and churned earth. The man took her by the wrist, helped her gently to her feet and dusted her off.

'It's becoming a habit, saving your life,' he said. 'But at least you've got your clothes on this time.' As far as Charlie could tell, she'd never met this man before. A combination of confusion and shock caused her to wobble violently and collapse back to earth. The man seemed to consider this for a moment, then joined her on the ground. He sat with arms wrapped around his knees, hands clasped. 'Excuse me for being personal,' he said, 'but that's a charming haircut.' He had a faint accent — German, maybe?

Charlie perked up and managed a smile. She wasn't going to die after all. This deluded stranger had seen to that. 'Thanks,' she said. 'If it hadn't been for you ...' That awful possibility didn't bear thinking about. Charlie took a closer look at her saviour. She still couldn't place him. 'Who are you? Have we met?'

'Am I really that forgettable?'

'No,' said Charlie. 'You're not. That's why it's so strange that I don't remember.'

He smiled. 'All right, I'll introduce myself again if I must. Karl Richter.' He extended his arm. She propped herself up shakily on one elbow and shook his hand.

'And who exactly do you think I am?' she asked.

'You're Samantha Carmichael. From Melbourne. Just visiting . . . although it's been a very long visit.'

'Oh, I get it,' she said, laughing. 'You've got me mixed up with my sister. She's Samantha.' Charlie nodded, pleased she'd resolved things in her own mind, if not in his. 'I'm Charlie. How exactly did you meet Sam?' She wanted to add, and why didn't she have her clothes on? No, she'd better direct that intriguing question to her sister. Not that she'd blame Sam. Charlie took a closer look at her mysterious saviour. He was pretty cute – slim, with long muscled legs and intelligent grey eyes. Mary insisted grey eyes were associated with water and wisdom. Their bearers might appear mild-mannered, she said, but in fact they possessed a hidden strength – the inexorable power of water; able in time to wear away even the hardest rock. Maybe Mum was right. Whatever the case, this man's quiet confidence was oddly alluring.

'Look,' said Karl. 'I'd love for us to have a good, long chat about how we met, and who we know, and who you might actually be. But it's not really the time.' He stood up, reached for her, and for a second time she took his hand. She'd always been a sucker for a man in uniform. This time she managed to remain on her feet. 'You okay to walk?' She nodded. 'Let's go then,' he said. 'Samantha, or Charlie, or whoever you are.'

'Where are we going?' she asked.

'To look at a bog.'

'You're kidding me.'

'I know sphagnum bogs don't get good press,' he said,' but they're really quite fascinating. Vital habitats filtering water into mountain catchments. Whole communities of flora and fauna depend on them – the whole ecosystem depends on them.'

'But . . . ' began Charlie.

He held up his hand. 'Considering that I keep saving your life, could you humour me, please?'

Charlie began to hop with excitement, trying to get a word in. 'You don't understand,' she said. 'I love bogs, particularly that bog.' She pointed down the hill. 'They're one of my very favourite places. Along with their frogs and lizards and snakes and things.'

Karl looked at her sideways. 'You've either hit your head or you're teasing me,' he said. 'Last time we met you didn't seem so keen on reptiles.'

'I told you,' said Charlie. 'That must have been my sister, Sam. Did she have a posh voice?'

'I suppose she did,' he conceded.

'Then she didn't sound like me exactly, did she?' It was surprisingly hard work, convincing him that she wasn't her sister. Had it been this difficult for Sam? Had people mistaken her as well?

'Maybe not. You just look so much alike.'

Charlie groaned. 'Never mind,' she said. 'Let's go.'

He nodded, apparently happy with that, and they walked down the hill to Corroboree Bog. Or at least to what had once been Corroboree Bog. Charlie sensed trouble even before she reached the wetlands. The slope had been eroded by the hoofs of cattle, exposing the fragile peaty soil to the elements. The expected summer carpet of marsh marigolds and orange everlastings was nowhere to be seen. Clumps of silver alpine daisies were grazed down to the ground. She glanced across at Karl. He wore a grim expression on his face.

When they reached the bog, what had once been a chain of pristine pools was little more than a wallow. The greenhood orchids were gone; the moss beds trampled. In some places pug holes had run together, creating little downhill channels, draining dry whole parts of the marsh. Karl began to take photographs.

'Look,' said Charlie. She bent down to where a small green frog was struggling to escape from a fresh cow pat. It had a broken leg. 'What are cattle doing back in the park?' she asked, as she went to rescue it.

'Wait,' said Karl. He took photos from every angle of the frogling trapped in the dung. 'There's a trial on,' he said. 'To test whether cattle reduce the risk of bushfires. Although so far, published and peer-reviewed research shows no statistically significant difference between grazed and ungrazed areas.' He spoke like she imagined a professor might speak, and his voice was strangely compelling. Karl pointed to the tiny injured frog that Charlie was releasing into one of the few undamaged ponds. '*Litoria spenceri* - the spotted tree frog,' he said. 'Critically endangered.'

Charlie was stunned. She'd never met anyone who even knew the common name of a frog, let alone somebody who could identify one by its Latin name out in the field, and who also knew its conservation status.

'My mission is to protect the habitat of your little frog friend . . .' He was on a mission? Like James Bond? Fantastic. She didn't know people actually had missions in real life. 'With the help of your keen eyes and these photos,' he patted the camera. 'I hope to get this grazing trial suspended.'

You had to love this bloke. 'I bloody well hope so,' she said.

'It's not just cattle, although they're the obvious culprits here.' Karl gestured to the looming mountain peaks. 'Balleroo is infested with feral pigs, deer, horses - we need to get rid of the lot.'

Charlie went quiet. All of a sudden she wasn't quite so gung-ho for Karl's mission. He went on taking measurements, pictures, water samples. He wandered off to the far side of the wetlands, talking into his iPhone. Charlie squatted down on a trampled bed of cushion plants, took an exercise book from her back pack, and started making her own notes and drawings. After a while Karl returned, a puzzled look on his face. 'What are you doing?'

'Writing a report,' she said.

'Who for?'

'Just for me.' Charlie looked up as he squatted beside her, his face close to hers, his expression more bewildered than ever. Karl wasn't the sort of man she normally went for, but she did love the accent, and he was handsome in a clean-cut sort of way. Of course, saving lives and knowing about frogs made him sexy even without all the other stuff.

'How did you get here in the first place?' he asked. 'I could see no car. Do you know that fire trail is closed to the public?'

'I rode here,' she said. 'My horse is tethered on the hill above the wetlands.' He looked surprised – displeased, even. 'Don't worry. He's more than thirty metres away from any watercourse, and I don't need a permit to ride in this area, do I?'

'No,' he said. 'You don't.' He gazed at her with a clear-eyed intensity that she supposed he usually reserved for endangered species. 'Just who exactly are you?'

'I told you. Charlie.'

'Charlie Carmichael?' he asked.

Charlie Carmichael. She might have been, if things had been just a bit different.

'I'm Charlie Kelly,' she said. 'Charlie Kelly from Brumby's Run.'

CHAPTER 31

Sam gave up, slipped from the yard, and returned to the house through the afternoon shadows. She and Whirlwind were at an impasse. Maybe it was time to ask Bushy for help.

Now Charlie was back, the time was fast approaching when she'd have to come clean with Bushy — come clean with the whole town, for that matter. It was a terrifying prospect, one she hoped could be put off for a few more days. Charlie had said she didn't want to go into Currajong yet, didn't want the curious eyes of the townsfolk upon her. That gave Sam a little breathing space; some time to figure out just how to go about her impossible confession.

Bushy, she'd decided, would be the easiest person to tell. Perhaps she'd start with him. She trusted Bushy. The morning after they'd taken the mare (she didn't use the word stolen, even to herself), Bushy had given his statement to the police, with Sam hovering nervously in the background. 'Kids,' he'd said, with a snort of derision. 'A bunch of them opened the gate. Saw them myself, I did.' He'd glanced at Sam and winked. 'Probably dared each other to get in the yard with that damned man-killer, and then turned tail and ran.' He spat a wad of tobacco at the ground. 'Bloody kids.'

'Bloody kids,' the sergeant had agreed, shaking his head in disgust. 'Wayne said the horse was branded?'

'That's right,' said Bushy. 'UV on the near shoulder, and a 9 on the off.'

'Well,' said the sergeant, with a quick look around, like he hoped that Whirlwind might just trot past or something. 'I suppose it'll be long gone by now.'

Bushy nodded sagely. 'Long, long gone.'

Sam had let out a sigh of relief, loud enough to draw the sergeant's attention. For a moment she was a rabbit in the spotlights, then he gave a wave and left.

'You may have bitten off more than you can chew with that mare,' said Bushy after the sergeant was gone. 'And if I were you, I'd alter those brands.'

Sam felt herself flush firehouse red. 'How do you mean?'

'It doesn't take much to change a 9 into an 8, or a U into an O, or a V into a diamond.' Sam opened her mouth to deny it, but what was the point? 'Let me know if you need me,' Bushy had said.

She needed him now. Whirlwind was eating well, and at least the mare wasn't actively trying to kill people any more. But that was the extent of her improvement. She was still fearful and hyper vigilant, and wouldn't let Sam anywhere near her. None of the standard tactics had worked. Sam free-lunged Whirlwind round her yard each evening, waiting for that precise moment when the mare would drop her head, relax her jaw – grow calm enough for an approach. That moment never came. It seemed that Whirlwind would rather drop from exhaustion than allow a human to lay a hand on her.

Condor trotted along at Sam's feet on her way down to the house. The big bird was missing Charlie, who still wasn't back from Balleroo. Sam tried her phone - turned off. What was Charlie thinking, going off on her own like that? Sam was sick of feeling responsible for her sister. Sick of cooking her nourishing meals, monitoring her medication, worrying about her. Why couldn't Charlie have just listened to the doctors, and to Mary? Why couldn't she have stayed in

Melbourne? Sam shook her head. There was no point thinking like that. Charlie was home, so she'd just have to make the best of it.

Sam had been waiting every day for Drew to drop round and casually sling his arm around Charlie, for him to rekindle their relationship, but so far it hadn't happened. Her sister seemed equally uninterested. But then Charlie wasn't well, and would still be angry with Drew, surely, for his betrayal. Sam might just be seeing what she wanted to see. She hadn't found the nerve so far to ask Charlie outright.

Sam was in over her head. Confused, unsure, living in a torment of duty versus desire. She couldn't go on like this. It was time to confront Charlie with her own feelings, and try to gauge just how much Drew still meant to her sister.

Sam had told Charlie that she was deferring her commerce course. Her sister had been touchingly pleased by the news. So had Mary. Even Sam's father hadn't seemed to mind. 'It's your decision, Sammy,' he'd said. 'That university isn't going anywhere.' She resisted the possibility that he just didn't care. Wasn't he sending her money? It was partly guilt money, she knew that. Dad had flown straight back to Dubai from France, but then *away* was his default setting. She was used to it, and the allowance was helping keep Brumby's Run afloat. That, and the payments going into Charlie's bank account from her mystery benefactor.

Her mother hadn't been so easy to convince. Faith had stayed on in Europe after the initial month that she'd originally planned to be away. She'd taken Mamie and her arthritis to the Mediterranean for the duration of the northern winter. When Sam broke the news about her gap year, Faith had cried and argued and threatened. 'I'm coming straight home to talk some sense into you.'

'You can't change my mind,' Sam had said, gritting her teeth. 'Don't bother coming unless you bring Pharaoh too.' Her mind was made up. There would be no leaving Brumby's Run, no leaving Charlie – no leaving Drew. He'd risked a lot the night he hijacked Whirlwind. It was crazy and dangerous, and he'd done it just the same. It was an act of love, she knew that, and Sam loved him in return.

Sam's mobile rang. It was Mary. 'Sweetie, how are you? How's Charlie?'

'Fine,' said Sam cautiously. 'We're both fine.' She never quite knew what to expect from Mary's phone calls.

'Can you put Charlie on?'

Sam thought quickly. Charlie was off riding alone in the mountains, but she couldn't tell Mary that. 'She's outside somewhere. I'll get her to ring you, shall I?'

'Outside? She's not overdoing it, is she? The doctor said she should take it easy.'

Tell her yourself, Sam wanted to say. I'm not your daughter's keeper. But instead she just asked 'When are you coming home?'

Mary launched into a list of what sounded suspiciously like excuses. '. . . so, it won't be until Carlos gets the car fixed. Will that be all right? Can you girls manage a while longer?' Sam toyed with the idea of saying, no, they couldn't. Would it make any difference?

Sam was beginning to see that Charlie was right about Mary. She'd been a devoted mother during the crisis, no doubt about that, but had lost focus pretty quickly once Charlie was on the mend. 'Mum was on her best behaviour at the hospital,' Charlie had said. 'Trying to impress you. She can never keep up the Mother Mary act for long. Once there's a man involved, I come second. Always did. Maybe it's an abandonment complex because my dad ran out on her. She always hangs on to blokes too tight.'

'We can manage, Mary,' said Sam. 'We can manage just fine. Talk soon.' Psychoanalysing her birth mother was all very interesting, but there was a dinner to cook. With Mary acting so flaky, it was probably just as well that she stayed away. Mothers were such problem creatures.

Sam gave Condor a piece of cheese, chased him out the back door, and put on one of Charlie's Sara Storer CDs. She'd become a fan of Storer's sweet, country sound, with a subtle steel in the lyrics.

Sam looked in the fridge. She'd make something simple and tasty, like warm chicken salad, with wild blackberries and fresh cream for afterwards. And maybe buttery garlic bread. She needed to fatten Charlie up, and fortunately her culinary skills had advanced a long way from boiled eggs and toast. They'd been her staple back home in Melbourne on the rare occasion she prepared a meal for herself. Faith had a chef, but Sam dared not tell Charlie, or she'd never hear the end of it.

Sam pulled chicken strips out to defrost and set about chopping fresh greens and slicing the French loaf. Time ticked by. Still no Charlie. Sam made garlic butter, all the while glancing at the door. Strands of anxiety wadded to a ball in her stomach. Where on earth was her sister?

CHAPTER 32

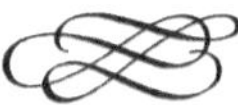

It was after seven before the back door slammed and Charlie limped in. 'Whatever happened to you?' asked Sam. 'Did you have a fall?' Charlie shook her head, but she looked worn out, covered in mud, with grazed elbows and a sunburned face. Sam fetched disinfectant and tissues, and began dabbing at the broken skin on Charlie's skinny arms.

'Ow!' she pulled away.

Sam persisted, taking Charlie's elbow gently in her left hand, and cleaning it with her right. 'You have to be careful about infection,' she said, 'or you'll end up right back in that Melbourne hospital.' Might not be such a bad thing, thought Sam uncharitably. 'Where have you been anyway?'

'Up in the wetlands, below the Snake Creek watershed.' Charlie pulled an exercise book from her backpack. 'Some idiot has let cattle into the park. They've destroyed Corroboree Bog, and probably all the others besides.' Her voice quivered with exhaustion, or emotion, or both.

Charlie opened the notebook and began to read. '*Damage ranges from flattened vegetation, numerous cow pats, large patches of bare ground, trampled and dislodged plants.*' She looked up. 'A lot of the sphagnum moss was shrivelled and dead.' She went on reading. '*Cattle have caused serious erosion, making tracks that connect and drain ponds. Half of the bog is completely dry. These drainage channels can spread the water-borne spores of Chytrid fungus.* That's the fungus killing off frogs worldwide, and do you know the worst thing?' Sam shook her head, feeling sick. 'I only found two frogs up there – one dead and the other injured. It'll probably die too. There should have been dozens.' Charlie's voice raised a frantic notch. 'These are spotted tree frogs I'm talking about. Protected frogs, critically endangered.'

'Whose notes are those?'

'Mine.'

Sam barely believed her. 'They sound very … technical.'

'Do they?' Charlie's downcast face brightened with pride. 'When the mobile library was in Currajong, I always used to read the Department of Environment field observations. I tried to copy their recording style, their terminology. I've got oodles of notes, starting from when I was eight — a ten-year ecological history of Balleroo National Park.'

Sam was stunned. She hadn't imagined that her sister had a scholarly side. Charlie had been hiding her light under a bushel.

Charlie's voice grew tremulous. 'I rode Tambo up there, and then this bull charged me, and then this ranger shot it, and then . . . ' She started to sob. 'Then I discovered the ruined bog.' Charlie slumped into a kitchen chair. Her sobs turned to all-out wails racking her frail frame.

'A bull? What on earth —?' Sam pulled up a chair and wrapped her arms around Charlie's shuddering shoulders. 'It's okay,' she murmured over and over, until her sister seemed spent.

'Do you know a bloke called Karl Richter?' asked Charlie. The sudden change in tack left Sam momentarily confused. She shook her head.

'His voice sounds a bit German or something,' said Charlie. Still nothing. 'You didn't have your clothes on.' Sam felt her jaw drop. The day in the mountains when they caught the brumbies. The snake in the pool. How did Charlie know about that?

'You mean that park ranger?'

Charlie nodded. 'He's the one who shot the bull and saved my life. He thought I was you, and said that at least I had my clothes on this time.' She looked like she was expecting an explanation. Sam didn't know quite where to start, but told the story as best she could, leaving out the bit where Karl said she looked fetching in her underwear. 'I can see how that happened,' said Charlie when she'd finished. 'I wondered if people might get us mixed up. Did it happen much?'

This was it, the perfect segue. This was the time to explain how everybody in Currajong thought she was Charlie. Sam got up, poured her sister an orange juice, took a deep breath and began. This time she left nothing out of the story. She took hold of Charlie's hands and told her about how it had started with an innocent mistake, of how shy and embarrassed she'd been in the beginning, of how awkward and difficult it was to challenge people's assumptions. Sam dropped Charlie's hands and walked to the window, as if out there she might find more courage. When she turned back around, her sister's eyes were wide. Sam averted her gaze, hung her head and told Charlie about how she'd got used to playing the part. Of how wonderful it was to feel accepted by the tight-knit Currajong community, of how she'd relished the solid sense of belonging. Of how she felt like she'd come home.

Charlie listened in silence. When Sam ran out of words, she hesitantly lifted her eyes to Charlie's. Her sister's face had sort of crumpled, fallen in on itself, blurred. It was horrible. Sam rushed to kneel before her sister and held her hands again. Charlie gulped, like she might choke. 'Didn't anybody notice it wasn't me?' she said, her voice wavering.

'Oh, yes.' Sam tried to reassure her. 'Of course.'

'Who?'

Sam almost lied, then thought better of it. There'd been too much lying already. 'Spike,' she said. 'And Drew, of course.'

'Who else?' Sam didn't speak. 'Who else?' said Charlie, her voice angry now, demanding. Sam cringed. Her sister's pain was palpable. 'I grew up in Currajong,' said Charlie. 'You? You've been to France,

America, England – all around the world. But do you know what?'
Sam shook her head. 'Before I got sick, before I went to Melbourne,
I'd never been farther than Wodonga in my entire life. Not bloody
once.' She rested her scrunched-up face in her hands for a moment.
'How do you think it feels, to realise that after a lifetime lived in this
town, nobody even knows who I am? To realise that I'm completely
interchangeable with the first damned stranger who waltzes into
Currajong and looks a bit like me?'

Sam felt like she'd been struck. She rose from her knees and sank
into the chair beside Charlie. There was a rap at the door and Drew
walked in, followed by Bess, wagging her tail. Charlie hit him with
both barrels. 'No one in this town knows who I am, do they Drew? I
could have died and nobody would have even noticed.'

Bess whimpered and backed out the door. Drew gave Sam a look
of thorough approval. 'You finally fessed up then.'

'Yes, she did,' said Charlie, her voice full of venom. 'My dear, loving
sister finally fessed up. It wasn't enough that she hit the jackpot the
day she was born and went off to live with a mega-rich family. It
wasn't enough that I had cancer and she didn't. No, she had to come
here, scavenge through what was left of my life, and pick the eyes out
of that as well.'

'You asked me to come . . .' began Sam.

Charlie turned on her. 'I didn't ask you play some bloody
masquerade. What am I supposed to do now? I can't show my face in
town. I'll be completely humiliated.'

'Hang on, Charlie,' said Drew. 'Don't be so hard on your sister. You
two are dead ringers. Even I was fooled at first, and nobody knows
you better than me.'

Charlie stood up and pointed an accusing finger at Sam. 'You said
that he knew you weren't me.'

'He did,' Sam said, silently cursing Drew for his candour. 'After a
few minutes, he did.'

Charlie collapsed back in her chair. She looked completely
defeated. Sam didn't imagine this was the sort of incident-free
recovery Professor Sung had in mind for her sister. Sam moved to

hug her, to try to comfort her, but Charlie's accusing eyes stopped her in her tracks. Sam hugged Bess instead, glad of the unconditional affection shining in the big dog's eyes. It was the *damned stranger* comment that had hurt the most. Was that how Charlie thought of her? It was true enough, though. They barely knew each other. In Charlie's shoes, she'd be just as wild. If only Sam hadn't let the charade drag on for so long. Well, it was over now, and the whole town would soon discover what a fraud she was. There was no way around it.

Sam felt faint. She hurried down the hall to the bathroom and dragged a wet washer over her face. Red, sore-looking eyes looked back at her from the mirror. She perched on the edge of the ancient claw bath, head in hands. What would Charlie say if she knew Sam was in love with Drew? Sam bit her lip. She could just hear Charlie shouting that Sam had stolen her boyfriend, along with everything else. And the awful thing was, it was true. However she cared to spin it to herself, no matter how innocently it had all begun – the facts were the facts.

Impassioned voices sounded from the kitchen. A horrible thought hit her. What if Charlie didn't want her to stay any more? The thought of leaving Brumby's Run made Sam sick with grief. She wouldn't do it. She flat-out wouldn't do it. This land was her heritage as much Charlie's, and Sam didn't intend to give up an inch of it without a fight.

The argument still raged in the kitchen. She could hear every word.

'You're an ungrateful bitch, Chaz,' said Drew. 'You always were.' His harsh words were tempered by the tone of their delivery - mockingly affectionate. 'Us letting your stock into the park was all that saved those poor buggers from starving to death. Anyway, they're back home now. Safe and sound and growing fat as butter.'

'It's too late,' said Charlie. 'The damage is done. It'll take years for those wetlands to recover — that's if they ever do.'

'What about your precious brumbies?' said Drew. 'I don't suppose they cause any damage, do they? I'm meant to let your cattle starve, but it's fine, apparently, for feral horses to trample all over the park.' It was a fair point, but Charlie ignored it.

'If my cattle were starving, it was because your father had the run of our best land,' she said angrily. 'I saw one of my cows today, with a scrubber bull above the bog. Stupid me, thought she must have escaped. I never thought you'd deliberately put cattle into Balleroo, Drew. How could you do that? It's a park, not a bloody paddock!' Her voice rose an octave. 'And my sister? Did she know about this?'

Sam went cold, knowing only too well Drew and his damned honesty.

'Absolutely,' said Drew. Of course he did. 'Sam helped me muster them in there. She did a fabulous job too,' he added, 'for a city girl.'

Why did Drew have to go and say that for? He was always so reckless with his words, so completely lacking in discretion. Sam heaved a big sigh. No, he was unfailingly truthful, that was all. Pity some of that honesty hadn't rubbed off on her. If she'd confessed to letting the cattle out in the first place, there'd have been no surprises for him to spring on Charlie.

'I should sue!' Charlie was yelling now. 'You had no lease any more. Why the hell didn't you just get your cattle off my land when I told you to?'

'It was actually your sister who told me to,' he reminded her, cool as a cucumber. 'And I had them out within a week. But the state *your* cows were in? They didn't have another week.' Everything sounded so reasonable, the way he explained it. 'Chaz.' His tone had changed to coaxing and kind. 'You should be thanking me instead of going off your nut. Did you bother to read the original lease contract?'

'No, why?' asked Charlie, still on the defensive, but sounding less sure of herself.

'Well, let me give you a little lesson in the law. Mary didn't have to sign any renewal. Dad was entitled to keep his cattle on Brumby's Run, keep on paying rent and still be a lawful tenant, because there's a thing called a periodic tenancy. It automatically renews itself each month, unless one of the parties gives notice.'

'Sam gave notice.'

'She's not a party to the agreement,' said Drew. 'She can't give notice. Neither can you – only Mary can. If anybody's going to sue for breach of contract, it's Dad.'

That choice piece of information provoked Charlie into a torrent of shouted insults. Drew returned fire with a few of his own. Bess whined and pushed her wet nose into the palm of Sam's hand. 'Well, girl,' she whispered, fondling the dog's big head. 'Time to face the music.'

Charlie lay down on a soft bed of everlastings in order to better examine the bizarre fungus. With seven scarlet arms, it certainly earned its name of the common starfish fungus. She wrinkled her nose and held her breath. It may have been beautiful, but *Aseroe rubra* was a member of the stinkhorn family and smelled of rotten flesh. Flies crawled around its glistening red heart, unwittingly collecting spores. Charlie took a few photos and made some notes.

In the week since Sam's stunning confession, Charlie had taken to going bush every day. Out here it didn't matter a jot what the townsfolk believed. It didn't matter a jot what any human being on the face of the earth believed. This grand wilderness was indifferent to the petty concerns of man. She stood up and stroked Whirlwind's shoulder. 'Time to go.'

The mare lifted her head for a moment from the sweet patch of snowgrass, then went on grazing. Charlie took hold of a handful of mane and swung onto her back. Whirlwind hardly seemed to notice. Charlie gently pressed her heels to her side. 'I said time to go.'

The mare tossed up her own heels in play and set off through the trees, trotting back along the creek, then down the hill towards the yards of Brumby's Run. Jarrang trumpeted a greeting to his daughter.

Whirlwind picked up speed, cantering straight for the hay shed. When they swept inside, Charlie jumped off into a pile of loose hay. Whirlwind lay down beside her and rolled. Then she stood up, shook herself, and snatched a big mouthful of oaten hay from right under Charlie.

'Cheeky thing.' Charlie tried without success to tug the hay away from the mare. Whirlwind chastised her with a shove of her nose, then settled down to feed, pawing occasionally to reach the grain that had slipped through the stalks. Charlie helped her for a while, searching out tasty seed heads and offering them to the mare's whiffling lips. When the mare lost interest, Charlie lay back in the fragrant hay bed, pulled her new smart phone from her pocket, and read over the messages from Karl.

After the sexy ranger had saved her life, he'd been sending her texts. Charlie had seven of them now, one for each day since they met. They contained fascinating accounts of his daily work in Balleroo. Each one finished with an obscure frog-themed joke that she didn't always fully understand. *What is the first book tadpoles read at school? Metamorphosis by Kafka*, or *Two frogs were sitting on Robinson Crusoe's back. One frog said, 'I have to go now, but we'll meet again on Friday.'*

Charlie reread the latest message, the one that finished with the silly cartoon instead of a joke; the one that had left her in no doubt about Karl's intentions. A man without a shirt was sitting on an examination table. The doctor was frowning and pointing to a screen that displayed two images, side by side. The first was labelled *Normal Sperm*. It showed lots of tadpole-like sperm swimming around. The second image was labelled *Your Sperm*. Here the sperm had developed into little frogs, and the doctor's response — *I take it there hasn't been any sex for a while?* Could there ever be a more charming pick-up line? Charlie closed her eyes.

She'd never imagined somebody like Karl would come along, somebody who so completely shared her love of the natural world. It was clear from his texts that he understood the vital role each living thing played in the ecology of the national park. He valued spiders and ants. He could not contain his excitement upon discovering a colony of southern forest bats. And, of course, there was his adorable passion for the Balleroo bogs. Karl had another highly desirable quality. He was an outsider. Right now, everyone belonging to Currajong was in her sights.

Charlie hated knowing that the town had mistaken Sam for her. She loathed the incestuous little community; the community that had failed her so badly. What Sam saw as some idyllic Shangri-La was really a suffocating hole full of ignorant, close-minded people who didn't give a damn. Well who cared? She didn't need them.

Charlie drifted off to sleep in the hay, dreaming of the tantalising possibilities of Karl Richter. She woke an hour later with Whirlwind snorting affectionately in her face. She really was an excellent companion. The mare knew how to just let her be. Sam, on the other hand, fussed and worried about her all the time: about her health, her diet, her mood. And she kept on apologising – for everything. She apologised for putting the cattle into the park. She apologised for digging up Mum's mint patch, mistaking it for weeds. She apologised for impersonating Charlie all over Currajong. Sam couldn't be in the same room with her at the moment without being sorry for something. It was annoying.

Charlie stroked Whirlwind's velvet muzzle. To give Sam credit, she did keep trying to put things right. 'We'll go around town, the two of us,' she'd offered, again and again. 'I'll explain to everybody who I really am.' But Charlie wasn't ready for that ordeal. She'd made Sam promise to let the status quo stand, at least for now. Stuff the town. Maybe she'd wait until her hair grew back, style it like Sam's, and just step back into her own life with nobody the wiser.

Flicka called from her paddock, with a *why aren't you paying me any attention?* sort of neigh. The mare was due to foal any day now. Her belly had dropped, her udder was full, and milk squirted from her waxed-up teats whenever she walked. Better go check in on her, give her a brush and a good feed. Whirlwind followed Charlie into the yard for a bucket of oats. The girl rubbed the mare's little horns for luck and closed the gate.

The first time she'd brushed Whirlwind's flowing forelock, Charlie had made the remarkable discovery of the two tiny horns. She could think of no rational explanation for them. Perhaps the old stories about magical brumbies were true after all? The protrusions were about three centimetres long, and dark grey, exactly like horn buds on a five-month-old calf. Charlie was dying to tell Sam, but if she did, she'd also have to admit that she'd been handling Whirlwind, and that might start an argument. Her sister could wait a bit longer for that startling piece of information.

Sam was already cooking dinner when her sister came in. Charlie's attention was fixed firmly on the screen of her phone and her cheeks were aflame. When she looked up, she was positively glowing with pleasure.

'You look pretty happy about something,' said Sam, reluctant to interrogate Charlie, but curious nonetheless.

Charlie raised an eyebrow and shot her sister a cheeky grin. 'You could say that.'

'Well, don't keep me in suspense?'

'Might as well tell you,' said Charlie. 'I don't like keeping secrets from my sister.'

Sam looked suitably contrite, and Charlie nodded approval. 'It's another text from Karl.' She looked in the oven, then washed up at the sink. 'You know, that new park ranger? We're going to hook up.'

Sam felt her face flush with hope, and a question burned in her mind. This was her chance. Come on girl, she told herself. Are you going to wait forever? 'How will Drew feel about that?' she ventured.

Charlie snorted with laughter. 'Drew? What's he got to do with it?' Sam was lost for words. Had she really had it so wrong for so long? Charlie looked suddenly shrewd. 'Speaking of Drew, it's pretty clear he's keen,' she said. 'Can't take his eyes off you.'

Sam met her sister's gaze, her expectant brown eyes, and wanted to deny everything. What sort of person was she? Just come clean, for goodness sake. 'I didn't know about you and Drew when it started,' she said. 'I really didn't.' This wasn't going well. She was sounding so defensive. 'Drew never said anything.' No, don't blame Drew — just tell the truth and apologise. 'I'm sorry, Charlie. I'm in love with Drew. You can't help who you fall in love with, can you?'

There, she'd said it. Sam's heart heaved in her chest and sticky tears ran down her face. It was hard to gauge Charlie's expression through blurry eyes. She took a deep, staggered breath; more of a sob, really. She should have done this long ago.

Charlie stood up and walked over to the kitchen bench. She plucked a big wad of tissues from the box, came back over and pulled her chair around so they faced each other. With utmost tenderness, Charlie dabbed tears from Sam's eyes, and wiped her cheeks. 'Sam,' she said softly. 'Why did you think I'd mind?'

'He was yours, wasn't he? Just like everything else here in Currajong.' She heard the cry in her voice. Great, now she was snivelling like a baby. 'It's like you said, I did take over your life. If you hate me, that's fair enough. Thanks to me you're stuck in this house, and you can't face anybody. I didn't have the courage to tell you that I wanted your boyfriend as well.'

Sam's eyes were streaming. For a long time Charlie didn't respond. Then she wiped Sam's face again, harder this time. Ow, that hurt.

'What a bitch,' Charlie said at last. 'You thought Drew was my boyfriend?' Sam nodded, a hot rush of shame burning her cheeks. 'And then you fell in love with him, and pretended to my face that nothing was going on?'

'Nothing was going on,' insisted Sam, but her sister wasn't listening.

'You're a piece of work, you know that?' Charlie hung her head. 'Have you slept with him?'

'Yes,' admitted Sam, knowing how it must sound. 'But only once.' Had she really said that? What was he? A car she'd taken for a test drive?

Charlie burst out laughing. 'I had you pegged as a self-righteous, sanctimonious miss goody two-shoes. Drew told me how you'd gone around town paying our bills, making things right. Everybody loves you, he said. That pissed me right off. And now I find out that you're actually a sneaky, slutty little coward, just like me.' Sam held her breath. 'And I bloody love you for it,' said Charlie with a broad smile.

'You do?' Her sister wasn't making any sense.

'Don't get me wrong,' said Charlie. 'If it was true about me and Drew, I'd be seriously bummed, but luckily for you, it isn't.'

'But Drew admitted it. He said Mary hated you two being together.'

'She did,' said Charlie. 'But that was ages ago. Drew hasn't been my main squeeze since I cheated on him with Spike.'

That last item of information required further scrutiny, but not now. 'That's not what you said on the phone,' protested Sam. 'You said that you and Drew were tight, remember? You said he was your boyfriend.'

'Maybe I was on too many meds,' said Charlie, dismissively. 'Maybe you misunderstood.'

'I didn't misunderstand anything.' Sam cringed at the pleading tone in her voice, but she couldn't stop herself. 'I've been sick with guilt over this.'

'Aww … poor, hard-done-by Sam,' said Charlie, pushing the corners of her mouth down into a clown frown. Did Sam deserve to be mocked? Probably. 'Here's some advice. A sure-fire way to avoid all that sickening guilt. Don't sneak around with your sister's boyfriend in the first place.'

'Drew wasn't your boyfriend. You just said that,' said Sam, before groaning at the stupid circularity of her own logic. May as well make Charlie's next point for her. It would save time. 'But I thought he was.'

'Exactly,' said Charlie with a smug smile. 'I'm the forgiving type. One more apology should do it. That will make one million and one.'

Charlie had outfoxed her and Sam was glad about it. 'I'm sorry.'

'Good,' said Charlie, with a satisfied nod. 'I'll accept that. Drew's not my type, anyway. I've gone off cowboys and found me an intellectual instead.' You had to hand it to her sister. She'd barely left the house, and she'd still managed to find a man. Charlie reached for Sam's phone where it lay on the table. She picked it up, and offered it to Sam. 'Call him,' she said. 'I'll clear out and check on Flicka … give you some space.'

Drew sat at the table in the kitchen, solemn-faced while Sam told her story; how she'd fallen for him, and pulled away because of a stupid misunderstanding — and how her feelings had never, ever changed. He listened in that intense, considered way he had, without interrupting. Finally she ran out of breath. Sam studied his face as if seeing it for the first time. His perfect nose, flared now with emotion. His penetrating green eyes, full of tenderness. His broad suntanned face and square chin, smudged with grease.

Still Drew was silent. Did she need to start all over again? Maybe she'd made no sense at all. One thing was certain; Sam was willing to explain herself a thousand times over if it would make him understand. But as she opened her mouth to speak, Drew stood up. Without a word he rounded the table and kissed her, long and deep and slow. She rose to meet him, throwing herself into his arms. Drew's hunger for her pulsed as strong as ever, and she laughed with the sheer delight of his response.

When they parted there was puzzlement as well as joy in Drew's expression. 'You sure did read me wrong,' he said, shaking his head. 'Why didn't you just ask me straight out?' She struggled to answer, struggled to find the right words to explain her monumental lack of faith in him. He shushed her and laid a forefinger across her lips. 'It doesn't matter. You were being loyal to your sister. There's no shame in that.'

'Bravo, bravo!' cried Charlie, applauding loudly. Neither of them had noticed her come in. They'd been lost in a world of their own. 'This is all very touching,' said Charlie, 'but Flicka's gone down. That foal's made up its mind to come.' Everybody scrambled out the door into the dusk. Sam had not witnessed the miracle of a birth before. It was to be a night of marvels.

CHAPTER 34

S am took a moment, on waking, to recall the momentous happenings of the previous night. She stretched and yawned, reaching for where Drew should have lain beside her in the bed. It was an unpleasant jolt to find herself alone. Then the fullness of last night's events returned, and she knew exactly where he'd be — up at the yards with Flicka and her newborn colt.

Sam pulled on T-shirt and jeans, feeling like the cat that ate the cream. She tiptoed down the hall to the kitchen, trying not to wake Charlie. They'd all had quite a night, and for a number of reasons, nobody had had enough sleep. Sam yawned, put on the kettle and cut up some carrots for Flicka. She made two cups of tea, one for her and one for Drew, and took them outside.

One for Drew. The significance of simply making Drew a morning cup of tea gave her goose-bumps. After last night there'd be no more guilt, no more divided loyalties. Their love was finally out in the open, free of misunderstandings, and best of all, it was graced with Charlie's approval. The safe arrival of Flicka's foal felt like a final blessing on their happiness.

'Good morning, Bess.' The dog smiled and thumped her tail on the dusty porch. 'Coming to see the baby?' Bess barked assent and followed her up to the yards.

'He's gorgeous,' said Sam. 'Absolutely gorgeous.'

'Yep,' said Drew, from his perch on the yard rail. 'He sure is something to brag about.' Flicka stood guard over a foal so perfectly formed, so finely chiselled, he didn't look real. His coat was a pretty silvery grey that Drew assured her would shed out to deepest black.

Sam held up a mug. 'Brought you some tea.'

'I can't believe he's a black. A direct throwback to Abbey,' said Drew, shaking his head. 'I have a beautiful black colt with a double Abbey cross in his pedigree. Do you know how hard it is to get your hands on a horse like that?'

'Correction,' said Sam. 'I have a black colt with a double Abbey cross.'

Drew jumped down from the fence and pulled her in for a kiss. 'You'll spill the tea,' she said. He took both mugs from her and balanced them on a post. Then he picked her up and spun her around and around until she was dizzy with laughter.

'Correction,' he said, retrieving his tea. '*We* have a beautiful black colt with a double Abbey cross.' The foal nickered on cue.

Sam steadied herself against a rail until she could no longer hear her heartbeat. 'I don't know who this Abbey is,' she said. 'What's so special about him?'

He looked like he didn't believe her. 'Everybody knows Abbey. He's a legend.'

She shook her head. 'Sorry, no.'

'By Radiant? Going way back to Radium?'

She shook her head again. 'Still nothing.'

'Crikey, Sam. This is important stuff. What do they teach you in Melbourne?' He looked so completely perturbed, Sam turned away to hide her smile.

'Tell me, then.'

'Abbey is a stock horse foundation sire. Big and black, born in 1955 up in New South Wales, in a stall behind the Willawarrin pub. I've been there. There's a photo of me standing outside.'

'You've been there?'

Drew looked embarrassed. How utterly charming. 'Kind of a pilgrimage, I guess.' He pointed to the foal. 'When I first laid eyes on that little bloke, I thought to myself, I bet that's exactly what Abbey looked like when he was born.' How she loved seeing him all fired up like this, brimming with enthusiasm, impatient to dive headfirst into the future – their shared future. 'You know, they almost cut Abbey as a yearling?' he said. 'Can you imagine that?'

'Cut?'

'Gelded. His dam and sire were both by Radium II, half brother and sister. They thought he was too inbred. Thank Christ they changed their mind. That horse won the Taree campdraft at just eighteen months old.' Drew slid through the rails and stroked the foal, an expression of immense pride on his face. 'Abbey won twenty-three campdrafts with the legendary Harry Ball in the saddle. The pair couldn't be beat, and Harry worshipped that horse.' The foal sucked at Drew's shirt and he let it chew his fingers.

'That's a lovely story,' said Sam.

'Tragic ending, though. Harry's on the Pacific Highway, coming back from the Warwick Rodeo with Abbey, when there's a terrible accident. Harry's killed. As a tribute to her husband, Harry's wife decides nobody will ever ride Abbey again. She sends him over to Theo Hill at Comara Station. That stallion went on to found the finest stock horse bloodline in Australia.' Drew knelt down. The foal sniffed his face and he blew softly into its nose. 'And to think Abbey blood runs through this bloke's veins, eh? It's a fair dinkum miracle.'

There was no doubt about it. Sam did have a rival for Drew's affection, but it wasn't Charlie. Drew was in love with the little colt. Sam smiled as he gave the foal a great hug and Flicka whinnied her disapproval. The mare gathered the baby up with her nose and urged him away. He obediently turned tail and buried his nose beneath his mother's flank for a feed, tail wagging merrily.

Sam finished her tea. 'I have to go to work.'

Drew spun her around and kissed her comprehensively. 'I'm going to hang around here for a bit,' he said. 'Try that imprinting stuff you were talking about.'

Last night Sam had told him about Dr Robert Miller's theory for imprinting foals. It was all about bonding with humans in the brief window of time straight after birth. Such foals began to see humans as fellow horses instead of predators. The deep trust they established in their handler often lead to miraculous training results. Sam smiled. She'd handed Drew the perfect excuse to spend all day with the new colt. Flicka laid back her ears as Drew tried to hijack the foal again.

Sam fed her the carrots. 'You'd think he'd done all the work himself, wouldn't you?' she said to the mare, before heading for the car.

Phoenix's piercing neigh greeted her as she came in sight of the show-ground. He knew her car. At first Bushy had put it down to coincidence, but he agreed now that the colt recognised the blue beetle, and even responded to its engine noise coming up the track. Sam parked and went to say hello to Phoenix. The young stallion performed excited pirouettes as she approached, and accepted the apple she offered with a regal nod of his head. Flicka's newborn foal was adorable, true – but no horse could replace the special place Phoenix held in Sam's heart.

Sam headed for Bushy's *kitchen*, the narrow porch between the horse wash bays and his room. She needed a big mug of his strong, sweet tea, and a plate piled high with hot buttered toast, chock-full of fat raisins. A sugar hit might chase away her weariness.

Sam told him about the foal, but instead of being excited, Bushy was uncharacteristically quiet. He stirred the tea and handed her a steaming mug, as his deep-set eyes searched her face. 'I'm glad you've got a little 'un at home. That fella's going to teach you a lot.' A faint smile. 'That's if Drew ever lets you near him.'

Sam grinned. 'He's head over heels, all right.'

Phoenix burst into a series of commanding neighs. 'How do you reckon that golden colt's been going?' asked Bushy.

'Phoenix? He's fabulous, doesn't put a foot wrong. Soft mouth, good transitions, great laterals. Awesome stop. He's good to catch and float. Opens and closes gates. Stands for the farrier. You can even crack a whip off him.'

'You're a fair hand with that whip these days.' Sam nodded, curious. She knew Bushy. He was gearing up to saying something important. Bushy finished a mouthful of toast. 'How'd you like to take Phoenix home?' he said. 'That horse could use some bush work.'

'Really?' Sam could hardly believe her good fortune. 'I can take him home to Brumby's Run?'

'That you can. Ryan suggested it himself, just this morning.' Sam's smile grew larger. This was truly wonderful news, so why did Bushy look so gloomy? 'You're to finish Phoenix for his new owner,' he said, gazing into his tea.

Sam's smile faltered. She couldn't make sense of Bushy's words. 'New owner?'

'I'm afraid that colt's been sold.'

Anger and panic formed a heavy stone in Sam's stomach. 'Unsell him then,' she said swiftly. 'I'll buy him, whatever the cost.'

Bushy shook his head sadly. 'Can't be done. Apparently the buyer's promised Ryan a major sponsorship. He can't afford to welch on the deal.'

No. It was impossible — impossible to contemplate that this could happen to her again. Sam reeled from the kitchen and pelted to the yard where Phoenix pranced about, impatient for his morning feed. The colt was heartbreakingly beautiful, haloed in morning sunshine, framed by the majesty of Maroong Mountain. But Sam's eyes were brimful of tears and she couldn't see him anymore. All she saw was the formless shape of her own loss.

The tail end of a bad dream slipped away, and Charlie woke up, knuckling sleep from her eyes. What a relief. This wasn't her hospital bed and she wasn't ill again. This was her own room at Brumby's . . . and someone was knocking on the door. She pulled on her clothes and ran down the hall. It was Karl.

The three weeks since she'd met Karl had been the most fascinating and rewarding weeks of her life. Nearly every day now, Karl swung by and collected her on his way up to Balleroo. He was conducting a field review on the impact of the grazing trial, and Charlie was helping him. She didn't know what was more exciting. Being involved in a serious scientific research program, or spending hours on end with Karl. With each day they spent together, Charlie felt more drawn to the quirky, sexy ranger.

She opened the door to Karl, offered him a dazzling smile, and grabbed her bag from the porch.

It had started with the texts. Then one morning Charlie had woken to the sound of a car coming up the track, had crept down the hall and peered out the bathroom window. A government vehicle and a khaki-clad figure stood in the drive : Karl.

Charlie stepped into jeans, leaving off her belt for once, letting them sit low on her hips. She gave a little shimmy. The mirror told her she looked good – no longer skeletal, but slim and healthy. The knock came at the door again. This time she opened it, to find Karl standing there, holding a cardboard box. He'd combed his sandy-blond hair and slicked it neatly back in an obvious effort to be presentable. With his boyish features, pressed khaki uniform and polished boots, Karl looked like an overgrown boy scout. Charlie almost expected a three-fingered salute and an admonition to be prepared. She tried to restrain herself, she really did, but laughter crept around her edges and spilt from her seams.

Karl looked perplexed, unhappy even. That wasn't what she wanted. Charlie slapped her hand resolutely over her mouth.

'Miss Kelly?' He inspected her face. 'It is Charlie Kelly this time? You have not transformed into another?'

'No, it's me. Charlie.'

He proffered the box. It looked heavy. 'For you.' She gestured for him to come in, and he put it down on the kitchen table. 'Open it.'

Inside were copies of government field notes for Balleroo, dating back to the nineteen fifties. Endangered species reports, flora and fauna surveys, bog water quality assessments, frog population counts. Charlie couldn't believe her eyes. It was a veritable treasure trove. 'Where did these come from?'

'The Department of Environment Library. I made copies.'

Charlie flipped through volume after precious volume. 'It must have taken forever.'

'It took some time, yes.' His eyes locked onto hers. 'Do you like them?'

'No.' His face fell. 'I *love* them.' She moved closer and pressed her lips against his cheek, sliding them at the last minute from his cheek to his mouth. He quivered and returned the kiss.

Then Drew had pushed in through the fly-wire door with impeccably bad timing. 'What's going on here?'

Karl seemed wary. Charlie introduced the men, then pulled Drew out the door. 'Haven't you got some cows to chase or something?'

Drew had put on his hat. 'Are you okay?'

'Of course I am. Now nick off, will you?'

'Your boyfriend?' Karl had asked her after Drew left. Charlie shook her head and Karl had smiled. 'Very good. May I see you tomorrow?'

'Yes Karl,' Charlie had said solemnly. 'You may.'

CHAPTER 36

Sam rose at first light to put the kettle on. The first week of April, and there was already a nip in the early morning air. Fog had crept down from the range overnight. Outside the window, trees loomed grey and amorphous in swirls of mist. Sam prayed it would clear to the sunny day promised by the forecast.

Charlie emerged from the hallway, pyjama-clad and yawning. The physical change in her sister these past six weeks had been nothing short of remarkable. She seemed taller. Her body had filled out, in spite of Sam's limited recipe range, and Charlie's own laziness in the kitchen. Her limbs, once skinny sticks, had grown ripe and smooth. Muscles were starting to define her upper arms and calves, rounding out the knobbly bits. Her sister no longer peered at the world through gaunt hollows. Clear amber eyes gazed from an angelic face, its heart shape enhanced by a newly defined widow's peak. Charlie's hairline curved back from the dark triangle in a way identical to Sam's own, exaggerating their resemblance. It was kind of flattering to think that people had mistaken her for this gorgeous girl. 'When are they supposed to get here, again?' asked Charlie, slipping bread into the toaster.

'Ten o'clock, and Drew will be over at nine to help saddle up. Is

Topsy's gear back up at the yards?' Charlie nodded. 'It's a miracle you found a crupper. That pony's got no wither at all. I lay awake half the night imagining the saddle, and the girl too, slipping straight over his head on the way home.'

Charlie applied slabs of butter and lashings of honey to the toast, then popped another round on. You couldn't fill her up lately.

'I'm still concerned about time,' said Sam. 'A twelve-year-old could slow us down more than we bargained for. Are you sure that track down to the creek isn't too steep for a child? I'll die if she falls off.' Sam started going through papers on the table. 'Where are those *waiver of liability* forms? Oh good, here they are. I wonder if we've got enough spares? People could make mistakes. Would it be enough for them to initial the correction, do you think? Or should we give them a completely new form? I think a new form, don't you, just to be on the safe side?'

Charlie plonked down tea and toast in front of Sam. 'Will you chill already?' She rolled her eyes and put still more bread into the toaster. 'It's only five people. We can do this standing on our heads.' Then she yawned and stuffed her mouth with honey toast.

Sam pressed a hand over her eyes and squinted them tight shut. Her sister was absolutely right. She needed to relax – although not quite as much as Charlie, perhaps. Charlie appeared to have gone back to sleep, hunched over her tea cup. Which was pretty remarkable, really, considering what a momentous day it was. Today, *Brumby's Run High Country Trails* welcomed its very first customers.

They'd put a test advertisement in the Currajong Gazette — *The majestic mountains of north-eastern Victoria abound with fascinating wildlife, ancient forests and stunning views. We offer rides through the heart of the high country. Explore spectacular Balleroo National Park. Visit historic huts, ride through unspoiled wilderness and breathe pure mountain air. An unforgettable horse-riding experience. Knowledgeable guides and horses to suit all abilities.*

Their target market wasn't locals, of course, but tourists. City slickers after an authentic bush experience. But for now it seemed sensible just to dip their toes in the water – run a few rides and see if they worked. If all went well, they'd launch an internet advertising campaign in the spring.

Charlie and Drew had done a good job planning the course of today's ride. It wound its way through the lush creek flats of Brumby's Run up to the national park entrance, where Drew had built an imposing bush-timber gateway. Then the track struck out through scattered candlebarks and peppermint gums growing close to the cliff face. It offered sweeping views across the range, all the way down to where Currajong nestled like a toy town beside the Merri River.

They passed several lookout points where riders and horses would have a chance to catch their breath, and allow any slowcoaches to catch up. The forest leg of the ride gave opportunities for spotting kangaroos, echidnas and perhaps even a rare brush-tailed rock wallaby or two. Near the end of the first hour, they would ford Snake Creek and stop for photos at scenic Bluff Falls. Platypus could usually be spotted in the ferny pools below the cascade, and eagles often soared above the escarpment. Then it would be just about time to head for home.

Their first clients were locals from nearby Tallangala, experienced riders all, and a perfect group for a test run. Sam had chosen their horses with great care: the smallest skewbald pony for the girl, the two creamy brumbies for the older aunts, and the pair of flaxen-maned taffies for the mother and father. Sam would ride Tara, a sensible brown mare. Charlie, of course, would ride Tambo, and Drew was coming along on Clancy.

They'd groomed the horses to within an inch of their lives. Their coats gleamed. Their manes lay combed and smooth. Even their hoofs were oiled and freshly trimmed. 'We're not off to the royal show,' Charlie had said, but she still seemed pleased at how well the horses scrubbed up, especially Tambo. She even helped Sam clean and polish the old tack that had been thrown in as a package deal with the Mitchell string.

There was something marvellously therapeutic about the process; sitting together in the kitchen, watching the ancient leather soak up warm oil applied with paint brushes — past differences forgotten. A final buff up with saddle soap completed the procedure. Bridles that looked like they'd never been cleaned in their life hung shining and supple. Buckles and bits gleamed. Saddles that had been covered in green grime came up almost like new.

Sam had been so looking forward to today; couldn't wait to show off their beautiful new horses and equipment. But now the day had actually arrived, nerves were getting the better of her.

'Would you go into town for more milk?' she asked Charlie. 'We mightn't have enough if they all want coffee.'

'We've got plenty of milk,' said Charlie, in the sort of tone one might use to reassure an anxious child. 'They'd need to drink about five mugs each for us to run out. And anyway, I don't go to town.'

'That's ridiculous,' said Sam. 'You can't just never go into Curra-jong again.'

'Why not?' Charlie licked honey from her fingers 'I've managed so far. Don't blame me. If you hadn't decided to steal my life, I wouldn't have to hide out here at Brumby's.'

Sam sighed and nodded. 'If that's what you want . . . and I suppose you're right about the milk.' She put the forms into a plastic sleeve and grabbed her hat from the hook near the door. 'I'm going up to feed the horses.'

Sam emerged into the chilly morning, wrapped her coat tight around her and looked skywards. Streamers of pastel blue showed beyond the mist, and a wan sun seemed determined to break through. Good, the day promised to be fine. A volley of neighs greeted her on her way up the hill, and Phoenix reared and boxed the air. Even the prospect of losing him wasn't enough to spoil her happiness today. Sam was firmly in denial on that score, and determined to believe in miracles.

She smiled and broke into a small dance, finishing with a twirl and curtsey as she reached the yards. A row of curious heads were lined up all along the rails. Jarrang snorted and turned his back on her fool-ishness. She laughed and plucked a sprig from a fragrant native mint bush that was blooming beside the yards. She buried her nose in its snowy-white flowers. They really were very beautiful, like tiny orchids. Trumpet-shaped, with splotches of colour – purple, red and yellow. She breathed in deep lungfuls of perfumed air, held the tiny bouquet aloft and bowed to her watchful, prick-eared audience. It would be impossible at that moment to feel any happier.

Sam took hold of the wheelbarrow and headed for the shed. Soon all the horses were happily munching their hay – all except for Whirl-wind. She sulked in the yard next to Jarrang's, refusing to touch her food while Sam was watching. 'You're just like Charlie,' Sam scolded as she poured a measure of oats into the mare's feed bin. 'You'll bite your nose off to spite your face.'

After feeding up, Sam went to the little room beside the hay shed that was to serve as their office. She stacked the liability-waiver forms neatly on the desk, and tested the mobile eftpos machine. She picked up a business card and read it out aloud. *Brumby's Run High Country Trails. Horses to suit all riders. Proprietors Charlie Kelly and Sam Carmichael.'* They were partners now, practically and legally.

Drew arrived at quarter to ten, and Sam and Charlie were ready for him. Horses brushed and saddled, forms waiting to be signed, helmets lined up on a bench. Sam had brought the portable butane cooker up to the office, and a bright new kettle was on the boil. Milk in an ice box, mugs and spoons in a row, shortbread biscuits for afterwards.

Charlie was trotting Topsy up and down the drive so he wouldn't be too fresh. 'Don't get him all sweaty,' yelled Sam.

Bess was barking now and Sam could hear a car. How exciting! Their first ever clients had arrived. She walked down to meet them, resisting the impulse to run. A pretty blonde child was hugging a happy Bess around the neck.

'Welcome to Brumby's Run,' Sam said, smiling. Everybody introduced themselves. Sam kept repeating their names in her head, to ensure she'd remember. The blonde girl was Meg Morgan. Her even blonder mother was Sue. Craig, her handsome father, reminded Sam of somebody, but she wasn't sure who. The two older aunties were Tracey and Mel. Five people wasn't too hard. How well would she manage with more?

'Are there brumbies?' asked Meg, eyes shining with expectation.

Sue hushed her. 'Don't mind Meg,' she said. 'My daughter's obsessed with those *Silver Brumby* books. I told her there wouldn't be real brumbies.'

'Oh, but there are,' said Sam, doing a quick mental calculation. Jarrang, Phoenix and Tambo. Whirlwind, the two creamies, and Flicka's newborn colt. 'We have seven brumbies,' she said. 'Two stallions, four mares and a foal.'

Meg exploded in questions, and Sam answered them as best she could. 'Can I ride one?' the girl asked eagerly as they walked up the hill to the yards.

'I actually had a lovely pony picked out for you.'

'Can't I ride a brumby,' begged Meg. 'Please?'

'My daughter's an excellent rider,' said Craig, ruffling the girl's hair. 'She's done five years of pony club, and has outgrown her Welsh Mountain pony. In fact we're looking around to buy something bigger. It would be a real thrill for Meg to ride a brumby.'

Sam considered her options. This was proving to be more difficult than she'd imagined. Their first clients hadn't even mounted, and already things weren't going according to plan. She compared the temperaments of the two creamies. They were equally quiet, especially if allowed to follow along in the middle of the string. Gemma was a little friendlier, perhaps more affectionate than Golden. Sam excused herself and went to talk to the others.

'The kid'll be fine on Gemma,' said Charlie.

'But we had the aunties on the brumbies.' Sam didn't like sudden changes of plan. 'Ruby might be too flighty, and the black mare, Jet? She likes the lead way too much. She wouldn't suit the aunties at all.'

'Simple,' said Charlie. 'Put an auntie on Tara, and you ride Phoenix instead.'

Sam considered her sister's suggestion. She hadn't ridden the golden colt out with the other horses before, but it was either that, or disappoint both the girl and her parents. 'Right, I'll get him ready. You guys have them sign the forms, and don't forget to offer them coffee, and ask them if they need the mounting block , and . . . ' But Drew and Charlie had already walked off, talking and laughing with the clients.

To say that Phoenix was keen would have been a monumental understatement. He trembled all over while Sam gave him a swift brush down. He neighed wildly while she saddled and bridled him. Then he danced down to meet the other riders. There was an audible gasp from the girl, and admiring glances all round.

'He's the most beautiful horse in the world,' sighed Meg. As if he understood, Phoenix redoubled his efforts to show off. All colts were full of themselves, but this was ridiculous. He frisked about so, that it took all Sam's skill just to mount. It was a bit like riding a pogo stick. He pranced and capered, seemed to hang suspended in space between strides, striking heroic poses in silhouette. He arched his neck and flirted with the mares, impressing everybody except his rider. Sam wrestled with the reins, trying without much success to make him pay attention.

They all set off up the hill. The plan was for Charlie and Drew to go up front, as they knew the way better than Sam did. If Charlie got too tired, she could simply go home. Sam would go last in line and keep an eye on the slower riders. At first Phoenix objected to the arrangement, tossing his head and jogging to try to overtake the leaders. But soon his herding instincts kicked in. Within a wild mob, the oldest mare travels at the front of the group and the stallion at the rear. By driving the mares ahead of him, he ensures that none stray, and they're less likely to be stolen by other males.

Phoenix enthusiastically threw himself into the role of mob stallion. He drove the group forward by running alongside the creamy mares in front of him, urging them on if they dawdled. Gemma and Golden had been raised in a wild brumby herd, and fell quickly in line with his demands. It was really very useful. The mares were a bit on the lazy side, and the bossy colt was saving their riders from having to constantly kick them on.

Golden stopped abruptly and ducked her head for a mouthful of grass. Phoenix snaked his head at her, swinging it from side to side like a threatening cobra and flattening his ears. The mare moved smartly forward.

'However did you teach him that?' asked Mel. Or was it Tracey? Sam had already gotten the aunties mixed up. 'You must be a wonderful trainer. I can't wait to tell my friend about you. She's wanting a horse for her daughter. I'll get her to give you a ring.'

Sam almost admitted to the woman that Phoenix had taken it upon himself to keep the group together. That Sam doubted she could stop him, even if she tried. But instead she just smiled and took the credit. 'Brumbies are highly intelligent and trainable,' she said. 'They make excellent saddle horses.'

'Well you've certainly sold us,' said the smiling auntie, and they all took off up the hill at a gentle canter.

The ride was a terrific success. Nobody fell off, for starters. Meg had no problems handling Gemma; in fact, all the horses behaved themselves beautifully. And it wasn't only the horses. At the lookouts, eagles wheeled overhead on cue. In the forest, wallabies bounded by. Echidnas waddled across the path and they spotted a koala and her baby up a tree. It was neither too hot nor too cold. A light breeze kept the flies at bay and Charlie didn't get too tired.

The falls were a big hit, offering plenty of photo opportunities, and a pair of obliging platypus playing in a shady pool. Phoenix seemed determined to go for a swim, barging into the shallows, scattering diamonds of spray with his forefeet. Sam pushed him on with all her might, but Phoenix wasn't listening. Any minute now he'd roll in the stream and make a complete fool of her. Just as his legs buckled, Drew was at her side, taking the colt's reins and urging him from the water. Then he was gone, cantering off with the panache of a movie hero and the easy grace of a man born in the saddle. Sam sighed with pleasure. To think that dashing man was in love with her.

They left the falls precisely at eleven-thirty as scheduled, and thanks in no small part to Phoenix, arrived back at the yards on time. Sam had enjoyed herself more than anybody, and couldn't quite believe that she was about to be paid for the privilege. Meg helped Drew and Sam unsaddle the horses, while Charlie handed around coffee and biscuits.

'Brumbies are awesome,' the girl announced, as they turned Phoenix out. 'Can I see the others?' Meg was looking past the hay shed, to where Jarrang and Whirlwind stood in adjoining yards. 'Are they brumbies too?' Sam nodded. 'Can I have a look?' asked Meg. 'Please?'

Sam hesitated, but the girl's enthusiasm was infectious. 'Come on, then.' She indicated for the girl to follow her. 'Just don't get too close. They're still quite wild.'

Jarrang barely deigned to notice them, but Whirlwind rushed the fence with her ears pinned. Meg took a few steps backwards. 'I told you not to get too close.' Sam laid a protective hand on the girl's arm.

'What's her name?'

'Whirlwind.'

'She doesn't look like a brumby.' Meg moved forward again. The girl seemed unfazed by the mare's aggression, and had an appraising eye that belied her youth. 'She's too big, for one thing.'

Sam agreed. Whirlwind was tall for a brumby. Undoubtedly Jarrang had sired her – they had the same presence, the same white stripes on their hoofs. But it was clear that none of the mares in Jarrang's captured herd were Whirlwind's dam. 'Whether she looks it or not, that mare was wild-caught just a few months ago.'

'I love her mane,' said Meg. 'It looks like it's been crimped. I could brush it all day.' Sam nodded. Whirlwind really did have an incredible amount of mane. But there was something odd about it, now that she looked closely. It was no longer snarled and tangled. Instead it lay in silky waves. The mare's tail, too, fell in a full, luxurious curtain to her dappled hocks.

'Do you know who she looks like?' Meg didn't wait for Sam to answer. 'Gandalf's horse in the Lord of the Rings movies. Shadowfax was magical – Gandalf's partner, not his servant. Whirlwind looks just like Shadowfax.'

Charlie strolled over and caught the tail end of the conversation. 'She does, doesn't she?'

'Don't ask me how,' said Sam, who was a fan of those movies. They'd showcased so many beautiful horses, and she'd read quite a bit about their equine stars. 'Shadowfax was played by a sixteen year old Andalusian Stallion named Domero,' she told Meg. 'He was trained to work at liberty, responding to off camera cues.'

'He was awesome,' said Meg with a dreamy smile.

Sam nodded. 'Yes, he was.'

'Can I pat Whirlwind?' asked Meg.

Sam was about to warn the girl away when her sister interrupted. 'Sure thing, kid.' Charlie slid through the rails and pressed her cheek against the mare's neck. 'Come on in.'

Meg opened the gate before a horrified Sam had the presence of mind to stop her. The child held out her hand. Whirlwind arched her neck, elegant ears angled forward and her eyes kind, accepting Meg's fingers on her mane with a gracious nod of her head. There was a certain import, a holiness about the interaction, that was evident to both horse and human.

'Shadowfax could understand the speech of men,' Meg told Charlie, whispering as if she was in the presence of royalty. 'He was fearless and faster than any other horse in Middle Earth. Nobody could ride him except for Gandalf. He would accept neither bridle or saddle, and carried Gandalf only by his own choice.'

'What?' said Charlie, 'like this?' She grasped a handful of mane and casually swung herself onto Whirlwind's broad back. The mare twisted her neck and snuffled Charlie's leg.

'Come out now, Meg,' said Sam, in a low voice, her heart thudding hard. With one last pat, Meg slipped back through the gate. Sam resisted the impulse to seize the girl and hug her tight to her chest. Should she be furious with Charlie, or in awe of her dazzling horsemanship? Sam understood now. Charlie was in a league of her own. Still, if her sister ever got out of that yard alive, Sam might kill her herself.

Meg sparkled with a kind of intense joy, chattering on about how much she'd loved the day. Her prattle blurred into white noise. 'Get off now, Charlie,' said Sam, trying to keep her voice calm. 'I think she's had enough.'

'No, wait,' Meg was saying. 'Wait!' The girl was pulling at Sam's sleeve now. 'My uncle's here. I want to show him how Charlie can ride Whirlwind without a saddle or bridle.'

Sam looked towards the main yards and her skin crawled with fear. Spike Morgan was lounging against a rail. This girl beside her with the shining eyes? This must be Spike's niece. What a fool she was, not to have made the connection. He'd recognise the stolen mare in a second. Bushy had altered her brand, but the new scar was still fresh, the deceit still apparent. They'd let a twelve-year-old child go into a yard with the horse that had killed Spike's best friend, not two months ago. It would be the end of the road for their business. There'd be charges of negligence and of theft . . . and it would be the end of the road for Whirlwind. Sam fought for breath.

'Uncle Spike,' yelled Meg, and ran off towards him.

Charlie started at the sound of Spike's name, and gave Sam a shocked glance. Her apprehension was shared by Whirlwind, who reared. Charlie leaned low over her neck and clung to her mane, becoming part of the beautiful mare. 'Open the gate,' she said urgently. Sam shook her head and began to protest, but her voice only came in strangled gasps. 'Just do it!' hissed Charlie. Sam said a prayer, opened the gate and closed her eyes.

CHAPTER 37

Whirlwind cantered calmly up the hill, with Charlie securely aboard. Sam's breath still came in shallow spurts, but with every second that passed, her hands unclenched a little. Unbelievably, it looked like they were going to be all right.

The mare had stunning movement. Extended and elevated, cadenced and harmonious. Sam imagined for one moment how her gait would wow judges in the dressage arena. Whirlwind and Charlie gained the brow of the hill, just as Meg arrived with Uncle Spike in tow.

'Afternoon, princess,' he said, with a cocky lift of an eyebrow.

Ever since the fateful buckjump competition, Sam had gone to extraordinary lengths to avoid Spike. He'd not pursued her. Perhaps because he'd lost the bet, the deal that they'd go on a date if Spike was crowned King of the Mountain. Drew had claimed that honour.

Of course, this was a ridiculously simplistic take on things. Spike would have to be a very concrete thinker indeed to believe a relationship could be governed by the same sort of rules as a poker game, and she could be picked up like the kitty. But for whatever reason, until now he'd stayed away.

Meg pointed up the hill, to where Whirlwind's grey rump was vanishing into the trees. 'Did you see her?' she asked her uncle.

'Too far away,' said Spike. Meg's face fell. 'Cheer up,' he said. 'There are other brumbies, aren't there?' He tickled her and made her laugh. 'Show me them instead.'

Sam sized him up, and saw no sign that he'd recognised the mare. Charlie's courage and presence of mind had undoubtedly saved Whirlwind's life.

Meg grabbed Spike's arm and pulled him away to look at the new foal. Sam waited until they'd moved off, then ran over to where Drew was saddling Clancy. 'What are we going to do?'

'I'll find her,' he whispered, and took off up the mountain. Breathe, Sam told herself. Just breathe. There was still a lot to do – take the money, for a start. Hand around coffee and biscuits, collect some feedback.

'You've quite a fan in my daughter,' said Sue, as they watched Meg drag Spike over to see Phoenix. Sam smiled at the compliment and invited her into the office. Sue took out her credit card and slipped it into the reader. It whirred and clicked, and a few seconds later Sam was handing over a receipt for the very first payment to Brumby Trails. It wasn't a lot - petty cash from her father's perspective. But for some reason it felt like she'd made a million dollars. It must be true what they said about appreciating things more if you worked for them.

Sam was suddenly ashamed to think of how often she'd taken money for granted. Not this time though. This time she'd earned it. Holding that humble credit card docket felt as good as acing her final exams, or being selected in the A team for the state dressage squad. No, it wasn't like that at all. It was ten times better.

The whistling kettle brought her back to earth 'Coffee?' Sam asked.

Sue nodded and took a shortbread. 'You really have got the perfect setup here.' she said. 'Now, which brumbies are for sale? Meg has her heart set on a filly, freshly broken. She's keen to train a horse from scratch.' For a moment Sam didn't follow. 'And that stunning palomino colt,' said Sue. 'How much is his stud fee? I'm retiring my barrel racing mare and would like to put her in foal.' Sam didn't know what to say. Sue misinterpreted her silence. 'Don't say he's already fully booked for next season?' She sounded so disappointed. 'I like your buckskin stallion too. He's beautiful, but I'm afraid I've fallen in love with the palomino.'

Think quickly now. Her first instinct was to say no, to explain that there were no horses for sale, no stallions at stud. But this woman was handing them a potential new income stream on a plate. Bushy had half a dozen young brumbies, green broke, but going well under saddle. And how she'd love to see a foal by Phoenix. Sam's head told her that Phoenix wouldn't even be here in spring, but her heart refused to believe it. 'I do have some young stock,' Sam said cautiously. 'But wouldn't Meg be better off with an older, fully schooled horse? It's not a great idea for two youngsters to be learning on their own.'

'I couldn't agree more,' said Sue, nodding. 'That's why I want Meg to have lessons. We'll leave her new horse at Brumby's Run on agistment, and I'll drive her here three times a week after school.' Sue dipped the biscuit in her coffee. 'Oh, and on weekends. What do you charge for a full day? Do you have some sort of school-holiday program? Meg might like to bring her friends along.'

'We can do that,' said Sam, trying to sound bright and confident. Trying not to show how overwhelmed she really was. She needed to talk to Charlie. However Charlie was off in the bush somewhere, riding an unbroken man-killer without saddle or bridle. So much for the promises she'd made to Mary about not letting Charlie overdo it, about keeping her safe.

'Good,' said Sue. 'I won't have a look at your sale horses right now, if you don't mind.' Thank goodness for that. There weren't any sale horses. 'I'll come back on my own later. We're wanting to surprise Meg.' Sue took a card from her purse. 'Here's my contact details. Why don't you just text me the price and particulars?' She scribbled on the back and handed over the card.

Sam looked at the list written there. Stud fees. Lesson fees. Agistment fees. This was too good to be true. 'Meg is interested in high-school riding. You don't happen to know of a local coach, do you? It's all barrel racing and campdrafting around here.'

'I'm a level one NCAS dressage coach,' said Sam, 'if that's any help.'

'That sounds marvellous.' Sue looked impressed. 'What does it mean, exactly?'

'It's a certification through the Equestrian Federation of Australia national coaching scheme. It means I'm qualified to teach beginners through to elementary level. I used to help coach the juniors of the state dressage squad.'

'Good heavens, you are a find!' Sue was absolutely beaming. 'There's a group of girls at the Tallangala Pony Club who are dead keen on dressage. Just wait until they hear I've found them a coach.'

Craig and the aunties came in for cups of coffee, laughing and joking and saying how much they'd enjoyed their ride. Sam took a second look at Craig. Although older and heavier, the resemblance to his brother Spike was obvious now. If only she'd picked it earlier. Sue kept up a steady stream of chatter, aimed mainly at her husband, talking up the idea of buying Meg a brumby. Sam imagined Sue normally got her way.

'We'll be in touch,' said Sue, as they rose to leave. 'Don't forget to text me.' Sam waved Sue's card gaily about, to show she'd remember. Sue glanced around and dropped her voice to a stage whisper. 'I'd like photos of your available horses, maybe a little bit about them – and the price, of course. I presume they're all registered in the brumby stud book, or whatever it is you call it?'

Sam nodded. As far as she knew, all Bushy's horses were eligible for listing with the Brumby Association. She could hurry it through if she had to.

'Perfect.' Sue took one last biscuit. 'We'd best get going.'

They all crowded out the door. Meg was describing the finer points of natural-horsemanship training to her uncle. Spike lit up a smoke and slouched against the rails. Buckjumping was as far from natural horsemanship as you could imagine. But then there'd been his impressive performance in the Bareback Challenge, cantering perfect circles without saddle or bridle, revving that silly chainsaw. He knew a thing or two about communicating with his mount. Sam took a good look at Spike. Objectively, he was gorgeous, but she was immune to his charms. Drew had it all over him. Spike sauntered over, and winked at her. 'You've done a top job, princess. Those horses look a million dollars.'

Sam gave him a smile of genuine gratitude, though she doubted he'd be so generous if he knew about Whirlwind. She said goodbye, and the group moved off to their cars, Meg bouncing about like an excited labrador puppy. Sam stood and watched until she was certain they'd all gone, then felt in her pocket. Where was her phone? It suddenly rang from the office, and she dashed to retrieve it. Drew. He'd found Charlie and she was fine. Was it safe to come home? Right, they wouldn't be long. Sam let out a deep breath, made herself a strong coffee and sat down to wait.

No rational explanation existed for what she was seeing. Charlie and Drew, companionably cantering their horses down the hill. Whirlwind stood like a rock while Charlie slipped off her back, and then the mare followed – followed – her sister into the yard.

Charlie started to groom her. Sam tiptoed to the rails and watched Whirlwind lean into the body brush, the way Pharaoh used to do. She blinked away the sharp sting of tears, wanting to berate her sister for forging this secret alliance behind her back. For making a fool of her. Then she thought of Drew. Charlie had no monopoly on secret alliances.

Sam started to say, 'You've got some explaining to do,' but stopped herself. It was exactly that kind of preachy attitude that had caused problems between them in the first place. No wonder Charlie hadn't been straight with her. So instead she said, 'It all went so well. The Morgans were thrilled.'

'Did they pay?' asked Charlie. Sam nodded. Her sister looked exhausted, completely done in, but completely happy at the same time. She waved Sam into the yard. Cautiously Sam ducked through the rails and approached the mare. Whirlwind showed no fear, no hostility. She allowed Sam to stroke her shoulder, her neck, her cheek. Miracles really did happen.

'Here, what do you make of this?' said Charlie, tugging at Whirlwind's flowing grey forelock. 'I've been dying to show you.' The mare obligingly lowered her head. Unbelievable.

Charlie took hold of Sam's hand and placed it under the forelock. What on earth? Beneath Sam's fingers were two bony bulges, like baby horns. Sam looked at her sister askance. Charlie grinned. 'Cool, isn't it? She actually is a demon horse.'

Sam had a closer look. No doubt about it — a pair of tiny horns grew from Whirlwind's forehead. Sam guessed the rodeo men wouldn't have noticed them. You'd have to lift her forelock first.

'This is amazing,' said Sam. A thought struck her from left field. 'She doesn't have warts under her tail, does she?'

'How did you know?' said Charlie. 'You can't see them unless you're right up close.' Sam ignored the reminder that, until now, she hadn't been able to get anywhere near the mare. Sure enough, there was a cluster of little warts at the base of her tail. It was beginning to make outlandish sense. Whirlwind's height and strength, her luxuriant mane and tail, her magnificent charisma.

'There is a breed of horned horse,' said Sam, slowly. 'Very rare, though. Impossibly rare.'

'Get out!' said Charlie.

'It's true. They're called Carthusian Andalusians. The most ancient equine stud book in the world. All descended from one grey foundation stallion, Esclavo. He had little horns and warts under his tail. Monks protected his bloodlines for hundreds of years. Esclavo was said to be the perfect horse; perfect in conformation and perfect in temperament. My dressage coach says Carthusians are the finest high-school mounts ever known.'

'Are there any left?' asked Charlie.

'Some,' said Sam. 'They're bred at a special stud farm owned by the Spanish government. Not much chance of running into one on Maroong Mountain though.'

'So these Carthusian horses,' said Drew. 'They're Andalusians, you said?'

Sam nodded. 'The oldest, purest strain of all.'

'But Jarrang is Whirlwind's father,' said Charlie. 'The same striped hoofs. That's no coincidence.'

'No, it's not,' said Drew. He'd been listening to their conversation with a thoughtful look on his face. 'Jarrang's her sire all right. A more interesting question is, who's her dam?' He ducked through the rails and headed for the hay shed. Sam chased after him, followed by Charlie.

'You know something, don't you?' said Sam.

'I might.' Drew was gathering biscuits of hay. 'But don't you think the horses deserve a feed first?'

They distributed the hay. It seemed to take forever. When they'd finished, the trio sat outside the office with the last of the coffee and biscuits.

'So?' asked Sam.

'There's a place that breeds those Andalusians over at Jindabyne. El Soldado Stud or something like that . . . Don Campbell's joint. A few years back they lost a filly. Real special she was, apparently. Imported all the way from Spain.'

'When you say lost, you mean what? Died?'

'No, I mean just what I said. Lost – or stolen more like it. Some mad brumby stallion came down and kicked the slip rails out of her yard during the night.'

They all sat for a bit without speaking. Sam guessed they were all thinking the same thing. That lost Andalusian filly was Whirlwind's mother. 'Did she have horns and warts under her tail?' asked Sam.

'How should I know?' said Drew, swigging his coffee. 'But if I were you, I'd be finding out.'

Late afternoon ambled through to evening. 'When will dinner be ready?' Charlie eyed the oven hungrily.

'Not for ages.' Sam slapped some cheese on a piece of bread and pushed it across the table to her sister, the events of the day still spinning in her head. 'Think we can really do this?'

'Hell, yeah!' said Charlie. 'Our own brumby stud. They'll be the next big fashion. We've already got the makings of a great herd. First we get Jarrang and Phoenix into the stud book.' Sam's heart lurched. She hadn't told her sister that the colt had been sold. 'And there's Whirlwind and the two creamies. In the meantime, we buy in some started brumbies from Bushy, school them a bit more and sell them as heritage horses.' Charlie was buzzing with excitement and energy. It was impossible to believe this was the shadow of a girl she'd first met in the hospital, all those months ago. 'We'll offer the Coalition an overflow sanctuary for freshly caught horses in return for being able to train up and sell some youngsters. We'll run the herd up near the park boundary and give brumby-spotting tours. Oh, and take in horses for training, charge agistment for them. We'll make a bloody fortune.'

'And what will we do in our spare time?' asked Sam, trying to keep a straight face.

'Don't,' said Charlie, giving her a playful punch. 'We can do it. You just watch us.'

Charlie watched Karl's face as they drove through the gate into Balleroo National Park, studying his profile. She liked the way his lightly tanned skin blended with his head of sandy blond hair. Sun had bleached the tips, giving him highlights, like a male model might have in a magazine. Karl took his eyes off the road and turned to smile at her. Those compelling slate-grey eyes contrasted with his fair complexion. He looked like he could read her mind.

She'd fallen hard for Karl. The man was in a class of his own, a different breed. There was the physical attraction, of course, but it was more than that. She loved the sexy hint of an accent in his voice, the clipped consonants and oddly formal rhythm of his speech. It conjured up images of exotic places and faraway lands. But Karl's most desirable quality — and she surprised herself with this one — was his mind.

Charlie had never met an environmentalist before. People generally considered her fascination with Balleroo curious at best, mad at worst. In school she was labelled a greenie, and suffered open hostility from kids whose families had been run off the alpine cattle leases they'd held for generations. She'd learned to hide her opinions.

She didn't have to hide anything from Karl. Miracle of miracles, he actually shared her views. For Charlie, discovering that a kindred spirit existed in her world was like discovering she wasn't the last person alive after a nuclear holocaust. Karl had done a university course in environmental science. He'd even won some sort of Young Conservationist of the Year prize in his last job on the New South Wales north coast. The award, apparently, was for dramatically reversing species decline, and increasing local support for grey-headed flying fruit bat colonies. 'You can't achieve good ecological outcomes,' he said, 'without bringing the community along with you.' Consensus conservation, he called it.

'You'll never get consensus in Currajong,' said Charlie.

Karl didn't share this view. He was an optimist. 'There are plenty of people like us,' he said, as they slowed to allow a kangaroo and her half-grown joey to bound across the road.

'Not around here,' argued Charlie. 'Alpine grazing's been going on for over a hundred years. It's a cultural thing. People say cattle reduce fuel for bushfires. They say they eat the weeds.'

'Not everybody.' Karl swerved to avoid a deep pothole. 'Some people say they spread the weeds.'

'The cattlemen don't, and they're the ones who count.'

'You'd be surprised.' Karl tossed her a pamphlet - the newsletter of an organisation called *The Ecological Farmers Network*.

'What's this mob on about, then?' asked Charlie.

'It's a progressive association of farmers, all sorts, cattle producers as well. They support environmental programs, especially those that protect biodiversity.' He turned off the road and headed up a corrugated fire trail. 'You know Ray Hardy? Runs cattle out at Jackson's Track?' Charlie nodded. 'He's a member. And Julie Wilson from the berry farm, and Frank Jones from Claremont Wines. Frank wants to do trips into Balleroo – combine them with fine dining and accommodation. He doesn't want cow pats all over the park. And there's Balleroo Bees, promoting alpine wildflower honey. And John Brooks from the trout farm. I could go on,' he said. 'They're all jumping on board.'

But Charlie would not be convinced. 'It won't be enough.'

'Do you know what I think?' said Karl. Charlie shook her head. He pulled the car over and trained his serious grey eyes upon her. 'I think you've got a chip on your shoulder. I think it's been there for a very long time and ...' He pointed to a tall candlebark. 'I think it's about the size of that tree.'

'As big as that?' She tried to laugh off his remark and failed. Instead her voice was small, barely recognisable. Where was her usual smart comeback when she needed it? Karl leaned over, took her face in steady hands, and kissed her with infinite care. It wasn't just a kiss. It was an article of faith, a reassurance, even a dare. A dare to let it all go, to heave the heavy chip away and walk lightly once more on the earth. A pledge that he would see her through, if she had courage enough to take the risk. The kiss of a man with a woman, not a boy with a girl, and it literally took her breath away. Karl stroked her cheek. There was something deeply intimate and reassuring about the caress.

'Are we good to go?' he asked. She nodded and he returned his hands to the wheel. She missed his touch already. The jeep continued up the mountain, turned left at a fork in the track and stopped abruptly. Dozens of red-and-white Herefords dotted the slope, cows with well-grown calves, ready for weaning.

'It's just like at the other sites,' he said, snatching up a notebook. 'Not a radio collar in sight.' They'd spent the last week tracking down the four hundred head Bill had put into the park. Their movements were meant to be monitored with GPS collars. So far, Karl and Charlie had not found one single beast fitted with a tracking device.

'What happens now?' asked Charlie.

Karl kissed her again, a brief, triumphant kiss this time. 'We have enough evidence,' he said, patting his camera. 'Let's shut this trial down.'

CHAPTER 39

'Y ou ready?' asked Charlie.

'Ready as I'll ever be.' This wasn't true. Sam felt like a deer in the spotlights. Today was the day she'd decided to come clean with the town. It was a natural progression. For months now, a bulldozer of truth had inexorably ploughed its way through her life, tearing down each lie. The charade Sam had acted out for the people of Currajong would be the final falsehood to fall.

Charlie parked the car outside the general store. Marjorie first. She was known for her big heart. 'What if she hates me for it?' Sam cringed at the pathetic tone of her voice.

'Too bad,' said Charlie. 'Just do it.'

'Right.' Sam took a second to steel herself to the task ahead. She waited until there were no customers in the shop, then braved the door.

'Charlie,' said Marjorie. She stopped cleaning the glass refrigerator doors and put down her spray bottle. 'What can I do for you?'

'Do you have a minute?' asked Sam.

Marjorie looked around at the empty shop. 'It sure looks that way.'

'I've got something to tell you.' Marjorie's gentle face softened.

'This probably sounds ridiculous, but … I'm not really Charlie. I've been pretending. To you, to everybody.'

Marjorie put on her most sympathetic smile. 'I know, love. I know.'

Sam had her next sentence ready to go, her mouth running ahead of her brain, trying to get the humiliation over with. 'My name is Samantha—' Sam stopped short. She must have misheard. 'You know?'

Marjorie leaned over and patted her hand. 'Yes, dear.'

'Since when?' It was almost a demand.

'Since the beginning. Would you like tea? Or coffee perhaps?' Marjorie put on the kettle. 'I only have instant, I'm afraid.'

'I don't understand,' said Sam. 'Why didn't you say something?'

'I didn't like to pry. I supposed you had your reasons, and you'd tell me in your own time — when you were ready. I've lived in this town all my life, dear. Most of us have. We all knew about Mary's babies and the terrible choice she had to make.' Marjorie walked to the front door and flipped the sign to *Closed*. 'You're very different from your sister. I guessed right away. I've been worried about Charlie. Such a kind girl, that one. Always came by to help me load up the deliveries of a Friday, because of my back. Is she okay?'

'Yes,' said Sam. 'Yes, she is. Would you like to see her? She's out in the car.'

'Well, bring her in, for goodness sake!' said Marjorie.

Sam went out to the car. 'Have you done it?' asked Charlie. Sam nodded. 'What happened?'

'Marjorie wants to see you.' Charlie looked scared stiff. 'Come on,' said Sam. 'It's going to be fine.' They pushed their way through the door together.

'Charlie.' Marjorie beamed and enfolded her in a motherly embrace. 'Welcome home.'

It was the same thing all over town. Wherever they went, people confessed that they already knew. 'Course I did,' said George at the produce store, with a gruff laugh. 'The new *not quite right* Charlie didn't have a clue. Our Charlie wouldn't have been silly enough to buy that damn Showstopper horse feed, when you can mix your own for half the price. Or buy a rubber mallet to drive in steel fence posts. Or ask if you could buy fencing wire by the metre.'

Sam felt her cheeks burn. 'Why didn't you say?'

'Wasn't any of my business, was it?' he said. 'I could see you were a good kid, and you must've had your reasons. I was just happy to know that other little baby of Mary's was okay; happy to know she'd finally come home to Currajong.'

Even Harry from the garage had known. 'You may be a loud-mouth bitch, Charlie, but I've got to hand it to you – you know your way around an engine better than my best apprentice. This one?' He gestured to Sam with a toss of his head. 'Wouldn't know a carburettor from a head gasket.' He wiped his greasy black hands on a rag. 'What's your name again?'

'Samantha. Or Sam. Call me Sam.'

Harry looked at her like she'd gone mad. 'I'd just as soon go on calling you Charlie,' he said, putting his head back under the bonnet. 'Seeing as I'm used to it.'

It was an extraordinary thing. Like the collective consciousness of the town had quietly chosen to embrace Sam for who she was, regard-less of names or labels. They'd accepted her on face value, not in place of Charlie, but in addition to Charlie. 'Come on,' said Sam. 'We've got one last visit to make.'

Sam and Charlie stood together in Bushy's kitchen. He regarded them with no hint of surprise. So he knew too. 'Let's have a cuppa.' His face cracked into a smile. They sat down on plastic chairs around a card table, while Bushy switched on the electric kettle. He took a cigarette from a metal tin, fetched three chipped mugs from hooks on the wall, and added sugar and coffee. 'Run out of milk, I'm afraid.'

'Bushy,' asked Sam. 'That very first day, did you—?'

'Oh, I knew all right.' He lit his cigarette and coughed twice. 'I'm no fool.' Charlie let out a whoop of laughter and Sam wanted to strangle her. 'You wasn't bad with them horses. You made a fair fist of it.' He blew a smoke ring and grinned, like he'd just heard a very funny joke. 'But you weren't no Charlie.'

'I don't understand,' said Sam in confusion. 'You'd never even met my sister.'

'Didn't have to.' He turned to Charlie. 'You've got a quite a reputation, young lady.'

Charlie bristled, instantly on the defensive. 'Do you think I give a rat's?'

'The finest young rider and trainer ever turned out of the district. That's the reputation I'm talking about.'

Charlie's jaw dropped. 'People actually say that?'

'My word, they do.' The humming kettle began to whistle. He flicked off the switch. 'And if you'd stop making so much noise yourself, you might be able to hear them.'

'Outside,' ordered Sam. Condor cocked his head and flew onto the kitchen table instead, scattering her papers to the floor. Sam didn't scold him. She hadn't been able to concentrate anyway. Her thoughts kept returning to the extraordinary events of yesterday. Sam gave the big black bird a crust and chased him out the back door. Then she gathered the forms from the floor and put them aside, giving up the pretence of doing paperwork. Sam was in no mood for quarterly income estimates and insurance policies. Instead she put on Kasey Chambers' latest album and gazed out the window to the luminous, blue mountains beyond.

Everything was perfect. At last there were no more secrets, no more misunderstandings or half-truths. Today was the first day of a new, authentic life here in Currajong. She had Charlie's confidence and affection. She had the unconditional acceptance of the town. And best of all, she had Drew's love. Sam felt capable of anything.

Phoenix's imperious neigh sounded from the yard, reminding Sam that everything wasn't perfect after all. Ryan had put the young stallion through his paces during the week, and pronounced him ready to go to his new owner. That wasn't going to happen, not if she could help it. What she needed was a plan. Maybe Dad could help? Outbid the buyer, make Ryan an offer he couldn't refuse? The sound of wheels on gravel distracted Sam from her reverie. Maybe it was Drew? If they put their heads together, they were bound to come up with a solution.

'Hello? Anybody home?' Sam froze. Faith was the last person on earth that Sam expected to walk into the kitchen.

'Mum, what on earth are you doing here?' Faith approached Sam with outstretched arms and enfolded her in a hug. For one lovely, fleeting moment, Sam was excited to see her mother. She had so much to tell her, so much to show her. Such a lot to brag about. But in almost the same instant images of Pharaoh crowded into her mind, hardening her heart. Sam pulled away. She hadn't forgiven her mother, not by a long shot.

'Darling, I told you I was coming.' Sam looked blank. 'On the phone . . . from Saint Tropez?'

'I didn't think you were serious,' said Sam. 'I told you not to.'

'Nonsense, Samantha. Surely I can visit my own daughter?'

Sam marshalled up a hundred responses in her head – clever ones, bitter ones, sarcastic ones – but couldn't blurt out a single line. 'Why didn't you ring first?' was the best she could manage.

Faith heaved a great sigh. 'I thought you might not agree to see me, Samantha.'

She was probably right. Sam stared at her mother, lost for words. Faith looked larger than life and utterly out of place in Brumby's little kitchen. You could tell she'd been in France. The French always over-dressed for everything. Whatever would Charlie make of her? Faith wore high heels, belted tailored trousers and a lavender blouse. Lavender for God's sake. The elegant ensemble was set off with a striped silk scarf and sparkling cluster earrings. Had Faith always looked so overdone? Or had Sam's own tastes been stripped bare in this remote place?

She wanted to run to her room, flee from this old life that was so unexpectedly catching up with her. Then a wild, hopeful thought struck her. 'You got Pharaoh back, didn't you? That why you're here.'

Faith's face fell. 'It's not possible, darling. I've tried my hardest. Pharaoh is not for sale.'

Sam was hollow with disappointment. 'I want you to go, Mum. I'm not ready to do this.'

'Not even a pot of tea?' asked Faith. 'I have . . . I have quite a lot to tell you.' She looked genuinely stricken at the prospect of having to leave.

Sam studied her mother's anxious, eager face and relented. 'Sit down, Mum.' Sam pulled out a chair at the kitchen table, half expecting her mother to turn up her nose at its cracked linoleum seat. But Faith nodded her thanks and sat down without complaint. Sam put on the kettle and sat down too. For a little while nobody spoke. 'You haven't told me what a dump this place is yet,' said Sam at last.

To Sam's surprise, Faith's eyes glistened with tears. She reached across the table and took Sam's hands tenderly in her own. 'I'm sorry about Pharaoh. That was so terribly, terribly wrong of me.' Her tone was unusually heartfelt. 'You may not believe this, Samantha, hurt as you are, but I miss him too. I will never stop trying to bring Pharaoh home.' Her mother's obvious contrition was very moving. Sam was confused, unsure of how to react. 'I do have something else to offer,' said Faith.

Sam cut her off. 'There's nothing else I want from you.'

Faith cast her an uncertain glance, then reached into her bag and produced a large, yellow envelope. 'For you, Samantha. Please, at least look at it.' Sam nearly pushed it back across the table unopened, but curiosity won out.

No, it couldn't be. At first she was too stunned to appreciate the significance of what she was reading. Registration papers declaring Phoenix to be a foundation sire of the Australian Brumby Studbook. She read on, not daring to believe. His owner was listed as Samantha Carmichael.

'Are you happy, darling?'

For a while Sam forgot how to speak. 'Oh yes,' she said, when she finally found her tongue. 'God, yes!'

'Then you must forgive me for Pharaoh,' said her mother. 'You simply must.'

This was classic Faith. Ordering forgiveness, like it was a new fragrance or something. But her mother's high-handedness could not detract from the pure joy of the occasion. 'Thank you,' said Sam, overwhelmed. 'I feel like I'm dreaming. How did you know about Phoenix?'

'Mary told me.'

Could Faith's visit become any more astonishing? 'But I thought you hated Mary?'

'We're very different people, that's true.' The kettle began its low whistle. 'But we share a powerful connection — you.' Sam turned off the kettle and sat back down. 'Samantha.' Her mother's tone became serious. 'I have some rather more difficult news for you.'

'What's wrong? Is Dad okay?'

Faith frowned. 'May I have some water?'

Impatiently Sam fetched her a glass. Through the kitchen window she saw Drew's ute pull up outside. She sat back down and fixed her eyes on Faith. 'Mum just tell me.' The tension became unbearable.

Faith took a sip, uttered a shuddering sigh and said at last, 'Your father and I . . . we've separated. We're getting a divorce.' The water in the glass rippled, betraying her unsteady arm.

'Oh, Mum, no,' Sam reached for her hand. 'What happened?'

'Your father has been unfaithful, Samantha. On more than one occasion it seems.' She shook her head sorrowfully. 'It's been a great trial for me.'

'Of course, Mum. Of course it has.' Sam squeezed her hand. 'We'll get through this together.'

'There's more,' said Faith. 'Much more. It's about … your father.'

'Mum, you already said that.'

Faith shook her head. 'I mean your real father, your biological father.'

Sam felt the blood rush to her head. The mysterious Robert Smith? Could she finally meet him? 'What have you found out? Do you know where he is? We think he's been sending money to Mary and Charlie ever since the transplant.'

'I don't doubt it.' Faith nodded as if it all made sense. 'He's a very wealthy man. A generous man as well.'

'So you know him?' Sam's hands were trembling.

'I do. We both know him, as a matter of fact.'

Faith seemed paralysed. A vile thought struck Sam. Bill Chandler - Bill was her father. Wealthy enough to be the secret benefactor. Living next door to Mary all these years. It had to be Bill. Thank God Drew was adopted. Otherwise, well, it didn't bear thinking about.

'Tell me the truth, Mum. I can take it.'

Sam steeled herself for the shocking confirmation, while Faith forced a smile. 'Your father is . . . well, he's your father and my husband — Victor Carmichael.'

Her mother's words made no sense. 'You mean Dad is really my dad?' Faith nodded. 'And Charlie's too?'

'It all came out in France,' said Faith. 'If you'd come, he'd have never confessed. He'd have been too ashamed. In any case, he told me the whole story … and now I'm telling you.'

Sam opened her mouth to speak, but Faith raised her eyebrows. 'Please, Samantha, don't interrupt me. I may not be able to start again.'

Sam nodded and Faith gave her a grateful smile. 'It's almost twenty years ago now. Your father was a cabinet minister. He undertook a tour of the Upper Murray, supporting some conservative party candidate in a by-election campaign.' She took a deep breath and appeared to be composing herself. 'He met Mary somehow.' Faith gulped her water. 'She was a girl of seventeen. Your father was forty.' The words hung in the room like a bad smell. 'He behaved very badly, Samantha. In every way. He gave the girl …' Faith looked suddenly shamefaced. 'He gave your mother a false name, but was careless with his phone number. When Mary discovered her pregnancy, she rang him and left messages. He ignored them. Can you imagine that? We'd been trying for years to have a child, and he ignores this poor pregnant girl. Mary rang him once a month until the babies . . . until you and Charlene were born. I suppose she was hoping he might help her, so she needn't relinquish one of her twins.'

'He didn't?'

'No, he didn't. Instead he did something monstrous. He organised to privately adopt one of the infants. It didn't matter which one, apparently. Your father wanted to give me a baby, you see. He knew how much I wanted one, and he loved me – in his own peculiar way. But he knew that I'd leave him if I discovered the truth.'

'So,' said Sam, reeling from the news. 'When I found out that I was adopted, he let me think he wasn't my real father, even though he was? Just so he didn't have to tell you the truth?'

'When he learned your sister was so terribly ill, the guilt was too much for him. He set up a generous monthly stipend for Charlie and Mary. He bought your sister a car. Our accountant raised the unexplained expenditure with me last week, and I confronted Victor.' Faith looked grim. 'There were other liaisons. My whole marriage has been a lie. The one thing real about it is you, Samantha, and so here we are.'

Sam's eyes filled with tears as she tried to take her mother's words in. How hurt Faith must feel. And how weird to learn her dad was, well, her dad. 'Is that everything?' she asked, suspecting more secrets.

'It's enough, don't you think?' Faith gave a shaky smile.

'So Dad really is my father, and he's Charlie's father too?'

Faith nodded. Sam slumped back into her chair. For the second time in months, her world had been utterly changed. Was nothing ever real?

Drew poked his head around the door. 'You two okay?'

Sam looked into his concerned face, into Faith's solicitous eyes. She thought of Charlie. How astonished she'd be by this news ... her news too. Whirlwind and Phoenix and the new foal —Sam's dream herd grazed peacefully in the shadow of Maroong Mountain. Who was she kidding? It didn't get more real than this.

CHAPTER 40

S am fussed about the kitchen, rearranging scones on the plate, pretending to be busy. Charlie got off the phone, her face ashen. 'He wants to meet me.' She looked so unsure, like a scared rabbit. She looked about twelve.

'What do *you* want to do?' asked Sam. 'That's the important thing.'

'I haven't a clue,' said Charlie. 'Part of me hates him – a big part.' Sam nodded. She felt the same way. 'But part of me is dying of curiosity. You know our father, Sam. You always have. I want that chance.'

It had been a week since Faith dropped her bombshell. Sam was almost as confused as Charlie. Dad was flying home. He was sorry, he said. Wanted to make amends. Wanted his wife back. Wanted to make it right — for his daughters, for Faith, for Mary . . . but how to atone for a lifetime of deceit? Sam's own brief charade paled beside her father's cruel folly.

Drew and Bill walked in, voices raised. 'Abbey's a bloody good bloodline,' said Bill. 'I'll give you that, but breeding brumbies?' He snorted. 'You need your head read.'

'We already have two top stallions, Dad, with bookings for next year's stud season. And Sam's dressage training a first-cross Andalusian-brumby mare, caught straight out of the park. Reckons she'll get her to Grand Prix standard without any trouble at all.' He helped himself to a scone. 'Remember when El Soldado Ranch lost that imported mare a few years back?'

Bill nodded. 'Don was ropeable. That mare was some special strain? A Carpathian, I think he said. He paid a fortune for her.'

'A Carthusian,' corrected Drew. 'And that lost Carthusian is the dam of Sam's mare. Don's been out to confirm it – and get this, he offered to buy her. Imagine that. Don Campbell wanting to buy a brumby. Not a bad foundation mare to start out with, eh?'

'I'll be the judge of that,' grumbled Bill.

'Come up to the yards and see for yourself then,' said Drew. 'We'll keep the new colt here at Brumby's Run though.' He gave his father a friendly punch. 'You're not gelding this one, Dad.'

That night a storm raged over the mountain. Sam couldn't sleep. She slipped from bed without waking Drew, wrapped herself in the fluffy bathrobe that was a present from her mother, and tiptoed down the hall. She could hear Charlie's steady breathing as she passed her bedroom, Bess's soft snoring in her basket by the fire.

Sam pushed open the back door and stood until she had her night eyes. Things began to take shape in the gloom. Condor squawked from his perch on the verandah, ruffled his feathers and tucked his head back beneath his wing. The wind roared through the tree-tops. Shadows shifted and shook. Lightning cracked and lit up the scene for just an instant, giving Sam a snapshot of the sheds and yards and the wild dark forest beyond.

When Sam slipped off her robe, it felt like she was shedding more than her clothes. She walked naked into the rain. This was hers – all this power and beauty and terror. This was her home. The pain of loneliness was a vague memory that seemed to belong to somebody else. And as she whispered a small prayer to the spirit of Maroong Mountain, something told her that she need never be alone again.

ACKNOWLEDGEMENTS

Thank you to A.B. 'Banjo' Paterson, whose wonderful poem *Brumby's Run* inspired this story.

Thanks to the team at Pilyara Press, especially Kathryn Ledson, Kate Belle and Sydney Smith.

Thanks to Kathryn Massey, president of the Hunter Valley Brumby Association, for her tireless work on behalf of the magnificent wild horses of Australia.

And finally, thanks to my patient family for their love and support.

CURRAWONG CREEK

THE WILD AUSTRALIA STORIES – BOOK 2

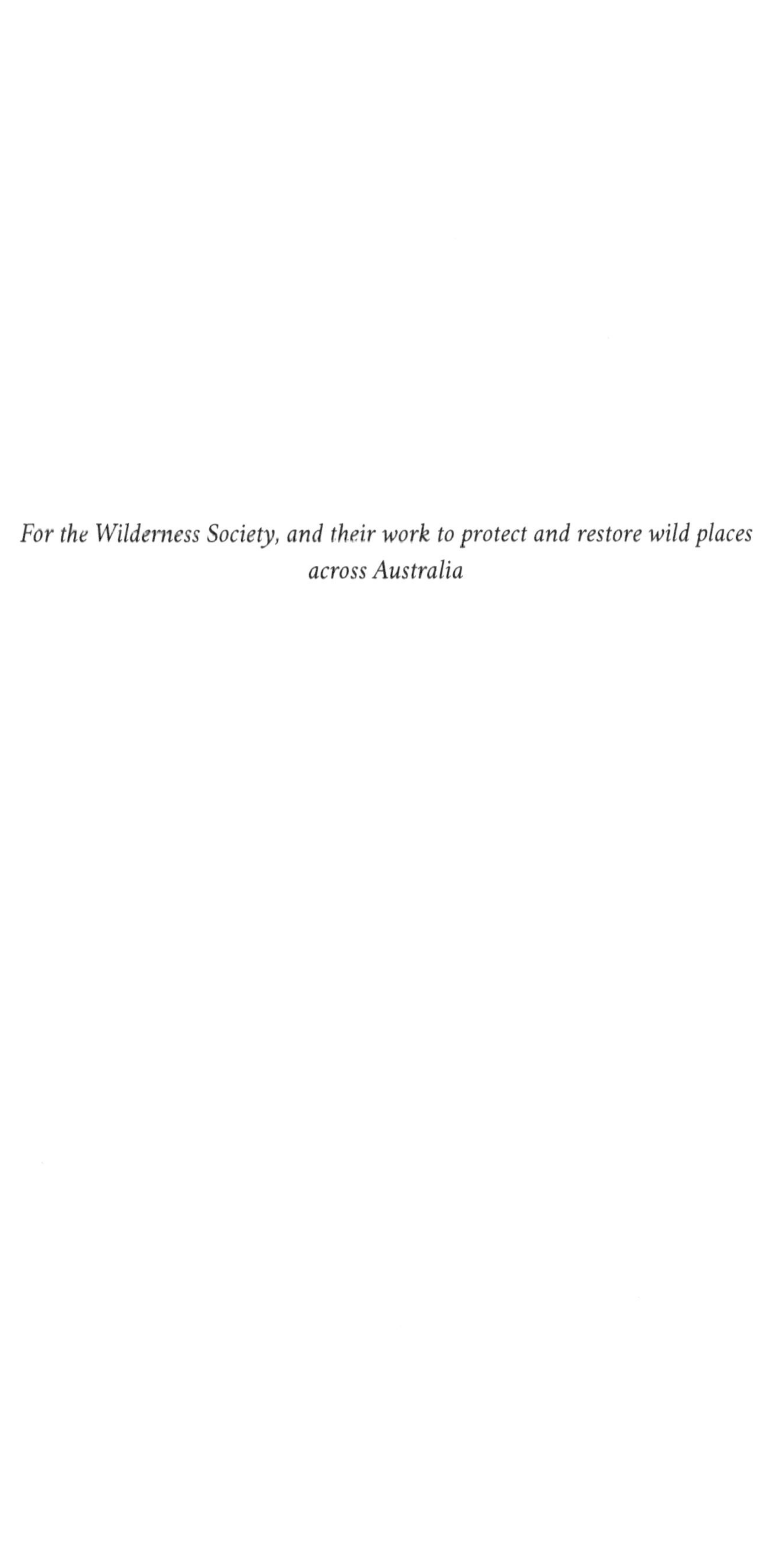

*For the Wilderness Society, and their work to protect and restore wild places
across Australia*

CHAPTER 1

Friday morning. Clare finished the interview and sized up her client. Too thin, junky thin. Red eyes, more than a hint of the shakes and she couldn't stop sniffing.

'I advise you to plead guilty,' said Clare. 'We'll present a plea in mitigation and ask for a bond or a community-based order. It will be better all round.' This week she'd seen too many cases just like this one. The young woman was going to make a bad impression on the court without even opening her mouth.

'Can we nick out for a smoke?'

'Of course.'

The boyfriend was already out the door, and the girl wasn't far behind. Clare started making notes on the file, then looked up. The little boy was still sitting there. Clare walked to the door and called after the two figures retreating down the hall. 'Haven't you forgotten something?'

The boy regarded her with solemn eyes, peeking from beneath cartoon-perfect lashes. An uncommonly pretty child in spite of his snotty nose and soiled, shabby clothes.

'Mummy and Daddy will be back soon.' Clare's voice was bright and encouraging, but the boy's expression didn't change.

'Daddy's dead,' he said in a small voice. His bottom lip began to quiver.

Oh. Tiredness and guilt washed over her, along with a feeling that she couldn't name. A vague dissatisfaction that had troubled her all week, each time she'd looked out of her narrow window to the view of the stunted coolabah tree, and beyond it, the barren car park. A *missing*. Or perhaps a *wishing* for something indefinable. Clare averted her gaze, both from the tree and the boy, and rifled through the files on the desk. What on earth was his name? It was hard to concentrate with him looking at her like that. She glanced down at the interview sheet. The mother was Taylor Brown. But that was it - no mention of the child at all.

'What's your name?' she asked.

He didn't answer. He just maintained that unsettling stare. It didn't matter. How long could it take to smoke a cigarette? Clare turned back to her work, reviewing her record of the interview so far. The plea in mitigation would be simple. Taylor had a depressingly familiar tale: growing up in a series of broken homes, women's refuges and foster care placements. She ticked all the boxes and was an addict to boot, although currently on a methadone replacement program. Clare reread the charge sheet. Theft of a bull terrier puppy. Cute, really. The rest wasn't so cute. Around three o'clock in the morning of May the second, police had stopped and searched her vehicle on Wickham Street in the Valley. They'd found drugs, a large sum of money and various stolen items. The boy had been unrestrained in the front seat. Clare looked up and surprised herself by imagining him with a puppy on his lap. Would the puppy have made him laugh? Put a smile on his serious face? Had Taylor wanted to see that smile?

Time ticked by … Her next appointment would be here soon. Clare daydreamed out the grimy window. A bird sat in her poor excuse for a tree. She'd never seen a bird there before. A currawong, big and black, with bright yellow eyes and startling white crescents on its wings. It looked straight at her and uttered a wild, ringing cry. The call sounded disturbingly out of place in a city carpark.

With a wrench Clare returned her attention to the boy. What was

Taylor's mobile number? The digits on the legal aid form were a series of uncertain scratches. A quick glance over the rest of the largely incomplete application, revealed her to be barely literate. Under *date of birth* Taylor had laboriously written her age instead — *twenty*. Only twenty years old. Good grief, how old could she have been when she had the kid? Clare began to key the digits into her phone, then stopped. There weren't enough numbers.

'Hey, come back here,' said Clare, as the little boy got down from the too-big chair and went to the door. 'Where do you think you're going?'

The child turned to face her. Pale blue eyes. A tangled lock of golden hair fell over his forehead. Pushing it aside with a thin hand, he said, 'Mummy,' and tugged at the door knob.

The phone rang. Clare automatically reached for it, then let her hand fall and hurried for the door instead. She guided him back to the chair, impulsively putting her hands around his waist and lifting him into the seat. He was light as a feather. She kneeled in front of him on the worn blue carpet. 'What's your name?'

His mouth moved to shape a word, ever so slowly. 'Jack,' he said at last.

The word was no more than a sigh. If her face hadn't been so close to his, her green eyes so close to his wide blue ones, she would have missed it. Clare loved the name Jack. It was her father's name, a father that she'd recently lost, way too early, to cancer.

'Stay,' she said, and reached once more for the phone. It stopped ringing. A knock came at the door. Thank goodness. 'Here's Mummy now,' said Clare.

But it wasn't Taylor. It was Debbie, the legal aid centre's one and only secretary. 'Just letting you know, Clare, your ten-thirty's here.'

'Could you have a look outside please?' said Clare. 'For a young woman, tall and thin, with long brown hair.' She nodded towards the boy. 'His mother — and a man. They went for a cigarette.'

Debbie retreated from the room, looking doubtful. She returned a few minutes later, shaking her head. 'I'm sorry. No sign.'

Clare frowned. She lifted Jack down from the chair, picked up

Taylor's file and took hold of the boy's small hand. 'Ask my next appointment to wait,' she told Debbie. 'I need to see Roderick.'

Clare finished speaking and watched Roderick stroke his bush of a beard with a forefinger, deep in thought. The child pressed in against her knees, pushing her pin-striped linen skirt up her legs. His skinny warmth radiated through her black tights. Eventually Roderick held out his hand for the file and she handed it over.

'Ring Child Protection and have them send somebody round to pick him up,' he said at last. Clare nodded and tried to prise the child from her legs.

Jack began to scream, a piercing cry that tore through the thin walls of the office.

'My next client …' she said through the noise. 'I have to go.' The more she tried to detach herself from the boy, the harder he yelled.

'Enough.' Roderick held up his hand. 'He obviously wants to stay with you.'

Clare let her hands fall from Jack's shoulders and the screaming ended as abruptly as it had begun.

Roderick picked up the phone. 'Debbie, send Clare's next one to me, and see if you can divvy up her morning slots between the rest of us.'

Clare looked confused. 'I don't understand.'

'You're looking after the boy until a social worker comes.'

Clare's mouth fell open. 'What do you expect me to do with a four-year-old kid?'

'I don't know, McDonald's maybe?' He fished a wallet from his pocket and plonked some money on the table. 'Get him a Happy Meal.'

Clare dragged herself from the room, with Jack still attached to her leg.

Debbie watched her struggle back towards her office. 'Adam rang,' she said. 'To remind you about the ballet tonight.'

Adam's sister was opening in the lead role of Queensland Ballet's production of Giselle. Clare secretly didn't like the ballet and was bored after ten minutes, but Adam loved it and tonight was apparently a very big deal.

Debbie smiled at the little boy. 'He's a sweetie.'

Clare grimaced as she finally made it to the office and slammed the door behind her.

The child was sitting in the too-big chair again, watching her with those wide eyes. Every now and then he looked out the dirty window. The currawong had flown, leaving the misshapen little tree looking even sadder than usual. Clare's arm ached from holding the phone to her ear. The department's intake worker was apparently on the other line, trying to tee up a place for Jack. 'Clare,' she said at last. 'I've found something. An experienced foster carer who lives in the same suburb as the boy's mother. It's a stroke of luck that we can keep the child within his community, don't you think?'

Clare bit her tongue. It hardly mattered. Taylor was transient. She'd listed her latest address as a caravan park, where she'd been for two weeks. What sort of a connection were she and Jack supposed to have with that particular community?

'The carer can take him this afternoon,' said the intake worker.

'We'll be waiting.' Clare hung up the phone. 'Good news, Jack. Let's get lunch to celebrate.'

The little boy didn't say anything. As she took his hand he looked out the window again. She followed his gaze to the bare tree. His hand felt warmer than before, and it nestled into hers like a baby bird in a nest.

The pimply-faced teenager behind the counter put a colourful cardboard box and a drink cup on the tray. They sat down at a corner booth. Jack pulled ineffectually at the tough plastic bag containing the Happy Meal toy, then handed it to Clare. She used her fingernail to poke a hole and extracted the small item inside: a fat, orange hog-like creature with tall black ears, a yellow nose and a fierce face, like it wanted to bite someone. Clare looked at the instructions. Its name was Tepig, and it was something called a Pokémon. According to the leaflet, its little ball of a tail was supposed to light up. Clare squeezed it a few times. Nothing happened.

Jack wiped sauce from his mouth, then leaned over and took the toy from Clare's hand. He put it on its back. Ah, there was a switch. Jack flicked it and Tepig's tail glowed purple.

'Well, what do you know?' Clare smiled at him. 'You're a pretty smart kid.'

Jack picked up a card that had fallen out along with the toy. It was some sort of trading card with a hologram of a bird on it. His eyes lit up and for the first time, he smiled. He pulled a dog-eared deck of cards from his pocket and proceeded to lay them out, side by side, on the table.

'What's that you've got there?' she asked.

Each card had a picture of an odd animal on it, twelve cards in all. The new card was the only one with a sparkly hologram and Clare guessed it was special. She felt ridiculously pleased about that. Jack handed her the paper cup that minutes ago had been filled with cola. His little box of food was empty as well. The burger and chips hadn't seemed to touch the sides going down. 'Same again?'

Whoever said looking after kids was hard? This was a breeze. Jack let her wipe his nose. 'How about I have a Happy Meal too?' she said. We'll get more cards and toys that way.'

Four Happy Meals later and they were both full. The table was littered with empty food wrappers, Pokémon figures and swap cards. Jack burped, then lay down on the bench seat and patted his tummy. Clare found herself copying him, stretching out on her back along the seat at right angles to his. The tops of their heads were almost touching. Jack reached backwards and touched Clare's face, an unexpectedly tender gesture. Then he started to tickle her. Clare laughed in surprise.

'Jack, no, people are looking—' However her inhibitions were no match for Jack's wriggling fingers. 'Stop,' she gasped, but it only spurred him on. Now he was giggling too – peals of musical laughter shaking his slight frame.

'Clare, is that you?'

Clare felt herself redden. Oh no … she knew that voice.

Clare sat up to find one of her fellow solicitors regarding her with an expression halfway between curiosity and distaste. What on earth was Veronica doing at McDonald's, of all places? The overpriced tapas bar down the road was more her style. Clare attempted to reclaim some dignity, straightening her skirt and running her fingers through her blonde bob. As she did, she noticed a pink smear on her shirt — tomato sauce.

'We're here for lunch,' Clare said, unnecessarily. 'Would you like to join us?' What a dumb thing to say. Jack's expression was one of rebuke. He was right of course; Veronica would spoil their fun. Veronica would spoil anybody's fun.

The woman was, as always, immaculate; clothed head-to-slender-ankle in Gucci elegance, balanced on high-heeled red Louboutins. Veronica had ambitions to be a trial lawyer. Next year she was reading at the bar with Paul Dunbar, one of Brisbane's top criminal barristers - essentially an apprenticeship. What Clare wouldn't do for such an opportunity. The only reason that she and Veronica were working in the same building was that Dunbar had a social justice agenda. He liked to see himself as a defender of the common man and often appeared for a reduced fee, or even pro bono, if the trial was high profile enough. Dunbar required his readers to spend twelve months as legal aid lawyers, believing that nothing blooded a future barrister better than the world of petty crime. So unlike Clare, Veronica was a reluctant champion of the underdog.

Her mouth twisted at Clare's offer to join them. 'I didn't come here for lunch.' She spat out the last word like lunch was something loathsome, like she'd never eaten lunch in her life and didn't intend to start now. 'I'm here to fetch you back. You're needed at the office.' Veronica's expression was faintly puzzled, as if she couldn't understand why anybody would need Clare for anything.

Clare wanted to say that she'd only come to McDonald's because of Jack, but stopped herself. It might hurt the little boy's feelings, and anyway, what did it matter what Veronica thought?

'Why didn't you just ring me?' asked Clare.

'Ringing you really would have been so much simpler,' agreed Veronica. 'Since I'm absolutely swamped with extra work today. But somebody – ' She took a phone from her bag and placed it on the table in front of Clare. 'Somebody forgot her mobile.'

Clare picked up her phone. She felt about as tall as Jack.

Veronica looked at the discarded wrappers from the four Happy Meals, at the sauce on Jack's sleeve and finally at Clare. 'Enjoy your … lunch,' she said, and swept from the restaurant.

As they walked back to the office, Jack volunteered his hand. It fitted so comfortably into her own. Clare gave it a pleased squeeze. For the first time she tried to imagine where he might be going. An experienced foster carer, that's what the intake worker had said. Jack should be okay with somebody like that, shouldn't he? Until his mother came back?

CHAPTER 2

The person from the Department of Human Services was waiting for them in Clare's office when they got back – a thin, young woman with frizzy black hair and a crooked smile. She introduced herself as Kim Maguire. 'And this must be John,' she said. 'Why don't we all sit down?'

'Jack,' Clare corrected her. 'His name is Jack.'

Kim pulled a thick bundle of papers from her briefcase and examined it, while Jack slipped from his chair onto Clare's knee.

'No, as I said, it's John. Definitely John.' Kim brandished a fat manila folder like a weapon. 'There's already quite a file on him.'

'The kid should know his own name, don't you think?' said Clare. 'And he told me his name is Jack.'

Kim's expression was pained. 'That's simply not possible, Clare. John is autistic, quite high on the spectrum.' She paused. 'He can't speak.'

This was so patently untrue that Clare found herself speechless. Kim stared at her and Jack, nodding and looking slightly sad. The silence dragged on until it became uncomfortable. Jack was looking out the window at Clare's coolabah tree again. He seemed to like trees. She wondered if the little boy had ever been beyond the city limits.

'He *can* speak,' said Clare. 'He told me his name. He told me his father was dead. Didn't you, Jack?' She could feel the child's small body stiffen, but he didn't answer.

'I have no information on file about John's father,' said Kim. 'But there is a wealth of information verifying his autism. Reports from clinical psychologists, doctors, social workers, childcare staff ...' The kid had really done the rounds. As Kim recited each category of professionals, she slapped a corresponding sheaf of paper down on the desk. 'John has been in care before. The last paediatrician to examine him said that with his level of disability, it's unlikely that he'll ever speak.'

'And what about his mother?' asked Clare. 'What does Taylor Brown say about her son?'

Kim shuffled through her pile of papers. 'Taylor reports that John has spoken, but her caseworkers indicate that she is an unreliable witness. Perhaps she understates the extent of her son's disability because she fears she'll be blamed for it.'

'He talked to me,' Clare repeated.

'And told you what?' said Kim. 'That his name is Jack, when it isn't? You must have imagined it, Clare. Files don't lie.'

Clare frowned. Records were only as good as the people who kept them — and from her own observations of the overworked, under-resourced, burnt-out workers of the child protection system, the people often weren't very good at all. A slipshod assessment or a wrong diagnosis could follow a kid around for years.

Roderick peered briefly into the room. 'Finished here, are we?' he asked. 'Ready to get back on the treadmill?'

Clare heaved a sigh, picked up the boy, whoever he was, and placed him on the chair beside her. She tried to be more objective. Jack had to leave no matter what, so they may as well both make the best of it.

'This lady is Kim,' she said stroking Jack's white-gold hair. Kim smiled her crooked smile. It occurred to Clare that, if she was a child, she might think Kim was a witch. 'She's going to take you to another nice lady, who'll look after you until Mummy's home.'

The boy shook his head violently and crawled back onto Clare's knee.

'Come along, John,' said Kim, in a cheerful voice. 'We're going to have a lovely time.' The boy picked up a heavy stapler and aimed it at Kim's head. His throw was surprisingly accurate. Kim shrieked as the stapler thudded into her temple. Her hand found the spot; blood showed on her fingers. Now the boy was screaming. He ran to the corner of the room and started to bang his head rhythmically against the wall. Bang … bang … bang. How could he do that? Surely it must hurt? When Clare tried to get close to him, he vomited up his lunch — a projectile stream that hit her skirt and dribbled down her tights.

In a truly impressive move Kim tackled him from behind, pinning his arms and holding him too close for his kicking feet to have much impact. The boy hurled himself backwards and struck her in the belly with the rear of his skull. Kim gasped like she'd been winded, but hung on grimly.

When Roderick rushed in, the boy was still yelling. Not crying, but yelling. Long, angry bellows, like an animal. Clare couldn't bear to watch. She ducked from the room and headed for the bathroom. The boy's cries reverberated through the walls. Clare pressed her palms to her ears. The row grew fainter and fainter until at last, all was quiet again. She checked herself in the mirror. What a mess. Her face was red. Her tangled blonde hair had sticky bits that refused to comb out, and there was pickle on her teeth. Clare dabbed ineffectually at the sick on her skirt with some damp toilet paper.

When she'd cleaned herself up as best she could, she ventured out, tiptoeing down the corridor back to her office. Overturned chairs and scattered files told the story. A suspicious puddle lay on the floor near the door. She picked up the bag of Happy Meal toys, along with Jack's special trading cards. He must have dropped them in the fight. Clare switched on Tepig. His purple light now shone pale and sad.

Debbie came in with a mop. 'Don't worry. Veronica's seeing your next customer.' She looked around and shook her head. 'He seemed like such a sweet boy. I wonder what happened?' Clare began to collect the rainbow of multi-coloured paper clips dotting the carpet. Yes, what had happened? The boy had been in care before. Where? How many times? Was that when the error-filled reports were made? Clare stood up, stepped over Debbie's broom, and went to see Roderick.

Roderick was on the phone when Clare entered his office. He waved her in and she sat down to wait. 'Still no sign, I'm afraid ... I know it's not an ideal arrangement for the child, but what do you expect us to do? Produce his mother out of thin air? Potentially she's unfit to retain custody anyway ... Of course, you'll be the first to know ... Bye.'

'Well?' asked Clare. 'What's the upshot?'

'You know what it's like, trying to put a kid like that with a regular foster carer.'

Clare shifted uneasily. 'What do you mean?'

'I means the placement fell through.'

'So, what happens to the boy?'

'They've found him some sort of short-term emergency housing.'

'He's four years old,' said Clare. 'You're not telling me he's going into a contingency unit?'

'Brighthaven.' Roderick shrugged. 'What can you do?'

'You're not serious?' But she could tell by the look on his face that he was. Contingency units were used as a last resort, usually for older children with multiple behaviour problems. One of her clients had been placed in Brighthaven a few days ago. Aiden: a troubled teenager, in and out of state care all his life — guilty of sex offences against younger boys. Brighthaven was a risky place for any child, let alone a vulnerable four-year-old.

'Jack did tell me his name,' she said. 'And Rod - Aiden's just been placed in Brighthaven.'

Clare watched his face as he made the connection: puzzled at first, then concerned and finally, pale. She handed him his phone. 'You call Kim and tell her to bring the boy back or I will.'

Roderick opened his mouth as if he was about to argue, then smiled. 'That attitude,' he said, 'is what makes you such a terrific advocate. You have until the end of the day to find him a new placement.'

Clare returned to her desk and began to make calls. One call. Two calls. Three …

Five o'clock. Déjà vu, all of them back in Clare's office. Jack sat on her lap again, clutching his bag of Pokémon toys. Kim finished her phone call and wrote something down on a notepad.

'Well?' asked Clare.

Kim looked grim. 'There is nowhere else,' she said. 'He must return to Brighthaven.'

Clare shook her head. 'I'll take him.' The words startled out of her mouth. 'For a little while,' she said. 'Until his mother comes back.'

Kim looked at Clare for a long time without speaking. 'A foster care assessment takes time,' she said at last. 'Months.'

'What about a kinship care assessment? Can you do that?' Clare already knew Kim could. Kinship assessments could be fast-tracked in emergencies, and only rough guidelines existed as to who a kinship carer might be. There was nothing to legally rule her out.

Kim frowned. 'It's a little unorthodox, seeing as you and John aren't related.' Another long pause. 'But the term *kinship* is a flexible concept. For the purposes of this assessment we can perhaps regard you as a person who shares a community connection with the child.'

'Perfect.' Clare could feel herself smiling and tried to arrange her face into a more professional expression. It was no use. She beamed as Jack wrapped his arms round her waist.

Kim gave Clare a probing look. 'Are you sure you want to do this? Jack has very complex needs. He belongs in a disability placement.'

'Do you have one of those?' asked Clare. They both knew she didn't. 'Just get on with it.'

'I've seen people like you before,' said Kim. 'You think that if you just love a child enough, you can cure him - make him normal. Love can't cure autism.'

'Who said anything about love? The kid needs a safe, temporary place to stay. You don't have one, so I'm offering. Nothing more, nothing less.'

'As long as you know what you're getting into. It will only be until we find John somewhere else, so don't get too attached.'

Clare nodded and Kim finally seemed satisfied.

'Okay, let's get started. I need to be finished by six,' Kim said. 'We've got tickets to the football. The Brisbane Bears elimination final.' Her eyes lit up at the prospect, and she began crossing questions off on the form in front of her. 'That's not pertinent to you ... nor that ... okay. How do you propose to meet the needs of such a challenging child?'

Clare didn't have a clue. Kim believed the boy was mute and Clare knew he wasn't, so they didn't even agree on what those needs were. But Clare would play the game if it meant she could take Jack home.

'Suppose John shows aggression,' said Kim. 'What would you do?'

Clare tried to remember what she was learning at puppy school with her new dog, Samson. 'I'd try ignoring it. Provide no response, no talking, no eye contact. Oh, and I'd give positive reinforcement when his behaviour improved.' Clare had almost said that she'd give Jack a dog biscuit.

Kim looked impressed. 'Excellent. I see you've done some child psychology along the way. That will be a great help.'

Clare nodded and smiled.

'What else might you try?'

'Um ... Redirecting. I'd distract him with a toy when he starts to get agitated and refocus him on a calming activity.' Kim beamed, and ticked off a series of boxes. The puppy training technique for children was working like a charm.

'What about discipline?' asked Kim. 'What are your thoughts?'

'No physical discipline, obviously,' She wracked her brains for some more canine tips. Of course, crate training. 'Time out, perhaps?' said Clare. 'Or a naughty chair?'

Kim moved on to easier questions. Stuff about the layout of her flat, and where Jack would sleep. For some reason, when asked about relationships, Clare didn't mention Adam. Was it because they hadn't been dating for that long? No, a year was long enough. It was more that she didn't want Kim talking to him. Adam wouldn't approve of her impulsive decision any more than Roderick had when she'd suggested it. *'You know the golden rule,'* he'd said. *'Don't get involved. A lawyer who breaks that rule is less effective professionally, loses objectivity, can't function. You know all this, Clare. Let it go, will you?'*

'I'll let it go,' she'd responded. 'Just as soon as you tell me you've found somewhere safe for Jack.'

As the assessment continued, Clare wasn't entirely forthcoming about Samson either. German shepherds had a bad reputation with some people, so Samson was magically transformed into a cuddly labrador pup.

'Before we proceed any further, you should see this.' Kim handed Clare a few stapled pages titled *Report by Specialist Children Services on John Brown.*

Her eyes ran down a daunting litany of behavioural problems listed by the clinical psychologist. *Repeated and severe head banging, extreme tantrums, food obsessions.* Clare took a deep breath. *Hitting others, hitting himself, screaming, spitting, biting, bed-wetting, soiling.* What on earth was she getting herself into? *John has failed to develop language. He only communicates through yelling or by inflections of grunting (animal noises). His mother reports that John never cries. Given his diagnosis of mid- to high-range autism, he may never learn to talk.* Perversely, this piece of misinformation cheered Clare up. Jack could definitely talk. If that part of the report was wrong, maybe the rest was too?

An hour later and the assessment was complete. 'You'll need to book him in for a general health check with your doctor.' Kim stood up. 'And get his vaccinations up to date.'

'Of course,' said Clare. That reminded her - Samson was due for his next set of shots too.

'There's funding available for child care,' Kim continued. 'You can arrange that yourself. Just make sure I sign off on it once it's organised.'

Clare hadn't thought so far ahead. What about that crèche just around the corner from home? Jolly Juniors? No, Jolly Jumbucks. And it was right opposite Samson's doggy day-care. She could drop them both off on her way to work. How long would those places care for Jack in one stretch, she wondered? Whole weekends, maybe? As long as they did late nights so she could still go out with Adam. He wouldn't be able to stay at her place for now, not unless he jumped through some hoops, like submitting to a police check, and she couldn't imagine him doing that. But perhaps, despite her misgivings, he might actually warm to the little boy? It was hard to say with Adam.

Kim handed Clare a business card with her phone number and an after-hours contact. 'For emergencies,' she said. 'There's a spare car seat in my boot. I'll just go get it. And I'll give you a ring in a day or two; see how you're getting on.'

As Kim went to shake hands, she reached past Jack, who was still perched on Clare's knee. The boy bit Kim on the arm. Clare could see his little teeth marks, opposing white crescents on Kim's pink skin. Jack growled low in the back of his throat.

'Good luck,' said Kim, rubbing her arm and frowning. 'You'll need it. I'll meet you outside with the car seat.'

Clare nodded her thanks as Kim left the room. Had she lost all perspective? Lost all judgement? Was she just flattered that Jack seemed to like her and nobody else? She stroked his hair and he snuggled into her shoulder. Clare hugged him tight. What did it matter if her motivation was flawed? All that mattered was that Jack stayed safe and happy until Taylor came back. 'Come on,' she said, taking his hand. 'Let's go home.'

CHAPTER 3

The phone rang as they were almost out the front door.

'For you.' Debbie held her hand over the receiver and whispered, 'It's Adam.'

Oh no - the ballet. It took Clare a second to choose a white lie. 'Adam, sorry, my phone's been off.' Clare took a deep breath. 'I'm sick, Adam … yes, a pretty high temperature … it just came on so quickly. Apologise to your sister for me, won't you? Perhaps Heather could go instead? … Yes, I know you don't need me to organise your social life … No, don't come round. I want an early night.' She could see Kim through the window, holding the car seat and looking cross. 'Got to run.'

Clare ended the call. She'd almost added *I love you* but had thought better of it. Letting Adam down like she had, then lying to him? These weren't especially loving things to do. And anyway, they were at that awkward stage of their relationship. Clare ignored the little voice that suggested the *awkward* stage was lasting a long time. Adam told her that he loved her in the heat of the night, but the phrase hadn't yet passed his lips when the sun was up. Clare had once tested the water with a lunchtime *I love you* and had been met with stony silence. She'd almost died of embarrassment.

With a relieved wave to Debbie, she and Jack were out the door. Kim helped her fit the car seat and hurried off. Clare struggled to strap the wriggling boy in. He slapped her in the face. 'Ow,' she said. 'Stop that.' This was already harder than she thought it would be.

A few minutes later, they were climbing the stairs to her flat. Clare unlocked the door and Jack trailed in after her. At least he'd let go of her leg. 'Home sweet home,' she said. 'What do you think?'

Jack marched into the kitchenette. He dropped his bag of toys, opened the fridge and began pulling out the contents. Bread, cheese, chocolate, carrots, half a tomato, lemons. He tipped over a milk carton. The liquid dripped onto the grey slate floor. He took a few bites from the cheese, a few bites from the chocolate and then dropped them in favour of bowling lemons along the tiles.

'Jack, no.' Clare retrieved the carton and dabbed at the white puddle with a sponge from the sink. Jack bowled a lemon at her legs. Clare caught it, put it on a high shelf and collected the others. When she tried to wrest the last piece of fruit from Jack's grasp, he screamed and hurled it at her face. Clare dodged just in time. If her reflexes hadn't been so swift, she would have had a black eye. It left her shaken. 'You'll make quite a wicket keeper one day.'

Jack ran into the minimalist, open-plan lounge room, bounced off the treadmill in the corner, then flung himself down on the white Georgetti couch. Not so white any more, not since Samson. She groaned. Samson. She'd forgotten all about him. She'd have to ring doggy day care. Maybe Helga could drop him off?

Clare sat down and the little boy hid his head under Samson's old blanket. 'Jack?' She lifted the corner. 'Jack?' He peered back at her, his expression blank. Pale skin, red tired-looking eyes. She picked up the remote and turned on the television, flicking through until she found a children's channel. Strange cartoon animals appeared out of magic balls, shooting fire and water and battling each other.

'Hey,' she said. 'Jack, look, it's a Pokémon. It's Tepig.' Sure enough, an animated version of the funny orange pig was running around on the screen. Jack peeped out from under the blanket. 'Do you want some milk?'

He nodded.

Clare pushed the glazed coffee table against the couch. She went into the kitchen and picked up his bag of toys before pouring a glass of milk. Skim. It was all she had in the fridge. That and Chablis. Clare took Jack the drink and the bag of Pokémon. He rewarded her with an uncertain smile, the first since McDonald's. She pulled up a chair next to him. He drank down the milk, curled up and promptly fell asleep. With a great, relieved sigh, Clare pulled Samson's blanket up to his chin. She sneaked back to the kitchen, poured herself a generous amount of wine and sat down to think. The fog of emotion was clearing, allowing a little more clarity of thought. The enormity of what she'd done was finally hitting home and it was giving her a headache.

Her phone rang. Clare scrambled to retrieve it from her handbag before the jazzy tune woke Jack. It was Helga, director of doggy day-care, a veritable Valkyrie when it came to defending the rights of her canine charges - sometimes even from their misguided owners. This was, apparently, one of those times. 'Samson is still waiting to be collected, Clare. May I remind you that this is becoming an all too regular occurrence.'

'I'm sorry,' said Clare. 'Could you perhaps keep him overnight?'

'A dog is a living, breathing, emotional being, Clare. Not some object that you can keep in the cupboard until you feel like playing with him.'

Clare's cheeks burned. 'Sorry. I'm not really set up for a dog.' She regretted the remark as soon as it had passed her lips, although it was true enough. Managing a German shepherd puppy in an upmarket, second-floor apartment was difficult to say the least.

'Then why did you get one?'

'Samson was my father's dog. I only took him on a month ago, when Dad died suddenly.'

There was a long pause before Helga spoke. 'My condolences,' she said. 'You should consider rehoming him.'

'No!' Clare's raised voice caused Jack to stir in his sleep. 'Dad loved that dog. He'd never forgive me.'

'Don't sacrifice Samson on the altar of your guilt,' said Helga. 'Puppies who spend too long in kennels can suffer long-term damage. Aggression, separation anxiety, depression – an inability to properly bond. Particularly with a dog as large and strong as Samson, the risk must not be overlooked.'

'I'll do better, I promise,' said Clare. 'But I honestly can't come and get him tonight. Could you … could you perhaps drop him off?'

Another long pause. 'Will I see Samson at obedience school this week?' asked Helga. 'You missed last Sunday's session.'

That was blackmail. 'Yes,' she said. 'Of course. We'll be there.'

'Very well, Clare. I'll drop him off around seven.'

'Thank you, Helga.' Clare switched off her phone. Adam was out for the night so he wouldn't ring. In any case, the last thing she wanted was to talk to anybody. Clare pulled a stool up to the breakfast bar, sat down and drained her wine glass. She squeezed her eyes shut, trying to ward off the growing ache in her skull. It had been a very long Friday and the weekend wasn't panning out quite like she'd planned.

CHAPTER 4

Clare opened her eyes. It took a moment to position herself in the new day. That's right, it was Saturday. Her tongue was furry, a sure sign she'd been drinking. But her head barely ached, which meant she hadn't overdone it. Good. A glance at the clock. Eight o'clock already? Samson would be busting.

Clare yawned and headed for the lounge room. She remembered about Jack just as the stink hit her nose and the chaos came into view. Samson was in the kitchen, scoffing cornflakes and milk from her Venetian glass fruit bowl, which was on the floor. The dog acknowledged Clare's presence with a wag of his tail.

She rescued the bowl. Jack sat cross-legged on the tiles beside Samson, the cereal box upended above his open mouth. A shower of golden flakes rained down on them both. But that wasn't the worst of it. In the lounge room, mounds of fluffy white stuffing spilled from the couch cushions. It looked like a fairy floss machine had spun out of control. Clare shrieked and hurried over to inspect the damage. It wasn't just the cushions; the upholstery was ripped too, a long tear down the back. The matching drapes were wet and stained where Samson had lifted his leg. Her bare foot squelched in something soft and warm. 'Eeew.'

Clare held her breath and changed direction, hopping for the bathroom. She sat on the edge of the tub, extended her smeared foot and turned on the tap as hot as she could bear it. The water turned brown and swirled down the plughole.

Her couch. Her beautiful, insanely expensive couch. It had been Adam's idea to buy an imported Italian sofa. It had cost almost as much as her car, and now it was ruined.

Samson had been an instant hit with Jack, and vice versa. Last night, before Helga even handed him over, the dog zeroed in on the sleeping child. Helga had followed the direction of his gaze, seeing the lump on the couch beneath Samson's blanket. Jack's head was just visible. 'A child?' Clare nodded. 'Children under twelve should not be left alone with dogs,' said Helga. 'You can never completely trust them.'

'But Samson is so friendly,' said Clare. 'I can't imagine him hurting anybody.'

'I meant the children,' said Helga. 'It's the children you can't trust.'

'I'll supervise Jack very closely,' promised Clare.

Helga cast one last, disapproving glance at Jack, gave Samson a consoling pat, then left them to it. But despite Clare's best efforts, it wasn't long before Samson jumped on top of the little boy. Jack woke up yelling. Clare dived for the dog's collar and tried to drag him off. Samson ignored her, didn't even seem to notice her tugging. He thoroughly licked Jack's face, tail thrashing with excitement. The little boy stopped yelling and threw his arms around the dog's thick ruff. Then he'd laughed – that pealing, musical laughter that had so surprised and delighted Clare at McDonald's.

The same laughter that she could hear now.

Clare turned off the tap, swung her legs out of the tub and returned to the lounge room, where Jack and Samson were playing tug-of-war with a tea towel. 'Samson.' The dog dropped the tea towel and bounced over to her.

She called him into the kitchen, encouraging him to lick the cornflakes and pools of milk off the floor. Clare picked up the empty cereal box. How would she tell Adam about the couch? He loved that couch, went on and on about its superb quality, its elegant craftsmanship. He waxed lyrical about Italian design, how it was unmistakable, but impossible to define. Its flair, its innovation, its beauty of line and function. You'd think it was his couch.

When she turned round to put the box in the bin, there was Jack on hands and knees beside Samson, licking the floor too. 'Oh, Jack, no.' She swept him up, and he wrapped his arms around her neck and grinned. Such a sweet smile for such a naughty boy. It was hard to stay mad at him.

Clare ran a bath, undressed Jack and wrinkled her nose. His little trousers were stiff with grime, underpants caked with faeces, jumper and T-shirt frayed at the seams. She half-expected to see bruises on his skinny body, signs of physical abuse. But apart from a few normal bumps and scratches, she found nothing. Thank goodness for that. She tipped some shampoo under the running tap to make bubbles - just like Grandma used to do for her. Jack tried to climb in. 'Wait.' Clare turned off the taps and watched him laugh and splash, catching great handfuls of suds and tossing them into the air. What a sweet kid. Taylor must be missing him terribly.

Clare gathered his discarded clothes, threw them into the washing machine and brewed herself a coffee. There was so much to do before Monday. Arrange child care. Buy Jack clothes, and a camp bed or something for the spare room. And she'd promised Helga she'd show up to dog training on Sunday morning.

The bell rang. Oh no, not Adam. Clare bundled Samson into the living room. 'Sit, Samson. Stay,' she said, without much hope. It wasn't the first time she'd regretted the absence of doors in her airy open-plan apartment. But to her surprise the dog cocked his head as if he was considering her request, then sank to his haunches. Clare whispered a quiet *thank you*, took a deep, steadying breath and answered the door.

A sigh of relief - it was Debbie. 'I've finished typing up that transcript.' She thrust a manila folder at Clare. 'Thought you might need it over the weekend.' A flimsy excuse for snooping. She peered past

Clare into the apartment. 'How are you getting on?' Clare wasn't quick enough and Debbie was in before she knew it. 'What's that pong?' Debbie's eyes widened when she saw the kitchen, widened more when she saw the lounge room and its clouds of stuffing. 'It looks like world war three. Did that little boy do all this?'

No, thought Clare. He had some help.

'Where is he?' asked Debbie.

'In the bath,' said Clare, but she was more interested in where Samson was. She couldn't see him.

Debbie explored further, peering first into the bedroom, then into the bathroom. She disappeared through the door. 'Is your dog supposed to be in here?'

Clare followed her. Samson and Jack were sitting together in the bathtub. Jack was emptying a bottle of shampoo onto the dog's back. A second empty bottle lay discarded on the floor, which was being swamped from foam waves made by Samson's wagging tail. Shining mountains of suds lay everywhere, casting thousands of tiny rainbows.

'That's right,' said Clare, trying to sound matter of fact. 'They're sharing. I've always believed in being water wise.'

It was afternoon before Clare finally had the flat shipshape. Kitchen spotless, bathroom mopped, carpet cleaned. Air freshener sprayed about. She'd stuffed as much filling back into the couch as she could, and binned the rest. Gaffer tape worked well to repair the ripped upholstery. Pity it didn't come in white. The couch looked a little deflated, but you'd hardly be able to notice, from a distance.

Jack's clothes were washed and dried. He'd cooperated when being dressed and eaten a sandwich without incident. She'd plonked him on the couch in front of the television, but now he and Samson were wrestling again. Clare glanced around at the order she'd reimposed. They were bound to mess it up all over again, so what was the point of being too picky? The apartment seemed suddenly crowded. Nowhere near big enough for a woman and a dog and a boy.

She called to her charges. 'Walkies.'

They headed for the park. Jack no longer hung onto Clare's leg - he hung onto Samson. And instead of pulling ahead, dragging Clare in his wake as he usually did, Samson matched the child's pace, slowing down when he lagged, waiting patiently for Jack to grasp his collar again. There was no doubt about it — far easier to walk the pair of them together, than to walk either of them separately.

A smiling, elderly couple came towards them. 'What a charming picture,' said the old lady. 'You must be so very proud.'

And suddenly Clare was. So very proud of Jack and Samson.

'Those two make quite a team,' said the old man with a grin, stopping to give Samson a pat. He reminded Clare of her grandfather. 'Every child needs a best friend like that. Your son's a lucky boy.'

Your son. They'd mistaken Jack for her son. Well, why not? She was twenty-seven now, more than old enough to have a four-year-old child, although she didn't feel old enough or responsible enough to be anybody's mother. She didn't even feel responsible enough to be a dog owner, and Helga apparently agreed with her. Clare's thoughts turned to Jack's real mother, Taylor. Just twenty-years-old. Where was she at this very minute? Had she eaten today? Was she thinking about her son?

They entered the park through a shady corridor of lilly pilly trees. Usually Clare headed for the Blue Dog reserve. The park had two large, fenced off-leash areas. Blue for big dogs, and red for smaller dogs and puppies under nine months. She'd started Samson off in the Red Dog reserve. He was a puppy after all, albeit a large one. But he'd mistaken his little companions for targets in a merry game of fetch, and had insisted on chasing and retrieving the smallest ones and proudly bringing them to Clare. Unharmed, thank goodness. Clare marvelled at how gently he'd placed the little wriggling dogs at her feet. The other owners hadn't been quite as appreciative. She'd retreated, red-faced, and from then on joined the assortment of labradoodles and other pooches roaming the big dog park.

Today she made a detour. Jack had spied the playground. He released his hold on Samson's collar and dashed off to the slides. Samson jumped and whined and dragged Clare after him. She hadn't paid much attention to the playground before. What a great place for kids, with its rockers and tunnels, bright blue bridges and spinning poles – even a sunken pirate ship. There were children playing and laughing in the sunshine. Clare used her hand to shade her eyes, and settled down with Samson in the shade to watch, her back against a fig tree. Jack was having a lovely time, swinging and bouncing and hiding. Every now and then he turned to look at her and she waved. For once Samson sat quietly beside her, eyes trained on Jack.

The park overlooked the picturesque Rainbow River. Clare turned to watch an elegant egret stalk among the reeds. The scene was strangely familiar. Red gums lining the river bank, shedding bark in colourful ribbons. The single, sharp alarm call of a native hen. Flotillas of ducks floating by, trailed by fluffy ducklings. Diving grebes. A shag on a rock, wings hung out to dry.

A tall tree stood on an island in the river. A distinctive tree. Prehistoric looking, with a domed crown, sharp, glossy leaves and giant, green pinecones the size of footballs. The sense of déjà vu grew stronger, and then it struck her. Currawong. The river bend at Currawong Creek, her grandparents' property on the Darling Downs. How long had it been since she'd thought of it?

Samson whimpered and rose to his feet. Clare soothed him with a few words and stroked his head absentmindedly. Memories flooded in. Endless summers. She and her brother leaving the house after one of Grandma's giant breakfasts and not coming home till dark. Clare could almost see Ryan now, sitting on the river bank with his line in the water, waiting for a bite. She smiled. As a girl, she'd always been too squeamish for fishing. If she was ever on the spot when Ryan caught something, her torrent of tears always convinced him to let it go. She preferred catching yabbies behind the bore head and keeping them as pets. Currawong's dam was full of the pretty blue crayfish. She drew back the lens of her mind's eye and a landscape appeared: the view from the old homestead across to the shining tower of the Southern Cross windmill and the dam. More of a lake, really. A shining expanse of sweet fresh water, fed by the Great Artesian Basin. A vast underground ocean, millions of years old. She'd written a story about it at school: a cross between *Journey to the Centre of the Earth* and *Alice in Wonderland*. A girl escapes from her bossy mother down a wombat hole to the shores of the Great Artesian Basin. She makes friends with the plesiosaurs that live there, grows a long neck and flippers, and she never goes home.

Clare hadn't been to Currawong Creek since she was a child. It was the only permanent home she could remember, a precious constant in an ever-changing world. With Dad in the military, she and Ryan had grown up as army brats. Their childhood had been shaped by the constant loss of friendships, by never having a hometown, or any place to belong. It was hard on them and on their mother. Clare must have been about eleven years old on that final visit to Currawong. It was the same summer that Mum had left them. Afterwards Dad had discouraged all contact with her side of the family. Clare had lost both her mother and her grandparents in one cruel blow.

She'd watched her father fight his way out from under the loneliness and grief, fight to obliterate the memories of their former life. And Clare had respected his wishes, all this time. The dreams of Currawong, its creeks and mountains, had slowly faded. Even when Grandma died they'd only sent flowers. That was ten years ago, and now Dad was dead as well. How was Grandad, she dared to wonder? He'd have to be at least seventy by now. Clare could still picture him, a pair of huge clydesdale horses in tow, crossing the stable yard to the cart shed.

Those clydesdales had seemed bigger than elephants when she was a child. But they were gentle giants and she couldn't ever remember being afraid. Not even when Ryan dared her to lead their pony, Smudge, under the belly of Rastus, Currawong's enormous stallion. Eighteen hands, he'd stood. Rastus had spooked and reared, a tonne of horseflesh looming above her, blotting out the sky. His platter-sized hooves had crashed to earth just inches from her head. But she'd known with calm certainty that Rastus wouldn't hurt her, that he would do everything to avoid her.

That was a lifetime ago. Those things had happened to a different person. After finishing school she'd studied law on her father's advice and built a career in the city.

She didn't have many friends, but that didn't bother her. Childhood experience had taught Clare that friendships didn't last anyway. It was an advantage that she didn't have a busy social calendar to distract from her professional ambitions. Her life up until now had suited very well.

Sixteen years had passed since she'd last seen Grandad. At first, each time a hot north wind blew, it had reminded her of Currawong and she'd ached for her grandparents, but she'd learned the knack of letting go. She'd built a fence around her heart, walling out the pain, growing into a self-contained, studious teenager who'd tried hard to please her father. In the end she'd hardly thought of them at all. Until today. It was only natural, she supposed, to think of family with her father's death so fresh. Grandad probably didn't even know that Dad was gone. Who would have told him?

Samson started to bark, then with an almighty tug he wrenched the lead from her hand, dragging her away from her recollections.

Clare jumped to her feet. The sun was still in her eyes and it was hard to see. She shielded her face with a hand and scanned the playground. Where was Jack?

'Jack,' she yelled. 'Jack!'

Clare sprinted down the hill after Samson. The dog ran straight as an arrow, and like an arrow, he seemed unable to deviate from his course. He ploughed straight through a group of children.

'Is that your dog?' asked a red-faced woman nursing a screaming toddler.

'I'm reporting you,' said another, comforting a crying child at the same time. 'Dogs like that should be put down.'

'So sorry,' called Clare, putting on a burst of speed. She was well out of earshot before anybody else had a chance to complain. Clare crested the hill and stopped to catch her breath. In the distance, at the far side of the barbecue area, stood a red and yellow striped marquee. Bunches of bright balloons were strung from poles. Someone was handing out plates to a line of waiting children, while parents milled about. Clare ran closer for a better look. She could see now. A colourful clown held aloft an elaborate, castle-shaped birthday cake. Candles in the shape of fluttering flags graced the towers and turrets, along with tiny chocolate cannons. Its moat, complete with candy swans, glinted in the sun. A truly magnificent creation. A work of art - and Samson was on a collision course with both the clown and the cake.

'Samson!' yelled Clare. She'd never get there in time. It was like being witness to a looming train wreck, and being powerless to stop it. Everything seemed to be happening in slow motion. Too late now. Samson bowled the clown over and the cake toppled majestically to the grass. Toy soldiers leaped from the battlements as it fell. The poor clown landed face down in the ruins, while kids ran screaming in every direction. All except one - Jack.

Jack had crashed the party, and had been standing in line with a plate. Now he trotted over to the smashed cake and, using both fists, started shovelling chocolate and cream off the ground, and into his mouth. One turret. A piece of blue moat. The drawbridge. Then Samson grabbed a mouthful of Jack's jeans. He began dragging the child back towards Clare by the seat of his pants, ripping the threadbare fabric.

'Help!' A woman tried to move towards Jack, but her stilettos sank into the grass. Clare guessed her to be the party host. 'Somebody help that little boy. That brute of a dog's got him.'

The clown dashed forward. Clare winced as he kicked Samson in the jaw, but the dog maintained his grip. The clown grabbed hold of Jack, and played a brief game of tug of war, until Jack sank his teeth into the man's clutching hand. The clown let go, yelling that he'd been bitten.

'Get back,' said the woman. 'That dog's dangerous. It just bit this poor man.'

'Not the dog,' wailed the clown. 'The boy. It was that f**king boy who bit me.'

Some kids gawked at him, open-mouthed. Others stared at each other and giggled. 'That clown's *ruuude*,' said one. 'He just said a bad word.' The parents looked even more horrified than before.

Clare skidded to a halt in the midst of the chaos, planting herself squarely between Jack and Samson and the angry horde. She held up her hands, palms out, and forced her face into a smile. 'I'm Clare,' she said. 'And little Jack here …' She placed a protective hand on his shoulder. 'He was lost. Thank goodness my dog found him.'

Samson barked and the crowd, as one, took a step back.

'He got a little carried away, that's all. A little too enthusiastic … a little over-affectionate.' She grabbed hold of Samson's trailing lead and picked up Jack. 'Very sorry about the cake. It was absolutely spectacular, by the way. Let me pay for it.' Clare put Jack down again and pulled her purse from the tote bag slung over her shoulder. 'I insist.'

'Do I know you?' asked the host.

Clare maintained her smile. It was beginning to make her cheeks ache.

'And you mean to tell me that's your boy?' The woman's tone was accusing.

Clare nodded. She could feel her smile fading.

'So, he was never invited?'

'No. Jack's a blow in, I'm afraid. I do apologise.'

A confused chattering of *I thought he was with you,* began among the guests. Clare unzipped her purse, plucked out the notes inside, around two hundred dollars' worth, and shoved them at the woman. Then the three of them made a run for it, Jack and Samson laughing and barking as they sped away. Back on the street, Jack's sticky hand sneaked into hers. The same damned question niggled again. What had she got herself into?

CHAPTER 5

Clare woke to Jack jumping on the bed. She had a vague memory of him doing the same thing earlier on when it was barely light, and of her pulling the pillow over her head and going back to sleep. Clare groaned. Sunday morning, but not like any Sunday morning she could remember. She was used to suiting herself, waking in her own time, at her own pace. She sniffed. There was a sickly, sweet odour in the air. Clare glanced at the clock on her bedside table. Why couldn't she see the time? She raised herself up on one elbow. A large tumbler was in the way, brimming with something that looked suspiciously like urine. What on earth?

Jack bounced off the bed, picked up the glass in both hands and offered it to her, slopping its pale contents over the doona. She recoiled and sniffed again. Wine, stale wine. He'd been in the fridge. 'Jack, no.' What if he'd been drinking it himself? She imagined Kim's reproachful face as they pumped Jack's stomach in the emergency room.

Clare prepared to tell him off, but something in his expression puzzled her, gave her pause. It was an expression she'd not seen on his face before. Eager, hopeful … shyly proud. Clare was trained to get into people's heads, discover their deepest motivations. How else could you portray them sympathetically to a magistrate? Everyone had a reason for what they did. The trick was to pick it. And then it hit her – Jack wasn't being naughty. He wanted to please her by bringing her the wine. Heaven knows she'd swilled enough of the stuff last night. Another evening of drinking alone, she thought ruefully. How was a four-year-old supposed to know that a beverage she'd enjoyed so much last night, would be repulsive to her in the morning? It was touching really. Thank heavens she hadn't scolded him.

Clare took a sip, trying not to screw up her face. 'Thanks, Jack.' He flashed a swift smile and scampered from the room. Clare fell back on the pillow, still tired. Her tongue was thick and furry. She hadn't brushed her teeth last night. Neither had Jack. Jack didn't even have a toothbrush. What sort of a foster mother was she? With an immense effort she threw off the doona. The room smelled like a bar. She glanced at herself in the mirror. Lank, tangled hair that needed wash-ing. Dark rings beneath bloodshot eyes. Her white T-shirt had a big brown stain down the front, courtesy of last night's tub of chocolate ice-cream. Lovely.

Clare emerged from her bedroom to find Jack asleep on the couch in front of cartoons. It was funny how he could just fall asleep like that. One minute a bundle of energy, the next minute, dead to the world. By the looks of things he'd been up half the night. There were no books left on the shelf. Instead they were strewn over the floor, together with a mangled loaf of bread, its soft middle scooped out. Crumbs everywhere. Biro and lipstick scribbles on the wall. A lidless tub of melted ice-cream on a chair. Double rows of spice jars marched like little soldiers along the artificial turf of Samson's doggy loo, flanking a procession of Pokémon toys.

No serious damage. You couldn't really blame the kid, she thought, considering there wasn't much for him to play with. She'd have to fix that, buy some toys. Put things up high. Fit some childproof locks. Samson whined from his crate. Normally on Sunday she took him on a morning walk to the park. She thought back to the chaos of yester-day. No, the park was off limits for the time being. Anyway, with Jack flaked out on the sofa, she couldn't really leave the flat at all. How on earth did full-time parents manage? She was stuck at home unless she woke him up, and that might be disastrous. As Dad used to say, best to let sleeping dogs lie. Samson would need to use his inside toilet this morning.

Clare cleared away the spice jars, and the toys, and the tiny mirrored elephant with the raised trunk that stood in pride of place on top of the wooden wee post. She dumped them in a sink of hot, soapy water. She fetched the key to the padlock and released Samson from his crate. The dog bounded obediently to the patch of fake grass. He didn't squat like a puppy any more to empty his bladder. Instead he lifted his leg, half-missing the fake tree trunk and leaving a mustard coloured spray pattern on the wall. Oh dear. She'd bought the Supersize Pooch model, but the poky contraption looked like it was designed more for a poodle than for a German shepherd.

Samson trotted into the kitchen and fetched his lead from the hook. Clare shook her head. 'Not this morning.' She poured herself a coffee and sat down in a chair by the window. Samson cocked his head and inspected her face, confirming she was serious. Then he leaped for the treadmill, evenly positioning his great paws, quivering a little with anticipation. He gave a soft whimper. Clare put her forefinger to her lips. 'Shh … not now. You'll wake Jack.' Samson trotted to the sideboard, stood on his hind legs and picked up the remote control in his mouth. He dumped it in Clare's lap. She hadn't realised dogs were so clever.

'Okay, just on slow.'

The dog repositioned himself with a joyful wag of his tail. The treadmill beeped twice and ground into action. Clare kept a close eye on Jack, but he didn't stir. Samson watched her as he padded along the rubber belt, ears pricked, his eyes pleading. She knew that look. He whined again. He'd bark soon if he didn't get his way. She sped up the treadmill until Samson was galloping along, and wondered suddenly what her grandfather would make of it. She recalled a timeless scene – driving down the winding lane to Merriang as a child, sitting high and proud beside Grandad in the sulky, as he cracked the carriage whip above Baron's broad back. Currawong's energetic pair of dalmatians, Pongo and Perdita, leading the way to town, tails aloft, getting all the gossip with their twitching noses. By comparison, Samson here, toiling away on a stainless steel treadmill in a second-floor apartment was a sad and sorry sight. She felt a rush of sympathy for him. Helga was right - this was no life for a dog.

A knock came at the door and Samson leaped from the treadmill in a flurry of barking. His voice was growing deeper and louder every day. What if it was Mr Jacobs, the secretary of the building's body corporate? Strata management had given her permission to keep a dog. Luckily they hadn't asked about the breed. Samson must be pretty close to breaking the *peaceful enjoyment* noise provision by now, and it was Sunday morning for Christ's sake. Why couldn't he just shut up?

Clare opened the door. It wasn't Mr Jacobs. Worse than that, it was Adam. Clare shook her head in disbelief. How could it be Adam? The first time in the entire twelve months of their relationship that he'd dropped by unannounced, and she just happened to look a wreck. And the place was a mess; utterly trashed. It wasn't fair.

Samson growled and Adam backed up a fraction.

'I'll put him away.' Clare grabbed Samson's collar and dragged him off to his crate.

'Feeling better?' Adam asked from the doorway. 'You missed a real treat on Friday.' He flashed his handsome smile, but she didn't respond. 'I tried to ring' he said, 'but your phone's turned off.'

He searched her face with his piercing grey eyes. Sunday morning, and Adam was still the picture of style. White oxford shirt with rolled-up sleeves exposing smooth, tanned forearms. Her favourite Borrelli boot-leg jeans, the ones with the hand-stitched, twisted seams. A razor-straight part in his, dark flicked-back hair. His mouth was straight too, and the bridge of his nose. Everything about him was sharply defined.

Clare, by contrast, was a frump. She needed to shower, to change, to wash her hair. She needed to make Adam go away and come back in half an hour. She needed for him not to go into the lounge room and expect to sit down on the couch. Clare ducked into the bathroom and dragged a brush through her hair. Not that it would help much. Combed greasy didn't look much better than tangled greasy. She spared herself by not looking in the mirror.

Jack ran in and clamped onto her leg.

'Clare?' Adam's voice was uncertain, but he'd obviously moved from the doorway into the lounge room. 'Clare? Who's the kid?' She froze, as if she might thereby evade detection, '...and what happened to the couch?'

Clare looked down at Jack's anxious, upturned face and gave him what she hoped was a reassuring smile. Dogs could sense your mood, that's what Helga said. Maybe kids could, too? She didn't want Jack to think there was anything wrong. And anyway, was there anything wrong? Not really. Her vanity was taking a bit of a hit, that was all. Clare took a deep breath, picked Jack up and went into the lounge room.

Adam stared at them, a confused expression on his face. 'The dog was bad enough, Clare. But a kid? And who demolished the apartment? Were you robbed?'

'This is Jack,' she said, pushing the little boy forward. 'He's the son of a client who's-' She'd been about to say *who's done a runner.* 'A client who's unable to look after him this weekend.'

'Isn't that a bit ... unorthodox?' said Adam. He knew very well that it was. He was a barrister, a rising star. Clare couldn't imagine what he must think about her getting so personally involved with a client. It was about as unprofessional as you could get.

'There were no disability placements available,' she said. 'You can't put such a little boy into a residential unit. He'd be eaten alive.'

She realised her mistake at once.

'Disability?' said Adam. He leaned close and peered at Jack, like he was a bug under a microscope. 'What the hell's wrong with him then?'

Jack spat in his face. Adam recoiled and plucked a tissue from the box on the shelf. 'Dirty little bugger,' he said, wiping his cheek. 'He could have AIDS or anything.'

'Would you please not talk about Jack like that,' said Clare. 'He's not deaf.'

'Okay then. He's not deaf, so what is he? What's wrong with him,' asked Adam again, this time from a safe distance.

Jack ran to the couch and hid beneath Samson's blanket. 'They say he's autistic,' said Clare. 'But I think they're wrong.' She could hear the defiant tilt in her voice.

Adam indicated the ruin all around. 'The flat looks like this and you think they're wrong. *You* do. You — who've had so much experience with children.'

She hated it when he got sarcastic like this.

'Didn't you tell me just last week that you couldn't stand kids? That you didn't have a clue about them? And now you're a f**king expert?'

She wished he wouldn't swear like that in front of Jack. 'This is different,' she said. 'There was nobody else. Jesus, Adam. It's just for a weekend.'

'So that's why you couldn't come on Friday' said Adam. 'You weren't sick at all, were you?' She didn't deny it. He snorted. 'Not much of a relationship if we can't be honest with each other.' It was the first thing he'd said that she agreed with.

They stared at each other in silence for a few moments. Adam frowned then said, 'Sorry. Can we start again?' He slipped an arm around her waist, kissed her cheek, her ear, the nape of her neck. Clare yielded a little. What did she expect? He'd had no more to do with children than she had. No nieces, no nephews. She loved him for his dry wit, his brilliant mind, his ambition, not for his parenting skills 'I've missed you,' he said.

She'd missed him too. It was a whole month since she'd spent a weekend at his South Bank apartment, a month since Samson had moved in. She loved Adam's place, with its panoramic views of the tranquil Brisbane river. You could see the botanical gardens from the balcony, the golden glow of Brisbane's CBD at night. The riverfront restaurant precinct was a short stroll away, Southbank just a two-minute ferry ride. Clare looked at Samson, whining in his crate. Helga or no Helga, she needed to find a good kennel where he could spend his weekends.

Adam kissed her mouth with searching lips. Clare waited for the hot, insistent pull of him to kick in, the delicious hunger for more. But the kiss was a fizzer. Nothing. Well, how was she supposed to feel romantic with Jack peeking from the couch and with Samson keeping up an indignant whine? She pulled away. Adam threw up his hands.

'Lisa brought down the house with her performance in Giselle,' he said pointedly. 'Thanks so much for asking.'

'If I'd told you about Jack, you wouldn't have understood.'

'No,' he said. 'I wouldn't have. The reasons we don't get involved with our clients is first-year law stuff. This – ' he gestured around the apartment – 'This … situation you've got yourself into. It has conflict of interest written all over it.'

Clare was suddenly weary. He was right, of course. She'd been a fool, but a willing one. And she still was.

Adam ran his hand across the tear in the back of the couch, a stricken expression on his face. Then he peered at Jack again. 'Roderick must be ropeable.'.

'He's not happy,' she said. 'But he didn't go off at me like you just did. Christ, Adam, it's only temporary.'

'Fine,' said Adam. 'It's clear I won't be able to talk any sense into you.' He looked at the shambles all around and grimaced. 'Call me when you get yourself sorted.' He turned to go, paused when he reached the door, and came back into the lounge. He kissed her on top of her head. 'Spend next weekend at my place,' he whispered. 'Put the dog in a kennel, find somewhere else for the kid if, God forbid, he's still here, and come home with me on Friday. Okay?'

She nodded and watched him leave. As soon as he'd gone, Jack released Samson from the crate. The two of them started a rowdy game of chasey, racing round and round the beleaguered couch. Clare slumped down among its dishevelled cushions. She glanced at the clock. Time to get ready for Helga's doggy obedience class. What a shame there wasn't one for kids too.

. . .

Clare arrived at Centennial Reserve, a huge expanse of well-kept parks and playing fields. She was on time for once, and sat Jack down on a shady bench with a good view of the class. 'Stay,' she said, without much hope. Then she joined the line of dogs and owners. Samson and Clare were in the *beginner basics* class, but several grades of training were taking place simultaneously. Next door were the agility dogs. They were doing some sort of trial, and had quite an audience. Their arena looked just like a children's playground, complete with colourful equipment, and Jack couldn't seem to take his eyes off it. Neither could Clare.

She watched a dog prance down the course beside his owner. A pitch-black German shepherd – a grown up version of Samson. Before long he was leaping over obstacles and into tyres, shooting through brightly striped tunnels and balancing on boardwalks. He teetered on a seesaw, scaled walls and finished by weaving between a line of purple poles at breakneck speed. So clever. Clare wanted to applaud.

She was less enthusiastic about the next performance. It started off well enough. A graceful standard poodle, sailing over jumps and bounding into stripy tunnels. 'Be mindful of your dog's mood. Always watch his ears,' boomed Helga. But Clare was too busy watching the neighbouring arena to pay much attention to Samson's ears. Samson tugged on his lead just as a ripple of laughter rose from the crowd.

Oh no — please, no. Jack had escaped his bench and was crawling into the tunnel after the poodle. Samson plunged forward and Clare was so distracted that she dropped the lead. He took off after Jack. Here we go again, she thought.

The crowd cheered and clapped as they were all put through their paces. First the poodle and its handler, both trying to ignore the odd turn of events. Then Jack, crawling and seesawing and climbing the equipment with surprising alacrity, copying the poodle's every move. Then Samson, fearlessly pursuing Jack over and under and through every obstacle. And finally Clare, bringing up the rear, calling ineffectually to her charges.

How humiliating. Helga sent them all packing.

Clare had found a dog friendly café on the far side of the park, ordered ice creams and milk shakes, and sat down to lick her wounds. But for some reason, the embarrassment wasn't as bad as she'd expected. Maybe she was just getting used to it. Clare slurped the last of her milkshake, making Jack giggle. Clare hadn't had a milkshake since she was a kid. She'd forgotten how delicious they were. Grandma used to make the best malted shakes, with creamy milk fresh from Angel, their jersey house cow. Angel gave twenty litres of foaming white milk a day, more than enough for her calf and the household combined. Clare had loved Angel's little calves, honey coloured with pretty dished faces. They had the longest, blondest lashes imaginable, framing the biggest, brownest eyes. Just like Bambi. Jack would love them too.

Clare shook her head, chasing away the idea. What was with her? Why was she thinking about the farm so much? Jack let Samson lick his ice-cream, but Clare was prepared for it. She had a second one ready, gave it to Jack, and allowed him to share the first with the dog. It worked a treat. From now on, rather than scold Jack for giving his food to Samson, she'd have something he was allowed to share.

Another little boy arrived with his mother, and started playing with Matchbox cars at a nearby table. Jack stared and got off his chair. 'Sit, Jack,' said Clare. After a moment's indecision, he sat back down and quietly ate his ice-cream. Yes! Clare could hardly believe it. She felt a surge of triumph. Maybe she was finally getting a handle on the kid. It had been a hell of a day, and it was still only lunchtime. But now, sitting in the sun with a surprisingly compliant child and a tired, happy dog, smiling at the other mothers, watching Jack's delight as sparrows stole crumbs from beneath the tables – right now, all seemed well with the world.

Come on Jacky,' she said. 'You've been good. Let's go through the car wash.'

CHAPTER 6

The weekend with Adam never eventuated. It was three weeks now, since Jack had turned Clare's life upside down, and there was still no sign of Taylor Brown. Jolly Jumbucks didn't do weekends. They didn't even do late nights. They closed, in fact, at six o'clock.

Jack hadn't settled well into their kindergarten program. Despite the cheerful sign out the front, proclaiming the place to be *A Worry Free Home Away From Home*, Clare spent her workdays rigid with anxiety, fearing that every phone call might be from the dreaded centre manager. And unfortunately, a lot of them were. Jack was soiling himself. Jack had thrown yet another tantrum. Jack had hurled his food, and everybody else's, at the Happy Elves - the ridiculous name they gave the mostly teenage kindergarten assistants. Jack had bitten another child. Jack was hoarding all the toys. He'd made them into a giant pile and then perched in defiance on top of them, in some sort of heroic last stand. He was screaming and spitting and snapping at anybody who came near.

Adam was no support, although he had calmed down about her having Jack. There'd been some mid-week lunches, and one stolen afternoon at his place, but he didn't visit her flat any more. Adam said

340

it was because he didn't want to upset Jack. 'Don't worry about me,' he'd say. 'I'm snowed under with work at the moment anyway. We'll wait until you find somewhere for the boy.'

The weeks dragged on. At first she was grateful for Adam's patience, then surprised and in the end even a little suspicious of it. He still rang her most nights after Jack went to bed. She used to love his phone calls, full of wonderful stories about triumphs and mistakes in the court room. Lately though, any talk of mistakes left her cringing. Clare had made more mistakes in the last three weeks than she had in her entire legal career. And on top of that, she'd been late for work nearly every day.

Dropping Jack off at child care was a long, drawn-out process. Painful too. Jack clung to her, wailing at the top of his lungs, holding on with surprising strength. When the centre staff intervened, Jack transformed from a clingy child into a violent ball of rage. Clare hadn't yet managed to get away in under half an hour. At work she'd missed a few deadlines, prepared a few substandard briefs that she knew wouldn't pass muster, and then stayed up all night redrafting. In between everything else, she was reading an assortment of child psychology and parenting books, as well as keeping up with case law. Once, the grey light of morning had crept through the window blind before she was through. And there was no catching a quick sleep between sunrise and eight o'clock any more. Jack always woke at the crack of dawn and rattled Samson's crate to make him bark. Clare couldn't risk that. So she had to get up, no matter how tired she was.

Inexplicably, the little boy was a delight in the early morning: cooperative, cute, endearing even. Jack loved getting dressed in the new clothes that she'd bought him. He inspected himself in the mirror, seemingly fascinated by his different reflections. He loved his bowl of cocoa pops, followed by rounds of buttery vegemite toast. Clare was following suit -so much quicker and easier to make them both the same breakfast. Tasty too, and only temporary. So what about Adam's organic berries and yoghurt.

It was after breakfast when the trouble began. Jack didn't want to leave the flat. He'd been okay on day one. Not too bad on day two, but by day three he'd figured it out. Leaving the flat in the morning meant going to child care. So after breakfast Jack hid under the bed, or climbed into the bathtub, or wedged himself beneath the couch. When Clare finally extracted him, which of course she had to do, he'd throw the mother of all tantrums. He'd wet himself, necessitating a change of clothes. But how to dress a kicking, screaming four-year-old? Samson would hide in his crate and Clare felt like joining him. Heaven knows what the neighbours thought. She was exhausted before she even left the apartment.

Friday morning. Roderick poked his head in. 'Clare - my office.'

What now? Clare sighed and followed him down the hall.

He gestured for her to sit down. 'Coffee?'

She nodded and he put on the jug. It must be very bad news if he was making her coffee. 'I've heard from Taylor. She wants to know how her son is.'

'That's marvellous,' said Clare.

'She called him Jack by the way.'

'That's what I told Kim.'

'Yes,' said Roderick. 'You did.' He was being unusually reticent.

'Where is Taylor?' asked Clare.

'Living in Ipswich with a new partner. Some sort of boarding house. She didn't say exactly.'

'What about her court date? It's next week. Do you think she'll turn up?'

Roderick poured her a coffee, then sat on the desk and nursed his own. 'She said she would.' He seemed deep in thought.

'Shall I represent her then?' asked Clare. 'Jack will be over the moon. When does Taylor want to collect him?'

'That's the thing.' He gazed out the window for a moment before turning to look at her. 'She doesn't.'

Clare looked blank. She must have heard him wrong. 'What do you mean, she doesn't?' Clare waited for Roderick to explain, but he only shrugged. 'You mean she doesn't want her own child?'

'Taylor's in a difficult position,' he said. 'There's her new boyfriend, for starters. Belts her apparently, and a junkie to boot. I'm afraid that under his influence Taylor has lapsed from the methadone program.' Roderick took a sip from his mug. 'She's actively using again, Clare. The girl has enough sense to know she can't look after her son right now.'

'Where does she think Jack is?' asked Clare. 'Does she even care?'

Roderick gave her a reproachful look. 'Of course she cares. If Taylor didn't voluntarily surrender the child at this stage, the department would be under an obligation to take him from her. She knows that.' He downed the rest of his coffee in one gulp. 'And as to your other question, Taylor believes her child is in a caring foster home. Which is the case, isn't it?'

'But I thought that you didn't approve?' said Clare. 'That you thought it was stupid and unprofessional to take Jack on?'

'I did, I did,' he said. 'But I've changed my mind. Don't forget, my young Sam's the same age as Jack. Nobody wants to see a child that young go into a residential unit. You have a good heart, Clare, a fearless heart, and you've already saved Jack from great harm. You're not afraid to put yourself on the line. The least we can do is back you.' He smiled. 'If you must know, we've all been very moved and humbled by what you've done.'

Clare processed his words. That was all very well, very flattering. But it still left the little issue of Jack.

There was a knock at the door and Veronica came in without waiting for an invitation. She looked at Clare then back to Roderick. 'More problems?' she said with a smile.

Clare glared at her. Why couldn't anybody else see the woman for what she was?

'Whatever it is Ronnie, it can wait,' said Roderick. 'I'm not quite finished here.'

Veronica cast Clare a pitying glance and withdrew. She probably thought Roderick was chewing her out for something. If only she'd barged in a few seconds earlier in time to hear all the compliments.

'I assume you're prepared to keep the child until a more suitable placement is found?' said Roderick.

Clare didn't know what to say. Taylor loved Jack. Clare didn't know exactly how she knew it. She just knew it. And Jack loved his mother. Clare had always believed that Taylor would return for her son sooner rather than later. That her leaving had been some kind of aberration, some kind of desperate, last-ditch measure to cope with an impossible living situation. Taylor would come to her senses, and then Clare could refer her and Jack to the variety of excellent support services linked to the legal aid centre: crisis accommodation, counselling and health care. If Taylor had an abusive partner, there were refuges and domestic violence outreach workers. If she wanted help to manage Jack, Clare could make parenting classes and child psychologists available. If she needed to get back on track with her methadone program, Clare could help there too. There was so much she was ready to do, that she wanted to do, for Jack and Taylor. And now?

'Truth is, I'm having a tough time of it.' Clare disliked the tone of defeat in her voice. 'Jack hates being in child care. It was bad enough for the poor kid when his mother disappeared. Now it feels like I'm traumatising him all over again every morning when I leave It makes me late, distracts me, hurts him ... '

Roderick popped a half-empty packet of Tim Tams onto the table. 'Have one,' he said. 'Go on.'

She extracted a chocolate biscuit. He was being so amenable. For some reason it made her nervous. 'You have some time off owing, Clare,' he said. 'God knows you've only taken one holiday in three years. You've always staffed our Christmas skeleton roster. You're never sick.' What was he saying? 'Take some leave, Clare, until they find somewhere else for Jack. It shouldn't take long. A week or two...'

'So you don't want me...?'

Roderick held up his hand. 'There'll be none of that. I want you working here more than you know. But will it kill you to take a break when you're owed it?'

Clare thought the suggestion through, trying to put aside the idea that this was just a nice way to get rid of her. But Roderick was as straight as they came. She could trust him. 'How's Kim going with finding Jack a new home?'

'She's been a bit vague,' said Roderick. 'Apparently they're expecting a disability placement to open up soon.'

'He doesn't need a disability placement,' said Clare. 'There'd be so many more options available if they looked in the pool of general foster carers.'

'Clare,' said Roderick in a soothing voice that got her back up straightaway. 'We lose our objectivity when we get too close.' What was it with the royal *we*? 'You said yourself, not ten minutes ago, that Jack has some very challenging behaviours.'

'He's four years old,' she said, 'and he's just lost his mother. What do you expect?'

Roderick tapped his finger on the desktop. 'Does he speak?'

'Of course he does. I already told you that.'

'The average four-year-old asks over four hundred questions a day,' said Roderick. 'I know our Sam does. What did Jack ask you today? Or yesterday? What did he say?'

Clare was about to launch into her answer. About how Jack always asked for strawberry ice-cream because he liked it better than vanilla or chocolate. About how he wanted her to read *The Poky Little Puppy* before bed. About how he complained when she switched the television over from cartoons to the news at seven o'clock. 'I want cartoons,' he'd said just last night. But when she thought about it, when she *really* thought about it, she realised that Jack had said no such thing. Clare even surprised herself with this revelation. She knew strawberry was his favourite flavour because he gave chocolate or vanilla to Samson. She always read him *The Poky Little Puppy* before bed because he threw the other books on the floor. He asked her not to switch channels by running off with the remote control.

She wracked her brain to come up with examples of him speaking.

'Jack tells me when visitors come,' she said at last. But that wasn't strictly true either. What Jack actually did was rush to the door with Samson and bark. It was a game, Clare knew that. A copying game. But she dared not tell Roderick that the only verbal communication the child had made during his fortnight's stay, apart from screaming, was to make animal noises.

It appeared Roderick could read her mind. 'File notes say the boy is completely non-verbal,' he said. 'Taylor's been getting a payment available only to parents of disabled children."

'You've got to be kidding me,' said Clare. 'That payment's far more generous than the regular single parent benefit. Can't you see what's happened? She's gone along with a misdiagnosis to get more money.'

'Wherever the truth lies,' said Roderick, 'Jack is a special case, wouldn't you agree?' Clare had to nod. 'And finding him a suitable placement will take time.' She nodded again, begrudgingly. 'Well, Clare, the offer's there. Take a break until this matter is resolved.'

Clare considered his words. Maybe he was right. She did need a holiday. She was sleep-deprived, strung-out. She'd lost weight. What a luxury it would be to forget about work for a while. And how good for Jack? No day care. He could stay home all day with her and Samson. They could take drives to the beach or into the country. She could let them both off the leash. By the time the child had a new placement, he'd be calmer, more settled. More able to cope.

'I'll think about it,' she said. 'I'll seriously think about it.'

'Capital.' Roderick was beaming. A genuine, open, inclusive smile. The sort that made you want to be around him. 'Just in case, I'll send somebody in and you can bring them up to speed on your cases. Ronnie perhaps?'

'No,' said Clare quickly. 'Not Veronica. She was just telling me yesterday how snowed under she is.'

Roderick looked surprised. 'Really? I thought her workload was a touch on the light side. Much lighter than yours, Clare. I'd better look into that.' He fixed her with encouraging eyes. 'Our extra funding is in. That young bloke Davis starts next week, so we won't be down a solicitor. It's the best possible time for you to take leave.'

As Roderick talked, Clare found she'd made her decision. A weight seemed to lift from he, and she smiled. 'Relax boss. You've convinced me.'

'That's more like it,' he said, sounding pleased with himself. 'I reckon Isaac's our man. He's in court this morning, but I'll send him round to you when he gets back. Now, get out of here.'

'You'll let me know when there's any news?' said Clare.

Roderick nodded. 'And don't worry about Taylor . . . I'll represent her myself.'

Clare returned to her office. She was lighter, happier than she'd been. Roderick's praise had left a warm residual glow, and everything about her decision felt right. She launched into her day with renewed enthusiasm, pulling out manila folders, going through the most important points that she needed to brief Isaac about. Clare liked Isaac. He was competent and compassionate. She trusted that he'd act in her clients' best interests while she was away.

The phone rang - Roderick again. 'Do me a favour, Clare? The annual Bar Association lunch is on today. I'm supposed to go, but you know how I hate those functions.'

Clare knew all about the lunch. Adam had promised ages ago to take her and she'd been really looking forward to it. That lunch was one of the high points of Brisbane's legal calendar, a supreme networking opportunity. A place to be seen. But then on Monday Adam had cancelled on her. Apparently he had an appearance that day at Dalby court; an assault or something. Dalby was way out west, not too far from Currawong Creek, her grandfather's place. Odd, how little reminders of Grandad kept popping up. Clare hadn't even known that Adam worked the country court circuit, but she supposed a young barrister couldn't refuse briefs - not even a rising star like Adam. He could afford to miss the lunch. As Paul Dunbar's junior, his career was right on track. But for Clare it had been a definite disappointment.

'Take my place today, will you?' asked Roderick. 'They'll bang on a slap-up meal, and you'll have the chance to sound out Justice Cameron before you take that break. He's had his eye on you.'

'Really?' said Clare. 'Don't you normally send Ted to these things?'

'I don't want to send Ted,' he said. 'I want to send you.'

Clare experienced a shiver of excitement and pride. 'Thanks, Rod,' she said. 'I'd love to go. You can count on me.'

Brisbane's Riverview Hotel. The concierge wore a gold braided uniform. Clare told him her name and he ticked it off the list, directing her to the first floor. She made straight for the ladies room. Good, it was empty. She inspected herself in the full-length mirror. For once she approved. The fact that she'd dropped a kilo or two meant her business suit fitted like a glove. Better than it ever had. She looked sexy even, in a sensible, corporate sort of way. Stress must be good for her.

Clare smiled at her reflection, inspected her hair, her make-up, her teeth. Her dark suit contrasted with her blonde bob. The look was serious, but stylish. And for the first time in days she wasn't thinking about Jack. But of course, that wasn't true, was it? She had to think about him, in order to congratulate herself for not thinking about him. Clare shook her head. Today was a career-building exercise, no room for foolishness. She exited the gleaming marble bathroom and followed the signs to the hotel's Grand Ballroom. Tables were already filling up with guests. Impeccably clad waiters dispensed warm bread rolls and jugs of water, bobbing with ice cubes and lemon slices.

The man at the door led her to a table set for six, positioned near the front of the room. Clare couldn't believe her luck. Justice Cameron was at the very next table. It was too perfect. Clare pulled out her chair to sit down and the judge turned around.

'Just the person I wanted to see.' Justice Cameron spoke in a low voice to the man beside him, and he swung around too and beamed at her. It was Paul Dunbar. She'd never actually met him before, but she recognised him at once. Paul Dunbar was the city's most notable criminal barrister, and its most flamboyant as well. He wore a purple shirt, a polka-dotted bow tie and sported a magnificent handlebar moustache, a la Merv Hughes. The moustache, in combination with his massive bald head, made Dunbar look somewhat like a walrus.

'Frank and I were just talking about you, Ms Mitchell,' Dunbar said. 'Discussing your dazzling advocacy.' He twirled his moustache between thumb and forefinger. 'There's been a lot of talk in Chambers about the Fenwick case. Bringing the teacher in like that, at the last minute? You practically turned the tables on the rules of evidence.' He slapped his broad thigh. 'Had the jury eating right out of your hand. I hear the prosecutor went so red at the *not guilty* verdict that he popped a vein. That's the way to nail a trial,' he said. 'With a bit of panache.' His sweeping arm gesture resulted in a firm clout to the head of the judge. 'Ha,' said Dunbar. 'Take that, Frank Cameron. For all the trouble you've caused me in your estimable court.'

'Thank you, Mr Dunbar,' she stammered.

'Call me Paul, please.'

Clare felt herself flush as red as the aforementioned prosecutor. She *had* pulled off a coup in the Fenwick trial. Roderick had almost not let her have the case. If their client hadn't been so emotionally attached to her, he would have farmed it out to one of his pet barristers. But the girl wouldn't have testified for anybody else. She only trusted Clare. Clare spent many hours overtime, settling her, reassuring her, even going to her house when her nerve threatened to fail. That was crossing the line between counsel and client, but it had paid off. The girl ended up being an astonishingly compelling witness. Such a standout victory in a high profile case was bound to attract attention, but she'd never imagined somebody like Paul Dunbar would sit up and take notice. She wished that Veronica had been there to hear Paul Dunbar praise her like that.

'Your Roderick and I go way back,' said Paul. 'At law school together, we were. Best friends for years.'

Clare already knew that. Roderick had given Veronica her job at Fortitude Valley Legal Aid as a favour to Paul. The two always helped each other out with career paths for their protégés. Paul got to his feet and sat down on the vacant chair beside Clare. 'You have ambitions then, Ms Mitchell? Ambitions to go to the bar?'

'Well, yes,' she said. Too softly. She had to be more assertive. 'Yes,' she said again, this time owning the word.

Paul took a fat wallet from his pocket and extracted a business card. 'Call me,' he said, 'if you'd be interested in working together. I'd enjoy a dynamo like you as my reader.'

Clare took the card and stared at it dumbly.

Paul looked right, then left, then lowered his voice to a conspiratorial whisper. 'Truth is, the person I've lined up to read with me next year isn't quite ready ...' He trailed off, but the implication was plain enough. Clare almost felt sorry for Veronica.

A waiter placed two bottles of wine on the table, and Paul helped himself to the red. He poured himself a generous glass and another for Clare. She was stunned by the sudden turn of events. It had had the feel of a set-up. A splendid set-up, certainly, but a set-up just the same. Roderick, being so solicitous, giving her time off, insisting she take his place at the lunch. This had been planned. By Paul and Roderick, and maybe by Justice Cameron as well. They'd talked it over, maybe many times. Over drinks, or in chambers, or at the Counsellor's Club. It was overwhelming. Clare was thrilled right down to her toes. She knew she had a goofy grin on her face. Hardly becoming. She tried to arrange her face into some semblance of decorum.

Paul looked her up and down. 'You're pleased then?' Her mouth was suddenly too dry to speak. 'Don't try to hide it,' he said. 'Passion makes the difference between an outstanding advocate and a merely adequate one.' He heaved a great belly laugh, as if at a hilarious, private joke. 'Oh, it will get you into trouble at times, there's no doubt. But without it? Without that ability to reach deep and yank the emotional guts out of a jury? Without that, a barrister can never achieve true brilliance.'

Justice Cameron rose from his chair and caught Clare's eye. 'That passion he's talking about? It doesn't just work on juries. He's ripped my guts out in court more than once. Nobody sums up a case like Paul here. Now if you don't mind, I have someone to see.'

Clare said goodbye and turned her attention back to Paul. 'I just want to clarify - you're offering to take me on as your reader next year?'

Paul plucked an old-fashioned fountain pen from his pocket, scribbled the proposal onto a napkin, and presented it to her with a flourish.

Clare could have kissed it. This was proof of merit, proof of a life lived with passion. If only Adam could have been here. He'd said much the same thing, that it was her passion that set her apart from his previous girlfriends. For all Veronica's good looks and style, she had about as much passion as a snail. No, that wasn't true. Clare had watched a documentary on snail's mating habits. She'd seen them writhing together in a copulation that could last for hours. Veronica didn't even have as much passion as a snail.

Clare was basking in a soft, warm glow when Paul excused himself. He gave his moustache a few dramatic twirls. 'Once more unto the breach, dear friends,' he proclaimed to the room in general, and then charged off to talk to a man at the bar.

Three other people sat down at the table. Clare didn't know them and, in any case, they immediately became engrossed in private conversation. Left to her own devices she had a quiet moment to digest her news. Going to the bar with a man like Paul Dunbar as her mentor. Something her father had dreamed of for her, and now she couldn't tell him. It was a bitter pill. She could tell Adam though. She wanted to ring him then and there. Tell him they'd be working in the same chambers next year. She looked around the rapidly filling room. Was there time to duck out? No, better not. She might miss something.

Clare buttered a bread roll and was nibbling at it absentmindedly, when someone sat down beside her. She stared in disbelief. Adam. He'd come after all. He'd made an effort to rush back from Dalby. He'd understood how important this lunch was to her. For a moment she wondered how he knew she'd be there. Of course, Roderick. Roderick had told Adam where she was and he'd come to surprise her. Maybe he already knew about her news. All of Clare's doubts about him melted away. He'd just proved how much he cared, and warmth rushed through her.

But when she looked into his eyes, Clare didn't like what she saw there. His face, it was all wrong. She'd expected him to seem smugly satisfied that he'd surprised her - that was his usual way. But instead he looked uncomfortable, guilty even. Clare slipped her hand into his. 'Adam, what's wrong?'

Now he was positively squirming. A woman came up behind them. She leaned over the back of Adam's chair, a hand on each shoulder, and gave him a long, lingering kiss, low on his cheek. Veronica slipped into the seat beside him. Clare snatched her hand away from his. Veronica studied them both and comprehension dawned in her eyes. The only gratifying thing about the whole, appalling situation was that she looked as stunned as Clare felt.

They both turned to glare at Adam. He played it very cool, greeting Clare. 'It's good you made it,' he said, a perfect smile on his face.

No thanks to you. The room grew hot and airless. Her leg cramped. Perspiration trickled down her neck, inside her shirt. Clare wanted to scream, but instead she put on a smile as forced as his own, gaining confidence from Veronica's dumbfounded expression. For once it wouldn't be *her* left standing on the back foot. 'How nice to see you,' she said sweetly.

Adam turned his attention to Veronica. Clare strained her ears, listening to their furious whispers. Adam spoke in a low murmur, but

Veronica was unable to keep the strident tone from her voice. *'What's she doing here?... hand on your arm ... must have known ... deliberate humiliation ...'* Adam lapsed into sullen silence. Clare was all too familiar with this particular defence strategy, and it was gratifying to think it wasn't reserved especially for her.

What should she do? Leave? This was her first impulse. Take the high road? She could stay, hide how gutted she really was and outlast them. She didn't want to fight with Adam in public. She should leave, shouldn't she? But how would that look to Paul Dunbar? And by staying, at least she got to see what happened next.

Adam turned back to her, and embarked on a far-fetched explanation of how he came to be at the Bar Association lunch, instead of at the Dalby Court House. Clare briefly closed her eyes. She wasn't listening to his words, rather she was listening to the meaning behind the words. Did he really think he could explain his way out of this? She wiped her forehead with a napkin and glanced at Veronica. Did he take them both for fools?

Adam finally gave up talking and sat between the two of them, staring into middle distance. A waiter served the soup.

Clare's decision to say nothing was weakening, and the desire to make Adam suffer was growing hot and insistent. Was Veronica aware of their twelve-month liaison? Possibly not. No, almost certainly not. Clare was a particularly private person. Roderick may not even have known about her and Adam. Debbie knew, of course, but Veronica would never deign to chat to a secretary. If she didn't know the full extent of their relationship, if her anger was based only on a hunch ... then it wouldn't take much for Adam to talk himself out of trouble and back into Veronica's good books. He would get away with it.

But before she could formulate a plan, Veronica leaned across in front of Adam, and fixed Clare with anguished, perfectly plucked brows. 'Are you screwing him?'

Clare took a bottomless breath and her opinion of Veronica went up a few notches. This was a woman who knew how to cut through the bullshit.

'Yes,' said Clare, 'For about a year, now.' She threw Adam a long, accusing stare. He dropped his head to his hands and the table went quiet. The other people didn't know where to look. She tried to imagine Veronica naked with Adam, but mercifully the image wouldn't come.

Clare's phone rang, making her jump. For a moment she wondered who might be calling, but she should have known. Jolly Jumbucks, of course. This time Jack had surpassed himself. He'd bunkered in beneath the stairs and held the entire staff at bay for fifteen minutes with a cache of fire extinguishers he'd discovered there. Clare found herself impressed that Jack had figured out how to use the devices. Then again, they weren't that complicated. All you had to do was pull the pin, rather like a hand grenade, then press the lever.

She imagined a blizzard of foam, burying the Happy Elves in soft white drifts. This was it, surely. Jack's last chance at Jolly Jumbucks, gone. No matter. She didn't need them any more.

Clare sat back, took a long, objective look at Adam, then stood to leave, praying her legs would not betray her. She stepped away from the table, paused and stepped back. She leaned down, brought her mouth close to Veronica's cheek, as if for a kiss. 'He's a good lay at first,' she said in a loud stage whisper. 'But he wears off.' Then she excused herself to the room in general, and walked out with head held high.

Clare picked a delighted Jack up from Jolly Jumbucks, barely hearing the manager's long-winded account of the boy's wrongdoings, and why he wasn't welcome any more. She had a far warmer reception from Helga. 'You should collect Samson early more often. It would do you both the world of good.'

Clare drove in silence, numb, like she'd been cut with a very sharp knife and was waiting for the pain to set in. By contrast, the two in the back were in high spirits. She drove them beyond the city limits, found a stretch of bushland and set them free. Jack ran along a river, splashed after fish in the shallows, threw sticks, skipped stones. Nobody here to report them for anti-social behaviour. No signs saying keep that dog on a leash or stay off those gardens or don't climb the trees. Not a sign in sight. Not another person in sight, for that matter. Just them and the bush. Jack spotted some horses in a paddock and took off down the slope to investigate, with Samson at his heels. But for once their impetuous bolt didn't cause her stomach to lurch in fright. Out here, there were no roads, no shops, no stranger-danger. Clare could let them go. She sat down on a stump to watch.

It was a pearl of an afternoon. From her perch on the hillside she had a spectacular view across to Moreton Bay, a shining, azure crescent in the distance, merging with a deep blue sky. Somewhere a currawong called. Paddocks stretched out along the river flats below. Jack ran to the fence with Samson and put an outstretched arm through the wire. A horse grazing nearby raised its head, stared at them for a few moments, then ambled over. Clare stood up in readiness to sprint down the hill if Samson went in for the chase. But dog and horse simply touched friendly noses. Good on you, Samson. Clare was proud of him.

Jack amused himself by tugging at long grass on his side of the fence and collecting green bunches to give to the horse. It accepted these offerings with a gracious, bowed head and whiffling lips. Half an hour later, Jack still hadn't budged from the fence. When it was time to go, Clare had a battle to tear him away, and he really cried. Not yelled. Not his usual angry screams, that sounded more like a roaring animal than a child. No, he cried, with real tears. It was a breakthrough, she knew that.

Clare stretched out on the couch and flicked on the television. Her strategy had been to tire the pair out, and it had worked like a charm. Jack was asleep. Asleep in his own room for once. Samson was asleep too, curled up at the foot of Jack's bed, and it was only seven o'clock.

Clare's phone rang. It was Debbie. 'I can't believe it.' Her voice was high and excited. 'What Adam did, I mean. I've heard all about it.'

Clare sighed. Of course she had. Who knew why? Who knew how? But Debbie had the uncanniest nose for gossip. She launched into a protracted appraisal of Clare's relationship with Adam, founded on nothing, apparently, but the odd snippet or two of news that Clare had carelessly let slip at work. And the once or twice that Debbie had met Adam at the office. Hardly a sound basis for judgement. It was surprising then, how accurate Debbie's assessment actually was. 'Ooh, you just can't trust blokes like him.' How right she was. 'I could tell the minute I saw him,' Debbie said on the phone. 'It's the eyes that give them away, every time. Kind of shifty.'

Clare tactfully refrained from reminding Debbie that she'd swooned over Adam's grey eyes just last week. They'd been *dreamy* then. Now they were shifty. Clare smiled. They agreed on that much, at least.

Clare fobbed Debbie off as kindly as she could, and tossed the phone in the direction of the coffee table. It slid along the smoked glass top and onto the floor. Exhaustion washed over her, and she left it where it fell. There was a nature documentary on the telly. A weasel chasing a rabbit. Clare always cringed at moments like these. She decided she was barracking for the rabbit this time. She didn't always barrack for the prey animal. It depended on the day she'd had. She never did if pictures of the predator's hungry young were shown prior to the hunt.

This rabbit didn't have much going for it. A rough crevice in a cliff served as a temporary hiding place, but it wouldn't fool the hungry weasel for long. And worst of all, it was a dead end. The weasel sniffed out the refuge and prowled about for a few moments, sizing things up. Then it dived for the rabbit. Clare jumped. Jeez, were her nerves ever shot! But to her surprise and delight the rabbit flung itself skywards, somersaulted in mid-air and scampered to freedom, having cheated death by inches. The thwarted weasel seemed to shrink in embarrassment, as if it knew that the cameras were upon it. Clare made up her mind then and there to never be the rabbit again.

The documentary ended and advertising took over the screen. Clare's eyes glazed over. Her gaze wandered to the painting on the wall above the television. A pair of harnessed clydesdales stepped out with power and grace. The figure of a man wearing overalls, her grandfather, followed behind them, treading the furrows made by the hand-held plough. An old farmhouse with a wide verandah stood in the background. Clare had owned the painting for many years - so many years that she'd ceased to really see it. *Days of Gold* had followed her around all through her student days , from shared houses to cramped flats, to this wall right here. She almost hadn't hung it. The painting's warm, earthy tones hardly went with twenty-first century minimalism. Clare looked at it, as if for the first time. Mum wasn't a bad artist. She'd captured the spirit of the great horses in the angle of their erect ears, in their arching necks and straining shoulders. She'd caught the care in Grandad's lined face.

Clare's phone rang. She retrieved it from the floor and checked the caller ID. Adam. Clare switched it off. If she never heard Adam's voice again, it would still be too soon. Her afternoon in the country with Jack and Samson, watching the river flats and the horses, had done something towards healing her heart. Some small thing. Just as well she'd found out about Adam before she got in any deeper. Now she just wanted to forget about him, to escape the memories, to get away from Brisbane.

Maybe there was a way. Clare went into the bedroom. After Dad's funeral her brother Ryan had helped pack up the house. They'd put most of what was worth keeping into storage, but she had retrieved a few items.

Clare found the step-ladder and heaved down a crate from the top of the wardrobe. There, beneath dad's car manuals, lay a taped-up box marked *Currawong Creek*. She was almost too scared to open it. Clare fetched herself a glass of wine and perched it on her dressing table. Then she broke the seal and removed the objects from the box one by one. She laid them on the bed. Photos of beautiful clydesdale horses wearing championship sashes. Some baby clothes tied with lace. Mum's old school reports. Memories tumbled back thick and fast. A black and white currawong feather. The cracker for a stock whip. Some large nuts in a little box. Bigger than Brazil nuts, but Clare couldn't remember their name. She lifted out two brown paper packages with cancelled stamps. Posted to her father's address, but both still unopened. One was marked *for Ryan Mitchell*. The other was for Clare.

She broke the seal with an unsteady hand. Inside was a letter from her grandfather.

My dearest Clare,

I am writing to let you know that Grandma passed away last week. I'm sure your father has told you. It's been a very sad time, but don't worry about me. I'm holding up okay. Grandma always loved you and your brother very, very much. Right up until the end, she would talk so proudly of you both. Here are some small things she wanted you to have. If you ever have time to come to Currawong Clare Bear, I would be so happy to see you.

All my love,

Grandad XXOO

The letter was dated seven years ago. In a panic Clare leafed through what was left in the box. More unopened mail for her and Ryan. She tore an envelope and pulled out a card. It had a Dalmatian dog on the front and *Now You're 14* in glittery writing. A twenty dollar note fluttered out when she opened it. *Happy Birthday Clare* it said. *From your loving grandparents.* There were dozens of letters. Dozens of letters that her father had kept from his children.

A wave of heartache threatened to drown her. Clare knuckled the tears from her eyes and looked inside the package from her grandfather. A locket with a photo of her and grandma inside. An opal ring. A kitchen journal that looked vaguely familiar. It was filled with hand written recipes and pressed flowers. In an instant she was a child again, scouring the paddocks of Currawong Creek with Grandma, searching for pretty leaves and blossoms. Clare gazed at the faded flowers, held between pages of recipes for salmon bake, savoury mince, pavlova and scones. Here was a sprig of coolabah blossom, still retaining its creamy colour. She thought of the sad little coolabah tree growing outside her window at work, and choked back sobs.

Clare scrabbled around in the box until she found what she was looking for. Her father's small green address book. She flipped through it until she found her grandfather's number. With trembling fingers she punched it into her phone.

'Grandad? It's me, Clare.'

CHAPTER 8

Jack hit the little girl sitting next to him on the head with the whip. She burst out crying. 'Come on, sweetie,' said Clare, dragging Jack out of the stagecoach by his arm. 'Sorry,' she called, as a man holding a camera stormed over. She hurried Jack away. So much for the happy snap.

When the department gave her permission to take Jack on a holiday, Kim had asked for a photographic record of the trip. Something Jack could share with Taylor when he saw her. They'd reached Toowoomba, an hour and a half west of Brisbane, and the Cobb & Co Museum had seemed like the perfect stopover. It would set them in the mood for Currawong.

The museum housed over fifty horse-drawn vehicles, including sturdy drays and farm wagons of the sort pulled by Grandad's clydesdales. They told the story of European settlement on the Darling Downs. The original Cobb and Co coaches, including the last coach which ran from Yuleba to Surat in 1924, were the pride of the collection. Clare had given Samson a quick walk, a drink of water and put him back in the car. Then she'd taken Jack's hand and headed for the entrance to the museum. The visit had been a disaster from the minute they passed through the gate.

Jack had made a beeline for a stand where a wizened old saddler with a bushy white beard was giving a leatherwork demonstration. He was plaiting what looked like the thong of a whip. Jack had clambered up a wall display of belts and bridles, toppling the whole thing to the ground. Then he'd snatched a stock whip and run off.

The old man barely looked up from his task, but his lips cracked into a thin smile. 'You need a kelpie to round up that one, love.'

Clare stared after Jack. Damn. She'd have a fight getting that whip off him. 'I'll buy it,' she said. Thank goodness she could still see Jack in the distance, climbing up onto a dray. No Samson to keep tabs on him now.

The saddler put down his work, taking his time and extended his arm. 'I'm Sid.'

Clare shook his hand impatiently.

'That young feller of yours, he's picked a good 'un,' said the man, in a slow drawl. 'Six-foot, twelve-strand kangaroo. For its weight, roo hide's the strongest leather in the world.' He lit a hand-rolled cigarette and continued. 'A whip's like a chain, love. The more links in a chain, the smoother it runs. Likewise, the more strands a thong has the more supple it moves.'

'That's very interesting, Sid,' said Clare, trying to keep one eye on Jack. 'How much do I owe you?'

But Sid would not be hurried. He stood up and fished a whip from among the leather goods scattered in the dust. 'Now this little number,' he said, shaking it, coiling it and offering it to Clare, 'is the right size for your boy. Red hide, three-foot, four-plait. It's cowhide, better for beginners. Heavier than roo, puts more weight into the belly of the whip. Makes it easy to crack.' The man demonstrated by cracking it loudly, three times in succession. 'Hear that? That's a mini sonic boom.' Sid cracked it once more for good measure. Jack turned and looked in their direction. Then he came pelting back. The man waited for him to arrive, then put on a bit of a show. A crowd gathered around. Jack was mesmerised, eyes large as Frisbees.

Sid held out the smaller whip to the boy. 'Want to swap, snowy?'

They made the exchange, then Sid gave Jack an impromptu whip cracking lesson.

After five minutes, Jack made his whip ring out like a rifle shot. Then again, with a grin as wide as his face. Sid was grinning too. He kneeled down and showed Jack the parts of his whip. 'You've got the handle, and the flick. The flick gives the whip shape and speed. And this long plaited lash part? That's called the thong.' He pressed each part as he described it into the palm of Jack's hand. 'This slotted leather loop is the fall. It connects to the cracker. That's the bit at the end that goes bang.'

Jack was fascinated. Clare hadn't seen him listen like that before. Afterwards, he set about practising his whip cracking, causing people to give him a wide berth. She gave Sid a grateful smile and helped him put right the display stand. Then she paid him for the whip. 'Much obliged,' he said, and returned to plaiting his leather.

'Come on, Jack,' she said hopefully. 'Let's look at something else.' But the visit was all downhill from there. She tried taking him to the toilet, but instead he pulled down his pants and peed up against a carriage wheel in front of everybody. He brandished the lash and threw his drink bottle at a boy in the café. Clare had hoped for some nice photos of Jack in the charming children's area, *The Coach Stop*. Here kids could play in a pint-sized general store or take a ride on a full-size replica horse, or even dress up and pretend to ride a Cobb and Co coach through the outback. But every time she tried to take the shot, Jack was frowning or belting somebody with the stock whip.

'I give up,' she said, and they headed for the car park.

Jack and Samson greeted each other like long lost friends and chased each other in ever widening circles. Samson bailed up a young couple, barking and jumping. Oh no, now Jack was barking too. Clare raced off to retrieve them, burning with embarrassment. She apologised and bundled her wayward charges back into the car. It seemed like she'd apologised more times in the last month than she had in her entire life.

Samson had taken a chunk out of the back seat upholstery. Of course he had. The dog panted and grinned at her, as if to say *that'll teach you to leave me behind*. Clare took off down the road, wheels spinning on gravel. Samson laid his head on Jack's knee and the pair promptly fell asleep as if nothing had happened. She could use a very strong coffee right about now, but she dare not stop at a shop. She dare not leave the car. Whatever had possessed her to embark on a four-hour road trip with those two?

Clare settled in for the drive. It took some time to escape Toowoomba's sprawling outskirts and catch her first glimpse of Gowrie Mountain. This distinctive, flat-topped hill was a perfectly preserved extinct volcano. She'd explored its lofty slopes with her grandfather as a child. He'd shown her the funnel-shaped opening of the crater. The great hole where molten lava erupted long ago to fill the valley below.

Childhood memories crowded in thick and fast, and Clare's anxiety slipped away along with the miles. This was easy driving. Up until now, Warrego Highway had required all of her concentration. It had been raining as she approached the eastern face of the Great Dividing Range. Parts of the road had recently been washed away and the crumbling bitumen and potholes had kept her on constant alert. The rich, volcanic farmlands of the Lockyer Valley were known as Brisbane's salad bowl, its fertile hinterland. But Clare had found it hard to admire the scenery. Some years ago, dozens of people had perished here. A tropical cyclone combined with a deep rain trough had sent a deadly, seven-metre wall of water surging through the valley. An inland tsunami. She'd shivered a little as the windscreen wipers worked harder. The sense of foreboding didn't lift until they'd left the floor of the basin and started the steep climb up to Toowoomba.

Now they were waving goodbye to the town and heading for Dalby, following the railway line. Clare turned on the radio. Static, apart from a country music station. It would do. Simple chords and *he done me wrong* lyrics suited her mood. Signs warned drivers to beware of road trains: monstrous trucks hauling equally monstrous trailers, some bound for Darwin more than three thousand kilometres away. Paddocks grew bigger and bigger, stretching away to the horizon.

The sun came out to celebrate the first day of spring. Driving to Currawong was like going back in time. Clare hadn't seen these black soil plains since childhood, but they felt familiar. The landscape was dominated by rolling hills, patchworked with lush green pasture and spring crops. Local dirt roads intersected the highway. They stretched away into the distance, crisscrossing bushy ridges and winding creeks. Roads with evocative names like Jumbuck Way, Stagecoach Track and one with a simple signpost saying Stock Route. Tumbledown wool sheds and rusted machinery lay scattered in paddocks, remnants from a bygone era of exploration and settlement. They passed water tanks and farmhouses and silos, big and small. Proud windmills stood dotted across the farmlands, raising the life-giving waters of the Great Artesian Basin. It comforted Clare to see their silhouettes. She loved the bottle trees too, with their signature swollen trunks and dense, evergreen crowns. Cattle dozed in their shade. The Downs retained its solid, well-remembered sense of place.

There was one feature of the landscape though, that she didn't remember. In some paddocks, haphazard arrangements of odd machinery squatted on squares of bulldozed ground. They weren't connected to the iconic windmills and bore heads. In fact the two never appeared within cooee of each other. Irrigation systems, perhaps? She'd never seen anything like them before, but things must have modernised out of sight in the last sixteen years. Some were no more than ugly collections of pumps and wheels and gauges. Others had storage tanks and tall, thin chimneys like giant flues, with pale flames peeking from the top. Solar panels mounted on stands, seemingly attached to nothing, powering who knew what? Pipes appeared and disappeared into nowhere, and strange dams of dark red water had been scoured into ground made bare for hundreds of metres around. Stout, steel-panelled fences guarded these installations. More than sufficient to keep out the odd, inquisitive cow or kangaroo who didn't heed the yellow hazard signs. The occasional outline of taller towers loomed on the horizon, well off the road, like oil rigs in the desert. Except this wasn't the desert. This was the finest agricultural land in the continent. What was so much industrial equipment doing in this peaceful, rural place?

A crop-dusting plane flew low overhead. She would have liked to show it to Jack, but he wasn't awake. An hour passed. Approaching Dalby now, and still Jack and Samson slept. Clare amused herself by trying to identify crops along the road. She could pick the wheat and corn. The paddocks of baby sunflowers. By summer their iconic, dinner-plate blooms would stand metres tall, bright faces following the sun across the sky. Fresh shorn sheep and fat cattle grazed beside swathes of sorghum. Or was it barley? Did they even grow sorghum at this time of year?

There was a time when she would have known. Once she could pick them all: chickpeas, mung beans, millet, soy – crops of all kinds. Grandad had taught her and Ryan their various growth habits and seed row widths. If the Lockyer Valley was Brisbane's salad bowl, the Darling Downs was a prime food bowl for the whole of Australia. It had been great fun, riding in Grandad's old truck, trying to pick out all the different crops and types of trees. Clare suddenly missed Ryan. He'd followed in Dad's footsteps, joined the army straight from school and married young. Their communications had grown less and less personal, their visits farther apart, and now she rarely saw him. His fault or hers? She supposed they were equally to blame. After all, she hadn't told Ryan about Jack, or about this trip to see their grandfather after so many years.

Clare slowed as she came into Dalby, and glanced into the back seat. Two terrors still asleep. She could have died for a coffee, but stopping might wake them. They passed the racecourse and approached a bridge surrounded by parklands. It all flooded back. A day in Dalby with her mother and grandparents - a picnic in the park. Playing chasey with Ryan round an engraved bluestone pillar. The memory was clear as a Condamine bell. Grandma's voice, explaining to them about the monument, a tribute to Cactoblastis, the humble caterpillar that had eradicated a plague of prickly pear in the 1920s.

Such happy days. Days of sunny summer holidays and intact families. Days of Mum with Dad, with all of them, and no concept of change that might lurk around corners. Of the gut wrenching gap Mum would soon leave in all their lives. It hit Clare then, a confusion of past and present loneliness, leaving her close to tears. Her mother was gone, and her father. Grandma too. Ryan as good as gone … and Adam. Now she returned alone to Currawong, to her grandfather. Her family had shrunk, through death and abandonment, to this one old man.

They crossed the bridge that spanned the swollen waters of Myall Creek, on its collision course with the Condamine River south-west of town. The Condamine drained the northern Darling Downs into the mighty Murray-Darling basin. The river gave its name to Condamine bells. Or bullfrog bells, as Grandad used to call them. He had quite a collection of the classic, square-mouthed cow bells, all strung up in the cart shed. Clare used to love running beneath them with a big stick, setting them pealing like it was her own, humble cathedral. Would they still be there, she wondered? Would she get to teach Jack that old game?

Dalby was a thriving country town with wide streets and plenty of pubs. Clare turned right across railway lines on its outskirts, leaving the Warrego Highway and heading north on the Bunya Road. An hour's driving and she'd be at Currawong Creek, turning into its century-old cast-iron gates. Sunshine gates, Grandad called them. Clare had loved to swing on those gates. She could see the word *SUNSHINE* wrought on the centre strut. And what was written above it? That's right - H. V. McKay. She'd chanted the name, over and over, as she played a complicated swinging game devised with Ryan. It had involved counting the number of swings you could do, in the time it took the windmill blades to turn ten times. It all depended on deter-mination and wind speed. Fancy remembering that. Grandma had said they were called Sunshine gates because of the McKay machinery company, which had made cultivators, swingle trees and horse yokes in the 1880s. They were famous for their Sunshine brand of harvesters and gates. But Grandad always said his gates were named for the sunshine itself, for the happiness they brought into the lives of people who entered through them. Clare had never doubted him for a minute.

It was a rough road to Merriang. The landscape grew hilly and wild. A pair of eagles spiralled high in the sky, causing her to crane her neck for a better view. Scatterings of gum trees turned into patches of forest: Myall, Cyprus and Wilga. She slowed down to negotiate a deep floodway, one of dozens that crossed the road. Clare was thankful that Jack and Samson slept through it all. She wanted time to herself, time to think about seeing her grandfather again. How would he look, she wondered, after all this time? Her memory was of a lean, tanned man with smiling eyes. An old man, though he'd only been in his fifties. She didn't have a clue what he might look like at seventy. It frightened her to think of him as aged and frail.

Soon the Bunya Mountains loomed in the windscreen. They rose abruptly from the surrounding flood plain, dominating the landscape. Someone stirred in the back seat. Clare glanced behind to see Jack yawning, eyes still sleepy. She pulled the car well off the road and let the pair of them loose. Samson bounded about in circles and Jack chased after him, or sometimes vice versa. A simple game, but one of which they never seemed to tire. Clare smiled. It suited her well enough. All she had to do was sit on a tree stump and watch. It really was astounding how good Samson was with Jack. The dog seemed to have in mind an invisible safety zone, outside of which the boy was not allowed to stray. If he tried, Samson lured him back with engaging moves, bowing low on his forelegs, tail raised and wagging – an irresistible invitation to play. Sometimes he used his body to physically shepherd Jack home.

Clare checked her phone. Two thirty - they'd be there by three. What perfect timing. Jack was usually on his best behaviour just after a sleep. Though Jack's golden time, for what it was worth, wouldn't last long. They'd better get a move on. With Samson's help she bundled Jack back in the car. She tried calling Grandad again, but had to leave a message. Oh well. She'd see him in person soon enough. Her foot was heavy on the throttle as they flew through the little town of Merriang. Past the general store, the pub, the post office. Not far now.

The road to her grandfather's place was officially and inexplicably named Railway Road. Inexplicably, because the nearest railway was eighty kilometres away. Grandad had removed the road sign long ago, together with one marking it as a scenic route. *The last thing I need are a bunch of bloody tourists taking pictures,* he'd said. Grandad replaced the old sign with one of his own, renaming the road to Currawong *Clydesdale Way.* And that's how it had stayed. On a few occasions council workers had reinstalled the correct sign, but it had received short shrift. And now, all these years later, it was still Clydesdale Way that Clare turned the car into.

The road aimed them straight at Bunya's peaks. The view of them left her mouth dry and her body breathless. Clare shrugged off the irrational, mounting fear that she wouldn't be able to find Currawong, that she might not recognise the driveway. That she'd have to turn around and go home. She had no idea why this thought unsettled her so. It had been such a long time. She had every excuse, sixteen years of excuses. But to miss the turnoff would be like saying her childhood hadn't mattered. It would be like saying the happy times weren't worth remembering. Only the dreadful days after Mum left.

Clare shivered. She hadn't expected the visit to affect her this deeply. It was turning a self-possessed professional woman into someone she didn't recognise and wasn't sure she liked. Of course she'd know the turn off. What could have possibly changed, way out here?

CHAPTER 9

Twin Bunya pine trees marked the gateway, just as she remembered. Clare was sick with anticipation as Jack began to yell.

'Almost there,' she said.

Samson whined at the sound of her voice — a voice strained and thick with emotion. The Sunshine gates were closed. The old *Curra-wong Creek* sign hung on the rail, with the same weathered image of a draft horse etched into its timbers. Beside it, however, hung two new signs. One read *Merriang Veterinary Surgery*. That was different – and a disagreeable reminder that time hadn't stood still.

The second sign, however, was much more troubling. A yellow triangle proclaimed *Warning Notice* in bold red letters. It went on to say *All common law rights to enter are expressly withdrawn. Admittance by invitation only to any persons and entities. Otherwise trespass applies.* The last bit was the most disturbing of all. *HCA 1991 171 CLR 635 F.C. 91/004.* Clare frowned. Why on earth would Grandad be citing a Full Bench decision of the High Court on his gatepost? It was bizarre.

Clare opened the gates and drove in, drinking in the view. Framed by the dramatic backdrop of the Bunya Mountains, the old farmhouse still looked like something from a pioneer movie. Things may have grown a little more dilapidated. The fences more sagging, the track more rutted than she remembered. But this was without doubt the cherished holiday home of her childhood. There was Grandma's garden … and the cart shed … and the training paddock - its driving course marked out with rusty forty-four-gallon drums. Jack spotted a pair of clydesdales dozing in the yards beside the shed. He squealed with delight and banged on the car window. More horses grazed beyond the yards, on the green pine-sprinkled slopes that rose towards the mountains. Here was something Clare hadn't fully remembered – Currawong's breathtaking beauty.

A little choke caught in Clare's throat, as an aristocratic pair of dalmatians trotted down the drive to meet them. Pongo and Perdita? No, of course not. The playmates of her youth would be long gone. It wasn't them, but Clare was delighted by that sweet, foolish notion.

'Samson - shush.' He was barking in her ear, attention fixed on a row of three ugly demountable rooms perched in a paddock to the left. They looked like they'd accidentally fallen off a truck and someone would be back for them any minute. A roughly graded square of gravel lay out the front, with a battered jeep parked there. A lonely-looking crow sat atop a home-made sign, that rather grandly pronounced this to be the *Merriang Veterinary Clinic - Client Car Park*.

It would be nice to walk up to the house – let the dogs all get to know each other on the way. Clare parked beside the jeep under the shade of a coolabah tree, a tree she remembered climbing with Ryan when it wasn't so tall. Compared to her weedy carpark specimen back in Brisbane, this coolabah was in robust good health. Tall and spreading, its shimmering canopy fragrant with the scent of eucalyptus. She climbed from the car and stretched muscles grown stiff from the long drive.

A clydesdale horse in an adjoining paddock raised its head and nickered to her. Then it plodded across to hang its massive neck over the fence for a pat. She gingerly stroked its broad, white blaze, having not touched a horse since that last day at the farm. Clare pressed her face to its nose. She'd read that people loved or hated certain smells because of the context in which they'd first encountered them. She was sure she loved the old-fashioned scent of lavender because it reminded her of Grandma's garden. Clare breathed in the horse's familiar, comforting smell and knew she'd come home.

Samson was barking louder now. She turned to see Jack's little hand waving out the back window. The dalmatians were standing nearby, noses raised, curiously sniffing the air. They looked friendly enough. It was the other dog that bothered her. A big blue heeler, crouched between her and the car. Where on earth had it come from? She stared at the dog as a rumbling growl rose in its throat. Samson stopped barking and the dalmatians turned around, as if to watch the show. The dog dropped down on its belly, like a lion about to launch an attack. 'Good boy,' she said, trying to smile. 'Good dog.' Did its hackles rise or was it her imagination?

Clare didn't like heelers. One had bitten her last year, launching itself from the darkness one night when she was walking with Adam. It had ripped through jeans, through skin, through muscle, and left her lame for weeks. This dog looked just like that one.

According to Helga, dogs perceived eye contact as a challenge. Clare wrenched her gaze away and waited a moment. When she looked back at the dog, it commando-crawled closer and growled louder. Clare screamed. A small scream, true – not much more than a squeal — but it was enough to set the dog off. It rushed at her, barking wildly, tail lashing from side to side.

Clare climbed the tree. She didn't quite know how she did it. One minute she was standing on the ground, rigid with fear. Next minute she was astride a broad branch, peering down like a possum with the heeler leaping and snapping below. There was little danger of falling. She was wrapped round that trunk so tight, she might as well have been welded on. Getting down, on the other hand, might present some problems.

Clare took the risk of reaching into her pocket for her phone. A bull ant chose the same moment to crawl over her fingers. She screamed again - a proper scream this time - and flung her arm out, propelling the ant and her brand new iPhone into mid-air. She groaned as she watched the phone spin in the sunlight, then plummet to the ground. Where had it landed? There, near that stick. Its sparkly case, studded with tiny Swarovski crystals, glinted in the light. The case was a present from Adam. Hand-stitched Tuscan leather with a waterproof, polycarbonate core, designed for extreme impact protection. His taste for high-end goods had paid off this time.

The heeler stopped its insane barking, turned around ... sniffed the ground. Clare held her breath. Maybe it was leaving? No, it seemed instead to be searching for something, scratching around in the leaf litter. A horrible thought struck her. Please no — not her phone. Then he had it. Damn Adam! Damn his glittery, leather case, which had turned her new iPhone into a highly visible chew toy.

The dog picked it up and trotted back to the base of the tree. He lay down, tail wagging. 'Drop it,' yelled Clare. 'Drop it, you stupid dog.' Then a sickening crunching sound.

The heeler spat out the phone and redoubled his efforts to snatch her from her perch, growling and jumping. The dalmatians trotted over to join in the chorus, and Samson too from the car - all barking at the top of their lungs. Clare looked hopefully at the modest little clinic. If someone was inside, surely they'd hear the racket? 'Help,' she shouted. 'Help ... help.'

A man's head appeared out of the window. 'Red,' he called, barely making himself heard above the commotion. 'Get here.' The heeler spun around and galloped off, its feet raising tiny plumes of dust.

Clare took a relieved gulp of air and almost lost her balance. The dalmatians kept on barking, but their hearts didn't seem to be in it any more. She could hear Jack yelling, his hand still waving out the open window like a pale, fluttering bird. Any minute now the man would come out. What would she say? She must look pretty silly, sitting halfway up a tree. No, she mustn't think like that. The heeler belonged to the man in the building, that much was obvious. He'd left a vicious dog at large ... let it rush a visitor. When the other heeler had bitten her, she'd been unable to identify its owner. This time would be different. This time, the owner would have to take responsibility for his negligence.

Minutes ticked by. Where was he, anyway? Why hadn't he come

out? The dalmatians gave up and trotted back up the drive to the house. Not much chance of Grandad hearing her. He'd been a bit deaf even when she was a child.

Clare tried to assess just how high up she really was. How the hell had she climbed so far? Must be four metres at least. She'd break a leg if she tried to climb down. There was nothing for it but to wait for the idiot to come out. Would he have a ladder? He'd need a ladder to get her down. Probably not much call for one in a vet clinic. He'd have to go up to the house and borrow one. The sting of impending tears pricked the back of her eyes. Clare sniffed them back. This was not how she'd wanted to meet Grandad.

Clare waited and waited. Every now and then a loud thud came from the demountable, and an occasional shout. What on earth was happening in there? Jack had settled into a harsh singsong wail. She could see him rocking in rhythm with his own cries, slamming his seat back and forth. Thank God the car was in the shade, and the window was open. He wouldn't be too hot. Would he?

Clare had promised Taylor to keep Jack safe. Taylor didn't know about the promise, of course, but that didn't matter. Clare had made it just the same, and she always kept her promises. It was a habit she'd cultivated to differentiate herself from her mother. Her mother's promises were like autumn leaves – bright and beautiful in the beginning, but fading to nothing in the end. Just a rotting mess to be trodden underfoot or swept away. Clare's promises weren't like that. Or were they? She'd hauled Jack out to the middle of nowhere and left him stranded in a car. That wasn't keeping him safe.

Beads of sweat formed on Clare's forehead. She wiped them away with the back of her hand and squinted into the blinding sunshine. No more yelling or barking came from the car now. It was disturbingly quiet. Each second seemed to take an hour. To play a waiting game in this heat was to play a very dangerous game indeed. Clare manoeuvred herself into a new position. A precarious position, but from here she might be able to reach the next branch with her foot. She looked down again. Not so much of a branch, really. More of a twig. It was curious how the branches she'd scaled in panic on her way up looked far too flimsy to bear her weight on the way down.

Clare took a deep breath. Hugging the trunk, she lowered her body, extended her right leg and fumbled for a foothold. Clare wasn't much of a physical risk-taker. She'd made some brilliant gambles in court and they'd paid off, but they were always carefully calculated. More importantly they didn't pose actual danger to life or limb.

Clare didn't like heights. She didn't bungy jump or parachute or hang glide. The older she grew, the more cautious she'd become. But the urgency of Jack's need outweighed her fear. Her foot found purchase and she gingerly lowered herself onto the branch below. So far so good. The bough felt sturdy enough underfoot.

Clare found herself a metre closer to the ground than before. She sized up the next branch with more confidence, and steeled herself to step off, to make that leap of faith. It was then she felt the tickle on her wrist. A spider the size of a saucer crawled onto her forearm. Clare willed herself to hang on regardless, but it was no use. Her reflexes weren't listening to her brain, and suddenly she was hurtling towards the ground. She closed her eyes.

Clare landed hard. The momentum of the fall slammed her head forward into a stump. Stabbing pain ricocheted round her body as the wind was knocked out of her. She fought for air, fought against the suffocating horror of empty lungs. Blood ran from her nose and lip. She tasted it on her tongue.

When Clare could breathe again, she struggled to her feet and stumbled to the car. She wrenched open the doors and stood panting and apologising to Jack and Samson. For once, the dog didn't erupt from the car in an explosion of energy. He just looked at her with those deep brown eyes, his velvet brow wrinkled in concern. Jack too, was uncharacteristically quiet — large-eyed and staring. Heat exhaustion perhaps?

Then Clare caught her reflection in the car window. Her blood-smeared face. Her tangled hair and intense, wild eyes. So that was it. They were scared of her. Clare tried to smile, but it hurt her face. She smoothed her hair into some sort of order, combed out leaves and twigs with her fingers. A small spider abseiled from her forehead to her nose on a thread of silk. She cast it away with a flick of her fingers. Jack opened his eyes a little wider. Was she shaking? Clare steadied herself, though her legs felt like straw, and tried the smile again. 'It's all right,' she said. 'I'm here now.' It seemed to work. Samson's ears relaxed and Jack gave a familiar protest yell. The dog's huge tongue swept over the boy's face and he burst into laughter. Good, they were okay.

Clare wasn't so sure about herself. Her ankle ached. She'd skinned her hands and knees. She had a fat lip. Was her nose broken? She pinched it gently and wiggled it a little, but she couldn't tell. The last time she'd felt this sore was after falling off a bolting Smudge in this very paddock. For some reason the thought cheered her up.

With a little encouragement, Jack and Samson tumbled from the car and embarked on their inevitable game of chasey. Her previous concern for their welfare was morphing into anger at the man in the vet clinic. What if she'd broken her leg in the fall? What if she'd been knocked out, or worse? What if she'd been unable to rescue Jack from the car? The possibilities didn't bear thinking about.

Clare stalked towards the clinic, Jack and Sampson romping along after her. She spread arms in a protective gesture designed to keep them behind her, and took hold of Samson's trailing lead. The heeler was still around somewhere, and the thought gave her a chill. Only the strength of her outrage made her bold enough to open the door.

An urgent voice sang out. 'Quick, get in here – and close that door.'

Just as she suspected. The heeler must be outside somewhere, ready to attack. She grabbed Jack by the hand and pushed inside, slamming the door after her.

An extraordinary sight confronted her. Waiting room chairs lay scattered and upturned. Shelves stood dragged away from walls, their contents spilled to the floor. No wonder the man hadn't come to her aid. He was struggling in the corner, wrestling with a snake – a python, to judge by its enormous size. The creature's length was wrapped around his body. 'Grab its tail,' he yelled. 'Grab its tail!'

Was he mad? Clare stood statue still, trying to make sense of the scene. But before she could manage to, Jack had darted forward and wrapped both hands around the snake's twitching tail.

'That's right,' said the man. 'Now hang on while I get his front.' He dived for the reptile's head, which had escaped his hold and was snaking out towards the window ledge. Its purple tongue flicked in and out, tasting the air. Samson started barking. Clare tied him to a cupboard and wished she could do the same to Jack.

'Jacky,' yelled Clare. 'Come away!' He ignored her. Instead he hugged the creature tighter to his body, while the tip of its prehensile tail twined around his wrist.

The man grasped the snake's neck, and brought its head up next to his own. Reptile and man regarded each other for a moment. Then in an awful, mesmerising dance, that involved passing the snake's head rhythmically from hand to hand and around his back, he unwound the snake from his torso. Clare hated herself for thinking it, but his actions were oddly sexy.

Finishing his dance, the man's tanned face cracked into a smile. 'I'm Tom, by the way. Tom Lord, the new vet. Help me get her into the surgery, will you?'

'Are you insane?' said Clare. 'Aren't you going to take it outside?'

'Not a chance,' Tom said. 'Not when I went to so much trouble to catch her.'

'You caught it?' said Clare. 'I thought it caught you.'

Jack was doing a surprisingly good job, helping manoeuvre the snake through the door and onto a stainless steel table. Tom wrestled its head into a rubber funnel attached to a plastic tube. The tube was in turn attached to some sort of machine. 'Press that button,' the vet said, looking straight at Clare and pointing to a red switch. The snake flipped, almost knocking Jack over. Clare was paralysed with fear. Tom raised his voice a notch. 'If you want me to put this snake to sleep, you'd better bloody well press that button. That red one.'

Clare hesitated for a moment longer, then pressed it. She felt unaccountably sorry for the snake.

'Will it be quick?' asked Clare. 'And painless?'

'Relatively so. I'm using Isoflurane.' Tom adjusted the tube. 'It's gold standard for anaesthetising reptiles and there's no oesophageal or tracheal irritation. That's the problem with most of these gases.'

Clare was touched. How many people would care enough to humanely put down a snake? She waited with bated breath. For a little while, nothing happened. Jack still hung on, and the snake seemed as recalcitrant and active as ever. 'It can take a few minutes. She doesn't breathe as fast as a mammal.' The vet flashed Clare a killer smile. 'Won't be long now.' He was really quite good-looking, in a rough and ready sort of way. Sandy blond hair worn in a no-nonsense, almost military, buzz cut. Rugged tanned features. The material of his blue scrubs strained across broad shoulders and outlined the arch of his upper back.

The snake sagged in the middle. 'Get that wooden board in the corner and lay it on the table.' Clare obliged, and he laid the front third of the snake across it. The vet gently disengaged Jack's arms from their death grip. 'Good job,' he said. Jack beamed with pride. The snake looked lifeless.

'Why the board?' asked Clare.

'Metal tables suck heat from reptiles and she's weak enough already. Wood will keep her that little bit warmer.'

Weak? The snake was more than weak. It was dead, wasn't it? Why would you want to keep a dead snake warm?

Jack was watching the man's every move with rapt attention. Clare had never seen him so focused. It had certainly been an adventure for him. The thought that it might not have turned out as well as it did made Clare shudder. Tom scrubbed forearms and hands, pulled on surgical gloves, then stopped and stared at Clare as if seeing her for the first time. 'Something's happened to your face,' he said. 'It's all puffed up and bleeding. You'd better let me look at that afterwards.'

. . .

Clare felt her nose and ignored his comment. Jack was patting the snake. It was good for children to learn about life and death through animals. For her it had been Grandma's chickens. Collecting eggs one morning, she'd found a hen lying quite still in the nest box. It took some time for Grandma to convince her that it wasn't just asleep. For the first time she'd seen what *dead* looked like. Clare overcame an instinctive reluctance to touch the snake. She stroked its body, surprised by the skin's dry silken texture. Its scales, reflected in the light, took on a transparent violet glow, dazzling in its brilliance.

Tom followed her gaze. 'Beautiful, isn't she? Gets her name from that purple sheen. *Amethystine python*, although most people call them scrub pythons. Not nearly as poetic.'

'It's enormous. How long do you think?' asked Clare.

The vet sized up the reptile. 'Four metres, maybe? But she's just a tiddler. I've seen ones up north go eight and a half.'

Jack gave the python a shake.

'Sorry, darling. It won't wake up,' she told the little boy in a consoling voice.

'That's right, mate,' said Tom. 'It won't, thanks to this little beauty.' He inserted a thin tube into the snake's mouth and tied it in place. 'This goes down her trachea,' he said. 'It's what she'll breathe through. I'm running oxygen and isoflurane down it so she'll stay asleep, like your mum said. But don't worry. She's going to be fine afterwards. Now, let's get her x-rayed.' The vet wheeled the table across the room, positioned it beneath the arm of a tall, grey machine, and heaved the prone reptile onto her back.

'You mean the snake's not dead?' asked Clare.

'I should hope not,' said Tom cheerfully.

'I thought you were …' Clare stopped, unwilling to admit her mistake, but Tom didn't appear to be listening. Jack was still stroking the snake. She sprang for him and gathered the child protectively in her arms. Her reward was a head-butt in the face. Jack squirmed free and returned to the snake's side.

Tom glanced up. 'She's completely harmless' he said, then added with a grin, 'Right now.' Clare didn't know how to respond. She became curious about the procedure this strange man was performing. His hands expertly massaged the reptile's belly as if feeling for something. His large fingers were surprisingly tender, as they made their way down the body, probing gently as they went. 'Aha.' He disinfected a section of pale belly scales, then made a short incision. By now Clare was as fascinated as Jack.

'Don't worry,' said Tom. 'She can't feel a thing.' He mopped away a small amount of blood. 'There's the problem.' The final slice of the scalpel revealed three dimpled spheres lined up along the reptile's gut. What were they? Eggs? With a pair of tongs Tom eased one of the objects out. It wasn't an egg at all. It was a golf ball.

'How in heaven's name?' said Clare.

'Old Harry used them as decoy eggs in the hen house. They encourage the new pullets to lay in their nest boxes. Those chickens weren't the only ones fooled. Madam here thought she was onto a good thing.'

Harry. Clare's grandfather.

Tom eased out a second ball. 'This morning Harry found the nest empty, and her in the corner with a bellyache. He put two and two together and called me.' Tom took out the final ball and lined it up beside the others. They were covered in mucous and blood. The sight made Clare sick.

Tom prepared to suture the wound. 'Come on, Jack,' she said. 'Time to go.' The boy shook his head violently.

'Hold on. I'll be with you in a minute.' Tom indicated Samson. 'He's a fine-looking dog. What seems to be the problem?'

For a moment Clare didn't understand. 'I'm not here as a client-'

'Snake,' said Jack.

Clare caught her breath. Had she imagined it?

'A special kind of snake,' said Tom. 'A python.'

'Python,' said Jack.

'That's right. You've got a smart kid here.'

'He spoke,' whispered Clare, mainly to herself. 'Jack spoke.'

Tom tied off the stitches and eased the tube from the snake's throat. 'So you're Jack,' he said, giving him a warm smile. 'And what's your mum's name?'

'I'm Clare,' she said, still stunned that Jack had spoken.

'Clare ... Harry's granddaughter? I didn't know you had a son.'

She nodded. The nod was for the first bit. It was a nod for, *Yes, I'm Harry's granddaughter*, not for, *Yes, I have a son*. She opened her mouth to clear up the misunderstanding, but Tom was talking again. 'The old man's been waiting for you all day. Never seen him so excited. You didn't have to stop in and say hello to me first.' Clare sighed. Tom really was exasperating. He coiled the sleeping snake into a pet crate, then swung Jack into the air. The little boy giggled with glee. 'I'll come up to the house with you two. Update Harry on his snake.'

She should say no. She should tell him to take his ugly portable buildings and his snakes and his vicious dogs and leave her alone. Maybe it was the shock of Jack speaking, or maybe she had concussion from falling out of the tree, but for whatever reason, she allowed Tom to carry Jack out the door.

CHAPTER 10

Time had stood still. The cream and green cupboards, the matching enamel stove, the battered timber table top – all just as they had once been. Clare might have been eleven-years-old again. The funny thing was that she couldn't have recalled a single thing about that kitchen if you'd asked her an hour earlier. But now? Now she recognised each tiny detail.

'Harry,' called Tom, still holding Jack aloft. 'Got something for you.'

Her grandfather emerged from the hallway. Unlike the kitchen, he had changed. The few strands on his head were white now. His clothes hung loose on a skinny frame and the years showed on his lined face. But he still stood tall, unstooped, and when he saw Clare, his smile was as warm as ever.

'Well, look at you,' he said, taking her in, not seeming to notice her dishevelled hair and bruised face. 'My little Clare all grown up and quite a beauty, wouldn't you say so Tom?'

For some ridiculous reason, Clare found herself waiting on Tom's response. She turned her head away a fraction in embarrassment.

'That I would, Harry,' came the answer. 'That I would.'

Clare bit her lip. The man had some hide.

. . .

Harry strode over and embraced Clare, holding her for the longest time.

Clare blinked back tears. What a precious sensation, to be encircled in her grandfather's protective arms. It was a feeling to hold on to. 'I'm sorry about your dad,' he said.

She felt a shaft of shame. '*And I'm sorry about Grandma,*' she wanted to say. '*I'm sorry for not being here, for not caring enough,*' but the words were like a weight she couldn't lift.

'And who have we here?' asked Harry.

'This is Jack,' said Clare. 'The little boy I was telling you about.'

Comprehension dawned on Tom's face. 'So he's not yours then?'

'I'm his temporary foster parent.'

'I'll bet that's quite a story.' Tom's smile broadened. 'She's got a dog too, Harry. He's outside. A black German shepherd pup.'

'Well, bring him in,' said her grandfather. 'The more the merrier.'

Tom put Jack down. 'I'll fetch him.' The little boy followed Tom out the door, ignoring Clare's call. 'He's fine with me,' said Tom. 'We'll be back in a jiffy'.

Clare hesitated, then nodded and let Jack go. She was too worn out to argue. Truthfully it was a relief to abdicate responsibility, even if it was just for a minute, even if it was to that insensitive idiot.

Being alone with her grandfather left Clare a little tongue-tied. It had been easier with Tom there, helping the conversation along, but now she felt the gulf of years between them. What to do? What to say? They were strangers.

Harry put an ancient kettle on the cast iron range and indicated for her to sit. Clare sensed an awkwardness in him too. He fussed about the kitchen while they waited for the others to come back. Clare was on to her second cup of Grandad's strong, sweet tea, when Samson poked his head in the door. She froze. The blue heeler was right behind him, a deep growl in its throat. She jumped to her feet, tipping over her chair and retreating against the wall.

'Don't mind Red,' said Harry, with a chuckle. 'He's daft. Growling's his way of saying hello.'

Grandad sounded like the daft one. The dog advanced, a snarl on its lips. Clare edged around the wall towards the hallway. Thank god Jack was still outside.

Harry gave her a bemused look. 'That snarl? … that's just him smiling. I told you he was daft. People get the wrong idea.' As if to prove Grandad's point, the heeler jumped up and licked his hand, still making the rumbling sound. 'See? He's like a cat purring.'

Clare began to relax. Had she really got it so wrong? The heeler turned his attention to her now and she steeled herself to stand still. He licked her toes where they poked through her sandals, making her flinch. He looked up and whined. She tried to imagine his bare-toothed snarl as a grin. 'Hello, boy,' she said hesitantly, smothering a squeal as the heeler jumped up for a pat.

Grandad was rummaging round in a cupboard. 'There are biscuits somewhere.'

Samson and Jack tumbled inside and played chasey around the kitchen table. The heeler joined in the fun, growling and snarling and wagging his tail. Clare composed herself and sat down just as Tom came in. He took a seat beside her and watched the game, shaking his head. 'Red sure is one, crazy mixed-up dog.' He glanced up, laughing, and caught her watching him. She flushed a little, hoping it didn't show. 'Let me take a look at those cuts to your face,' he said.

She shook her head.

'What happened?' he asked. 'You come a cropper off a horse?'

She nodded. Anything to avoid admitting that she'd climbed a tree to escape his stupid, smiling dog, and had promptly fallen out of it.

Grandad produced a packet of Iced VoVos, offered one to Jack, and shook the rest onto a plate. Clare took one and examined it. Pink fondant icing atop a wheat biscuit, a strip of strawberry jam running down the middle, and the entire thing dusted with coconut. She turned it over. The back still bore the fancy moulded design that she remembered from childhood. A memory of sharing these same biscuits around this same table hit her so powerfully that Clare half-expected Grandma to walk in the door.

'You were right about the python,' said Tom, helping himself to a biscuit. 'I just cut three golf balls from her belly. Had a hard time holding her, but these two were a big help.' He stood up and dusted crumbs off his shirt. 'Better get back to it. You coming to the meeting tonight, Harry?'

'Planned to,' said Harry, 'but I wouldn't miss the first evening with my granddaughter, not even for the cakes.'

'Righto,' said Tom. 'I'll fill you in tomorrow. Never know your luck — I might bring you back a lamington.' He waved an expansive good-bye, and left with Red trotting at his heels.

'What's it about?' asked Clare. 'This meeting?'

'Nothing for you to worry about.' Samson sat at his feet, squirming and smiling as Grandad rubbed his ears. 'How about I find this scoundrel of yours a bone and the lad some toys, eh?' His face, alight with pleasure, already looked ten years younger.

Why had she left it so long between visits? They'd lost too many years - years that should have been filled with love, and family, and a sense of belonging. All of it sacrificed to her father's bitterness, and the altar of her own ambition.

Harry emerged a few minutes later with a huge cardboard carton. He put it on the kitchen floor and called Jack over from where he was watching flies buzz at the window. Clare drew in a quick breath. Here was a treasure trove of memories: a wind up jack-in-the-box that used to frighten her, a fleet of hand-carved trucks, a wooden skittle set. Jack started gathering together the Matchbox cars.

Samson picked up a worn rag doll in his mouth. It wore a purple dress that Clare remembered Grandma knitting. Harry took an enormous marrowbone from the fridge and offered it to Samson. 'This'll suit you better.' He rescued the doll, and Samson took the bone into the corner. Clare watched the boy and the dog, both of them relaxed and happy in a way that just didn't happen back at her apartment — like they'd broken free of something.

Clare gazed around the kitchen. Sixteen years of memories held in its walls and she didn't know what they were. She could guess. Grandma cooking her famous roasts. Grandad dancing her around the table. Card games and flower pressing. Writing and wrapping all those unopened cards and presents. Grandad taking over the cooking as Grandma got sick. Boiled eggs and cups of tea. Chicken soup and toast. Clare could guess, but she didn't know. She wanted to ask her grandfather about it, but she couldn't. Not yet. Not when she looked at the door and realised just how long it had been since Grandma had walked through it.

'Do you ever hear from Mum?' she asked.

He gave her a heavy-hearted smile. 'Not often, love. She's all caught up in her own world. No time for her old dad.' Or her children, thought Clare. But who was she to judge? She'd been just as bad, abandoning Harry for all these years ... and Grandma. That was unforgiveable. She was suddenly horrified to think she'd never see her again, as if the dreadful finality of her grandmother's death had only just hit home. Guilty tears pricked at her eyes, but all that she could see in Grandad's eyes was love.

Clare spent a magical afternoon showing Jack around. They pushed each other on the tyre swing in the garden. They played the giant xylophone of Condamine bells in the cart shed until her ears rang. They collected eggs from the chook house and picked the first broad beans of spring. They climbed on the haystack and practised whip cracking. The little boy was entranced by each activity. 'That's a fine stockwhip,' Grandad said, when he came to find them. Clare told him an edited version of their day at the Cobb & Co museum. It turned out he knew the saddler. 'I thought it was one of Sid's.'

Grandad and Jack took the horses some carrots, while Clare returned to the house to make up Ryan's old bed in the verandah room. When she opened the curtains, spectacular orange trumpets of winter-flowering flame creeper crowded against the rusted fly wire.

Childhood memories lay in ambush around every corner. Memories that made her ache with both sadness and happiness.

Later Clare helped Grandad prepare the roast: a plump leg of lamb nestled among potatoes and carrots, pumpkins and parsnips. She could already taste the rich, dark gravy made in the pan. Clare prepared fruit for the pie. The kitchen was redolent with the aroma of hearty country cooking. Quite a contrast to her own, where the microwave was the only appliance to get a regular workout.

After dinner Clare stood at the bedroom door while Grandad read Jack a tattered copy of *Where the Wild Things Are*. The little boy dropped off to sleep, clutching his stock whip, before the sun had fully set behind the mountains. She smiled as her grandfather kissed Jack's cheek and closed the curtains. Samson hopped onto the foot of the bed and turned beseeching brown eyes on Clare.

'Leave him,' said Grandad. 'The lad has a right to his dog.'

He turned out the lamp and followed Clare back down the hall. She'd only been at Currawong for a few hours, but already the distractions of Brisbane and the pain of her recent breakup seemed a world away.

She helped Grandad tidy the kitchen and do the dishes, mulling over the events of the afternoon. Her thoughts kept returning to the remarkable way Jack had responded since he'd been at the farm, and of how he'd actually spoken. If you didn't know any better, Jack would have almost seemed like a normal little boy today. Grandad pulled an old Scrabble set from a bookshelf. 'I won't be quite so easy to beat these days,' she teased.

'We'll see,' he said. The tension between them was slipping away.

To her surprise, Grandad trounced her - twice. 'I'm done,' she said, standing up. 'You're too good for me.'

He gave her a heartfelt hug. 'It's a great joy having you here, Clare.'

'It's a great joy being here,' she said, smiling at the pet name she'd forgotten about. 'I've missed you, missed this place. Funny thing is, I didn't even realise how much until today.' She reached for his hand. 'Goodnight, Grandad.'

'Goodnight, love.'

Clare tiptoed down the hall and looked in on Jack. Moonlight streamed through a crack in the curtains, spotlighting his pillow. The little boy looked serene, his features relaxed in sleep. Samson stretched and thumped his tail. 'Goodnight, you two.'

She slipped into her room, slipped into her old bed. The moon sailed high outside her window, bathing the familiar space in a soft light. The giant bunya pine, standing guard in the yard, cast a reassuring silhouette against the luminous sky. Clare drifted off to sleep, overcome by the strangest notion – the notion that returning to Currawong might be the wisest decision she'd ever made.

Grandad placed a steaming plate of scrambled eggs before her. Jack was already shovelling great spoonfuls into his mouth, while Samson sat beside him, wolfing up the inevitable spills. A knock came at the door. 'It'll be Tom,' said Grandad, with a chuckle. 'That boy can smell breakfast a mile off.'

Clare ran her fingers hurriedly through her hair. She hadn't expected to see anybody so early.

Tom came in and sat down beside Jack. Clare looked warily around. Friendly or not, she was still not a great fan of Red, but there was no sign of him. Soon they were all hoeing into the biggest breakfast Clare could remember. Piles of buttered toast. Bacon, tomato and grilled mushrooms the size of her hand.

'Harry grows them in bags of compost under the house,' said Tom, taking a second helping. 'Bloody beautiful, they are.'

Clare imagined how horrified Adam would be at the cholesterol-laden spread, and then took another slice of bacon.

Tom was playing spider fingers with Jack in between mouthfuls, threatening to pounce whenever the little boy reached for his spoon, generating a storm of giggles.

'How was the meeting?' asked Grandad.

'Got a bit out of hand at the end,' said Tom. 'A few blokes turned up that were on Pyramid's side. Reckoned we were just scaremongering, trying to spoil things for them.' He reached across for more toast, brushing against Clare's arm in the process. She was acutely aware of his touch; the warmth of his skin. 'Pyramid offers generous compensation for each well per year, as well as an up-front fee. If you host say, twenty wells, that's big money. Can't blame people for being tempted.'

'No, I suppose you can't,' said Grandad with a sigh. 'The almighty dollar always wins out in the end, eh?'

'Maybe,' said Tom, tousling Jack's hair, and pushing his chair back from the table. 'And maybe not. Look at Pete Porter. He makes a good income from his wells, but he'd get rid of them in a heartbeat, given half the chance. Those for Pyramid were outnumbered ten to one by the rest of us. It's not hard to see which way the tide of community opinion is running.' He washed up his plate, gave Clare a nod and left.

'What wells?' asked Clare.

'Coal seam gas wells,' said Grandad. 'Pyramid Energy reckons the biggest field in Australia lies right under Merriang. They've taken out exploration licenses for the whole region.'

'Natural gas?' asked Clare.

'There's nothing natural about it.'

'And what … they want to put wells here at Currawong Creek?' He nodded.

'Is that what the sign on the gate's all about?'

'Yep.' There was a grim set to his jaw. The subject was apparently closed. 'Thought I'd take the young fellow yabbying.' He stood and collected up the empty plates, scraping the scraps into the chook bucket. 'And don't worry, love. I remember you've got a soft spot for the little snappers. We'll let them go afterwards. What do you say, Jack? Do you want to catch some yabbies? Maybe we'll dig out that old aquarium and you can keep a few as pets, just like your mum used to do.'

'I'm not his mother,' corrected Clare.

'Course you're not,' said Harry, taking some steak from the fridge and cutting a few tiny slivers. 'My mistake.' The little boy bounced from his chair and grabbed Harry's arm. Clare studied him as he tried to drag her grandfather outside.

Should she let them go? 'Jack …' She stopped, not wanting to say too much while the little boy was listening. 'He runs away,' she said at last, 'and tantrums … unless he's with Samson.'

'The dog looks after him then?'

She nodded. 'And Grandad, Jack can't speak - except he did, once, with me, and then again yesterday with Tom.'

Harry looked at her without surprise, his expression matter of fact. 'I expect the lad will talk when he's good and ready,' was all he said, and the pair headed for the door.

'I'll join you in a bit,' she called after them. 'Watch Jack around the dam, won't you?' Clare fetched her laptop and checked without much hope for internet access. Nothing. Tom must have Wi-Fi. Surely you couldn't run a modern vet clinic without it?

Through the window, she saw her grandfather make his way across the yard, bucket in hand, while Jack and Samson chased each other in a wide arc around him. Pongo and Perdita trotted ahead. Apparently the same names had been used for different dogs in the family for fifty years. Ever since Grandma read Dodie Smith's classic novel, *101 Dalmatians*, there'd been a Perdita and Pongo at Currawong. Tradition played no part in the life Clare knew in Brisbane. She was oddly appreciative of finding it alive and well out here at the family farm.

Clare packed up her laptop and made her way down the drive to the clinic, where a couple of cars were parked. A short girl with three border collies stood by the surgery door, along with a red-faced man sporting a comb-over. He was holding two buckets labelled *Henry's Honey*.

'Hello,' said Clare.

'Hello,' said the girl shyly. Clare waited nearby, shifting from foot to foot. The man nodded a greeting, then proceeded to cast odd glances her way, as if he didn't quite approve of her being there. At last the door swung open. Tom turned the little sign in the window from *Closed* to *Open*, then stared past the others to Clare. He smiled, crinkling the little laugh lines at the corners of his mouth.

'Here you go,' said the man, offering the buckets.

Tom looked puzzled. 'What's this, Henry?'

'Thought it might do as a trade for what's left on my bill,' he said and marched inside, followed by the girl, the border collies and finally Clare.

The room was still a mess from the previous day. Shelves were once more in place against the walls, but their contents had been jammed back in haphazard piles. Stacks of books, brochures and journals spilled from the reception desk, almost burying the ancient computer. The collies roamed about the room, poking curious noses under cupboards and onto shelves. Their girl made no attempt to control them. Instead she waited patiently beside a sign saying *All dogs to be on a leash*. Maybe the snake wasn't entirely to blame for yesterday's mayhem after all. It could just be the natural state of affairs around here. Clare moved closer to the desk and discovered a wireless modem behind a box of horse worming paste. Good, that solved her communications problem.

'What am I supposed to do with all this honey?' asked Tom,

'There's loads you can do with honey, besides eat it of course,' said Henry. 'Use it as a facial, hair conditioner, antiseptic, and my missus swears by it for treating rough elbows.' He turned to leave.

'Wait,' said Tom. 'I don't think …'

Henry held up his hand. 'No need to thank me doc,' and with that he ducked out the door. An old gentleman arrived next, with a bald cockatoo wearing a little knitted jumper. Clare wondered if he was going to try and trade it as well.

The *If I Could Talk to the Animals* tune rang out, and Tom found his phone under a box of catnip. Who did he think he was? Dr Doolittle? She shook her head in disgust. How on earth did the clinic even function? She'd never seen anything so unprofessional in her life. Perhaps it would be better to come back later.

As Clare turned to go, a hand touched her arm. She looked up into Tom's clear blue eyes. Summer sky blue. 'Can I help you?'

'I want to get online.'

Tom's hand remained on her arm. It was rough-skinned like a farmer, and long-fingered like an artist. 'Be my guest. There's no password,' he said and disappeared into the consulting room with the collie girl.

The cocky spread its bald wings and said, *Hello stranger.* Clare laughed and said hello back. It answered her with a wolf whistle and a little dance.

'Buddy's always been a flirt,' the old man said fondly. The bird nuzzled his cheek.

Tom emerged from the consulting room, followed by the girl and her dogs. 'All up to date now,' he said. 'That C5 vaccination covers Canine Cough as well, so they'll be right to go into kennels in a couple of weeks.'

'Can I have two tick collars as well, please?' asked the girl.

Tom looked around at the cluttered shelves. 'Now where did I put them?'

Clare spotted a box labelled *Excel Tick Control Collars* behind a stack of dog toys. She retrieved the box, placed it in a more prominent position, then took out two packets and handed them over. Tom looked impressed. The girl paid the account and he turned his attention to Mr Cockatoo man.

'Paddy, if you'd like to come in ...'

'I'll not be dragging this out,' the man said in a thick Irish brogue. 'Do you have those test results?' Tom nodded. 'And you wouldn't go beating around the bush with me, would you doc?'

Tom's expression softened. 'I think we both knew, Paddy, but the test confirmed it. Buddy has PFBD ... psittacine beak and feather disease.'

The old man scratched the bird's neck and it bounced with pleasure. 'There's no cure, is there now?' Tom shook his head. The man's face had crumpled alarmingly. 'My wife Betty, bless her heart, found Buddy here as a wee nestling, the week we lost our son Patrick to the pneumonia. In the middle of our back paddock, Buddy was, with never a tree in sight. I think a crow must have dropped him, but Betty said he'd fallen from heaven. She nursed him day and night till he was well. I used to tease her - tell her she loved that bird more than me.'

Buddy bobbed his head and called out, 'Betty, Betty, Betty.' They all smiled.

'That was forty years ago now, if it was a day.' Clare was enthralled. 'Betty was a church-going woman, so she was. One morning she told me that God had spoken to her in a dream. *I will lend you this magic bird*, he'd said to her, *for you to love while he lives and mourn when he dies.*' Paddy's voice held a world of sadness. 'She said the Lord gave us Buddy to comfort us after Patrick.'

A chill fell on the room, and it dawned on Clare that something awful was about to happen. She felt the prickle of tears behind her nose. 'And comfort us he did, for all those years, and then kept me company when I lost Betty. He's been a great joy, Buddy has - my truest friend.'

'I can give you a cream ...' began Tom.

Paddy shook his head. 'No, no ... he wants to fly, you see. He tries so hard, I can't bear to see him always disappointed ... and he'll get sicker, won't he? I've read enough to know.'

Tom pressed his lips together and followed Paddy into the consulting room. Clare gulped and tried to compose herself. Thank goodness there were no other clients. The silence screamed as she waited for Tom to finish, waited for it to be over. At last they emerged. Paddy carried a small bundle wrapped in a towel. Clare began to cry. The old man put a wrinkled hand on her shoulder. 'Thanks for your tears, lass,' he said solemnly, and then he was gone.

'Hey, now,' said Tom. 'I thought you were a tough city lawyer. It was the kindest thing.'

'There's nothing kind about taking away a lonely old man's best friend,' managed Clare between sobs.

'No,' Tom said. 'I suppose not.' He boiled the electric kettle in the corner and poured her a cup of coffee. 'Stay and use the internet.' Tom grabbed what looked like an old-fashioned doctor's bag from behind the counter. 'You have the place to yourself.'

Clare said goodbye and tried to pull herself together, but the old man's face haunted her. How utterly bereft he must be. Now she was alone, Clare could no longer sniff back the tears. She laid her head on the desk and wept like a child.

When she was finally spent, Clare washed her face at the sink and peered in the mirror. Swollen, bloodshot eyes peered back. She looked as bad as she felt. Clare gulped down the lukewarm coffee and opened her laptop. No emails from work of course. That felt very strange. In fact there were hardly any emails at all, at least nothing personal. Clare checked Facebook. She hadn't been on the site for a long while and wasn't up to date with anything. She'd been so preoccupied lately. Between Dad's illness, her work and Adam, she'd allowed friendships to take a back seat. The embarrassing truth was that nobody seemed to have missed her.

She pushed aside the emptiness of that thought, made another coffee and googled coal seam gas on the Darling Downs. Dozens of websites popped up and she combed through the opposing views. It was a hot-button issue, no two ways about it, but Clare's legal training obliged her to put aside the hype and concentrate on facts. The first fact required no research. Under Queensland law, all resources below ground were the property of the state. Providing miners had the correct permits, farmers could not refuse them access to private land, no matter how many High Court decisions they quoted on their front gates.

Coal seam gas, she discovered, was just natural gas – mainly methane – extracted from coal seams deep below the ground. It was a low carbon energy source, producing half the greenhouse gas emissions of coal. As Tom had mentioned that morning, there was an upfront advance to landholders with wells, followed by annual payments. Companies were legally obliged to make good any damage caused, and surrounding land could still be used for cropping and grazing.

For the first time Clare considered how Grandad might be travelling financially. From what she remembered, his clydesdales used to give demonstrations at agricultural shows and were hired out for gypsy caravan holidays. He sold yearlings, stood stallions at stud, broke in horses to harness and ran a few steers. How much of that, she wondered, was he still capable of? He was old now. His back remained straight, but he was thin and so much frailer than she remembered. In some lights there was an odd translucency to his skin, as if his tan disguised an underlying pallor. The property too showed signs of neglect. Sagging fences. Stands of lantana and other weeds that Clare couldn't identify. The house could use a coat of paint. It might well be worth having a few ugly gas plants at Currawong Creek if it meant Grandad could take it easy.

The waiting room phone rang. Clare hesitated for a moment before answering it.

'Thank goodness the doc's come to his senses and hired an assistant,' said the caller. 'You have a job in front of you, my girl, trying to organise that one. Anyway, let him know Mrs Potts has an egg-bound budgie.'

Clare took down the message. 'When can you bring it in?'

'Oh, I don't drive, dear. Doctor Tom comes to me. It's so much easier that way.'

Easier for who? thought Clare, but dutifully noted the woman's phone number. She packed up her laptop and escaped the clinic before the phone could ring again.

Clare walked back up to the house, but there was nobody there. How was Jack getting on, she wondered? Maybe she shouldn't have let him go off like that with Grandad. She went to find them, heading down through the veggie patch towards the dam. Past the old tyre swing in the garden. Her mother used to tell her wonderful stories while pushing her on that swing. Stories of strong independent princesses. Princesses who won battles and slew dragons, without a Prince Charming in sight. Past the stack of old bricks that Ryan had piled up by the tool shed long ago. She couldn't believe it was still there. He'd named it *The Stone Table*. They used it to play *The Lion, the Witch and the Wardrobe* games. He'd been Aslan and she'd been Jadis, the evil White Witch. They'd reenacted scenes from the book. She'd regularly tried to sacrifice him on the bricks, with varying degrees of success. Past their old cubby. It wasn't in too bad a shape. Maybe she'd fix it up for Jack.

Clare detoured down a grassy track that led to Currawong Creek. It opened onto a familiar expanse of winding water, more of a river really. Here were the red gums, bunya pines and reedy shallows of memory. This was the scene she'd recalled back at Koala Park. Back on that awful day when she'd lost Jack and they'd retreated from the reserve in disgrace.

The sound of laughter drew her back up the path. Grandad, Jack and the dogs were returning from the dam. 'The yabbies weren't biting, but we haven't come back empty-handed. Show her, Jack.' Jack proudly showed Clare their bucket. It was filled with enormous eggs. 'I finally found their nest, with the help of your shepherd pup,' said Grandad, fondling Samson's head. 'There'll be goose egg omelettes for breakfast tomorrow.'

They put the eggs in the kitchen and sat out on the verandah with cups of tea. Samson was helping Jack collect sticks. The little boy assessed each one carefully, then either discarded it or added it to his pile. 'What's the difference?' Clare said. 'They're all the same. A stick's a stick.'

'To you maybe,' said Grandad. He nodded when Jack balanced another stick on his pile, as if he agreed with the choice. A breeze blew out of nowhere and Grandad turned his head to meet it, staring into the distance and sniffing the wind. 'Storm on the way.' Clare studied his weathered face in profile. They'd lost so much time. In some ways Grandad was as big a mystery to her as Jack was.

A week now at Currawong Creek, and Clare could feel the cares and anxieties of Brisbane slipping from her like an outgrown skin. She yawned and cleared away her dishes. Jack and Samson had already headed out with Grandad, leaving Clare to enjoy a lazy breakfast. No phone, no email, no need to do anything at all in particular. She'd been spending her days playing with Jack, or weeding Grandma's veggie patch or exploring the house and sheds. Sometimes she simply sat in the garden, reading a book selected from Grandma's well-thumbed *Collection of Modern Classics*. Jane Austen, Charles Dickens, Sir Arthur Conan Doyle - the dusty hallway bookshelves were stacked high with all sorts of gems. A copy of *Treasure Island* that Grandad used to read, putting on a silly pirate voice. Mum's *Golden Treasury of Poetry*, its spine mended with packing tape. A photo album. On the cover was a shot of Clare riding Smudge. Mum stood proudly by her side, holding the pony's reins. Clare had flipped slowly through the old pictures, stroking each page, closing her eyes to help summon memories. Here at Currawong, the past wasn't gone. The present was crowded with it.

Clare found Jack and her grandfather seated on picnic chairs by the dam, throwing bread to a gaggle of grey geese, and drinking lemonade. The day was picture-perfect. Water sparkling like diamonds. The sun sailed in a blue sky between islands of cotton-wool clouds. The morning air had a special clarity that seemed to bring the Bunya mountains close enough to touch.

A lone horse in the adjacent paddock trotted over to the fence to say hello. He was of a monstrous size, with an arched crest and proud, high-stepping gait. 'Is that your stallion?' asked Clare. 'He looks a bit like Rastus.' Jack moved towards the fence and Clare protectively blocked his way.

'Well picked,' said Grandad. 'That's Goliath. Last stallion standing at Currawong Creek. Same bloodlines as Rastus and just as gentle. He'll do your boy no harm.'

'Aren't some stallions dangerous?' asked Clare.

Grandad stood up stiffly and went over to stroke the horse's nose. 'Any stallion worth his salt is bound to be high-couraged,' he said. 'But Goliath hasn't a mean bone in his body. He'd do almost anything for me without the slightest argument.'

Jack darted past Clare, ran to the fence and joined in patting the horse. 'The lad's not scared,' said Grandad. 'He's got the knack, you see. Not everybody does. I've seen grown men try to hide their fear of stallions with a show of bravado - a loud voice, and perhaps a whip for defence. They may trick others, they may even trick themselves, but they'll never deceive a horse. That stallion decides that since the man has no confidence in himself, there must be something wrong with the man, and stallions don't suffer fools lightly. That's when they get dangerous.' Clare edged forward and willed herself to be brave. Goliath nuzzled her cheek with utmost gentleness, while Grandad beamed at them both.

Back at the dam, two yabbies sat in the bucket. She'd forgotten how beautiful they were – flawless satin shells, dappled with soft beige, and brandishing electric blue claws. Jack was entranced by the little crayfish. He'd been at Currawong for just a week, but his attention span already seemed to have stretched. Grandad took Jack's hand and moved him a little way down the bank, then threw a baited string in the water. 'Hold this,' he said. Jack did as he was asked. Amazing.

Samson sat down next to him, ears cocked forward, watching the rippled surface as intently as any human yabby hunter. Grandad returned to Clare wearing a thoughtful expression. 'What's the lad's story?'

It was a relief to pour it all out. Not just about Jack, but everything else that had happened since the day Taylor Brown turned up at the office. How could Clare have predicted the profound effect Jack's arrival would have had on her life?

'That's some story,' said Grandad. 'Did he break your heart, this Adam feller?'

Clare was floored by the question. A broken heart was such an old-fashioned, sentimental concept.

'Yes,' she said at last. 'I suppose he did.'

Grandad leaned across and kissed her cheek. 'He never deserved you then, love. I can promise you. You're well out of it.'

How good it was to be affirmed like that? Since Dad died, there was nobody who cared enough to say such things. Clare suddenly missed her mother. She turned and wrapped her arms around her grandfather's bony shoulders.

He held her very tight for a moment, then pointed to Jack. 'The pup's been a help there?'

Clare nodded. 'Without Samson I probably would have given up on Jack. You have no idea what he's been like because, for some reason, he's all of a sudden on his best behaviour. But the kid was expelled from kindergarten for God's sake.' Her grandfather chuckled. 'It wasn't funny,' said Clare.

He moved to Jack's line and, with infinite slowness, began to haul it in. 'No, I guess it wasn't.'

A little kingfisher landed on the pump house to their left. It was a colourful bird, with a cobalt blue back, buff-orange breast and violet streaks along its flanks. In a flash it dived into the dam at their feet, and carried away the squirming yabby off Grandad's string. 'Good luck to you,' Harry said. 'At least the little snappers will make someone a good supper.' He re-baited the line and threw it back into the water. 'If I were you,' he said, 'I'd ask Tom about the lad. Tom has a certificate in equine therapy, or some such thing. Worked with kids back home in the Hunter Valley.'

'He doesn't seem very responsible,' she said. 'I don't want Jack getting hurt.'

'I'm telling you, love, Tom ran groups at *Riding For The Disabled*. Worked wonders with those children apparently.' Really? Clare considered her grandfather's words. Tom might be a blockhead, but he did have a way with Jack.

'It won't hurt you to talk to him,' urged Grandad.

'I will,' she said, cutting herself a piece of string. 'Just as soon as he's back from his rounds.' She checked the watch Grandad had given her. It was her grandmother's and she loved it. Plus it was the only way to tell the time now her iPhone was defunct. Still early. She held up the string to check its length, and Grandad gave it an approving nod.

'Now,' she said. 'I just need some bait.'

CHAPTER 13

'Gee up,' Tom told the grey mare. 'I have someone for you to meet.' He led Fleur down the hill to where Harry and the little boy stood beside the stockyard with Clare. There was straw in Clare's hair. She must have been collecting eggs, fossicking through the hay shed where Harry's hens stubbornly continued to lay, instead of in their nest boxes in the chook house. The tousled look suited Clare – her windswept, shoulder-length bob both messy and stylish at the same time. He couldn't help thinking it was how she'd look straight out of bed.

'This is Fleur,' said Tom, bringing the big horse to a halt. She nickered a greeting. Age had not detracted from the mare's natural air of nobility and she arched her snow-white neck as proudly as if she was back in the show ring.

'What is she?' asked Clare. 'Not a clydesdale.'

'Fleur's a percheron,' said Harry. 'A draft breed originally from France. They're used a lot over outback station mares to put size and strength into stock horses. Add a bit of toughness.'

Fleur stood just sixteen hands, on the short size for a draft horse, but she was quality through and through: short-coupled, strong of top line and straight of bone. Her legs were clean and free from feather and her eye was kind.

'She's a nice sort of mare,' said Tom.

'Supreme Champion at Royal Sydney Show three years in a row.' Harry's voice swelled with pride. 'One of her foals is the drum horse for Victoria police. The national vaulting team has two more.' He stroked her neck. 'This old girl's done well by me, but her breeding days are over. Sent her off to Macca's new stallion two years in a row and she never came in season. Wouldn't have a bar off him.' He chuckled. 'Reckon she's telling me she's done.'

'Haven't you got something smaller?' Clare was trying to hold Jack back from climbing into the yard.

'Sorry, love,' said Harry. 'Fleur's the smallest horse at Currawong. But she's gentle as the day is long, is Fleur. I trust her and Tom with your lad, love, and I'd tell you if I didn't.'

Clare did not look convinced. 'Jack's not going to ride her,' said Tom. 'Not if you don't want him to.'

'What exactly will you be doing then?'

'I have a diploma in Equine Facilitated Learning.' Tom threaded a piece of long grass around his fingers as he talked. He noticed Clare watching his hands. 'There's plenty of clinical evidence that being around horses changes our brainwave patterns, calms them down. Horses can help kids to stop fixating on negative events in their past. EFL works particularly well for kids with autism - kids who find it hard to communicate. Can we see how Jack likes it?'

It was already pretty clear how Jack was going to like it. Clare was struggling to hold him back.

She nodded and let him through. 'How does just being with a horse do all that?'

Jack approached and stroked Fleur's shoulder. The mare bent her giant head in greeting.

'Horses mirror people,' said Tom. 'Reflect back their emotions. Don't let her size fool you; at heart Fleur's a prey animal so she wants to feel safe. If Jack is fearful, she'll be fearful. That's the challenge: in order to get Fleur to cooperate, Jack must first overcome any fears himself. Horses are good at picking up on human emotions, so he'll have to modify his own behaviour in order to get the horse to cooperate. He has to be calm and reasonable to put her at ease. This teaches him that his behaviour affects others. It's a great communication aid.' Clare looked a bit happier. 'That's the theory anyway. There's a mystical side to it that I swear no theory will ever explain. Shall we give it a try?'

Clare nodded, though he could tell she wasn't convinced. 'Calm and reasonable? I'd try anything for calm and reasonable. Although, I admit, just being at Currawong has already worked wonders.' She smiled at Jack, who was hugging Fleur's front leg. 'Good luck, Jacky.' She blew him a kiss.

'You're going to help me work with Fleur today, all right?' Tom said to Jack.

The boy nodded, eyes shining.

'Now hold this rope in your right hand, which is this hand, and stand there by her shoulder.' He positioned Jack correctly. Fleur stood steady as a rock. 'Before we start, I want you to say hello to your horse, okay?' Jack nodded. 'I want you to say *Hi Fleur.*'

'Hi Fleur,' said Jack softly. He didn't quite get the L, but it was a good attempt. Tom heard Clare's sudden intake of breath.

'Say, *How you doing?*'

'How you doing?' said Jack, with a bit more confidence.

'Good. Now gather up the rope — that's how you're going to lead her.' The boy was following his instructions to a tee. 'Now I want you to say *walk on* and then we're going into that big yard over there.'

'Walk on,' said Jack.

'Say it like you mean it,' called Harry.

'Walk on,' Jack said more firmly. For the next ten minutes he led Fleur around the ménage, learning how to change direction, halt her, even to back her up. It was quite a sight - the mighty mare and the tiny boy, acting in concert. It always amazed Tom to see the natural affinity kids had with horses. Clare was taking photos from the wings. In no time Jack had Fleur circling him on a lunging rein: the horse, the whip and the rope making sides of a perfect triangle.

'Let him jump her,' said Harry. 'Give the lad a real thrill.'

Clare was looking worried again. Harry came into the yard and began to set up cavaletti – low jumps made of crossover end pieces and a centre pole. 'Just the one,' said Tom. 'But make it two poles high.' He took the rope from Jack's hands. 'You're going to watch me and then do what I do. Okay?'

'Okay,' replied the boy.

'You're going to step over this and then Fleur's going to follow you.' Tom led the mare over the cavaletti and gave the rope back to Jack. 'Do you think you can do that?'

Jack nodded and copied Tom, struggling a little to get over the low jump. Fleur followed obediently, stepping over the poles. Everybody clapped and Jack grinned from ear to ear. Tom swapped the lead rope for a lunge rein. 'Now what I want you to do is ask Fleur to walk in a circle … that's the way. This whip you're holding isn't to hit her with, it just makes your arm longer.'

Fleur encountered the cavaletti at the perimeter of the circle and dutifully stepped over. 'Great,' said Tom, a protective hand on Jack's shoulder. 'Now, let's ask her to trot. Just raise your whip and say *trot on* in a loud voice.'

'Trot on,' said Jack.

'A bit louder.'

'Trot on!'

The mare broke into a cadenced trot. This time when she came to the jump, she gathered herself as if in slow motion, rose up on her powerful hindquarters and made a great leap, towering over not just Jack, but Tom as well. It was a truly magnificent sight. The ground trembled at her landing and Jack's eyes were saucer-wide. A look of pure joy and astonishment lit up his face, as cheers rose from the sidelines.

'Well done,' Tom said. 'That was fantastic, but it's enough for one day. I want you to lower the whip and ask Fleur to stand up.'

'Stand up,' said Jack, and the great mare came to a graceful halt. She swung around to face them, ears pricked as if asking, *what now?*

'Go and say thank you. Tell her she's a good girl.'

'I've got carrots,' called Clare, slipping through the rails. 'Offer them on the flat of your hand. That's right.'

'Good girl,' said Jack. 'Good girl.'

Fleur lowered her head, graciously taking the titbit with gentle lips. Jack threw his arms as far as they could reach around her neck in a fierce hug. Tom patted the little boy on the back. This had gone better than he could have imagined. He'd even impressed himself.

'I'm speechless,' said Clare. 'How was that even possible?'

'I tell you, this stuff really works,' said Tom. 'There's nothing better than to bring a child like this together with a horse like that - and just watch the magic happen.'

'I don't know how to thank you,' said Clare. 'That was truly amazing.'

Tom thought quickly. What did he have to lose? 'Let me take you to dinner at the pub tonight,' he said. 'That's if Harry's okay to watch Jack?'

'Go on, you two,' Harry said. 'I'm happy to mind the lad.'

What a break. Harry approved. It would have been a major obstacle otherwise.

Now for Clare … she took her time answering. 'Okay, you're on.' She held his gaze for a long moment.

Tom grinned, picked another blade of grass and threaded it between his fingers. On first meeting Clare had seemed so uptight. She'd reminded him of the professional girls he'd met back in Sydney, caught up in their appearance and their careers; searching for their next step up the ladder. Not his type at all. But he'd misjudged her. This girl had a heart, taking on a little kid like Jack. That set her apart for a start. And of course the fact that she was drop dead gorgeous didn't hurt any.

Harry was looking at him. Tom turned his head, and tried to stop thinking about what Clare's skin might feel like. Better not rush this. He'd made that mistake before. Clare was all class, and Harry's grand-daughter to boot. Take it slow, he told himself. Take it slow. 'Pick you up around seven?' She nodded and Tom led Fleur away, impatient for the evening to come.

. . .

Clare finished her rather gelatinous chocolate mousse and took a deep, contented breath. She'd almost had too much to drink. It was a bad habit she'd got into. Lawyers drank a lot; it was embedded in the culture. Wine with lunch, beers after work, a tokay or two in chambers. Adam always seemed to be swigging back scotch, and he kept a case of French sparkling wine at his place, just for her. She couldn't remember a time she'd been to bed with him when she was completely sober. But she didn't want to think about Adam now. Her grandfather barely drank, and she'd been aiming for an alcohol-free few weeks, but tonight the temptation had been too much. She was already onto her third wine. Tom was becoming more fascinating by the minute.

'Have you considered the possibility that Jack's not autistic?' asked Tom.

Her mouth went dry. Finally somebody agreed with her. She told Tom about the string of professionals confirming the boy's autism. She told him how, at the beginning, she'd disbelieved the diagnosis. She told him about the nightmare few weeks with Jack in Brisbane, and how she was beginning to believe she'd imagined Jack's first few words – until today. She told him about Taylor Brown, and her addiction, and about the stolen bull terrier puppy, and how she knew that Taylor really loved Jack, but that she didn't want him back.

'Jack's lucky to have you,' Tom said.

Clare wasn't good at receiving praise. Instead of accepting the compliment, she was inclined to argue the point.

'Lucky? Since I've had him he's been kicked out of child care, got lost, been locked alone in a car and now I'm sending him into yards with giant horses.'

'Locked alone in a car?' asked Tom. 'When was that?'

Clare finished her wine and asked for another one. Tom went to the bar and returned with a riesling and a beer. He was drinking light. She launched into the falling-out-of-the-tree story.

Tom looked genuinely horrified. 'I had no idea.'

'That was the problem,' she said.

They both burst out laughing. A droplet of beer shone on his lower lip and she wanted to dab it away. He wiped a finger around his dessert bowl like a kid and sucked it.

'Is your waiting room always so chaotic?' she asked.

'Afraid so,' he said. 'I've got no experience at all running my own practice. Used to work for a big clinic in the Hunter Valley. They took care of everything, but I wanted to go out on my own. Merriang was all I could afford, but it's a start. There's plenty of work.'

'Well, you can't go on like you are,' she said boldly. 'The place is a total shemozzle.'

He spread his arms wide. 'Guilty as charged, your Honour.'

Clare sipped her wine. 'Why did you ask me if I thought Jack might not be autistic?'

'He doesn't fit the profile,' said Tom. 'He makes good eye contact, he listens, he can focus on a task. He can certainly form attachments, at least with animals. Look at him and Samson.'

'He head bangs,' said Clare. 'He bites, he rages, he can't make friends, he won't talk.'

'Ah,' said Tom, brandishing his beer. '*Won't* is the operative word here, not *can't*, wouldn't you say?' He looked very handsome when his eyes lit up like that. Full of life, pulsing with energy. She wanted to kiss him. 'Have you heard of selective mutism?' Clare shook her head. 'It's an anxiety disorder, different to autism. Kids *can* talk, but for some reason they don't.'

'Wouldn't the paediatricians and psychologists have picked that up?' said Clare.

'Apparently not. They say Jack has no language, right?' She nodded. 'But we know that's not true. You, me, Harry - we've all heard him talk. What does his mother say?'

'Taylor used to say he could speak, but it seems like nobody believed her. They put her on a higher welfare payment because of Jack's disability, so I think she gave up trying to convince people.'

'Maybe. The problem can worsen until the child never speaks to anyone at all, even to close family members. Whatever the case, Jack's been misdiagnosed, pure and simple.'

It all made perfect sense. 'What causes selective mutism?' asked Clare. 'And how come you know so much about it?'

'Lots of things can cause it,' said Tom. 'But from what you've told me of Jack, trauma's the most likely culprit. You say he's been in care before?'

'More than once,' said Clare, 'and he's only four years old.'

'That could do it. Repeated separation trauma. A teenage mother with addiction problems, and he's probably suffered at the hands of her boyfriends as well. You said there'd been domestic violence?' She nodded. 'It's a wonder he can speak at all.'

All the pieces seemed to fit. How could so many professionals have missed it? 'And the other part of my question. How come you know about selective mutism?'

'A crash course in child psychology as part of my EFL diploma.'

'You've no idea how good it feels to hear all this.' The riesling and the relief and the proximity to Tom all combined in a thoroughly delicious way. Clare relaxed into the evening. Conversation flowed as easily as the wine. She told stories about Jack and Samson in Brisbane that made him laugh. They swapped jokes. Tom opened about his life. Never married. No kids. Divorced parents. A sister somewhere. His hand rested near hers on the table, close enough that she could almost feel it.

He reached across and covered her fingers with his own. An aching tug of desire ambushed her. Suddenly she couldn't breathe, couldn't think. 'Clare, I was wondering ...'

She wanted him to take her to bed, then and there. She wanted him beside her, wanted his unfamiliar flesh to erase all trace of Adam. His eyes locked onto hers, and he gently stroked her wrist with his thumb. The sensation was electric. 'If Harry doesn't mind ...'

'Yes?' she urged. 'Go on.'

'Could you help out for a few hours in the clinic tomorrow?'

Clare slumped a little, and offered him a weak smile.

'Oh,' she found herself saying. 'Okay.' She felt heat climbing her cheeks, and the night spiralled around her. How drunk was she exactly? And how had she read him so wrong?

Tom's phone rang. 'It's Harry. Jack's acting up. I suppose we'd better go.'

Clare nodded, hoping her disappointment didn't show. There was nothing in Tom's voice to match the path his thumb had made across her wrist.

Sun streamed through the window. Clare looked at the time and groaned. She must have forgotten to set her alarm. She dragged herself from bed and into the shower. Why had she ever agreed to help Tom out today? Why had she drunk so much, might be a better question? Last night Tom had seemed irresistible. The *beer goggles* effect no doubt. Still, she'd promised, and it was just this once.

In the kitchen Grandad presented her with an omelette. 'Sorry,' she said. 'Don't have time,' Clare drained her mug of tea and downed a couple of headache tablets.

'Good luck, love,' said Grandad.

She waved goodbye to Jack, who was dipping toast soldiers into his soft-boiled egg.

Clare walked down to the clinic while lazy kookaburras chortled a belated dawn chorus. A car was parked out front. She opened the door and cautiously edged inside, on the look-out for snakes and biting dogs.

Tom emerged from the consulting room in faded blue scrubs. Maybe they were a size too small, maybe they'd shrunk, but for whatever reason they were too tight a fit. They emphasised his narrow hips and broad shoulders. They emphasised the bulge at his crotch.

A young woman in a revealing halter-neck top was standing at the counter, holding a shivering teacup chihuahua. 'What can I do for you, Dallas?' asked Tom.

'Tiny has a rash.' The little dog dived in between the woman's ample breasts and peeked out nervously. 'Would you take a look?' She made no effort to extract her pet. 'Don't be scared. He won't bite.'

What an outrageous flirt! Tom was looking everywhere except at Tiny.

Clare stepped forward. 'Here, let me help,' She removed the chihuahua and presented it to Tom, answering his grin with one of her own.

'Who are you?' asked Dallas, clearly peeved.

'This is Clare,' said Tom. 'She's helping out in the surgery.'

Dallas looked Clare up and down. Tom mouthed a silent *thank you* behind her back and examined the dog. 'Flea dermatitis,' he said, parting the little dog's fur. 'I can give you a spot on treatment for that.'

The door opened and a man entered with a pair of kelpies.

'Never mind.' Dallas snatched Tiny from Tom's arms. 'I'll buy it at the produce store. *They* won't charge through the nose.' She swept out as a fat woman came in with a little pink pig and set it down on the floor. It proceeded to run around the room squealing, pursued by the barking kelpies. The piglet sought refuge under a cupboard.

Tom looked perplexed. 'Is it sick, Martha?'

'Not at all, Doc. It's in lieu of payment.' she said. 'What with milk prices down, we're a bit short this month. Thought a nice piglet might do the trick instead. He'll grow into a fine, fat porker for you.'

Clare helped the man haul off the kelpies, while Tom retrieved the piglet. 'Thanks Martha, but...'

'No worries, Tom,' said Martha. It was hard to hear over the screaming pig and barking dogs.

Another man came in with two bleating lambs. Tom gave Clare a helpless look.

She took a deep breath and pushed her way through the throng to stand behind the counter. She'd seen Debbie take control of an unruly waiting room back at the legal aid centre plenty of times. How hard could it be?

'Everyone with animals requiring treatment, please take a seat.' Tom gave her an encouraging smile and tried to hand the piglet back to Martha, who dodged and frowned.

'From now on,' Clare added, 'this clinic will be conducted on a cash or account basis only.'

Everybody started talking at once. 'Is this true, Tom?'…'Who is this woman?'…'But you took six geese from Bob Barker just last week.'

'Quiet!' called Tom. 'She's absolutely right. As of today, terms of trade are strictly cash or account.'

'And who is she? 'asked Martha, pointing an accusing finger.

'Clare is my new assistant,' announced Tom, with only the slightest waver in his voice. 'And what she says, goes.' Martha glared, but this time she accepted the piglet back when Tom offered it to her.

People looked a little stunned and began filing out. In the end, only the man with the kelpies remained. Tom heaved a great sigh and positioned a chair behind the counter for Clare. 'You're a godsend,' he whispered, before escorting his client into the consulting room.

A steady trickle of patients arrived throughout the morning. A tabby cat needing stitches. A diabetic pug. An angora goat with impacted baby teeth. This was more fun than she'd expected.

When the last client said goodbye, Clare was almost sorry her shift was over.

Tom washed up and made two mugs of coffee. 'You were magnificent, you do know that?'

'Was I?'

'This last month I've been paid in everything from duck eggs to tractor tyres.' He shook his head. 'See that painting?' A framed portrait of a heeler hung above the counter. 'That's Red, painted in settlement of an account for an alpaca caesarean.'

A familiar snarl sat on the lips of the dog in the painting.

'It's a good likeness.' Clare sipped her coffee. 'Why did you do it?' she asked. 'Accept payment in kind, I mean?'

Tom laughed and shrugged. 'Guess I'm a soft touch. Felt sorry for one old codger and word spread like wildfire.'

'Well, enough's enough,' she said. 'From now on it's cold, hard cash … and don't give anybody an account who's not good for it.'

'Right,' he said with a boyish smile. Clare looked at him sideways. Charming, but not very convincing. Tom was too kind for his own good. She had to admit though, it was refreshing after the dog eat dog world of Brisbane petty crime. Maybe she'd work at the surgery for a few more days — help him to stick to his guns.

CHAPTER 15

Tom topped up the teapot while Harry plonked a dish of pancakes down in the middle of the kitchen table. 'Eat up.' Tom put a pancake on his plate, and another one on Jack's. Where was Clare? He'd hoped they could walk down to the clinic together.

It was a week since Clare had started doing mornings at the surgery. Two hours, that's all it was, roughly from nine until eleven, but already she'd brought a degree of order to what was formerly chaos.

So far Jack hadn't been a problem. There was nothing the little boy enjoyed more than spending time with the horses, so Harry took him along on his morning paddock rounds. When Harry was done, or Jack had had enough, the pair would come by the clinic. Harry would always take Jack into the room serving as the hospital ward. Here lived the inpatients, and animals recovering from surgery. You never quite knew what you'd find. Cats and dogs were commonplace, but there were more unusual patients as well. Cleo the scrub python was still there. Being cold-blooded, reptiles were slow to heal, and it would be at least another week before her stitches came out. There was a barn owl with a broken wing, a flying fox with barbed-wire fence injuries and a koala with chlamydia, all waiting for pick up by local wildlife carers. When Jack had finished looking around, Clare would finish up and head back to the house with Jack and Harry.

It had been a wonderful, if frustrating, week. Tom was falling hard for Clare. It seemed he couldn't properly think about anything else. She moved about the clinic, blonde hair neatly pinned up, exposing the long sweep of her graceful neck, the ridge of her clavicle, the curve of her throat. They'd be discussing the best time for Mrs Madden to bring in her sick peacock, when he was really imagining the taste of her polished skin. He sometimes stole little brushes against her. Once he got so distracted by the soft swell of breasts peeking from her open-necked shirt, that he forgot about the syringe he was holding and stabbed himself in the hand. At least he'd be immune to cat flu now.

There'd been no repeat of that night at the pub, when Clare's smile had been so full of promise. The memory of her hand in his wouldn't let him go, yet no similar opportunity had since presented itself. The following night Harry had some kind of turn. He insisted he was fine, and went about his daily chores the next morning, but Clare didn't want him to worry about babysitting Jack at night any more.

'What sort of a turn?' he asked her.

Clare furrowed her perfect brow for a second. 'He got up from the table and sort of lost his balance. Said he was seeing double. It was a minute or so before he was right, and then he complained of being tired. It's not like Grandad to get tired, is it? And I imagine it's even more unusual for him to complain about it.'

'That's true enough,' Tom said. 'Harry's no whinger.'

Since then, Clare had insisted her grandfather have early nights. The old man had argued no end about it, but Tom could see that deep down he was pleased that she cared. Now Clare was no longer free to go out in the evening. He could go to her for dinner, of course, cadge an invitation. But when he'd leased the site for the clinic, Harry had included breakfast in the deal. Tom had been up at the house for his morning meal almost every day for six months now. It might be a bit of a stretch turning up for dinner as well.

Then there were his living arrangements. Tom lodged with

Bonnie Black, a young widow in town. Her interfering mother, Blanche, stayed over so often that she might as well have lived there too. Tom had moved in to discover that Blanche had appropriated the spacious spare room, and that he'd been relegated to the verandah.

It was fully enclosed with insect screens, but mosquitoes still managed to get in. Tom had patched up any obvious holes. He'd tried everything: repellent, insect spray, mosquito coils left to burn all night. Nothing worked. If anything his efforts seemed to attract them, and he was forced to sleep with a sheet pulled over his head, listening to the frustrated drone of the little bloodsuckers, inches from his ear. Occasionally they dive-bombed him, inserting their proboscis right through the thin linen, and he would be covered with itchy red welts by morning. On top of that, there were the cane toads. God knows how they got in, but each morning he'd find at least a couple of the ugly creatures somewhere.

Once he'd woken up to one beside him on his pillow, like something from the Princess and the Frog fairy tale. But even if he was looking for a prince, he wouldn't be kissing this frog. The skin of *Bufo marinus* oozed a poison that irritated skin and burned the eyes. Tom hadn't heard of deaths in humans, but their venom was potent enough to kill dogs and cats, along with any unfortunate wildlife that consumed it. Quolls, goannas, dingoes – he'd seen them all succumb to this toxic invader. What would Clare think of waking up next to a cane toad? Even if she was free, and a romantic pub dinner led to something more, he couldn't bring her home.

Clare came into the kitchen and sat down beside him. She reached for the golden syrup with a slim, lightly-tanned arm. Her singlet top exposed the delicious curve of neck and shoulder, the sheen of her skin, damp from the kitchen's clammy heat. He imagined how her breasts might look, minus their flimsy wrapper.

'If you don't like my pancakes, just say so,' said Harry. The old man's words brought Tom back to earth with a crunch, and he heaped up his plate. 'Don't do me any favours,' snorted Harry. He drained his tea and thumped the mug in the sink. 'Come on, Jack,' he said. 'We've got horses to feed.' The little boy scrambled from his chair and raced out the door after him.

'What's got into Harry?' asked Tom. He had an uneasy suspicion that the old man somehow knew of his daydreams.

'He hasn't been sleeping —' began Clare.

Tom's phone rang. A new client, Willow Moore, was apparently waiting for him down at the clinic. 'Minnie's in labour,' said an urgent voice, 'and I think a pup's stuck. She's been trying for hours, but nothing's happening.'

'Be right there,' said Tom.

Clare pushed back her chair. 'I'll go change.'

Tom sprinted down the hill. A tattooed young man dressed like a Goth waited beside an ancient mini minor. A tearful teenage girl, dressed all in black and carrying a shoebox, rushed to the clinic door as he approached. Tom fumbled in his haste to turn the key. As soon as he stepped inside he could tell something was wrong. A few pamphlets lay on the floor. A tin of cat food had rolled beneath a shelf and the broom had fallen over. The door to the hospital ward stood wide open. Damn, he must have forgotten to check it last night. He hurried in to see what creature might have escaped.

Cleo. The scrub python's cage was empty, and the box that had contained Ginger, a geriatric guinea pig, was on its side. He'd been in overnight with pneumonia. The prognosis had been poor, even with saline, antibiotics and a steroid injection. Tom searched in vain through the spilled straw. No rodent.

Tom returned to the waiting room, keeping one eye peeled for the wayward snake. Willow stood clutching the shoe box, her facial piercings glistening with tears. 'Where's the patient?' he asked. A tortured squeal came from the box. Willow offered it to him with trembling hands. Inside was a distressed piebald rat. Tom heaved a great sigh. It was going to be one of those days.

Tom gently took the rat from Willow. It was a warm morning but Minnie felt cold, a sure sign of shock. Her breathing was rapid and shallow, and her ears and mucous membranes were pale. Blood oozed from beneath her tail, and every now and then she squealed in pain.

He fetched a heating pad and laid the little creature on the examination table.

'Blade said you'll just do a caesarean and then she'll be fine,' said Willow, her expression hopeful.

'Did he just?' Tom looked up to see the Goth boy in the doorway. Curse Blade for raising such unrealistic expectations. Rat caesareans were notoriously difficult, and he didn't have the right small-scale implements. On top of that, it wasn't feasible to deliver the young and then repair the uterus. A full hysterectomy would be necessary, meaning Minnie wouldn't be able to produce milk even if the babies could be saved. Without a foster mother, her pinkies would not survive.

'I'd like to try something first —' began Tom, then froze. Cleo was gliding along the floor behind the unsuspecting Willow, a telltale guinea-pig-sized bulge in her body. She slid behind the bags of dog food in the corner. He took a deep breath. On the bright side, at least he knew where she was. 'Oxytocin injections can stimulate a tired uterus to contract,' he said, trying hard to concentrate. 'First I'll x-ray Minnie to check there's no extra-large pup stuck in the birth canal, otherwise strong labour could rupture her uterus.' Willow crossed her legs and turned white. 'Perhaps you should wait outside,' said Tom. The girl nodded and left. Tom quickly x-rayed the rat, keeping one eye on the corner. Good. They were normal-sized pinkies, well positioned, and only five of them. Now to take a guess at dosage.

Clare came in looking cool and collected. Tom saw a flash of flickering tongue and pale scales as the snake slid across the room and disappeared behind the filing cabinet. He tried to remain calm. Should he tell Clare? No, he just couldn't do it. He'd scare her again for starters, and look like a complete incompetent to boot.

Clare pointed to Minnie. 'What's that?'

'Pet rat in labour.'

Clare made a face. 'Don't take too long. You've got a Mr Baker with his bassets at nine for vaccinations.'

Tom groaned. Brian Baker always insisted on having Tom express his dogs' anal glands, whether it was needed or not. 'Better out than in,' he'd say in a satisfied voice, then head for his car, offering no help at all. With most dogs it was a simple enough exercise, but not with Brian's bassets. They howled and leaped and growled, making the procedure downright dangerous for everyone involved. On top of that, Brian's bassets were simply the smelliest dogs in the world. The place always stank to high heaven after their visits. Clare couldn't be there for that. She'd never be able to think of him in a romantic way again. He'd have to find a way to get rid her.

Tom injected Minnie with the oxytocin, feeling a twinge of sympathy for the tiny rodent and hoping her exhausted frame could withstand the strain of renewed contractions. He placed her and the heating pad in a box, took it to the hospital ward and then went to talk to Clare. He'd taken a few steps when he returned and fastened a lid on the box, just in case Cleo had designs on Minnie for breakfast.

Clare was behind the counter entering treatment notes into the computer. 'You should set some time aside to catch up on these,' she said in a chastising tone. 'There's quite a backlog.'

'Never mind that,' he said. 'I was thinking, since it's such a lovely day … Why not take Jack for a drive in the Bunya Mountains?' I can manage here.'

She shot him a puzzled look. 'It's such a busy morning. Are you sure?'

'Absolutely. Go enjoy yourself.'

Clare went through the appointment list. 'You've got the Baker bassets, some crazy man who thinks his wife is poisoning their siamese cat, a boxer with toothache, a newfoundland with indigestion, a kitten with a rash, a litter of puppies for vaccinations, a lame goose, and there are bound to be walk-ins.'

He looked out the window. Oh no — Brian Baker was pulling up with his dog trailer. Tom dashed for the door and waylaid him as he was unloading his hounds.

'Sorry, I'm flat out right now,' said Tom. 'Tricky labour. An emergency caesarean might be all that can save the pups. Can we do this tomorrow?'

'Course we can, Doc,' said Brian, juggling a tangle of excited basset hounds. 'Course we can.' He chuckled. 'Don't suppose you vets know what will land on your doorstep next, eh?'

'Got it in one, mate.' This was going to be simpler than he thought.

A voice from behind startled him. It was Willow. 'How's Minnie?'

'She's had an injection to restart her labour,' he said, hoping the girl wouldn't somehow put her foot in it. 'Come and we'll check on her now.' Willow nodded, her expression taut with nerves, and started to follow him back to the clinic.

'Don't worry, love,' Brian called out after her. 'The Doc here will save them pups, and their mum too.'

Willow gave him a grateful smile. 'I hope so. Minnie's my favourite rat.'

CHAPTER 16

Clare went back to entering patient notes on the computer, trying to ignore the tattooed teenage boy sneering at her from across the room. Where was Tom? And why would he want her to leave on such a busy morning? He was acting very strangely, even for Tom.

She hadn't been so confused about a man for a long time, maybe never. Clare thought back to her early days with Adam. His dazzling advocacy had been the talk of Brisbane's legal set, and she'd been more than a little star-struck when the hot-shot young barrister had asked her out. Feeling flattered wasn't a good way to start off though. It had set the pattern for their whole relationship. Her trying to impress, feeling not-quite-good-enough. Him acting superior.

Tom was very different. Adam always looked for an angle and Tom took people as he found them. Adam earned top dollar and Tom was paid in piglets. Adam had a killer streak and Tom saved the lives of snakes and pregnant rats. He was rough and ready, true, but she had to admit he did exude a sort of raw, unconscious sexuality. Clare suddenly imagined him pulling her in close, in tight, and kissing her with hard, searching lips.

A soft, scraping sound in the corner interrupted her daydream.

She peered under the shelves. Was that something moving?

Tom and the pierced girl came back in and headed straight for the ward. A man with a bevy of basset hounds burst in after them. That must be Brian Baker, their first appointment for the day. Clare couldn't stop staring. She'd heard of people growing to look like their animals, but in this case the resemblance was astonishing. Brian had his dogs' same sagging cheeks and long face. His nose was large and shiny and his lids drooped over red, rheumy eyes. His expression, however, wasn't hangdog like his bassets. It was angry.

'I won't be fobbed off, Doc,' said Brian. 'Not for a bleeding rat.' Pierced girl burst into tears and Brian looked abashed. 'Sorry love, but they're vermin. What do you want to go around saving vermin for? It's bloody crazy. I just spent a fortune at my place exterminating the little buggers.' Brian noticed Clare, seeming surprised to see her. He looked to the crying girl and then back to Clare, took off his hat and wrung it between his hands. 'No offence meant, mind.'

The girl cried harder, and his face softened. 'It really is your pet then is it, this rat?'

'I love her.' The words were little more than a sob, but they lent the girl a delicate vulnerability. Beneath the piercings, she suddenly looked about twelve

'You do, do you?' asked Brian in astonishment. 'You love this rat?'

Willow nodded, choking back tears. 'Minnie's my heart rat.'

'Well, I'll be.' He plucked a box of tissues from the counter and offered it to her. 'Can't believe I'm saying this,' said Brian, shaking his head, 'but I sure do hope the Doc can help you out, love.'

'Clare?' Tom's voice came from the ward. 'Can I have you, please?'

She found Tom hovering over a shoebox, looking pleased. Clare peeked inside. Two tiny pink babies were squirming and squeaking on the paper towel. Minnie was holding another in disturbingly human-like hands, nibbling at it with little pointy teeth. 'She's not eating it?' asked Clare, horrified.

Tom put a reassuring hand on her shoulder. His touch made her momentarily forget all about the rat. 'She's cleaning it,' said Tom, 'and eating the afterbirth. Rats are devoted mothers.'

A scream and a barking chorus erupted from the waiting room. Willow rocketed in. She'd gone very pale. 'There's a snake!'

Clare glanced at Cleo's cage. Empty.

Tom shoved the shoebox at the panicky girl. 'Here Willow, take Minnie. She needs a midwife.'

Willow became suddenly brave, oohing and aahing over the babies. 'I won't let that big old snake get you.'

Tom grabbed a long pole with a deep hook and emptied out a rubbish bin, then went back into the waiting room. Clare tentatively followed him. Cleo was apparently holed up beneath a cupboard, to go by the basset pack milling around in full cry. The noise was deafening.

'Get them out of here,' yelled Tom. Brian didn't seem to hear him. 'Get them out,' he shouted, louder this time, and pointed to the door. Tattooed Blade helped Brian drag the dogs outside.

Tom expertly hauled the python out. There was a suspicious bulge in her sleek lines. Tom manoeuvred the hook roughly to the middle of her body, lifted her in one smooth motion and deposited her in the bin. Soon Cleo was safely back in her cage.

'Cool,' said Blade, now hovering in the inner doorway. 'I like snakes. What's that bump in it?'

'Ginger, the guinea pig,' said Tom in a strained voice. 'Previously my patient.' He rubbed his forehead. 'Now his six-year-old owner will be traumatised and her mother will probably sue.'

Clare's jaw dropped. She'd seen the weeping, golden-haired girl when Ginger had arrived yesterday morning. '*I don't care what it costs, just fix the bloody thing,*' her mother had said, showing a distinct lack of affection for her daughter's pet, but a healthy respect for her daughter's temper. '*Melody will have a fit if it dies.*'

Tom checked in on Minnie, who was birthing her fourth baby. Blade's sneer had vanished. Instead he wore a broad grin, like a proud father. Even Clare felt a warm glow as Minnie groomed her newborn pups.

'My sister's got guinea pigs,' said Blade. 'What colour was this Ginger? Sort of reddish-brown?' Tom nodded. 'Short haired?' Tom nodded again. A look of comprehension dawned on his face. 'Boy or girl?' asked Blade.

'Boy,' said Tom. 'A large, reddish-brown male guinea pig.'

Blade gave him a sly smile.

'You can't,' said Clare. 'It's completely unprofessional. Completely unethical.'

'I'll be back.' Blade dashed off.

'Please don't look at me like that,' said Tom, before escaping outside. She looked through the window. He was crossing the car park to where Brian was tying his bassets to the side of his trailer. The two men began an animated conversation. What were they saying? They'd been speaking for a minute or two, when Brian burst out laughing - a loud, raucous sound that made Clare jump. For some reason he was pointing to the surgery, bent over with mirth. She ducked out of sight and went to see how the rat count was going.

'Five,' said Willow, her voice bursting with delight. 'I think she's finished.'

Clare had changed her opinion of little Minnie. At first she'd wrinkled up her nose and agreed with Brian. Why would anybody want a rat as a pet? But now she had a sneaking admiration for the new mother. Minnie had arrived near death, exhausted, her frail body wracked with pain. She'd endured the cramping agony of forced labour, without the benefit of pain relief. Clare's cousin had gone through an oxytocin-induced labour with her second child. She said the artificial contractions were infinitely stronger, more frequent and more painful than natural ones.

Yet Minnie had valiantly rallied from her ordeal, and was crouching over her babies to encourage suckling, despite her own weariness. The mother's devotion was inspiring. It gave Clare a whole new appreciation and sympathy for rodents.

Tom had come back inside and was talking to a beaming Willow. 'You have quite a rat there.'

He looked very handsome – the sun catching copper tones in his hair, and a warm smile on his face. Clare's heart missed a beat. Life at Currawong Creek was becoming more interesting by the minute.

Marlene Price produced her credit card to pay the bill, while Melody stroked Ginger -mark two. 'Ginger must like the food here,' the girl said to Clare, hugging the guinea pig close to her cheek. 'He's grown so big and fat.'

Tom held his breath. Would Clare give the game away? She looked uncomfortable, but said nothing.

'Look, Mummy,' said Melody. 'Ginger's all better now.'

Marlene shrank away from the creature with a look of distaste on her perfectly-made-up face. 'Thank goodness for that.' She favoured Tom with a smile. 'I would never have forgiven you, Tom. Not if you'd let my daughter down.'

Tom avoided Clare's eyes. He mumbled something about *just being here to help* and escaped outside with his veterinary bag to where Brian was waiting.

'Thanks for levelling with me, Doc. The rascals do pong a bit when you squeeze their glands.' He presented the first dog for vaccination. 'Wouldn't want to offend the little lady, eh? Might scare her off. You reckon that catching hook of yours would work on women as well as pythons?' Brian was greatly amused by his own joke.

'All done,' said Tom, giving the dog a friendly slap on the rump. 'Next.' Two more cars pulled into the gravel road. 'Won't be long,' called Tom, keeping his tone cheerful.

Clare arrived, looking confused. 'Why aren't you treating the dogs inside?' she asked.

'Easier and quicker out here, love,' said Brian. Tom shot him a grateful glance.

'It's so busy this morning,' said Clare, gesturing to the new arrivals. 'Are you sure you don't need me to stay?'

'Of course he needs you, love,' said Brian 'Tell her, Tom.'

'On second thoughts,' he said, 'I could use a hand.'

Clare smiled, and hurried back to the clinic. Brian winked. 'That one likes you,' he said. 'She's got that lovelorn look in her eye.'

Really? Clare *had* looked pleased when he asked her to stay. He watched her go, her loose hair swaying in time with her hips.

'Put your eyes back in your head, Doc,' said Brian, as he pulled another dog over to be treated. The basset hound jumped up and licked Tom's face with her broad ribbon of a tongue. 'Violet here'll get jealous.'

It was after twelve o'clock before they were done with morning surgery. Harry had dropped by with Jack and seemed in no hurry to leave. Thank goodness the old man was in a better mood today. Jack was making friends with a little boy named Timmy, whose mother, Bronwyn, was getting her six-week-old kelpie pups their first shots.

'I've never seen that,' Clare whispered to Tom, as the kids chased each other round the car park. 'He's normally violent with other children.'

'Well, he's doing fine at the moment.'

They watched the boys collecting gumnuts and making piles on the porch. Jack was examining a particularly large gumnut, obviously a prize. Clare gasped as he added it to Timmy's pile. 'He's sharing,' she said. 'That's impossible.'

'Currawong seems to agree with your boy.' A fancy took him as he watched her sweep a stray lock of hair from her forehead. 'My next job's at a pony stud. Worming, checking broodmares, that sort of thing. Would you and Jack like to come along?'

She gazed at him with cool green eyes. He couldn't see anything remotely lovelorn about them.

'Yes,' said Clare. 'We'll come.' Tom tried to hide his excitement. 'I used to have a pony here at Currawong when I was a kid.' She interrupted Harry's conversation with Bronwyn. 'Smudge. Remember Smudge, grandad?'

'Top little mare,' said Harry. 'Only lost her last year.'

'Really?' said Clare, looking stricken. 'I should have been here … should have said goodbye.'

'No matter,' said Harry. He looked suddenly weary. 'What's done is done.'

'You must bring Jack round some time to play,' said Bronwyn.

'I'd love to,' said Clare. 'Jack doesn't have any friends.'

Bronwyn nodded. 'It's hard when you live in the country. There aren't always kids the same age nearby. It's so great you and Jack have come to stay.'

Tom waited for Clare to protest that indeed she wasn't staying, that in a week or two she'd be back in Brisbane. But instead Clare just looked at Tom and smiled. He loved that smile, the way her cheeks grew round, and dimpled just a fraction. 'Jack likes it here,' she said finally, 'and so do I.'

'Is the Brady stud your last job?' asked Harry. Tom nodded. 'Why not take Clare and Jack for a picnic in the mountains afterwards? You'll be half-way there. I'll make sandwiches, and throw in a packet of bikkies and a bottle of Buderim ginger beer.' He slapped Tom affectionately on the back. The weariness seemed to have passed.

'How about it, Clare?' Tom searched her face and she flashed him that gorgeous smile in answer.

'Let's go pack a feast then, eh?' said Harry. He leaned a little on Clare as the three of them headed up to the house.

Tom watched them go, Clare's slim figure framed by the tall old man and the little boy. He felt the hairs stand up on the back of his neck. Tom didn't know how or why, but he knew with sudden certainty that these three people would utterly change his life.

CHAPTER 18

'The Bunya Mountains are a national park,' said Tom. 'No dogs allowed.'

Clare held her breath. Jack usually panicked at being separated from Samson. This time he just hugged the dog goodbye and climbed in the car.

'He finally trusts that Samson will be here when he gets back,' said Tom.

During the journey Jack sat calmly in his seat and stared out the window. No head banging, no screaming, no hitting himself.

'Look Jacky,' said Tom. 'Kangaroos.' Sure enough a mob of forester kangaroos bounded from the roadside scrub, keeping pace with the car.

'Kang-a-roos,' said Clare, slowly and deliberately. 'Now you say it.'

'Kang-a-roos, kang-a-roos, kang-a-roos,' Jack chanted.

Clare was at once thrilled and exasperated. 'Why does he only talk when no one's watching? It's like having some magical animal that nobody else can see.'

'We're not *nobody*. Neither's Harry,' said Tom. 'We'll vouch for the kid.'

'But you're not in Brisbane, are you?' said Clare. 'You're not in Kim Maguire's office. She's impossible. It would take a miracle for me to convince that woman that Jack can talk.'

'He still has a way to go,' Tom pointed out. 'I've only heard single words so far.'

'Jack can string a sentence together when he wants to. The first thing he said to me was *Daddy's dead.*'

Tom shot her a concerned look. 'Is he?'

'I've no idea.'

They turned into an impressive gateway and drove beneath a wrought-iron arch featuring a pair of prancing ponies. Tom got out to open the gate. It bore a sign identical to the one at Currawong. The yellow triangle proclaiming *Warning Notice* in bold red letters. The one withdrawing common law rights to enter the place. She'd seen the same notice on just about every paddock gate along the way.

'Those signs are useless,' said Clare. 'Freehold titles in Australia provide that all minerals are reserved for the Crown.'

'I'm no lawyer,' said Tom. 'So I won't argue with you. But we have advice that there's a loophole in the law. The Government must prove there are minerals on your land, and they can't do that unless you let them in to do the preliminary exploration. It's worked so far. The coppers in Dalby told me they can come through an open gate regardless of the sign, but can't open one. That's why we always keep our gates closed. They can't even deliver a summons past our signs unless a felony has been committed under the Crimes Act and a warrant issued.'

'What helpful police you have around here,' said Clare, as they drove between neat post-and-rail paddocks.

'That's because they're all on our side.' Tom pulled up in front of a low-slung shed, divided into loose boxes. A pony popped his head over a stable door and Clare did a double-take. It looked just like her Smudge. Jack began banging his head, eager to escape the car. 'Come on, you two,' said Tom. 'There's work to do.'

They were greeted by a cheerful middle-aged woman with kind

eyes and a neat grey bun. 'I'm Anne Brady.' The woman shook Clare's hand. 'And you must be Harry Macleod's granddaughter.'

'This pony,' said Clare, going over to its stall. 'It looks just like one at Currawong when I was little.'

'That's Smudge's grandson, Sparky,' said Anne. 'He's been on lease to a lady out Kingaroy way, but apparently her girl's lost interest.'

Clare stroked Sparky's grey velvet nose. Jack ran over and the pony nibbled his hair. The little boy burst into a fit of joyful giggles. His laugh was infectious and soon everybody was smiling. Clare looked around. More ponies were scattered across the green paddocks: mainly greys, but with a sprinkling of blacks and chestnuts.

'See you've got yourself one of our signs,' said Tom.

'My word,' said Anne. 'Those Pyramid blokes were over at Bert Jordan's place last week, having a friendly chit-chat.'

'Bert let them in?' asked Tom.

'Poor old bugger didn't know any better. Invited them for a cup of tea even. Very charming people, apparently. Looked like farmers. Wore farmers' hats and farmers' shirts.'

'I'll give him a ring,' said Tom, 'Ask him to one of our meetings.' He headed off with his vet bag towards the yards.

'Neville will help you,' Anne called out after him. 'I'll stay and talk with Clare.'

Clare picked some grass and let Jack feed it to the pony. 'What breed is he?' asked Clare.

'Sparky's an Australian pony, same as all the others here.'

'I didn't know Australia had its own breed of pony,' said Clare.

'The studbook was founded way back in 1931,' Anne said. 'All sorts went into the mix: Timor ponies, small Arabians, Welsh mountains – even the odd brumby or two I suspect. We've ended up with a quality, homegrown pony with a sweet character all of its own … and perfect for children, I might add.'

Clare admired Sparky's classic head, his alert ears and large dark eyes. 'He sure is beautiful.'

While Tom wormed the yearlings and checked their teeth, Anne looked out a box of toys for Jack. 'I had these for my grandchildren when they visited from Sydney. It doesn't happen much,' she said with a wistful smile. 'They'll have grown out of them by now anyway.'

Clare sat down with Anne at an outdoor table, while Jack investigated the box. 'Tepig!' he cried, seizing a figurine. Unbelievable. The child only talked in front of people who expected him to. Clare recognised the toy at once: the piggy body, the tall black ears, the yellow nose. But this was no cheap plastic Happy Meal toy. This was sturdy and as big as a grapefruit, its tail painted permanently purple. The joy on Jack's face was a delight to see. He soon ferreted out a variety of other Pokémon toys.

'Take the box home with you,' said Anne.

'I couldn't —' began Clare.

'Please,' she said. 'I can't think of a better place for it.'

Clare looked into Anne's generous, smiling eyes, thinking about how long she'd spent climbing the career ladder, where everything came with strings attached, where there was always a *quid pro quo*. But here was Anne simply giving, with no expectation of anything in return. It didn't matter that it was just a carton of secondhand toys; Clare couldn't have been more moved. Out of the blue, tears came. 'Thank you,' she said. 'You're very kind.'

Anne squeezed Clare's hand, then knelt down on the ground to play with Jack. 'Pokémon,' she said, making a procession through the grass with the toys.

Jack snatched one of them up, ran to Clare and plonked it down on her knee. 'Pokémon,' he said, eyes alight. He climbed up and gave her a bear hug, while she kissed his hair. Could this really be the same child she'd first met in Brisbane? Maybe she wasn't so bad at this mothering caper after all.

'He's adorable,' said Anne. 'Harry never said he had a grandchild.'

Clare was about to say *Jack's not mine,* but a perverse desire kept her silent. A sudden, fierce, hopeless desire for Jack to actually *be* hers. To properly belong. To permanently belong. Tom's arrival rescued her from having to respond.

'All done,' he said, putting his bag in the ute. 'The palomino needs his wolf teeth out before you put a bridle near him, though.'

Jack climbed into the car and Clare placed the carton of toys beside him.

'Score,' said Tom when he saw Jack's loot. He and the little boy high-fived each other.

'When did he learn to do that?' asked Clare in wonder. Jack was certainly full of surprises.

The Bunya Mountains were an island of distinctive, basalt peaks, the remains of ancient volcanoes, cut off from the rest of the Great Dividing Range. They rose abruptly from the surrounding plains, as if dropped intact from some far wilder place. It was a sacred feeling to leave the open farmlands and enter the forest - like stepping into the stillness of a cathedral from a busy street. Narrow winding roads offered mountain panoramas and breathtaking views across the southern plains. Hoop pines and myrtle dominated the lower slopes, but the vegetation changed as they climbed. Soon dome-shaped bunya pines raised their majestic heads above the sub-tropical rainforest canopy. Sunbursts of golden king orchids graced their trunks. It was overwhelming, Clare discovered, to find herself back in this primeval forest; back in the place she'd so loved as a child.

'Bunya pines are living fossils,' said Tom. 'They're found in geological records dating way before the Jurassic.' He glanced at Jack. 'Dinosaurs, Jacky, you like dinosaurs?' The boy grabbed a toy brontosaurus from the box and marched it up and down his car seat. 'Well, dinosaurs just like your Bronte were snacking on these kind of trees two hundred million years ago.' Tom grinned at Clare. 'It's hard to get your head around, isn't it?'

'I had no idea these pines were so old,' said Clare. Until now they'd been simply a symbol of childhood happiness. Now she felt their significance reaching right through the ages, to long before humans existed, to beyond the dawn of history.

Jack began to bang his head on the car seat. 'He needs to wee,' said Clare.

Tom found a safe place to pull over. 'September's not bunya nut season, but I still wouldn't hang around. Their cones are dinosaur-size too, bigger than footballs, and you're a goner if you cop one on the head.'

Clare already knew that. These mountains had been her grandparents' favourite picnic spot. They'd always told her and Ryan that it was a magical place. Back then, Clare had believed them.

She took Jack from the car and looked around. They were deep inside the cool forest here, hidden from sunlight. She gazed up at the ancient trunks, towering one-hundred-and-fifty-feet tall. They remained the dark, mysterious trees of childhood fantasy. This was an Enid Blyton enchanted wood, full of portals and blurred boundaries. A tawny wallaby peered at her from among the ferns, as Jack peed against a rock. Its bright eyes regarded her with primal wisdom. She half-expected it to speak in this charmed place. Something was calling to her, as clear as a clarion bell. Call it intuition, call it magic – call it love. She didn't know what it was, but its impossible message was plain. *Stay* it said. *Stay at Currawong. Stay in the foothills of these magic mountains. With Grandad, with Jack ... with Tom. Let nothing tear you away.*

Jack took her hand. 'Clare,' he said. She shivered as he tugged her towards the car. It was almost as startling as if the wallaby had spoken. She laughed out loud, picked Jack up and spun him around and around in excitement. Tom leaned out the window, a curious look on his face.

'Jack said my name,' called Clare. 'He said my name.' Until that moment she hadn't realised how much she'd longed for that. It was as if Jack had finally claimed her.

She bundled the giggling, wiggling child back in, struggling to clip up the straps of his car seat. Tom leaned over the back seat to help. Sunlight flickered across his features, and Clare unexpectedly found herself kissing him, full on the lips. A kiss like she'd never known, all heat and breath and surprise. A wonder kiss. A Tom kiss.

When she pulled away there was shock and pleasure on his face. With superb comic timing, Jack clapped a hand over his mouth and widened his eyes. It was impossible not to laugh, but when Clare met Tom's gaze, behind his amusement, she saw exactly what she'd hoped to see. Hunger for more.

CHAPTER 19

'There's nothing to talk about,' said Clare, debating whether or not to hang up on Adam.

'Look, I did the wrong thing, and for that I'm sorry. But Veronica just about threw herself at me. I won't apologise for being flesh and blood.'

'I don't want you to apologise, Adam. It doesn't matter any more.'

Clare sat in the hallway alcove, gazing out the dusty window overlooking the yards. She ran her fingers across the heavy handset of the old phone. Her mother had used this same phone to make urgent, whispered calls to someone on that very last visit to Currawong - not to Clare's father. She and Ryan had tried to listen in, tiptoeing down the hallway towards her, but a squeaky floorboard had always given them away.

'When are you coming back to Brisbane?' asked Adam.

'One, it's none of your business, and two, like I said, it doesn't matter.'

'Not to you, maybe.' There was a note of real pain in Adam's voice. 'Paul Dunbar dismissed me. I'm no longer his junior.'

Clare thought she must have misheard him. 'But you're his *golden boy*.'

'Not any more.' There wasn't a trace of pretense in his voice.

She let her fingers slide over the carpet, felt the news in her gut, even after what he'd done. 'Why? What happened?'

'What do you think happened?' He let the question hang. 'Congratulations on your own appointment, by the way. Paul Dunbar's reader – quite a coup. Seems Paul's a bit of a white knight.'

'I don't understand.' The feeling in her stomach was growing stronger.

He spelled it out. 'Paul said that, considering how I'd treated you, it wouldn't be fair expecting you to work alongside me.'

So that was it. Her public denunciation of Adam at the Bar Association lunch. Who would have thought Paul would take her side so strongly? She couldn't help feeling flattered, but she hadn't meant to cause the collapse of Adam's brilliant career. Some short-term embarrassment was all she'd hoped for. The Brisbane legal fraternity was a small world and Paul Dunbar was its shining star. Get on the wrong side of him and it could be a long climb back up the ladder.

'That's dreadful,' she said. 'I'm truly sorry. But what do you expect me to do about it?'

Adam hung silent on the end of the line for the longest time. 'Nothing,' he said, his voice softer now. 'Nothing except listen. The truth is, I still love you, Clare.'

She drew her breath in, watched the squares of sunlight on the carpet, how the old faded pattern disappeared beneath the glare. This was crazy. Adam had never once told her he loved her when they'd been together – outside of the bedroom, that was.

'Let me finish, please Clare. I know I hurt you, and that you probably don't want me back in your life.'

'Got it in one,' she said.

'I deserved that.' Adam had never sounded contrite before. 'But my life's a train wreck right now. I'm asking for your friendship, that's all. For you to keep the lines of communication open. I've hit rock bottom, Clare. I really have, and I miss you. Your warmth, our walks. I even miss you dragging me around those weekend farmer's markets. Where am I supposed to get my organic pomegranate juice now?'

She smiled, relenting a little, tracing her finger over the wallpaper roses the way she did as a child. A friendship with Adam - was it possible?

'Please,' he said. 'Have a heart.'

'Okay. You win … friends.'

He breathed what sounded like a relieved sigh.

'What are you going to do?' she asked him.

'Go back to corporate law, for now. Even though it's boring as batshit.'

'At least it's a job.'

'If you can call it that.'

Clare didn't respond. She wasn't a fan of self-pity.

'Don't worry,' said Adam. 'I'll bounce back. I'll be downing scotch in the Barrister's Bar before you know it.'

'Of course you will,' she said. 'Look, I've got to go.'

'Goodbye, Clare … and thanks for listening.'

CHAPTER 20

Sunday morning and something was up. All through breakfast, Tom had looked like the cat that ate the cream. Clare studied Grandad. To go by the grin on his face, he was in on it as well. Clare helped Jack to another sausage. 'Okay, you two. What gives?'

'Never you mind, Clare Bear,' said Grandad. It was the first time he'd used his old pet name for her. Clare felt like she was about ten again. 'You always were too inquisitive for your own good.'

Something about the name caught Jack's fancy. He climbed onto her lap, put his nose against hers and stared into her eyes. 'Clare Bear, Clare Bear, Clare Bear,' he chanted in a deep voice that made her laugh. When Jack went back to his seat, he looked around as if searching for something. The little boy lifted the cloth and peered beneath the table. 'Samsam stole my sausage.'

They all froze. Clare looked first at Tom, then at Grandad. Jack had spoken a complete sentence.

Tom hurried to a bag that sat on the floor in the corner and pulled out a video camera. He aimed it at the little boy. 'What did Samson do, Jacky?'

'Samsam stole my sausage.'

Clare felt the soft swish of Samson's tail. The dog had been hiding under the table all along.

Tom took another sausage and placed it on his own plate near the edge of the table. Samson's nose poked from under the cloth, and in a flash the sausage was gone. Jack pointed and giggled. Tom kept the camera trained on his face. 'What did Samson do just then?' he asked.

Jack was bobbing up and down with excitement. 'He stole *your* sausage.' Grandad did the same thing. Once again the sausage disappeared. Jack's mouth dropped open and his eyes grew large with fun. 'Samsam stole Grandad's sausage.'

Emboldened by the success of his sneak attacks, Samson emerged from underneath the cloth, put his giant paws on the table, and helped himself to the whole plate. Jack was beside himself with delight. 'Samsam stole *everybody's* sausage!'

Clare crouched down and threw her arms around the neck of the surprised dog, in one mighty hug.

Tom was studying the video camera. 'Got it.' He showed Clare the footage of Jack. There it was, captured for anybody to see, audio and all. The little boy's voice sounded clear as a bell. 'Look, Jack,' said Tom.

The child stared at the screen in wonder. He stabbed it with his finger. 'Jack,' he said, his voice small and uncertain. He searched Clare's face for reassurance. Clare released Samson from her arms. The dog jumped boldly up at the table, eyeing off the rounds of toast this time.

'Get out of it,' growled Grandad, and shoved him down. Samson slunk off, realising that for some reason his charmed breakfast-stealing life was over.

'Here's your answer,' said Tom, holding up the camera. 'The department won't be able to argue with this sort of evidence.'

That was true, it was wonderful, but a question still burned in Clare's brain. 'How did you know that would happen? I saw you before. You were pleased before Jack even spoke. And why do you just happen to have a video camera?'

Tom didn't answer her. She looked at Grandad who was showing a sudden interest in his shoes.

'It'll all be clear in a minute,' said Tom, stowing the camera in his bag and slinging it over his shoulder. 'Come on.' He took Clare's hand. 'I have a surprise.' He tousled Jack's snowy head. 'You too.' Tom led them out of the house, past the barn to the stockyards.

Clare couldn't believe her eyes - Smudge. Her old pony was dead, she knew that, but the pretty, dappled-grey imposter standing in the yard was the spitting image.

'Recognise him?' asked Tom. 'It's Sparky. I bought him for Jack.' If Clare hadn't already been keen on Tom, this extraordinary, unexpected gift might well have been the clincher. It was like being a kid again, seeing the pony there. Like having a boundless, bright future stretching before her and not a care in the world. She wanted to climb onto Sparky's back, bury her face in his neck and inhale his warm, equine scent.

'That pony's a dead ringer for Smudge,' said Grandad. 'It's almost like the old girl's come back.' He rubbed his eyes and turned away. Were those tears?

'Come on in, Jacky,' said Tom. He opened the gate with one hand and beckoned the boy inside the yard. His other hand held the camera. He was videotaping the meeting. So that's what the camera had been for.

Jack approached Sparky with care, just like he'd been taught to do. The pony bent his head and snorted softly, inspecting the little boy with his muzzle. Jack flashed Clare a brilliant smile. He stroked the pony's crest, running his tiny fingers through his thick mane. With Fleur, even on tiptoe, he could barely reach her shoulder.

'Sparky certainly is more his size,' said Clare. 'I won't mind Jack riding him.'

'Not so fast,' said Tom. 'Riding's the last thing I'll teach him, not the first. These two need to get to know each other, learn how to connect on the ground. They need to build a relationship. Riding will just be the icing on the cake.'

'You're the expert,' said Clare. 'But if Jack's not riding Sparky, maybe I will. Right now I have an urge to take him for a swim in the dam.'

Tom smiled and gave her the video recorder. Then he took a head collar, showed Jack how to fit it, and snapped on a leading rein.

'Shall we get started?'

The little boy nodded and a sunny smile lit up his face. He looked particularly angelic today. No two ways about it, Tom was a miracle worker. Or maybe it was the horses, or the dogs, or just the space? There was room here at Currawong. Room for Jack to be himself, room for him to grow.

Clare thought back to her cramped apartment, to the television that ruled the lounge room. She thought of Samson and the wretched inside doggy loo with its fake tree. She pictured the treadmill, with Samson running on the spot like a mad thing. Running and running and never getting anywhere. No place for a dog … or for Jack. Maybe it was no place for her either.

Yet it was merely a matter of time before Samson would be back on the treadmill. Clare's dream job awaited her in Brisbane, in just a few months' time. She was living a fiction here, building a fanciful future upon the shifting sands of an overactive imagination. Or more ridiculous still, built on a delusional encounter with an enchanted forest. She could just imagine Roderick's face when she told him that magic trees had told her to stay here at Currawong – to stay here with Tom and Jack. *Jack isn't your child*, he'd say, and he'd be right. What was the point of giving him a pony? Just like Clare and Samson, he'd soon be back in Brisbane. With his mother. With Taylor.

Where was Taylor, anyway? Roderick had promised to call the minute there was word. An unspeakable hope slipped into Clare's consciousness from where it had been lurking at the edges of her mind. Maybe Taylor would never come back.

CHAPTER 21

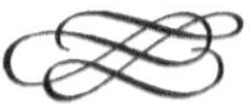

'Are you sure you'll be all right?' Clare asked for the tenth time.

'Positive,' snapped Harry. 'Now you get along to that meeting and see if somebody can't talk some sense into you.'

Clare sighed. Her grandfather had been impossible today. They'd argued. She'd been trying to point out the advantages of at least allowing Pyramid Energy to drill some test wells at Currawong. Clare had done her research, even visiting Pyramid's office in Dalby to clarify a few points. Under the *Petroleum and Gas (Production and Safety) Act 2004* and the *Petroleum Act 1923*, the miners held all the cards. Providing they produced a current authority to prospect and had issued a notice of entry, Pyramid had every legal right to enter Currawong. But what Grandad didn't seem to understand was that they also had statutory responsibilities. They had to provide compensation for well heads and minimise environmental impacts. There were strict regulations with respect to fencing, stock and weed control. Surrounding land could still be used for grazing and a duty of care existed for land rehabilitation at the completion of drilling. If Pyramid were coming in anyway, it made more sense to work *with* them than to fight them. And according to the company's landholder liaison officer in Dalby, there was no doubt they were coming in. He'd shown her the map. Currawong and its immediate surrounds were coloured red – an area estimated to be of high production value.

But talking to her grandfather was like talking to a brick wall. 'They'll ruin the place,' he said. 'Pollute the air, the ground, the water, just like at Quimby Downs. Pete Porter's had wells there for two years now. Won't even let his dog drink from the bore any more … and he's been crook for ages.'

Grandad was going to blame every coincidence on the presence of the wells, that much was obvious. But she hadn't put it to him as bluntly as that. She'd chosen her words very carefully. 'The wells are constantly monitored,' Clare had said, hoping to reassure him. 'Not just by Pyramid, but by external government inspections. I think you're worrying about nothing.'

Grandad had snorted. 'Nothing? Is it nothing that Pete's packed up and gone to live with his daughter in Dalby? He's been my neighbour at Quimby Downs all my life. Best friend a man could ask for. Built the house with his own two hands. Brought up six children, nursed his wife there until she died. Thought the only way he'd leave his land was in a box, same as me. But no – he's gone. Driven out by those bloody gas wells.'

It was no use. He wasn't listening. She'd tried a different tack. 'The compensation payments might actually make it easier for you to stay on at Currawong.'

'I don't want their bloody compensation payments!' He was shouting now. 'I just want to be left alone. Your grandmother would turn in her grave to hear you talk like that.'

He'd glared at her like she was the enemy. That last remark had cut deep. Was this really about the gas wells? A pool of guilt lurking just below the surface bubbled up. For the last sixteen years all she'd done was leave him alone. Was he having a go at her? Clare hated upsetting her grandfather like this, but it was no use him putting his head in the sand. The gas wells were coming whether he liked it or not. 'If I promise to get together the best, most up-to-date information on the pros and cons of what Pyramid's proposing,' said Clare, 'will you at least read it?'

He'd looked suddenly cagey. 'Go along with Tom to the *Shut the Gate* meeting tonight. I'll mind Jack. Keep an open mind and see what you make of it. Do that for me, and I promise to read whatever you want. Deal?'

'Deal,' she'd said. It seemed like a fair arrangement.

It was almost seven o'clock when Tom marched in the door. 'Thought I'd never get away tonight. That Mrs Potts would talk the hind legs off a donkey. Reckon I could recite the pedigree of every one of her budgies by now.'

Jack pulled at Grandad's sleeve and pointed to the top of the kitchen dresser. The old man reached up, took down a board game and set it on the table. 'What do you say?' he asked the little boy.

'Ta,' said Jack, pulling off the lid.

Grandad beamed at Clare, and ruffled the boy's hair. 'He's coming along in leaps and bounds, this one.'

'He certainly is,' said Clare. She kissed her grandfather's cheek. 'Are you sure you wouldn't rather go to the meeting instead?'

He held up his hand. 'A deal's a deal. And to tell you the truth, I've been a bit crook today. I'd just as soon stay home and play *Snakes and Ladders* with Jacky.'

'Crook how?' asked Clare. 'What's wrong?'

'I'll live,' he said. 'Get her out of here, will you, Tom? Jack and me are busy.'

'Wait.' She ducked into the bathroom to brush her hair in front of the mirror.

'The lass won't be a minute,' she heard Grandad say. 'Probably putting on her face.'

'If she didn't do a thing,' said Tom, 'she'd still be streets ahead of the rest.'

Grandad chuckled appreciatively and Clare emerged, feeling both embarrassed and pleased. Tom saluted and took hold of her hand in an almost proprietary way. Grandad took in the gesture with a long, considered stare and Clare held her breath until he cracked a smile.

'See you, Jacky,' she said, waving goodbye as Tom pulled her out the door.

The meeting was at the Merriang Soldiers Memorial Hall on the outskirts of town, a small weatherboard building with a gabled porch like a Californian bungalow. The car park was overflowing, and they had to park up the street.

'It's a good turnout,' said Clare.

'The local MP's coming,' said Tom. 'Gordon McCrae. We hope he'll take our fight to parliament.'

Inside, chairs had been set up facing the stage. A document tray full of fat envelopes stood on a card table by the door. It was labelled CSG *Submissions*. An elderly lady in front of them dropped an envelope into the tray. Basildon Bond, the same elegant brand of stationary her grandmother had used for letters and thank you notes. It was addressed in ink, a graceful, flowing hand. Another man dumped a box file beside the tray. Tom slipped an envelope from his own pocket and added it to the pile.

A teenage girl was playing John Williamson's *True Blue* on a piano in the corner. In proper bush fashion, benches and tables groaned with plates of sandwiches and cakes. An urn bubbled beside the sink in the kitchen.

'We should have brought a plate,' said Clare. 'Why didn't you tell me?'

'I'm not in the habit of bringing one,' said Tom, popping an Anzac biscuit in his mouth. 'I'm in the habit of taking one home.' He ate another biscuit. 'I love these things.'

'Don't,' said Clare, and found a seat. Tom squeezed in beside her. 'Is that another biscuit?' she asked.

'There's always too much food,' he mumbled, his mouth crammed full. 'I'm doing them a favour.'

The piano stopped and a man brought a microphone and stand onto the stage and people began to take their seats. A loud buzz of conversation came from the back of the hall. Clare turned to see what it was about. An unassuming middle-aged man, grey at the temples, had arrived, and was clearly the centre of attention. That must be Gordon McCrae, the MP.

A young man with dreadlocks, who couldn't have been more than twenty-five, thanked everyone for coming, and the crowd greeted him with an enthusiastic round of applause. 'We'll get housekeeping matters out of the way first,' he said, 'and then Gordon will talk about why he's here. He's vowed to take your questions into parliament.' There was a little cheer.

'Who's the hippy?' whispered Clare.

'Gavin Butler, the group convener.'

'He doesn't look like a farmer.'

'He's not,' said Tom. 'Gavin's an artist – a painter. This gas business has led to some strange bedfellows. Farmers and greenies both want to do the right thing by their land. There's more sense in them teaming up than fighting, I guess. And it's not just the greenies. There's both sides of politics here as well.'

Clare was impressed. This kind of community consensus was rare. Only a powerful groundswell of protest would fuel it. Maybe there was more to the gas wells than she'd imagined?

Now Gordon McCrae began to speak. He gave some background about where things stood politically, and the leverage of independents in the current house. The audience listened politely, although there was a grim set to many of the faces. 'There's plenty of power in the cross bench,' he said, 'So let's use it.' A general nod of approval came from the crowd. 'Now, I'd like to hear from you folks who've come along tonight,' said Gordon. 'I've done my own research, discussed it with the bigwigs on both sides of the house. Sat on a parliamentary committee or two on the subject. What I want now is some anecdotal evidence about what it's like out here on the ground. So ... stories please folks.'

One by one people stood and spoke. Clare knew better than to be swayed by emotional rhetoric. There was plenty of that on show. But some accounts were genuinely disturbing: bores losing pressure, groundwater tasting of metal and salt, sick stock and failed crops.

Some people claimed health impacts, too. Reports of nose bleeds, and sore eyes and rashes. How much was truth, she wondered, and how much was paranoia?

After almost two hours, Gavin closed the meeting. The MP stepped down from the stage to enthusiastic applause and cries of 'You tell 'em Gordon,' and 'We're depending on you, mate.' The crowd descended on the refreshments at the back of the hall and Tom joined them. Clare hovered at the edges, observing. Nobody approached her, even though she recognised quite a few people. Anne Brady for instance, and the basset man, Brian Baker. They all seemed too preoccupied to make idle chit-chat with a virtual stranger.

Tom caught her eye and separated himself from the cake table. 'Try these rum balls.' She shook her head. Tom tempted her, holding a chocolate sphere to her lips. She couldn't resist snapping at it. He pulled the sweet away, teasing. Clare got it on the third try and Tom went back for more.

People were still lining up to put their case to Gordon. The relentless fears they held were beginning to unnerve her. She studied the poster of a gas plant beneath storm clouds that was pinned to the wall. The odd machinery squatted, alien and strange, over a familiar patchwork of crops. A sinister image, carefully designed that way. Clare knew all this, but found herself swayed nonetheless. It wouldn't take much for her to embrace their alarm.

Clare caught Tom's eye. He swallowed two dainty sandwiches at once and made his way back to her. 'Can we go?' she asked. Tom nodded and said some swift goodbyes. Then taking her elbow he guided her out the door. How different he was to Adam. Half the time with Adam she'd felt like she was just tagging along, a bit of an afterthought. She hadn't realised quite how unimportant he'd made her feel, until she had Tom for comparison. By contrast, his need for her was plain.

'That was pretty intense,' she said when they were back in the car.

Tom slung his arm around her shoulder and pulled her close. 'You want to see intense?'

He kissed her slow and hard, then cradled her face in his hands.

Butterflies stirred in her stomach, but a curious group of people passing on the footpath caused Clare to pull away. She wished she hadn't. The sky was darkening outside. She could hear Tom shifting in his seat and the sound of their breathing. Why had she moved away? What if she'd put him off?

'The night's still young,' said Clare. 'Shall we go back to your place?' Tom didn't respond.

Oh. Had she been too forward? She tried again.'Grandad won't mind if we don't go straight home.' His hands were on the wheel now, instead of on her. Perhaps he was just overwhelmed. Her skin, where he'd touched her, felt alive.

Finally he spoke. 'My place is no good.'

Why was he suddenly playing hard to get? The anticipation of his touch in the dark made her bold, and she slid her hand onto his knee. Tom's expression was hard to read in the fading light.

'What are we waiting for,' he said at last, and turned on the ignition. The wheels spun on the gravel roadside. In a few minutes they pulled up outside a raised bungalow, a typical Queenslander, with flower beds and an ornamental woven-wire fence. The gabled iron roof was framed by a pale sunset. She didn't know what she'd expected, but it wasn't this. She tried to imagine absent-minded, disorganised Tom pruning the roses, and failed.

They walked up the twilight path and the porch light switched on as if by magic. Timber steps led to a verandah swathed in flowering jasmine. The air hung heavy with its sweet fragrance. 'This is lovely,' said Clare, taking his hand. Tom pulled her into the shadows and kissed her until every nerve in her body screamed for more. She drank in his warmth, his strength, the delicious force of his desire, and her head swam like she'd had too much wine.

As his fingers found the buttons of her shirt, Clare caught a movement out of the corner of her eye. A huge toad leaped from the darkness and snapped up a beetle near her shoe. She let out an involuntary scream.

'I've got it,' said Tom. To her horror, he scooped up the creature and vanished inside, leaving her alone on the verandah. Clare tentatively pushed through the screen door just in time to see Tom disappear into the kitchen at the end of the hall.

'Get that bugger out of here,' yelled a voice, a female voice.

Who was here? Clare tiptoed down the corridor and peeked into the kitchen. A pretty young woman was standing with her back against the fridge. A slight muffin top spilled over the waistline of her low-slung jeans. Wavy blonde hair tumbled to her waist and generous breasts spilled from a tight boob-tube. Who was she?

Tom stood with the toad held out like a sacrifice. The creature lay acquiescent in his hands. 'You're not putting that thing in the freezer,' the woman said defiantly. 'Mum nearly had a heart attack when she found that other one.'

Time for some answers. 'Hello,' said Clare, entering the kitchen and introducing herself. She offered her hand, but the girl just eyed her suspiciously. 'Tom,' said Clare, indicating the young woman with a slight nod. 'I haven't had the pleasure…?'

'This is Bonnie. Bonnie … Clare.' Bonnie. The name sounded more like a collie than a person. 'This is actually Bonnie's home,' said Tom. 'I just rent a room.'

So that was it. His peculiar behaviour all made sense now. 'Ahh …' said Clare. 'You didn't tell me.' She made no effort to hide the edge of rebuke in her voice. Tom shrugged and looked a little helpless. 'I'm sorry —' he began, but was cut short by a scream. A middle-aged woman barged into the kitchen, eyes blazing.

'Get that infernal creature out of here,' she shouted. 'I went for the ice-cream last night and found two of them things instead. Stiff as boards, they were. What do you want with frozen toads anyway? Are you doing some sort of mad experiments?'

Clare stifled a laugh. 'I've run out of *Hop Stop*,' said Tom. 'Cooling toads in the fridge overnight, followed by freezing, is the next best way to kill them.'

'Fridge?' said the woman, a look of mounting revulsion on her face.

'You can't put them straight into the freezer,' said Tom, in his most reasonable voice. 'Exposing fully conscious toads to extreme temperatures causes painful ice crystals to form in their skin. It's not humane.'

The woman's horror turned to mirth. 'Humane?' she said with a cackling laugh. 'My George doesn't worry about being humane. He practises his golf swing on the little bleeders.'

The toad squirmed. 'You're putting it in the fridge?' said Clare.

'Not any more, he's not,' said Bonnie.

'The toads don't know they shouldn't be here,' said Tom, calming his amphibian charge by flipping it over and rubbing its belly. The toad appeared to fall asleep. 'Ultimately, all the damage they do is our fault for introducing them. We have to get rid of them, true, but we have to show them as much compassion as we would any other animal.'

The older woman looked pointedly at Bonnie. 'I always said he was a little loopy.'

Tom retreated, complete with cane toad, and Clare followed him out the back door. 'That was interesting,' she said, failing to restrain a giggle. 'Not quite how I expected the evening to turn out, but interesting just the same.'

'I should have said,' mumbled Tom. 'About Bonnie, I mean.'

'Yes, you should have.'

He took the toad to the car, found a cloth bag in the back and placed the unfortunate creature inside. 'I'll drop it off at the surgery after I take you home.' Clare nodded. They sat for a bit, while stars wheeled above them in a show of celestial brilliance. The desire she'd felt when he kissed her in the shadows was undiminished, in spite of the strange scene in the kitchen. Clare reached for him, but he shrank away.

'I can't touch you,' he said in a strangled voice. 'My hands, they're starting to sting. I must have triggered her poison glands.'

'You mean the toad? How do you know it's a she?'

'Size,' he said. 'The females are bigger.' Tom uselessly wiped his hands on his trousers, then settled them back on the wheel. 'I'd better get you home.'

Clare nodded, then leaned over and carefully kissed his cheek.

'Tom,' she said, while buckling her seat belt. 'You really … really need to get your own place.'

It wasn't much past ten when Clare got in, but Grandad had already gone to bed. Clare crept into Jack's room, just like she'd done each night since she'd been at Currawong. Almost a month now. It was hard to believe that she'd once seen Jack as an imposition.

She softly scolded Samson, who was stretched out beside the child, sharing his pillow. Jack was squashed up against the wall, one arm flung over the dog's neck. 'Come on you. Back where you belong.' A sheepish Samson commando-crawled backwards, down to the foot of the bed. Clare rearranged the little boy's sleepy limbs, and repositioned his head more comfortably. Jack's fine white-gold hair lay like a silky halo on his pillow. How long it was getting now. He'd need a haircut soon. There was that little place in town with the funny name, but where did she stand on that? Would Taylor mind? Did Clare have the right, as his carer, to take Jack to *Click Go The Shears*? A sharp stab of resentment caught her by surprise. Why should she have to agonise over something so simple, so ordinary? For almost two months now she'd been Jack's mother in every sense of the word, hadn't she? She'd even left her job, sacrificed her life in Brisbane to bring Jack to this place of healing.

A small voice whispered that this wasn't quite true, that she was rewriting history. *You came to Currawong because you were curious*, it said, *and because Adam cheated on you.* She tried to ignore the voice, but it grew more and more insistent. *You have no real place in Jack's life*, it whispered. *It's futile to think along those lines. You're his temporary carer, nothing more.*

That was the law and nobody understood it better than she did. Taylor could come back at any time. If she'd made a fair fist of improving her life, Jack would be hers. And that, of course, was just how it should be. Clare would take the job with Paul Dunbar and her sojourn at Currawong would end. Whatever was going on with Tom would probably end too. She stood there in the dark, still feeling

Tom's touch on her skin, his lips on hers. Maybe Jack's social worker had been right all along. Getting attached to Jack was a recipe for heartache. And maybe getting attached to Tom was just as risky. Her picket-fence fantasy of staying in Merriang, of settling into some kind of life with Tom and Jack, was just that – a fantasy. An idyllic silly dream. Wasn't it?

She sat down on the edge of Jack's bed as a wild, hopeful notion took hold. To hell with her job. To hell with Taylor. If she could keep Jack she would. If she could stay here with him and Grandad … and Tom, she would. She'd stay and build a new life, a different future. Jack stirred in his sleep. Clare swept the little boy's hair off his face, and her imagination took flight. It wasn't an impossible dream, after all. It could really happen. She was suddenly sure that she and Tom would make it. It was early days, and she didn't have much evidence, but her heart was shouting that he was the one. Not the carefully protected heart of her past, but one that had broken free of its safeguards: a heart that longed to recklessly love this boy, this man, this place. A heart that hoped Taylor would not return to claim her son.

CHAPTER 22

The ringing phone jolted Clare from sleep so abruptly, that her dream remained vivid, the horror still real. She'd been miles beneath the earth, swimming in a warm underground ocean. Jack was there too, on the beach, laughing and throwing sticks into the shallows for Samson. A tranquil scene. But while they played, the waves changed direction, breaking at an unnatural angle to the shore. It was then she saw it – a dark stain in the distance, expanding at incredible speed. She'd called to them, but Jack had merely waved and cast a stick into the waves. Samson bounded after it, swimming strongly out to sea. 'Jacky, no!' But like a flash the child was in the water too, dog paddling towards the stain. The black water assumed a concave shape – a monstrous, roaring vortex, swallowing all before it. Samson and Jack vanished down its gaping throat. A primal scream broke from her lips. The whirlpool had sucked the ocean dry, and left her standing in a desolate wasteland. Nothing left but pale skeletons dotting the slimy seabed.

The phone call summoned her home. Clare shook her head, still groggy from sleep, and looked at the time on her alarm clock. Six o'clock in the morning. Who'd be ringing this early? She stumbled out to the hall.

'Jesus Christ, Clare … You're a hard woman to get hold of.'

'Roderick?' It was preposterous to hear her boss's voice coming from the clunky old Currawong phone. A worm turned in her stomach.

'Don't sound so surprised, Clare. You're on the Darling Downs, not on the rim of the known world.'

Clare didn't know what to say. She was fond of Roderick. More than fond. His encouragement and passion had inspired her ambition for the bar. But she didn't want to hear from him now. Not now. Not here.

'Great news,' he said. 'Taylor's back.'

It was like he'd punched her. 'That's good,' she managed. 'How *is* Taylor? How'd she go in court?'

'She's well and truly headed in the right direction,' he said. 'Good behaviour bond and a treatment order. We've found her safe housing, she's dumped the violent boyfriend and, best of all, she's back on the methadone program.'

'You've been busy,' was all Clare said.

'It's all gone far better than we could have hoped. I reckon our Miss Taylor Brown is a fine contender for getting that kid back.'

Clare's hand trembled. She couldn't hold the phone steady. Bile rose in her throat, while some far distant part of her begrudgingly acknowledged the girl's achievements and commitment to her son.

Clare subjected Roderick to a searching inquisition, desperate for every detail. Roderick mainly met her barrage of questions with silence. Finally he said, 'Settle down, Clare. I've already breached Taylor's confidentiality by telling you what I have. Let's not compound the offence, eh?'

'Of course,' said Clare. 'Sorry.'

'Will keep you posted. I don't mean to raise your hopes too soon. Taylor's got a way to go yet.' She could almost hear him beaming. 'Meanwhile, how about sending me through some photos of John for his mum? And the department's organised for Taylor to go down there for a visit, so just make sure I can contact you, okay. Is this landline the best number to get you on? And what the hell happened to your mobile? It's like you dropped off the face of the earth.'

If only thought Clare. 'My mobile's kaput.' Not a bad thing either. She liked not having a phone, liked not being at everybody's beck and call. 'It fell out of a tree and broke and there are no phone shops in Merriang, but you'll always get me on this number.'

'I will, will I?' said Roderick. 'That's funny ... because I've rung you half a dozen times in the past week. Some old bloke always answers. Your grandfather, I'm guessing? I left messages, but you never get back to me. Why else do you think I'm ringing you so goddamn early in the morning?'

Clare felt a warm flush of love for Grandad. He should have told her about the calls – of course he should have — but she knew why he hadn't. He'd wanted to keep her and Jack close. They were co-conspirators now.

'Grandad's forgetful.'

'That's not good enough, Clare. I need to be able to reach you. And what sort of an excuse is my phone fell out of a tree? It's about as believable as the dog ate my homework.'

Perfectly believable, thought Clare. After all, a dog had eaten her phone.

'You *will* get me on this number,' she said. 'I'll have a word to my grandfather.'

'You do that, Clare,' said Roderick.

There was an uncomfortable pause. 'How's the new guy doing?' she asked. 'Davis. Filling my shoes all right?'

'About that Clare ... It's almost November and we're losing you to Dunbar next year anyway.'

'Yes .'

'I could offer Davis a full-time position now. He's not you, Clare, but he's good. I'd be happy to have him on the team. What do you say?' Clare didn't say anything. 'It will solve next year's staffing problems, and give you time to ease Taylor back into a parenting role.'

His words wrenched at her. It hurt, no doubt about it. Hurt that Roderick had replaced her so easily. But of course he was right. One way or another she was leaving Fortitude Valley Legal Aid. She should be grateful that her position would be so swiftly and capably filled. What was it that Grandad had said the other day? *Nobody's indispensable.* Nobody but Grandad, she'd wanted to say. Clare could no longer imagine life without his warmth and wisdom.

'When's Taylor coming?' she asked.

'That's why I've been trying to ring,' said Roderick. 'She's coming tomorrow, Clare —Thursday. Thank god I finally got hold of you. There'll be hell to pay if Kim Maguire organises this access and it falls through. Stay by the phone, won't you? She'll be calling this morning.'

'Of course,' mumbled Clare and they said goodbye. Clare sat down on a kitchen chair and tried to put herself back together. Part of her was proud of Taylor – in awe of her. How difficult it must have been, struggling alone with her addiction, battling on for the sake of her son. *Her* son. Jack was Taylor's son, Clare told herself. Taylor's son.

CHAPTER 23

Thursday morning. Clare stared at her scrambled eggs with no appetite. She pushed them around her plate, then gazed out the window. The sun shone, but to the north an odd shelf of grey clouds had obscured the Bunya range.

Jack was biting his vegemite toast into the shape of a gun. 'Bang,' he said, and shot her. 'You're dead.'

'Have you told the lad yet?' asked her grandfather. Jack looked up.

She shook her head miserably.

'Want me to do it, love?' Grandad asked.

'No,' said Clare, her voice sharper than intended. 'Of course not.' She hated the look of disapproval on Grandad's face. Currawong and guilt so often seemed to go hand in hand, even if the guilt was self-inflicted. Jack pushed his plate away and hopped down from the table, still clutching his toast gun.

'Bang,' he said, and chased Samson out the door. If only Tom was here. Clare didn't quite know why, but it would have been easier to tell Jack with him around. But he'd left at daybreak to vaccinate dairy cows at Oakey, and wouldn't be back until after lunch. Taylor would be here by then. One o'clock, that's what Kim had said. Taylor had got hold of a car somehow and had permission to take Jack out for the afternoon. Clare could barely let herself think about it. What if Taylor was using after all? She might be high, or drunk. She might shoot up with Jack in the car. She might crash … She might leave with him and never come back.

'I'm driving out to check the brood mares. Want me to take the lad as well? Once you tell him about his mother, that is. Give you some time to yourself?'

'No,' said Clare swiftly. 'I'm spending this morning with Jack.'

Grandad wrapped his arms around her in a fierce embrace. 'Things will work out, love. I'm only as far as the two-way if you need me.' He whistled and Samson cannoned back into the kitchen, followed by the dalmatians. 'Come on, you lot,' said Grandad, and they all vanished out the door.

Clare had half-expected Jack to answer Grandad's whistle, along with the dogs. She glanced at the time. Nine o'clock. Taylor would have begun her long drive to Merriang. She couldn't put off telling Jack about his mother's visit any longer. Kim Maguire's warning echoed in her ear: '*A child like John probably won't understand when you tell him, but it's still wise to prepare for some acting out, just in case.*'

Jack would understand all right. Clare was woefully unprepared to deal with the situation and, for once, she'd listened carefully to what Kim had to say. '*Access visits can trigger a child's repressed feelings of anger, sadness and despair, all associated with separation, and loss of their parents. This may manifest in tantrums or anxiety. John might be hyperactive and agitated, or conversely quiet and depressed.*'

Great. In other words, anything could happen. That was a big help.

Clare finished her tea. Breakfast dishes could wait. It was time to get it over and done with. The day was bright, with a scattering of high cloud and the scent of jasmine on the breeze. An early chorus of crickets thrummed in the garden, and a courting currawong piped a tune. Such a perfect day, such a pervasive sense of peace. Surely nothing could go wrong on such a day. Maybe she was blowing Taylor's visit out of proportion.

'Jack,' called Clare. 'Ja-cky.' He wasn't building roads in the load of builder's sand that Grandad had dumped beside the stable for him. He wasn't in the feed room looking for mice. He wasn't in the cart shed making cubbies, or playing in the hay, or hunting for eggs in the hen house? Where was he? The big gates across the drive were securely closed. Maybe he was inside after all. But as Clare turned back towards the house, something made her stomach lurch. The little garden gate leading to the paddocks hung open. A spidery fear crept up her spine. 'Jack!' Clare ran out the gate, screaming his name.

Sparky … that's where he'd be. She ran down to the day yard. Jack's pony dozed in the shade of a myall tree, his satin coat twitching at flies, but the little boy wasn't with him. If only Samson was here. She searched the stables, the stockyards, the turnout paddocks. Nothing. She combed the nearby fields at a run, startling the grazing clydesdales, causing them to frisk away with their big, slow-motion trots and lumbering hooves. Not a sign. With lungs bursting, with breath rasping in shallow, painful spurts, Clare sprinted to the dam. No — not that. Not her dream.

'Jack!' She yelled for him so hard and so long and so often, that her voice grew hoarse and faded to a husky whisper.

Wrenching herself from the search, Clare pelted back to the home-stead. She slammed in through the door, allowing herself one wild, hopeful sweep of the house before calling her grandfather on the two-way. Then she called Tom. Then she called the police, the rural fire service, the state emergency people. Lastly she called Kim Maguire and left a brief message. 'It's Clare Mitchell. I've lost Jack.'

Clare sat slumped in the kitchen chair, staring out the window into the middle distance.

'What was Jack wearing?' asked Grandad. He took pen and notepad from a sideboard drawer, along with a large sheet of heavy, folded paper, its edges curled and yellowed with age.

'A long-sleeved blue T-shirt with penguins,' said Clare. 'Blue cotton trousers with yellow stripes and black elastic-sided boots.'

Grandad noted it down and then spread the old survey map of Currawong out on the kitchen table. 'You head west on the quad bike, out the laneway and up this hill.' He pointed to the map. 'I'll take these eastern paddocks along the creek.'

Clare licked her lips, but they wouldn't stay wet. Currawong Creek began high in the Bunya watershed. In places it flowed dark and deep between steep banks and its course was choked with snags. So much danger for a little boy lost. The creek, the dam, the snakes. The wild dogs and dingoes ... the vast, indifferent Australian bush.

'I'll keep Samson with me,' he said. She was about to protest, when it dawned on her: Grandad wanted Samson because he was searching the creek paddocks. In her mind's eye, the dog stood barking at a small figure floating face-down, wedged between rocks, pale hair fanned out on the water.

'Don't forget to take the two-way,' said Grandad. A vehicle pulled up outside the house, then another. Neighbours rallying to help. It felt so good to see them there. 'You get going,' he said, nodding towards the cars in the driveway. 'I'll fill them in.'

A group of five riders on horseback arrived, along with a boy on a motorcycle. Clare ran down to the cart shed for the bike, while Grandad held Samson's collar. The dog leaped and barked and whined - straining to race after her as she roared out the gate and up the hill towards the Bunya range. Clare scanned the ground for tracks, scanned the trees for movement, scanned the horizon - praying to see the boy's slight silhouette against the sky.

She checked the time. Quarter past ten. Taylor would be here in a few short hours. Where would Clare find the words to tell the young mother that her precious four-year-old son was lost and alone in the bush? Where would she find the strength?

'Harry to Clare ... Harry to Clare.' The two-way crackled to life, making her jump. Clare was clumsy in her haste, sweaty hands fumbling with the receiver. 'Grandad, any news? Have you found him?'

'No, love, no luck yet, and I've bloody well gone and lost Samson as well. Was up in the front paddock near the road, when the dog just took off through that scrubby bit and I couldn't keep up.'

'Near the road?'

'That's right.'

'Do you think he picked up on Jack's scent?'

'Might have done, love. I just don't know,' he said, unable to disguise the despair in his voice.

'I'm coming home, Grandad.'

The Dalby State Emergency guys had arrived by the time she got back. Clare gave them a description of Jack and his clothes. She was going inside to fetch a photo when Samson came galloping down the drive, barking his head off.

'That's Jack's dog,' said Clare. 'I think he wants us to follow him.'

'What,' said one bloke. 'Like Lassie?'

'Yes,' shouted Clare, over her shoulder. She was already pelting down the drive. 'Just like Lassie.' Samson led them out to the road. The emergency vehicle pulled up beside Clare, whose heart was bursting in her chest, trying to keep pace with the racing dog. She climbed in, gasping for breath, terrified she might lose sight of him. Samson detoured through an open, steel-framed gate leading into a paddock on the other side of the road. Not a farm gate, more like one you'd find in a commercial enterprise. Beyond the gate lay some sort of earthworks, an expanse of bulldozed ground in the middle of open pasture. The dog suddenly vanished from sight. One minute he was tearing across the rough, broken ground, and next ... he was gone.

The wheels sank into the soft earth, losing traction. Clare leaped from the car and ran to where she'd last seen Samson. And there, standing below her in a shallow pit, arms locked around the dog's shaggy neck ... there was Jack. Clare felt a lightness in her limbs: weightless, unanchored. She slid down the steep bank and swept the little boy into her arms. Jack looked at her reproachfully, face smudged with dirt. 'You lost me.'

Clare nodded, smiling through her tears. 'But I've found you now.'

Jack scrunched shut his eyes and buried his face in her shirt.

'I won't lose you again, Jacky,' she said. 'I promise.'

Clare rushed into the bathroom with a towel and clean clothes for Jack. Tom was back, sitting on the edge of the ancient, clawed bath, washing Jack's face and helping him to build a bubble bath tower. The little boy was giggling and squealing as if nothing out of the ordinary had happened at all.

Tom stood and gave Clare a swift kiss. 'I'll clear off. Give you some time to talk with Jack.' Clare nodded absently, still in a daze, barely registering Tom's lips against hers, the burn of them. She hoisted Jack from the tub and wrapped him in a towel. Please let the clock on the wall be fast. It couldn't be one o'clock already. She had not told Jack about his mother's visit yet.

It hadn't helped that she'd been on the phone to Kim Maguire for half the morning. Clare had rung her the minute she'd found Jack. She'd meant it to be a brief call, informing Kim of the good news. She'd hoped recriminations could wait. No such luck.

'What happened today is completely unacceptable,' Kim had said. There was an air of exaggerated outrage about her words, but Clare could hardly disagree. 'I'm writing a full incident report as we speak.'

You'll enjoy that, thought Clare. People like Kim were much more at home filing forms than dealing with people.

'And I have a great many questions,' said Kim.

Clare had spent a humiliating half hour admitting her neglect, only to discover that Kim's concern was more for herself, than for Jack. 'You've betrayed my faith in a major way, Clare. You've exposed the department, and potentially me, to a law suit.'

Should Clare argue? Should she point out that Jack was back home and had suffered no harm? Should she advise the social worker that, having properly placed the child with Clare, she was not responsible for breaching any duty of care? Not like when Kim had tried to place Jack at Brighthaven. That was a textbook case of failure to protect.

But Clare knew how to play this game. 'I can't tell you how sorry I am, Kim,' she'd said. 'You bent over backwards to accommodate me, rushed through the kinship assessment. You've been so wonderful, and then I go and cause you all this grief.'

Kim sounded mollified. 'Can you tell me what steps you'll take to ensure John doesn't wander away again?' As Clare talked about child-proof gate locks and not allowing Jack outside unsupervised she pictured Kim ticking off the boxes. Kim asked if there was a garage door that allowed access to the street. She'd clearly forgotten that they were talking about a country property, where you couldn't even see the street from the house. She'd also forgotten that Clare had a dirty, tired, frightened little boy to deal with, one who was currently rocking on her lap. 'Well goodbye, Clare.' At last. 'Thank God you found the child before his mother arrived.'

That was one thing, at least, that they both agreed upon.

The dogs were barking now, signalling a visitor. She glanced out the window in time to see Taylor emerge from a battered blue Holden station-wagon. Surely that thing wasn't roadworthy? Tom greeted Taylor and waylaid her with conversation. Good, that would buy her some time. Clare finished dressing Jack and sat down on the bath-room floor beside him. 'Listen to me, Jacky. We have a visitor ... Mummy's here.'

The little boy stopped trying to climb back into the bath and just stared, his eyes large. Why on earth hadn't she told him earlier, given him some time to get used to the idea? Clare ran through the possible reactions she'd been warned to expect. For some reason, the one reaction she wasn't prepared for was one of unbridled joy. Jack ran from the room. Clare scribbled Grandad's landline and mobile numbers on a piece of paper and followed the boy outside.

Jack was already wrapped in his mother's arms. The four dogs romped around them, but Taylor didn't seem to be the least bit perturbed. Clare took a closer look at the young woman. She looked much healthier than the first time they'd met. Her long chestnut hair was clean and brushed. Her face, once so pale, was flushed pink with pleasure. Her limbs were a little rounder, her face a little fuller ... her eyes, still hard, but much brighter. And right now those eyes glowed with unmistakable love and pride as she gazed at her little son.

Taylor looked up as Clare approached. '*So* sorry my kid ran off on you. He can be a little bugger like that.'

Clare was stunned. It was an absurd apology. She was the one who'd lost Jack. It had all been her fault. Nevertheless, the girl sounded perfectly genuine, heartfelt even. But there was something much more confusing. How did Taylor know about Jack's disappearance in the first place? Both Clare and Kim had hoped to keep that quiet.

'Where'd you find him?' Taylor directed that question to Tom.

He ruffled Jack's hair. 'Clare will fill you in.' With a nod, he left. She tried to make sense of it. Tom? Tom must have told Taylor that she'd lost Jack. He'd handed Taylor a powerful weapon to use against her, something even that witch Kim Maguire hadn't been prepared to do.

'Come inside,' said Clare. 'I'll make you a coffee and explain what happened.' If she could just convince the girl to spend her visit here at Currawong.

'Nah,' said Taylor. 'It doesn't matter.' She put Jack down and lit a cigarette. 'We're going to the circus.'

'What circus?'

'Toowoomba, was it? I love Jacky's hair. It's long now, isn't it? He looks like a little girl.'

'Toowoomba?' Clare's mouth went dry. Toowoomba was more than two hours away. 'You can't …' started Clare, brain scrambling to find a logical excuse for keeping Jack home.

'He's my son,' said Taylor, eyes narrowing. There was a new edge to her voice. 'I can take him if I want.'

'Of course,' said Clare, forcing herself to smile. 'It's been such a long drive, that's all. I thought you might like a coffee first … or maybe a cold drink?'

It wasn't working. Taylor looked wary now. 'No thanks,' she said, avoiding eye contact.

Clare pulled the piece of paper from her pocket and handed it over. 'You can get me on these numbers,' she said. 'My old one won't work. I lost my mobile.'

'Same here,' said Taylor. 'I always lose them things.'

'You don't have a phone?' asked Clare, feeling sick. 'But what if I need to talk to you?'

Taylor shrugged and shoved the piece of paper into her pocket. She dropped the smouldering butt of her cigarette to the ground and trod on it.

Such a filthy habit. Clare bit her tongue, trying to keep track of where the butt lay on the drive, so she could retrieve it later.

'I'd better go,' Taylor said.

Clare's hands tightened into fists. It was intolerable to think this girl could just strap Jack into that deathtrap of a car and drive off. Clare looked to Jack. Maybe he wouldn't want to go? Maybe he would fight and scream to stay.

'Bye bye, Clare.' Jack waved and climbed into the car with heart-breaking alacrity.

Taylor's eyes lit up. 'He's talking? Does he talk much?'

'More and more each day,' said Clare.

'Cool,' said Taylor. She secured Jack in his seat, then turned back to Clare. Her hard eyes softened. 'Very cool.'

'Samsam,' called Jack. The dog leaped into the car and took up his customary position beside Jack, on the cracked linoleum back seat.

Taylor stroked his head. 'Can we take the dog ?' she asked. 'That'd be fun. Jacky loves dogs.'

'No,' snapped Clare. She dragged her hands through hair, limp with sweat and desperation. Take it easy, she told herself. If you're not careful you'll make things worse. 'Samson better stay here,' said Clare. She meant to sound bright and upbeat, but her voice was wavering. 'They wouldn't let a dog into the circus.' For a moment Taylor looked like she wanted to argue the point. Then she turfed Samson out of the car. Jack whined and began to bang his head. Taylor shoved a lollipop in his mouth then climbed into the driver's seat.

'When will you be back?'

'See ya.' Taylor turned the key and the engine sputtered to life.

'I need to tell you about his routine.' Clare could hear the desperation in her own voice. 'Jack needs to be home by six.'

Taylor lit another cigarette, wound up her window and took off down the hill, wheels spinning on the gravel. Samson launched off after them and Clare grabbed his collar just in time. The dog howled. Clare choked back a sob. She'd broken the solemn promise she'd made to the little boy less than two hours ago. She'd promised not to lose him again, and yet now, for the second time that day, Jack was gone.

Clare sat at the kitchen table with Samson's head cradled in her lap. How many hours to fill? The minutes crawled by. Clare checked the clock so frequently that sometimes no time seemed to have passed at all. The worst thing was that Taylor hadn't given any indication of when she'd be back – or even *if* she'd be back. Clare fought back tears. A huge chunk of her seemed to have vanished into a vast black hole, along with the child. This must be how it felt to have your legs amputated, or your house burn down. The shaft of sunlight streaming through the open window dimmed and then disappeared altogether. Clare shivered and hugged herself. Jack didn't even have his jumper.

Grandad came in, hung his hat on the peg by the door, then pulled up a chair opposite. 'Jack's mother came for him, then? When's he due back?'

'Tonight sometime,' mumbled Clare.

Grandad reached across the table for her hand. 'It'll work out, love. The lad will be home in no time.'

'You don't know that, Grandad. Taylor might never come back. This is killing me, and all you can do is say stupid things about something you know nothing about.' She stood and paced the room. For a moment she didn't realise that she'd translated her mean-spirited thought into words.

Grandad withdrew his hand and slumped a little in his chair. He rubbed his brow as if warding off a headache. 'You might give me a bit more credit,' he said. 'I've done my fair share of waiting for people.'

Clare swallowed hard. He was right. Grandad had been waiting for his daughter - Clare's mother - for a very long time. Waiting for Ryan … waiting for her.

'I'm sorry.' She sat back down. 'I didn't mean it.'

'I know you didn't, love.' He extended his hand again, and this time she took it. 'We're all on tenterhooks. I'll make you a cup of tea. That always helps.'

Clare gazed into her grandfather's worried eyes and felt ashamed. This was hard on him too. She had no monopoly on loving Jack. Today had been one heart-wrenching drama after another, and yet she'd barely given a thought to how Grandad was feeling.

Clare threw her arms around him, kissing his rough cheek. He smelt comfortingly of horses and sweat. 'How about I make you one instead.' She was rewarded with a smile. She loved the way his hollow cheeks filled out when he smiled. He was suddenly a young man again, with a twinkle in his eye.

Now Samson licked her hand. His expression was one of almost human concern. Maybe she should stop worrying about Jack and start appreciating what she still had. Grandad, Samson … Tom. But did she really have Tom? He'd betrayed her, blurted out to Jack's birth mother, of all people, how Clare had lost her son. How she'd let him wander away. There was one good thing, though. Jack was no longer in care on a voluntary basis. She was grateful that Kim had moved so quickly on that front. The state of Queensland was now Jack's legal guardian, and Taylor would be technically kidnapping her son if she failed to return him to Currawong.

Clare made the tea, scalding her hand with steam in the process. A glance out the window showed Tom's jeep, still parked down the hill outside the surgery. 'I'm going for a walk,' she said, handing Grandad his tea. His smile had vanished, replaced with a look of great weariness. 'Won't be long.' Clare kissed him again, called Samson, and headed out the door.

Despite the sunshine, a cold breeze had blown in from nowhere. Swirling twigs and fallen leaves formed sad little willy-willies, which died as soon as they began. Clare rubbed her goose-bumped arms. Tom wasn't at the clinic. A *closed* sign hung on the surgery door and a chain stretched across the car park entrance.

Samson padded restlessly about, whining and sniffing the breeze. She crouched beside him, burying her face in his dark ruff, thinking about when he first came to her. She'd only taken him on from a sense of duty to her dead father. When Samson had first arrived back in Brisbane, he'd seemed like such a silly pup: destructive, demanding, annoying. On more than one occasion Clare had wished him gone. And now? Now she adored him, and between the two of them, Samson seemed by far the cleverest and wisest.

The dog pricked his ears. Clare heard it too, the thrum of an approaching car. She checked her watch. Only two o'clock, but perhaps Taylor had changed her mind and was bringing Jack home early. Her heart made a joyful leap and she ran for the Sunshine gates. But as the vehicle came into view, Clare's hope died. It was her grandfather's tray-back truck, with Tom at the wheel. Clare reached him as he got out to open the gate.

'I want to talk to you.' She was shouting, but she didn't care.

'You okay?' asked Tom.

'No,' said Clare. 'I'm not. I want to know why you told Taylor about me losing Jack?'

'Righto,' he said, climbing into the cab. 'We'll talk at the house. Want a lift?' Clare shook her head. Tom leaned across and opened the passenger door. 'Are you sure?'

'Certain.' Tom frowned, slammed the door shut and took off up the track, with Samson racing along beside. Clare trudged uphill, a growing ball of fury inside her. It was as if he didn't care at all that Jack was gone, didn't care that he might never come home. It was as if he didn't care about her. When she reached the house, Tom was unloading the truck like nothing was wrong. Jack was gone and he'd gone shopping. Unbelievable.

'Look out below.' He turfed a roll of chicken netting to the ground. There were more rolls of wire and some panels of steel fencing.

Grandad came out of the house with his mug of tea and gave them a wave. 'Hope you put that stuff on my account, Tom.'

'No way, Harry. This lot's on me.'

Clare couldn't believe it. Now they were both behaving like nothing was wrong. She wanted to scream. Tom manoeuvred the steel panels to the edge of the truck. She hadn't seen him in a singlet before, and the strength of his arms and upper body was on display. If she hadn't been so furious, she would have been impressed. 'I asked why you told Taylor about me losing Jack.'

Tom straightened his back and wiped his brow. 'I assumed she already knew ... that you'd told her.'

'And give her ammunition to use against me?' said Clare, itching for an argument. 'Why the hell would I do that?'

'First,' he said in a measured voice, 'I didn't know it was a fight between you two. And second, I thought you'd told her because she's his mother, and has a right to know what happens to her kid.'

'He's got a point, love,' Grandad said.

Clare shook her head in disbelief. Tom was one thing, but her grandfather? Whose side was he on?

Tom went back to work as if the matter was closed.

For the first time Clare focused on what was being unloaded from the truck. A tall chain-link gate, about two-metres high. The sort you might find in a factory fence or a dog run. Beneath the gate lay dozens of tall pine posts. Grandad emerged from the cart shed with a post-hole digger and long-handled shovel. Tom jumped off the truck and kicked a roll of tall wire mesh towards the sagging, garden fence.

For a few moments she couldn't make sense of what she was seeing, and then it hit her. While she'd been moping around, imagining worst-case scenarios, blaming everybody else and feeling sorry for herself, they'd been planning to build a fence. A fence to keep Jack safe. Such a simple thing. Such a simple, loving practical thing to do. It left her completely overwhelmed.

Tom caught her eye and smiled. Clare smiled back and threw herself into the work at hand. No more simmering in an emotional stew. It felt so much better to be doing something constructive. Nobody talked much. Tom took a few calls from clients, but after determining they weren't emergencies, he postponed their appointments or asked them to go elsewhere. By the time Grandad declared afternoon smoko, the new fence was half-finished.

An unfamiliar car turned in the gate, and for a moment Clare's heart leapt with hope. 'That's just my mate, love,' said Grandad, looking almost guilty that it wasn't Jack. 'He's come to lend a hand.'

The visitor looked familiar. It was Sid, the wiry old whip man with the bushy white beard – the saddler from the Cobb & Co Museum at Toowoomba. He recognised her straight away. 'I should have known your boy had something to do with Harry. He had too keen an eye for them whips.'

Sid pulled some cold beers from an esky and handed them around. Clare took one, letting the bitter bubbles slide down her throat, letting the tension drain away. A high wind had swept the curtain of cloud from the Bunyas, framing their timeless peaks with a backdrop of infinite blue. An eagle soaring high overhead somehow put things into perspective. Eagles had hunted these same hills for thousands of years. One person's problems didn't amount to very much in the grand scheme of things.

Clare sat down in the sun, her back against the cart shed. Her arms ached and her shirt was damp with sweat, but the beer tasted good and things suddenly didn't seem so dire after all. Not sitting out here in the sunshine, watching gangly foals play hide and seek around their patient mothers. Sid was telling some story about driving an eight-horse hitch back in the fifties, while Grandad shook his head. 'You're dreaming,' he said. 'That was never more than a six-horse outfit.' Then Grandad's phone rang and, for once, he heard it. Everybody froze. Clare held her breath while he fumbled a little in answering it. 'I'll just get her for you ... Taylor,' he mouthed.

'Hello?' said Clare. Don't ask if everything's all right. Don't act worried.

'My car's buggered,' said Taylor. 'Me and Jack won't be back till tomorrow.'

Clare's stomach dropped like a lift with a broken cable. 'Are you both okay?'

'Yeah.' Taylor sounded uncertain. Clare could hear a child screaming in the background. 'Jack's being a little turd, that's all.'

'Where are you?' asked Clare. 'I'm coming to get you.'

'Nah, don't worry.' The screaming stopped. 'We'll be right.'

'I'd better come,' urged Clare. 'You don't have permission for overnight access. Jack's on a guardianship order. The department might issue a warrant.'

'No, that's all sorted,' said Taylor. Now Clare could hear a rhythmic thumping sound. 'Kim said I'm allowed to keep him.'

That couldn't be true. Either she'd misheard Taylor or the girl was lying. 'Where are you?' This time she couldn't hide the panic in her voice.

'I don't know the name,' said Taylor. 'It's real nice, but.' There was a loud crash and a cry. 'Got to go.' And that was that. Clare longed to crawl down the phone. She ignored the curious expressions of the others, and rang Kim. Damn it, an answering machine.

She was about to leave a message when Kim picked up. 'Clare? I was about to call. Taylor's car broke down and won't be fixed until the morning. I found some funding for her to stay at a motel in Toowoomba.'

'What motel?'

'You know better than that, Clare.'

'Just tell me, and I'll go get John. What if she doesn't bring him back?'

'Apparently Taylor calls him Jack, Clare. From now on, you should use the name favoured by his mother.' Clare had neither time nor energy to point out the absurdity of this last statement. 'You don't have to worry about her bringing the boy back,' said Kim, reading Clare's mind. 'Taylor's doing much better, but she still finds it difficult to parent her son. He's proved to be quite a handful, and she hasn't coped very well.'

'Is he all right?'

'I think Taylor's the one who's not all right. She's been glowing in her praise of you though, Clare. Says you've done wonders with the child. Says she doesn't know how you do it. His behaviour at the beginning of the access was apparently impeccable … but Taylor said it wore off, and she blames herself. Frankly, I think she'll be secretly glad to give him back.'

Clare could have cheered. 'That's wonderful.' Bless Jack and his disruptive heart.

'How is it wonderful that Taylor can't manage her son?' asked Kim. 'She's made some positive changes in her life and was understandably hopeful of regaining custody. I'm afraid this access has been a disappointing reality check for her.'

And a welcome reprieve for me, thought Clare. 'Jack does have some extremely challenging behaviours.'

'Don't I know it,' said Kim. 'You're a braver woman than me. I've no doubt that Taylor will return the boy tomorrow. Call if there are any problems.'

Clare handed Grandad the phone, then pressed her palms against her eyes, gathering her thoughts. 'Well,' said Grandad. 'Don't keep us in suspense.'

'Taylor's car broke down.' Clare took a steadying breath. 'She and Jack are staying in Toowoomba overnight and they'll be back tomorrow. She's had a lot of trouble handling him, and said some really nice things about me. Apparently she can't wait to bring him home!'

Grandad's face spread into a slow smile. 'I told you it would work out, didn't I?' She gave him a quick kiss. 'Tom, why don't you take Clare out somewhere? Help take her mind off things. She's such a worrier. Takes after her grandmother, I guess.'

'But we haven't finished here,' said Tom.

'Sid's the fastest damned fencing contractor in Queensland,' said Grandad. 'Between him and me, we'll be done in no time.'

Clare glanced at Tom. His eyes held an invitation, and all the feelings that had been swamped by the day's dramas flooded back. In her body was a low ache, a longing to be with him, somewhere shady and cool. A longing for his touch on her skin.

'Go on,' said Grandad. 'Off you go.'

'What will we do?' Tom asked her. 'Anything you want.'

'Let's go riding,' said Clare, the desire seeming to come from nowhere.

'Riding it is,' said Tom. 'Great idea. You ride Sparky and I'll take Fleur.'

'Sparky?' she said. 'I want to ride Fleur.'

'Well, I can't ride a pony,' said Tom. 'My feet would touch the ground. Are any of your clydies saddle-broken, Harry?'

'There's the stallion, Goliath. Although he hasn't been ridden in a while.'

'How'd he be riding out with a mare?'

'Level-headed enough, as long as the mare wasn't in season.' Harry chuckled. 'Then you'd have a job on your hands.'

'Goliath?' Sid slapped his thigh in amusement. 'Your feet won't touch the ground on that fella. He must stand eighteen hands.'

'Are you game, Tom?' Harry asked.

'My oath.' He grinned at Clare. 'We're going to have a ball.'

CHAPTER 25

Clare scaled the stockyard rails and scrambled onto Fleur's broad back. This was the first time she'd been in the saddle since childhood, and she was a little unsure. Fleur seemed impossibly high. 'Give it some time, Clare Bear,' her grandfather told her, rubbing the mare's cheek. 'You were always a terrific little rider. Gutsy as well. It'll come back to you.' She leaned down to stroke Fleur's broad neck. Tom strapped on a saddlebag, then hopped around on one leg trying to mount Goliath, who refused to stand by the fence. He was a mountain of a horse, rich bay in colour, with a wide blaze, magnificent feather and four tall white socks. It looked like Tom was trying to mount an elephant.

Grandad disappeared into the cart shed and emerged with an old wooden mounting frame. Tom scaled its steps and was finally aboard. He sat his horse with the easy grace of a man at home in the saddle. Straight back. Strong thighs. Steady fingers, firm on the reins, but soft on the mouth — the embodiment of *good hands*. Goliath pranced sideways, muscles rippling beneath his satin skin, ears pricked and head held high.

Tom's expression was one of calm control and Clare saw him in a whole new light. Man and horse moved with the grandeur and grace of a medieval knight and his charger. Grandad opened the gates, a look of pride on his face, and they moved off down the drive. Clare was tentative at first. It was a long way to the ground, and she wasn't exactly sure what her mare wanted to do or how to read her signals. But while she was busy thinking things through, her body was responding all by itself. Call it muscle memory, call it intuition: she didn't know, but once she got used to it, riding on the Percheron mare's broad back seemed as comfortable and familiar as sitting in an armchair.

They reached the Sunshine gates, which were closed, of course. They were always closed these days. Clare gave Tom a rueful smile. 'Someone's going to have to get off.'

'Maybe not.' Tom manoeuvred his giant horse parallel to the gates. It was obvious the pair spoke the same language. In a few moments he'd swung the catch and, barely shifting in his seat, hauled the gate open.

Goliath arched his neck and Tom waved them through. 'Very gallant,' Clare whispered to Fleur, with a smile. Tom expertly closed the gate. They headed out onto the road and turned right. The horses walked abreast to start with, but the stallion's long legs and impatience soon saw him forge ahead. Clare urged Fleur into a timid trot to catch up. Late afternoon sunlight fell in dappled patterns across the road. Goliath shied at the shadows, but Tom easily kept his seat. Thank goodness Fleur had more sense. 'I love riding this horse,' said Tom, turning in the saddle and parking his right palm on the stallion's round rump. 'I absolutely love it. It's like floating on a couch in the clouds.' Clare nodded agreement. Fleur's gait was also slow, smooth and easy, yet there was something thrilling about sitting astride this magnificent mare. Clare was riding tall, and couldn't remember the last time she'd had so much fun.

The road rose before them in a gentle incline. 'Let's trot,' said Tom.

Clare shortened her reins a little, and pressed her heels to Fleur's side. Goliath began calmly enough, but soon he was pulling and tossing his great head.

'Can we canter?' asked Tom.

Clare took a deep breath. 'Go ahead.' The stallion took off, and Fleur followed suit. Clare gave an involuntary scream. Exhilarating and scary, to thunder down the road on these huge horses, manes and tails streaming, plate-sized hooves pounding, striking sparks from the road like fire from flint stones. A pure, physical adrenaline rush, the likes of which she couldn't remember. Really good sex perhaps, or an important, improbable victory in court. Fleur put on a sudden burst of speed, almost leaving her behind. She gasped and laughed and tried to find her rhythm … there it was. Grandad said it would come back, and he was right. The knowledge was latent not lost, how to meld with her horse and read its mood.

Tom wheeled Goliath about. The mighty stallion half-reared in a shaft of sunshine and the sight took Clare's breath away. Even Fleur looked impressed. She nickered and pranced, sidling up to Goliath against Clare's instructions. The horses touched noses. Fleur squealed and pawed the ground while Clare laughed and tugged at the reins. 'Where are we going?' she asked, breathless.

'It's a surprise,' and Tom swept away. Clare and her mare followed like they were drawn on a string. Tom turned into the gate leading to the mysterious earthworks where Jack had got into trouble that morning. The horses plodded across the soft ground. Clare dared not look into the pit. She half-expected to see Jack there, his clothes dirty and his face streaked with tears. Real tears. He'd learned to cry at Currawong.

'What is this place?'

'Pyramid's building a new waste water pond,' said Tom. 'Quimby Downs already has thirteen coal seam gas wells.' Quimby Downs. Where had she heard that name before? 'Harry was gutted when Pete left.' That was it. Grandad's friend. The one who'd raised six kids and lost his wife. The one who said he'd been driven out by the gas wells.

'So nobody lives here any more?'

Tom shook his head. 'Pete still runs a few head of brangus breeders. Harry and I keep an eye on them for him, but he doesn't take the cattle side of things too seriously now. The wells give him a guaranteed annual income.'

Fleur ducked her head to snack on a patch of fresh grass. Clare gave her mare a loose rein. 'That would be one good thing at least, if the wells come to Currawong,' she said. 'Grandad won't have to work so hard. He can sit around and listen to the cricket, or go on a holiday while the money just rolls in.'

Tom moved his stallion close to Fleur. 'Do you know why Pete moved out?'

'Not exactly.'

'Come on,' said Tom, heading up the hill. 'I want to show you something.'

Tom dismounted his horse in one sure, swift movement, then helped Clare down. His hands encircled her waist as she slipped from Fleur's back. It was a shock to feel them, rougher than expected, in firm control of her descent. Clare's heartbeat quickened. She landed a little awkwardly, and stumbled into the mare's warm neck. For a fleeting moment she was sure she felt Tom's hard body pressed against her, his breath on her neck. But when she turned around, he was leading Goliath into a large stockyard, its rails overgrown with willow jasmine. The stallion tore eagerly at the long grass, while Tom unbuckled his girth and hauled the mighty saddle from his back.

'What are you doing?' asked Clare.

Tom unstrapped the saddlebag and took out a bottle of champagne and a huge punnet of strawberries. He held them up to her, eyebrows raised. Clare laughed and tugged Fleur across to the yard. Soon the horses were both unsaddled and grazing contentedly.

'This is such a lovely place,' said Clare. The timber homestead's pretty portico led to a wide verandah. A profusion of purple flowering bougainvillea almost obscured the decorative white balustrade. Above the front door, a stunning fanlight of etched, coloured glass depicted a sunrise. 'How could Pete bear to leave?'

'How, indeed?' said Tom. 'Pete built this house out of pit-sawn timber. He felled the cedar and blackwood himself, up in the Bunya Mountains. See there?' Tom pointed to the roof. 'You can still see original hand-cut shingles beneath the corrugated iron.' Clare murmured her admiration. 'Wait until you look inside. It's a real showpiece.'

Clare didn't doubt it. 'The house is truly beautiful,' she said. 'I want to live here myself.' Fantasies of her and Tom came to mind, sitting out on the porch at twilight, sipping wine and watching Jack play.

'You might think differently after you see this.' Tom led her along the side of the house. A vegetable plot, rampant with weeds, stood across the path to her left. They stopped beside an outside tap, with a simple garden hose attached.

Clare looked around. What was she was supposed to see? 'It wouldn't take much to clear out those weeds and start growing vegetables again,' she said.

Tom frowned, retrieved the end of the hose from under a yellow daisy bush and turned on the tap. The faint waft of chemicals replaced the fragrance of bougainvillea on the breeze. Tom took a cigarette lighter from his pocket. He gripped the garden hose and held it at arm's length. Then, holding the lighter beneath the arc of water escaping from the nozzle, he flicked it on. Clare couldn't believe what she was seeing. A tongue of fire flashed from the end of the hose. It erupted like dragon's breath right before her eyes. The impossible flame, liquid and sinuous, licked along the water arc, transforming it into a burning bow. 'No way!' The unnatural spectre flared steadily in the late-afternoon sunshine. It was more than a minute later when Clare told Tom to turn it off.

'How is that even possible?' asked Clare.

'The bore's contaminated with natural gas, mainly methane. Two years ago Pyramid fracked half the wells on Quimby Downs.'

'Fracked?' asked Clare.

'Hydraulic fracturing. It's used to speed up the flow of coal seam gas from underground. They pump a mixture of water, sand and chemicals at high pressure into the gas-bearing formation below the water table, fracturing the strata. It causes little earthquakes that open up pathways for gas to flow out of the rock and into a well ... or a bore.'

'But I went to Pyramid's office in Dalby,' said Clare, still over-whelmed by what she'd seen. 'They insisted that less than four percent of their wells had been fracked.'

'Who knows?' said Tom. 'But Pete's wells were.'

'They said it was safe.' Clare cringed. How foolish and naïve she must sound.

'For Christ's sake, Clare. They're drilling straight through the aquifers of the Great Artesian Basin. They're injecting millions of litres of water and hundreds of tons of chemicals each time. They say these sites are sealed, but the pressure's staggering. There've been cases where fracking has split concrete bore casings and even sheared right through them. Who knows where the bloody gas and chemicals go?' He kicked the tap, frustration evident in his rigid shoulders and clenched jaw.

Clare put her hand on his arm. 'I'm sorry.'

Tom shook his head, as if to chase away the anger. 'Let's go inside,' he said. 'Have that picnic.'

Late afternoon was drifting into evening. They sat in Quimby's lovely old dining room, eating strawberries and drinking warm champagne. Clare took in the pressed metal ceilings, the carved fireplace surround, the intricate shutters gracing wide casement windows. There was no air of decay; it was more like the homestead was holding its breath — waiting for its family to come home. Clare ran admiring fingers across the table's polished surface, making a wavy line in the dust. 'Handmade,' said Tom. 'Like just about everything else at Quimby. The top's carved from a single slab of hoop pine. You'd never get a tree that size these days.' Clare topped up her glass. 'Let's go sit on the comfy chairs.'

They moved to the lounge room, sitting side by side on the couch. 'Tell me what happened here,' she said.

Tom poured her the last of the wine. 'Not long after the wells arrived, Pete noticed an odd taste to the water. When he filled the sink to wash dishes it fizzed like Alka-Seltzer and smelled funny. He didn't want to drink it of course, so he complained to Pyramid. The company came and confirmed the contamination, and then, you know what they did? Installed methane alarms in and outside of his house. A red light warned him not to go inside if the levels rose too high.'

Clare forgot to breathe. 'You mean there's gas in the house?'

'It's safe enough,' said Tom. 'I checked the meters when we came in.'

'They're still here?'

'Of course,' he said. 'If the alarms weren't here, we wouldn't be here either.'

'Pete could sue.'

'No, he can't. Pyramid gave him a bucket of money and had him sign a confidentiality clause. They trucked clean water to Quimby Downs and monitored the alarms. According to the terms of their agreement, that amounts to making good the damage. Fact is, there's no way to fix this. When it rains, gas bubbles up through the puddles. And yet when Pete left, they said it was his choice.'

'So this beautiful old homestead just goes to waste,' said Clare. 'It's a crime.'

He pulled her across to his lap. She relaxed against his body, feeling his energy pulse through her. The hairs stood up on the nape of her neck, as Tom kissed her there. His teeth grazed her skin, and she trembled. This felt downright dangerous.

As she sank back into his chest, a loud, imperious neigh sounded from outside. Tom pushed her aside, with a quick apology, and headed for the door.

'I don't believe it,' she heard him say.

Clare followed and looked past him. 'Oh my lord. Are they doing what I think they're doing?'

'Yep,' said Tom. 'They sure are.'

'Shouldn't we stop them?'

'If you want to get in the middle of that,' said Tom with a grin, 'you're a braver person than I am.'

I t was a truly magnificent sight - Goliath rising in slow motion. There was no doubting his immense strength as he reared on pillar-like hind legs and landed with surprising precision on Fleur's broad back. The impact of the stallion's bulk on the smaller mare was considerable. Fleur staggered forwards a few steps, before managing to steady herself. She braced against the powerful grip of the stallion's forelegs upon her flanks, and his swift forward thrusting.

Tom glanced at Clare. She stood open-mouthed, transfixed by the spectacle. In a minute the mating was over. The stallion rested for a moment on top of his mare, then dismounted. Fleur assisted him by stepping forwards and sideways. The pair companionably nibbled each other's wither, in a gesture of equine, post-coital affection.

'That was so quick,' said Clare, with a faint, teasing smile 'Poor Fleur.' She touched his arm and smiled, face a little flushed, moist lips parted. That was it. Tom pulled Clare close, sensing in her the same anticipation. He tipped back her head and closed his mouth over hers. Clare's soft lips moved against his. She tasted of strawberries and smelled of saddle soap. Tom was instantly hard. His breath grew tight and urgent.

Desire made him reckless. Tom pulled her from the porch and

down into the garden, ignoring her half-hearted protests. He lowered Clare to the grass, praying he wasn't rushing things, praying she wouldn't say no. Tom stared into her smiling green eyes. His head swam with longing, light-headed, desperate to see her naked and willing beneath him.

Where was his brain? He wrenched himself away. Slow down, for goodness sake. 'Clare …' His voice sounded hoarse. She shushed him with a forefinger to his lips, pulse fast at her soft, white throat. Then she undid the top button of his shirt. Yes. He flung off his clothes and stripped Clare, impatiently, like he was opening a present. Everything about her was more than he had expected: her breasts more luscious, her skin smoother, her waist narrower than in his fantasies. Her beauty stopped him in his tracks.

Clare knelt up and slipped her slim arms around his neck. Tiny golden hairs stood erect on her skin, gleaming in the light. 'If I were you,' she said, 'I'd kiss me.' He pulled her to him, lips pressing against her mouth as she yielded to his shape. God, she was lovely. He had the strangest sensation of their bodies dissolving, melting into each other. When he entered her, they both cried out, and she arched her back to drive him deeper. The smell of their combined heat mixed with the scent of bruised leaves and crushed earth. It blended with the heady perfume of bougainvillea and jasmine. Here was paradise on earth.

Afterwards, they lay for the longest time, entwined in each other's arms. He traced the shape of her breast with his finger, astonished by its perfect form. 'I love you,' he said.

Clare raised herself on an elbow. 'What did you say?'

'I love you.'

'You can't,' she said. 'Not yet. We barely know each other.'

'Do you usually have sex with people you barely know?'

She punched him lightly on the arm. 'You know what I mean.'

'I don't actually,' he said. 'I feel I know you very well. We've seen each other every day for weeks now.' He kissed her, and his desire stirred again. 'Anyway, haven't you heard of love at first sight?'

'You didn't fall in love with me at first sight. You barely even noticed me. You left me stuck up a tree.'

'I'm a vet,' he said. 'I've taken an oath. My patient's welfare is paramount.'

Clare smiled. 'An oath?' She sat up and pulled on her shirt. 'I thought the Hippocratic Oath was for doctors.'

'It is,' he said. 'But we vets have our own.' He placed her hand on his heart. 'Being admitted to the profession of veterinary medicine, I solemnly swear to use my scientific knowledge and skills for the benefit of society through the protection of animal health, the relief of animal suffering...'

She moved her hand from his chest and placed it over his mouth. 'Enough.'

He burst out laughing.

'Okay, I believe you have an oath,' said Clare. 'But I don't believe you love me.' She gathered up her clothes and retreated to the house.

Tom lay back in the grass and stretched, every inch of his body deliciously spent. He rested his head in his hands and closed his eyes. Life had never been sweeter. Clare would learn to trust him. It was merely a matter of time.

CHAPTER 27

'Sit down, Tom.'

It was unprecedented, having lunch with Harry in town like this. It made him nervous. How could the old man know about Tom's tryst with his granddaughter yesterday? Had Clare told him? What other explanation for this meeting could there be?

He sat at a table by the window of the only café in Merriang, while Harry ordered at the counter. Big bay windows overlooked the creek. Barely a trickle. After last year's horrendous floods, they'd had an unusually dry winter. Now, more than a month into the wet season and still no real rain. If not for the bores, drilling down into the infinite waters of the Great Artesian Basin, this year's summer crops would be in serious trouble.

A jeep sped down Merriang's main street, narrowly missing Milly, the café's tiny terrier. She had a dangerous habit of sunning herself on the road. The jeep hadn't slowed a whisker. Traffic in sleepy little Merriang wasn't usually so fast, or so ruthless.

Leila, who owned the shop, rushed outside and scooped the dog up in her arms. 'Bastards,' she said, giving Milly a hug. 'A few seconds later, Doc, and my Milly here might have needed you.'

'Keep her off the road,' said Tom. 'The traffic's only going to get worse around here.' As if to prove his point, a convoy of Pyramid water tankers roared past, heading for the gas fields at Laredo. Tom imagined the vast, hidden aquifers, far beneath his feet. He could almost feel their ebb and flow.

'Tom,' said Harry. 'Tom.' This time more sharply. 'Where's your head, son?'

Maybe it was the unkind glare of noonday sun on his face, etching each wrinkle and line into sharp relief. Maybe it was the odd pallor under his weather-beaten skin. Whatever the reason, Harry looked much older than usual - looked every bit of his seventy-three years.

Leila brought over coffee for Tom and a pot of tea. 'Pies are on their way.'

'We'll have them outside please, Leila,' said Harry, getting to his feet. 'I could use a smoke.'

Tom couldn't believe his ears. Whatever had prompted Harry to take up smoking again after thirty years? When quizzed, all he said was, 'It's one of life's pleasures. Surely, at my age, a man's entitled to his pleasures.'

'Not if that man wants to live long,' said Tom. They settled themselves at a sunny outside table. Harry produced a tobacco pouch and began rolling a cigarette. Tom couldn't stand the suspense any longer. He was ready to defend his relationship with Clare. 'Quit stalling, Harry. What do you have to say to me here that you couldn't say back at the house?'

The pies arrived, surrounded by mounds of golden chips, but neither Tom nor Harry touched them. Harry struck a match. He lit the cigarette and leaned back in his chair, enjoying the first long draught. Then he smoked the whole cigarette slowly and without a word. Each puff was taken with such deliberate care that it added a curious import to the occasion. Tom wasn't going to hurry him again. The old man could take his time.

'Remember that trip I took to Brisbane last month?' said Harry at last. 'Well, it wasn't to go meet with the bank, like I said. It was for some tests.' Harry stubbed out his cigarette. 'There's something on my brain. Some kind of tumour.' Harry read the question on Tom's face.

'No mate, there's nothing they can do. I could spend the next few months in hospital, sick as a dog, with radiation treatments that won't work anyway. Or I can stay here, in the place that I've loved all my life, and enjoy each day I have left with my granddaughter and her boy. Those two coming … well, it's a blessing I never expected before I died. Sometimes I feel my Mary looking down, fairly weeping with joy about them being here.'

Tom was numb from the news. He poured Harry a cup of tea with an unsteady hand.

'Now son, what would you choose? Tell me. Currawong or the hospital?' Harry took a big bite of his pie.

'And there's no chance they're wrong?' asked Tom, his breath hardening in his chest.

'No, mate,' said Harry. 'I've had my second opinion. More pessimistic than the first. But on the plus side, I'm not in much pain yet. Some headaches … they'll get worse apparently. I feel dizzy sometimes. Confused, lose my legs. The steroid tablets help with that, though they make me cranky. Best news is, this tumour could take me one day in my sleep, when I don't even know it.' Harry finished his pie. 'Can't barely taste a bloody thing any more,' he grumbled, then used the serviette to wipe his mouth. 'So, Tom, now you know the score, you can answer my question. Currawong or the hospital?'

What could he say? He was a vet. One of the advantages of being a companion animal, he'd always thought, was the opportunity of a peaceful death before remorseless suffering set in. It was more than most people got. More than Harry would get. His throat was tight with emotion, and for a moment he couldn't catch any air. Affection for the old man rose up in a warm wave that threatened to wash him away. If Harry had asked him for a decent dose of horse tranquiliser at that very moment, he would have given it to him. 'How long?'

'Six months, if I'm lucky.'

Tom had never smoked, but he suddenly wanted one of Harry's roll-your-owns. 'Harry,' said Tom. 'You have to tell Clare.'

There was no reading Harry's face, not a flicker of emotion. He rolled another cigarette, lit it and took a bottomless drag, like he was smoking a joint. He expelled it from his lungs in neat smoke rings and cracked a smile. 'I'd love to show Jack that trick,' he said with a chuckle. 'But it's not kosher these days, is it, mate?'

Tom shook his head. 'No, Harry, it's not.' He skulled his coffee. 'We were talking about Clare.'

'You're fond of my granddaughter, aren't you Tom? How fond?'

'I love her,' he said simply.

Harry looked well satisfied. 'Give us some time, Tom. The truth will be out in the open soon. Give us this special time together, before the grief sets in. I dare say it'll be brief enough.'

What could Tom say? Who was he to take something so important away from Harry? And anyway, he was right. Why break Clare's heart ahead of time? He bit his lip. 'Okay, Harry. You have your time.' He reached over and grasped the old man's hand. 'Anything you need, it's yours,' he said, his voice breaking. 'Anything at all.'

A welcome, familiar twinkle came into Harry's eye. 'You going to eat that pie, lad?'

Tom pushed his plate across, and idly took a chip. The food lodged in his throat, choking him. He forced it down.

'What about Fleur, eh?' said Harry. He hoed into the flaky pastry. 'Here I am wasting my time, sending her over to Macca's horse, when all along she's got a thing for Goliath. Or maybe there's something more than methane in the water over at Quimby, eh Tom?'

Tom gave him a sharp look. Was that a dig at him? He decided to change the subject. 'Looks like you'll be getting yourself a clydie-percheron colt next year. Could be nice cross.'

'You'll have to look after that little 'un for me,' said Harry. 'I won't be around to see it.'

Oh. What a fool he was. 'I'm sorry —' Tom started to say.

Harry held up his hand. 'The reality hasn't sunk in for you yet. God knows, it takes a while. I don't want you walking on eggshells around me. Promise?'

Tom felt the unfamiliar stab of tears behind his eyes. 'Promise.'

'There's something else I'd like from you,' said Harry. 'Other than your pie.' There was that twinkle again. 'I want you to come and live at Currawong. There's plenty of room, and Clare will need somebody when I go. You are serious about my granddaughter, aren't you son?'

'I'm going to marry her,' said Tom.

Harry raised his eyebrows. 'Does Clare know?'

'Not yet,' Tom said with a grin. 'It's early days. Wouldn't want to scare her off.'

Harry nodded approvingly. 'Take it slow, Tom. Take it slow.' He stubbed out his cigarette. 'Will you do it then? Will you move into the house?'

'Just try and stop me …'

Harry let out a long relieved sigh. 'Come on then, lad. Let's get back to Currawong. See if Clare has got little Jack back. I can tell you, Tom, that girl's going to need you more than ever if Taylor takes the boy away.'

Tom nodded. It would hurt Clare to lose Jack now. It would really hurt, but he'd be there for her. Harry could depend on him to stay right by her side.

CHAPTER 28

Clare sat out on the verandah, watching the sun rise towards its zenith, grasping for a handle on her seething emotions. Vignettes of her and Tom together in the garden at Quimby Downs crowded her mind.

Samson stood on watch beside her. Jack still wasn't back. Clare ignored the kernel of fear buried deep in her belly, buried behind the images of her and Tom and the sweet smell of the grass beneath them. Nothing would go wrong today. Jack would be home soon, she just knew it. The phone in the hall rang. Clare tripped over Samson in her rush to answer it. Hallelujah, it was Taylor.

'We're just about to leave Dalby,' said Taylor.

Dalby was an hour away. It still seemed like forever to wait, but in the mood Clare was in, it was easy to stay positive. They were on their way home, that was the main thing.

'How's Jack?' asked Clare.

'He's okay.' Taylor sounded doubtful. Was that a child yelling in the background? 'He's been naughty though … in a shop. Can you speak to the lady?'

'Hello?' An unfamiliar voice came on the phone. 'I'm Jane Palmer. I own the gift shop in Main Street, Dalby. There's a little boy here who's done some damage. Broken quite a lot of china. My husband has had to restrain him to let his mother make this call or else there'd be nothing left intact in the store.' The woman stopped talking, giving Clare time for the information to sink in. 'His mother says you know her?'

'Yes,' said Clare swiftly. 'Yes, I know her.'

'She says you might be prepared to pay for the damage and the stolen item. Otherwise, I'm calling the police. I'm afraid she allowed the boy to leave with a ceramic figurine hidden beneath his shirt.'

Taylor was on a good behaviour bond. A theft charge would be a breach of that order. It would be so easy to put her back in court. So easy to put Taylor out of contention for custody. But that wasn't the way that she wanted to win Jack. 'Yes, of course. I'll pay. Let me fetch my credit card.' Ten minutes and five hundred dollars later, Clare hung up the phone. It didn't matter about the money. All that mattered was that Jack came home and, from the sound of things, that was what Taylor wanted too. Clare turfed the dogs from the kitchen and took some cold meat from the fridge. A few biscuits on a plate wouldn't be enough. Taylor would need something more substantial before she began the long drive back to Brisbane. Clare pulled out lettuce, some tomatoes, and began buttering slices of bread.

Tom. A momentary lapse in concentration and the insistent idea of him almost chased Jack from her thoughts. Sex with Tom had been mind-blowingly amazing. Clare considered herself a woman of the world. She'd had her fair share of lovers. Adam had been the best of them – up until yesterday. Adam was experienced and considerate in bed. He took an immense degree of pride in his work, for that was how he approached it. More than once, when their relationship hit a rough patch, Adam's talent in the bedroom had brought her back to him. Hands down the best make-up sex she'd ever had. The best sex she'd ever had, for that matter.

But now? Now Clare knew she'd just been going through the motions. Adam was a skilled technician, nothing more. By contrast, sex with Tom was a wild, multi-dimensional ride, her lust and emotions tangled together so tightly that they could not be undone. Never before had she so truly inhabited each inch of her body. A constant, all-consuming desire for him ran through her veins, blotting everything else out. At times it even blotted out her yearning for Jack. And to top it off, in the soft afterglow, Tom had said that he loved her. He'd confessed it so earnestly, so early, so convincingly. He'd taken her completely by surprise. No matter how involved Adam was in the moment, no matter how many times an *I love* you was ripped from his ecstatic body, there had always been a time of him pulling away afterwards. How she'd craved for Adam to say those three words and really mean them. How she'd hoped it might be more than sex and convenience.

But Tom? Tom turned her inside out with emotional and physical passion, then calmly announced that he loved her, as if it was the most normal thing in the world. She hadn't believed it at the time. It had been too soon, too unexpected, but she tingled now at the memory. This is what she'd been missing. A straightforward, genuine man who wore his heart on his sleeve. A man who rejoiced in simple animal pleasure, then fell in love just as naturally. Clare laughed out loud with the sheer delight of it all.

The phone rang again. What sort of trouble had Taylor got herself into now? But it wasn't Taylor. It was Adam. Adam, who thought himself such a stud in bed. Adam, who didn't actually have a clue about the rapturous, satisfying experience that was top sex. She banished another image of the sunlight on Tom's bare back, and tried to concentrate on the call.

'How are things?' She guessed already that things weren't good. There was a side of Adam she hadn't seen before - a fragile, needy side. His text messages invariably described how low he felt and begged her to come back to Brisbane. *We could try again*, he'd say. *This time will different.* Clare had ignored them. They weren't in the spirit of 'staying friends'. Time to end this pretense; it was only giving him false hope. Still, part of her would miss talking to him. It offered a window on the world back in Brisbane, a chance to catch up on the latest legal news. Currawong was heaven on earth, no doubt about it.

She loved the space and the silence, but she remained curious about her old life.

'How's your new job?' she asked.

'Boring as watching two flies crawl up the wall.' He snorted. 'God, I miss it, Clare ... the challenge of the courtroom. The thrill of it. Pyramid have got me monitoring compliance, advising on law changes that might impact their business, drafting contracts, that sort of thing. It's deadly dull."

Clare froze. Pyramid Energy? Adam was working for the enemy? 'What are you doing right now?'

'Redrafting confidentiality clauses on their contracts with land-holders. Strengthening penalties. By the time I'm finished, those poor saps will be tied down so tight they won't be able to tell their mother what they had for breakfast without being sued.'

She felt her jaw tense. *It's not Adam's fault*, she told herself. It's his job. In the same circumstances she'd do the same thing. If she hadn't been to Quimby Downs, that was. If she hadn't seen the water there turn to liquid fire. If she didn't know that a man named Pete Porter, her grandfather's dear old friend, was living out his twilight years in effective exile. Forced from the graceful homestead he'd built with his own hands, forced to leave his land, his livelihood, his community, his connections ... and threatened with loss of his compensation payout if he complained.

The dogs began to bark. Was Jack home? 'I have to go,' said Clare.

'So soon? When the hell are you coming back to Brisbane? I miss my job, Clare, but I miss you more.'

Absence, apparently, really did make the heart grow fonder. Or was it merely Adam's ego still smarting from their breakup? But she didn't ask him to stop calling. She didn't ask him to stop his lovelorn texts. It was just too intriguing, him working for Pyramid. So instead she said, 'Good to hear from you, Adam. Don't be a stranger.'

Jack burst in the door and hurled himself into her arms. She fell to her knees and embraced him, speechless with delight. Samson arrived and covered them both with doggy kisses. Jack squealed and hugged him tight. 'Samsam,' he declared, and turned to Taylor. 'Mummy,

Samsam.' The young woman stood uncertainly in the doorway. She looked like she'd been crying.

'He's happy to see you,' said Taylor. It was part observation, part accusation. Clare wrested herself away from Jack, leaving him wrestling on the floor with Samson. 'That's a nice dog,' said Taylor. 'I like dogs. So does Jack.' She took out a packet of cigarettes. 'Can I smoke?'

It was ironic. Taylor had run off to have a cigarette when they'd first met and Clare had wound up with Jack. How grateful she was for that now. Maybe Taylor would do it again. Go out for a cigarette and not come back. Part of Clare wanted that, a big part, but then she looked at the girl's drawn face. She looked utterly exhausted. 'Go on,' said Clare. She looked for a saucer in the kitchen dresser to use as an ashtray, and found something unexpected: a proper ashtray. It was tucked in behind Grandad's little teapot, the one he used when making a cuppa just for himself. She put it on the table. Taylor gave her a nervous smile and lit up. Clare pulled out a chair, indicating for Taylor to sit. 'Coffee?' After a few moments hesitation, the girl nodded and took a seat. 'Are you hungry?' Clare put on the kettle and took the plate of sandwiches from the fridge.

'I think he missed your dog.' Taylor pulled a small, pottery German shepherd dog from her bag. 'Now I know why he took this.' She pushed the figurine towards Clare. 'It's yours now.'

Clare poured two coffees and sat down. 'Thank you.' She ran a finger down the little dog's smooth back.

'I saw that hot guy again down the drive. Tom. Why's he got a rifle?' asked Taylor.

'He's a vet,' said Clare. 'My grandfather has an old cow that's sick…'

'So, what, he's going to shoot it?' asked Taylor.

'He's going to put it out of its misery.'

'That poor cow.' Taylor looked like she was going cry.

'There's something I want to ask you,' said Clare softly. 'Jack's father … is he dead?'

Taylor nodded, her expression hard to read. 'An overdose. Jacky found him … He was only two, he wouldn't remember.'

The little boy heard his name and ran over, cheeks rosy with excitement. 'Bikkies?' Clare took a tin down from the cupboard and gave the boy two malt-o-milks, one for Samson and one for himself. 'Ta,' said Jack, and began playing keepings off with Samson, who seemed determined to get both biscuits. She offered the tin to Taylor, who took two as well and dipped one in her coffee.

'Now there's something I want to ask you,' said Taylor. 'How do you do it - get him to behave so well I mean? What's the trick?'

The question caught her off guard. 'It's not that simple,' said Clare. How to describe in a few sentences the fraught process that had underpinned Jack's progress? So much had been trial and error. All the puzzling and problem-solving. All the time and thought and gentle boundary setting. Samson and Currawong and Tom's amazing equine therapy - with maybe a bit of magic thrown in. All these things had played their part.

'Jack was real good when I picked him up,' said Taylor. 'Talking and everything. But he went crazy at the circus, yelling and kicking people. By this morning he'd stopped speaking. I couldn't get him to do anything. Then he trashed that shop …'

'I think it's mainly this place,' said Clare. 'All the room … and he loves Samson, and the other animals.'

Taylor nodded. 'I always wanted to get him a dog.' She butted out her cigarette and took a sandwich. 'I told you he liked dogs, didn't I?'

'You did,' agreed Clare.

'Could you teach me how to do it?' asked Taylor.

'Do what?'

'Get Jack to do what I say?'

'I said it's not that simple.'

'You just don't want me to know,' said Taylor. 'You don't want me to have Jack.'

There was plenty of truth in that last bit, but Clare felt obliged to protest.

Jack came over and climbed on her knee. 'Don't fight,' he said and pinched Clare's lips together.

'You tell her, Jacky,' said Taylor, looking pleased with her son.

Jack ducked under the table and appeared on Taylor's knee. The girl tried to cuddle him, but he hit her in the face and ran off. Taylor's face fell and Clare's heart went out to her. 'I didn't know much about kids at first either,' she said, 'but I did read a lot about parenting.' Clare went into the lounge room and came back with a book. She gave it to Taylor. '*Transforming the Difficult Child*. You can have it if you like.'

Taylor's face lit up with pleasure. 'So this taught you how to get Jack to behave?'

'It was a big help,' said Clare.

'I'm not usually that great with books,' said Taylor. 'But I'll read this one. I don't care how long it takes me.'

Clare couldn't help but like this girl.

'I'd better get going,' said Taylor. 'Can I take some sandwiches?'

Clare stood up and packed two rounds of sandwiches in a paper bag. She threw in some biscuits, a banana and a boxed juice. Taylor needed someone to look after her almost as much as Jack did.

'Um, can I borrow some petrol money? Twenty dollars would do.' Clare found her bag and handed over a fifty. 'Thanks,' said Taylor. 'Bye, Jacky. Mummy has to go.'

Jack ran over and wrapped himself about her leg, just like he used to do with Clare. 'I'll see you soon, Jacky. Be good now. Maybe Mummy could ring you up and tell you a bed-time story one night?' She opened up the little boy's clenched fist and put her lips to the palm of his hand. 'Put this kiss under your pillow for when you need it.' She closed his fingers. Jack stared at his hand for a second and then punched her.

Taylor looked pleadingly at Clare, who helped her disengage the little boy. Jack ran to the corner, where he began to rhythmically bang his head against the wall, accompanied by an angry singsong wail. 'Just go,' said Clare. Taylor disappeared out the door, face white as a sheet. A few seconds later the old Holden coughed to life and roared off. Taylor must have lost her muffler somewhere. Clare went to sit on the floor beside Jack. He hadn't behaved like this in weeks, but she knew better than to interrupt him until he calmed down. Every time his head hit the wall, she flinched.

Samson trotted over, whining his displeasure. Firstly he squeezed in between her and Jack, and then between him and the plasterboard, so that the little boy's head thumped into his soft back instead of against the hard wall. 'Good boy,' said Clare, stroking Samson's fur. A few head bangs later, Jack collapsed against Samson and started to cry. Proper crying, with proper tears. Clare heaved a big, relieved sigh. She knew how to help Jack back from this. She'd done it before. Her thoughts turned to Taylor driving home to Brisbane, smoking and eating sandwiches. Clare imagined her reading the book. She suddenly wished she hadn't felt so sorry for Taylor, wished she hadn't given her that book. What was it her father had always told her? Yes, that was it. No good deed goes unpunished.

CHAPTER 29

Swathes of sweet-scented wattle perfumed Bronwyn's bush garden. Bright blossoms abounded: magenta callistemon, scarlet grevilleas and a colourful collage of day lilies. High up in the air, Clare could hear the refrain of a butcherbird piping a tune; on the ground, the buzz of bees on nectar-laden flowers. Merriang in late October was truly glorious.

Clare sat out on the verandah with Bronwyn, watching Jack and Timmy play in the wading pool. Samson kept leaping in and out, showering the boys with water and provoking squeals of delight. 'I hope you don't mind me bringing Samson along.' They both smiled as Jack tipped a bucketful of water over the dog's head. 'Those two are inseparable,' said Clare. Samson shook himself in a rainbow of spray, showering Jack with water all over again. Jack screamed with laughter, and chased Samson from the pool.

'I can see that,' said Bronwyn. 'Timmy loves Samson too. He'll miss him when you go back to Brisbane.' She indicated the fresh pot of brewed coffee on the table. Clare poured herself a cup.

'I'm not going back.'

Bronwyn gave her a searching look. 'But that job you were telling me about. That dream job … You can't just turn your back on it.'

'Why not?'

Bronwyn stared.

'Go, on.' Clare didn't mean to sound defensive, but that was how it was coming out. 'Tell me why I can't turn my back on that job?'

Bronwyn's mouth gaped, but for a few moments nothing came out. She twisted a stray lock of dark hair in her fingers. 'I wanted to go to university, you know. I wanted to study fine arts. Had fantasies about being some sort of designer.'

'What happened?' asked Clare.

'The course was too expensive. Dad sent me to the agricultural college in Dalby instead. I met Jordy, got married and landed right back on the land where I started. I'm not complaining, mind you. I love it here, but part of me always wonders what would have happened if I'd moved to Brisbane after school and studied art.'

Clare sipped her coffee. Was Bronwyn right? Would she regret her decision to stay? Sometimes it did seem like a mad choice, to throw away all that Paul Dunbar offered. Then she thought of Jack and Tom and her grandfather, and she was sure that leaving Currawong would be the truly mad choice.

'Everybody's different,' said Clare. 'And I didn't say it was an easy decision, but we can all play the *what if* game. Maybe you'd have been miserable studying in Brisbane. Maybe you'd have been deliriously happy. How will you ever know? One thing's for sure, you wouldn't have Timmy.'

'I know,' said Bronwyn, 'And of course I wouldn't be without him, or Jordy. But to tell you the truth, I was pretty jealous when I heard of your brilliant career. I was so impressed by your ambition.'

'I think it's easier for us than for our mothers,' said Clare. 'Mine studied accounting and always wanted a career. I think she resented having me and Ryan because we got in the way. Mum left us when I was eleven.'

Bronwyn whistled. 'That's tough.'

'It was different for her generation. She thought she was a failure for *just* being a mother,' said Clare. 'I'm not like her. I don't have anything to prove.'

'I never thought about it like that,' said Bronwyn. 'It came as a shock, that's all, to think that someone like you would rather have my sort of life.'

Timmy and Jack ran over and helped themselves to homemade muffins.

'Merriang can't be that bad after all, eh?' said Bronwyn.

'No,' said Clare, taking a muffin before the kids finished them. 'Merriang is paradise.'

Bronwyn was beaming now. 'I should appreciate what I've got,' she said. 'Don't take any notice of me. It sounds like I'm trying to talk you into leaving, when that's the last thing I want.'

'Isn't it funny,' said Clare, 'how we always think the grass is greener on the other side? She topped up her coffee cup. 'Tom's moving into the homestead tomorrow.' Bronwyn shot her a smile as if to say, *Well, that explains everything.*

Sunday morning, and she and Tom would be living under the same roof by nightfall. Clare had been gearing up to ask whether he could come and stay, but before she did, her grandfather had made the offer. *I've given the back room to Tom,* he'd said. *It makes sense for him to be here.* She could have kissed him. The thought of having Tom so close all of the time sent a quiver through her. Clare poured herself a cup of tea. 'Want another cuppa, Grandad?'

'No thanks, love. Got a bit of a headache. I'm going to have a lie down.'

He'd had too many headaches lately. Clare took her tea onto the verandah as Tom's jeep came up the drive. He'd already made a trip to bring his things over from Bonnie's. He certainly travelled light. One suitcase, two green garbage bags full of who-knew-what, and a dog kennel. But then he'd gone out again for some reason. Red bounced along the path ahead of Tom as he climbed the steps to the verandah. He carried a big bucket and a bag of groceries.

Clare followed him into the kitchen. 'What have you got there?'

'Where's Jack?' he asked.

'Digging in the sandpit with Samson.'

Clare looked into the bucket on the floor. It contained a pile of large nuts, like the ones she'd found in the Currawong box at the top of her wardrobe.

'Boiled bunya nuts,' said Tom. 'I'm cooking bunya nut pie for dinner, but I need Jacky.'

'Why?' asked Clare.

'You'll see,' said Tom. He went back to the jeep and returned with a big hammer and a small mallet. 'You haven't lived until you've made bunya nut pie, Currawong style.' He pulled an ancient cookbook from the shelf. It was one of Grandma's, with favourite pages still encased in plastic sleeves. He flipped to the page he wanted, then unpacked the grocery bag: onions, leeks, broccoli, sweet potato, carrots, and cream. 'Harry showed me the recipe,' he said, 'It's all in the preparation.' He chose a knife from the block and expertly sliced a carrot. Impressive. The man could cook as well. Tom took some eggs from the fridge. 'Duck out to the veggie patch and get me a capsicum and some tomatoes will you...? And mushrooms. See if Harry's got any under the house. About two cupfuls.'

Clare fetched the old wicker harvest basket her grandmother once used. She touched his shoulder as she passed him and felt a familiar tug of desire. Tom looked so at home in Currawong's kitchen, and she loved how well he fitted in, but part of her longed for it to be just him and her. Between Jacky, Grandad and the surgery, it was difficult to steal time alone.

Clare returned with the fresh garden vegetables and got to work on the chopping board, casting the odd sneak peek at Tom. She loved the way his tongue poked out slightly when he concentrated. She loved his steady hand as he brought down the knife on a sweet potato. For a while they sliced and diced in companionable silence. Occasionally Tom pointed to a line in the recipe, and Clare wordlessly set about the indicated task. She put the leeks, broccoli and sweet potatoes on to steam.

'I'll go get Jacky.' said Tom. 'We'll need him for this next bit.' Clare washed the sharp knives and put them away, wondering how a four-year-old could help. And what were the hammers and nuts for? A few minutes later Jack and Samson burst through the door, with Tom chasing after. They were all laughing, even Samson. The dog, tongue lolling, wore a distinctly self-satisfied grin.

Jack's attention was drawn to the big bucket by the door. Tom took down a heavy cast-iron pan from the shelf. He cleared the sink, then tipped out a cascade of nuts into it. Next, he played some sort of magic trick, extracting a nut from behind the little boy's ear. Jack's face glowed with delight. 'Nothing up my sleeve,' Tom said, and another nut materialised from Jack's pocket. Now Clare was laughing too. Tom gave her a swift kiss and, with great ceremony, placed a single nut onto the worn, timber tabletop. 'Now watch me,' said Tom. He hefted the big hammer and smashed it down on the unsuspecting nut with an enormous bang. Jack squealed and Clare screamed. The shell lay splattered around its smashed heart. Tom picked out the bits of kernel and threw them into the pan.

Grandad emerged from the hall. 'What the bloody hell's going on?' he said. 'I'd just nodded off.'

Tom chose another nut with a flourish, put it on the table and gave it the same treatment. '*Only way to make bunya nut pie.* Isn't that what you said, Harry?'

Grandad chuckled. 'Did you boil them well, son?'

'Boiled them to billy-o,' said Tom.

'Go on,' said Grandad. 'Do another one.' Tom obliged. Bits of shell skimmed along the floor, providing Samson with a lovely game. The dog slid along the floorboards after the woody pieces, pouncing and wolfing them down. 'That's one way to get your fibre,' said Grandad.

Clare captured Samson by his collar and hauled him outside. When she returned, Jack was standing on a chair at the kitchen table, a look of glee on his face, and brandishing the small mallet in his hand. Tom deposited a nut in front of the little boy. 'Drum roll, please.' It didn't seem right to teach the little boy to bash things with hammers. Clare started to speak, but Tom held up his hand for silence. 'Objection dismissed,' he said with mock solemnity. 'Think of it as an exercise in hand-eye coordination.' Clare smiled, felt her stomach flip over again at the sight of Tom, and held her tongue. Jack was poking the nut with his mallet; it skittered around the table. Tom observed for a while, then put his own nut on the table. Jack stopped to watch him smash his target to smithereens, then, with a determined glare, planted both hands firmly along the handle of his mallet.

'Keep your eye on the nut,' advised Grandad.

With a sweep of his arms, the little boy scored a bullseye, caving in the hard shell and exposing the creamy white kernel beneath.

'Bravo, Jack,' cried Grandad. 'Bravo. That's the same technique your uncle Ryan would use — the double-fisted slammer.'

A memory crept into Clare's consciousness. A memory of Grandad and Ryan, jumping and shouting and slamming away in the kitchen. She tried to catch hold of the recollection; it threatened to slip away like a half-remembered dream. There, she had it again. She was a child, with her hands over her ears and a big grin on her face. Grandma was there too, laughing until she cried, but always a little shy to pick up the hammer.

'I want a shot,' said Clare.

'Good on you, love,' said Grandad.

Tom placed a nut in position. She lined it up and delivered a killer blow, splitting the shell in one shot, and leaving the kernel exposed and intact. It took more force than she'd expected.

Grandad clapped. 'That's the way. Not too hard. Not like this mad bugger.' He pointed to Tom. 'There's nothing much left after he finishes. And not too soft, or you'll never get through it.'

She gave him a thumbs up. This was a lot of fun. 'More nuts,' she said. Soon she and Jack were yelling and thumping and laughing. Grandad and Tom were an enthusiastic audience, rescuing the kernels and throwing them into the pan.

Grandad took the hammer and held up a nut. 'I name this nut *Pyramid Energy*.' Bang, it was gone.

'Let me,' said Clare. Soon she was smashing her way through all the people and institutions in life of which she did not approve.

Tom raised his eyebrows. 'You have a long hit list.'

'And I haven't finished yet,' she said, through tears of laughter. 'I name this nut *Adam*.' Bang. I name this nut *Veronica*.' Bang.

Was that the phone? Its ring was barely audible over the noise. She ran into the hall. 'Hello?' Nobody spoke, but there was somebody on the end of the line. She could hear them breathe. 'Hello? Who's there?'

'Clare? Is that you?' It was hard to hear over all the banging but she'd recognise that prim, self-righteous voice anywhere. It didn't make any sense, but Veronica was on the phone. *I just smashed you to bits*, Clare wanted to say, but restrained herself.

'Yes,' said Clare.

A long silence ensued. 'I found this number in Adam's phone,' said Veronica at last. 'I didn't know whose it was.'

Clare tried to make sense of Veronica's words. Why would she ring an unknown number she'd found in Adam's phone? And why did she have Adam's phone in the first place? Then it struck her. Of course. Veronica was still seeing him. Here was Adam, professing his undying love for Clare in every phone call, when he was still screwing around with Veronica.

'I'm wondering,' said Veronica, 'considering your very public breakup with Adam, why there have been a number of calls between his phone and this number … your number.' There was a challenge in her voice. 'It's not been one-sided. Recently you've matched him, call for call.'

Of course Clare had. She'd been trying to get some dirt on Pyramid Energy, so far without success. 'I'm not seeing Adam, if that's what you're wondering,' said Clare. 'Not after what he did.' She couldn't resist a little dig. 'I wouldn't be so stupid.'

'No, I suppose you wouldn't,' said Veronica, her voice bitter, 'but I, evidently, would.'

Clare almost felt sorry for her.

'Is he … is he pursuing you?'

'Yes,' said Clare. 'He is. At first he just asked if we could stay in touch.'

'Because he's so depressed and needs a friend,' said Veronica.

'Why yes. Then he said he loved me and what a mistake you'd been. He'd only been with you–'

'Because I threw myself at him and, hey, he's only human.'

'That's right,' said Clare. 'I guess he said the same thing about me?'

'Precisely. I can't believe I fell for it. I really can't believe it.'

A huge shout came from the kitchen, followed by a tremendous bang.

'What on earth's going on there?' asked Veronica.

How odd that particular explanation would sound. 'It's a bit hard to describe,' said Clare, 'but don't worry, everything's fine.' Veronica hung on the end of the phone without speaking. 'What about you?' said Clare. 'Are you okay?'

'I will be,' said Veronica. 'Once I get back at the bastard … like you did.' This conversation was getting more and more intriguing . 'There were times I wasn't fair to you, Clare. I'm sorry.' Clare gasped. Veronica was famous for never apologising. 'Truth is, I was jealous. You're such a natural in court. You're brilliant.'

'This is insane,' said Clare. 'You always went out of your way to make me feel like an idiot.'

'I said I'm sorry,' said Veronica. She sounded genuine; even the tone of her voice had changed. 'I want you to forgive me for being such a bitch. I imagine you're the kind of person who can do that, Clare, the kind that's gracious in victory. And it's been a comprehensive victory, hasn't it. Adam, Paul Dunbar … even Roderick. You're always the favourite.'

'Veronica —'

'Call me Ronnie. It's what my friends call me.'

'Okay … Ronnie. This was never a competition.'

'No … I suppose not,' said Ronnie, with an unhappy sigh. Clare took a deep breath. What other astounding things might her newfound friend say next?

'I was so in love with Adam that I couldn't see straight. Thoroughly, stupidly, blindly in love. I won't be able to sleep until I settle the score with that pig,' she said. 'And don't go all holier-than-thou on me, Clare. You swung some serious payback yourself. You destroyed his career. I do so wish *I'd* had that privilege.'

Clare was about to say that she hadn't planned it that way, that she'd behaved on an impulse, when she bit her tongue. Perhaps she could turn this bizarre situation to her advantage?

'Ronnie.' The nickname sounded wrong on her lips: too casual, too friendly. 'Adam's working for a coal seam gas company that wants to put wells on my grandfather's land. Under ordinary circumstances there's nothing Grandad can do to stop it.' Words spilled from her mouth as if they had a mind of their own. 'I've been pumping Adam for anything that might put a spanner in the works. Some sort of corporate non-compliance maybe, something that might trigger the unconscionable conduct provisions – whatever might slow the process down, or better yet, stop it altogether.'

'So that's why you've been calling him,' said Ronnie. 'Any luck?'

'Not yet,' said Clare. 'Listen.' Her tone was urgent and low. 'You want to get revenge? Then help me and my grandfather. Dig up some dirt on Pyramid Energy and leak it to me.'

'You mean spy on him?' asked Ronnie.

'That's exactly what I mean.'

'You're on.' The answer came clear and unambiguous, just as the ruckus in the kitchen reached a crescendo. 'What *is* that?' asked Ronnie.

'Hold on,' said Clare. 'Promise me you won't hang up.' She rushed down the hall and slammed the door. It would be impossible to draft a battle plan on the house phone. Too many curious ears. What she needed was some privacy. Tomorrow she'd drive to Dalby and get a new mobile. 'It'll be tough,' she told Ronnie. 'You'll be playing a charade. You said you love Adam.'

'I thought I did, yes. How foolish can a person be?'

'Don't do this if it hurts you,' said Clare. 'I shouldn't have asked.'

'It will hurt more if I don't do it,' said Ronnie. 'Now, tell me more about these gas wells …'

CHAPTER 31

Tom put down the phone. 'Why is it,' said Tom, his voice raised in frustration, 'that the minute a vet touches an animal, he's held personally responsible for every bad thing that happens to it from that moment on? That was Ray Sharp. Yesterday I treated a cow of his that'd been sick for two weeks. Two bloody weeks. I almost told him to ring his neighbour instead, the one that had been doling out free but completely useless advice ever since the cow went down. I get there and can see straight off that she's going to die. They've pulled her dead calf using a bloody tractor and then left her all this time with a torn uterus.'

Clare put the kettle on. She hated hearing these stories. The life and death of a production animal could indeed be a brutal one. But she knew how much it helped Tom to have a sounding board. He felt for each and every one of his patients, no matter how hopeless their case, no matter how close to the end of their life they might be. It was one of the reasons that she loved him. The bell over the door rang. Another client on an already busy Thursday surgery.

'The cow was in shock,' he continued. 'Covered with flies … her body racked with infection.' Clare put her hand on his arm. 'I told him straight out that she'd die. *Let me put her out of her misery*. But no. To hear Ray tell it, that poor cow that he'd left untreated for weeks — that cow suddenly meant the world to him. So I did what I could: painkillers, intravenous fluids, anti-inflammatories, antibiotics.' Clare pressed a coffee into his hand. 'That was him on the phone. The cow died last night. He says I must have killed her, so he's not paying the bill. Next time I'm at the produce store, it'll be *I hear one of Ray's best cows had calving trouble. He got you out and it died.'*

Clare wrapped her arms around Tom's neck and kissed him. Even here, with him in scrubs and clients waiting, she still felt the sizzle when their skin touched. 'Nobody with any sense listens to Ray.'

'Maybe so, but unfortunately there's a heap of folks without any sense around here.'

She smiled. 'Lucky you happen to have a waiting room packed with sensible people then.' He gave her a wry grin and called in the next patient.

Clare was settling down to the thankless task of sending out bill reminders, when the phone rang. Ronnie again. It was two weeks now since that first conversation about Adam. Since then they'd been in constant touch, partly to discuss industrial espionage strategy, and partly because Ronnie needed a friend, and friends were apparently a bit thin on the ground back in Brisbane.

It was still hard for Clare to get her head around it. That the stylish and sophisticated Veronica Fisher had been jealous of her. This new Ronnie was embracing their fledgling friendship. She'd even forgiven Clare for snatching the Paul Dunbar readership out from under her. 'You're better than me, right now anyway, but I won't give up,' she'd said. 'I'm going to stick it out at the Valley for another year ... see what happens after that.' Clare was impressed. She was even more impressed with Ronnie's enthusiasm for her new role as a spy.

Clare took her call in the hospital ward, under the curious gaze of an epileptic poodle and a sick swan. 'I've hit pay dirt,' said Ronnie. 'Something that will knock your socks off.'

'Fantastic,' said Clare. 'What have you got?'

'A risk management report Adam used to draft gag clauses in settlement agreements. It's backed up by over a hundred cases of contamination and other damage caused by fracked wells.' Clare sucked in a quick breath. 'Listen to this. *Pyramid Energy must be protected from liability for aquifer contamination caused by recent surface spills and operations underground.* And this. *The fluids involved contain heavy metals, toxic minerals, chemical additives and known carcinogens.* I'm telling you, this stuff is gold.'

'How'd you get it?'

'I stayed at his place last night. Adam left his laptop on when he went for a run. It was all there: the report, PDFs of each case file, everything.'

Clare couldn't help it. She pictured his South Bank apartment. Adam going for his seven o'clock run by the river. The laptop set up by the window with the view to the gardens. But instead of her being there, waiting for the customary gourmet dinner for two which would arrive at precisely eight o'clock – instead of her, there was Ronnie. Ronnie in her place, scrolling through Adam's documents, glancing at the door, slipping in a memory stick to save the damning evidence of Pyramid's treachery.

'Are you okay?' asked Clare.

'I don't know yet. Part of me is over the moon, and the rest of me wants to cry.'

'What are you going to do now? Can you bear to stay with Adam a bit longer? If you dump him now, he'll guess.'

'I suppose you're right. It might be fun to stick around and watch the fallout.'

Tom came in, followed by an elegant Afghan hound. 'Will you weigh Fatima please?'

She held up her hand for him to be quiet. 'Can you email the info through to me?' Clare asked Ronnie.

'Done,' she said. 'It's on its way.'

'I owe you one, Ronnie,' said Clare. 'More than one, actually.' She sank back in her chair, giddy with excitement and disbelief.

Tom regarded her curiously. 'You okay?' he asked. 'Should I be jealous of this Ronnie character?'

She jumped up and slapped a kiss on him. 'No,' said Clare. 'You should be thanking *her* instead. And don't use the internet for a bit. I'm expecting a big download.'

That evening, Clare lay in bed, trawling through the information Ronnie had sent her. It really was too good to be true. Tom made an effort to tempt her out, even once tried to get into bed with her, but she chased him off. She only had eyes for the report – the report that laid out Pyramid's long-term concerns about public health, pollution and potential compensation claims. Examples were given, backed up by detailed case studies. A school located in a heavily drilled area with asthma rates ten times the state average. A well site blowout that spewed methane for sixteen hours. A drunken dozer driver who accidentally released thousands of litres of chemical-laced wastewater into nearby creeks. Wells contaminated by methane and benzene. The list was endless and she knew just who to give it to.

Clare skimmed through the conclusion. *Area managers will project pollution catastrophe scenarios for their regions to ensure Pyramid has sufficient insurance to cover the costs of these types of events ... comprehensive, iron-clad confidentiality clauses will be used in settlement agreements to gag potential claimants.* She lay back in bed, listening to the night time serenade of frogs on the dam. Her dream came back to her, the one where a black stain had fouled the prehistoric waters of the Great Artesian Basin before the vortex drained it dry. That nightmare would never come true. Not if she could help it.

Grandad poked his head around the door. 'Not often you hit you hit the sack before me, Clare Bear. Is everything all right?'

Clare jumped out of bed and hugged him tight. 'Everything's better than all right,' she said. 'Everything's perfect.'

The next morning Clare began calling. Gordon McCrae had been surprisingly accessible. Less than an hour of ringing around and she had the man himself on the phone.

'I have a leaked Pyramid Energy report,' she told him, 'documenting a cover-up of contamination in the Darling Downs gas fields.'

'Email me the material,' said Gordon. 'I'll be in touch if there's anything in it.'

Clare did as he asked, then sat down to wait. Gordon was a busy man. He might not look at the documents straightaway. It might take weeks for him to get back to her. Maybe she should go directly to the media. She tried to distract herself by tackling one of Grandad's half-finished crosswords. *Another word for blessing?* Seven letters ... with D as third and last letter? The phone rang just as she penciled *godsend* into the squares.

'Clare Mitchell?' It was Gordon. 'That report you sent me ... it makes very disturbing reading. I'll be raising it in parliament next week.'

'Will it stop the expansion of the gas fields?'

'There's every chance,' he said. 'When people see this, it'll be a brand new ball game.'

Gordon rang off. Clare sat for a while, trying to grasp the implications of what he'd told her. Every chance, he'd said. There was also every chance that Pyramid would trace the leaked documents back to Adam. She felt a twinge of regret, but then hardened her heart. It couldn't be helped. Adam had made his bed ... let him lie in it.

Clare went to find her grandfather. He was in the lounge room, going through stud records. 'Grandad? I think you'd better sit down.' She waited until he was settled in his favourite old armchair. Claire took a place on the frayed couch and launched into her news.

The story was hard to tell. She was leaving bits out, some of them on purpose, and talking too fast. Her grandfather listened in silence, occasionally tugging at his ear. 'So,' she concluded, 'Gordon McCrae says there's a good chance that this could stop the gas wells.' Clare wet her lips and waited, wound tight, awaiting his response.

A slow smile crinkled across his face. 'I can't believe you did this,' he said, his voice quivering. 'For me, for Currawong.'

Clare felt a catch in her throat. The emotion in her grandfather's voice overwhelmed her. If she could do this, if she could save Currawong, it would be some kind of atonement. She sat on the arm of his chair and buried her face in his shoulder.

When she looked up there was a joyful light in his eyes. 'I'll not ask you how you came by this report,' he said. 'There are some things a grandfather shouldn't know about his granddaughter, eh?'

She gave him a grateful smile. God, how she loved this old man.

CHAPTER 32

Sunday morning, first day of November. Spring sauntered towards summer, but it was still cold this early at Currawong, lying as it did in the shadow of the Bunya range. Early sunbeams streamed in the window, bathing the room in a cool, golden glow. Clare stretched, then snuggled back beneath the blankets

Tom's silly secret knock came at the door, and he slipped in. He wore satin boxers sporting a serpent design, and carried a plate of mangos, sliced checkerboard fashion, and a damp facecloth. He sat on her bed and they feasted on the luscious fruit in silence, exchanging glances. Juice ran down her chin. Occasionally he stroked her face and décolletage with firm sweeps of the washer, lingering on the swell of her breasts. He kissed her mouth, tasting of sweetness and sun and sin. She shivered. Jacky could burst in the door any minute. That was the only reason Clare didn't pull Tom into her bed then and there.

In some ways, having him under the same roof was more frustrating than having him at Bonnie's. He was always so tantalisingly close. Sunning himself half-naked on the lawn after a swim in the dam. Working with Jack and Sparky in the ménage, a look of calm concentration on his rugged face. Playing fetch with Red. Swinging in after work in his sexy scrubs – it didn't matter; Clare had the permanent hots for him, and he for her. But the old Currawong homestead wasn't a big house. It didn't have thick walls. It didn't offer much privacy. Their rendezvous were limited to when Grandad took Jack out on morning paddock rounds or late at night, when they hoped the others were asleep.

Even then, they couldn't be certain of uninterrupted time together. Grandad might be away for ten minutes or two hours; he was notoriously unpredictable. 'The old bugger's doing it on purpose,' complained Tom once, while putting on his trousers, hopping around on one leg and swearing. Then there were the *walk-ins* at the surgery. Depending on how urgent the case or how pushy the client, these often ended up at the house when the surgery was closed.

So far their close encounters had happened mainly in the cart shed, among the hay bales, beneath the massive, gleaming harnesses hanging on the wall. They closed the high timber doors for privacy and to keep the curious dogs at bay. Tom's bare body, the sight and scent and feel of it, was inextricably linked in Clare's mind to summer gardens and the warm smell of hay and saddle leather. They had swift, silent, urgent sex in the dark. It was about as far as it could be from the slow, sensuous lovemaking that Clare craved. But even so, these hurried trysts with Tom were more exciting than anything she'd known before. Without fail they left her restless and hungry for more.

Tom's fingers slipped the strap of her singlet from her shoulder, just as Jack rocketed in the door, followed by his shadow, Samson. The pair leaped onto the bed and Jack started his favourite tickling game. Clare took refuge beneath the covers and Tom rescued her by hoisting Jack aloft, so his wriggling fingers couldn't reach. 'I think she deserves a Sunday sleep-in,' said Tom. 'How about I take you for a ride on Sparky?'

'My pony,' yelled Jack. 'My pony.'

Clare emerged from beneath the blankets and whispered a thank you.

'No worries,' said Tom. He gave her a quick kiss and shepherded the little boy and his dog from the room.

That old adage about it taking a village to raise a child made perfect sense to Clare now. You needed other people to share the load: Grandad, Tom, Bronwyn and Timmy — even Samson. They preserved her sanity, and Jack needed extended family and friends around as much as she did. Each person showed the child a different way of being in the world. How did she ever think she could have managed him all by herself in Brisbane, just her and the Happy Elves? It seemed so stupid to her now. She yawned, snuggled back down onto her pillow and closed her eyes. Life was good.

Later, over breakfast, Clare watched Grandad. He seemed years younger. The furrows had fallen from his face and been replaced with smile lines. Gordon McCrae and that leaked report was all he could talk about.

'I'm mighty grateful to you, love. Mighty grateful,' he said for the umpteenth time. Simple words for so heartfelt a sentiment. 'You've given me a whole new lease of life.' He piled an extra helping of bacon on his hot, buttered toast.

'Happy to help,' she said, feeling a warm glow of pride. She gave her grandfather's bony shoulders a big bear hug, then stood him at arm's length to examine his face. 'Have you been smoking?' The faint, acrid smell of cigarettes clung to his clothes.

'Won't lie to you, love. Sid gave me a packet of Drum. Just been having the odd one every now and then, I swear.'

'The *odd one* is one too many,' said Clare. 'After all the effort you said you put into giving up. Maybe that's why you're getting those headaches.'

'Funny thing is,' said Grandad, 'the fags seem to help.'

'Don't give me excuses,' she said, unable to stay stern. 'You're old enough to know better.'

'That I am, love,' he said, with a chuckle. 'Where's Jacky?'

'Having a lesson on Sparky.'

Grandad scowled. 'Well, tell Tom to get the lad back here,' he said. 'I'm handling Bessie's new foal today. It'll be a real treat for the boy.'

'Sorry,' she said firmly. 'Jack's got a play date with Timmy. I'm really looking forward to spending the morning with him.' She shook her head. 'Between you and Tom, I barely get a look-in with that boy.' Her grandfather looked so put out, she gave him a kiss.

'That's enough of that lovey-dovey stuff.'

'Nonsense,' said Clare. 'You lap it up.'

He put his gnarled old hand over hers, where it rested on his shoulder. 'That I do, love' – a smile breaking through his frown – 'That I do.'

Out the window, a sparkling early summer day beckoned; fairy floss clouds floating in a sea-blue sky. Clare finished packing her bag and went out the screen door, just as the hall phone rang. Should she leave it? No, Grandad only heard the phone half the time these days. An important mare was coming to stud today. It might be the owners asking for directions. When on earth was Grandad going to get hearing aids? She ran back in. Grandad sat oblivious, lost in the latest *Heavy Horse World* magazine, newly arrived from the UK.

But when Clare answered the phone, she wished she hadn't. 'Kim?' A dart of fear pricked her happy mood. 'How are you?'

'We need to talk.'

Clare had never known good news to follow such a phrase. She braced herself.

'I've been approached by a solicitor representing Taylor Brown. She's suing for custody of Jack.'

It didn't make any sense. 'But he's on a twelve-month guardianship order.'

'She's challenging it.'

'On what basis?'

'On the basis that her circumstances have changed and that the child will no longer be at risk in her care.'

Clare didn't trust herself to speak. If a single word came out of her mouth, she was bound to break the golden rule when dealing with Kim: don't show how much you care.

'There's another thing, Clare, another basis upon which she's challenging the order ...'

'What?' asked Clare. Kim hung silent on the phone. 'Tell me.' She'd almost shouted that time.

'Taylor is challenging your own fitness to care for Jack.'

'Based on what?' She could hear the anger in her voice, but there was no stemming the rising tide of outrage.

'She's alleging neglect and inadequate supervision. Taylor's lawyer …' The sound of rustling papers. 'Sarah Chapman her name is. A most unpleasant woman.'

Chapman. Clare felt coldness creeping through her. 'That's absurd,' said Clare. 'Jack's made astonishing progress here. You can't possibly let him go back to Taylor.' She caught herself in time. 'Not yet, I mean. You can't let him go back to Taylor, yet. It would be devastating for him.'

'You did lose the child, Clare. And for several hours. From what I understand there was quite a search … dozens of locals. Police. State emergency personnel. And Jack was found almost a kilometre away.' She let her accusations sink in. 'It doesn't sound so absurd to me.'

'Anything else?' said Clare. 'Perhaps I've tortured Jack for fun or used him for target practice.'

'I wouldn't joke about it,' said Kim. Her tone had turned icy. 'As a matter of fact, there is more. Guns. Taylor said there were men with guns. Don't you think you might have mentioned them?' It was apparently Kim's turn for sarcasm.

Clare racked her brain to determine what she could possibly mean. 'There was one man,' she said. 'One man with one gun. A vet. He had to shoot a sick cow. It's a farm after all.' She was beginning to panic now. 'And my grandfather has a rifle, but it's kept in a locked gun cabinet. Of course it is … I guarantee it is.'

'It's alleged there are dogs too, Clare. Large, dangerous, uncontained dogs at the farm where you have Jack. Heelers and German shepherds. Not a labrador puppy in sight.' Kim's words were clipped and cross.

Taylor was making Currawong sound like a place straight out of the wild west. Clare felt her teeth grind together. Betrayed. Utterly betrayed. She'd taken in this young woman's son. She'd protected him, nurtured him, healed him ... loved him. Clare glanced desperately around her, searching the pretty, papered walls for some comfort. She tried to imagine Currawong without Jack, and the joy of her new life leaked away. She'd turned herself upside down for Taylor Brown. Sacrificed her home, her career, her whole life in Brisbane.

'I do hope that rifle *is* safely stored, Clare.' Kim's voice had grown anxious. Not for Jack's welfare, Clare guessed, but for her own. She took a deep breath and tried to get some sort of perspective on the situation. For all Kim's blustering, they were in this together. If Currawong was such an unsuitable home for Jack, it was Kim who'd put him there. By covering her own back, Kim was likely to cover Clare's as well. She needed to calm down and pump Kim for more information.

'Clare,' said Kim. 'Clare?'

'I'm here,' she managed. Thank goodness Taylor or, more precisely, Taylor's pit bull of a lawyer, didn't know about Tom's early equine therapy work with Jack. It wouldn't matter that Fleur was the gentlest horse in the world. The fact of it would be enough – a four-year-old handling a horse that weighed close to a ton.

'I'm a little surprised by your reaction,' said Kim. 'I expected you to be upset by the allegations, naturally ... although I'm afraid they all seem to be true.'

Here it comes, thought Clare.

'But I didn't expect you'd be so anxious to hold on to the boy. I feel you've become too attached. Way too attached. The aim of this exercise has always been to return Jack to Taylor's care. You know that perfectly well, Clare.'

'Are you going to fight it?' asked Clare, no longer trying to disguise the emotion in her voice. 'Is the department contesting Taylor's challenge?'

'Yes,' said Kim. Clare let out a great, relieved sigh. 'We don't believe your misconduct warrants a quality of care investigation. And we're not yet convinced that Taylor is stable enough to resume custody. Although Clare ...' Kim's voice had hardened. 'If Taylor stays on her current course, there's no doubt that she'll eventually regain the care of her son. And that is exactly as it should be.'

'Of course.' Clare squeezed her eyes closed until her vision swam with spots. 'When will …'

'There's a hearing on the first of December. Jack has an appointment with a court-based psychologist on the fourteenth of November, so have the child available on that day. And Clare … no more incidents, okay?'

'No more incidents,' agreed Clare. 'Promise.'

Kim's voice blurred into white noise. She couldn't lose Jack. She just couldn't. The mere prospect made her tremble. Thank goodness for Tom. She needed him now, needed to confide her fears – needed the shelter of his arms.

CHAPTER 33

Jack was a natural. He sat tall in the saddle while Sparky circled at the trot on a lunge rein. A broad grin split the little boy's face as soon as he spotted Clare. 'I can trot,' he yelled, startling Sparky into a canter. Jack squealed with delight, sitting his pony with ease, keeping an eye on Clare to make sure she was watching.

'Slow him down,' said Tom.

Jack expression became determined. He sat down hard, struggling to gather the reins in his tiny fists. Sparky broke back into a fast trot and the boy bobbed up and down in time with the rhythm of his pony's hammering hooves.

'Tom,' called Clare.

He flashed her a swift, proud smile, then turned back to his pupil. 'Walk on.' But instead of the easy transition Clare expected, Sparky swung towards Tom and came to an abrupt halt, throwing the little boy onto his neck. Jack clung on like a monkey, winding his fingers into the pony's flowing silver mane. For a moment Clare's heart was in her mouth. But then Jack regained his balance, grinned like a Cheshire cat and turned his grip into a great, big hug. Sparky tossed his head and Clare remembered to breathe again. There was no doubting Jack's guts, and his courage made her brave. Sharing her

522

news with Tom would help too. What was it Grandad always said? *A trouble shared is a trouble halved.*

Tom lifted Jack down and the little boy ran to her, eyes shining. 'Did you see me?' he said. 'I galloped.'

'Cantered,' said Tom, leading Sparky over. He looked at Clare as if she might scold him for it. 'The canter was a bit of an accident.'

Clare lifted Jack's helmet from his head and smoothed a stray lock of hair. 'Yes, I saw you. You were fantastic, and so was Sparky … and so were you, Tom.' Jack hugged her leg for a moment, and then tried to climb back into the saddle.

'No, that's all for now,' said Tom, hoisting the boy off the pony. 'Come and help me unsaddle him.'

Force of habit made Clare brace for the tantrum that used to so often follow the word *no*. The yelling and hitting. The small taut body hurling itself to the ground. But instead Jack calmly positioned himself at Sparky's near shoulder and took charge of the reins like Tom had shown him. 'Walk on,' said Jack, and led his pony off towards the stable. Tom walked by his side and Clare trailed after them. She longed to tell Tom about Taylor's custody grab. Ached to vent about her outright lies. But it was impossible with Jack there.

'I need to take Jacky to the house now,' she said. 'Then I'll come back. There's something I want to tell you.'

'No way,' said Tom. 'Feeding and grooming Sparky is as important a part of Jack's therapy as riding. More important, actually. It cements the bond between them.'

'Just this once,' she said. 'I *really* need to talk to you.'

Tom's phone rang and Clare groaned. 'So you have both feet but no head,' he said. 'Which way are the hoofs flexed? Do they point down or up … down? Good, it's not a breech birth then.' He took Sparky's reins from Jack, handed them to Clare with an apologetic shrug, and continued his conversation. 'I'm on my way. In the meantime make the mare stand and walk. This will help the foal slide back into the womb a little and make it easier to reposition.' Clare combed Sparky's mane with her fingers. 'She's up? Good work. Wash and lubricate your arm anyway, in case I'm not there in time. If she goes down and starts straining again before I arrive, you'll have to help her with directions from me over the phone. Okay? Hopefully it won't come to that.'

'I know, I know,' said Clare. 'You've got to go.'

'The life of a country vet,' called Tom over his shoulder as he sprinted down the hill.

'Well, Jacky.' The little boy hugged her. 'It's just you and me, kid.'

It wasn't until after dinner that Clare finally found herself alone with Tom. All day she'd struggled alone to cope with the idea that Taylor might soon reclaim Jack. Clare had toyed with telling Bronwyn in the morning. She'd almost confided in Grandad on countless occasions during the afternoon, but each time she'd bitten her tongue. How would she bear Bronwyn's sympathy or her grandfather's very own grief at the thought of losing the little boy? It was Tom she needed, Tom who'd understand. So instead she'd waited, each second seeming to take an hour.

Sid arrived in the afternoon to check out the new foals, and then disappeared to the pub with Grandad. Clare fed Jack his dinner, listening for Tom's footstep on the porch. He arrived in time to read Christopher Robin to Jack, while she washed up. At last the little boy was asleep, and there they were, out on the verandah, with beers in their hands. It had been a dreary day, a gloomy one, but for a single, magnificent moment, the sun flared bright on the horizon. It rimmed the dark clouds in dramatic crimson. In almost the same moment it mellowed and lost its hold on the sky. Stray rosy rays slanted across the ancient Bunya range, like they must have done for aeons past. Clare usually loved this mysterious interlude between night and day, this transition point between worlds. But tonight it unnerved her, with its promise of imminent change. What she really wanted was for nothing to change - nothing at all.

Tom put down his drink. His expression was intense and searching. ' I can tell something's wrong. Spill.' That was all it took to release the torrent. Clare launched into her story, blurting it out in a great stream-of-consciousness flood of emotion that left her hollow and exhausted.

'Come here.' His voice was low and commanding and his arms opened wide. This was it, what she'd waited for, what she'd longed for during all that grey, slow day. The moment of release, the moment when, together, they'd hatch a plan to keep Jack. Clare sat on his lap, in his arms, a lonely, needy child herself, letting the tears wrack her body until they were spent. Tom's firm, warm presence calmed her. He swept a damp lock of hair from her face and she managed a smile. He kissed the tip of her nose. 'Clare,' he whispered. 'Everything will be all right.' His words were salve to an open wound.

'I suppose next you're going to tell me to stay positive.'

'I might,' he said, stroking her brow. 'If it helps.'

'Go on then,' she said interlacing her fingers with his. 'Tell me how the power of positive thinking will help us.'

'Well …' he said. Why was his tone suddenly tentative? She wanted strength and certainty from him, not hesitation. 'This might be the best thing, in the long run.'

'You're wrong there,' she said. 'You might think an early hearing will give us more security, but it won't. The best thing would be for Taylor not to challenge at all and let the original twelve month order run its course.'

'Best for who?' he asked. 'Just exactly who would that be best for?'

The hair on the back of her neck bristled. Clare untwined her fingers and sat up. She couldn't quite grasp the point he was making. 'Best for Jack of course. What are you getting at?'

'Don't you mean best for you?'

She struggled to understand him, to twist his words into some recognisable form.

'Surely,' said Tom, 'what's best for Jack is to be with his mother.'

With infinite slowness she disengaged her body from his. 'Say that again?'

He tried to fold her to him but she was unbending as glass. Even her heart felt brittle and hard, as if it might shatter at the next beat.

He drained the last drop of his beer. 'If Taylor gets back on track, why shouldn't she have her child?'

'How long have you got?' said Clare, still not sure she'd heard him right. 'Taylor shouldn't have her child because if she *is* back on track, which I highly doubt, it's only been for about five minutes. Because in these last few months of stability, Jack has improved in extraordinary leaps and bounds, and doesn't deserve to be thrown back into chaos. How would it be for him to lose his grip on all this progress, and slip back into mutism and violence and self-harm? Because he's not a toy that belongs to Taylor. He's a real live little boy. Because she can't keep having turns with him, while his childhood and any chance of a normal life slip away.'

'But if she really changes.' Tom couldn't even look at her.

'Do you know what happened at Timmy's party last week? Somebody spilled the sugar bowl, and guess what Jack did?' Her pulse was hammering. 'He took a straw, made a line of sugar on the table, and tried to snort it.'

'But if she gets clean, and goes to those parenting classes and seeks counselling.' He stood and paced the verandah. 'If she finds a safe place to live and gets Jack some sort of therapy ...'

The pain in Clare's chest spread through her body. 'He already has a safe place to live,' she said. 'And as for therapy, where's he going to find anything that comes close to Currawong? To Grandad and the animals ... to you? That's the therapy Jack needs and you damn well know it. For God's sake, Tom. Jack found his father dead from an overdose when he was only two year's old. What sort of mother is Taylor to let that happen?'

In the pale porch light Tom's jaw grew stiff. 'I'm sorry, Clare, but the bottom line is that kids should be with their families. Bringing a child into your home doesn't make you a mother, any more than standing in a stable makes you a horse. How would you feel if somebody took your child?'

Clare backed towards the door. Why was he saying this?

'I love you, Clare,' Tom said, looking lost. 'More than anything. If Jack goes home to Taylor, we'll get through it.'

He loved her, did he? The warmth of the night was suddenly oppressive. The mocking laughter of a late-calling kookaburra was aimed straight at her heart. *You stupid, gullible fool,* it cackled. Clare wanted to wring the bird's neck.

She ran through the darkening house to her room. Tom's footsteps followed. They echoed after her on the floorboards, and she dared not turn around, dared not look into his treacherous face. She reached her room, slammed the door and sat down shaking on the bed. *Knock, knock … knock, knock.* His tap came soft and insistent. *Knock, knock … knock, knock, knock.* Harder this time.

'Honey … Let me in.' The doorknob began to rotate.

Clare sprang up and wrenched open the door. 'Fuck off, Tom,' she hissed. 'Just fuck the hell off.' She banged the door shut and flung herself on her bed, but she didn't cry. She wouldn't cry. That was the sort of unguarded emotional response that had got her into trouble in the first place. Instead she bit her lip until it bled, and knuckled away a few mutinous tears. In the acute silence, she listened for the sound of retreating footsteps. It took an agonising few minutes, but finally she heard them. Tom was gone, and that's exactly how it was going to stay.

For a long time Clare lay where she fell. She buried her face in the pillow of the high feather bed, twirling threads of pink candlewick between her fingers. She loved Currawong's old beds. They were soft like clouds. It enraged her to think that Tom would sleep in one that night. He didn't deserve it. She fought back a sob. Just as well Grandad wasn't home. It would be so tempting to tell him about Tom, and she didn't want to do that when she was angry. Grandad wasn't well, and he'd need Tom now that she was leaving Currawong.

Building a life in the country with Tom had been an impossible romantic dream, nothing more. Her place was in Brisbane, where her hard-won career awaited her. Thank heavens she hadn't burned her bridges with Paul Dunbar. Thank heavens she hadn't thrown away her future on a schoolgirl crush. She tried to sit up but the deep, sinking mattress held her fast, held her like a trap.

Clare struggled to her feet as Sid's car pulled to a stop in the yard.

Grandad was home. She couldn't tell him, not yet, but she had to confide in someone. If she kept this heartache to herself she'd burst. Not Bronwyn; there was no way she'd hear a bad word spoken about Tom and that went for most of the town. No, she needed someone who wouldn't take sides, someone who'd experienced their own share of disappointment lately. Someone who would relate to the sort of betrayal that Taylor and Tom had heaped upon her. Of course ... she needed to talk to Ronnie.

Saturday morning, and they were all gathered in the kitchen. Grandad wore a face Clare hadn't seen before. The face of a stoic, of a man who could endure any hardship without complaint. Was that the expression he'd worn at Grandma's funeral? Clare hated seeing it, hated knowing that she was the one who'd put it there.

Jack was dragging their bags back down the hall. 'Stop it,' she said, her voice raised more than a notch. She wanted to scream. Jack screamed instead, and hurled something at her head. A smooth river stone he always kept in his pocket. She ducked just in time. Even Samson was misbehaving. He'd been ratty all morning, picking fights with the peaceable dalmatians and refusing to come when called. Right now he was skulking under the table, lips parted in a sour snarl whenever Red approached. Clare didn't relish the idea of sharing a long car trip with either of them.

Tom stood by the door, hat in hand. Clare avoided his gaze. Another look at his anguished, handsome face and all her resolve might crumble away. Since her announcement yesterday, Tom had campaigned fiercely to make her change her mind about leaving. He'd been unrelenting. He wanted her, he said. He needed her, he loved her. His life would be empty without her. How sweet these words would have sounded just a few days ago. But now? Now they were like needles in her heart. Tom stubbornly refused to say the only thing that mattered.

'Sure you won't stay, love?' asked Grandad. 'Me and Tom'll be lost without you lot.' Something passed across Grandad's face, some sort of shadow. He pulled out a chair and sat down, seeming suddenly frail. Clare braced against the wrench in her guts. 'No,' she said. 'I can't stay.'

Jack leaped onto Grandad's knee and glared at her. 'I won't go,' he yelled. 'I won't bloody go.'

Grandad hugged him briefly, got to his feet and put the little boy down. 'Don't talk like that,' he scolded. 'Clare will bring you back for a visit soon. Won't you love?'

She couldn't bear to look at them. 'Yes.' Clare inspected her shoes. 'Of course.'

'Come on then,' said Grandad, giving Jack a smile. 'Time to go.'

Tom stepped forward, hoisting the little boy aloft, carrying him to the car and strapping him in. 'See you, champ.' Tears glistened in Jack's eyes like silvery snail trails, pasting his lashes together. Samson took his place on the seat beside him. The little boy had already begun his rhythmic head thumping, eyes shut tight, lost in some other world.

'Goodbye love.' Clare embraced her grandfather, and he stroked her hair. 'I'm coming to that court hearing about Jacky,' he said. 'No arguments. Just tell me when it is.'

'You don't have to.'

'I'll hear none of your back talk,' he said firmly. 'I'm coming, and that's that.'

'Thank you, Grandad.'

When she turned to go, Tom was by her side. On an impulse she extended her hand. He seized it with such force it hurt. His eyes bored into her, as if he could make her stay by sheer force of will. They held each other's gaze for the longest time. Was there nothing more to say? Would it really end this way?

Tom opened his mouth and closed it several times, like he was struggling to find the right words. She hung on the moment, waiting, watching his Adam's apple bob up and down. He rubbed his hand through his hair. 'Goodbye Clare.'

'Bye Tom.' Clare swallowed hard and drove away without a backward glance.

CHAPTER 34

She'd hoped to slip into *Fortitude Valley Legal Aid* that first morning unnoticed. No such luck. 'You're back,' squealed Debbie, running out from behind reception to give Clare a hug. 'And you've even got yourself a tan,' she said. 'It looks so natural.'

'That's because it *is* natural,' said Clare. She pulled up the short sleeve of her shirt, exposing the white skin.

Debbie looked horrified. 'I'll take you to *Bronzilicious* at lunchtime,' she said. 'They'll even you up, no worries. And there's a Supa-Dark tanning-bed special on – buy ten sessions, get ten free. You'd look great with a proper tan.'

Clare smiled and thanked her for the advice. It was somehow reassuring to discover that Debbie hadn't changed. Isaac emerged from the corridor with a fat manila folder under his arm and a familiar frown creasing his broad forehead. He did a double take at the sight of her, and broke into a grin. 'So you're back.' A fresh-faced young man that she didn't recognise came out of her old office. Isaac introduced him as Davis. Clare inspected her replacement. He looked about fifteen. She must be getting old.

'I'm back part-time until the end of the year,' she said, shaking Davis's hand. Ronnie walked through the glass doors, fabulous in a dark, geo-print dress that looked both chic and corporate at the same time. At first, the expression on her flawlessly made-up face was as snooty as ever, but when she saw Clare it changed to a pleased smile. 'Let's do lunch,' whispered Ronnie.

Clare nodded. 'You're on, but right now I want to speak with Roderick.' And with that she escaped down the hall.

Roderick looked tired. There was nothing unusual about that, but there was something else behind his eyes. Uncertainty maybe? Misgivings?

'How's Jack?' he asked

'He's having some trouble adjusting to being back,' she said. 'For that matter, so am I.'

He nodded, as if she'd given him the right answer.

'He's made such big strides these past few months,' Clare said.

'Where is he today?'

'In a new day care place. It offers a therapeutic program for kids with emotional problems …' She trailed off. Roderick was studying her face. 'Jack doesn't like it,' she said, 'but it's an improvement on Jolly Jumbucks, and it's only three days a week.' Why was he looking at her like that?

'Well, we can certainly use the help leading up to Christmas,' he said. 'Young Davis is good, but he's green.'

He paused, as if expecting her to say something. But what?

'You know who's been a real turn up for the books?' he said. Clare shook her head. 'Ronnie. You wouldn't know her, not since that business with Adam Grant. She's been twice as hardworking and ten times as clever. I'm afraid I underestimated her.'

Exactly what *business with Adam* was he talking about? How much did Roderick know?

He was smiling at her now. 'Why the change of heart, Clare?' His voice was kind, concerned. 'Last time we spoke you were determined to stay up country till next year. You said you were so happy you mightn't ever come back, remember?' He picked up a perfectly sharpened pencil and tested its point with his finger. 'What changed?'

'That's none of your business.' Clare felt anger flushing her face. Then she stood up, horrified that she'd spoken like that to her old friend. 'I'm sorry,' she said, 'but I'd rather not talk about it.'

'That much is obvious.' Roderick's manner became businesslike. He patted a fat pile of folders on the desk. 'Overflow files we could use a hand with. Nothing too complicated.'

Clare picked them up.

'I've partitioned off the large storeroom and put a desk in there. It doesn't seem right to turf Davis from his office.'

'That's perfectly all right,' she said, but her voice was not quite steady as a wave of longing for Currawong overcame her. Part of her wanted to apologise to Roderick, collect Jack and Samson and find her way back to Clydesdale Way and through the Sunshine gates. But instead she turned on her heel and left. There was no going back – not now.

Clare threw herself into work, rating the files before her in order of priority. She made brief notes on each one, appraising the probable strength of the cases and flagging folders where, at first glance, a guilty plea seemed appropriate. This preliminary sorting stage was something she normally enjoyed, a kind of legal lucky dip. You never know what interesting cases you might come across. But today she found the process tedious. Her mind kept turning to the looming custody hearing. What would Taylor's lawyer do and say? How would Jack's psychological assessment go? What sort of witness would Taylor make?

By the time Ronnie knocked on her door at lunchtime, Clare had only worked through half the files she should have. Ronnie flicked through the documents in her out-tray with a curious eye. 'My, we are in a bad mood, aren't we?'

'What do you mean?' asked Clare.

'According to you, in each of these cases our client is guilty as charged and should cop a plea. Remind me never to appear before you if you decide to switch sides. Her Honour, Clare Mitchell - the hanging judge.'

Clare threw her a sarcastic smile. 'Do you want to have lunch or not.'

'Absolutely. I wouldn't dream of getting on your bad side,' she said in mock fear, tapping the pile of files on the desk. 'Not after seeing these.'

They sat down on the chrome and glass chairs at the tapas bar. Adam would have loved it here, Clare thought. Just as she suspected, the menu was wildly overpriced.

'Shall I order for you?' asked Ronnie, with a faint look of pity. Clare nodded. 'The drinks too?'

'But I don't drink at lunchtime,' said Clare.

'You must,' said Ronnie, 'or you'll offend Chef Diego .'

And that apparently was that. Ronnie clicked her fingers at the waiter. 'Miguel, we'll have the champinones al ajillo, the clams, patatas aioli, chorizo sausage and the dancing flamenco.'

'Very well, Madam.'

'And some Basque cider to begin with.' Ronnie snapped the menu shut.

'We only have an hour,' protested Clare.

'That's plenty of time. And lunch is on me, by the way.'

As the clams arrived, their conversation turned to men. 'So Adam never suspected that you leaked the Pyramid report?' asked Clare. 'I was worried for you.'

'Adam didn't have a clue. He did suspect *you* however, but couldn't quite figure out how you managed it.'

'Well he'll figure it out pretty quickly if he sees us together.'

'Don't worry, Adam's gone,' said Ronnie. 'Pyramid traced the leak to his computer. He offered to resign without entitlements in return for them not pursuing a breach of contract claim. Right now, Adam's working at his uncle's practice at Bankstown in Sydney.'

Clare raised her brows and whistled. She tried to imagine Adam as a humble solicitor in a down-market suburban shopping strip, and failed. 'What sort of practice?'

'Wills, tax, conveyancing,' said Ronnie. 'Oh, and family law.' Neither of them could stifle their laughter. 'What about you?' asked Ronnie. 'You and your vet patched things up yet?'

'Tom?' Clare shook her head. 'No.'

'So it's all because of his attitude to Jack?'

'I suppose it is,' said Clare, finishing her cider, and starting on a crisp dry white that had miraculously appeared before her.

'I don't understand,' said Ronnie. 'You never struck me as the maternal type.'

'With respect, counsellor,' said Clare. 'I don't think I struck you as much of anything.'

'Well, I think you're crazy,' said Ronnie. 'To give up a scrumptious man because he thinks a boy belongs with his mother?' She shook her head. 'He's probably right about that, Clare. And how on earth will you combine motherhood with being a barrister?'

Clare put the last mushroom on a piece of bread, 'I have no idea,' she said. 'No idea at all.' She ate the bread and finished her wine. The waiter put a little plate of sausage in front of her. 'If I eat this,' she asked, 'do I have to have another drink, yes? Tell me,' said Clare, as Ronnie pointed out an item on the wine list to Miguel. 'Why do you care so much that I get together with my *scrumptious vet?*'

'Isn't it obvious?' said Ronnie. 'If *you* make a tree change to play house with Dr Doolittle, *I* get your job with Paul next year. Although it was actually my job to begin with, so we'd simply be restoring the status quo, wouldn't we?' Ronnie's hair had come loose from its sleek chignon and her fingers were not quite steady on her glass.

'Yes, we would,' said Clare, slowly and thoughtfully. 'It was your job, and I did take it from you, and you've been very, very nice about it.'

Ronnie brushed her hair back from her face and picked up her glass. 'I propose a toast,' she said. 'To our unlikely friendship ... and to being back late in the office.'

They clinked glasses. 'He's been calling,' said Clare. 'Tom. Calling, texting, emailing …'

Ronnie raised her exquisite brows. 'And?'

'And I've been ignoring him.'

Ronnie rolled her perfectly made-up eyes. 'You could at least *talk* to the poor man.'

'No' said Clare, recalling Tom's heartbreaking words. *What's best for Jack is to be with his mother.* 'There's nothing to say.'

CHAPTER 35

Clare had been back in Brisbane for two weeks, and it was finally the day of Jack's pre-hearing assessment with the court psychologist. She was a bag of nerves. For the first time her dubious, self-taught parenting abilities would be clinically assessed. Not only that, she'd be seeing Taylor for the first time since the young woman's visit to Currawong.

Clare took a deep breath, then knelt down on the floor to extract Samson from the chewed-up-land under the bed. She grasped his collar and dragged him out. Damn, she'd caught her skirt on something and brought the hem down. She tied the dog to the table leg and quickly pinned it up. Next job was to extract Jack from under the battered couch. Ouch … she'd kneeled on the pin. Biting her lip, Clare reached under and tried to grab him. Jack kicked out and began to wail. 'Please, Jacky, give me a break.' She pulled him out by his shirt, feeling guilty and justified all at once. She was already late. What was she supposed to do?

With practised precision she slung her bag over one arm, tucked the little boy under the other, and groped for Samson's lead. The quick-release knot Grandad had taught her allowed her to free the dog one-handed. Very useful that. Clare hitched Jack up higher and reached awkwardly for the doorknob with her left hand. This couldn't go on. She needed a house. A place with a yard and a swing and a lemon tree. She intended to spend the weekend searching for just such a house. Maybe then she wouldn't feel like it was her and Jack against the whole world. Maybe then they'd be happy again. She took one last look around the chaos that was her flat, and backed out of the door.

The waiting room was airy and spacious, with floor-length windows that let in the light, and a well-equipped play area. Jack was on edge, choosing a toy, then discarding it moments later. He glanced at Clare often, as if he thought she might sneak away while he wasn't looking. How many times, she wondered, had he been through this sort of thing before?

Clare was on edge too. She'd had a long, sleepless night to rehearse her fears. What would happen when Taylor walked in?

The glass had turned the room into a hothouse full of emotion. A young woman approached the doors and Clare held her breath, but it wasn't Taylor. Maybe she wouldn't show. Jack began to jig from one foot to the other, like he needed to wee. Clare swooped and encouraged him towards the toilet, but he wouldn't move. When Clare turned around, Taylor was standing behind her.

'Jacky,' cried Taylor. The little boy made an excited beeline into his mother's arms.

'Hello, Taylor,' said Clare.

'You can go now,' said Taylor. 'The shrink wants to see me and Jacky, not you.'

'I think you'll find she wants to talk to both of us.' Clare sat back down.

Taylor glared at her, and cuddled Jack harder. He pulled away and Taylor looked stricken. Jack began to line up wooden cars along a pattern in the carpet, but his mother made no attempt to join in. When Jack gave her a car, she tried to pull him back onto her lap. He threw the car at her.

'You've turned him against me,' said Taylor.

Clare remained silent. Unnoticed by Taylor, a middle-aged woman had emerged from a side door and was quietly watching them. 'You must be Taylor Brown,' she said, with a kindly smile. 'I'm Stella Martin, a court-appointed psychologist. And this is your son Jack?' Taylor nodded. She looked well. She'd put on weight again and had some colour in her cheeks. 'If you two would like to come with me,' said Stella.

'Come on Jacky,' Taylor said hopefully. 'We're going to speak to this nice lady.'

Jack looked like he was in two minds. After an interminable pause, he followed Taylor into the room and Stella closed the door.

Clare stared out the window. The sun was pitiless, blazing uninterrupted against the glass. What was happening behind that door? Oh, to be a fly on the wall. It seemed to take hours before they emerged. 'So, you're Clare,' said Stella, offering her hand. 'Do you happen to have an extra pair of pants? Jack's had a little accident.'

'Yes,' said Clare. It felt like a test. 'Yes, of course. I always carry a spare, just in case.' She fossicked around in her bag and produced a small pair of jeans. Taylor was glaring at her.

'Would you help Jack change please, Clare, and then meet me in there?' Stella pointed to the room she'd just come from. Thank god Jack hated being wet these days. Clare waved the pants at him and he followed her promptly to the bathroom.

When they emerged, Taylor was sitting in the waiting room. 'We'll be some time,' Stella said to her. 'Do you want to say goodbye now?'

'I want to have a visit with my son when he comes out,' said Taylor.

'I'm going back to work after this,' said Clare. 'I'm afraid there won't be time.'

'Work?' said Taylor, looking puzzled. 'I thought you'd be taking Jacky back to the farm. He likes it there. He's got a dog.'

Clare wanted to strangle her. *Yes,* she felt like saying. *He does like it there, and so do I. But since you told everybody that Currawong was a violent death trap, crawling with armed men and dangerous dogs, I've had to make other arrangements.*

'I'm living back in Brisbane now,' said Clare. 'Come on, Jack.'

The boy didn't move. He'd been watching the exchange between Clare and his mother with a defiant look on his face.

Taylor must have sensed a mutiny. She called Jack herself. 'Come to Mummy, sweetie. Come and say goodbye.' To Clare's horror, Jack climbed onto his mother's knee. Taylor beamed at Stella, who was watching the scene with great interest. Any minute now she'd start taking notes. Stay calm, don't make this into a contest. Clare waited with a fixed smile on her face, while Taylor and Jack played a tickling game. It was stupid and immature to be jealous, but she couldn't help it.

'We really must get on,' said Stella at last. 'Clare?'

What was she supposed to do? Drag the boy from his mother's arms? She dared not call him again, in case he refused to come. What did she do when Samson ignored her? Of course, she offered his ball. Clare took Jack's box of Pokémon from her bag. 'I thought we might show Stella your toys,' she said. 'But I can't remember this one's name.' She extracted a figure and took a few steps towards Stella's office. Jack looked torn. 'It's Pikachu, isn't it?' asked Clare.

'No,' said Jack, unable to resist correcting her. 'That's Squirtle.' He struggled from Taylor's grasp and ran to Clare. She offered the box to him. He rummaged through it until he found a little yellow figurine. '*This* is Pikachu.'

'You'd better come, Jack, in case I get it wrong again,' said Clare. The child took her hand. Taylor looked close to tears.

'Good,' said Stella brightly. 'Let's get started.'

Stella watched Jack arrange his Pokémon toys on the desk. 'He spoke,' she said, sounding puzzled. 'I didn't see anything about him speaking in his file.'

'That's because his file's wrong,' said Clare. She took an iPad from her bag. 'Take a look at this.' It was the video of Jack at breakfast. *'Samsam stole my sausage,'* he said, clear as a bell.

Jack peered at the screen. 'That's me,' he said with a broad grin.

Clare smiled too. For a shutter-blink of time she wished Tom was there to share the moment. The mutinous desire sneaked in before she could cast it aside.

The rest of the assessment went just as well. Jack liked Stella and wanted to teach her about his Pokémon. She was a willing student, putting Jack in an amiable mood. Clare answered all the psychologist's questions as reasonably as she could, keeping a firm lid on her emotions. By the time Stella escorted them out, Clare was pretty sure she'd made an excellent impression.

'You manage him very well,' said Stella, with genuine admiration in her voice. 'Jack has made astonishing progress in the few months he's been with you.'

Clare allowed a wave of warm relief to wash over her.

'He could even be at the point where his mother might manage him,' said Stella. 'With a little help, of course. What do you think? You know the child better than anybody.'

Clare's smile died on her lips. Surely not? Surely this woman wasn't suggesting that Jack's improvement was a reason to hand him back to Taylor? 'I don't know,' Clare mumbled, trying not to let her misery show. 'I'm sorry, but I'm late for work.' Stella nodded and waved them goodbye.

Great. She thought she'd managed so well during the assessment. But she might have just shot herself in the foot instead.

CHAPTER 36

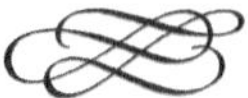

Friday afternoon. Clare checked the clock. Home time at last. During the last two weeks she'd performed her duties, represented her clients, gone through the motions – but her heart wasn't in it any more. The crawling days, the restless nights, the ever-present burn of tears and loneliness. Clare had never been more miserable. She missed Tom. His absence stung her every hour of every day. Bed was no comfort any more, and neither was work. Where had her drive gone, her energy, her commitment? Clare listened to her clients' sad stories. She listened to their tales of alcoholic fathers and disabled mothers, and could barely muster an ounce of sympathy. How was she supposed to present a plea of mitigation to the magistrate, when she wasn't convinced of its merits herself?

The drunk drivers and drug users, the teenage car thieves and shoplifters that she used to have sympathy for? Now she saw them as foolishly bent on self-ruin, destroying their loved ones' lives in the process. Their anguished parents and grandparents, their neglected children – all of them collateral damage in a desperate, downward spiral. Thank goodness the job was only three days a week. How would she ever manage full-time in this frame of mind? How could she possibly do her clients justice? She tried not to think about the life of a criminal barrister that awaited her next year. That was full-time. That was more than full-time. It was an all-encompassing career choice, a commitment that would entail a complete lifestyle change. Where would there be room for Jack, even if she could hang onto him?

Clare shook her head to clear it, squeezed her eyes shut against the sting of tears. 'I'm out of here,' she told Debbie as she hurried past the desk. What a relief to get outside. The day was bright and hot, the sky an empty, punishing blue, but the city buildings hid the sun. Heat shimmers rose from bitumen and cement. Late-afternoon shadows lengthened across the road and crept up the facades of skyscrapers, as if trying to climb out of the concrete jungle and escape across the rooftops. The city felt like a prison.

She clicked the remote on her key ring. The roll-a-door to the basement car park glided up and she hurried to her car. Damn Jack, damn Currawong – damn Tom. He'd made her feel like a fish out of water in her own life. *We've only been city creatures for a few hundred years*, he'd said one night, staring up at the stars. *That's just a blink of evolutionary time.* He was right. She didn't belong here in Brisbane any more, but she didn't belong back there either – not while Tom took Taylor's side. Not while he expected her to hand over Jack without a fight.

Clare fumbled with her car keys and they slipped to the ground. This tiny frustration was almost enough to tip her over the edge. She wanted to weep. The phone rang. Tom again. Clare didn't answer it. Instead she dug the heels of her hands into her eyes until it hurt. She had to pull herself together. The hearing was only a week away. She daren't lose courage now. Jack was depending on it.

Harry offered Tom a second scoop of curried lamb, but he waved the pot away. 'You have to eat,' said Harry, piling up the plate anyway. 'Christ almighty. Anyone would think it was you with the cancer.' He took a second pot from the stove and ladled out sticky rice without asking permission.

The two men ate in silence, growling at the dogs in turn each time they poked their noses through the kitchen door. 'You have to speak to the lass,' said Harry at last.

'I've tried ringing,' said Tom miserably. 'She won't answer.' They both picked at their meals again. '*You* could, Harry,' he said hopefully. 'You could talk to her.'

'Don't put me in the middle. I can't tell her what she needs to hear.' Harry took another mouthful, staring belligerently at Tom. 'You're the one who needs to grow a backbone.'

Ever since Clare left, a pall had descended on Currawong. Nothing Tom did gave him pleasure any more. His patients weren't so bad. At least they let him get on with the job. It was their owners that he couldn't abide. He hauled himself from bed each morning, dreading having to make small talk, thrown by the simplest, *How are you, Tom?* He'd never been one to abide pretence. His natural instinct was to answer the question honestly. How was he? He was gutted, that's what he was. He missed Clare so badly, it was a constant physical ache. Nothing seemed worthwhile without her. Each day was empty - a dreary matter of going through the motions.

Inevitably his dreams were of Clare. The unbearable thing was that in these dreams things always worked out. Either she'd never left, or she came back, or he rescued her from bears that had shredded her clothes ... and the dream then turned deliciously X-rated. However weird the scenario, they always ended up living happily ever after.

How appalling then to wake up each morning and, like in a perverse version of Groundhog Day, have to confront his heartache all over again. Consequently he didn't want to sleep. He watched movies late into the night or played online computer games, building himself a gorgeous avatar lover who looked suspiciously like Clare. He drank too much bourbon, hoping it might provide a respite from dreaming. It didn't, but it did provide him with a sore head in the morning. Life had become a living nightmare.

He'd misjudged things badly, he saw that now. Expecting Clare to see things from his point of view, without giving her any basis for doing so. And why the hell should she anyway? Her life wasn't his life. How could she possibly appreciate the danger of taking a child from his mother the way he did?

'Tom,' said Harry. 'I reckon it might be easier for you to talk to me, kind of a practice run.'

'I can't.'

Harry pulled out his tobacco pouch and rolled a cigarette. There was a certain gravity in the air, like something important was about to happen. 'This is difficult for you, Tom, I can see that.' Harry stood stiffly and rummaged through the pantry. 'Here it is.' He pulled out a velvet-lined display box and placed it on the table. It contained a dusty bottle of whisky. 'My old dad won this fifty years ago at the Royal Sydney Show. Currawong horses took out every championship in sight that year, including Grand Champion Stallion. First and last time that honour's gone to a clydie, I reckon.' He smiled to himself, like he was remembering. 'I've been keeping it all these years ... don't know what for. Whisky ages in the cask, not in the bottle.' Harry removed the cork and gave it an appreciative sniff.

'It's already been opened,' said Tom. 'There's some missing.'

'That happens with old spirits,' said Harry. 'They evaporate. Dad said it was the angels taking their share. Anyway, I reckon this one's ripe. Fetch some glasses, will you, lad?'

'What's going on, Harry?'

'Just a little talk, lad.' Harry poured them both a drink. 'Just a little talk.' They both took a sip, then another. 'I knew your father,' said Harry. 'He was a hard man, by all accounts. But he was a damn fine vet, almost as good as you are.'

Where was this leading?

'I never knew much about your mother, though,' Harry said.

Tom felt the bile rise in his throat.

'Why is that, Tom? Is she dead?'

'No, she's not dead,' said Tom at last. 'But she may as well be.'

Harry lit his cigarette and drew in deeply. 'I want you to tell me about her. You wouldn't deny a dying man, would you now, Tom?'

What could he say? He barely had the words. But maybe Harry was right, maybe he should try to find them. Tom raised his glass and took a big swig. The smooth, sweet liquor went down easily. 'When I was eight years old my folks split up. Me and my older sister Karen went to live with Mum. It was what we wanted, but Dad wouldn't have it. He got a lawyer and went for sole custody of us both. That lawyer must have made my mother look pretty bad because he won the case. Dad sent us to boarding school. What was the point of taking us off Mum, just so he could send us away? Mum remarried and I barely saw either of them after that.' Tom took another drink.

'I'm sorry to hear it,' said Harry. 'Look at me, son.'

Tom met the old man's gaze.

'Do you know what I think, no? Oh, I think you do,' said Harry. 'I think you know exactly what I think. You want Jack to live with his mother because of what happened to you. But Jack's not you, Tom. You're not being fair to either him or my granddaughter.'

'Maybe you're right.'

'There's no *maybe* about it,' said Harry. 'And there's no maybe about the fact that Clare needs some support right now, whatever that court decides. If you love the girl, and I think you do, she should hear that story for herself.'

'She won't take my calls.'

'Where there's a will, there's a way.'

'She won't listen to me.'

'That,' said Harry, 'is because, up until now, you haven't said anything worth listening to.'

CHAPTER 38

Clare waved Jack goodbye and slipped out the childcare centre door. She collapsed back into the car. Samson laid his great head on her shoulder, and she stroked his muzzle. 'Why the hell we're fighting so hard to keep that child is a mystery to me,' she said. 'Maybe we should just let Taylor have him. It would serve her right.' Samson pulled away, as if he disapproved.

Jack had been more impossible than ever that morning. Clare had learned long ago that the boy was an emotional barometer. She'd tried to act as if today was a normal day, but she hadn't fooled him. Consequently it had taken longer than usual to coax him into the car. It had taken even longer to pry him out of it and then there was the painful leaving scene, where he clung to her and yelled at the long-suffering staff at the Pinocchio Centre. On her way out she'd knocked over an entire shelf of books. She was all too familiar with that feeling – when things just wouldn't stop falling.

Clare straightened her back, checked the time and started the car. Her eyes ached from lack of sleep. She was running late already and she still hadn't dropped off Samson. How on earth did other women manage? Clare shook her head to clear it. She had to pull herself together or she'd be a mess at the hearing. 'Wish me luck,' she said to

Samson as she fastened her seatbelt. 'Today could be the most important day of our lives.'

Clare wasn't late after all. A high-speed dash through Brisbane's streets saw her arrive ahead of time. She sat on a chair outside courtroom number seven and observed the hustle and bustle going on around her. She wasn't used to being on this side of proceedings. She wasn't used to being out of control. She hated waiting around for complete strangers to decide about her life. This must be how it felt for her clients. How it felt for Taylor, those other times she'd lost Jack.

Clare kept an eye on the lifts, scanning the faces that emerged. Here came Sarah Chapman, checking her watch. She caught sight of Clare. Normally the two women would have exchanged pleasantries, maybe talked a little about the day's cases. Today, however, Sarah acknowledged her with the briefest nod. Clare checked her watch again. Taylor still wasn't here. A no-show would almost certainly decide the case in the department's favour.

To her surprise, Ronnie emerged next from the lift, looking like a fashion plate for the young professional on the ladder to success. 'What are you doing here?' asked Clare. 'Do you have something on today?'

Ronnie sat down, crossing her feet in their chic Jimmy Choo boots. 'I do,' she said. 'I have a colleague to support, even if that colleague is demented.'

Clare's spirits lifted. She reached over and squeezed Ronnie's perfectly manicured hand. It was good to have a friend by her side.

Now key players were arriving thick and fast. The department lawyer, Grace Carter, came over and introduced herself. Grace was a plump, efficient-looking young woman. Until today, they'd only ever talked on the phone.

'Have you seen the psychologist's report?' asked Clare.

Grace nodded. 'Based on that assessment, today could go either way. She's given you a glowing carer recommendation, but she's also given the mother full marks for improving her circumstances. Taylor has safe, supported housing. She's passed every drug screen, and she's stuck with the methadone program so faithfully that the doctors have lowered her dose. She's participated in parenting classes and, as far as we can tell, she's cut off all contact with the violent boyfriend. And she's in counselling.'

Oh. Taylor had jumped through every hoop the department had presented her with. Clare couldn't help it. There was that grudging admiration again.

'On the plus side for us, Jack has now been in care for a cumulative total of eighteen months. It means he's a candidate for a stability plan.'

An SP was an official plan for long term out-of-home care for a child. 'If only we had one of those,' said Clare.

Grace whipped a document from her wallet. 'We do,' she said. 'Here's your copy. You really should have seen this before, but there just wasn't time. It was only finalised this morning, courtesy of Kim Maguire. I trust there's nothing in there that you disagree with?'

Clare read the pages. The plan proposed, among other things, that Clare become Jack's long-term carer, and that he be kept on a guardianship order for now, with a planned transition to permanent care. There was provision for Taylor to have generous access. Clare couldn't believe it. Kim had really come through for her. *Transition to permanent care.* The prospect was too good to be true. 'No,' said Clare. 'There's absolutely nothing that I disagree with. This is wonderful.'

'Right,' said Grace. 'I was hoping Kim could be here as a witness, but she's giving evidence in another case. Instead I have a comprehensive affidavit from her for the court. Kim speaks glowingly of you, by the way. But don't get your hopes up,' warned Grace. 'We're still in for an uphill battle, and Magistrate Jackson is known to be sympathetic to birth parents.'

Clare groaned. Not Joe Jackson. She usually cheered when she wound up in his court, but that was when she was acting for the other side. Clare recalled the time she'd won back custody of twin girls for their single mother on her latest release from jail. Even she hadn't expected to win that one. The three-year-olds had been in a stable, loving placement for two years. Their foster parents had wept at the decision. It made her ashamed now to think about how she'd treated them.

Ronnie helped herself to the document in Clare's lap. 'Permanent care?' she asked in astonishment. 'Is that really what you want?'

'Yes,' said Clare, keeping her eye on the lift. 'It's what I want more than anything.'

Clare wasn't only on the lookout for Taylor. Her grandfather had promised to come. Of course she'd told him not to bother. She'd told him that it was too far for him to drive, especially with those dizzy spells of his, and she'd meant it, but a big part of her still hoped she might see him walk through that door. And then there he was, large as life, clutching his hat, looking out of place in the windowless hall. His bewildered expression transformed into a sunny smile the moment he spotted her.

Clare leaped to her feet. 'Grandad, you shouldn't have.'

'Yes, I should have,' he said, embracing her.

Clare introduced him to Ronnie, wondering what she'd make of him.

'How do you do, Mr MacLeod.' Ronnie looked him up and down. 'I love your style. Pure R. M. Williams. That look's very in right now.' She glanced over at Clare. 'Perhaps you could give your grand-daughter some fashion tips.'

Taylor still hadn't arrived and Clare allowed herself to hope. They were first on the list. If she didn't show soon, it would be game over.

Then it happened. The lift door opened, framing two people inside. Clare's heart faltered. Taylor … and Tom. What on earth? She turned, open-mouthed, to her grandfather.

'Don't start, love,' he said. 'Tom drove me up here.' Grandad was speaking in the tone that he used for nervous, young horses. 'He spotted Taylor in the lobby and they got talking.'

Taylor noticed Clare. They eyed each other warily, and then Tom spotted her too. What would he say? What would she say? But she needn't have worried; he didn't approach her.

Clare felt sick. Her heart ached at the sight of him, but she couldn't stop staring. Devastatingly handsome in a charcoal suit and tie. The tailored clothes emphasised his height, his square shoulders, his lean hips. Her body responded to him in spite of herself. She folded her arms across her chest. The only thing worse than Tom not being there to support her, was him being there to support Taylor.

'It's not what you think,' said her grandfather.

'Good,' said Clare as she stood up. 'Because if it's what I think, Tom's a dead man.' She marched off down the corridor to compose herself. Sarah called Taylor over. Clare moved closer - close enough to overhear the barrister's last-minute instructions to her client. She eavesdropped shamelessly, but Sarah wasn't giving anything away.

'You'll be asked to take the stand,' said Sarah. 'You can either swear on the bible, or simply swear that you'll tell the truth. Answer all questions honestly. If you don't understand a question, ask for it to be repeated. If you still don't understand, ask for the Magistrate to make the question clearer. Address him as *Your Honour* or *Sir*. I'll ask you questions first, then the other lawyer will cross-examine you. Okay?' Taylor looked like a scared rabbit, but she nodded and the case was called.

Grandad stood up. 'We can't go in,' said Clare. 'You're not a party, and I'm a witness.' Her grandfather sat back down.

Tom came over. 'Hello, Clare.'

'Tom.'

'Can we talk?' he asked.

'No,' she said, powerfully aware of his physical presence. Damn that man. She had to keep her wits about her for the stand.

'Leave her be, son,' said Grandad. 'It'll keep.'

Tom gave her one last, longing look, and then sat down a few seats away.

Ronnie's eyes widened and a knowing smile played on her lips. 'You weren't kidding,' she said. '*Scrumptious* is an understatement.' She sneaked another peek at Tom. 'I might pack up and go bush for him myself.'

Clare ignored Ronnie and concentrated on calming down. She could *feel* Tom, though she couldn't look at him. For a moment she thought she could smell him too: a kind of warm, open air, animal scent She forced her mind away from him. Time slowed, along with the beat of her heart. She was intensely present in each moment, like in a meditation. When they called her, she'd be ready.

The sound of the clerk saying her name startled her. Surely it wasn't time yet? It was too soon. With a pat on the back from her grandfather and an unexpected hug from Ronnie, Clare entered the court. Grace met her on the other side of the door.

'There's been a change of plan,' she whispered. 'His Honour wants to speak with you.'

What was Grace talking about? Either Clare was giving evidence, or she wasn't. Taylor stood in the witness box with a defiant tilt to her chin. She glared at Clare. Whatever this was, it didn't look pretty.

His Honour Joe Jackson was a cheerful, middle-aged man, with grey hair and fine principles. He was one of the more progressive magistrates on the bench, and liked to pursue what he regarded as a social justice agenda. In other words, he was a bit of a sucker for the underdog. That normally suited Clare just fine, but not today.

'Ms Mitchell,' he said. 'Always nice to see you in my court, whatever the circumstances.'

'Thank you.' She sized up the situation. To her surprise, Sarah Chapman looked furious. That had to be good.

'Ms Brown has a rather novel proposal. If it should prove acceptable to both parties, it would allow for this matter to be settled with a consent order.'

Whatever was he talking about?

'If you wouldn't mind reiterating your request?' he asked Taylor.

Taylor looked at the Magistrate in confusion. 'Tell us again what you want, Ms Brown,' said Jackson. 'We're all waiting with bated breath.'

Taylor slowly turned her gaze to Clare. Nobody else, just Clare. Her voice, when she finally spoke, was resolute. 'I love my son,' she said. 'Don't get me wrong, he's the best thing that ever happened to me. The truth is, though, I haven't always been the best mother to him. I've always tried. I've tried my heart out for that little boy. I'm still trying.' She stopped.

'Go on,' said Jackson, gently. 'Tell Ms Mitchell what you told me.'

'I hate her,' said Taylor, and Clare forgot to breathe. 'She's a stuck-up bitch. But I know she loves my son … and I know he loves her too.' Taylor wiped her eyes and looked at Jackson. 'That's probably why I hate her, eh?'

Jackson smiled. 'Quite possibly.'

She returned his smile, and it seemed to give her courage. 'The fact is, Clare's good for Jack. He's talking and everything. I love hearing him talk. He only talks when he's happy.' She turned back to Jackson. 'So I was thinking, 'cause I do love him so much, that I might give him to her.' Clare's breath returned in a heady rush. 'But I'll only do that if Jack can live with her at that farm. He likes it there. He's got dogs and a pony. I want him to have a pony. And I'd have to be able to see him at Christmas and birthdays and holidays and stuff.'

'Well,' said Jackson, beaming. 'As you've now heard for yourself, Ms Mitchell, this is an unusual request indeed. I've never made a consent order before that has been conditional upon the child having a pony.' There was laughter from the court, and Clare felt tears beginning to slide down her face. 'Ms Mitchell, I believe you're poised to take up a position at the bar next year. That would of course be incompatible with Ms Brown's request. Should you wish, we will continue with the hearing. But know that if you are agreeable, I'll have the relevant order prepared forthwith.'

'Yes,' said Clare, smiling through her tears 'Yes, absolutely yes.'

'Then I think we have reached an agreement.'

Sarah could no longer contain her outrage. 'With respect, Your Honour cannot make an order that directs Ms Mitchell to remain at a certain address. Nor can you direct her to give the child a pony.' More laughter. 'I don't think my client understands this.'

'That's very true, counsellor.' Joe Jackson turned to Taylor. 'I can't direct Ms Mitchell to remain at this farm indefinitely. You would have to take it on trust, and of course you would always be free to apply for a variation of the order, should circumstances demand. So, what say you?'

'Sure,' said Taylor. 'I'll trust her.' Sarah threw her papers in the air.

Clare wanted to hug Taylor and never let her go, but the girl looked on guard. Better take things slowly. This was going to be a steep learning curve for the both of them

It was only when they were all directed to rise, and were filing from the courtroom, that she thought of Tom. She was going to be living at Currawong again. How on earth was that going to work?

CHAPTER 39

They were an odd assortment, all gathered in Clare's untidy apartment. Jack and Samson in the lounge room, attempting a game of tug-a-war with an old tea towel. Taylor on her knees, getting in their way, trying to cuddle each of them in turn without much success. Clare smiled. A lap dog and a baby doll would suit Taylor better.

Ronnie and Grandad were perched on bar stools in the kitchen, talking a dime a dozen. Who would have guessed they shared a love of antiques? For the first time ever, the place felt like a real home. Clare cleared the clutter away in the kitchen, until she could reach the huge coffee machine squatting in the corner. A present from Adam that she'd barely used, but it might impress Ronnie.

She plugged it in and tried to remember the instructions. 'Don't worry about that, love,' said her grandfather. 'A cuppa will do me fine.'

'Tea?' asked Ronnie. 'Yes, tea sounds like fun. Do you have one of those pots?'

For a moment Clare didn't know what Ronnie meant. 'You mean this?' She extracted a large and very beautiful old teapot from the back of the cupboard, a present long ago from her mother.

Ronnie clapped her hands. 'Perfect. We'll have a tea party, shall we?'

'If you like,' said Clare, abandoning the monstrous coffee machine and putting on the kettle instead. 'It won't be all that traditional. I think you're supposed to have scones and jam at a tea party, not take-away pizza, but we can pretend.'

Tom was standing at the window, staring out across the city lights. He'd barely spoken a word since the court case. Was he unhappy with the outcome? If he was, he was the only one. What was it, she wondered, that he'd wanted to say to her earlier on?

Grandad made himself useful, finding plates and distributing slices of pizza. Clare took a marrowbone from the fridge, banishing it and Samson to the training crate.

'That's cruel,' said Taylor, patting the dog through the wire, and feeding him bits from her plate.

'Come on, Jacky,' said Grandad. 'Sit up. How about some garlic bread as well.'

'Pizza,' yelled the little boy, climbing up onto a bar stool. How happy he looked. How content, to have all the people who loved him together in this one place.

'Clare,' said Ronnie, in a wheedling tone. She didn't look entirely at ease, balancing a plate of greasy take-away on her knee, but she was making a valiant attempt to cope. 'What a brave decision you made today. I do so admire you.'

'Do you now?' said Clare sweetly. She held the teapot aloft. 'Tea?'

'Please.' Clare had been stringing this out all day. It was kind of fun, torturing Ronnie. 'When do you think you might talk to Paul?'

'Paul?' asked Clare.

'Oh, come off it,' snapped Ronnie. 'You won't be at the bar with Dunbar next year. Why don't you just tell him? You have an obligation Clare, to tell him this very day. And you must ask him if he'll consider me as your replacement. The job's truly mine, in any case. You stole it right out from under my nose.'

Clare grinned. This was the Ronnie she knew and loved. It was time to put her out of her misery. From the corner of her eye, Clare noticed Tom watching her. Shirt sleeves rolled up. Collar open. He looked very handsome in the soft reflected light at the window. It emphasised his rugged features, his unkempt hair, his watchful eyes. He looked a little wild.

'Relax,' Clare told Ronnie. 'I've already spoken to Paul. He's very happy for your old arrangement to stand. In fact, he wants to meet you for dinner tomorrow night to finalise things.'

Ronnie's expression collapsed into a teary mess, mascara running, smearing her face as she dragged her knuckles across her eyes. She clutched at Clare's hand. 'You're my truest, dearest friend,' she said, sounding slightly unhinged. 'This job is my every dream come true. You have no idea. I'd cheerfully sell my grandmother for this chance. I'd even have stayed another year in the Valley, if Paul had insisted.'

'Thank goodness it didn't come to that,' said Clare. The irony was lost on Ronnie, whose hands fluttered in the air like startled birds as she repeated her thanks.

Clare studied Ronnie's exalted face. It told her something rather surprising, something she was very glad to learn. She didn't really want the job, at least not the way Ronnie did. Ronnie had a fierce, uncompromising hunger for it. She wouldn't have given it up for anything. How hard, then, must it have been for her to forgive Clare and offer her friendship? In spite of Adam, in spite of Paul. They may have started out as co-conspirators, but their connection had blossomed into something far deeper. This was a friendship that would stand the test of time.

Moments later Ronnie was on her mobile, ordering buckets of home-delivered champagne. 'And a bottle of whisky?' She looked at Grandad, who was thoroughly enjoying himself. 'Single malt?'

He nodded, and Ronnie smiled. She cast her eyes around the room one more time, and her gaze settled on Jack. 'And a bottle of non-alcoholic sparkling wine, suitable for a small boy.' She beamed at Clare, apparently pleased with herself for being so child friendly.

'How about I take Jack and Samson for a walk?' said Tom, who had mysteriously appeared at Clare's shoulder.

'If you like,' she said coolly.

Taylor gave up trying to braid the back of Jack's hair, and came into the kitchen. 'Are you going with Tom?' she asked Clare. 'On the walk?'

'No,' said Clare.

'Why not?' asked Taylor.

'I have guests,' said Clare shortly. She turned away to collect the empty mugs, and began to stack them in the dishwasher.

Taylor pouted and took another piece of pizza. 'I should have made you two get married.'

'What?' Clare dropped a teacup. It shattered on the floor. Taylor ignored it. 'Tom's nice. Jack would like having him for a dad.'

'Taylor,' said Clare. 'Whatever do you mean?'

'I mean,' said Taylor, with exaggerated emphasis, as if Clare was a bit slow, 'I should have made you two get married, like I made you go and live back at the farm with Jack.'

'You didn't make me go live at the farm,' said Clare. 'I'm choosing to live there.'

Taylor giggled. 'I did too. And I could've made you marry him. I reckon you love my son that much. Tom should've thought of it when he thought of the other idea.'

Clare's hands went clammy. 'What other idea?'

'I've got a job,' said Taylor, inexplicably changing the subject. 'Out west. They're going to train me to drive those monster trucks at a mine.'

Tom bent down to release Samson from his crate. 'Don't you move,' commanded Clare. She grabbed Taylor's arm and marched her over to Tom. The room went quiet. 'Go on, Taylor,' said Clare. 'Finish your story.'

'The Newstart Centre lined me up for the job weeks ago. I wanted to tell Sarah that you could keep Jacky, I really did, but she was so gung-ho about everything. I was scared she'd think I didn't love him … so the case sort of kept rolling along.'

'Go on,' said Clare again. Everybody had moved closer to listen. 'Well, I was so confused this morning,' said Taylor. 'What was I supposed to do? If I told people about the job, they'd think I was a bad mother. But if I got Jacky back, I couldn't take the job, could I? I want it that bad. I've never had a job before. I think it would make Jacky proud of me.'

'I think so too, love,' said Grandad. Taylor shot him a grateful look. 'Anyway, Tom saw me crying in the lobby.' Taylor faltered again.

'For God's sake, just spit it out,' said Ronnie.

'Don't you get it?' said Taylor. 'Today was all Tom's idea. I told him that I wished Jacky could live at the farm with you. So he said, why don't I tell the judge? He said nobody would think that I didn't love Jacky. So I did. I wouldn't have been brave enough if it wasn't for him.'

Clare wet her lips with her tongue. 'And ...?'

'And I was just thinking, since Tom loves you and all, it would have been nice if I'd made you get married as well, and then Jack could have a daddy ... as well as a pony.'

'Tom,' said Clare. 'Is this true?'

Tom nodded, his gaze bold and unapologetic. It put her unexpectedly on the back foot.

'Taylor told me she wanted Jack to live with you at Currawong, and I suggested she tell the judge. Simple as that.'

'And you didn't think to tell me?' said Clare.

'I tried. You wouldn't listen. By the time the case was over, you already knew. What would have been the point?'

Clare shook her head in disbelief. She ran over the events of the day in her mind. It was true – he had asked to talk to her. 'And what's this about us getting married?'

He held out the palms of his hands. 'Now that's a new one on me.'

Clare tried to digest all she'd heard. Did the end justify the means? It was true that Taylor had held her over a barrel today, but the end result was that she had Jack. And though she was loath to admit it, it looked like she had Tom to thank. Clare turned to confront Taylor, who was sitting on a bar stool looking miserable.

'You think I'm a bad mother, don't you,' said the girl, before Clare had a chance to speak. 'To want the job so much.'

'No,' said Clare. 'I don't think that at all. But I also don't think you should be keeping secrets and ... and blackmailing me.'

'Steady on, love,' said her grandfather. He'd gone all protective of Taylor, and it irritated Clare.

'What business is it of yours, if and who I marry?' asked Clare. 'And wherever did you get the idea that Tom loves me?'

'He told me,' said Taylor. 'Not that he had to. Blind Freddy could see it a mile off. I don't think you know how lucky you are. You've got a farm, and horses and dogs. You've got Tom and he's a hunk, by the way, in case you haven't noticed. You've got Harry. He's the sweetest old man in the world … You even have my son. But instead of being happy, you're storming around like you're mad at everybody.' It was the longest speech Clare had ever heard Taylor make. 'I think you should thank your lucky stars.'

Jack crept over. He climbed the bar stool and nestled into his mother's lap. Taylor folded him in her arms and kissed his hair.

'You know what?' said Clare. Taylor shook her head. 'I think you're right.'

It was the going away party she'd missed the first time round, all her legal aid colleagues gathered together after work on her final day. Roderick thumped the table. 'Will everyone please charge your glasses.'

Clare helped herself to a glass of riesling from the cask and poured another one for Ronnie. Her friend took a sip and made a face. 'The only thing worse than this wine is having to listen to one of Roderick's speeches,' she whispered.

Clare giggled. Ronnie was right. He did go on a bit. She nibbled a cracker topped with gherkin and cheese, while Roderick cleared his throat. 'As we gather to farewell our colleague, Clare, I'm reminded of words spoken by Brutus in Shakespeare's Julius Caesar. *There comes a tide in the affairs of men, which taken at the flood leads on to fortune.* Such a tide has swept Clare from us. We hope that for her, the flood will lead to something better than it did for Brutus and Cassius …'

A sprinkle of laughter. Debbie looked confused. Ronnie looked bored. Clare would miss these people, these friends. She gazed out the window to the wizened coolabah tree. It was her friend too. She wished she could spirit it away with her, back to Currawong. She wished she could set it free. Ronnie dug her in the ribs just as Roderick finished. '... So I ask you to be upstanding and drink to Clare and her future.'

It was growing dark when Clare finally waved goodbye and headed for the car. She clicked the key to unlock it and sat awhile in the dark. Then she got out again, retraced her steps and slipped around the side of the building to her coolabah tree. It stood forlorn on a patch of dead grass, narrow leaves trembling in the breeze. Silhouetted against the sunset, its spindly branches looked like crooked hands reaching skywards, begging for release. Clare ran her finger down its rough furrowed bark. She scanned its sparse canopy until she found what she was looking for. There, at the tip of a low hanging bough. Clare reached up and plucked a drab bunch of grey-green gumnuts. She collected a few more from the ground. 'Don't worry,' she told the tree, before she turned to go. 'Grandad will know just what to do with these.'

CHAPTER 40

Clare awoke in her own bed, in her own little room back at
Currawong. The candlewick spread, the pretty lamp, the lacy
curtains - nothing ever changed in this space. It could have been her
first night back at the homestead, and all that had happened these past
few months might well have been a dream. It was both a comforting
and unsettling thought. She was certain of one thing though. Last
night with Tom had been no dream.

Clare stretched, cat-like. What time was it anyway? The bunya
pine in the yard already cast a shadow on the window. She checked
the wind-up alarm clock beside the bed. It was later than she thought.

A knock came at the door. 'Breakfast's up, sleepy head,' said
Grandad. Clare hopped out of bed, and into jeans and a T-shirt. She
pulled a comb through her tousled hair, slipped on sandals and was
ready to go. It took her two minutes. How different from her mornings back in Brisbane, juggling Jack and Samson and traffic: juggling
everybody's expectations, including her own. She'd been exhausted
before she began. The contrast made her smile.

'What's this?' asked Clare. Beside the bacon and eggs, the buttery
toast and the jar of vegemite, was a big bowl of fresh summer fruits.

'Who said you can't teach an old dog new tricks,' said Grandad. 'I learned a thing or two those few days I stayed with you in Brisbane. I learned that I like fruit for breakfast.' He turned to where Jack was chewing on bacon rind. 'I'm going to make you a nice fruit salad, lad.' He searched around in the fridge. 'Now where'd I put that yoghurt?'

Jack pulled a face and escaped out the door, where Samson was patiently waiting for him. The dog gave a joyful bark and the two of them ran off.

Clare smiled and looked round for Tom. Last night they'd spent a magical evening; forgiving, re-joining, falling in love all over again. Grandad had thoughtfully retired early, leaving them to share chips and beer and cherries out on the verandah. They'd talked until way after midnight. About their childhood and families. About their hopes and dreams and the things that made them who they were. They'd reconnected with a deeper understanding.

Mother Nature had turned on a spectacular show, as fork lightning cracked over the Bunyas, dazzling the eyes. A deafening boom of thunder had made Clare jump against him, and Tom had snatched her in his arms. She'd almost cried out at his touch, at how much she wanted him.

Afterwards they'd sneaked down to the surgery and made sweet, slow love. The pair of boobook owls in the recovery room provided the soundtrack — a duet of low, rhythmic mating calls. Clare had stumbled back to bed in the pale light of picaninny dawn, knowing life didn't get any better.

'Where's Tom?' asked Clare.

Pregnancy testing cows at Kingaroy.' Clare smiled, wondering how Tom was managing on hardly any sleep. 'I thought we might spend the day together,' said Grandad. 'Just you, me and Jacky. We could go for a drive into Dalby, maybe have a picnic at Myall Creek. Or what about a carriage ride into Merriang and lunch at the pub. Fleur could use a bit of a run? What do you say?'

'They both sound perfect,' said Clare. 'You choose.'

'A carriage ride it is then,' said Grandad.

'There's something I want to ask you first,' said Clare. She fetched the gumnuts she'd collected from her coolabah tree in Brisbane, and spread them on the table. 'Can I grow these?'

She watched as he put on his glasses and examined the woody pods. Was it her imagination or had he grown more frail? Yes, he had. It was easier to spot after being away for a few weeks. The skin on his hands looked thin enough to tear with a touch, and his eyes seemed sunken. They retained their old sparkle and warmth, though, and he still had a spring in his step.

'What are they?' asked Grandad. 'Black box? Coolabah …?'

'Coolabah,' she said.

'First thing,' he said, 'is to stick them in a paper bag under the verandah until the nuts release their seed.' He picked up a gum nut she'd taken from the ground and rolled it between his fingers. 'This is a good'un. Some trees hold their nuts way past the first year. With these older ones, you're sure the seed is ripe.'

'Wait.' Clare grabbed a pen and paper.

'Plant the seed in pots with a mixture of peat and sand. Stick them in the fridge for six weeks so they think its winter. Then just take them out and keep them moist. You'll have a fine crop of coolabah seedlings before you know it.'

Clare finished writing down the instructions, then leant over and kissed him. 'Thanks Grandad. I knew I could count on you.'

The phone rang and for once Grandad heard it. Clare cleared away the gumnuts and poured herself a cup of tea, idly listening to the conversation. She put down the teapot. Something was wrong, she could hear it in his voice. 'You buggers will come onto this land over my dead body,' he said, his voice thick with anger. The phone slammed down. It took some time for him to emerge from the hall.

'We'll have to take a rain check on that carriage ride. Those Pyramid bastards are on their way.' His hands closed into fists. 'Going ahead with some exploratory wells, they said. Reckon they've got the paperwork, and I can't do nothing about.'

A flush of guilt scorched her face. She'd been so caught up in her own problems, she'd forgotten about his. 'Oh, Grandad, I thought we'd put an end to all that.'

'So did I, love,' he said. 'Gordon tabled that report of yours in parliament last week and the vote's today. He's crunched the numbers. It'll be close, but it should get through. If it does, he reckons there'll be a moratorium on new wells. But if those buggers get their toe in the door before the vote, they might just get away with it.'

'The vote's today? Surely we can stall them for one day?'

'Buggered if I know how. There's a whole convoy on its way.'

Clare took his arm and smiled. 'I wasn't a student activist for nothing,' she said. 'Ring around. See who can get over here straightaway. Ask them to bring chains and padlocks. We're going to stage a protest.'

'Blimey,' said Grandad, looking more cheerful. 'Why didn't I think of that?'

More than two hundred people turned up, with tractors and cultivators and graders – anything that could block access to the Currawong track. A party atmosphere developed. Women served sandwiches. Someone had brought along balloons for the children. An eclectic collection of farm dogs milled around, some circling each other, stiff-legged, manes up and spoiling for a fight. But one word from an owner was generally enough to stand them down. They soon sorted out a pecking order and formed a rough pack. Samson and Red, Pongo and Perdita – they all joined in.

Clare, along with Bronwyn and a few others, sat chained to the Sunshine gates. She was enjoying herself, reliving the student sit-ins of university days. 'There's nothing like a bit of civil disobedience,' she said. Jack and Timmy thought it was great fun and demanded to be chained up too.

'Not today,' said Bronwyn firmly. 'Maybe next time.'

Clare laughed. 'Chaining children to fences might be going a bit far.' Another truck joined the blockade. 'Let's hope the press get here before Pyramid does. Otherwise they'll never get through.' Vehicles were already parked ten deep.

'It's about time we put up a fight,' said one man, and doffed his hat to the chained women. The hairs on the back of Clare's neck stood up, and a shiver of pride ran through her.

'Have you got that radio?' she asked.

Bronwyn handed over a big, battery-powered Sangean. 'I've set it to the broadcast of parliament.' The modulated voice of an ABC announcer rang clear in the still air. News on the hour of bomb blasts and earthquakes and rebellion in faraway places. Then the droning voice of MPs debating some bill about tariffs.

'Parliament's sitting late tonight,' said Clare. 'It could be ages before we know.'

The sound of a distant motor stopped the general chatter. Not a loud motor. Certainly not trucks in convoy. A car rounded the bend. 'They're from the local paper,' said someone. Good. This was all going according to plan. A young man and woman got out.

'How do you reckon they'll spin it?' Clare asked.

'Are you kidding?' said Bronwyn. 'That reporter—' she pointed to a pretty woman conducting interviews. 'Her parents are here. Her grandparents too. I think we can bank on good press.'

Clare smiled for the photographer.

Now a new, more menacing sound - the rumble of heavy vehicles. Once more the chatter stopped, and heads turned as one. Truck after truck crested the horizon. It was an army. 'Action stations,' shouted an earnest young man who looked vaguely familiar. She had it, Gavin Butler the artist, local president of Shut the Gate, minus the dread-locks. An uneasy calm settled on the crowd as they waited for the trucks to come.

Ten minutes later the lead vehicle grumbled around the corner. It bore gold emblazoned Pyramid Energy logos and looked brand new. 'That's the first bulldust that bumper's seen,' someone said. Grandad threaded his way through the throng to meet the convoy, flanked by two burly farmers.

Clare was too far away to hear, but if she peered sideways, she could see what was going on. One thing was certain. It was a heated exchange. Wild arm gestures, muted yells, the threatening revving of engines. Gas company trucks were lined up along Clydesdale Way, unable to turn into the blockaded track. Dogs, attracted by the noise, charged back from the gully where they'd been chasing rabbits. Petty differences forgotten, they were united now against a common enemy. They charged at the strangers as a single barking, snarling pack. It was a frightening sight. The Pyramid Energy man leaped into the cabin, losing his hat in the process. Red seized the hat, ripped it to shreds and settled down to eat it.

The man handed Grandad some papers through the window. Grandad tore them up. After twenty minutes of shouting, the man gave up. He reversed from the track. Three farm vehicles instantly took his spot. Now the drive was completely blocked, allowing the trucks nowhere to turn round. They had no choice but to rumble off along Clydesdale Way.

A cheer rang out. Clare caught a movement down on the road. Tom's jeep was approaching the rear of the convoy. It squeezed through on the inside, barrelled past the trucks, nosed into the Currawong track and parked. The barricade parted to let him through. Clare scrambled to her feet.

Tom sprinted towards her, weaving through the vehicles with a proud grin on his face. Clare stood attached to the gate, laughing and waiting for him. Tom looked her up and down as she pulled against her chains. 'Now why didn't I think of that?'

'Very funny,' said Clare, rattling the links. 'Now, who has a key?'

The crowd took their country time going home. Those that hadn't wandered up to the homestead, promised to return when the sun went down. The sweet scent of victory lay heavy in the air.

Tom had discovered a case of beer under the house, and Clare and Bronwyn were trying to fit a few more cans into the drinks fridge. 'That's it,' said Clare, straightening up. 'There's no more room.'

A man came in with a bag of ice and tipped it into the concrete laundry trough. 'Problem solved,' he said. 'You two shoot through. I'll finish here.'

Clare thanked him, and they headed for the kitchen where celebrations were in full swing. Where was Grandad? Ah, there he was, deep in conversation with a man she didn't know, a man bent with age … a man who appeared to be crying. Bronwyn followed her gaze. 'That's Pete Porter,' she said. 'He lost Quimby Downs to the wells five years ago. If only we knew then what we know now, we might have been able to help him.'

'I've seen that homestead,' said Clare. 'It's gorgeous, such a waste.'

'Even if they clean up the gas leaks, he'll never live there again,' whispered Bronwyn. 'I'm friends with his daughter. She says he has lung cancer.'

'How sad,' said Clare. 'I wonder if Grandad knows.'

They joined Tom out on the twilight verandah, watching the children play chasey in the dusk. 'Where's the radio?' said Clare. 'Surely there'll be news by now.' Bronwyn ducked inside to fetch it.

Parliament had finished and the political roundup begun. *The illness of the Member for Morton, Craig Jones, and the refusal of the Opposition to grant the Government a pair, has caused an unexpected result in parliament today. The move for an immediate moratorium on coal seam gas exploration has failed. Instead the matter will be referred to a parliamentary joint committee. It could take many months for this body to bring down its findings. In the interim, mining companies can continue their activities unhindered.*

No! Clare's throat closed. The day had seemed such a success. The community had rallied so fiercely. Had it all been for nothing? Would all their hearts break?

Clare slipped inside to find Grandad. He sat at the kitchen table with Pete Porter and a couple of other old rabble-rousers, laughing and drinking and telling stories. Tom's reassuring form pressed against her back, his steady arms encircled her and she turned to meet his gaze. In that bittersweet moment they reached an understanding. They wouldn't tell him, not yet. Let him have his celebration.

But they weren't the only ones listening to the radio. A hush rippled through the crowd as the result filtered through. Her chest ached as Grandad received the news.

After a moment of raw disbelief, of sheer sorrow, he composed himself and become strangely philosophical. He raised his eyes to meet hers. They were full of concern.

'Never mind, love,' he told her, patting her hand. 'Things will work out.'

Wasn't that just like Grandad? Putting everyone else's feelings ahead of his own. Clare didn't known know what to say. They'd played their last card. It was too awful to think Currawong might end up like Quimby Downs: poisoned and polluted, a paradise lost. Tears welled up and she hung her head.

'Clare?' She turned to her grandfather and forced a smile. He studied her face. 'I said never mind. Don't you trust your old grandad?'

She kneeled beside his chair and laid her head against him, like a child. 'I trust you, Grandad. I trust you more than anyone else in the world.'

'There's my girl.' He stroked her hair with gnarled fingers. 'It's almost Christmas. I plan to make our first Christmas together one to remember. What do you say? Will you help me?'

'Of course I will,' she said. 'I'd do anything for you.'

He smiled. 'Then cheer up. We're not finished yet.'

It was a forlorn hope. Clare's stomach clenched with sadness, with the pain of disappointing him.

She took hold of his hands. 'I'm sorry,' she said, wiping tears from her eyes.

'You did your best,' he said. 'What do you have to be sorry for?'

Her body felt cold. The room and the people receded into a fog until the world consisted only of her and Grandad. 'I'm sorry for Grandma, for Smudge ... for not being around these last sixteen years.'

A soft look of comprehension crept over his face. 'Listen to me. Mary and I, we knew how your dad felt after our Patty left him. You were just a child, Clare. You and Ryan. None of it's your fault.'

'I wasn't a child forever,' she said. 'And I still didn't come.'

His eyes crinkled into the kindest smile. It spread over his face, into his eyes and spilled across the room. 'Forgiven and forgotten.' He kissed her fingers. 'That's water under the bridge, you hear?' Clare nodded, feeling lighter. His words had lifted a heavy, guilty stone from her heart.

'Thank you,' she said. 'I don't deserve it.'

'I'll tell you what you do deserve, my girl.' He sounded suddenly stern. 'You deserve to forgive yourself.'

CHAPTER 41

The laziness of Christmas afternoon had claimed them all. Taylor lay on the couch with Red on her lap. The heeler had taken a shine to her and vice versa. That dog was nothing but a big sook. He reclined on his back between the girl's knees, eyes closed in bliss as she rubbed his tummy.

'Isn't he cute?' Taylor must have found Clare's old box of dolls beneath the house. Red now wore a frilly, buttercup-yellow bonnet, tied firmly under his chin. Tom chuckled and took a photo. Such a perfect day. Clare wished it might never end.

As an added bonus, there'd been the thrill of a phone call from Ryan. What a pleasure to hear his voice. At Clare's insistence Grandad had filled him in on the Pyramid problem. They'd talked for ages. Ryan had seemed genuinely angry, and keen to help if he could. He'd promised to visit soon. It was good to feel like they were, in some small way, part of a united force again.

Even the phone call from Mum hadn't been as difficult as usual. Clare had given a potted version of the last few months, and her mother had seemed more interested in Clare's life than usual. Or was it that she herself was being more forthcoming, more ready to share things? When Dad was alive she'd had to pick sides.

Clare had hung up the phone, and tried to picture her mother in Currawong's kitchen, sharing in the festivities. Where was she anyway? Why wasn't she here? Clare had made up her mind to find out. Maybe, in the future, she'd be able to mend the broken pieces of her family.

Grandad caught sight of Red in his bonnet and roared with laughter. Clare studied his face. For the last ten days he'd gone about his business as if nothing was wrong. If anything, he had more energy than before. How to explain it? Denial, she guessed. He was in denial. The trucks wouldn't roll into Currawong until January. This brief hiatus, this space between the old year and the new – this was a very special time for them all. A golden time, before the ratbags ruined everything.

Grandad had cooked the traditional dinner himself, in spite of the heat. 'It's not dinner,' Clare had pointed out. 'Why does everybody call Christmas lunch *dinner?*'

'Pipe down,' Grandad had growled. 'Your grandmother called it dinner, and that's good enough for me.' He'd been ably assisted by Tom, and also by his old mate Sid who had no living family and was a holiday houseguest. Sid wore a Santa hat, and with his bushy white beard he was a dead ringer for Father Christmas. Roast meat, both beef and lamb, all the veggies, gravy, plum pudding, brandy custard and two trifles, one with wine and one without for Jack. Clare wasn't allowed to do anything but sip champagne. He and Sid called out 'Ducks on the pond!' whenever she tried to help with the cooking. It was an old shearer's catchcry, used when a woman approached that exclusively male domain, the shearing shed. For some reason it now seemed to apply to the kitchen.

'Don't you dare,' warned Clare, when it looked like Tom might join in the shout.

Taylor had arrived on Christmas Eve like a child in wonderland. Had she ever experienced an old-style family Christmas before? Clare doubted it. Every aspect appeared to be so fresh and new for her, and it was a great pleasure to watch. Decorating the tree, wrapping the presents, singing the carols, pulling some early bonbons – she was more wide-eyed than Jack. The pair's innocent delight had put extra smiles on all their faces. Last night Taylor had snuggled down on a mattress in the corner of Jack's room, refusing to take her son's bed.

After light's out, Clare had heard them giggling and playing and jumping around, like two kids at a sleepover. When all went quiet she'd peeped in. The camp bed had been moved next to Jack's, and the young mother lay curled up in sleep beside her son. It was a touching scene. Red and Samson stretched out at their feet, the girl's face so angelic in repose, so much like Jack's. Clare had smiled before closing the door, thinking once again that Taylor needed fostering almost as much as Jack did. But she'd be off to her new job in a few days' time; a job which had in fact made Jack very proud, just as his mother had hoped. 'Mummy drives *monster* trucks,' he kept saying, spreading his arms wide.

'She's very clever then, isn't she?' Clare would say.

Jack would nod solemnly and run off to tell someone else.

Another car arrived. All day, an odd procession of vehicles had been arriving, delivering little and not so little presents for Tom. Beer, biscuits, fruit cakes, honey – these were the common fare. But some gifts were more unusual. One client gave him a box of bullets, another a hand-crafted bridle, another a hat and Drizabone, another a rifle to match the ammunition. And Martha had finally managed to offload that pig.

Jack had squealed with delight when he saw it. 'It's Babe. I love him.' The little boy locked arms around the animal's neck. My how that piglet had grown, but Tom hadn't the heart to say no. They'd put it in the day yard next to Sparky, and the two had become instant friends. Her grandfather had shaken his head. 'Why'd you have to go and give Jacky that *Babe* movie, love? I watched it with him last week. How the heck am I going to put that pig on a spit now?' Red received two dog beds and enough treats to last him for a year. Jack got Matchbox cars, a disturbing arsenal of toy guns, and bags of Christmas lollies, which Taylor helped him demolish.

Clare went outside to see what new gift had arrived. But it wasn't a gift. It was Pete Porter, Grandad's old friend from Quimby Downs. A thin, middle-aged woman helped him from the car. 'I'm Faye.' She extended her hand. 'Pete's daughter. Apparently Pete's staying here for a few days? Hope you're expecting him. I didn't like imposing like this on Christmas day, but he insisted on coming.'

'Will you stop fussing, Faye,' said Pete. 'I organised it with Harry last week.'

Faye shot Clare a helpless glance. 'Your medicine's all packed. You will take it on time, won't you? Perhaps if I give it to Clare, she could help you?'

Pete shuffled over to his daughter, and rested his hands on her shoulders. His back might be bent, but it was clear that in his youth he'd been a tall man. 'I'm perfectly capable of looking after myself.' He kissed Faye's cheek. 'It'll do you good to have a break.' He pulled out his wallet and handed her a bank card. 'Take a trip to the Gold Coast on me, do some shopping, live a little.'

She managed a wan smile. 'You sure you'll be all right?'

He kissed her again. 'I'm sure.'

Faye threw her arms around him. 'I love you, Dad.'

'Not as much as I love you,' he said. She pulled back and wiped away a tear. 'Now, now, love. That'll do. You're the best daughter a man could be blessed with,' he said. 'You go and have some fun, for Chrissake.'

'Well, goodbye,' Faye said.

'Goodbye,' said Clare. 'And try not to worry. We'll look after him.'

Pete watched his daughter drive away with an expression of immense satisfaction. Harry put a drink in his friend's hand and said, 'Who's up for a game of backyard cricket?'

'Me, me,' called Jack.

'Righto,' said Grandad. 'The kid has terrific aim,' he told Pete. 'Hits the wicket nearly every time.'

Clare winced. Jack was a good shot all right. Ever since he'd scored that bullseye with the stapler in the centre of Kim's forehead, Clare had learned to duck when he was angry. It was heartening that the boy's talent for braining people had finally found a sporting outlet.

After the game, Sid, Pete and her grandfather sat out on the verandah, beers in hand. Grandad was twisting a new cracker for Jack's whip. Clare came back into the kitchen, where Tom was making himself a meal of leftovers. 'They're *all* smoking,' she whispered. 'I can't believe it. Pete's got lung cancer.'

'I suppose he doesn't think things can get much worse then.' Tom opened his arms and she melted into him. 'He's staying?' Clare nodded. 'That's it then,' he said. 'With Taylor, and Sid and now Pete, it's a full house. I'll be bunking down in the surgery tonight.'

He didn't sound like he minded, and neither did she. Their future stretched invitingly before them. They had all the time in the world.

After dinner Clare had a closer look at her presents. She put on the outfit Ronnie had sent her. All carefully coordinated: skirt, top, jacket, bag, shoes and jewellery. Not that she had any use for high heels in Merriang. Tom was more admiring of the saddle Grandad had given her, his finger tracing its intricate stitching and embossed pigskin seat. She inspected the gold, heart-shaped locket from Tom. It contained a picture of Jack with her grandfather. Clare squeezed the lid shut. It felt cool and solid in her hand and was the best present of all.

She jumped up and wandered around the crowded, festive homestead, taking snapshots with her heart. It had been a truly magical day, a day when Currawong had turned into a real life Shangri-La. What about tomorrow?

Tom shivered and pulled the covers up to his chin. For a moment he couldn't place where he was. One thing was certain though, he'd had a night of it. His head was sore, his back was sore and his tongue was furry. He opened his eyes a crack. The sharp light of summer poured in the window.

He lay on a blow-up mattress in the corner of the surgery, his home for the past week. Not so blow-up any more. His spine lay hard against the floorboards, and why couldn't he feel his legs? He propped up on his elbows. Red lay spread-eagled over the end of the mattress, a dead weight. 'You've got me confused with that pushover, Taylor Brown.' He kicked at Red, who smiled and wagged his tail as if to say, *Don't worry. I know you didn't mean it.* 'Get out of here,' growled Tom. A second kick convinced the dog he was serious.

Tom linked his hands behind his head, and fell back with a sigh on his pillow. New Year's Day, and he'd be back in his own bed tonight. Sid was giving Taylor a lift to Toowoomba this morning, where she'd catch a train to start her new life. He checked his watch. Past nine, they'd have already left. He hauled himself to his feet, drained a glass of water and gazed out the window. The coming year held some nasty surprises, what with Harry's illness and the spectre of gas wells at

Currawong. But it also held the promise of a glorious future with Clare and Jack. He weighed up the odds. They were in his favour.

What was that noise? The door opened a fraction. Clare. She slipped into the room and pulled her oversize T-shirt over her head. Naked except for underpants, her face flushed with desire. He was instantly hard. Wordlessly she locked the door and joined him on the floor.

Afterwards she lay with her head cradled in his arm. 'Marry me,' he said.

She sat up, a shocked expression on her lovely face. 'Is this Taylor's idea?'

He pulled her to him. 'Yes,' he said, 'but it's a good one.' They wrestled together on the floor, laughing and kissing until he was hard all over again. The second time surpassed the first. Clare could joke all she liked, but she'd say yes in the end. It was written in the stars. 'Come on,' she said, jumping to her feet. 'Let's get up to the house, or we'll miss breakfast.'

'So Taylor's gone,' said Tom, finishing his cold toast.

'Sid took off with her at seven o'clock this morning,' said Clare. 'I thought she'd never get up in time. She almost missed her lift.'

'She's not a morning person,' said Tom.

Clare laughed. 'I've come to love Taylor, don't get me wrong. But I think she's almost more trouble than Jack.'

Tom poured himself another cuppa. 'Pete still here?'

She nodded. 'Hasn't *he* given Grandad a new lease of life? They're like two naughty schoolboys.'

Grandad came in the back door, followed by Jack and all four dogs. 'Keep this lot here, will you? Me and Pete are heading over to Quimby. He wants to take a look around.'

'Would you like me or Tom to come along?' asked Clare.

'No thanks, mother hen,' he said. 'Us old blokes can take care of ourselves.'

He wrapped her in a hug that took her breath away. Grandad was becoming more sentimental every day. She drew in his scent, warm and familiar, the smell of the earth. How she loved him.

'You two have fun,' she said. What would it be like for Pete, seeing his old home again? The gracious homestead that he'd built with his own two hands, falling into disrepair. The grounds and garden fast returning to the wild. Surely it would tear him in two? She was struck by an overwhelming urge to go with them, in spite of any protests.

It seemed her grandfather could read minds. 'You're not coming.' His voice had taken on a commanding tone, and suddenly she was a child again. He looked her up and down, a satisfied expression on his face. 'You coming back like you did, love, and bringing little Jack … it's been a blessing. There's much of your mother in you,' he said, 'and of your grandmother. I see the resemblance each time I lay eyes on you.'

The mention of Mum was so unexpected it made Clare miss her. 'If you should speak to your mother … if you should speak to Patty, tell her how much I love her. How much Grandma and I always loved her. Tell Ryan that too.'

'I will,' she said. 'Now go before you make me cry.'

'In a minute.' He sat down and patted his knee. Jacky was there in a flash. 'Now you be good for Clare,' he said. 'And look after that pony while Pete and me are gone - and Babe the pig too.' The boy nodded gravely and something seemed to pass between them. Samson trotted over and put his head on Jack's knee. 'Keep an eye on my boy for me,' he told the dog, fondling his ears.

Pete tooted the horn of the truck. 'Will you be back for lunch,' asked Clare.

'I don't think so,' said Grandad.

'What will you do for all that time?'

Grandad shushed her, with a finger to his lips. 'Secret men's business.'

Clare laughed, but Samson erupted into a frantic flurry of barking. He stood in the doorway, forefeet spread, barring the way.

'Here now,' said Tom. He slipped a leash on the agitated animal and pulled him aside. Grandad put on his hat, took one last, lingering look around the kitchen and was gone.

What was it, she wondered, that was bothering Samson? Was it the same, indefinable thing that was bothering her?

'This is our first family ride together,' said Clare. She loved saying the word *family*. She loved how it sounded. She loved that that's what they were now. Tom rode Martini, a blue-roan clydesdale filly, sweet-tempered and pretty as a picture. According to Grandad, she was a rare throwback to the Queensland stallion, Hillend Macgregor — a champion during the war. Not that it meant anything to Clare. Maybe she should study the Currawong bloodlines? Yes, she should learn more about breeding these magnificent horses; carry on the family tradition, so to speak.

Martini was only a green-broke two-year-old, but already she stood sixteen hands high: a gentle giant with the heart of a lamb. Little Sparky had a crush on her. Tom barely needed to hold the pony's lead rope, he followed so faithfully at Martini's side. Jack sat his pony with assurance, listening to Tom's occasional instructions, his tiny tongue extending slightly from his lips in concentration.

Clare stroked Fleur's dappled neck, and the mare snorted in pleasure. Jack's aptitude never ceased to amaze her. Had it really only been five months since they'd first met in her office? Hard to reconcile the memory of that traumatised child with this smiling, confident little boy. 'Canter, canter, canter,' he yelled. Tom touched his heels to Martini's sides and she broke into a lumbering, yet graceful, trot. Fleur followed suit and Sparky was forced to canter in order to keep up with the two-time pace of the heavy horses. Jack's grin was a joy to see.

A currawong arrowed across the perfect arch of the cloudless summer sky. Here, in this high corner paddock, they were well and truly in the foothills of the Bunyas. To the left lay groves of brigalow: elegant wattles boasting high, silvery canopies. No breeze stirred their branches. Scattered patches of bright green vines showed in the gullies, remnants of subtropical rainforest that had occupied the brigalow lands millions of years ago. Swathes of pale-gold summer grass bent beneath the horses' drumming hooves, only to spring up behind them. Soon this heavenly hillside might be lost, a bombsite of roads and wells and wastewater dams, all carved into the rich black soil. Her grief, her grandfather's grief, cast a shadow over the golden morning.

They paused at the crest of the ridge. So silent. Spread before them, peaceful paddocks of grazing clydesdales, Currawong's main herd. Goliath wheeled and reared low, acknowledging the horses on the hill. She looked to the north. In the distance, Quimby Downs stood bathed in sunlight. Clare caught her breath. What a magnificent sight.

It was then she heard it. A faint boom, a distant explosion. Thunder? But the sky was a flawless blue. Her imagination? There came the sound of faraway barking. The horses pricked their ears and held their heads on high, staring in the direction of Quimby Downs. Clare glanced at Tom. His eyes narrowed. 'Look.' Flickers of bright flame flowered around the distant homestead and a thin pillar of smoke rose in the still air. Tom leaped from his horse, scooped up Jack and somehow remounted with the child in his arms. 'Come on,' he said, and thundered back to Currawong with Clare in swift pursuit.

Clare sat out on the verandah. A subdued Jack played at her feet, lining up his Matchbox cars in neat, obsessive rows. Samson stood chained to the rail, statue still, his gaze fixed to the north.

A second fire truck hurtled down the road, then another. A police car followed soon after. She fingered her phone. Why didn't someone ring? Harry was her grandfather, after all. She had more right to know than anybody. Samson raised his nose and howled to the heavens, the most mournful sound. Why couldn't the bloody dog shut up?

It was another half hour before the phone finally rang and Tom's shaky voice came on the line. 'I'm sorry, honey,' he said. 'Harry and Pete … they didn't make it.'

Jack was her saviour, all that dreadful morning. Staying strong for the children, such a cliché, such a fundamental truth. Giving the little boy a bath, making his lunch, going through the motions. It kept her sane until Bronwyn arrived with Timmy, freeing Clare to take the short trip to Quimby Downs.

Tom met her at the gate. They embraced for the longest time, gathering strength for whatever was next. 'What happened?' asked Clare.

'I don't know,' said Tom. 'I just don't know.'

The homestead was gone, razed to the ground, a smouldering ruin of timber and tin. The outbuildings were gone too. Behind the house, a fire still burned with a steady flame, cordoned off with crime scene tape. The earth all around was blackened in a wide circle. Was that where Grandad and Pete met their death? Clare headed towards the spot and was waylaid by two police men. She identified herself, feeling numb and oddly composed, 'If it's any comfort, your grandfather and his friend would have died instantly,' said one of the officers.

'What happened?' asked Clare.

'We think gas leaked from the domestic well and exploded inside the pump house. There's no putting out that fire now.' They all stared at the unearthly flames, burning bright on the scorched ground as if by magic. 'I understand there's a history of methane contamination at Quimby Downs?' asked the officer. 'Did your grandfather smoke?'

Her first instinct was to say no, but that would be wrong. He'd been smoking lately. He'd even given up trying to hide it. 'Yes,' she said. 'He smoked, and so did Pete.'

The officer nodded and made a note. 'Maybe they lit up in the pump shed,' he said to his colleague.

'The homestead,' said Clare. 'What happened to the homestead?'

'My guess is the wind blew burning embers into the roof,' said the officer.

Clare was in a daze. She recalled the vertical plume of smoke, rising straight as an arrow to heaven. There was no wind that morning. *Secret men's business.* 'Oh Grandad', she whispered. 'Whatever have you done?'

'If only Grandad could see this,' said Clare, waving the newspaper in Tom's face.

'Who's to say he can't?'

Clare gave him a swift kiss. 'Listen.'

The deaths of Darling Downs farmers Harry Macleod and Pete Porter in a gas explosion have shocked all Queensland, and galvanised a state-wide campaign against the coal seam mining industry. Pyramid Energy stands accused of non-compliance with dozens of environmental and safety regulations. It's alleged the company bullied owners of contaminated land into signing compensation agreements with unconscionable non-disclosure clauses. Today the State Government announced a suspension of all ongoing activities and permits relating to coal seam gas mining, and a moratorium on new exploration projects.

Tom smiled. 'Currawong's safe then.'

'It gets better.' Clare smoothed out the creases in the paper with trembling hands.

A bill was introduced into Canberra's lower house last night, calling for the Great Artesian Basin to be included as an environment of national significance. This would give the Federal Government broad powers to intervene for its protection. In the light of the recent Queensland tragedy, this proposal received bipartisan support.' Clare clasped a hand to her chest. Her mother, Ryan, everyone at the funeral service had prayed for this. In death, Grandad had finally brought the family to a common purpose.

'That's fantastic news,' said Tom. 'Unbelievable, fantastic news.' He handed her the funeral urn. 'Now let's get this show on the road.'

Clare waved goodbye to Bronwyn, who was supervising Jack and Timmy in the sandpit, and climbed into the jeep. They drove in silence for a while. 'Grandad loved Jack.'

'Yes,' said Tom.

'I wish you'd told me he was dying.'

Tom shot her an anguished glance that broke her heart.

'I've forgiven you,' she said, laying her hand on his knee. 'You know I have. Do you know what Grandad said to me on New Year's Eve?' Tom shook his head. 'He said that watching Jack blossom had been the greatest gift. He said he wished he could pay that gift forward somehow.' Tom stayed silent. 'Maybe I can do it for him,' said Clare.

'Go on.'

'That course in equine therapy that you did?' she said. 'I'm going to do it too. Let's turn Currawong into a place of healing for other kids like Jack.'

Tom turned to her with a brilliant smile. 'Harry would like that just fine.'

Clare and Tom approached the entrance to the rainforest walk. Seen from the outside, this bunya pine forest was a forbidding place: ancient trees standing shoulder to shoulder, limbs entwined as if barring the way. A curtain of vines and prickly plants stood bathed in sunlight at the jungle's edge, protecting the forest, keeping the drying winds and summer heat at bay.

They slipped inside. Domed pine canopies reached to the sky, while elephant-like buttresses held fast to the dappled earth. Each tree was a bridge between worlds. It had been this way since time immemorial, a place where all sorts of magical and dangerous things might happen. Their footsteps made no sound on the soft earth as they walked to the waterfall. A seedling sprouted from the stump of a long-dead forest giant. Death and regeneration went hand in hand in this place.

Clare stood on the ferny bank and scattered the ashes on the water. They dissolved in the dark stream, as it leaped from its course and shattered in a rainbow of spray on the rocks below. Grandad wasn't gone. He lived here now, where she could always find him. She took Tom's hand. With a silent prayer, Clare retraced her path and stepped from the shadows into the light.

ACKNOWLEDGEMENTS

Thanks to the team at Pilyara Press, especially Kathryn Ledson, Sydney Smith and Kate Belle.

I must thank my talented writing buddies of The Little Lonsdale Group for their help and support. Thanks also to the Darklings, a writing group formed while we were all together at Australia's National Writing Centre known as Varuna - The Writer's House. Varuna sent me on a magical writing residency to the Tyrone Guthrie Centre in Ireland where I completed this manuscript.

Thanks to my agent, Clare Forster of Curtis Brown Australia.

And finally, thanks go to my patient family for putting up with a distracted writer in their midst. A special thank you to my son Matthew, for always being willing to brainstorm ideas.

ABOUT THE AUTHOR

Bestselling Aussie author Jennifer Scoullar writes page-turning fiction about the land, people and wildlife that she loves.

Scoullar is a lapsed lawyer who harbours a deep appreciation and respect for the natural world. She lives on a farm in Australia's southern Victorian ranges, and has ridden and bred horses all her life. Her passion for animals and the bush is the catalyst for her bestselling books.

Visit Jennifer's website to enter the monthly prize draw! If you enjoyed this book and have a moment or two, please leave an online rating or review. Reviews are of great help to authors.

www.jenniferscoullar.com

www.ingramcontent.com/pod-product-compliance
Lightning Source LLC
Chambersburg PA
CBHW030655190726
48286CB00001B/28